外国语言文学学

金莉 许钧

外国文学理论

主 编
金莉 陈榕

外语教学与研究出版社
北京

图书在版编目（CIP）数据

外国文学理论：汉文、英文 / 金莉，陈榕主编. -- 北京：外语教学与研究出版社，2024.7（2024.12重印）. --（外国语言文学学科核心课程系列教材 / 金莉，许钧总主编）. -- ISBN 978-7-5213-5430-0

I. I106

中国国家版本馆CIP数据核字第2024K0P317号

出 版 人	王　芳
项目策划	张　阳
责任编辑	张　阳
责任校对	屈海燕
装帧设计	锋尚设计
出版发行	外语教学与研究出版社
社　　址	北京市西三环北路19号（100089）
网　　址	https://www.fltrp.com
印　　刷	北京九州迅驰传媒文化有限公司
开　　本	787×1092　1/16
印　　张	23.5
字　　数	641千字
版　　次	2024年7月第1版
印　　次	2024年12月第2次印刷
书　　号	ISBN 978-7-5213-5430-0
定　　价	79.90元

如有图书采购需求，图书内容或印刷装订等问题，侵权、盗版书籍等线索，请拨打以下电话或关注官方服务号：
客服电话：400 898 7008
官方服务号：微信搜索并关注公众号"外研社官方服务号"
外研社购书网址：https://fltrp.tmall.com

物料号：354300001

总主编的话

国务院学位委员会第六、七届外国语言文学学科评议组履职先后十年，在全体成员的积极努力下，做了许多工作，包括：外国语言文学学位授予和人才培养一级学科简介的撰写，外国语言文学学科目录的调整，外国语言文学一级学科硕士点、博士点基本条件的确定，外国语言文学学科发展报告的撰写，外国语言文学学科重要学术期刊的认定，外国语言文学学科核心课程的确定与指南的撰写，以及外国语言文学一级学科博士点的评审等。对于外国语言文学学科的建设而言，这些工作都很重要。其中有几项尤为关键：一是确立了学科发展的五大方向，具有前瞻性，为新时期外国语言文学学科的创新发展指明了方向，同时也为外国语言文学学科拓展了广阔的发展空间；二是在外国语言文学一级学科博士点的增补工作中，具有全局观，为全国外语学科的总体布局与重点突破做了战略性的安排；三是确定了外国语言文学学科核心课程，并编写了课程指南，为外国语言文学学科的研究生培养做了具有指导性的基础工作。

为了加强研究生课程建设，提高研究生培养质量，国务院学位委员会第三十四次会议决定，组织各学科评议组编写《学术学位研究生核心课程指南（试行）》。这项工作是在2018年开始组织落实的。第七届外国语言文学学科评议组在2018年7月与12月，分别在湖南师范大学和对外经济贸易大学召开会议，商议并部署外国语言文学学科核心课程指南的编写工作。根据外国语言文学学科五大方向的建设与发展的实际情况，评议组决定这项工作要坚持守正与创新的原则，稳妥推进，先行确定外国语言学、外国文学、翻译学三大方向各建设两门核心课程，分别为外国语言学理论、外国语言学研究方法、外国文学理论、外国文学研究方法、翻译学概论和翻译研究方法。比较文学与跨文化研究和国别与区域研究方向将根据各高校外语学科的实际发展状况，适时确定并推出核心课程。

先行确定的六门课程主要包括基础理论课和专业课，体现了外语学科三个方向的基础理论与专门知识。从六门课程的名称，我们就可以清晰地看到，这套教材所聚焦的是理论与方法这两个最为核心的层面。研究生培养需要着力于思维方法与能力的培养，而基本理论的掌握和科学研究方法的使用是其根本的保证。为了有力地促进外国语言文学学科的建设与发展，在外语教学与研究出版社领导的积极建议和大力支持下，第七届外国语言文学学科评议组决定在编写核心课程指南的基础上，把我们的工作再推进一步，组织有关专家编写外国语言文学学科核心课程教材，确立了前沿性、针对性与指导性的编写原则，确定了各课程教材的主编人选和编写框架。

核心课程指南的编写工作，除了学科评议组全体成员的积极参与，还得到了北京外国语大学、湖南师范大学和对外经济贸易大学部分专家的支持，在此向各位委员和专家表示衷心的感谢。我们还要特别感谢外国语言文学学科核心课程各教材的主编和编写专家，感谢你们积极承担这一具有开创性的工作，并付出艰辛的努力。最后，我们要感谢外语教学与研究出版社的大力支持。

金　莉　许　钧

2023年3月

编写说明

《外国文学理论》旨在服务外国文学理论的研究生课程教学。对于外国语言文学一级学科外国文学方向研究生而言，学习外国文学理论有着十分重要的意义。它能有效地帮助学生了解外国文学的理论知识体系，掌握文学研究的主要方法，培养批判性思辨能力，拓展理论视域，为学生进行文学批评与文论研究打下良好基础。《外国文学理论》以《学术学位研究生核心课程指南（试行）》为编写依据，以从古希腊时代到21世纪的外国文学理论的发展史为脉络，以不同时期的不同文学理论流派为主要内容，以文学理论核心概念为关键词，对外国文学理论进行系统介绍，帮助学生从理论角度深化对文学的认识，提高文学批评实践能力，促进学生的理论素养、专业视野、思辨能力和学术创新能力的全面提升。

教材特色

一、强调对外国文学理论文本进行原典阅读

外国文学理论著作思辨性强，语言难度系数大，无论是古希腊罗马时代先哲的著作，还是当代理论家，如拉康、德里达等人的著作，阅读起来均较为艰深。对于外国文学方向的硕士和博士研究生而言，阅读原典既是理论基本功养成的必需要求，也是增加对文学理论的感性认识、触发原创性思考、激发思辨性批判的起点。

二、聚焦外国文学理论的知识体系，既展现其传承性，也反映其前沿性

本教材紧扣外国文学理论两千五百年的发展历史，关注不同历史文化语境中重大理论流派的涌现，选取从古希腊时代到21世纪的理论著作中有典型代表性的篇目进行呈现和评介，既帮助学生认识到文学理论发展的源远流长，亦帮助学生了解文学理论前沿的动态。

三、重在呈现外国文学理论的立体图谱

本教材聚焦主要外国文学理论流派，对代表性理论家和经典理论作品撷取其精华进行展示，使学生能够透彻理解外国文学理论的关键词和核心议题。同时，本教材也重视展现理论内部的对话性——这种对话性体现在不同的流派对相同的文学理论议题的关注与回应，也体现在相同的流派内部的观念差异、思想共鸣与交锋。本教材亦鼓励学生以主体立场参与到理论的研讨之中。

教材构成

本教材由十四章组成，按照历史传承和时间顺序排列，包含从公元前5世纪到21世纪的与文学相关的重要理论流派的介绍和重点理论家的代表作的选读等。

各章具体内容结构如下：

- **概述**

厘清本章所聚焦的文学理论思潮的历史文化语境，介绍其发展脉络、核心议题、代表人物和重点作品，亦展现其内部的不同声音的交织与争鸣。

- **主要文本阅读**

精选四篇代表性选文。每篇选文前面设置选文简介环节，作为阅读引导。选文后设置思考题和讨论题。思考题帮助学生更好地回顾选文要义。讨论题鼓励延伸阅读和独立思考，可以作为课程小组讨论的题目，也可以作为课外小论文的题目。

- **补充文本选摘与评述**

每章补充选摘三篇拓展性选文。为了便于呈现重点，补充文本后设置选文评述环节，简要综述三篇选文的内容和进行议题延伸。

- **关键术语释例**

列出与本章内容密切关联的两个核心术语，对其进行简明扼要的介绍，同时力争展现这些核心术语内涵的动态发展。

- **推荐书目**

列出对更为深入了解本章讨论的理论流派和代表性理论家具有参考意义的重要入门指南、经典研究论著和前沿学术著作。

选材原则

本书选材以经典性为原则，选取九十八篇代表性理论著作的英文选文，内容丰富且具有典型性。其中，主要文本阅读部分共五十六篇，每章四篇。选材重视经典性、重要性和普及性，紧扣文学理论核心议题和关键词。补充文本选摘与评述部分共四十二篇，每章三篇。因为教材篇幅所限，补充文本仅选摘精华部分，提供核心段落的原文阅读。对于硕士研究生而言，补充文本有助于学生通过"管中窥豹"的方式拓展学术视野，也有助于使课堂议题更为丰富。对于博士研究生而言，补充文本与主要文本之间是有机整体，建议学生"按图索骥"寻找这些文献，进行全文阅读，从而更好地了解理论文本之间的对话性和理论议题的复杂性。

本书选文众多，均出自权威版本，选入教材时力求保持原文的风貌。另外，一些著作有较长的副标题。为了方便读者阅读，中文译名仅保留主标题，英文标题仅首次出现时列出全称。特此说明。

教学建议

全书共设十四章，加上课程介绍和期末考试，可以满足一个学期的教学安排。本教材也适用于一个学年两个学期的课程设置。建议第一学期的教学内容覆盖前七章（每章内容分两周授课），包括经典文论部分和现当代文论部分的前三章，即"俄国形式主义与英美新批评""精神分析与神话原型批评"以及"西方马克思主义"。建议第二学期的教学处理后七章内容，围绕20世纪下半叶出现的文学理论研究本体论转向、历史转向和文化转向等理论进程，以及性别、种族、生态等重要议题进行授课。

外国文学理论的资源是在一次又一次的文学理论流派的浪潮中，由一代又一代的理论家的贡献积累而成。因此它有着极其丰饶的积淀，也有着长青的生命力。编写《外国文学理论》是一项极具挑战性的任务。编者希冀借此呈现外国文学理论发展的积淀和绵延，反映文学理论思辨性的活力以及勾勒21世纪当下文学理论的最新动态。期待《外国文学理论》能够引领外国文学方向的研究生领悟文学理论的传承，感受理论的魅力，唤起理论的自觉，体会文学研究的探索之趣。

金 莉 陈 榕

2024年6月

目 录

第一部分 经典文论

第一章 古希腊罗马文论·····2
主要文本阅读
柏拉图：《理想国》
亚里士多德：《诗学》
贺拉斯：《诗艺》
朗吉努斯：《论崇高》

补充文本选摘与评述
高尔吉亚：《海伦颂》
昆体良：《演讲术原理》
普罗提诺：《九章集》

第二章 从中世纪、文艺复兴到新古典主义·····26
主要文本阅读
阿奎那：《神学大全》
但丁：《致斯加拉大亲王书》
锡德尼：《为诗辩护》
高乃依：《论三一律，即行动、时间和地点的一致》

补充文本选摘与评述
薄伽丘：《异教诸神谱系》
杜贝莱：《保卫与发扬法兰西语言》
德莱顿：《论戏剧诗》

第三章 从启蒙主义到浪漫主义·····49
主要文本阅读
休谟：《论趣味的标准》

席勒：《审美教育书简》
华兹华斯：《〈抒情歌谣集〉序言》
爱默生：《诗人》

补充文本选摘与评述
莱辛：《拉奥孔》
施莱格尔：《〈雅典娜神殿〉断片集》
雨果：《〈克伦威尔〉序言》

第四章 从现实主义到象征主义 75
主要文本阅读
丹纳：《〈英国文学史〉序言》
左拉：《实验小说》
詹姆斯：《小说的艺术》
马拉美：《文学的进化》

补充文本选摘与评述
托尔斯泰：《什么是艺术？》
王尔德：《谎言的衰朽》
叶芝：《诗歌的象征主义》

第二部分 现当代文论

第五章 俄国形式主义与英美新批评 102
主要文本阅读
什克洛夫斯基：《作为手法的艺术》
埃亨巴乌姆：《"形式主义方法"的理论》
布鲁克斯：《释义异说》
维姆萨特、比尔兹利：《意图谬见》

补充文本选摘与评述
艾略特：《传统与个人才能》
雅各布森：《主导因素》
燕卜荪：《含混七型》

第六章　精神分析与神话原型批评 127

主要文本阅读

　　弗洛伊德：《创造性作家与白日梦》

　　荣格：《论分析心理学与诗歌的关系》

　　拉康：《镜像阶段》

　　弗莱：《文学的原型》

补充文本选摘与评述

　　布鲁姆：《影响的焦虑》

　　穆尔维：《视觉快感与叙事电影》

　　卡鲁斯：《无法言说的经历》

第七章　西方马克思主义 153

主要文本阅读

　　霍克海默尔、阿多尔诺：《启蒙辩证法》

　　阿尔都塞：《意识形态与意识形态国家机器》

　　威廉斯：《马克思主义与文学》

　　詹姆逊：《政治无意识》

补充文本选摘与评述

　　卢卡奇：《平衡的现实主义》

　　葛兰西：《狱中笔记》

　　伊格尔顿：《马克思主义与文学批评》

第八章　结构主义与叙事学 179

主要文本阅读

　　列维-施特劳斯：《神话结构研究》

　　巴特：《神话学》

　　热奈特：《叙事话语》

　　费伦：《体验小说》

补充文本选摘与评述

　　索绪尔：《普通语言学教程》

　　巴赫金：《小说的话语》

　　瑞安：《故事的变身》

第九章　后结构主义与后现代主义 ······ 206
 主要文本阅读
  德里达：《人文科学话语中的结构、符号和游戏》
  福柯：《什么是作者？》
  利奥塔：《定义后现代》
  鲍德里亚：《拟像与仿真》
 补充文本选摘与评述
  德曼：《阅读的寓言》
  德勒兹、瓜塔里：《千高原》
  哈琴：《后现代主义诗学》

第十章　接受理论与读者反应批评 ······ 233
 主要文本阅读
  姚斯：《作为文学理论的挑战的文学史》
  伊瑟尔：《文本与读者的互动》
  霍兰德：《交互式批评》
  费什：《这个课堂有文本吗？》
 补充文本选摘与评述
  伽达默尔：《真理与方法》
  罗森布拉特：《读者·文本·诗歌》
  詹塞恩：《我们为什么读小说》

第十一章　女性主义 ······ 258
 主要文本阅读
  西苏：《美杜莎的笑声》
  肖瓦尔特：《走向一种女性主义诗学》
  胡克斯：《女性主义理论》
  巴特勒：《性别麻烦》
 补充文本选摘与评述
  波伏娃：《第二性》
  吉利根：《不同的声音》
  艾哈迈德：《过一种女性主义的生活》

第十二章　后殖民主义 …… 284

主要文本阅读

　　萨义德:《东方学》

　　巴巴:《文化的位置》

　　斯皮瓦克:《庶民能说话吗?》

　　莫汉蒂:《再访〈西方视野之下〉》

补充文本选摘与评述

　　法农:《黑皮肤,白面具》

　　阿希克洛夫特、格里菲斯、蒂芬:《逆写帝国》

　　杨:《后殖民存留》

第十三章　新历史主义与文化研究 …… 310

主要文本阅读

　　怀特:《元历史》

　　格林布拉特:《文艺复兴时期的自我塑造》

　　霍尔:《编码/解码》

　　赫伯迪格:《亚文化》

补充文本选摘与评述

　　蒙特罗斯:《新历史主义》

　　德赛图:《日常生活实践》

　　布尔迪厄:《区分》

第十四章　生态批评与后人类主义 …… 336

主要文本阅读

　　布伊尔:《环境批评的未来》

　　哈拉维:《赛博格宣言》

　　班内特:《活力物质》

　　摩尔:《生命之网中的资本主义》

补充文本选摘与评述

　　海勒斯:《我们何以成为后人类》

　　拉图尔:《面对盖娅》

　　胡根、蒂芬:《后殖民生态批评》

第一部分
经典文论

第一章
古希腊罗马文论

概述

古希腊是西方文明的重要发源地。大约在公元前1200年，来自北方的部族迁入爱琴海边的希腊诸岛，他们通过航海和贸易等形式与周边地区互动，与埃及文明、小亚细亚文明等接触、碰撞，逐渐孕育出古希腊文明。到了公元前500年左右，古希腊文明进入黄金时代，西方文学理论便诞生于这片文明的沃土。

首先，古希腊璀璨的文学成就为文学理论的萌芽提供了天然的滋养。早在公元前8世纪前后，古希腊神话便随着游吟诗人的吟诵传遍希腊诸岛，荷马在此基础上创作了《伊利亚特》和《奥德赛》。古希腊时代也是诗人辈出的时代，代表人物有《工作和时日》和《神谱》的作者赫西俄德以及女诗人萨福。随着希腊文明的发展，从祭祀和节日庆典发展而来的戏剧也迎来了它的黄金时代。公元前5世纪，古希腊戏剧达到辉煌的顶峰，涌现出悲剧大师埃斯库罗斯、索福克勒斯、欧里庇得斯和喜剧大师阿里斯托芬。神话、诗歌和戏剧等文学高度融入古希腊人的文化生活，对它们的观察和思考自然而然地出现："文学为什么会有打动人心的力量？""史诗和戏剧哪个更伟大？""什么样的戏剧让人哭？什么样的戏剧让人笑？它们各有什么样的特征？"就这样，文学理论在丰富的文学实践基础上得以萌生和发展。

与此同时，古希腊的城邦政治也为文学的繁荣以及文学理论的诞生创造了条件。古希腊诸城邦中雅典的影响力最大。雅典实行民主制，重视公民权，公民高度参与政治讨论，所以，以辩论、说服、鼓动人心为目标的修辞术是当时的显学。而"什么样的语言具有感染力？""演讲术的要素是什么？"这样的问题导向了文学理论有关语言、修辞和文体的思考。同时，这些思考也默认一个共同的前提：文学具有社会能动性，参与对价值观的形塑。

西方文论在此时的古希腊诞生还有得天独厚的条件：这是个文学家辈出的

时代，也是哲学家辈出的时代。西方哲学奠基人柏拉图（Plato）和亚里士多德（Aristotle）都来自这个时代。以"爱智慧"为目标的哲学关注事物的普遍规律，勇于探究事物的本质。"文学的本质是什么？""文学的意义是什么？"对这些问题的追问赋予古希腊文学理论思辨的深刻性。

在以上诸因的共同作用下，古希腊文学理论蓬勃发展。最早的议题之一围绕文学之"术"——修辞术——展开，讨论的是文学的"技术性"问题，即文学是如何运用语言的魅力影响人们的观点、操控受众的情感的。代表性人物是当时极负盛名的雄辩家高尔吉亚（Gorgias）。他认为雄辩的力量来自有技巧的语言，称诗歌是带韵律的言说，能够引发痛苦与欢乐等复杂情感，令人对他人的幸与不幸感同身受，使其思想被影响和塑造。

柏拉图和亚里士多德则认为语言之"术"是文学性的表层，需要追问其核心——文学的本质是什么？其意义是什么？柏拉图在《理想国》（*Republic*）中指出，文学艺术的本质是摹仿（mimesis）。这种观念源自柏拉图哲学的"理式说"（the Platonic forms）。柏拉图认为，在变化中的多样性的物质性的现实世界之上，有超越性的范式性的永恒的理式世界。文学所摹仿的是现实物质世界，方式是镜子式的再现，所以映照出的是现实世界的虚像，和柏拉图心目中的真善美的理式世界隔着层层距离。在柏拉图时代，"智者学派"（the Sophists）影响力很大，他们认为真理是相对的，提出"人是万物的尺度"，用修辞术推广各自信奉的观念。柏拉图基于"理式说"的文学观期待文学能够反映何为善、何为正义等永恒真理。柏拉图充分认识到文学的感染力，在《伊安篇》（*Ion*）中指出诗人受神灵附体式的灵感启发，进入创作迷狂的状态，其诗作的魅力如同磁石，会经由诗人、吟诵者和表演者，一环一环将磁力传递给听众。但是，他认为文学不应该仅仅满足于煽动人的情感、呼应人的欲望，因此在《理想国》中提出除非诗人能够证明他们能承担起教化民众的责任，否则就应将他们驱逐。

亚里士多德虽然是柏拉图的学生，却反对柏拉图"理式说"的超验性，将目光聚焦在生活在世间的人们。在《诗学》（*Poetics*）中，他指出模仿是人类本能，是人类了解世界和学习知识的方式之一。他认为文学的摹仿对象是行动中的人，如此一来，文学的意义就不再局限于柏拉图所说的对理式的劣等摹仿，而在于捕捉与再现真实世界的具体的人的生命体验。亚里士多德还提出文学和历史各有擅场，历史记录已发生的个别性的历史事件，文学可以描绘符合事物发展规律的可能性事件，文学由此也和哲学一样，可以反映世界普遍规律。他非常关注文学实践，在对古希腊文学作品的细致解读基础上进行理论总结，在《诗学》中分析了何为悲剧、何为喜剧、何为史诗，对悲剧情节构成和人物要素进行了提炼，深刻影响了西方戏剧的发展。此外，从《诗学》中还可以看到，亚里士多德对文学的教化功能的理解比柏拉图复杂。他承认文学的重要意义在于道德教化，但是也认可人的智性与心理需求，认为观看悲剧有益于增进智识、澄澈心境、陶冶情操、满足心理学意义上的情感宣泄与疏导——以上因素构成了亚里士多德的"卡萨西斯"（Catharsis）概念的复杂内涵。

伯罗奔尼撒战争之后，以雅典为首的希腊诸城邦逐渐走向衰落，但其文化影响力却向地中海和中东地区广泛辐射，历史进入"希腊化时期"。公元前2世纪前后，罗马崛起，逐渐取代马其顿王国。最终，罗马将希腊收入版图，也将希腊文明烙刻进了罗马的文化传承。因此，古罗马文论始终处于与古希腊理论的对话之中，这构成了古罗马文论的"古典性"的由来。但古罗马文论也有自己的语境：一是基于古罗马人的务实性；二是古罗马进入帝国阶段后，重视等级制的规范，不再鼓励大胆的思想探索。所以古罗马文论更重形式，更重实践技巧，缺乏古希腊时代形而上的思辨色彩。此外，受当时盛行的伊壁鸠鲁主义、斯多葛主义等的影响，古罗马文论有折中主义的倾向。

古罗马文论的重点之一也是修辞术。在罗马共和国时代，演讲被视为政治人至高无上的精神活动，修辞术被用于澄清观念、宣扬立场、赢得人心。西塞罗（Cicero）在《论选材》《论演说家》《论雄辩的种类》等著作中，强调修辞术的重要性。相比于柏拉图的担忧，即修辞术对形式的倚重会让它偏废对真理的追求，西塞罗认为，在真正意义的修辞术中，真理、美德和优雅的言说不可分割，修辞术凝结人类智慧，可以在国家政治中发挥重要作用。进入罗马帝国阶段，帝制取代民主政治，修辞术的政治意义衰落。昆体良（Quintilian）有感于此，写作了十二卷的《演讲术原理》（*Institutio Oratoria*），主张以修辞术为核心建构人文教育体系。他勾勒出如何从童年开始，通过写作、文科知识学习和德性的培养，循序渐进地教育出合格的演讲家。他的演讲家教育其实是公民教育，对西方教育学有重大影响。这种教育观也符合他所强调的文学语言的社会责任：修辞术的核心是德性，无德者的雄辩对社会有害。

古罗马古典主义的代表性理论家是贺拉斯（Horace）。他推崇希腊文学，主张奉其为经典，希冀用古希腊文明的丰厚传承为相对贫瘠的罗马文明提供标尺和范本。他和柏拉图一样，认为文学具有教育功能，在《诗艺》（*The Art of Poetry*）中提出应"寓教于乐"：好的诗既要有益于思想，也要有趣味和魅力，"既劝谕读者，又令他喜爱，才能符合众望"。他吸收了亚里士多德的摹仿论的精髓，肯定文学对人的关注，在此基础上提倡文学描摹的典型性、合理性和真实性，人物言谈举止应该符合各自身份，不能有悖于常识和惯例。从中也能看到贺拉斯所秉持的"合式原则"（the principle of decorum）。该原则主张措辞恰如其分，强调风格和内容的一致性，以整体和谐为美。贺拉斯的"合式原则"与他受伊壁鸠鲁主义影响有一定关系，也体现了他的古典品味，综合形成了其理性主义审美观，对后来的新古典主义有重大影响。

古罗马时期最具原创性的理论家是朗吉努斯（Longinus）。他的《论崇高》（*On Sublimity*）既关心修辞与文体，辨析崇高风格的来源，也是一部探讨文学何以伟大的理论著作。朗吉努斯提出崇高文体须具备五要素：思想、情感、修辞、措辞和结构。它们相辅相成构成有机整体，但是其核心是思想与情感，即崇高是"伟大心灵的回声"，以强烈激昂的情感震撼和牵动听众，引领他们进入灵魂升腾的崇高境界。此前古希腊罗马文论的重点是摹仿论，讨论的是文学与世界之间的关系。朗吉努斯是文学表现论的鼻祖，他的天才论、自然论以及超验性倾向在启蒙主义和浪漫主义中得到了强烈的呼应。

同样具有超验性的是普罗提诺（Plotinus）的新柏拉图主义（Neoplatonism）文学观。普罗提诺改造柏拉图的"理式说"，提出世界的本源是无限的永恒的至善的"太一"（the One）。太一因其自身的圆满"流溢"而出，阶梯式地构成了理智层面、灵魂层面和可感世界。他认为人的灵魂仰望理智的理式世界，向往太一的神圣，但是被肉身拖累，易被可感世界的假象所迷惑。在《九章集》（*The Enneads*）中，普罗提诺指出，艺术家的灵魂能够内观到理智美，以它为理想，雕琢粗糙的质料，使其成为美的艺术品。艺术不是对自然物的摹仿，而是对美的理式的再现和分有。普罗提诺的思想融合了理性主义和东方神秘主义，与基督教神学也有共通之处，是中世纪美学与19世纪浪漫主义的思想动力之一。

古希腊、古罗马的文学理论是西方文学理论的源头。其对文学的语言、修辞、文体、文类、社会意义的讨论反复被后来的理论家所引用、辨析、补充和深化。而它所关注的核心问题"文学的本质是什么？"更是成为西方文学理论的核心议题，在之后的两千五百年的漫长时间里，激励着一代代理论家根据各自的社会时代语境和思想史传承，给予新的回应。

主要文本阅读

柏拉图：《理想国》

| 选文简介

柏拉图的《理想国》是一部政治哲学著作，写作特点是对话体。柏拉图以老师苏格拉底为核心人物，通过苏格拉底与雅典人的日常讨论，展现城邦的理想构想。柏拉图意识到文学有巨大影响力，是不能忽视的议题，所以借苏格拉底与格劳孔的对话，对文学的本质和功能进行了阐释。选文的议题反映柏拉图的"艺术的本质是摹仿"的核心观点。柏拉图以"床"为喻，指出工匠造床，描摹的是神创造的唯一范本——"床"的理式；画家画床，以世间之床为底本，是对"理式"隔着两重距离的拙劣再现。描摹世间百态的诗人和画床的画家一样，只会这种等而下之的摹仿。诗人们貌似传达真理，实则靠艺术效果遮蔽无知。而且诗人越是懂得如何取悦观众，越是能操弄情感、败坏人性。柏拉图关注文学与知识、真理和至善的关系，将文学艺术的意义定位在其教化功能。

From *Republic*

Plato (ca. 427-ca. 347 B.C.)

"It's fairly clear," I said, "that all these fine tragedians trace their lineage back to Homer: they're Homer's students and disciples, ultimately. And this makes it difficult for me to say what I have to say, because I've had a kind of fascinated admiration for Homer ever since I was young. Still, we should value truth more than we value any person, so, as I say, I'd better speak out."

"Yes," he said.

"And you'll listen to what I have to say, or rather respond to any questions I ask?"

"Yes. Go ahead and ask them."

"Can you tell me what representation basically is? You see, I don't quite understand its point myself."

"And I suppose I do!" he said....

"...Our usual position is, as you know, that any given plurality of things which have a single name constitutes a single specific type. Is that clear to you?"

"Yes."

"So now let's take any plurality you want. Would it be all right with you if we said that there were, for instance, lots of beds and tables?"

"Of course."

"But these items of furniture comprise only two types—the type of bed and the type of table."

"Yes."

"Now, we also invariably claim that the manufacture of either of these items of furniture involves the craftsman looking to the type and then making the beds or tables (or whatever) which we use. The point is that the type itself is not manufactured by any craftsman. How could it be?"

"It couldn't."

"There's another kind of craftsman too. I wonder what you think of him."

"What kind?"

"He makes everything—all the items which every single manufacturer makes."

"He must be extraordinarily gifted."

"Wait: you haven't heard the half of it yet. It's not just a case of his being able to manufacture all the artefacts there are: every plant too, every creature (himself included), the earth, the heavens, gods, and everything in the heavens and in Hades under the earth—all these are made and created by this one man!"

"He really must be extraordinarily clever," he said.

"Don't you believe me?" I asked. "Tell me, do you doubt that this kind of craftsman could exist under any circumstances, or do you admit the possibility that a person could—in one sense, at least—create all these things? I mean, don't you realize that you yourself could, under certain circumstances, create all these things?"

"What circumstances?" he asked.

"I'm not talking about anything complicated or rare," I said. "It doesn't take long to create the circumstances. The quickest method, I suppose, is to get hold of a mirror and carry it around with you everywhere. You'll soon be creating everything I mentioned a moment ago—the sun and the heavenly bodies, the earth, yourself, and all other creatures, plants, and so on."

"Yes, but I'd be creating appearances, not actual real things," he said.

"That's a good point," I said. "You've arrived just in time to save the argument. I mean, that's presumably the kind of craftsman a painter is. Yes?"

"Of course."

"His creations aren't real, according to you; but do you agree that all the same there's a sense in which even a painter creates a bed?"

"Yes," he said, "he's another one who creates an apparent bed."

"What about a joiner who specializes in making beds? Weren't we saying a short while ago that what he makes is a particular bed, not the type, which is (on our view) the real bed?"

"Yes, we were."

"So if there's no reality to his creation, then it isn't real; it's similar to something real, but it isn't actually real. It looks as though it's wrong to attribute full reality to a joiner's or any artisan's product, doesn't it?"

"Yes," he said, "any serious student of this kind of argument would agree with you."

"It shouldn't surprise us, then, if we find that even these products are obscure when compared with the truth."

"No, it shouldn't."

"Now, what about this representer we're trying to understand? Shall we see if these examples help us?" I asked.

"That's fine by me," he said.

"Well, we've got these three beds. First, there's the real one, and we'd say, I imagine, that it is the product of divine craftsmanship. I mean who else could have made it?"

"No one, surely."

"Then there's the one the joiner makes."

"Yes," he said.

"And then there's the one the painter makes. Yes?"

"Yes, agreed."

"These three, then—painter, joiner, God—are responsible for three different kinds of bed."

"Yes, that's right."

"Now, God has produced only that one real bed. The restriction to only one might have been his own choice, or it might just be impossible for him to make more than one. But God never has, and never could, create two or more such beds."

"Why not?" he asked.

"Even if he were to make only two such beds," I said, "an extra one would emerge, and both the other two would be of that one's type. It, and not the two beds, would be the real bed."

"Right," he said.

"God realized this, I'm sure. He didn't want to be a kind of joiner, making a particular bed: he wanted to be a genuine creator and make a genuine bed. That's why he created a single real one."

"I suppose that's right."

"Shall we call him its progenitor, then, or something like that?"

"Yes, he deserves the name," he said, "since he's the maker of this and every other reality."

"What about a joiner? Shall we call him a manufacturer of beds?"

"Yes."

"And shall we also call a painter a manufacturer and maker of beds and so on?"

"No, definitely not."

"What do you think he does with beds, then?"

"I think the most suitable thing to call him would be a representer of the others' creations," he said.

"Well, in that case," I said, "you're using the term 'representer' for someone who deals with things which are, in fact, two generations away from reality, aren't you?"

"Yes," he said.

"The same goes for tragic playwrights, then, since they're representers: they're two generations away from the throne of truth, and so are all other representers."

"I suppose so."

"Well, in the context of what we're now saying about representation, I've got a further question about painters. Is it, in any given instance, the actual reality that they try to represent, or is it the craftsmen's products?"

"The craftsmen's products," he said.

"Here's another distinction you'd better make: do they try to represent them as they are, or as they appear to be?"

"What do you mean?" he asked.

"I'll tell you. Whether you look at a bed from the side or straight on or whatever, it's still just as much a bed as it ever was, isn't it? I mean, it doesn't actually alter it at all: it just *appears* to be different, doesn't it? And the same goes for anything else you can mention. Yes?"

"Yes," he agreed. "It seems different, but isn't actually."

"So I want you to consider carefully which of these two alternatives painting is designed for in any and every instance. Is it designed to represent the facts of the real world or appearances? Does it represent appearance or truth?"

"Appearance," he said.

"It follows that representation and truth are a considerable distance apart, and a representer is capable of making every product there is only because his contact with things is slight and is restricted to how they look. Consider what a painter does, for instance: we're saying that he doesn't have a clue about shoemaking or joinery, but he'll still paint pictures of artisans working at these and all other areas of expertise, and if he's good at painting he might paint a joiner, have people look at it from far away, and deceive them—if they're children or stupid adults—by making it look as though the joiner were real."

"Naturally."

"I think the important thing to bear in mind about cases like this, Glaucon, is that when people tell us they've met someone who's mastered every craft, and is the world's leading expert in absolutely every branch of human knowledge, we should reply that they're being rather silly. They seem to have met the kind of illusionist who's expert at representation and, thanks to their own inability to evaluate knowledge, ignorance, and representation, to have been so thoroughly taken in as to believe in his omniscience."

"You're absolutely right," he said.

"Now, we'd better investigate tragedy next," I said, "and its guru, Homer, because one does come across the claim that there's no area of expertise, and nothing relevant to human goodness and badness either—and nothing to do with the gods even—that these poets don't understand. It is said that a good poet must understand the issues he writes about, if his writing is to be successful, and that if he didn't understand them, he wouldn't be able to write about them. So we'd better try to decide between the alternatives. Either the people who come across these representational poets are being taken in and are failing to appreciate, when they see their products, that these products are two steps away from reality and that it certainly doesn't take knowledge of the truth to create them (since what they're creating are appearances, not reality); or this view is valid, and in fact good poets are authorities on the subjects most people are convinced they're good at writing about."

"Yes, this definitely needs looking into," he said.

"Well, do you think that anyone who was capable of producing both originals and images would devote his energy to making images, and would make out that this is the best thing he's done with his life?"

"No, I don't."

"I'm sure that if he really knew about the things he was copying in his representations, he'd put far more effort into producing real objects than he would into representations, and would try to leave behind a lot of fine products for people to remember him by, and would dedicate himself to being the recipient rather than the bestower of praise."

"I agree," he said. "He'd gain a lot more prestige and do himself a great deal more good."

"Well, let's concentrate our interrogation of Homer (or any other poet you like) on a single area. Let's not ask him whether he can tell us of any patients cured by any poet in ancient or modern times, as Asclepius cured his patients, or of any students any of them left to continue his work, as Asclepius left his sons. And even these questions grant the possibility that a poet might have had some medical knowledge, instead of merely representing medical terminology. No, let's not bother to ask him about any other areas of expertise either. But we do have a right to ask Homer about the most important and glorious areas he undertakes to expound—warfare, tactics, politics, and human education. Let's ask him, politely, 'Homer, maybe you aren't two steps away from knowing the truth about goodness; maybe you aren't involved in the manufacture of images (which is what we called representation). Perhaps you're actually only one step away, and you do have the ability to recognize which practices—in their private or their public lives—improve people and which ones impair them. But in that case, just as Sparta has its Lycurgus and communities of all different sizes have their various reformers, please tell us which community has you to thank for improvements to its government. Which community attributes the benefits of its good legal code to you? Italy and Sicily name Charondas in this respect, we Athenians name Solon. Which country names you?' Will he have any reply to make?"

"I don't think so," said Glaucon. "Even the Homeridae themselves don't make that claim."

"Well, does history record that there was any war fought in Homer's time whose success depended on his leadership or advice?"

"No."

"Well then, are a lot of ingenious inventions attributed to him, as they are to Thales of Miletus and Anacharsis of Scythia? I mean the kinds of inventions which have practical applications in the arts and crafts and elsewhere. He is, after all, supposed to be good at creating things."

"No, there's not the slightest hint of that sort of thing."

"All right, so there's no evidence of his having been a public benefactor, but what about in private? Is there any evidence that, during his lifetime, he was a mentor to people, and that they used to value him for his teaching and then handed down to their successors a particular Homeric way of life? This is what happened to Pythagoras: he wasn't only held in extremely high regard for his teaching during his lifetime, but his successors even now call their way of life Pythagorean and somehow seem to stand out from all other people."

"No, there's no hint of that sort of thing either," he said. "I mean, Homer's associate Creophylus' cultural attainments would turn out to be even more derisory than his name suggests they are, Socrates, if the stories about Homer are true. You see, Creophylus is said to have more or less disregarded Homer during his lifetime."

"Yes, that *is* what we're told," I agreed. "But, Glaucon, if Homer really had been an educational expert whose products were better people—which is to say, if he had knowledge in this sphere and his abilities were not limited to representation—don't you think he'd have been surrounded by hordes of associates, who would have admired him and valued his company highly?..."

"I don't think anyone could disagree with you, Socrates," he said.

"So shall we classify all poets, from Homer onward, as representers of images of goodness (and of everything else which occurs in their poetry), and claim that they don't have any contact with the truth? The facts are as we said a short while ago: a painter creates an illusory shoemaker, when not only does he not understand anything about shoemaking, but his audience doesn't either. They just base their conclusions on the colors and shapes they can see."

"Yes."

"And I should think we'll say that the same goes for a poet as well: he uses words and phrases to block in some of the colors of each area of expertise, although all he understands is how to represent things in a way which makes other superficial people, who base their conclusions on the words they can hear, think that he's written a really good poem about shoemaking or military command or whatever else it is that he's set to meter, rhythm, and music. It only takes these features to cast this powerful a spell: that's what they're for. But when the poets' work is stripped of its musical hues and expressed in plain words, I think you've seen what kind of impression it gives, so you know what I'm talking about."

"I do," he said.

亚里士多德:《诗学》

选文简介

亚里士多德的《诗学》现存二十六章,讨论了摹仿论、喜剧、悲剧、史诗等议题,其中对悲剧的讨论篇幅最重。亚里士多德指出,悲剧包含六个要素:情节、性格、思想、言语、歌曲和戏景。选文部分重点讨论了悲剧情节的复杂性、悲剧的人物论和悲剧的效果。亚里士多德认为戏剧情节有简单与复杂之分:简单的情节是连续性的和单线程的,变化缺少起伏感;复杂的情节则随着事件的推进,或引发幡然醒悟,或导致惊变突转。好的悲剧往往有复杂的情节。观看悲剧时,看到一个身居高位的人因为某种失误而导致的命运沉降,会唤起观众内心的怜悯与恐惧。亚里士多德的悲剧论承认人类情感的合理性,反对理性对情感的过度压抑,但是他的悲剧观的底色依然是理性主义的,有道德劝谕功能:通过观看帝王将相的人生沉浮,观众获得了对人生更透彻的理解,从而理性看待个人命运。此外,观剧过程中,负面的情感得以宣泄,有利于人们保持心灵的平静。

From *Poetics*

Aristotle (384-322 B.C.)

Among plots, some are simple and some are complex; for the actions, of which plots are representations, are evidently of these kinds. By "simple," I mean an action which is, as we have defined it, continuous in its course and single, where the transformation comes about without reversal or recognition. By "complex," I mean an action as a result of which the transformation is accompanied by a recognition, a reversal or both. These should arise from the actual structure of the plot, so it happens that they arise either by necessity or by probability as a result of the preceding events. It makes a great difference whether these [events] happen because of those or [only] after those.

A reversal is a change of the actions to their opposite, as we said, and that, as we are arguing, in accordance with probability or necessity. E.g. in the *Oedipus*, the man who comes to bring delight to Oedipus, and to rid him of his terror about his mother, does the opposite by revealing who Oedipus is; and in the *Lynceus*, Lynceus is being led to his death, and Danaus follows to kill him, but it comes about as a result of the preceding actions that Danaus is killed and Lynceus is rescued.

A recognition, as the word itself indicates, is a change from ignorance to knowledge, and so to either friendship or enmity, among people defined in relation to good fortune or misfortune. A recognition is finest when it happens at the same time as a reversal, as does the one in the *Oedipus*. There are indeed other [kinds of] recognition. For it can happen in the manner stated regarding inanimate objects and random events; and one can recognize whether someone has done something or not done it. But the sort that most belongs to the plot, i.e. most belongs to the action, is that which we have mentioned: for such a recognition and reversal will contain pity or terror (tragedy is considered to be a representation of actions of this sort), and in addition misfortune and good fortune will come about in the case of such events.

Since recognition is a recognition of people, some recognitions are by one person only of the other, when the identity of one of them is clear; but sometimes there must be a recognition of both persons. E.g. Iphigeneia is recognized by Orestes as a result of her sending the letter, but it requires another recognition for him [to be recognized] by Iphigeneia. These, then, reversal and recognition, are two parts of plot. A third is suffering. Of these, we have discussed reversal and recognition. Suffering is a destructive or painful action, e.g. deaths in full view, agonies, woundings etc....

After what we have just been saying, we must perhaps discuss next what [poets] should aim at and what they should beware of in constructing plots, i.e. how tragedy will achieve its function. Since the construction of the finest tragedy should be not simple but complex, and moreover it should represent terrifying and pitiable events (for this is particular to representation of this sort), first, clearly, it should not show (1) decent men undergoing a change from good fortune to misfortune; for this is neither terrifying nor pitiable, but shocking. Nor [should it show] (2) wicked men [passing] from misfortune to good fortune. This is most untragic of all, as it has nothing of what it should; for it is neither morally satisfying nor pitiable nor terrifying. Nor, again, [should it show] (3) a thoroughly villainous person falling from good fortune into misfortune: such a structure can contain moral satisfaction, but not pity or terror, for the former is [felt] for a person undeserving of his misfortune, and the latter for a person like [ourselves]. Consequently the outcome will be neither pitiable nor terrifying.

There remains, then, the person intermediate between these. Such a person is one who neither is superior [to us] in virtue and justice, nor undergoes a change to misfortune because of vice and wickedness, but because of some error, and who is one of those people with a great reputation and a good fortune, e.g. Oedipus, Thyestes and distinguished men from similar families. Necessarily, then, a plot that is fine is single rather than (as some say) double, and involves a change not from misfortune to good fortune, but conversely, from good fortune to misfortune, not because of wickedness but because of a great error by a person like the one mentioned, or by a better person rather than a worse one.

An indication [that this is so] is what is coming about. At first the poets recounted stories at random, but now the finest tragedies are constructed around a few households, e.g. about Alcmeon, Oedipus, Orestes, Meleager, Thyestes, Telephus and the others, who happen to have had dreadful things done to them, or to have done them. So the tragedy which is finest according to the [principles of the] art results from this structure....

The second[-best] structure is that which some say is first, the [tragedy] which has a double structure like the *Odyssey*, and which ends in opposite ways for the better and worse [persons]. This [structure] would seem to be first because of the weakness of the audiences; the poets follow the spectators, composing to suit their wishes. But this is not the pleasure [that comes] from tragedy, but is more particular to comedy. There the bitterest enemies in the story, e.g. Orestes and Aegisthus, exit as friends at the conclusion, and nobody kills anyone else.

That which is terrifying and pitiable can arise from spectacle, but it can also arise from the structure of the incidents itself; this is superior and belongs to a better poet. For the plot should be constructed in such a way that, even without seeing it, someone who hears about the incidents will shudder and feel pity at the outcome, as someone may feel upon hearing the plot of the *Oedipus*. To produce this by means of spectacle is less artful and requires lavish production. Those [poets] who use spectacle to produce what is only monstrous and not terrifying have nothing in common with tragedy. For we should not seek every [kind of] pleasure from tragedy, but [only] the sort which is particular to it. Since the poet should use representation to produce the pleasure [arising] from pity and terror, it is obvious that this must be put into the incidents.

Let us consider, then, what sorts of occurrence arouse dread or compassion in us. These sorts of action against each another necessarily take place between friends, enemies or people who are neither. If it is one enemy [who does the action] to another, there is nothing pitiable, whether he does it or is [only] about to do it, except in the suffering itself. Nor [is it pitiable] if the people are neither [friends nor enemies]. But when suffering happens within friendly relationships, e.g. brother against brother, son against father, mother against son or son against mother, when someone kills someone else, is about to, or does something else of the same sort—these are what must he sought after.

[The poet] cannot undo the traditional stories, I mean e.g. that Clytemnestra is killed by Orestes or Eriphyle by Alcmeon; but he should invent for himself, i.e. use the inherited [stories], well. Let me explain more clearly what I mean by "well."

The action may arise (1) in the way the old [poets] made people act knowingly, i.e. in full knowledge, just as Euripides too made Medea kill her children. Or (2) they may be going to act, in full knowledge, but not do it. Or (3) they may act, but do the dreadful deed in ignorance, and then recognize the friendly relationship later, as Sophocles' Oedipus [does]. This is outside the drama; but [they may do the deed] in the tragedy itself, as Astydamas' Alcmeon or Telegonus in the *Wounded Odysseus* [do]. Again, fourth beside these [ways] is (4) to be about to do something deadly in ignorance [of one's relationship], but to recognize it before doing so. Beside these there is no other way; for the act is necessarily either done or not done, and those who act either have knowledge or do not.

Among these [ways], (1) to be about to act in full knowledge, but not do, it is the worst. For this is shocking and also not tragic, as there is no suffering. For this reason nobody composes in this way, except rarely, e.g. Haemon against Creon in the *Antigone*. (2) To act is second[-worst]. (3) To act in ignorance, but recognize [the relationship] afterward, is better. This has nothing shocking in it, and the recognition is astonishing. (4) The last [way] is the best. I mean e.g. the *Cresphontes*, where Merope is about to kill her son, but does not kill him and recognizes him; the *Iphigeneia*, where [it is the same for] the sister and her brother; and the *Helle*, where the son is about to hand over his mother but recognizes her. This is why, as we said a while ago, tragedies are not about many families. [The poets] sought to produce this sort [of effect] in their plots, and discovered how to not by art but by chance; so they are obliged to concern themselves with those households in which such sufferings have happened.

As for the structure of the incidents, and what sort of plots there should be, let this suffice.

Regarding characters, there are four things at which [the poet] should aim.

(1) First and foremost, the characters should be good. [The tragedy] will have character if, as we said, the speech or the action makes obvious a decision of whatever sort; it will have a good character, if it makes obvious a good decision. [Good character] can exist in every class [of person]; for a woman can be good, and a slave can, although the first of these [classes] may be inferior and the second wholly worthless.

(2) Second, [they should be] appropriate. It is possible to be manly in character, but it is not appropriate for a woman to be so manly or clever.

(3) Third, [the character should be life-]like. This is different from making the character good and appropriate in the way already stated.

(4) Fourth, [the character should be] consistent. If the model for the representation is somebody inconsistent, and such a character is intended, even so it should be consistently inconsistent....

In the characters too, exactly as in the structure of the incidents, [the poet] ought always to seek what is either necessary or probable, so that it is either necessary or probable that a person of such-and-such a sort say or do things of the same sort, and it is either necessary or probable that this [incident] happen after that one.

It is obvious that the solutions of plots too should come about as a result of the plot itself, and not from a contrivance, as in the *Medea* and in the passage about sailing home in the *Iliad*. A contrivance must be used for matters outside the drama—either previous events which are beyond human knowledge, or later ones that need to be foretold or announced. For we grant that the gods can see everything. There should be nothing improbable in the incidents; otherwise, it should be outside the tragedy, e.g. that in Sophocles' *Oedipus*.

Since tragedy is a representation of people who are better than we are, [the poet] should emulate the good portrait-painters. In rendering people's particular shape, while making them [life-]like, they paint them as finer [than they are]. So too the poet, as he represents people who are angry, lazy, or have other such traits, should make them such in their characters, [but] decent [too]. E.g. Homer [made] Achilles good as well as an example of stubbornness. [The poet] should guard against these things, as well as against [causing] reactions contrary to those that necessarily follow from the art of poetry.

贺拉斯：《诗艺》

选文简介

贺拉斯的《诗艺》是致罗马贵族皮索父子的诗体书信，讨论了创作的素材选择、规范，以及创新性和人物塑造等文学议题，也讨论了写作的责任和艺术追求等有关作家养成的议题。他反对语言的炫技，认为有光彩的思想更为重要，提倡以判断力为指导的创作，鼓励写作者多读经典，观察社会，积累人生经验，勤于练笔写作，让天分和勤奋相辅相成。选文译自《诗艺》开篇。贺拉斯认为整体的和谐会为作品增色；描写应注重恰到好处，得体妥帖；选词应具时代性；刻画人物时，须捕捉年龄、性别和社会身份的典型特征。以上观点遵循古典原则，强调"合式"的理性；亦可见现实主义色彩，重视对生活的观察和再现。贺拉斯认为好的作品不能从艺术的空想中诞生，它需要作家深入到自己的时代之中，了解社会上具有鲜明特点的各类人物，用有生命力的语言刻画生活世界。

From *The Art of Poetry*

Horace (65-8 B.C.)

Unity and Consistency

Imagine a painter who wanted to combine a horse's neck with a human head, and then clothe a miscellaneous collection of limbs with various kinds of feathers, so that what started out at the top as a beautiful woman ended in a hideously ugly fish. If you were invited, as friends, to the private view, could you help laughing? Let me tell you, my Piso friends, a book whose different features are made up at random like a sick man's dreams, with no unified form to have a head or a tail, is exactly like that picture.

"Painters and poets have always enjoyed recognized rights to venture on what they will." Yes, we know; indeed, we ask and grant this permission turn and turn about. But it doesn't mean that fierce and gentle can be united, snakes paired with birds or lambs with tigers.

Serious and ambitious designs often have a purple patch or two sewn on to them just to make a good show at a distance—a description of a grove and altar of Diana, the meanderings of a stream running through pleasant meads, the River Rhine, the rainbow: but the trouble is, it's not the place for them.

Maybe you know how to do a picture of a cypress tree? What's the good of that, if the man who is paying for the picture is a desperate ship-wrecked mariner swimming to safety? The job began as a wine-jar: the wheel runs around—why is that a tub that's coming out? In short, let it be what you will, but let it be simple and unified.

Skill Needed to Avoid Faults

Most of us poets—father and worthy sons—are deceived by appearances of correctness. I try to be concise, but I become obscure; my aim is smoothness, but sinews and spirit fail; professions of grandeur end in bombast; the overcautious who fear the storm creep along the ground. Similarly, the writer who wants to give fantastic variety to his single theme paints a dolphin in his woods and a wild boar in his sea. If art is wanting, the flight from blame leads to faults. The poorest smith near the School of Aemilius will reproduce nails and mimic soft hair in bronze, though he has no luck with the over-all effect of his work, because he won't know how to organize the whole. If I were anxious to put anything together, I would as soon be that man as I would live with a mis-shapen nose when my black eyes and black hair had made me a beauty.

You writers must choose material equal to your powers. Consider long what your shoulders will bear and what they will refuse. The man who chooses his subject with full control will not be abandoned by eloquence or lucidity of arrangement.

As to arrangement: its excellence and charm, unless I'm very wrong, consist in saying at this moment what needs to be said at this moment, and postponing and temporarily omitting a great many things. An author who has undertaken a poem must be choosy—cling to one point and spurn another.

As to words: if you're delicate and cautious in arranging them, you will give distinction to your style if an ingenious combination makes a familiar word new. If it happens to be necessary to denote hidden mysteries by novel symbols, it will fall to you to invent terms the Cethegi in their loincloths never heard—and the permission will be granted if you accept it modestly—and, moreover, your new and freshly invented words will receive credit, if sparingly derived from the Greek springs. Is the Roman to give Caecilius and Plautus privileges denied to Virgil and Varius? Why am I unpopular if I can make a few acquisitions, when the tongue of Cato and Ennius so enriched their native language and produced such a crop of new names for things?

Fashions in Words

It always has been, and always will be, lawful to produce a word stamped with the current mark. As woods change in leaf as the seasons slide on, and the first leaves fall, so the old generation of words dies out, and the newly born bloom and are strong like young men. We and our works are a debt owed to death. Here a land-locked sea protects fleets from the North wind—a royal achievement; here an old barren marsh where oars were piled feeds neighboring cities and feels the weight of the plough; here again a river gives up a course that damaged the crops and learns a better way. But whatever they are, all mortal works will die; and still less can the glory and charm of words endure for a long life. Many words which have fallen will be born again, many now in repute will fall if usage decrees: for in her hand is the power and the law and the canon of speech.

Meter and Subject

Histories of kings and generals, dreadful

wars: it was Homer who showed in what meter these could be narrated. Lines unequally yoked in pairs formed the setting first for lamentations, then for the expression of a vow fulfilled though who first sent these tiny "elegies" into the world is a grammarians' quarrel and still *sub judice*. Madness armed Archilochus with its own iambus; that too was the foot that the comic sock and tragic buskin held, because it was suitable for dialogue, able to subdue the shouts of the mob, and intended by nature for a life of action. To the lyre, the Muse granted the celebration of gods and the children of gods, victorious boxers, winning race-horses, young men's love, and generous wine. If I have neither the ability nor the knowledge to keep the duly assigned functions and tones of literature, why am I hailed as a poet? Why do I prefer to be ignorant than learn, out of sheer false shame? A comic subject will not be set out in tragic verse; likewise, the Banquet of Thyestes disdains being told in poetry of the private kind, that borders on the comic stage. Everything must keep the appropriate place to which it was allotted.

Nevertheless, comedy does sometimes raise her voice, and angry Chremes perorates with swelling eloquence. Often too Telephus and Peleus in tragedy lament in prosaic language, when they are both poor exiles and throw away their bombast and words half a yard long, if they are anxious to touch the spectator's heart with their complaint.

Emotion and Character

It is not enough for poetry to be beautiful; it must also be pleasing and lead the hearer's mind wherever it will. The human face smiles in sympathy with smilers and comes to the help of those that weep. If you want me to cry, mourn first yourself; *then* your misfortunes will hurt me, Telephus and Peleus. If your words are given you ineptly, I shall fall asleep or laugh. Sad words suit a mournful countenance, threatening words an angry one; sportive words are for the playful, serious for the grave. For nature first shapes us within for any state of fortune—gives us pleasure or drives us to anger or casts us down to the ground with grievous sorrow and pains us—and then expresses the emotions through the medium of the tongue. If the words are out of tune with the speaker's fortunes, the knights and infantry of Rome will raise a cackle. It will make a lot of difference whether the speaker is a god or a hero, an old man of ripe years or a hot youth, an influential matron or a hard-working nurse, a traveling merchant or the tiller of a green farm, a Colchian or an Assyrian, one nurtured at Thebes or at Argos.

Choice and Handling of Myth

Either follow tradition or invent a consistent story. If as a writer you are representing Achilles with all his honors, let him be active, irascible, implacable, and fierce; let him say "the laws are not for me" and set no limit to the claims that arms can make. Let Medea be proud and indomitable, Ino full of tears, Ixion treacherous, Io never at rest, Orestes full of gloom. On the other hand, if you are putting something untried on the stage and venturing to shape a new character, let it be maintained to the end as it began and be true to itself....

Let me tell you what I and the public both want, if you're hoping for an applauding audience that will wait for the curtain and keep its seat until the epilogue-speaker says "Pray clap your hands." You must mark the manners of each time of life, and assign the appropriate part to changing natures and ages. The child, just able to repeat words and planting his steps on the ground with confidence, is eager to play with his contemporaries, gets in and out of a temper without much cause, and changes hour by hour. The beardless youth, his tutor at last out of the way, enjoys his horses and dogs and the grass of the sunny Park. Moulded like wax into vice, he is surly to would-be advisers, slow to provide for necessities, prodigal of money, up in the air, eager, and quick to abandon the objects of his sudden love. Soon interests change: the grown man's mind pursues wealth and influential connections, is enslaved to honor, and avoids doing anything he may soon be trying to change. Many distresses surround the old man. He is acquisitive, and, poor man, daren't put his hand on what he has laid up; he is afraid to use it. He goes about his business timidly and coldly, procrastinating, letting things drag on in hope, lazy yet greedy of his future; he is awkward and grumbling, given to praising the days when he was a boy and to criticizing and finding fault with his juniors. Years as they come bring many blessings with them, and as they go take many away. To save yourself giving a young man an old man's role or a boy a grown man's, remember that your character should always remain faithful to what is associated with his age and suits it.

朗吉努斯:《论崇高》

选文简介

《论崇高》是断简残篇，据考证有三分之一篇幅的佚失。作者朗吉努斯的生平也缺乏明晰的历史记录。从作品提供的线索看，朗吉努斯生活在公元1世纪前后。他在《论崇高》中批评当时的社会风气：人们重物质享乐，安于现状；加之帝国制度的政治管控严苛，人们缺乏进取精神，思想怠惰，文化活力不足，与希腊时代形成鲜明对比。朗吉努斯反对将这个时期文学的沉沦完全归咎于时代精神使然，认为人可以超越时代，在艺术创作中摆脱思想奴役和自我束缚。从选文中可以看出，朗吉努斯提倡崇高的文风，鼓励人们向伟大作家学习，向壮阔自然学习，以伟大的思想和高贵而激昂的情感为其精神内核，以精当的措辞和比喻等修辞为文学手法，创作出令人升腾的崇高作品，追求艺术、思想与人生的更高境界。

From *On Sublimity*

Longinus (first century A.D.)

Preface

My dear Postumius Terentianus,

You will recall that when we were reading together Caecilius' monograph *On Sublimity*, we felt that it was inadequate to its high subject, and failed to touch the essential points. Nor indeed did it appear to offer the reader much practical help, though this ought to be a writer's principal object. Two things are required of any textbook: first, that it should explain what its subject is; second, and more important, that it should explain how and by what methods we can achieve it....

You have urged me to set down a few notes on sublimity for your own use. Let us then consider whether there is anything in my observations which may be thought useful to public men. You must help me, my friend, by giving your honest opinion in detail, as both your natural candor and your friendship with me require. It was well said that what man has in common with the gods is "doing good and telling the truth."

Your education dispenses me from any long preliminary definition. Sublimity is a kind of eminence or excellence of discourse. It is the source of the distinction of the very greatest poets and prose writers and the means by which they have given eternal life to their own fame. For grandeur produces ecstasy rather than persuasion in the hearer; and the combination of wonder and astonishment always proves superior to the merely persuasive and pleasant. This is because persuasion is on the whole something we can control, whereas amazement and wonder exert invincible power and force and get the better of every hearer. Experience in invention and ability to order and arrange material cannot be detected in single passages; we begin to appreciate them only when we see the whole context. Sublimity, on the other hand, produced at the right moment, tears everything up like a whirlwind, and exhibits the orator's whole power at a single blow.

Your own experience will lead you to these and similar considerations. The question from which I must begin is whether there is in fact an art of sublimity or profundity. Some people think it is a complete mistake to reduce things like this to technical rules. Greatness, the argument runs, is a natural product, and does not come by teaching. The only art is to be born like that. They believe moreover that natural products are very much weakened by being reduced to the bare bones of a textbook.

In my view, these arguments can be refuted by considering three points:

(1) Though nature is on the whole a law unto herself in matters of emotion and elevation, she is not a random force and does not work altogether without method.

(2) She is herself in every instance a first and primary element of creation, but it is method that is competent to provide and contribute quantities and appropriate occasions for everything, as well as perfect correctness in training and application.

(3) Grandeur is particularly dangerous when left on its own, unaccompanied by knowledge, unsteadied, unballasted, abandoned to mere impulse and ignorant temerity. It often needs the curb as well as the spur.

What Demosthenes said of life in general is true also of literature: good fortune is the greatest of blessings, but good counsel comes next, and the lack of it destroys the other also. In literature, nature occupies the place of good fortune, and art that of good counsel. Most important of all, the very fact that some things in literature depend on nature alone can itself be learned only from art....

The Five Sources of Sublimity; The Plan of the Book

There are, one may say, five most productive sources of sublimity. (Competence in speaking is assumed as a common foundation for all five; nothing is possible without it.)

(1) The first and most important is the power to conceive great thoughts; I defined this in my work on Xenophon.

(2) The second is strong and inspired emotion. (These two sources are for the most part natural; the remaining three involve art.)

(3) Certain kinds of figures. (These may be divided into figures of thought and figures of speech.)

(4) Noble diction. This has as subdivisions choice of words and the use of metaphorical and artificial language.

(5) Finally, to round off the whole list, dignified and elevated word-arrangement.

Let us now examine the points which come under each of these heads.

I must first observe, however, that Caecilius has omitted some of the five—emotion, for example. Now if he thought that sublimity and emotion were one and the same thing and always existed and developed together, he was wrong. Some emotions, such as pity, grief, and fear, are found divorced from sublimity and with a low effect. Conversely, sublimity often occurs apart from emotion. Of the innumerable examples of this I select Homer's bold account of the Aloadae:

> Ossa upon Olympus they sought to heap; and on Ossa
> Pelion with its shaking forest, to make a path to heaven—
> and the even more impressive sequel—
> and they would have finished their work...

In orators, encomia and ceremonial or exhibition pieces always involve grandeur and sublimity, though they are generally devoid of emotion. Hence those orators who are best at conveying emotion are least good at encomia, and conversely the experts at encomia are not conveyers of emotion. On the other hand, if Caecilius thought that emotion had no contribution to make to sublimity and therefore thought it not worth mentioning, he was again completely wrong. I should myself have no hesitation in saying that there is nothing so productive of grandeur as noble emotion in the right place. It inspires and possesses our words with a kind of madness and divine spirit.

(1) Greatness of Thought

The first source, natural greatness, is the most important. Even if it is a matter of endowment rather than acquisition, we must, so far as is possible, develop our minds in the direction of greatness and make them always pregnant with noble thoughts. You ask how this can be done. I wrote elsewhere something like this: "Sublimity is the echo of a noble mind." This is why a mere idea, without verbal expression, is sometimes admired for its nobility—just as Ajax's silence in the Vision of the Dead is grand and indeed more sublime than any words could have been. First then we must state where sublimity comes from: the orator must not have low or ignoble thoughts. Those whose thoughts and habits are trivial and servile all their lives cannot possibly produce anything admirable or worthy of eternity. Words will be great if thoughts are weighty....

Digression: Genius versus Mediocrity

...

What then was the vision which inspired those divine writers who disdained exactness of detail and aimed at the greatest prizes in literature? Above all else, it was the understanding that nature made man to be no humble or lowly creature, but brought him into life and into the universe as into a great festival, to be both a spectator and an enthusiastic contestant in its competitions. She implanted in our minds from the start an irresistible desire for anything which is great and, in relation to ourselves, supernatural.

The universe therefore is not wide enough for the range of human speculation and intellect. Our thoughts often travel beyond the boundaries of our surroundings. If anyone wants to know what we were born for, let him look around at life and contemplate the splendor, grandeur, and beauty in which it everywhere abounds. It is a natural inclination that leads us to admire not the little streams, however pellucid and however useful, but the Nile, the Danube, the Rhine, and above all the Ocean. Nor do we feel so much awe before the little flame we kindle, because it keeps its light clear and pure, as before the fires of heaven, though they are often obscured. We do not think our flame more worthy of admiration than the craters of Etna, whose eruptions bring up rocks and whole hills out of the depths, and sometimes pour forth rivers of the earth-born, spontaneous fire. A single comment fits all these examples: the useful and necessary are readily available to man, it is the unusual that always excites our wonder.

So when we come to great geniuses in literature—where, by contrast, grandeur is not divorced from service and utility—we have to conclude that such men, for all their faults, tower far above mortal stature. Other literary qualities prove their users to be human; sublimity raises us toward the spiritual greatness of god. Freedom from error does indeed save us from blame, but it is only greatness that wins admiration. Need I add that every one of those great men redeems all his mistakes many times over by a single sublime stroke? Finally, if you picked out and put together all the mistakes in Homer, Demosthenes, Plato, and all the other really great men, the total would be found to be a minute fraction of the successes which those heroic figures have to their credit.

思考题

1. 柏拉图认为艺术的本质是什么？他如何利用画家画床的例子来解释他的立场？
2. 柏拉图指出，虽然人人爱荷马，但是荷马不配享有崇高的声誉，不配做雅典城邦的精神导师。柏拉图为什么这样说？你认同他的观点吗？
3. 亚里士多德如何区分简单情节和复杂情节？他为什么主张好的悲剧其情节应具有复杂性？他认为悲剧主人公应该具备什么样的特点？
4. 贺拉斯推崇文学的"合式原则"。请结合选文谈及的结构、语言、人物塑造等议题，对其进行解释。
5. 朗吉努斯如何定义崇高？他认为崇高有哪些要素？其中最重要的要素是什么？

讨论题

1. 柏拉图的文学观和亚里士多德的文学观都属于摹仿论范畴，但是彼此存在明显差异。请在阅读选文以及查阅课外资料的基础上，讨论两者的异同，简单分析原因。
2. 柏拉图、亚里士多德、贺拉斯和朗吉努斯都认为文学应具有教化的功能。请从中选取两位理论家，对他们的文学教化观进行比较。

补充文本选摘与评述

高尔吉亚：《海伦颂》
From "Encomium of Helen"

Gorgias (ca. 483-376 B.C.)

If speech (*logos*) persuaded and deluded her mind, even against this it is not hard to defend her or free her from blame, as follows: speech is a powerful master and achieves the most divine feats with the smallest and least evident body. It can stop fear, relieve pain, create joy, and increase pity. How this is so, I shall show; and I must demonstrate this to my audience to change their opinion.

Poetry (*poiēsis*) as a whole I deem and name "speech (*logos*) with meter." To its listeners poetry brings a fearful shuddering, a tearful pity, and a grieving desire, while through its words the soul feels its own feelings for good and bad fortune in the affairs and lives of others. Now, let me move from one argument to another. Sacred incantations with words inject pleasure and reject pain, for in associating with the opinion of the mind, the power of an incantation enchants, persuades, and alters it through bewitchment. The twin arts of witchcraft and magic have been discovered, and these are illusions of mind and delusions of judgment....What reason is there, then, why Helen did not go just as unwillingly under the influence of speech as if she were seized by the violence of violators? For persuasion expelled her thought—persuasion, which has the same power, but not the same form as compulsion (*anankē*). A speech persuaded a soul that was persuaded, and forced it to be persuaded by what was said and to consent to what was done. The persuader, then, is the wrongdoer, because he compelled her, while she who was persuaded is wrongly blamed, because she was compelled by the speech. To see that persuasion, when added to speech, indeed molds the mind as it wishes, one must first study the arguments of astronomers, who replace opinion with opinion: displacing one but implanting another, they make incredible, invisible matters apparent to the eyes of opinion. Second, compulsory debates with words, where a single speech to a large crowd pleases and persuades because written with skill (*technē*), not spoken with truth.

昆体良：《演讲术原理》
From *Institutio Oratoria*

Quintilian (ca. 30/35-ca. 100)

Since then the orator is a good man, and such goodness cannot be conceived as existing apart from virtue, virtue, despite the fact that it is in part derived from certain natural impulses, will require to be perfected by instruction. The orator must above all things devote his attention to the formation of moral character and must acquire a complete knowledge of all that is just and honorable. For without this knowledge no one can be either a good man or skilled in speaking, unless indeed we agree with those who regard morality as intuitive and as owing nothing to instruction: indeed they go so far as to acknowledge that handicrafts, not excluding even those which are most despised among them, can only be acquired by the result of teaching, whereas virtue, which of all gifts to man is that which makes him most near akin to the immortal gods, comes to him without search or effort, as a natural concomitant of birth. But can the man who does not know what abstinence is, claim to be truly abstinent? or brave, if he has never purged his soul of the fears of pain, death and superstition? or just, if he has never, in language approaching that of philosophy, discussed the nature of virtue and justice, or of the laws that have been given to mankind by nature or established among individual peoples and nations? What a contempt it argues for such themes to regard them as being so easy of comprehension! However, I pass this by; for I am sure that no one with the least smattering of literary culture will have the slightest hesitation in agreeing with me....

...On the other hand, there is no need for an orator to swear allegiance to any one philosophic code. For he has a greater and nobler aim, to which he directs all his efforts with as much zeal as if he were a candidate for office, since he is to be made perfect not only in the glory of a virtuous life, but in that of eloquence as well. He will consequently select as his models of eloquence all the greatest masters of oratory, and will choose the noblest precepts and the most direct road to virtue as the means for the formation of an upright character. He will neglect no form of exercise, but will devote special attention to those which are of the highest and fairest nature. For what subject can be found more fully adapted to a rich and weighty eloquence than the topics of virtue, politics, providence, the origin of the soul and friendship? The themes which tend to elevate mind and language alike are questions such as what things are truly good, what means there are of assuaging fear, restraining the passions and lifting us and the soul that came from heaven clear of the delusions of the common herd.

普罗提诺：《九章集》
From *The Enneads*

Plotinus (ca. 204/205-270)

On the Intellectual Beauty

It is a principle with us that one who has attained to the vision of the Intellectual Beauty and grasped the beauty of the Authentic Intellect will be able also to come to understand the Father and Transcendent of that Divine Being. It concerns us, then, to try to see and say, for ourselves and as far as such matters may be told, how the Beauty of the divine Intellect and of the Intellectual Cosmos may be revealed to contemplation.

Let us go to the realm of magnitudes:— suppose two blocks of stone lying side by side: one is unpatterned, quite untouched by art; the other has been minutely wrought by the craftsman's hands into some statue of god or man, a Grace or a Muse, or if a human being, not a portrait but a creation in which the sculptor's art has concentrated all loveliness.

Now it must be seen that the stone thus brought under the artist's hand to the beauty of form is beautiful not as stone—for so the crude block would be as pleasant—but in virtue of the Form or Idea introduced by the art. This form is not in the material; it is in the designer before ever it enters the stone; and the artificer holds it not by his equipment of eyes and hands but by his participation in his art. The beauty, therefore, exists in a far higher state in the art; for it does not come over integrally into the work; that original beauty is not transferred; what comes over is a derivative and a minor: and even that shows itself upon the statue not integrally and with entire realization of intention but only in so far as it has subdued the resistance of the material.

Art, then, creating in the image of its own nature and content, and working by the Idea or Reason-Principle of the beautiful object it is to produce, must itself be beautiful in a far higher and purer degree since it is the seat and source of that beauty, indwelling in the art, which must naturally be more complete than any comeliness of the external. In the degree in which the beauty is diffused by entering into matter, it is so much the weaker than that concentrated in unity; everything that reaches outward is the less for it, strength less strong, heat less hot, every power less potent, and so beauty less beautiful.

选文评述

这里摘选的三篇选文，分属古希腊和古罗马两个时期，前两篇的主题是主要文本阅读部分未深入论及的修辞术。第一篇《海伦颂》是古希腊文学理论的发端作品之一。高尔吉亚在文中为因引发特洛伊之战而饱受诟病的海伦辩护，指出如果她的私奔是被巧言所说服，这不是她的过错，因为技巧高超的演讲术可以操纵思想，对人进行精神劫持。高尔吉亚的潜台词是：不存在绝对真理，只存在被语言确立的立场。这是柏拉图十分反对的观点。为此他写了《高尔吉亚篇》，托身苏格拉底，假想与高尔吉亚论战，批评修辞术是舌辩之术，空有华丽外表，没有价值内涵。

第二篇选自《演讲术原理》。昆体良融合高尔吉亚和柏拉图的观点，既重视修辞术中语言的力量，同时，为了回应柏拉图的批评，提出德性是修辞术的灵魂。如果要讲的是公正、勇气等重要议题，唯有具备这些品质的人才能讲出深度，且拥有打动人心的真诚。

第三篇选文出自《九章集》，可以和柏拉图的《理想国》选文进行对照阅读。作者普罗提诺是古罗马哲学家、新柏拉图学派的创立者。他不关注修辞术等与文学实践密切相关的议题，而是继续追问柏拉图式的问题——什么是艺术的本质？他指出，美不在质料里，而在创作者的脑海中，它源自灵魂所分有的理智美。这种理智美属于更高的神的境界，是纯粹而完满的。虽然普罗提诺认为人类受灵魂的局限，面对质料的制约，无法在艺术品中彻底再现理智美，但他对艺术家的能动性和价值予以肯定，认为艺术家不是柏拉图所批评的不懂装懂的摹仿者，而是将美赋予质料的创造者。

关键术语释例

1. **摹仿（mimesis）**："摹仿"是文学和美学的基础概念，体现艺术反映论的立场，本质更接近于"再现"与"表征"，不能被简单地理解为"模仿"和"复制"。对于艺术描摹与反映的是什么，理论家们的见解不同。柏拉图认为艺术只能呈现变动中的现实世界的浮影，无法反映永恒的"理式"，所以他对艺术摹仿持否定态度。亚里士多德的摹仿论则主张艺术可以再现行动中的人，反映他们在世俗世界中的命运，由此肯定了摹仿论的现实主义意义。德国学者埃里希·奥尔巴赫的《摹仿论》是20世纪最重要的摹仿论理论著作，对从荷马史诗、《圣经》到《到灯塔去》的西方文学的摹仿论传统进行了深入细致的阐释。

2. **情节（plot）**：在叙事作品中，"情节"是事件展开时所遵循的顺序。率先关注情节概念的理论家是亚里士多德。他在《诗学》中指出情节是一系列相关事件的有机组合，它是悲剧的灵魂，将人物的行动和戏剧中的事件统合成连贯的整体。英国小说家E. M. 福斯特在1927年出版的《小说面面观》（*Aspects of the Novel*）中区分了"情节"与"故事"（story）的差异：故事依从自然时间，呈现事件的完整顺序；情节则是按照因果律对事件的进程所进行的重构。所以，"国王死了，然后王后死了"，这是故事；而"国王死了，然后王后死于哀伤"，这是情节。当代文论对情节的讨论更为深入，涉及对情节的要素、情节的驱动力、情节中的叙事顺序、情节的连贯性原则、传统情节论与后现代主义元小说的关系等的探讨。

推荐书目

Bychkov, Oleg, and Anne Sheppard. *Greek and Roman Aesthetics*. Cambridge: Cambridge University Press, 2010.

Ford, Andrew. *The Origins of Criticism: Literary Culture and Poetic Theory in Classical Greece*. Princeton: Princeton University Press, 2002.

Highet, Gilbert. *The Classical Tradition: Greek and Roman Influences on Western Literature*. Oxford: Oxford University Press, 2015.

Kennedy, George A. *The Cambridge History of Literary Criticism. Vol. 1: Classical Criticism*. Cambridge: Cambridge University Press, 1990.

Laird, Andrew. *Ancient Literary Criticism*. Oxford: Oxford University Press, 2006.

Levin, Susan B. *The Ancient Quarrel Between Philosophy and Poetry Revisited: Plato and the Greek Literary Tradition*. Oxford: Oxford University Press, 2000.

Russell, D. A. *Criticism in Antiquity*. Berkeley: University of California Press, 1981.

陈中梅:《柏拉图诗学和艺术思想研究》。北京:商务印书馆,1999年。

第二章
从中世纪、文艺复兴到新古典主义

概述

欧洲中世纪的时间跨度很长,始于5世纪后期西罗马帝国灭亡,以15世纪中期东罗马帝国灭亡为其尾声。因为中世纪居于古代和近代之间,夹在古希腊罗马古典文明的辉煌和文艺复兴的璀璨之间,长期以来,人们对中世纪的刻板印象是它受宗教禁锢,是停滞僵化的"黑暗时代"。事实上,它不是历史的停滞期,而是在变化生成之中。没有中世纪,就不可能有近现代欧洲的强盛。中世纪早期(5世纪到10世纪),欧洲经历蛮族入侵、帝国分裂的战乱动荡之后,社会日趋稳定,封建制度渐见雏形;中期(10世纪到13世纪)社会繁荣,人口增加,财富汇聚,城市兴起,教育振兴,中产阶级出现;晚期(13世纪到15世纪)虽有危机重重,如黑死病肆虐、英法陷入百年战争、罗马教廷的权势受到挑战,但社会经济、生产技术、高等教育等加速发展,为近代欧洲腾飞做好了准备。

中世纪对欧洲文化的贡献也不应被低估。这一时期确立了以基督教为中心的西方信仰体系,在哲学和神学领域涌现出奥古斯丁(St. Augustine)、阿奎那(Thomas Aquinas)、司各脱(John Duns Scotus)等代表人物。这一时期在思想史上的意义也十分重大,对信仰、理性、自然、自由意志等议题的讨论融入了欧洲文明的基因。在学术领域,中世纪继承了拉丁传统,重视古典学研究,由语法学、修辞学和逻辑学"三大学问",加之天文、几何、算数和音乐四科实践技艺,组成了"自由七艺"的人文学术基础。中世纪文论所携带着的正是以上神学、哲学和古典学的多重印痕。

中世纪的诗学研究以注释、总结、补充等方式围绕古典传统开展延伸性讨论。早期富尔根蒂尤(Fabius Planciades Fulgentius)在《维吉尔作品的道德哲学注释》中通过注释的方式,结合语文学和修辞学,细读维吉尔《埃涅阿斯纪》中的历史隐喻，分析主人公的命运如何呼应人类从诞生、成长到死亡的历程，以人性为桥梁，对接古典传统和基督教传统。加洛林文艺复兴时期的阿尔昆（Alcuin）在《修辞学》中对西塞罗和昆体良为代表的古罗马时代的修辞术进行了综合总结，加入了修辞术与基督教美德相结合的内容。文索夫的杰弗里（Geoffrey of Vinsauf）撰写了《新诗学》，其新意之一是突破贺拉斯《诗艺》的古典摹仿论，主张带有新柏拉图主义色彩的创作论，先由心灵勾勒出诗歌的完整结构，再用语言进行表达。因此，诗歌的素材安排不必因循自然顺序，艺术次序比自然次序更高雅。需要注意的是，杰弗里虽然颠倒了摹仿论中艺术和自然谁离真理更近的排序，将艺术置于自然之前，肯定艺术自有规则，但是他要求心灵构筑"完整的结构"，这种理念先于艺术的创作论，仍属于中世纪古典传统的理性论。

中世纪的世界以信仰为中心，因此文论的另一核心命题是如何在基督教框架下理解文学。拉丁教父时代的思想集大成者奥古斯丁受柏拉图思想影响，认为文学煽动低级欲望，阻碍人们运用理性把握上帝的真理，因此在《忏悔录》中，他将自己对文学心醉神迷的欣赏视为需要忏悔的内容，但他也认同柏拉图的"美是理式"的观点，而且将美的"理式"与基督教信仰中的上帝相关联，认为上帝是最高的美，是一切感性事物的本源，通过感性事物的低级美和有限美，人可以观照或体会到上帝的至美和至善。以上观点淡化了美学和宗教的分野，为审美和艺术的合法性预留了空间。此外，奥古斯丁对高级美和低级美、无限美和有限美的区分，暗示着艺术可以超越现实世界，容纳神秘主义、象征主义的文学想象。

中世纪经院哲学理论家阿奎那则深受亚里士多德影响。亚里士多德指出事物成形需要动力因。阿奎那将万物本源归于上帝，视其为自然造化的动力因、宇宙第一推动力。阿奎那的美学观也追随亚里士多德的摹仿论，提出上帝创造自然，自然体现上帝的完美理性设计，人类在艺术创作中应以上帝为师。要想领悟神的技巧与启发，应以自然是其所是的方式模仿自然。这种艺术反映论在符合古典理性规范的前提下体现了现实主义的倾向。

中世纪基督教文论的另一焦点是《圣经》及其奥义的阐释，方法论结合了古典语文学、修辞学和基督教神学。保罗（St. Paul）认为解读《圣经》时，需要区分字面义和深层内涵，即区分"字句"与"精意"。在《新约·哥林多后书》中，他指出上帝"叫我们能承担这新约的执事，不是凭着字句，乃是凭着精意。因为那字句是叫人死，精意是叫人活"。早期基督教神学家奥利金（Origen）吸纳犹太教释经学传统，提出"正如人有肉体、灵魂和精神，上帝为拯救人类所设的经文亦如是"，从而形成《圣经》文本的肉体——字面意义、灵魂——道德意义、精神——奥义的分类法。奥古斯丁讨论了《圣经》的寓意何以能够超越字面义，认为语言依赖有形的符号，而神无所不在，没有形体，所以语言无法彻底捕捉神意和真理。但奥古斯丁反对越过字面义解读经文的神秘主义倾向，认为释经应以文本为依托，通过渐进的体悟来领会语言传达的真理。阿奎那在《神学大全》（*Summa Theologica*）等著作中关注《圣经》语言的多义性，从受众的角度切入该议题，指出多义性的目标是让神的言说由浅入深，面向不同层次的听众传达适合其理解能力的意义。深刻的道理用浅显的语言说出来，普通人也听得懂，虔信者则可以揣摩出其中的深意。总体而言，中世纪的释经传统以肯定神的权威声音来支持《圣经》的文学元素和表意多重性，但也承认语言具有表意不确定性，成为阐释学的重要源头之一。它追问的文本复义现象在20世纪也成为解构主义的讨论焦点。

1453年，东罗马帝国灭亡。在东罗马帝国最后的动荡年代，逃离故国的学者们携带古希腊典籍进入意大利，带来了文艺复兴的火种。从14世纪到17世纪上半叶，这火种漫卷欧洲。文艺复兴是开启欧洲现代性进程的关键，但它不是与过去断裂的新生，而是多重力量交汇的渐进性历史进程：在宗教领域，改革的呼声撼动天主教权威，新教萌芽与发展；欧洲各国手工业和商贸蓬勃发展，市民阶级壮大，世俗社会的分量越来越重；高等教育体系日益完善，人文学科和科学技术共同发展；印刷术让普罗大众有了受教育的可能，也为民族语言的普及做出了贡献；地理大发现带来全球化进程的加速，东西方的交融催生新的思想……世界经历着转变：从人倾听神的律令，到人与神对话，乃至在基督教框架下人与人展开世俗对话。文艺复兴希冀从古希腊罗马的异教文明中寻找出路，突破基督教的僵化体系。它吸纳了古希腊的人本主义思想，扭转了宗教禁欲风气，歌颂现世生活，追求神、自然与人的统一，在艺术领域鼓励想象和创造。

但丁（Dante Alighieri）的文学创作和文艺理论都体现了中世纪向文艺复兴的渐进转变。他是中世纪后期最伟大的诗人，也是新时代的开启者。他的《神曲》通过寓言的方式，展现了人类精神追求的进程。他在《致斯加拉大亲王书》（"Letter to Can Grande della Scala"）中指出，他写《神曲》是为了体现"随着一层天升到另一层天……真福在于认识真理之源"。他的真理观符合中世纪神学观，视上帝为终极真理。然而，如果我们从但丁阐释《神曲》的方法论来看，他在用阿奎那解读《圣经》的多义释经法来阐释他所写的《神曲》的内涵。神的言说和诗人的文学创作之间的距离消弭了。其人本主义思想闪现着文艺复兴时代的光芒。

对比但丁，薄伽丘（Giovanni Boccaccio）在世俗化道路上走得更远，他拆解了基督教为排除异教文化遗产而竖起的藩篱。但丁因为荷马、柏拉图、贺拉斯等是异教徒，在《神曲》中把他们划入了地狱第一层。薄伽丘却在《异教诸神谱系》（*Genealogy of the Gentile Gods*）中把他们引入受神恩普照的世界，提出只要具有共同的人性，便可共享神性之光。他认为异教诗人介于神与世人之间，他们用诗歌表达的也是真理。薄伽丘还关注文学艺术创作的虚构性，反对将虚构视为缺陷和谎言，认为有意义的虚构是言说真理的方式之一。但是薄伽丘也有他的时代烙印，他认为诗歌是哲学的婢女，在真理性的等级阶梯上，神学高于哲学，哲学高于诗歌。

意大利学者卡斯特尔维特罗（Lodovico Castelvetro）在《亚里士多德〈诗学〉的通俗诠释》中则激进地划掉了诗歌的真理属性，转而关切诗歌令普罗大众喜爱的世俗功能。他指出，历史记录世间事，体现神的意志；科学受理性的统摄，反映客观世界；只有诗歌允许诗人进行虚构，诗人就本质而言是创造者。他认为诗性虚构不能背离常识、胡编乱造，但是也必须能给人以新奇感。他对新奇感的强调需要结合他的诗歌目的论来理解：他提出诗歌创作以提供愉悦娱乐为唯一目的。这一观点偏离了文学教化论的基督教诗学正统。

探索诗歌本质，为诗歌争取合法性的还有英国的菲利普·锡德尼爵士（Sir Philip Sidney）。他和戏剧家莎士比亚属于同一时代，是当时影响力较大的散文作家和诗人。在《为诗辩护》（*An Apology for Poetry*）中，锡德尼重提诗歌寓教于乐的教化作用，这是中规中矩的古典立场。但他直接将诗歌的历史追溯到人类文明的源头，认为诗歌比哲学更早承担起传达真理的使命，是物质世界最初的光明给予者，连主张驱逐诗人的柏拉图也在用诗性之美传达他的哲学思考。因此，锡德尼认为诗人启智宣德，比道学家、历史学家和哲学家更胜一筹，诗人是"学问的君王"。随着文艺复兴的发展，诗歌不仅摆脱了柏拉图的指责和基督教神学的贬低，而且从文艺复兴早期薄伽丘小心翼翼为诗歌争取来的"哲学的婢女"的位份，跃升为锡德尼所赞颂的世俗诸学科的无冕之王。

文艺复兴时期，除了为诗歌艺术进行的辩护，还有为民族语言和民族文学进行的辩护。中世纪的欧洲统一在基督教信仰之下，但由历史、习俗、文化、语言各不相同的众多民族构成。文艺复兴时期，神权统治有所削弱，世俗世界中的民族国家意识逐渐增长，加之印刷术推动民族语言的普及，用自己的语言写自己的文学的民族主义呼声越来越高。但丁在《论俗语》中指出，俗语是自然形成的语言，意大利应在其各地各异的俗语基础上建设理想的、统一的、光辉的意大利民族语言，来取代脱离大众生活的拉丁语。薄伽丘也是坚定的民族语言的支持者。他认为但丁已经做出了好榜样，指出但丁提升了作为方言的意大利语的地位，他对意大利人的重要性，就如同荷马之于希腊，维吉尔之于拉丁世界。法国的杜贝莱（Joachim du Bellay）在《保卫与发扬法兰西语言》（*The Defense and Illustration of the French Language*）中也反对盲目崇拜希腊、拉丁语言，鼓励法语文学创作，认为法兰西终会形成自己的伟大文学传统。

然而，在文艺复兴时代后期，神学约束力的衰减推动了世俗欲望的过度膨胀，要走出神权铸就的囚笼的人们面临转型带来的精神危机，文学创作水准下降，夸张的情节、泛滥的情感、华丽的语言成为风尚。因此，17世纪中叶之后，新古典主义（Neoclassicism）兴起，批评家重提古典传统和文学教化功能，反对放纵情感，推崇肃穆简朴的风格，要求严格遵守文体规范。

此时的"古典"转向，重新举起柏拉图、亚里士多德和贺拉斯的旗帜，但暗中有新意，将古典的理性对接笛卡尔式的近代理性，用理性取代信仰，使之成为艺术的首要原则。这种"新古典"还有深层的社会政治动因。从意识形态角度而言，新古典主义歌颂传统、理性和秩序，亦服务于君权为首的国家权威，将中世纪对神权秩序的维护转化为对世俗社会君主制的等级秩序的支持。

以法国诗人布瓦洛（Nicolas Boileau）为例。他是这一时期影响力最大的理论家，也是法兰西学院院士，深受法王路易十四的看重。他花费数年心血撰写的《诗的艺术》看似贺拉斯的《诗艺》的长篇翻版，但布瓦洛将贺拉斯的"合式"论改造为"理性"论，认为艺术的价值来自理性的光芒。他所推崇的高贵的文体、典雅的文字、规范的结构、界限分明的体裁以及作品整体的有机比例均衡都是理性原则的体现。

布瓦洛崇尚理性，主张向古典学习，他的保守主义立场让他成为彼时古今之争中崇古派的领军人物。在太阳王路易十四治下，法国崛起，正在成为欧洲强国，因此国内对民族文学何去何从的讨论十分热烈。尚今派认为新生的法国应抛弃传统束缚，拥抱自己的新文学。布瓦洛则认为尚今派推崇的新文学虚张声势，内涵肤浅，文辞铺张。他主张法国文学应该符合伟大文学的恒久标准。他崇尚经典，也歌颂王权等级。

"三一律"就是受到法国新古典主义瞩目的古典标准之一。亚里士多德在《诗学》中曾言及戏剧情节的完整性和一致性原则。文艺复兴时代的卡斯特尔维特罗为了反对中世纪神秘剧的混乱情节和离奇时空设置，提出戏剧中的行动需要在单一空间和有限时间内完成，行动、时间、地点三个要素组合成"三一律"。新古典主义时期，三一律被奉为戏剧金准则。高乃依（Pierre Corneille）的《论三一律，即行动、时间和地点的一致》（"Of the Three Unities of Action, Time, and Place"）是对这一原则的深入阐释。三一律要求戏剧的情节安排合理，较为真实地再现生活，约束了艺术表现的无度发挥，有利于凝练戏剧效果，这些是它的优点。但是在新古典主义教条下，它变成了衡量优秀戏剧的唯一标尺，这是矫枉过正。高乃依在剧作中灵活处理，突破了三一律的某些限制，因而受到了同时代批评家的严厉指责。他写《论三一律，即行动、时间和地点的一致》既是对该原则的总结，也有自辩之意。

英国新古典主义者受法国影响较大，也崇尚理性原则，但更具折中色彩。被塞缪尔·约翰逊赞誉为"英国批评之父"的约翰·德莱顿（John Dryden）在《论戏剧诗》（*An Essay of Dramatic Poesy*）中指出：戏剧是对人性的正确生动的反映，它要表现人的种种激情与脾性，以及人所臣服的命运的变化；戏剧的目的是给人类提供愉悦和教诲。这是比较温和的理性立场。此外，德莱顿积极倡导诗歌采用韵文写作，认为像英雄双韵体那样的格律令诗歌典雅、有力且内敛。他还批评莎士比亚用词不够考究，比喻较为奔放。但是他没有因此而否认莎士比亚的天才。相反，他认为莎士比亚的戏剧比遵守三一律的法国戏剧更伟大，描摹出活生生的人，弃置雕琢技艺的小道，成就艺术的大道。

亚历山大·蒲柏（Alexander Pope）是德莱顿的后辈，但保守色彩反而更浓。他信奉"存在巨链"观（Great Chain of Being），认为上帝是宇宙的神圣设计师，安排万物生灵，令它们在存在巨链中各守其位，造化出秩序井然的自然。蒲柏认为艺术所描摹的是这种闪烁着神的理性的自然。为了倡导理性，蒲柏在《论批评》中主张发扬批评的功能，树立正确的文学风气，向荷马等伟大作家学习，将古典的神髓化入英国文学的创作。但他也提出当代作家是未来文学经典的缔造者，背负着继承传统的重任，也承担着开创性的使命。

从中世纪到文艺复兴再到新古典主义时代，以神为中心的世界渐渐变成了以人为中心的世界。西方文论在经历基督教近千年的深入影响后，自15世纪到18世纪，迎来了文艺复兴的人性解放和新古典主义的理性回归，在基督教信仰和古典人文传统的根基上，开启了带有早期现代性色彩的新思考。

主要文本阅读

阿奎那：《神学大全》

| 选文简介

阿奎那在《神学大全》中讨论了基督教信仰的诸多议题，每个议题下设若干小问题，每个问题均由四部分组成：1)"质疑"，列举反对声音；2)"反论"，列举支持己方观点的经典著作；3)"正解"，阐述己方立场和理由；4)"释疑"，逐条回应"质疑"的反对意见。以下选文出自《神学大全》第一集第一卷的第一题"论圣道的性质和范围"。选文中的第九问"《圣经》是否应该使用隐喻?"讨论了《圣经》的诗学特征和真理言说之间的关系。反对者批评《圣经》的隐喻是诗歌手法,不宜传达圣道,会遮蔽真理,而且隐喻中的浅显意象也缺乏神圣性。阿奎那捍卫隐喻在《圣经》中的使用,认为它有利教化。他认为,上帝的启示不会因为借助可感知的表象进行传达而失去光芒,它只会令真理可亲可近。第十问"《圣经》中的同一个词是否具有多重含义?"则讨论了《圣经》语言的复义性。阿奎那认为《圣经》语言承载两层含义:字面意义和精神意义。精神意义又可细分为寓言意义、道德意义、奥秘意义。以字面义为基础,深意层层递进,立体言说真理。

From *Summa Theologica*

Thomas Aquinas (1225-1274)

Ninth Article
Whether Holy Scripture Should Use Metaphors?

We proceed thus to the Ninth Article:—

Objection 1. It seems that the Holy Scripture should not use metaphors. For that which is proper to the lowest science seems not to befit this science, which holds the highest place of all. But to proceed by the aid of various similitudes and figures is proper to poetry, the least of all the sciences. Therefore it is not fitting that this science should make use of such similitudes.

Obj. 2. Further, this doctrine seems to be intended to make truth clear. Hence a reward is held out to those who manifest it: *They that explain me shall have life everlasting*. But by such similitudes truth is obscured. Therefore to put forward divine truths by likening them to corporeal things does not befit this science.

Obj. 3. Further, the higher creatures are, the nearer they approach to the divine likeness. If therefore any creature be taken to represent God, this representation ought chiefly to be taken from the higher creatures, and not from the lower; yet this is often found in the Scripture.

On the contrary, It is written: *I have multiplied visions, and I have used similitudes by the ministry of the prophets*. But to put forward anything by means of similitudes is to use metaphors. Therefore this sacred science may use metaphors.

I answer that, It is befitting Holy Writ to put forward divine and spiritual truths by means of comparisons with material things. For God provides for everything according to the capacity of its nature. Now it is natural to man to attain to intellectual truths through sensible objects, because all our knowledge originates from sense. Hence in Holy Writ spiritual truths are fittingly taught under the likeness of material things. This is what Dionysius says: *We cannot be enlightened by the divine rays except they be hidden within the covering of many sacred veils*. It is also befitting Holy Writ, which is proposed to all without distinction of persons—*To the wise and to the unwise I am a debtor*—that spiritual truths be expounded by means of figures taken from corporeal things, in order that thereby even the simple who are unable by themselves to grasp intellectual things may be able to understand it.

Reply Obj. 1. Poetry makes use of metaphors to produce a representation, for it is natural to man to be pleased with representations. But sacred doctrine makes use of metaphors as both necessary and useful.

Reply Obj. 2. The ray of divine revelation is not extinguished by the sensible imagery wherewith it is veiled, as Dionysius says; and its truth so far remains that it does not allow the minds of those to whom the revelation has been made, to rest in the metaphors, but raises them to the knowledge of truths; and through those to whom the revelation has been made others also may receive instruction in these matters. Hence those things that are taught metaphorically in one part of Scripture, in other parts are taught more openly. The very hiding of truth in figures is useful for the exercise of thoughtful minds, and as a defense against the ridicule of the impious, according to the words *Give not that which is holy to dogs.*

Reply Obj. 3. As Dionysius says, it is more fitting that divine truths should be expounded under the figure of less noble than of nobler bodies, and this for three reasons. Firstly, because thereby men's minds are the better preserved from error. For then it is clear that these things are not literal descriptions of divine truths, which might have been open to doubt had they been expressed under the figure of nobler bodies, especially for those who could think of nothing nobler than bodies. Secondly, because this is more befitting the knowledge of God that we have in this life. For what He is not is clearer to us than what He is. Therefore similitudes drawn from things farthest away from God form within us a truer estimate that God is above whatsoever we may say or think of Him. Thirdly, because thereby divine truths are the better hidden from the unworthy.

Tenth Article
Whether in Holy Scripture a Word May Have Several Senses?

We proceed thus to the Tenth Article:—

Objection 1. It seems that in Holy Writ a word cannot have several senses, historical or literal, allegorical, tropological or moral, and anagogical. For many different senses in one text produce confusion and deception and destroy all force of argument. Hence no argument, but only fallacies, can be deduced from a multiplicity of propositions. But Holy Writ ought to be able to state the truth without any fallacy. Therefore in it there cannot be several senses to a word.

Obj. 2. Further, Augustine says that *the Old Testament has a fourfold division as to history, etiology, analogy, and allegory.* Now these four seem altogether different from the four divisions mentioned in the first objection. Therefore it does not seem fitting to explain the same word of Holy Writ according to the four different senses mentioned above.

Obj. 3. Further, besides these senses, there is the parabolical, which is not one of these four.

On the contrary, Gregory says: *Holy Writ by the manner of its speech transcends every science, because in one and the same sentence, while it describes a fact, it reveals a mystery.*

I answer that, The author of Holy Writ is God, in whose power it is to signify His meaning, not by words only (as man also can do), but also by things themselves. So, whereas in every other science things are signified by words, this science has the property that the things signified by the words have themselves also a signification. Therefore that first signification whereby words signify things belongs to the first sense, the historical or literal. That signification whereby things signified by words have themselves also a signification is called the spiritual sense, which is based on the literal, and presupposes it. Now this spiritual sense has a threefold division. For as the Apostle says the Old Law is a figure of the New Law, and Dionysius says *the New Law itself is a figure of future glory*. Again, in the New Law, whatever our Head has done is a type of what we ought to do. Therefore, so far as the things of the Old Law signify the things of the New Law, there is the allegorical sense; so far as the things done in Christ, or so far as the things which signify Christ are types of what we ought to do, there is the moral sense. But so far as they signify what relates to eternal glory, there is the anagogical sense. Since the literal sense is that which the author intends, and since the author of Holy Writ is God, Who by one act comprehends all things by His intellect, it is not unfitting, as Augustine says, if, even according to the literal sense, one word in Holy Writ should have several senses.

Reply Obj. 1. The multiplicity of these senses does not produce equivocation or any other kind of multiplicity, seeing that these senses are not multiplied because one word signifies several things; but because the things signified by the words can be themselves types of other things. Thus in Holy Writ no confusion results, for all the senses are founded on one—the literal—from which alone can any argument be drawn, and not from those intended in allegory, as Augustine says. Nevertheless, nothing of Holy Scripture perishes on account of this, since nothing necessary to faith is contained under the spiritual sense which is not elsewhere put forward by the Scripture in its literal sense.

Reply Obj. 2. These three—history, etiology, analogy—are grouped under the literal sense. For it is called history, as Augustine expounds, whenever anything is simply related; it is called etiology when its cause is assigned, as when Our Lord gave the reason why Moses allowed the putting away of wives—namely, on account of the hardness of men's hearts; it is called analogy whenever the truth of one text of Scripture is shown not to contradict the truth of another. Of these four, allegory alone stands for the three spiritual senses. Thus Hugh of St. Victor includes the anagogical under the allegorical sense, laying down three senses only—the historical, the allegorical, and the tropological.

Reply Obj. 3. The parabolical sense is contained in the literal, for by words things are signified properly and figuratively. Nor is the figure itself, but that which is figured, the literal sense. When Scripture speaks of God's arm, the literal sense is not that God has such a member, but only what is signified by this member, namely, operative power. Hence it is plain that nothing false can ever underlie the literal sense of Holy Writ.

但丁：《致斯加拉大亲王书》

选文简介

但丁的《致斯加拉大亲王书》写给给予他支持和庇护的斯加拉大亲王，介绍《神曲》中的主题、主角、形式、目的、题目和哲理。在讨论《神曲》的意义时，但丁指出《神曲》字面意义是亡灵的境遇，神秘寓言意义（寓意、道德和奥秘三重意义的统称）则是指人们运用自由意志采取行动后，终将善恶有报。他分析了《神曲》的文类归属，指出它是喜剧，始于黑暗的地狱篇，但结尾是沐浴天恩的天堂，总体意义是"要使生活在这一世界的人们摆脱悲惨的境遇，把他们引到幸福的境地"。虽然但丁的释义方法显然承袭阿奎那，但是这种释读法的性质已变，解读《圣经》的方法被运用于解读文学作品。阿奎那看轻诗歌，贬低它只能传达字面意义，认为唯有《圣经》有丰富的深层内涵，而但丁通过解析《神曲》展现出史诗也可传达神启和哲思。

From "Letter to Can Grande della Scala"

Dante Alighieri (1265-1321)

As the Philosopher says in the second book of the *Metaphysics*, "As a thing is with respect to being, so it is with respect to truth"; and the reason for this is that the truth concerning a thing, which consists in the truth as its subject, is the perfect image of the thing as it is. And so, of all things which have being, some are such that they have absolute being in themselves, others such that their being is dependent upon a relationship with something else: they exist at the same time with something which is their correlative, as is the case with father and son, master and servant, double and half, the whole and the parts, and many other such things. Because such things depend for their being upon another thing, it follows that their truth would depend upon the truth of the other; not knowing the "half," its "double" could not be understood, and so with the other cases.

Therefore, if one should wish to present an introduction to a part of a work, it is necessary to present some conception of the whole work of which it is a part. For this reason I, who wish to present something in the form of an introduction to the above-mentioned part of the whole *Comedy*, have decided to preface it with some discussion of the whole work, in order to make the approach to the part easier and more complete. There are six questions, then, which should be asked at the beginning about any doctrinal work: what is its subject, its form, its agent, its end, the title of the book, and its branch of philosophy. In three cases the answers to these questions will be different for the part of the work I propose to give you than for the whole, that is, in the cases of its subject, form, and title, while in the other three, as will be clear upon inspection, they will be the same. Thus these first three should be specifically asked in a discussion of the whole work, after which the way will be clear for an introduction to the part. Let us, then, ask the last three questions not only about the whole but also about the offered part itself.

For the clarification of what I am going to say, then, it should be understood that there is not just a single sense in this work: it might rather be called *polysemous*, that is, having several senses. For the first sense is that which is contained in the letter, while there is another which is contained in what is signified by the letter. The first is called literal, while the second is called allegorical, or moral or anagogical. And in order to make this manner of treatment clear, it can be applied to the following verses: "When Israel went out of Egypt, the house of Jacob from a barbarous people, Judea was made his sanctuary, Israel his dominion." Now if we look at the letter alone, what is signified to us is the departure of the sons of Israel from Egypt during the time of Moses; if at the allegory, what is signified to us is our redemption through Christ; if at the moral sense, what is signified to us is the conversion of the soul from the sorrow and misery of sin to the state of grace; if at the anagogical, what is signified to us is the departure of the sanctified soul from bondage to the corruption of this world into the freedom of eternal glory. And although these mystical senses are called by various names, they may all be called allegorical, since they are all different from the literal or historical. For allegory is derived from the Greek *alleon*, which means in Latin *alienus* ("belonging to another") or *diversus* ("different").

This being established, it is clear that the subject about which these two senses play must also be twofold. And thus it should first be noted what the subject of the work is when taken according to the letter, and then what its subject is when understood allegorically. The subject of the whole work, then, taken literally, is the state of souls after death, understood in a simple sense; for the movement of the whole work turns upon this and about this. If on the other hand the work is taken allegorically, the subject is man, in the exercise of his free will, earning or becoming liable to the rewards or punishments of justice.

And the form is twofold: the form of the treatise and the form of the treatment. The form of the treatise is threefold, according to its three kinds of divisions. The first division is that which divides the whole work into three canticles. The second is that which divides each canticle into cantos. The third, that which divides the cantos into rhymed units. The form or manner of treatment is poetic, fictive, descriptive, digressive, and transumptive, and it as well consists in definition, division, proof, refutation, and the giving of examples.

The title of the work is, "Here begins the Comedy of Dante Alighieri, a Florentine by birth but not in character." To understand the title, it must be known that comedy is derived from *comos*, "a village," and from *oda*, "a song," so that a comedy is, so to speak, "a rustic song." Comedy, then, is a certain genre of poetic narrative differing from all others. For it differs from tragedy in its matter, in that tragedy is tranquil and conducive to wonder at the beginning, but foul and conducive to horror at the end, or catastrophe, for which reason it is derived from *tragos*, meaning "goat," and *oda*, making it, as it were, a "goat song," that is, foul as a goat is foul. This is evident in Seneca's tragedies. Comedy, on the other hand, introduces a situation of adversity, but ends its matter in prosperity, as is evident in Terence's comedies. And for this reason some writers have the custom of saying in their salutations, by way of greeting, "a tragic beginning and a comic ending to you." And, as well, they differ in their manner of speaking. Tragedy uses an elevated and sublime style, while comedy uses an unstudied and low style, which is what Horace implies in the *Art of Poetry* where he allows comic writers occasionally to speak like the tragic, and also the reverse of this:

Yet sometimes even comedy elevates its voice,
and angry Chremes rages in swelling tones;
and in tragedy Telephus and Peleus often lament
in prosaic speeches....

So from this it should be clear why the present work is called the *Comedy*. For, if we consider the matter, it is, at the beginning, that is, in Hell, foul and conducive to horror, but at the end, in Paradise, prosperous, conducive to pleasure, and welcome. And if we consider the manner of speaking, it is unstudied and low, since its speech is the vernacular, in which even women communicate. There are, besides these, other genres of poetic narrative, such as pastoral verse, elegy, satire, and the hymn of thanksgiving, as could also be gathered from Horace in his *Art of Poetry*. But there is no purpose to discussing these at this time.

Now it can be explained in what manner the part I have offered you may be assigned a subject. For if the subject of the whole work, on the literal level, is the state of souls after death, in an absolute, not in a restricted sense, then the subject of this part is the same state, but restricted to the state of blessed souls after death. And if the subject of the whole work, considered allegorically, is man, through exercise of free will, earning or becoming liable to the rewards or punishments of justice, then it is evident that the subject in this part is restricted to man's becoming eligible, to the extent he has earned them, for the rewards of justice.

And in the same manner the form of this part follows from the form ascribed to the whole. For if the form of the whole treatise is threefold, then the form in this part is twofold, that is, the division into cantos and into rhymed units. This part could not have the first division as its form, since this part itself is [a product] of the first division.

The title of the book also follows; for while the title of the whole book is, as was said earlier, "Here begins the Comedy, etc.," the title of this part is, "Here begins the third canticle of Dante's *Comedy*, etc., which is called *Paradise*."

Having settled these three questions, where the answer was different for the part than for the whole, it remains to deal with the other three, where the answers will not be different for either the part or the whole. The agent, then, in the whole and in the part, is he who has been mentioned above; and he is clearly so throughout.

The end of the whole and of the part could be multiple, that is, both immediate and ultimate. But, without going into details, it can be briefly stated that the end of the whole as of the part is to remove those living in this life from the state of misery and to lead them to the state of happiness.

The branch of philosophy which determines the procedure of the work as a whole and in this part is moral philosophy, or ethics, inasmuch as the whole and this part have been conceived for the sake of practical results, not for the sake of speculation. So even if some parts or passages are treated in the manner of speculative philosophy, this is not for the sake of the theory, but for a practical purpose, following that principle which the Philosopher advances in the second book of the *Metaphysics*, that "practical men sometimes speculate about things in their particular and temporal relations."

锡德尼:《为诗辩护》

选文简介

锡德尼书写《为诗辩护》的现实契机是回应斯蒂芬·高森题献给他的《罪恶的学堂》。高森在书中批评诗歌腐化人心,指责诗人是社会的蛀虫。锡德尼未在《为诗辩护》中提及高森,但从题目可以看出他旗帜鲜明地反对高森的立场。从文学传统看,《为诗辩护》回应的是柏拉图对诗歌的批评。锡德尼反对柏拉图的"理式—自然—艺术"的等级排序,认为人类受上帝的眷顾,排序在自然造物之前,能感应神启、言说真理。本节选文的中心议题是诗歌的创造力。锡德尼认为文学所创造的世界,比自然世界更为丰富:"她(自然)的世界是铜做的,只有诗人给予我们的世界是金子做的。"诗人能够创造典型的人物,为世人提供榜样,也能用瑰丽想象创造自然中不曾存在的崭新形象,"自由地在自己才智的黄道带里游走"。锡德尼认为真正的诗人擅长思考,探索人类能做什么、应该做什么,通过诗歌引领人们亲近善、了解善,既怡情又传道。

From *An Apology for Poetry*

Sir Philip Sidney (1554-1586)

But now, let us see how the Greeks named it, and how they deemed of it. The Greeks called him a "poet" which name hath, as the most excellent, gone through other languages. It cometh of this word *poiein*, which is "to make": wherein, I know not whether by luck or wisdom, we Englishmen have met with the Greeks in calling him a *maker*: which name, how high and incomparable a title it is, I had rather were known by marking the scope of other sciences than by my partial allegation.

There is no art delivered to mankind that hath not the works of nature for his principal object, without which they could not consist, and on which they so depend, as they become actors and players, as it were, of what nature will have set forth. So doth the astronomer look upon the stars, and, by that he seeth, setteth down what order nature hath taken therein. So do the geometrician and arithmetician in their diverse sorts of quantities. So doth the musician in times tell you which by nature agree, which not. The natural philosopher thereon hath his name, and the moral philosopher standeth upon the natural virtues, vices, and passions of man; and "follow nature" (saith he) "therein, and thou shalt not err." The lawyer saith what men have determined; the historian what men have done. The grammarian speaketh only of the rules of speech; and the rhetorician and logician, considering what in nature will soonest prove and persuade, thereon give artificial rules, which still are compassed within the circle of a question according to the proposed matter. The physician weigheth the nature of a man's body, and the nature of things helpful or hurtful unto it. And the metaphysic, though it be in the second and abstract notions, and therefore be counted supernatural, yet doth he indeed build upon the depth of nature. Only the poet, disdaining to be tied to any such subjection, lifted up with the vigor of his own invention, doth grow in effect another nature, in making things either better than nature bringeth forth, or, quite anew, forms such as never were in nature, as the Heroes, Demigods, Cyclopes, Chimeras, Furies, and such like: so as he goeth hand in hand with nature, not enclosed within the narrow warrant of her gifts, but freely ranging only within the zodiac of his own wit.

Nature never set forth the earth in so rich tapestry as divers poets have done—neither with pleasant rivers, fruitful trees, sweet-smelling flowers, nor whatsoever else may make the too much loved earth more lovely. Her world is brazen, the poets only deliver a golden. But let those things alone, and go to man—for whom as the other things are, so it seemeth in him her uttermost cunning is employed—and know whether she have brought forth so true a lover as Theagenes, so constant a friend as Pylades, so valiant a man as Orlando, so right a prince as Xenophon's Cyrus, so excellent a man every way as Virgil's Aeneas. Neither let this be jestingly conceived, because the works of the one be essential, the other in imitation or fiction; for any understanding knoweth the skill of the artificer standeth in that idea or foreconceit of the work, and not in the work itself. And that the poet hath that idea is manifest, by delivering them forth in such excellency as he hath imagined them. Which delivering forth also is not wholly imaginative, as we are wont to say by them that build castles in the air: but so far substantially it worketh, not only to make a Cyrus, which had been but a particular excellency, as nature might have done, but to bestow a Cyrus upon the world, to make many Cyruses, if they will learn aright why and how that maker made him.

Neither let it be deemed too saucy a comparison to balance the highest point of man's wit with the efficacy of nature; but rather give right honor to the heavenly Maker of that maker, who, having made man to his own likeness, set him beyond and over all the works of that second nature: which in nothing he showeth so much as in poetry, when with the force of a divine breath he bringeth things forth far surpassing her doings, with no small argument to the incredulous of that first accursed fall of Adam, since our erected wit maketh us know what perfection is, and yet our infected will keepeth us from reaching unto it. But these arguments will by few be understood, and by fewer granted. Thus much [I hope] will be given me, that the Greeks with some probability of reason gave him the name above all names of learning. Now let us go to a more ordinary opening of him, that the truth may be more palpable: and so I hope, though we get not so unmatched a praise as the etymology of his names will grant, yet his very description, which no man will deny, shall not justly be barred from a principal commendation.

Poesy therefore is an art of imitation, for so Aristotle termeth it in his word *mimesis*, that is to say, a representing, counterfeiting, or figuring forth—to speak metaphorically, a speaking picture; with this end, to teach and delight. Of this have been three several kinds. The chief, both in antiquity and excellency, were they that did imitate the inconceivable excellencies of God. Such were David in his Psalms; Solomon in his Song of Songs, in his Ecclesiastes, and Proverbs; Moses and Deborah in their Hymns; and the writer of Job, which, beside other, the learned Emanuel Tremellius and Franciscus Junius do entitle the poetical part of the Scripture. Against these none will speak that hath the Holy Ghost in due holy reverence.

In this kind, though in a full wrong divinity, were Orpheus, Amphion, Homer in his *Hymns*, and many other, both Greeks and Romans, and this poesy must be used by whosoever will follow St. James' counsel in singing psalms when they are merry, and I know is used with the fruit of comfort by some, when, in sorrowful pangs of their death-bringing sins, they find the consolation of the never-leaving goodness.

The second kind is of them that deal with matters, philosophical: either moral, as Tyrtaeus, Phocylides, and Cato; or natural, as Lucretius and Virgil's *Georgics*; or astronomical, as Manilius and Pontanus; or historical, as Lucan; which who mislike, the fault is in their judgments quite out of taste, and not in the sweet food of sweetly uttered knowledge. But because this second sort is wrapped within the fold of the proposed subject, and takes not the course of his own invention, whether they properly be poets or no let grammarians dispute; and go to the third, indeed right poets, of whom chiefly this question ariseth, betwixt whom and these second is such a kind of difference as betwixt the meaner sort of painters, who counterfeit only such faces as are set before them, and the more excellent, who, having no law but wit, bestow that in colors upon you which is fittest for the eye to see, as the constant though lamenting look of Lucretia, when she punished in herself another's fault.

Wherein he painteth not Lucretia whom he never saw, but painteth the outward beauty of such a virtue. For these third be they which most properly do imitate to teach and delight, and to imitate borrow nothing of what is, hath been, or shall be; but range, only reined with learned discretion, into the divine consideration of what may be, and should be. These be they that, as the first and most noble sort may justly be termed *vates*, so these are waited on in the excellentest languages and best understandings, with the foredescribed name of poets; for these indeed do merely make to imitate, and imitate both to delight and teach, and delight to move men to take that goodness in hand, which without delight they would fly as from a stranger, and teach, to make them know that goodness whereunto they are moved: which being the noblest scope to which ever any learning was directed, yet want there not idle tongues to bark at them.

高乃依:《论三一律,即行动、时间和地点的一致》

选文简介

《论三一律,即行动、时间和地点的一致》中,高乃依讨论了戏剧中行动、时间和地点三要素的一致性原则。行动一致性要求"应该只有一个令观众安心的完整行动",喜剧中不必设置重重阻隔,悲剧也不必危机不断,但是主要行动中可以有相互呼应的各个独立行动,它们组合在一起,制造悬念,推动情节发展。时间一致性要求戏剧情节的时长尽量在一天之内,以贴合观众观剧的现实时间经验。地点一致性提倡让观众不必换景就能看完整部戏剧。高乃依在分析三一律时,经常以自己的剧本为例,也在此过程中,不断呼吁适度变通。比如,他对行动一致性原则异议较少,但是认为时长一天的原则可适度放宽;他认为绑定地点的原则太死板,应允许场景范围的扩大。高乃依反对教条主义,主张根据不同戏剧的具体需要调整三一律的执行标准。

From "Of the Three Unities of Action, Time, and Place"

Pierre Corneille (1606-1684)

The two preceding discourses and the critical examination of the plays which my first two volumes contain have furnished me so many opportunities to explain my thoughts on these matters that there would be little left for me to say if I absolutely forbade myself to repeat.

I hold then, as I have already said, that in comedy, unity of action consists in the unity of plot or the obstacle to the plans of the principal actors, and in tragedy in the unity of peril, whether the hero falls victim to it or escapes. It is not that I claim that several perils cannot be allowed in the latter or several plots or obstacles in the former, provided that one passes necessarily from one to the other; for then escape from the first peril does not make the action complete since the escape leads to another danger; and the resolution of one plot does not put the actors at rest since they are confounded afresh in another. My memory does not furnish me any ancient examples of this multiplicity of perils linked each to each without the destruction of the unity of action; but I have noted independent double action as a defect in *Horace* and in *Théodore*, for it is not necessary that the first kill his sister upon gaining his victory nor that the other give herself up to martyrdom after having escaped prostitution; and if the death of Polyxène and that of Astyanax in Seneca's *Trojan Women* do not produce the same irregularity I am very much mistaken.

In the second place, the term unity of action does not mean that tragedy should show only one action on the stage. The one which the poet chooses for his subject must have a beginning, a middle, and an end; and not only are these three parts separate actions which find their conclusion in the principal one, but, moreover, each of them may contain several others with the same subordination. There must be only one complete action, which leaves the mind of the spectator serene; but that action can become complete only through several others which are less perfect and which, by serving as preparation, keep the spectator in a pleasant suspense. This is what must be contrived at the end of each act in order to give continuity to the action. It is not necessary that we know exactly what the actors are doing in the intervals which separate the acts, nor even that they contribute to the action when they do not appear on the stage; but it is necessary that each act leave us in the expectation of something which is to take place in the following one.

If you asked me what Cléopâtre is doing in *Rodogune* between the time when she leaves her two sons in the second act until she rejoins Antiochus in the fourth, I should be unable to tell you, and I do not feel obliged to account for her; but the end of this second act prepares us to see an amicable effort by the two brothers to rule and to hide Rodogune from the venomous hatred of their mother. The effect of this is seen in the third act, whose ending prepares us again to see another effort by Antiochus to win back these two enemies one after the other and for what Séleucus does in the fourth, which compels that unnatural mother [Cléopâtre] to resolve upon what she tries to accomplish in the fifth, whose outcome we await with suspense....

The rule of the unity of time is founded on this statement of Aristotle "that the tragedy ought to enclose the duration of its action in one journey of the sun or try not to go much beyond it." These words gave rise to a famous dispute as to whether they ought to be understood as meaning a natural day of twenty-four hours or an artificial day of twelve; each of the two opinions has important partisans, and, for myself, I find that there are subjects so difficult to limit to such a short time that not only should I grant the twenty-four full hours but I should make use of the license which the philosopher gives to exceed them a little and should push the total without scruple as far as thirty. There is a legal maxim which says that we should broaden the mercies and narrow the rigors of the law, *odia restringenda, favores ampliandi*; and I find that an author is hampered enough by this constraint which forced some of the ancients to the very edge of the impossible. Euripides, in *The Suppliants*, makes Theseus leave Athens with an army, fight a battle beneath the walls of Thebes, which was ten or twelve leagues away, and return victorious in the following act; and between his departure and the arrival of the messenger who comes to tell the story of his victory, the chorus has only thirty-six lines to speak. That makes good use of such a short time. Aeschylus makes Agamemnon come back from Troy with even greater speed. He had agreed with Clytemnestra, his wife, that as soon as the city was taken he would inform her by signal fires built on the intervening mountains, of which the second would be lighted as soon as the first was seen, the third at the sight of the second, and so on; by this means she was to learn the great news the same night. However, scarcely had she learned it from the signal fires when Agamemnon arrives, whose ship, although battered by a storm, if memory serves, must have traveled as fast as the eye could see the lights. The *Cid* and *Pompée*, where the action is a little precipitate, are far from taking so much license; and if they force ordinary probability in some way, at least they do not go as far as such impossibilities.

Many argue against this rule, which they call tyrannical, and they would be right if it were founded only on the authority of Aristotle; but what should make it acceptable is the fact that common sense supports it. The dramatic poem is an imitation, or rather a portrait of human actions, and it is beyond doubt that portraits gain in excellence in proportion as they resemble the original more closely. A performance lasts two hours and would resemble reality perfectly if the action it presented required no more for its actual occurrence. Let us then not settle on twelve or twenty-four hours, but let us compress the action of the poem into the shortest possible period, so that the performance may more closely resemble reality and thus be more nearly perfect. Let us give, if that is possible, to the one no more than the two hours which the other fills. I do not think that *Rodogune* requires much more, and perhaps two hours would be enough for *Cinna*. If we cannot confine the action within the two hours, let us take four, six, or ten, but let us not go much beyond twenty-four for fear of falling into lawlessness and of so far reducing the scale of the portrait that it no longer has its proportionate dimensions and is nothing but imperfection.

Most of all, I should like to leave the matter of duration to the imagination of the spectators and never make definite the time the action requires unless the subject needs this precision, but especially not when probability is a little forced, as in the *Cid*, because precision serves only to make the crowded action obvious to the spectator. Even when no violence is done to a poem by the necessity of obeying this rule, why must one state at the beginning that the sun is rising, that it is noon at the third act, and that the sun is setting at the end of the last act? This is only an obtrusive affectation; it is enough to establish the possibility of the thing in the time one gives to it and that one be able to determine the time easily if one wishes to pay attention to it, but without being compelled to concern oneself with the matter. Even in those actions which take no longer than the performance it would be clumsy to point out that a half hour has elapsed between the beginning of one act and the beginning of the next....

As for the unity of place, I find no rule concerning it in either Aristotle or Horace. This is what leads many people to believe that this rule was established only as a consequence of the unity of one day, and leads them to imagine that one can stretch the unity of place to cover the points to which a man may go and return in twenty-four hours. This opinion is a little too free, and if one made an actor travel post-haste, the two sides of the theater might represent Paris and Rouen. I could wish, so that the spectator is not at all disturbed, that what is performed before him in two hours might actually be able to take place in two hours, and that what he is shown in a stage setting which does not change might be limited to a room or a hall depending on a choice made beforehand; but often that is so awkward, if not impossible, that one must necessarily find some way to enlarge the place as also the time of the action. I have shown exact unity of place in *Horace*, *Polyeucte*, and *Pompée*, but for that it was necessary to present either only one woman, as in *Polyeucte*; or to arrange that the two who are presented are such close friends and have such closely related interests that they can be always together, as in *Horace*; or that they may react as in *Pompée* where the stress of natural curiosity drives Cléopâtre from her apartments in the second act and Cornélie in the fifth; and both enter the great hall of the king's palace in anticipation of the news they are expecting. The same thing is not true of *Rodogune*: Cléopâtre and she have interests which are too divergent to permit them to express their most secret thoughts in the same place. I might say of that play what I have said of *Cinna*, where, in general, everything happens in Rome and, in particular, half of the action takes place in the quarters of Auguste and half of it in Emilie's apartments. Following that arrangement, the first act of this tragedy would be laid in Rodogune's antechamber, the second, in Cléopâtre's apartments, the third, in Rodogune's; but if the fourth act can begin in Rodogune's apartments it cannot finish there, and what Cléopâtre says to her two sons one after the other would be badly out of place there. The fifth act needs a throne room where a great crowd can be gathered....

The ancients, who made their kings speak in a public square, easily kept a rigorous unity of place in their tragedies. Sophocles, however, did not observe it in his *Ajax*, when the hero leaves the stage to find a lonely place in which to kill himself and does so in full view of the people; this easily leads to the conclusion that the place where he kills himself is not the one he has been seen to leave, since he left it only to choose another.

We do not take the same liberty of drawing kings and princesses from their apartments, and since often the difference and the opposition on the part of those who are lodged in the same palace do not allow them to take others into their confidence or to disclose their secrets in the same room, we must seek some other compromise about unity of place if we want to keep it intact in our poems; otherwise we should have to decide against many plays which we see succeeding brilliantly.

思考题

1. 阿奎那将《圣经》的语言意义分为四个层次，它们分别是什么？可以概括为哪两个主要层次？
2. 但丁如何阐释《神曲》的不同层次的意义？
3. 锡德尼如何理解诗人的创造性？他认为诗歌艺术和自然之间是什么样的关系？
4. 锡德尼在选文中指出诗人可以分为三类，分别是哪三类？锡德尼最推崇哪种诗人？为什么？
5. 请简述高乃依三一律的三大要素和基本原则。高乃依认为三一律中哪些是可以变通的要素？为什么？

讨论题

1. 请对比阿奎那的选文和但丁的选文，讨论但丁在何种意义上采用了阿奎那的理论，他的诗学在哪些方面有中世纪的特点，又在何种意义上昭示着文艺复兴即将到来。
2. 请参考第一章柏拉图《理想国》选文，解读本章锡德尼《为诗辩护》的立场，查阅相关资料，了解西方文论传统中诗歌与哲学之争的命题。

补充文本选摘与评述

薄伽丘：《异教诸神谱系》
From *Genealogy of the Gentile Gods*

Giovanni Boccaccio (1313-1375)

But, they may object, nature meant this gift for a useful purpose, not for idle nonsense: and fiction is just that—idle nonsense. True enough, if the poet had intended to compose a mere tale. But I have time and time again proved that the meaning of fiction is far from superficial. Wherefore, some writers have framed this definition of fiction (*fabula*): fiction is a form of discourse, which, under guise of invention, illustrates or proves an idea: and, as its superficial aspect is removed, the meaning of the author is clear. If, then, sense is revealed from under the veil of fiction, the composition of fiction is not idle nonsense. Of fiction I distinguish four kinds. The first superficially lacks all appearance of truth; for example, when brutes or inanimate things converse. Aesop, an ancient Greek, grave and venerable, was past master in this form; and though it is a common and popular form both in city and country, yet Aristotle, chief of the Peripatetics, and a man of divine intellect, did not scorn to use it in his books. The second kind at times superficially mingles fiction with truth...This form has been employed from the beginning by the most ancient poets, whose object it has been to clothe in fiction divine and human matters alike: they who have followed the sublimer inventions of the poets have improved upon them; while some of the comic writers have perverted them, caring more for the approval of a licentious public than for honesty. The third kind is more like history than fiction, and famous poets have employed it in a variety of ways. For however much the heroic poets seem to be writing history—as Virgil in his description of Aeneas tossed by the storm, or Homer in his account of Ulysses bound to the mast to escape the lure of the Sirens' song—yet their hidden meaning is far other than appears on the surface. The better of the comic poets. Terence and Plautus, for example, have also employed this form, but they intend naught other than the literal meaning of their lines. Yet by their art they portray varieties of human nature and conversation, incidentally teaching the reader and putting him on his guard. If the events they describe have not actually taken place, yet since they are common, they could have occurred, or might at some time. My opponents need not be so squeamish—Christ, who is God, used this sort of fiction again and again in his parables!

The fourth kind contains no truth at all, either superficial or hidden, since it consists only of old wives' tales....

I count as naught their condemnation of the fourth form of fiction, since it proceeds from no consistent principle, nor is fortified by the reinforcement of any of the arts, nor carried logically to a conclusion. Fiction of this kind has nothing in common with the works of the poets, though I imagine these objectors think poetry differs from it in no respect.

杜贝莱:《保卫与发扬法兰西语言》
From *The Defense and Illustration of the French Language*

Joachim du Bellay (ca. 1522-1560)

For languages are not born of themselves after the fashion of herbs, roots, or trees: some infirm and weak in their nature; the others healthy, robust, and more fitted to carry the burden of human conceptions; but all their virtue is born in the world of the desire and will of mortals. That (it seems to me) is a great reason why one should not thus praise one language and blame the other; since they all come from a single source and origin, that is from the caprice of men, and have been formed from a single judgment for a single end, that is to signify amongst us the conceptions and understandings of the mind. It is true that in the succession of time, some from having been more carefully regulated have become richer than others; but this should not be attributed to the felicity of the said languages, but to the sole artifice and industry of men. So then all the things which nature has created, all the arts and sciences in the four quarters of the globe, are each in their own way the same thing; but since men are of diverse wills, therefore do they speak and write diversely. In this connection I cannot sufficiently blame the foolish arrogance and temerity of some in our nation who, being in no wise Greek nor Latin, misprize and reject with a more than stoical haughtiness all things written in French; and I cannot sufficiently wonder at the strange opinion of some learned men who think that our vulgar tongue is incapable of good letters and erudition: as if an invention for language alone should be judged good or bad....

...And if the ancient Romans had been as negligent of the culture of their language when first it began to bud, certainly it would never in so short a time have become so great. But they, in the manner of good agriculturals, did first transplant it from a wild to a domestic place; then that it might the earlier and the better fructify, cutting off all around the useless twigs, in exchange for these did restore free and domestic branches, drawn in masterly fashion from the Greek tongue, which quickly were so well grafted and made like unto their trunk that henceforward they appeared no longer adopted but natural. Thence were born in the Latin tongue those flowers and those fruits colored with the great eloquence, the numbers, and the artificial binding together of phrases, all which things, not so much by its own nature as by artifice, every language is accustomed to produce. Therefore if the Greeks and the Romans, more diligent in the cultivation of their languages than we in that of ours, were unable to find therein, except with great toil and industry, either grace or number or finally any eloquence, should we marvel if our vulgar tongue is not so rich as it well might be, and thereby take the opportunity to misprize it as a vile thing and of little price? The time will come (maybe), and I hope for it with the help of good French fortune, when this noble and puissant kingdom will in its turn obtain the reins of sovereignty, and when our language (if with Francis the whole French language be not buried), which now begins to throw out its roots, will emerge from the ground, and rise to such height and greatness, that it can equal the Greeks themselves and the Romans, producing, even as they, Homers and Demosthenes, Virgils and Ciceros, just as France has sometimes produced her Pericles, Nicias, Alcibiades, Themistocles, Caesars, and Scipios.

德莱顿:《论戏剧诗》
From *An Essay of Dramatic Poesy*

John Dryden (1631-1700)

And this leads me to wonder why Lisideius and many others should cry up the barrenness of the French plots above the variety and copiousness of the English. Their plots are single; they carry on one design which is pushed forward by all the actors, every scene in the play contributing and moving toward it. Our plays, besides the main design, have underplots or by-concernments, of less considerable persons and intrigues, which are carried on with the motion of the main plot: just as they say the orb of the fixed stars, and those of the planets, though they have motions of their own, are whirled about by the motion of the *primum mobile*, in which they are contained. That similitude expresses much of the English stage, for if contrary motions may be found in nature to agree; if a planet can go east and west at the same time, one way by virtue of his own motion, the other by the force of the first mover, it will not be difficult to imagine how the underplot, which is only different, not contrary to the great design, may naturally be conducted along with it.

Eugenius has already shown us, from the confession of the French poets, that the unity of action is sufficiently preserved if all the imperfect actions of the play are conducing to the main design; but when those petty intrigues of a play are so ill ordered, that they have no coherence with the other, I must grant that Lisideius has reason to tax that want of due connection; for coordination in a play is as dangerous and unnatural as in a state. In the meantime he must acknowledge our variety, if well ordered, will afford a greater pleasure to the audience.

| 选文评述

在第一篇选文《异教诸神谱系》中,薄伽丘分析古希腊罗马神话传统,支持文学虚构。他将虚构故事分为四种。第一类是民间传说中以想象为主的虚构,以《伊索寓言》为代表性本文。这种虚构有其严肃的道德寓意。第二类是和真实混合在一起的虚构，虚构中隐含着神圣真意，《旧约全书》属于此类。第三类偏重历史性，以荷马史诗和维吉尔的《埃涅阿斯纪》为代表。第四类属于无原则的编造，缺乏内涵，他将其归为不值一提的老妪闲谈。薄伽丘所看重的诗性虚构应能激活想象力、扩展知识，让普通人体会到愉悦，让博学者洞察真理。

第二篇选自《保卫与发扬法兰西语言》。杜贝莱有感于当时民众对法语的轻视，指出法国作家既不是希腊人，也不是拉丁人，却以傲慢态度拒绝法语写作，殊为不智。法语和希腊语、拉丁语相比，传承单薄，这不是因为法语有缺陷，而是因为法国人对自己的语言和文学传统贡献太少。整个欧洲都用希腊语和拉丁语创作，才造就了希腊文学和拉丁文学的丰厚积淀。他期待法语能茁壮成长，在人们的日常使用中得到完善，相信法国文学也会孕育出属于自己的荷马、德摩斯梯尼、维吉尔和西塞罗。

第三篇选文出自德莱顿的《论戏剧诗》。《论戏剧诗》采用对话体，虚构了四位文人。他们谈古论今，品评戏剧创作的标准。其中尼安德（Neander）这个人物是作者德莱顿的化身。选文的主题是三一律。与本章中高乃依的选文进行对比阅读，可以看出德莱顿的民族主义倾向，也能看出英国新古典主义的灵活性。德莱顿指出，法国戏剧严格遵守三一律，每一场景紧扣单一情节；相比之下，英国戏剧枝蔓横生，有次要的情节和人物。但英国戏剧中，次要情节不影响主干情节的展开，依然符合三一律的基本准则，而且丰富的情节能够给观众带来更多乐趣，反衬出法国戏剧的呆板单调。德莱顿在序言中曾说他写《论戏剧诗》的目的之一是"维护我们英国作家的荣誉，使他们不受那些不义地偏爱法国人的人们的责难"。

关键术语释例

1. 寓言（allegory）：寓言最鲜明的特点是言与意之间的差距。这从它的希腊词根就能看出来：希腊文allos和agoreuein的意思是"以另一种方式说话"。寓言的字面意义对应着更为抽象的深层寓意。在古希腊罗马时代，人们阅读荷马史诗时，不仅被史诗的历史故事和冒险故事吸引，也关注故事的寓意。自基督教确立以来，对《圣经》的解读就和对文本寓意的发掘和对神的真意的探究相关。在文艺复兴时期，很多文学作品属于寓言文体，例如但丁的《神曲》和班扬的《天路历程》。在现当代文学中，卡夫卡、卡尔维诺、博尔赫斯等也喜欢运用寓言传达哲思和复杂含义。在现当代文论领域，形式主义关注寓意的深层内涵；解构主义关注寓意的复义性；西方马克思主义则关注寓意的意识形态功能。

2. 戏剧诗（dramatic poetry）：戏剧诗既包含诗体形式的戏剧，也包含有戏剧情节的诗歌。它的文学形式是诗，内容是有情节的叙事，有人物、情节、时间、地点等叙事要素。最早的戏剧诗始于公元前5世纪的古希腊戏剧，人们为了祭祀酒神，组成歌队，吟唱表演。荷马的《伊利亚特》《奥德赛》作为史诗也属于戏剧诗的文类。文艺复兴时期，戏剧诗中的经典既有但丁的史诗《神曲》，也有莎士比亚的戏剧。在当代，戏剧很少用韵文写作，所以诗体戏剧的传统逐渐式微，但是叙事诗在独白等艺术手法的运用上体现了戏剧诗的特点，T. S. 艾略特（T. S. Eliot）的《普鲁弗洛克的情歌》是例子之一。对于戏剧诗的理论探讨见于亚里士多德的《诗学》、德莱顿的《论戏剧诗》和狄德罗的《论戏剧诗》等。

推荐书目

Jones, Thora Burnley, and Bernard de Bear Nicol. *Neo-Classical Dramatic Criticism 1560-1770*. Cambridge: Cambridge University Press, 1976.

Marks, Emerson R. *The Poetics of Reason: English Neoclassical Criticism*. New York: Random House, 1968.

Matz, Robert. *Defending Literature in Early Modern England: Renaissance Literary Theory in Social Context*. Cambridge: Cambridge University Press, 2000.

Minnis, Alastair. *Medieval Theory of Authorship: Scholastic Literary Attitudes in the Later Middle Ages*. Philadelphia: University of Pennsylvania Press, 2012.

Minnis, Alastair, and Ian Johnson. *The Cambridge History of Literary Criticism. Vol. 2: The Middle Ages*. Cambridge: Cambridge University Press, 2009.

Norton, Glyn P. *The Cambridge History of Literary Criticism. Vol. 3: The Renaissance*. Cambridge: Cambridge University Press, 2006.

Preminger, Alex, O. B. Hardison, and Kevin Kerrane. *Classical and Medieval Literary Criticism: Translations and Interpretations*. New York: Frederick Ungar, 1974.

Weinberg, Bernard. *A History of Literary Criticism in the Italian Renaissance*. Chicago: University of Chicago Press, 1961.

陆扬：《文艺复兴诗学》。上海：上海交通大学出版社，2012年。

杨慧林：《圣言·人言——神学诠释学》。上海：上海译文出版社，2002年。

第三章
从启蒙主义到浪漫主义

概述

1784年，康德（Immanuel Kant）在《柏林月刊》发表文章《回答这个问题：什么是启蒙？》，开宗明义地指出启蒙是人们脱离自己所加之于自己的不成熟状态。而何谓不成熟？即不经别人的引导，就无法独立自由地运用自己的理性进行思考。康德将"理性"与"自由"这两个概念交融在了一起，与强调服从权柄与秩序的新古典主义理性形成了对比，肯定了人的主体性。"启蒙"的英文Enlightenment和法文Lumières都含有意表"光明"的词根，启蒙的光明洞穿了宗教的迷信蒙昧和王权制度的压迫本质，彰显出拥有生命权、财产权和自由权等自然权利的大写的人，照亮了人类历史进步的前路。在启蒙时代，天主教权威、专制王权、贵族特权等既定秩序被彻底摇撼，西方世界完成思想转型，正式步入现代社会。

启蒙时代崇尚自由平等，这一时期的文学理论也有相同特点，向新古典主义文论的贵族格调发起了挑战。法国启蒙思想家狄德罗（Denis Diderot）在《论戏剧诗》中提出，戏剧不应该拘泥于前人确定的规则和传统，而应追求真实。而他身处的时代的真实，不是古典剧里身着华服的贵族们的真实，而是普通百姓的平凡生活的真实。他基于同样的立场，指出现实不可能只有悲苦或者只有喜乐，应该在戏剧分类中增加一个介乎喜剧和悲剧之间的分类，即"严肃剧"。严肃剧是正剧，既有喜剧的自然、不故作高深，又有悲剧的道德意涵，展现人的美德和责任。古典戏剧论中有隐藏的阶级界墙：悲剧写帝王将相的悲情，喜剧以小人物为戏谑的对象。狄德罗拆除了这道界墙，用严肃剧的新文类来展现市民生活的真实境遇。

无独有偶，德国启蒙主义戏剧家莱辛（Gotthold Ephraim Lessing）也非常重视"市民戏剧"的概念。他在《汉堡剧评》中批评贵族和英雄虽能给新古典主义戏剧带来华丽气势，但他们高高在上，是他们的地位使他们的不幸显得重要。相反，能够叩击观众灵魂的是周围的普通人的不幸，它会令人感同身受。事实上，狄德罗和莱辛的戏剧观有诸多共同点：他们都认为戏剧应该展现普通人的生活；都主张用朴素通俗的语言表达真情实感；都强调情节安排应符合环境，不能牵强，等等。简而言之，狄德罗和莱辛是西方现实主义戏剧论的先行者。但他们在人物性格论上有分歧。狄德罗认为悲剧适宜表现个性，喜剧反映的是普遍性。莱辛反对这种二分法，批评狄德罗的"普遍性"原则将人物抽象成了概念，人物性格为主题和情节服务，丧失了作为个体的人的真实性。

英国启蒙文论的特点是拒绝唯理论和概念抽象，强调个人经验和建立在个人经验之上的集体共识，重视情感的力量，较多原创性的讨论集中在"审美趣味"这一联动情感与认知、个体性和社会性的议题，其思想史源头是始于弗朗西斯·培根、托马斯·霍布斯和约翰·洛克的经验主义哲学。经验主义反对理性的"天赋观念"论，提出人类知识起源于感觉，并以感觉的领会为基础。启蒙时期，沙夫茨伯里伯爵、弗朗西斯·哈奇森和休谟（David Hume）等纷纷对"什么是美？"这个问题产生兴趣。从经验论角度看，美感源自人的感官感知审美对象时内心体会到的愉悦感，所以美是个人感受。可是为什么人们能形成美学共识？比如：为什么人人都爱荷马，都爱莎士比亚？休谟的《论趣味的标准》（"Of the Standard of Taste"）回应了这个问题。休谟承认美感是情感性的、主观的、个人的，但他指出人类的感官机制具有同构性，"按照人类内心结构的最初条件，某些形式或品质应该能引起快感，其他一些则引起反感"。趣味的标准就建立在"人同此心"的原则上。虽然个人可能会受感官的敏锐度、智识的健全度、注意力的集中度等个体条件的制约而无法全然领悟美，但是人的社会属性会让他向往美，向往加入人类审美经验共同汇合而成的"审美共同体"。所以休谟重视批评家的作用，认为他们卓越的审美能力可以拉动社会趣味标准的提升。休谟指出，趣味敏感的人尽管很少，但由于他们见解高明、才能出众，以及受到普遍推崇，他们给予任何天才作品的赞语能够广泛传播，并成为一般性主导意见。艺术之美未必昭然若揭，需要能领悟它的人做发现者，引领风气之先。

事实上，英国启蒙文学理论家们普遍重视审美共同体的建构，乐于甄别、研讨和倡导时代的美学趣味。思想家埃德蒙·伯克（Edmund Burke）也在其列。他拓展了朗吉努斯的"崇高论"，提出"崇高"（the Sublime）与"优美"（the Beautiful）的对立审美范畴：前者建立在痛苦之上，后者则是或明快或柔和的愉悦。崇高之美厚重、庞大、黑暗、晦涩、粗粝，而优美之美柔和、精细、明亮、温和、和谐。伯克的崇高美以"强烈的情感"为标识，所联动的是人类的生存本能。当人类近距离面对危险（尤其是死亡威胁）却有幸能够免受伤害时，内心会涌起痛感与快乐交织的复杂情感，这是崇高审美的心理学基础。伯克崇高论的痛感美学和恐怖美学是彼时刚刚诞生的哥特小说这一文类的审美基调。

相比英法，德国进入启蒙时期较晚。此前它长期处于封建势力割据的状态，缺乏统一的国家意志，直到18世纪后半程才在一代雄主腓特烈二世统治时期，通过对外发动战争扩张领土、对内实行开明制度鼓励文化发展，跻身欧洲强国行列。因此，德国启蒙没有法国启蒙推翻王权的激进政治诉求。此外，德国启蒙对欧陆理性主义传统和新兴的英国经验主义采取了兼容并蓄的态度，主张沟通理性和感性，不肯偏废其一。这些都决定了德国启蒙的古典主义倾向。必须注意的是，这种古典性始终以启蒙为本质，反对因循旧制，主张思想解放，捍卫个人的主体性和自由。其中，最具影响力的是康德的美学观。在《判断力批判》中，康德提出审美"四契机"论：1）无任何利害关系的愉悦感；2）不涉概念的普遍性；3）无目的的合目的性；4）共通感的"必然性"。综合而言，康德美学是感性美学：他受休谟等经验主义者的启发，提出审美是个体的愉悦感，但具有社会心理学意义上的普遍性和共通感。康德美学是自由美学：无利害性、不涉概念和无目的性均显示出审美的非功利性和自由冲动。康德美学也沟通理性美学和道德美学，这源自他的欧陆哲学之根：无目的的合目的性暗合古典美学"天地有大美"的理性和谐和道德意指；共通感的"必然性"则隐含对人本主义"美的理想"的共同追求，美学共识不会违背道德意义上的普遍人性偏好。

康德是哲学家，他关心文学艺术之美的共性原则。席勒（Friedrich von Schiller）是文学家，他将阅读康德所获得的启示运用于时代反思，拓展了美学的文化与社会功能。席勒曾热切支持法国大革命，但法国大革命后期的暴力转向给他带来了幻灭感。他意识到民众虽被政治理念鼓动，但不知什么是真正的自由，当革命摇撼既有秩序时，民众急切渴望宣泄本能的冲动，致使国家陷入无政府状态。他意识到政治改革需要以人的道德素质的提升为基础，为此他撰写《审美教育书简》（*Letters on the Aesthetic Education of Man*），期待用审美教育孕育成熟的公民美德——人们进入美的王国，领悟什么是非他律的自律，自觉地与自由地运用自己的道德能力；人们通过审美实践，克服感性和理性的分裂带来的异化，抵达"人性的完整实现"的理想。在《论朴素诗和感伤诗》中，席勒从诗歌史角度再谈异化。他指出在古代，人类以天然本心悠然生活在自然之中，诗歌反映这种质朴的现实。到了近代，人类只能在感伤诗中怅然想象这种理想的统一性。席勒从启蒙进步史观出发，指出朴素诗是人类的童年之作，感伤诗更具思辨性，是人类文明发展的必然阶段。但他担心人的异化已成为他身处的时代的痼疾，这反映了他对启蒙现代性的保留态度。

实际上，在康德和席勒的时代，德国思想界一直存在对启蒙乐观主义的质疑之声，这些批评家和文学家聚拢在"浪漫派"的旗帜下，发出了欧洲浪漫主义运动的先声。德国早期浪漫主义本就是广泛意义上的启蒙思想的产物：爱自由、重创造、珍视艺术主体性。但它反对启蒙理性，拒绝用理性调和感性，认为冰冷的理性无法为包括艺术创造在内的人类生命实践提供指导。德国浪漫派排斥清晰、优雅、对称、秩序等审美原则，崇尚神秘、直觉和原始的蛮力。1798年，施莱格尔兄弟（August Wilhelm von Schlegel 与 Friedrich von Schlegel）以《雅典娜神殿》（*Athenaeum*）杂志为德国早期浪漫主义的主阵地，提出诗人的创作凭的是兴之所至，不必受制于任何狭隘规律的约束。他们遥望古希腊传统，认为那是人类的青春时代，人与自然、生活和艺术以神话为媒介融合在一起。新时代要想克服现代人的分裂，需要从古希腊传统中寻找启示，创造这个时代的"新神话"，书写浪漫诗的新章。他们意指的"浪漫诗"是一种"融汇诗"，诗人以想象为翼，穿越社会、自然、艺术之间的界墙，在诗歌里呈现有限与无限、有形与无形、物质与精神、个人与宇宙的交融。

德国浪漫派反思理性、反思现代性，这其实也是西方浪漫主义的普遍立场。启蒙的理性之光引领了法国大革命，但大革命后期的暴力专制令人大失所望。启蒙理性推动了科学技术发展，工业革命如火如荼地展开，但也带来了一系列时代新问题。自18世纪60年代以来，珍妮纺纱机、蒸汽机等纷纷登场，科技蓬勃发展带来社会巨变。工业革命提高了生产力，创造了前所未有的财富，促进了城市化进程，确立了资产阶级的领导地位，但工业革命也带来了传统有机社会的解体、人和人之间的疏离、对自然的过度掠夺、城市生活的异化、资本主义的残酷剥削与压迫等问题。为此，浪漫主义继承启蒙的自由平等理想，但反思启蒙理性观和进步观，呼吁建构人与自我、人与自然、人与社会间更为和谐的关系。英国、美国和法国受德国浪漫派牵动，也出现了各有特点的浪漫主义思潮。

英国浪漫主义的旗手是华兹华斯（William Wordsworth）、柯尔律治（Samuel Taylor Coleridge）、雪莱（Percy Bysshe Shelley）、济慈（John Keats）等诗人。华兹华斯为《抒情歌谣集》（*Lyrical Ballads*）所写的序言被视为英国浪漫主义的宣言。华兹华斯总结自己和柯尔律治的诗歌实验性尝试，主张突破诗歌内容、语言以及创作的古典主义限制。他指出诗歌应描写田园生活，反映普通人的人生境遇；诗歌应采用简单通俗的语言，使普罗大众也能读得懂；诗歌的创作冲动应源于真挚的自然情感的流溢，能打动读者的心灵。"自然"是这些纲领的题眼之一：浅显易懂的歌谣体描绘质朴田园理想，目标是抵制工业革命的机械论，修复现代性进程中人与自然被割裂的联系；抒情诗学倚重自然生发的情感，将诗歌从古典诗艺论的技术条框中解放了出来，文学创作自由、自然、不必刻意雕琢。华兹华斯描写山川自然与普通人的生活，表面看是摹仿论诗学——诗之镜中映出客观世界，内核却是表现论诗学——外部世界被人的心灵捕捉时的情感悸动和由此引发的沉思构成了诗歌生发的契机，内心情感谋求诗性的表达，诗人是感受者、凝思者、书写者、创造者。

《抒情歌谣集》的合作者柯尔律治和华兹华斯一样强调诗人的主体性，但他受德国哲学的影响很深，和华兹华斯的审美趣味存在差异，《古舟子咏》《忽必烈汗》等作品塑造出的世界神秘、高邈、奇幻瑰丽。他认为诗歌的神髓是想象力，提出想象力可以分为两种。"首级想象力"（primary imagination）是人类在感知和理解外部对象时的心智活动，它是先天的、自发的和重复性的，既源自人类有限的心灵，也关乎人类无限的创造力，是诗歌创作生生不息的生成动力。"次级想象力"（secondary imagination）则是首级想象力的回声，没有前者丰沛强大，但是人类的意志可以对其进行调度。所以诗人写诗时，会征用次级想象力，对不同的对象进行分解、重组、理想化和统一化等操作，使呆板的对象有了新鲜的活力。为此，他认同华兹华斯的诗歌创新性实验，但反对华兹华斯的平民化追求，认为刻意简单的语言会束缚想象力的翅膀。他赞美拥有超拔想象力的天才，认为他们不必受制于传统和规则，能够把司空见惯的事物表达出新意、激情和深度。

虽然华兹华斯和柯尔律治意见有分歧，但他们的诗人观都是自我中心论的。诗人济慈则另有新解，提出诗人应该具备"消极能力"（negative capability，或译为"延疑力""客体感受力"）。这是一种开放的心态，不妄谈真理，充满不确定性、神秘感和犹疑感。诗人不固执于自我，是万物也是空无，承载光明也包容暗影，具有拥抱世界和与万物融合的能力。济慈心目中的榜样是莎士比亚。莎士比亚以"无我"之姿，化身笔下的人物，创造出性格各异的鲜活形象。不执着于己，方能获得造化万物的创造力。

在大西洋彼岸，成立时日不久的美国则在19世纪30年代迎来了作为美国版浪漫主义的"超验主义"（Transcendentalism）思潮。超验主义受否定原罪论、主张基督人性论的新英格兰新教独神论派（Unitarianism）影响，同时还从德国哲学、英国浪漫主义、东方神秘主义吸收养分，生成了以自由、道德良知、理性直觉以及人的神圣性等为核心价值的超验主义思想体系，主张清除狭隘的清教思想的禁锢、修正社会发展的物质主义倾向、推动美国本土文化与文学的发展。爱默生（Ralph Waldo Emerson）是影响力最大的超验主义思想家。欧洲浪漫主义者普遍反对理性，认为它抹杀个性和想象力。爱默生也反对钳制思想的古典理性，笃信个人主义和自由，但受美国浓厚的宗教传统影响，不愿意放弃道德理性。为此，他嫁接德国启蒙哲学，提出理性是灵魂的最高能力，它不是简单的推理，而是直觉。凭借理性直觉，人们可以超越经验世界直抵精神世界。他还受新柏拉图主义的"太一"论启发，提出"超灵"（Over-Soul）说，指出超灵是充盈宇宙的力量，流溢出世界，每个人皆共有它的神圣性，能够与它互相感应，诗人是这其中的佼佼者。在《诗人》（"The Poet"）中，爱默生将宇宙视为整体，认为诗人领悟了其神秘的符号系统，获得了对人类经验的全面认识，书写着人、自然和宇宙的共鸣，因此也有资格为美国这方水土这方人进行代言。

埃德加·爱伦·坡（Edgar Allan Poe）却对超验主义这种高邈的哲思不感兴趣。在他看来，想要对抗这个时代的功利主义，有效方法是进入艺术与美的自治领地。在《诗歌原理》中，他提出"诗的唯一裁判是审美力"，认为美感是"尚在这世间的我们此刻还无力完全而永久地把握住的那些神圣的极乐狂喜"。他没有让诗歌承担席勒式的审美教育功能，提出诗人领悟美、书写美，是为了让世人有机会接近美。坡的唯艺术论在他的时代曲高和寡，却对19世纪后期的法国"唯美主义"产生了重要影响。

而19世纪前期的法国，批评家们反思曾经辉煌的新古典主义传统，在法国大革命失败后的保守主义威压下、在理想失落的彷徨中重新定义文学的意义。法国小说家夏多布里昂（François-René de Chateaubriand）主张"回头看"，强调基督教信仰对艺术的滋养，认为宗教能向人的心灵注入激情和朝气。现代人常怀忧郁，那是因为宗教点燃的激情会被现实社会的空虚浇灭，人们只能心怀忧伤地思慕天国理想。夏多布里昂的"忧郁美学"里有对中世纪的乡愁，认为现代人的空虚心灵需要神性指引。雨果（Victor Hugo）也关注基督教传统，但是落点在人性。他认为是基督教使人认识到自身的二重性：有灵魂也有肉体，有灵性也有兽性。他拒绝怀旧，主张各个时代都有自己的文学，提出诗歌发展三阶段的文学史观，即原始社会用抒情诗歌颂永恒，多神论时代用史诗传颂历史，近代用戏剧诗描绘人生。他认为近代戏剧受基督教双重人性论影响，以怪诞和崇高、惊悚和荒谬、悲剧性和喜剧性之间的对立为张力，既深刻又不让人压抑，兼具哲理的抽象性和形象的鲜活性。雨果反对古典主义对好人与坏人善恶分明的说教性刻画，他的浪漫主义人物观有阴影的深度和立体的复杂性。

简而言之，18世纪到19世纪上半叶是西方思想史上最富有活力的时期之一，法英德知识界之间既有同频共振，也有分歧对话，构成了启蒙主义和浪漫主义的"复数"特征。在文学理论领域，这种复数性特征也非常明显。我们或许可以将新古典主义时期的文论比喻为合唱团模式，批评家之间的异见构成高低声部之间的差异；启蒙时代到浪漫主义时期的文论则更像是同一片海里的浪花，批评家们不拘一格的创新探索是各自奔涌的浪，相互激发与推动，汇聚成层次丰富的潮声。

主要文本阅读

休谟：《论趣味的标准》

选文简介

休谟关注"趣味标准"的议题，是为了处理主观经验和客观价值之间的矛盾。审美趣味的差别无法用事实进行校准——因为艺术容许虚构。而且，美牵动的是每个人的本真的感受。既然人人平等，是否应该承认美无共识，只有个人标准？休谟对此予以否定回答。驳论很简单：二流诗人和弥尔顿之间的差距一望可知，可见美有标准。"两千年前，荷马取悦了雅典和罗马，如今在巴黎和伦敦仍受推崇。"任时代和社会变迁，荷马的荣耀依旧。好的艺术能够经得住时间考验——这是休谟趣味标准的外在规则。休谟还详细讨论了这个规则的内在依据——审美共识由人的感官决定。休谟将人的感官系统比作装满弹簧的精密机器：当小零件弹出时，机器无法正常运行。同理，有缺陷的感官无法领悟美的精细微妙。理想状态不易有，因此审美判断有差异。由于审美"是人类本性所能感受到的所有最美好和最纯洁的享受的来源"，所以休谟鼓励人们通过练习提升审美力。随着鉴赏经验的增加，感觉会澄清，判断会明晰，个人的趣味标准会提高，"以前似乎笼罩在物体上的迷雾消散了；感官在其运作中获得了更大的完善性"。

From "Of the Standard of Taste"

David Hume (1711-1776)

It is natural for us to seek a standard of taste; a rule by which the various sentiments of men may be reconciled; at least, a decision afforded, confirming one sentiment, and condemning another.

There is a species of philosophy, which cuts off all hope of success in such an attempt, and represents the impossibility of ever attaining any standard of taste. The difference, it is said, is very wide between judgment and sentiment. All sentiment is right; because sentiment has a reference to nothing beyond itself, and is always real, wherever a man is conscious of it. But all determinations of the understanding are not right; because they have a reference to something beyond themselves, to wit, real matter of fact; and are not always conformable to that standard. Among a thousand different opinions which different men may entertain of the same subject, there is one, and but one, that is just and true; and the only difficulty is to fix and ascertain it. On the contrary, a thousand different sentiments, excited by the same object, are all right: because no sentiment represents what is really in the object. It only marks a certain conformity or relation between the object and the organs or faculties of the mind; and if that conformity did not really exist, the sentiment could never possibly have being. Beauty is no quality in things themselves: it exists merely in the mind which contemplates them; and each mind perceives a different beauty. One person may even perceive deformity, where another is sensible of beauty; and every individual ought to acquiesce in his own sentiment, without pretending to regulate those of others. To seek the real beauty, or real deformity, is as fruitless an inquiry, as to pretend to ascertain the real sweet or real bitter. According to the disposition of the organs, the same object may be both sweet and bitter; and the proverb has justly determined it to be fruitless to dispute concerning tastes. It is very natural, and even quite necessary, to extend this axiom to mental, as well as bodily taste; and thus common sense, which is so often at variance with philosophy, especially with the skeptical kind, is found, in one instance at least, to agree in pronouncing the same decision.

But though this axiom, by passing into a proverb, seems to have attained the sanction of common sense; there is certainly a species of common sense which opposes it, at least serves to modify and restrain it. Whoever would assert an equality of genius and elegance between Ogilby and Milton, or Bunyan and Addison, would be thought to defend no less an extravagance, than if he had maintained a molehill to be as high as Tenerife, or a pond as extensive as the ocean. Though there may be found persons, who give the preference to the former authors; no one pays attention to such a taste; and we pronounce without scruple the sentiment of these pretended critics to be absurd and ridiculous. The principle of the natural equality of tastes is then totally forgot, and while we admit it on some occasions, where the objects seem near an equality, it appears an extravagant paradox, or rather a palpable absurdity, where objects so disproportioned are compared together.

It is evident that none of the rules of composition are fixed by reasoning *a priori*, or can be esteemed abstract conclusions of the understanding, from comparing those habitudes and relations of ideas, which are eternal and immutable. Their foundation is the same with that of all the practical sciences, experience; nor are they anything but general observations, concerning what has been universally found to please in all countries and in all ages. Many of the beauties of poetry and even of eloquence are founded on falsehood and fiction, on hyperboles, metaphors, and an abuse or perversion of terms from their natural meaning. To check the sallies of the imagination, and to reduce every expression to geometrical truth and exactness, would be the most contrary to the laws of criticism; because it would produce a work, which, by universal experience, has been found the most insipid and disagreeable. But though poetry can never submit to exact truth, it must be confined by rules of art, discovered to the author either by genius or observation. If some negligent or irregular writers have pleased, they have not pleased by their transgressions of rule or order, but in spite of these transgressions: they have possessed other beauties, which were conformable to just criticism; and the force of these beauties has been able to overpower censure, and give the mind a satisfaction superior to the disgust arising from the blemishes....

But though all the general rules of art are founded only on experience and on the observation of the common sentiments of human nature, we must not imagine, that, on every occasion, the feelings of men will be conformable to these rules. Those finer emotions of the mind are of a very tender and delicate nature, and require the concurrence of many favorable circumstances to make them play with facility and exactness, according to their general and established principles. The least exterior hindrance to such small springs, or the least internal disorder, disturbs their motion, and confounds the operation of the whole machine. When we would make an experiment of this nature, and would try the force of any beauty or deformity, we must choose with care a proper time and place, and bring the fancy to a suitable situation and disposition. A perfect serenity of mind, a recollection of thought, a due attention to the object; if any of these circumstances be wanting, our experiment will be fallacious, and we shall be unable to judge of the catholic and universal beauty. The relation, which nature has placed between the form and the sentiment, will at least be more obscure; and it will require greater accuracy to trace and discern it. We shall be able to ascertain its influence not so much from the operation of each particular beauty, as from the durable admiration, which attends those works that have survived all the caprices of mode and fashion, all the mistakes of ignorance and envy.

The same Homer, who pleased at Athens and Rome two thousand years ago, is still admired at Paris and at London. All the changes of climate, government, religion, and language, have not been able to obscure his glory. Authority or prejudice may give a temporary vogue to a bad poet or orator; but his reputation will never be durable or general. When his compositions are examined by posterity or by foreigners, the enchantment is dissipated, and his faults appear in their true colors. On the contrary, a real genius, the longer his works endure, and the more wide they are spread, the more sincere is the admiration which he meets with. Envy and jealousy have too much place in a narrow circle; and even familiar acquaintance with his person may diminish the applause due to his performances: but when these obstructions are removed, the beauties, which are naturally fitted to excite agreeable sentiments, immediately display their energy; and while the world endures, they maintain their authority over the minds of men.

It appears then, that, amidst all the variety and caprice of taste, there are certain general principles of approbation or blame, whose influence a careful eye may trace in all operations of the mind. Some particular forms or qualities, from the original structure of the internal fabric, are calculated to please, and others displease; and if they fail of their effect in any particular instance, it is from some apparent defect or imperfection in the organ. A man in a fever would not insist on his palate as able to decide concerning flavors; nor would one, affected with the jaundice, pretend to give a verdict with regard to colors. In each creature, there is a sound and defective state; and the former alone can be supposed to afford us a true standard of taste and sentiment. If, in the sound state of the organ, there be an entire or a considerable uniformity of sentiment among men, we may thence derive an idea of the perfect beauty; in like manner as the appearance of objects in daylight, to the eye of a man in health, is denominated their true and real color, even while color is allowed to be merely a phantasm of the senses.

Many and frequent are the defects in the internal organs which prevent or weaken the influence of those general principles, on which depends our sentiment of beauty or deformity. Though some objects, by the structure of the mind, be naturally calculated to give pleasure, it is not to be expected, that in every individual the pleasure will be equally felt. Particular incidents and situations occur, which either throw a false light on the objects, or hinder the true from conveying to the imagination the proper sentiment and perception.

One obvious cause, why many feel not the proper sentiment of beauty, is the want of that delicacy of imagination, which is requisite to convey a sensibility of those finer emotions....

It is acknowledged to be the perfection of every sense or faculty, to perceive with exactness its most minute objects, and allow nothing to escape its notice and observation. The smaller the objects are, which become sensible to the eye, the finer is that organ, and the more elaborate its make and composition. A good palate is not tried by strong flavors, but by a mixture of small ingredients, where we are still sensible of each part, notwithstanding its minuteness and its confusion with the rest. In like manner, a quick and acute perception of beauty and deformity must be the perfection of our mental taste; nor can a man be satisfied with himself while he suspects, that any excellence or blemish in a discourse has passed him unobserved. In this case, the perfection of the man, and the perfection of the sense of feeling, are found to be united. A very delicate palate, on many occasions, may be a great inconvenience both to a man himself and to his friends: but a delicate taste of wit or beauty must always be a desirable quality; because it is the source of all the finest and most innocent enjoyments, of which human nature is susceptible. In this decision the sentiments of all mankind are agreed. Wherever you can ascertain a delicacy of taste, it is sure to meet with approbation; and the best way of ascertaining it is to appeal to those models and principles, which have been established by the uniform consent and experience of nations and ages.

But though there be naturally a wide difference in point of delicacy between one person and another, nothing tends further to increase and improve this talent, than practice in a particular art, and the frequent survey or contemplation of a particular species of beauty. When objects of any kind are first presented to the eye or imagination, the sentiment, which attends them, is obscure and confused; and the mind is, in a great measure, incapable of pronouncing concerning their merits or defects. The taste cannot perceive the several excellences of the performance; much less distinguish the particular character of each excellency, and ascertain its quality and degree. If it pronounces the whole in general to be beautiful or deformed, it is the utmost that can be expected; and even this judgment, a person, so unpracticed, will be apt to deliver with great hesitation and reserve. But allow him to acquire experience in those objects: his feeling becomes more exact and nice: he not only perceives the beauties and defects of each part, but marks the distinguishing species of each quality, and assigns it suitable praise or blame. A clear and distinct sentiment attends him through the whole survey of the objects, and he discerns that very degree and kind of approbation or displeasure, which each part is naturally fitted to produce. The mist dissipates, which seemed formerly to hang over the object; the organ acquires greater perfection in its operations, and can pronounce, without danger of mistake, concerning the merits of every performance. In a word, the same address and dexterity, which practice gives to the execution of any work, is also acquired by the same means, in the judging of it.

席勒：《审美教育书简》

选文简介

《审美教育书简》收录了席勒于1793—1794年间写给资助者丹麦奥古斯滕堡公爵的二十七封信。席勒反对休谟的情感主义美学，认为以感性为基石的美受制于个人的和身体性的经验，缺乏精神的引领，而真正的美应该是感性和理性的平衡。席勒认为人具有被其生命的物质性所决定的感性冲动，以及被理性所决定的形式冲动。感性冲动不追求理想，只知道满足欲望；理性冲动无感受力，空虚苍白。因两者性质不同、无法调和，所以需要引入第三种冲动，即"游戏冲动"——它是感性冲动和理性冲动在互动中形成的平衡张力，是"活的形式"（living form），是审美的驱动力。选文中，席勒捍卫"美是游戏"的立论，指出人在审美的无功利的游戏中，摆脱了感性冲动的物质性和形式冲动的抽象性，将理想的形式赋予感性的材料，进行自由的创造，也体会到了完整的人性。在席勒看来，只有当人在完整意义上是人的时候，他才游戏；而只有当人在游戏时，他才是完整的人。

From *Letters on the Aesthetic Education of Man*

Friedrich von Schiller (1759-1805)

I am drawing ever nearer the goal toward which I have been leading you by a not exactly encouraging path. If you will consent to follow me a few steps further along it, horizons all the wider will unfold and a pleasing prospect perhaps requite you for the labor of the journey.

The object of the sense-drive, expressed in a general concept, we call life, in the widest sense of this term: a concept designating all material being and all that is immediately present to the senses. The object of the form-drive, expressed in a general concept, we call form, both in the figurative and in the literal sense of this word: a concept which includes all the formal qualities of things and all the relations of these to our thinking faculties. The object of the play-drive, represented in a general schema, may therefore be called living form: a concept serving to designate all the aesthetic qualities of phenomena and, in a word, what in the widest sense of the term we call beauty.

According to this explanation, if such it be, the term beauty is neither extended to cover the whole realm of living things nor is it merely confined to this realm. A block of marble, though it is and remains lifeless, can nevertheless, thanks to the architect or the sculptor, become living form; and a human being, though he may live and have form, is far from being on that account a living form. In order to be so, his form would have to be life, and his life form. As long as we merely think about his form, it is lifeless, a mere abstraction; as long as we merely feel his life, it is formless, a mere impression. Only when his form lives in our feeling and his life takes on form in our understanding, does he become living form; and this will always be the case whenever we adjudge him beautiful.

But because we know how to specify the elements which when combined produce beauty, this does not mean that its genesis has as yet in any way been explained; for that would require us to understand the actual manner of their combining, and this, like all reciprocal action between finite and infinite, remains forever inaccessible to our probing. Reason, on transcendental grounds, makes the following demand: let there be a bond of union between the form-drive and the material drive; that is to say, let there be a play-drive, since only the union of reality with form, contingency with necessity, passivity with freedom, makes the concept of human nature complete. Reason must make this demand because it is reason—because it is its nature to insist on perfection and on the abolition of all limitation, and because any exclusive activity on the part of either the one drive or the other leaves human nature incomplete and gives rise to some limitation within it. Consequently, as soon as reason utters the pronouncement: let humanity exist, it has by that very pronouncement also promulgated the law: let there be beauty. Experience can provide an answer to the question whether there is such a thing as beauty, and we shall know the answer once experience has taught us whether there is such a thing as humanity. But how there can be beauty, and how humanity is possible, neither reason nor experience can tell us.

Man, as we know, is neither exclusively matter nor exclusively mind. Beauty, as the consummation of his humanity, can therefore be neither exclusively life nor exclusively form. Not mere life, as acute observers, adhering too closely to the testimony of experience, have maintained, and to which the taste of our age would fain degrade it; not mere form, as it has been adjudged by philosophers whose speculations led them too far away from experience, or by artists who, philosophizing on beauty, let themselves be too exclusively guided by the needs of their craft. It is the object common to both drives, that is to say, the object of the play-drive. This term is fully justified by linguistic usage, which is wont to designate as *play* everything which is neither subjectively nor objectively contingent, and yet imposes no kind of constraint either from within or from without. Since, in contemplation of the beautiful, the psyche finds itself in a happy medium between the realm of law and the sphere of physical exigency, it is, precisely because it is divided between the two, removed from the constraint of the one as of the other. The material drive, like the formal drive, is wholly earnest in its demands; for, in the sphere of knowledge, the former is concerned with the reality, the latter with the necessity of things; while in the sphere of action, the first is directed toward the preservation of life, the second toward the maintenance of dignity: both, therefore, toward truth and toward perfection. But life becomes of less consequence once human dignity enters in, and duty ceases to be a constraint once inclination exerts its pull; similarly our psyche accepts the reality of things, or material truth, with greater freedom and serenity once this latter encounters formal truth, or the law of necessity, and no longer feels constrained by abstraction once this can be accompanied by the immediacy of intuition. In a word: by entering into association with ideas all reality loses its earnestness because it then becomes of small account; and by coinciding with feeling necessity divests itself of its earnestness because it then becomes of light weight.

But, you may long have been tempted to object, is beauty not degraded by being made to consist of mere play and reduced to the level of those frivolous things which have always borne this name? Does it not belie the rational concept as well as the dignity of beauty—which is, after all, here being considered as an instrument of culture—if we limit it to mere play? And does it not belie the empirical concept of play—a concept which is, after all, entirely compatible with the exclusion of all taste—if we limit it merely to beauty?

But how can we speak of mere play, when we know that it is precisely play and play alone, which of all man's states and conditions is the one which makes him whole and unfolds both sides of his nature at once? What you, according to your idea of the matter, call limitation, I, according to mine—which I have justified by proof—call expansion. I, therefore, would prefer to put it exactly the opposite way around and say: the agreeable, the good, the perfect, with these man is merely in earnest; but with beauty he plays. True, we must not think here of the various forms of play which are in vogue in actual life, and are usually directed to very material objects. But then in actual life we should also seek in vain for the kind of beauty with which we are here concerned. The beauty we find in actual existence is precisely what the play-drive we find in actual existence deserves; but with the ideal of beauty that is set up by reason, an ideal of the play-drive, too, is enjoined upon man, which he must keep before his eyes in all his forms of play.

We shall not go far wrong when trying to discover a man's ideal of beauty if we inquire how he satisfies his play-drive. If at the Olympic Games the peoples of Greece delighted in the bloodless combats of strength, speed, and agility, and in the nobler rivalry of talents, and if the Roman people regaled themselves with the death throes of a vanquished gladiator or of his Libyan opponent, we can, from this single trait, understand why we have to seek the ideal forms of a Venus, a Juno, an Apollo, not in Rome, but in Greece. Reason, however, declares: the beautiful is to be neither mere life, nor mere form, but living form, i.e. beauty; for it imposes upon man the double law of absolute formality and absolute reality. Consequently reason also makes the pronouncement: with beauty man shall only play, and it is with beauty only that he shall play.

For, to mince matters no longer, man only plays when he is in the fullest sense of the word a human being, and he is only fully a human being when he plays. This proposition, which at the moment may sound like a paradox, will take on both weight and depth of meaning once we have got as far as applying it to the twofold earnestness of duty and of destiny. It will, I promise you, prove capable of bearing the whole edifice of the art of the beautiful, and of the still more difficult art of living. But it is, after all, only in philosophy that the proposition is unexpected; it was long ago alive and operative in the art and in the feeling of the Greeks, the most distinguished exponents of both; only they transferred to Olympus what was meant to be realized on earth. Guided by the truth of that same proposition, they banished from the brow of the blessed gods all the earnestness and effort which furrow the cheeks of mortals, no less than the empty pleasures which preserve the smoothness of a vacuous face; freed those ever-contented beings from the bonds inseparable from every purpose, every duty, every care, and made idleness and indifferency the enviable portion of divinity—merely a more human name for the freest, most sublime state of being. Both the material constraint of natural laws and the spiritual constraint of moral laws were resolved in their higher concept of necessity, which embraced both worlds at once; and it was only out of the perfect union of those two necessities that for them true freedom could proceed. Inspired by this spirit, the Greeks effaced from the features of their ideal physiognomy, together with inclination, every trace of volition too; or rather they made both indiscernible, for they knew how to fuse them in the most intimate union.

华兹华斯:《〈抒情歌谣集〉序言》

选文简介

华兹华斯和柯尔律治合著的《抒情歌谣集》于1798年出版。该诗集因违反新古典主义原则而引起争议,所以华兹华斯为1800年诗集的第二版撰写了序言,以阐发自己的诗学立场。选文出自1802年版序言。华兹华斯在序言中表达了他的创作目标:用真实的日常语言表达普通生活中的事件和情境,用想象力使它们焕发光彩,培养自然的情感。华兹华斯在政治上持有同情下层人民的立场,描写乡村生活,使普通农人成为诗歌主角;他在文化上向往人与自然共在的有机生活;他在诗学上推崇淳朴有力的语言和真挚的情感表达。值得注意的是,序言中的"表现论"名句——"诗歌是强烈感情的自发流溢",后面跟着非常重要的限定句——"它起源于在平静中回忆起来的情感"。华兹华斯诗学的情感机制不是情不自禁的直抒胸臆,而是经时间的沉淀和反思的沉静,在某个触发相同的情感的际遇,任诗情自然流溢而出。此外,在诗歌语言方面,华兹华斯强调要用普通人的语言写作,反对生僻辞藻和抽象修辞,但是他不反对诗歌采用韵文写作。他认为保留诗歌精心设计的音步和韵脚可以为质朴平实的诗歌内容增添美学张力。由此可见,华兹华斯诗学主张"天然去雕饰",去掉的是新古典主义的矫饰浮华,追求的是经过艺术高度提炼的返璞归真。

From Preface to *Lyrical Ballads*

William Wordsworth (1770-1850)

The principal object, then, which I proposed to myself in these Poems was to choose incidents and situations from common life, and to relate or describe them, throughout, as far as was possible, in a selection of language really used by men; and, at the same time, to throw over them a certain coloring of imagination, whereby ordinary things should be presented to the mind in an unusual way; and, further, and above all, to make these incidents and situations interesting by tracing in them, truly though not ostentatiously, the primary laws of our nature: chiefly, as far as regards the manner in which we associate ideas in a state of excitement. Low and rustic life was generally chosen, because in that condition, the essential passions of the heart find a better soil in which they can attain their maturity, are less under restraint, and speak a plainer and more emphatic language; because in that condition of life our elementary feelings co-exist in a state of greater simplicity, and, consequently, may be more accurately contemplated, and more forcibly communicated; because the manners of rural life germinate from those elementary feelings; and, from the necessary character of rural occupations, are more easily comprehended; and are more durable; and lastly, because in that condition the passions of men are incorporated with the beautiful and permanent forms of nature. The language, too, of these men is adopted (purified indeed from what appear to be its real defects, from all lasting and rational causes of dislike or disgust) because such men hourly communicate with the best objects from which the best part of language is originally derived; and because, from their rank in society and the sameness and narrow circle of their intercourse, being less under the influence of social vanity they convey their feelings and notions in simple and unelaborated expressions. Accordingly, such a language, arising out of repeated experience and regular feelings, is a more permanent, and a far more philosophical language, than that which is frequently substituted for it by Poets, who think that they are conferring honor upon themselves and their art, in proportion as they separate themselves from the sympathies of men, and indulge in arbitrary and capricious habits of expression, in order to furnish food for fickle tastes, and fickle appetites, of their own creation.

I cannot, however, be insensible of the present outcry against the triviality and meanness both of thought and language, which some of my contemporaries have occasionally introduced into their metrical compositions; and I acknowledge that this defect, where it exists, is more dishonorable to the Writer's own character than false refinement or arbitrary innovation, though I should contend at the same time that it is far less pernicious in the sum of its consequences. From such verses the Poems in these volumes will be found distinguished at least by one mark of difference, that each of them has a worthy *purpose*. Not that I mean to say, that I always began to write with a distinct purpose formally conceived; but I believe that my habits of meditation have so formed my feelings, as that my descriptions of such objects as strongly excite those feelings, will be found to carry along with them a *purpose*. If in this opinion I am mistaken, I can have little right to the name of a Poet. For all good Poetry is the spontaneous overflow of powerful feelings: but though this be true, Poems to which any value can be attached, were never produced on any variety of subjects but by a man, who being possessed of more than usual organic sensibility, had also thought long and deeply. For our continued influxes of feeling are modified and directed by our thoughts, which are indeed the representatives of all our past feelings; and, as by contemplating the relation of these general representatives to each other we discover what is really important to men, so, by the repetition and continuance of this act, our feelings will be connected with important subjects, till at length, if we be originally possessed of much sensibility, such habits of mind will be produced, that, by obeying blindly and mechanically the impulses of those habits, we shall describe objects, and utter sentiments, of such a nature and in such connection with each other, that the understanding of the being to whom we address ourselves, if he be in a healthful state of association, must necessarily be in some degree enlightened, and his affections ameliorated.

I have said that each of these Poems has a purpose. I have also informed my Reader what this purpose will be found principally to be: namely, to illustrate the manner in which our feelings and ideas are associated in a state of excitement. But, speaking in language somewhat more appropriate, it is to follow the fluxes and refluxes of the mind when agitated by the great and simple affections of our nature....

...The subject is indeed important! For the human mind is capable of being excited without the application of gross and violent stimulants; and he must have a very faint perception of its beauty and dignity who does not know this, and who does not further know, that one being is elevated above another, in proportion as he possesses this capability. It has therefore appeared to me, that to endeavor to produce or enlarge this capability is one of the best services in which, at any period, a Writer can be engaged; but this service, excellent at all times, is especially so at the present day. For a multitude of causes, unknown to former times, are now acting with a combined force to blunt the discriminating powers of the mind, and unfitting it for all voluntary exertion to reduce it to a state of almost savage torpor. The most effective of these causes are the great national events which are daily taking place, and the increasing accumulation of men in cities, where the uniformity of their occupations produces a craving for extraordinary incident, which the rapid communication of intelligence hourly gratifies. To this tendency of life and manners the literature and theatrical exhibitions of the country have conformed themselves. The invaluable works of our elder writers, I had almost said the works of Shakespeare and Milton, are driven into neglect by frantic novels, sickly and stupid German Tragedies, and deluges of idle and extravagant stories in verse.—When I think upon this degrading thirst after outrageous stimulation, I am almost ashamed to have spoken of the feeble effort with which I have endeavored to counteract it; and, reflecting upon the magnitude of the general evil, I should be oppressed with no dishonorable melancholy, had I not a deep impression of certain inherent and indestructible qualities of the human mind, and likewise of certain powers in the great and permanent objects that act upon it, which are equally inherent and indestructible; and did I not further add to this impression a belief, that the time is approaching when the evil will be systematically opposed, by men of greater powers, and with far more distinguished success.

Having dwelt thus long on the subjects and aim of these Poems, I shall request the Reader's permission to apprize him of a few circumstances relating to their *style*, in order, among other reasons, that I may not be censured for not having performed what I never attempted. The Reader will find that personifications of abstract ideas rarely occur in these volumes; and, I hope, are utterly rejected as an ordinary device to elevate the style, and raise it above prose. I have proposed to myself to imitate, and, as far as is possible, to adopt the very language of men; and assuredly such personifications do not make any natural or regular part of that language. They are, indeed, a figure of speech occasionally prompted by passion, and I have made use of them as such; but I have endeavored utterly to reject them as a mechanical device of style, or as a family language which Writers in meter seem to lay claim to by prescription. I have wished to keep my Reader in the company of flesh and blood, persuaded that by so doing I shall interest him. I am, however, well aware that others who pursue a different track may interest him likewise; I do not interfere with their claim, I only wish to prefer a different claim of my own. There will also be found in these volumes little of what is usually called poetic diction; I have taken as much pains to avoid it as others ordinarily take to produce it; this I have done for the reason already alleged, to bring my language near to the language of men, and further, because the pleasure which I have proposed to myself to impart is of a kind very different from that which is supposed by many persons to be the proper object of Poetry. I do not know how, without being culpably particular, I can give my Reader a more exact notion of the style in which I wished these Poems to be written than by informing him that I have at all times endeavored to look steadily at my subject, consequently, I hope that there is in these Poems little falsehood of description, and that my ideas are expressed in language fitted to their respective importance. Something I must have gained by this practice, as it is friendly to one property of all good Poetry, namely good sense; but it has necessarily cut me off from a large portion of phrases and figures of speech which from father to son have long been regarded as the common inheritance of Poets. I have also thought it expedient to restrict myself still further, having abstained from the use of many expressions, in themselves proper and beautiful, but which have been foolishly repeated by bad Poets, till such feelings of disgust are connected with them as it is scarcely possible by any art of association to overpower....

I have said that Poetry is the spontaneous overflow of powerful feelings: it takes its origin from emotion recollected in tranquility: the emotion is contemplated till by a species of reaction the tranquility disappears, and an emotion, kindred to that which was before the subject of contemplation, is gradually produced, and does itself actually exist in the mind. In this mood successful composition generally begins, and in a mood similar to this it is carried on; but the emotion, of whatever kind and in whatever degree, from various causes is qualified by various pleasures, so that in describing any passions whatsoever, which are voluntarily described, the mind will upon the whole be in a state of enjoyment. Now, if Nature be thus cautious in preserving in a state of enjoyment a being thus employed, the Poet ought to profit by the lesson thus held forth to him, and ought especially to take care, that whatever passions he communicates to his Reader, those passions, if his Reader's mind be sound and vigorous, should always be accompanied with an overbalance of pleasure. Now the music of harmonious metrical language, the sense of difficulty overcome, and the blind association of pleasure which has been previously received from works of rhyme or meter of the same or similar construction, an instinct perception perpetually renewed of language closely resembling that of real life, and yet, in the circumstance of meter, differing from it so widely, all these imperceptibly make up a complex feeling of delight, which is of the most important use in tempering the painful feeling which will always be found intermingled with powerful descriptions of the deeper passions. This effect is always produced in pathetic and impassioned Poetry; while, in lighter compositions, the ease and gracefulness with which the Poet manages his numbers are themselves confessedly a principal source of the gratification of the Reader. I might perhaps include all which it is *necessary* to say upon this subject by affirming, what few persons will deny, that, of two descriptions, either of passions, manners, or characters, each of them equally well executed, the one in prose and the other in verse, the verse will be read a hundred times where the prose is read once. We see that Pope, by the power of verse alone, has contrived to render the plainest common sense interesting, and even frequently to invest it with the appearance of passion. In consequence of these convictions I related in meter the Tale of GOODY BLAKE AND HARRY GILL, which is one of the rudest of this collection. I wished to draw attention to the truth, that the power of the human imagination is sufficient to produce such changes even in our physical nature as might almost appear miraculous. The truth is an important one; the fact (for it is a *fact*) is a valuable illustration of it. And I have the satisfaction of knowing that it has been communicated to many hundreds of people who would never have heard of it, had it not been narrated as a Ballad, and in a more impressive meter than is usual in Ballads.

爱默生:《诗人》

选文简介

《诗人》是爱默生19世纪40年代初期的演讲稿,后收录到他的《散文二集》,于1844年出版。爱默生不关心诗歌的技艺,认为格律再妙也不是好诗。他珍视的是诗歌的精神引领作用,从超验主义泛灵论视角出发,主张用诗歌将沉沦于经验世界的功利和平庸的人们唤醒,恢复其世界原初的神圣性。在《诗人》中,他用激情澎湃的文字勾勒出诗人的理想形象:诗人是人类的代表,了解人类的所有经验,洞悉真理和艺术的奥秘;诗人是言说者和命名者,是负责呈现美的人——爱默生认为美创造出世界,人类也是美的造物,所以天生是诗人。可惜大部分人被生活遮蔽灵性,无法感应美,只有真正的诗人可以与宇宙精神交融,通过美与万物联通,为人、自然、宇宙吟唱。爱默生期待美国能出现这样的理想诗人,体察这片广袤土地上不同地域、不同阶层、不同职业的美国人的生活与经验,书写出属于这个新生国家的真正诗篇。

From "The Poet"

Ralph Waldo Emerson (1803-1882)

Those who are esteemed umpires of taste are often persons who have acquired some knowledge of admired pictures or sculptures, and have an inclination for whatever is elegant; but if you inquire whether they are beautiful souls, and whether their own acts are like fair pictures, you learn that they are selfish and sensual. Their cultivation is local, as if you should rub a log of dry wood in one spot to produce fire, all the rest remaining cold. Their knowledge of the fine arts is some study of rules and particulars, or some limited judgment of color or form, which is exercised for amusement or for show. It is a proof of the shallowness of the doctrine of beauty as it lies in the minds of our amateurs, that men seem to have lost the perception of the instant dependence of form upon soul. There is no doctrine of forms in our philosophy. We were put into our bodies, as fire is put into a pan, to be carried about; but there is no accurate adjustment between the spirit and the organ, much less is the latter the germination of the former. So in regard to other forms, the intellectual men do not believe in any essential dependence of the material world on thought and volition. Theologians think it a pretty air-castle to talk of the spiritual meaning of a ship or a cloud, of a city or a contract, but they prefer to come again to the solid ground of historical evidence; and even the poets are contented with a civil and conformed manner of living, and to write poems from the fancy, at a safe distance from their own experience. But the highest minds of the world have never ceased to explore the double meaning, or, shall I say the quadruple, or the centuple, or much more manifold meaning, of every sensuous fact; Orpheus, Empedocles, Heraclitus, Plato, Plutarch, Dante, Swedenborg, and the masters of sculpture, picture and poetry....

The breadth of the problem is great, for the poet is representative. He stands among partial men for the complete man, and apprises us not of his wealth, but of the commonwealth. The young man reveres men of genius, because, to speak truly, they are more himself than he is. They receive of the soul as he also receives, but they more. Nature enhances her beauty, to the eye of loving men, from their belief that the poet is beholding her shows at the same time. He is isolated among his contemporaries by truth and by his art, but with this consolation in his pursuits, that they will draw all men sooner or later. For all men live by truth and stand in need of expression. In love, in art, in avarice, in politics, in labor, in games, we study to utter our painful secret. The man is only half himself, the other half is his expression.

Notwithstanding this necessity to be published, adequate expression is rare. I know not how it is that we need an interpreter, but the great majority of men seem to be minors, who have not yet come into possession of their own, or mutes, who cannot report the conversation they have had with nature. There is no man who does not anticipate a supersensual utility in the sun and stars, earth and water. These stand and wait to render him a peculiar service. But there is some obstruction or some excess of phlegm in our constitution, which does not suffer them to yield the due effect. Too feeble fall the impressions of nature on us to make us artists. Every touch should thrill. Every man should be so much an artist that he could report in conversation what had befallen him. Yet, in our experience, the rays or appulses have sufficient force to arrive at the senses, but not enough to reach the quick and compel the reproduction of themselves in speech. The poet is the person in whom these powers are in balance, the man without impediment, who sees and handles that which others dream of, traverses the whole scale of experience, and is representative of man, in virtue of being the largest power to receive and to impart.

For the universe has three children, born at one time, which reappear, under different names in every system of thought, whether they be called cause, operation and effect; or, more poetically, Jove, Pluto, Neptune; or, theologically, the Father, the Spirit, and the Son; but which we will call here the Knower, the Doer and the Sayer. These stand respectively for the love of truth, for the love of good, and for the love of beauty. These three are equal. Each is that which he is, essentially, so that he cannot be surmounted or analyzed, and each of these three has the power of the others latent in him, and his own, patent.

The poet is the sayer, the namer, and represents beauty. He is a sovereign, and stands on the center. For the world is not painted or adorned, but is from the beginning beautiful; and God has not made some beautiful things, but Beauty is the creator of the universe. Therefore the poet is not any permissive potentate, but is emperor in his own right. Criticism is infested with a cant of materialism, which assumes that manual skill and activity is the first merit of all men, and disparages such as say and do not, overlooking the fact that some men, namely poets, are natural sayers, sent into the world to the end of expression, and confounds them with those whose province is action but who quit it to imitate the sayers. But Homer's words are as costly and admirable to Homer as Agamemnon's victories are to Agamemnon. The poet does not wait for the hero or the sage, but, as they act and think primarily, so he writes primarily what will and must be spoken, reckoning the others, though primaries also, yet, in respect to him, secondaries and servants; as sitters or models in the studio of a painter, or as assistants who bring building-materials to an architect....

The sign and credentials of the poet are that he announces that which no man foretold. He is the true and only doctor; he knows and tells; he is the only teller of news, for he was present and privy to the appearance which he describes. He is a beholder of ideas and an utterer of the necessary and causal. For we do not speak now of men of poetical talents, or of industry and skill in meter, but of the true poet....

This insight, which expresses itself by what is called Imagination, is a very high sort of seeing, which does not come by study, but by the intellect being where and what it sees; by sharing the path or circuit of things through forms, and so making them translucid to others. The path of things is silent. Will they suffer a speaker to go with them? A spy they will not suffer; a lover, a poet, is the transcendency of their own nature,—him they will suffer. The condition of true naming, on the poet's part, is his resigning himself to the divine *aura* which breathes through forms, and accompanying that.

It is a secret which every intellectual man quickly learns, that beyond the energy of his possessed and conscious intellect he is capable of a new energy (as of an intellect doubled on itself), by abandonment to the nature of things; that beside his privacy of power as an individual man, there is a great public power on which he can draw, by unlocking, at all risks, his human doors, and suffering the ethereal tides to roll and circulate through him; then he is caught up into the life of the universe, his speech is thunder, his thought is law, and his words are universally intelligible as the plants and animals. The poet knows that he speaks adequately then only when he speaks somewhat wildly, or "with the flower of the mind"; not with the intellect used as an organ, but with the intellect released from all service and suffered to take its direction from its celestial life; or as the ancients were wont to express themselves, not with intellect alone but with the intellect inebriated by nectar. As the traveler who has lost his way throws his reins on his horse's neck and trusts to the instinct of the animal to find his road, so must we do with the divine animal who carries us through this world. For if in any manner we can stimulate this instinct, new passages are opened for us into nature; the mind flows into and through things hardest and highest, and the metamorphosis is possible....

I look in vain for the poet whom I describe. We do not with sufficient plainness or sufficient profoundness address ourselves to life, nor dare we chaunt our own times and social circumstance. If we filled the day with bravery, we should not shrink from celebrating it. Time and nature yield us many gifts, but not yet the timely man, the new religion, the reconciler, whom all things await. Dante's praise is that he dared to write his autobiography in colossal cipher, or into universality. We have had no genius in America, with tyrannous eye, which knew the value of our incomparable materials, and saw, in the barbarism and materialism of the times, another carnival of the same gods whose picture he so much admires in Homer; then in the Middle Age; then in Calvinism. Banks and tariffs, the newspaper and caucus, Methodism and Unitarianism, are flat and dull to dull people, but rest on the same foundations of wonder as the town of Troy and the temple of Delphi, and are as swiftly passing away. Our log-rolling, our stumps and their politics, our fisheries, our Negroes and Indians, our boasts, and our repudiations, the wrath of rogues and the pusillanimity of honest men, the northern trade, the southern planting, the western clearing, Oregon and Texas, are yet unsung. Yet America is a poem in our eyes; its ample geography dazzles the imagination, and it will not wait long for meters. If I have not found that excellent combination of gifts in my countrymen which I seek, neither could I aid myself to fix the idea of the poet by reading now and then in Chalmers' collection of five centuries of English poets. These are wits more than poets, though there have been poets among them. But when we adhere to the ideal of the poets, we have our difficulties even with Milton and Homer. Milton is too literary, and Homer too literal and historical.

But I am not wise enough for a national criticism, and must see the old largeness a little longer, to discharge my errand from the muse to the poet concerning his art.

思考题

1. 休谟如何反驳"趣味无标准论"？他认为应该如何培养人的审美能力？
2. 席勒为什么说美是游戏？
3. 请解释席勒的《审美教育书简》选文中这句话的意涵："……只有当人在完整意义上是人的时候，他才游戏；而只有当人在游戏时，他才是完整的人。"
4. 请解释华兹华斯的《〈抒情歌谣集〉序言》选文中这句话的意涵："……诗歌是强烈感情的自发流溢，它起源于在平静中回忆起来的情感。"
5. 爱默生在《诗人》中主张诗人应该具备什么样的能力，以及承担什么样的责任？

讨论题

1. 休谟和席勒都关心审美议题，重视对审美能力的培养。他们的观点有什么相同的地方？又有什么区别？请在阅读选文的基础上，查阅课外相关资料，进行讨论。
2. 请分别总结华兹华斯的诗歌观和爱默生的诗学观，讨论二者在哪些方面反映了浪漫主义的特点。

补充文本选摘与评述

莱辛:《拉奥孔》
From *Laocoön*

Gotthold Ephraim Lessing (1729-1781)

Painting, with regard to compositions in which the objects are coexistent, can only avail itself of one moment of action, and must therefore choose that which is the most pregnant, and by which what has gone before and what is to follow will be most intelligible.

And even thus poetry, in her progressive imitations, can only make use of one single property of bodies, and must therefore choose that one which conveys to us the most sensible idea of the form of the body, from that point of view for which it employs it.

From this is derived the rule of the unity of picturesque epithets, and of frugality in the description of bodily objects.

...I find that Homer paints nothing but progressive actions, and paints all bodies and individual things only on account of their relation to these actions, and generally with a single trait. What wonder is it, then, that the painter, where Homer has painted, finds little or nothing for himself to do, and that his harvest is only to be gathered where history brings together a multitude of beautiful bodies, in beautiful attitudes, within a space favorable to art, while the poet himself may paint as little as he pleases these bodies, these attitudes, and this space?...

...For example, he wishes to paint for us the bow of Pandarus: a bow of horn, of such-and-such a length, well-polished, and tipped at both ends with beaten gold. What does he do? Does he give us a dry enumeration of all its properties, one after the other? No such thing: that would be to give an account of a bow, to enumerate its qualities; but not to paint one. He begins with the chase of the wild goat, out of whose horns the bow is made. Pandarus had lain in wait for him in the rocks, and had slain him: the horns were of extraordinary size, and on that account he destined them for a bow. They are brought to the workshop; the artist unites, polishes, decorates them. And so, as I have said, we see the gradual formation by the poet of that which we can only see in a completed form in the work of the painter.

施莱格尔:《〈雅典娜神殿〉断片集》
From *Athenaeum Fragments*

Friedrich von Schlegel (1772-1829)

Romantic poetry is a progressive, universal poetry. Its aim isn't merely to reunite all the separate species of poetry and put poetry in touch with philosophy and rhetoric. It tries to and should mix and fuse poetry and prose, inspiration and criticism, the poetry of art and the poetry of nature; and make poetry lively and sociable, and life and society poetical; poeticize wit and fill and saturate the forms of art with every kind of good, solid matter for instruction, and animate them with the pulsations of humor. It embraces everything that is purely poetic, from the greatest systems of art, containing within themselves still further systems, to the sigh, the kiss that the poetizing child breathes forth in artless song. It can so lose itself in what it describes that one might believe it exists only to characterize poetical individuals of all sorts; and yet there still is no form so fit for expressing the entire spirit of an author: so that many artists who started out to write only a novel ended up by providing us with a portrait of themselves. It alone can become, like the epic, a mirror of the whole circumambient world, an image of the age. And it can also—more than any other form—hover at the midpoint between the portrayed and the portrayer, free of all real and ideal self-interest, on the wings of poetic reflection, and can raise that reflection again and again to a higher power, can multiply it in an endless succession of mirrors. It is capable of the highest and most variegated refinement, not only from within outward, but also from without inward; capable in that it organizes—for everything that seeks a wholeness in its effects—the parts along similar lines, so that it opens up a perspective upon an infinitely increasing classicism. Romantic poetry is in the arts what wit is in philosophy, and what society and sociability, friendship and love are in life. Other kinds of poetry are finished and are now capable of being fully analyzed. The romantic kind of poetry is still in the state of becoming; that, in fact, is its real essence: that it should forever be becoming and never be perfected. It can be exhausted by no theory and only a divinatory criticism would dare try to characterize its ideal. It alone is infinite, just as it alone is free; and it recognizes as its first commandment that the will of the poet can tolerate no law above itself. The romantic kind of poetry is the only one that is more than a kind, that is, as it were, poetry itself: for in a certain sense all poetry is or should be romantic.

雨果:《〈克伦威尔〉序言》
From Preface to *Cromwell*

Victor Hugo (1802-1885)

In ancient times—if I may draw attention to something that the reader will already have deduced from the preceding pages—in ancient times, the Muse had been purely epic, and, in keeping with the old polytheism and the old philosophy, she had seen nature only from one side; when she imitated the world around her, she firmly rejected from art anything that didn't correspond to a particular type of beauty. That type was, at first, magnificent; but, as with anything that has been systematized, it ultimately became unrealistic, trite, and conventional. Christianity has led poetry to the truth. Like it, the modern Muse must look at things more loftily, and more broadly. She must feel that not everything in creation is "beautiful" in human terms, that there is ugliness alongside beauty, deformity next door to gracefulness, grotesquerie just on the other side of sublimity, evil with goodness, darkness with light. She must wonder whether an artist's limited, relative logic is preferable to the infinite, absolute logic of the Creator; whether a human being has the right to correct

God; whether Nature is made more beautiful by being mutilated; whether (so to speak) it is Art's job to cut up humanity, life, creation; whether anything can move better when its muscles and supports have been taken away; whether, in short, something is more harmonious when it is less complete. Then, keeping in view both the sublime and the ridiculous, influenced by the spirit of Christian melancholy and philosophic evaluation just mentioned, poetry must make a great, decisive step forward, a step that must change the whole face of the intellectual world like the shock of an earthquake. Poetry must resolve to do what Nature does: to mingle (though not to confound) darkness with light, the sublime with the ridiculous—in other words, body with soul, animal with spirit, since poetry and religion always have the same point of departure. Everything hangs together.

So a new concept, a principle unfamiliar to the ancient world, is introduced into poetry; and therefore a new form of art develops. (Add an extra component to an entity, and you change the whole entity.) The new concept is the grotesque; the new art-form is comedy.

This is a point that needs to be stressed, because, in my view, it's the crucial factor, the fundamental difference between modern art and ancient art, current art and extinct art, or (to use less precise but more familiar words) "Romantic" literature and "Classical" literature....

To return to the point, then, let's try to show that this fertile union of the grotesque with the sublime has been the origin of the modern spirit—so complex, so varied in form, so infinite in its creations (in striking contrast to the uniform simplicity of the ancient spirit); this must be our point of departure, if we are to describe the real and radical difference between the two systems.

选文评述

选文一摘自莱辛的《拉奥孔》。这是启蒙美学的名作，也是当代方兴未艾的媒介研究在理论溯源时必然要谈到的经典。《拉奥孔》讨论了文学与造型艺术这两种媒介在处理相同题材时的不同艺术手法。1755年，温克尔曼（Johann Winckelmann）发表了《对绘画和雕塑模仿希腊作品的思考》，指出古希腊雕塑《拉奥孔》中，被大蛇缠绕的拉奥孔父子没有露出挣扎求生的痛苦表情，是因为他们的心灵伟大而镇静。绘画和雕塑等用直接的方式呈现了古典艺术的准则——"高贵的单纯与静穆的伟大"。莱辛写《拉奥孔》，有一明一暗两个目的：从显性动机看，他立场鲜明地反对温克尔曼的古典美学观；从内在动机看，他反对温克尔曼对雕塑的推崇——作为戏剧家的莱辛要为文学正名，为文学家荷马正名。莱辛指出绘画雕塑等和文学的媒介性质不同：前者是空间艺术和视觉艺术；后者是时间艺术和听觉艺术。视觉艺术截取行动中最富有感染力的片段来加以呈现，它是静态的，以"美"为最高原则。文学的叙事是线性的，无法一时容纳整个场景，但是可以在时间中推动情节进展、展现人物变化、勾勒环境语境，它的最高原则是"真"。诗不如画美，但是创作自由度更高，能够体现人的历史和人的真实。

选文二出自施莱格尔的《〈雅典娜神殿〉断片集》。《〈雅典娜神殿〉断片集》共四百五十一条断片，对浪漫派诗学进行了全面呈现。选文是第一百一十六条断片，它概括了德国早期浪漫主义的文化纲领，提出浪漫主义诗歌是杂糅的、包容的、非功利的、生成性的、创造性的、未完成的。断片的书写方式反映以上特色。断片由一条条长短不一的句子组成，看起来类似格言，但本质不同：格言将意义凝固封闭在它的短句中；而断片的各条目之间互相激发，相互缠绕，意义不断生成。断片的文体形式在诗和散文之间摆荡，既有玄想，也有抒情，使感性和思辨融为一体。这些都符合浪漫派所推崇的自由、无限、未定性的审美标准。

选文三摘自雨果《〈克伦威尔〉序言》。它是浪漫主义黑暗美学的重要篇目。雨果反对新古典主义审美的单调标准，指出纯美的世界是虚假的、平庸的、缺乏新意的。既然神造世人时给予了他双重特性，文学世界也应该对此有所呈现。从审美角度而论，崇高优美属于经过基督教净化的灵魂，而怪诞反映人类的兽性。前者和谐，但范式单一；后者有局限性、较为偏颇，但千姿百态。文学不能对其进行二选一的割舍，否则就是对生命的阉割。他认为浪漫主义的现代精神就体现在它敢于将怪诞与崇高混为一体：肉体与灵魂、兽性与灵性、阴影与光明相互补充，"如此复杂，形式如此多样，创造如此无限"。

关键术语释例

1. **希腊精神（Hellenism）**：在文学和文化领域，Hellenism一般被翻译为"希腊精神"或"希腊主义"，指的是18到19世纪期间，欧洲启蒙运动和浪漫主义思潮对希腊传统的理想化想象。其倡导者是德国新古典主义批评家温克尔曼。他研究希腊文化，总结希腊精神，歌颂希腊人崇高而稳定的灵魂。温克尔曼影响了赫尔德、席勒、歌德等作家和思想家。在他们的共同阐释下，希腊成了启蒙者的精神故乡。在浪漫主义时代，对现代化进程感到焦虑的文学家们也在回望希腊，把它进一步塑造成未受现代文明侵扰的乌托邦。在德国浪漫派代表人物弗里德里希·施莱格尔心中，希腊是人类文明自然发展的黄金时代，理性与感性、自然和精神和谐共存。在诗人拜伦、雪莱、济慈的诗中，也时常能听到希腊精神的召唤。19世纪后期，马修·阿诺德（Matthew Arnold）在《文化与无政府主义》中对希腊精神与希伯来精神进行了比较，讨论了两希文明对塑造西方精神与文化世界的重要作用。

2. 抒情诗（lyric）：虽然人类在漫长的历史里一直在用诗歌抒情，"抒情诗"的文类概念直到18世纪末才随着浪漫主义而出现。1798年华兹华斯和柯尔律治出版了《抒情歌谣集》。此时，"抒情"仍是修饰"歌谣"这一诗歌体裁的形容词，但它意涵中的灵活度和抒情性随着《抒情歌谣集》的流行而为人熟知。19世纪初，歌德提出诗歌应根据它的自然形式分为三类：叙事诗、抒情诗和戏剧诗，抒情诗作为独立文类的合法性得以进一步确立。歌谣连同颂歌、十四行诗、赞美诗等也逐渐归于抒情诗的分类之下。但这种扩充也带来定义的难度。什么是抒情诗？常见的回答有篇幅短小、富有音乐性、表达个人感情。我们提及抒情诗，有时涉及以上一个元素，有时是以上几个元素的叠加。但总体而言，主观性是抒情诗的标识。抒情诗往往采用第一人称，以便展现心灵与自己的对话。但此处的"我"不一定是诗的作者，其设定是功能性的，经由主体性的自我表达传递感知、思考和领悟。

推荐书目

Abrams, Meyer H. *The Mirror and the Lamp: Romantic Theory and the Critical Tradition*. London: Oxford University Press, 1971.

Berlin, Isaiah. *The Roots of Romanticism*. Princeton: Princeton University Press, 2001.

Black, Jeremy. *A Subject for Taste: Culture in Eighteenth-Century England*. London: Hambledon and London, 2005.

Brown, Marshall. *The Cambridge History of Literary Criticism. Vol. 5: Romanticism*. Cambridge: Cambridge University Press, 2000.

Dupré, Louis K. *The Enlightenment and the Intellectual Foundations of Modern Culture*. New Haven: Yale University Press, 2004.

Engell, James. *The Creative Imagination: Enlightenment to Romanticism*. Cambridge, Mass.: Harvard University Press, 1981.

Ferber, Michael. *Romanticism: A Very Short Introduction*. Oxford: Oxford University Press, 2010.

Mattick, Paul, Jr. *Eighteenth-Century Aesthetics and the Reconstruction of Art*. Cambridge: Cambridge University Press, 1993.

Nisbet, H. B., and Claude Rawson. *The Cambridge History of Literary Criticism. Vol. 4: The Eighteenth Century*. Cambridge: Cambridge University Press, 1997.

张旭春：《浪漫主义、文学理论与比较文学研究论稿》。上海：复旦大学出版社，2013年。

第四章
从现实主义到象征主义

概述

　　始自18世纪末的浪漫主义携带自由与解放的力量，突破新古典主义的禁锢，到了19世纪上半叶，已经成为当时西方文学最强劲的潮流。与此同时，西方社会也在经历着日新月异的变化：从社会结构看，工业资本主义快速发展，贵族没落，资本家权力膨胀，中产阶级崛起，工人阶级的队伍不断壮大，阶级矛盾尖锐化；从价值体系看，达尔文主义给了动摇中的基督教信仰体系致命一击，但替代宗教的价值体系却未出现。此外，城市化进程已不可逆，城市人口急剧增加，城市的生产模式、消费模式和居住特点改变了人们传统的生活方式；科学技术不断跃升，铁路运输网、远洋汽轮、电报系统等给人们带来全新的时空体验……面对这些变化，关注超验的彼岸世界、神秘的他乡或者是田园诗性自然的浪漫主义，却越来越与时代脱节。在这样的时代背景下，现实主义文学思潮诞生。比较而言，浪漫主义强调想象力和自由，现实主义以真实为关键词；浪漫主义关心独立的个体，现实主义关心社会中的人；浪漫主义以自然与人有机关联的农业乌托邦和超验的理想世界等来抵抗现实世界的种种问题，现实主义则认为文学的价值在于直面社会现实，在针砭时弊的基础上呼吁改革。

　　19世纪西方现实主义继承了始于亚里士多德的广义现实主义的摹仿论传统，但它与长期占统治地位的古典摹仿论有本质区别：古典摹仿论受理性范式的制约，对生活进行拔高和提纯；现实主义主张呈现真实的社会，其先声是启蒙时代狄德罗和莱辛的市民戏剧论。从思想源流看，这一时期的现实主义文论呼应了同时代法国哲学家孔德（Auguste Comte）提出的实证主义。孔德反对启蒙抽象理性，认为它是空泛的坐而论道；他借鉴自然科学的实证范式，提出一切知识必须建立在来自观察和实验的经验事实基础之上，对人类社会和历史的研究也应如此。在《论实证精神》的开篇，孔德提出人类社会发展有三个阶段：神学阶段、形而上学阶段和实证阶段。19世纪的欧洲已经告别神学阶段和形而上学阶段的虚幻，进入实证阶段。孔德的实证主义主张观察人类社会的普遍秩序，总结各个发展阶段的不同规律，探索人类社会的进步方向，以经验克服抽象，以理性克服幻想，提倡务实有用，强调精确性和真实性。

反思浪漫主义，对古典主义的摹仿论进行扬弃，吸纳实证主义的思想动力，这些构成了现实主义文论的成因。19世纪现实主义理论家中不少是小说家，巴尔扎克（Honoré de Balzac）是其中的重要代表。巴尔扎克提出，故事家得是全才：应该是历史学家和戏剧家，应该有深刻的辩证法使描绘的人物活起来，还应该有画家的调色板和观察家的放大镜。他认为文学对世界的描摹离不开对世界的整体性把握，所以文学家需要有历史的眼光和思想的高度。但是，他反对文学受制于抽象历史规律，主张呈现人类心灵和社会历史的深入交织，所以他重视戏剧家的艺术张力、画家的艺术呈现力以及观察家对细节的入微把握。

巴尔扎克从文学家的视角关注现实主义的思想性和艺术性，丹纳（Hippolyte Taine）则从人文科学视角，对文学和艺术进行实证主义考察。丹纳深受孔德影响：孔德将自然科学范式引入对社会的考察，被誉为"社会学之父"；丹纳则将实证范式运用于文学艺术领域，总结艺术的哲学。此外，丹纳也受到了达尔文进化论的影响，借鉴物种适应环境的理论，思考人类艺术的制约性要素。综合以上原因，丹纳在《艺术哲学》中将美学类比为实用植物学：后者的研究对象是植物，前者的研究对象是人的作品；不同的土壤和气候孕育出不同的花朵树木，不同的民族心理、地域特点、社会构型、历史进程孕育出不同的文学。丹纳在考察文学史时，特别重视对种族、环境和时代精神这三个文学动因的分析，将作品、作家、文学运动放在其生成的客观条件中加以考察。在《英国文学史》（*History of English Literature*）中，他论述了莎士比亚、弥尔顿、雪莱等作家的作品如何反映英国的民族特性和各自身处的历史时期的时代精神。他的文学史观体现了历史主义与现实主义的结合。在相同原则基础上，丹纳提出以"特征性"为核心的艺术真实观，认为艺术家有权利对现实进行加工，突出特点，使艺术品能比实际事物表现得更清楚、更完整。

法国自然主义的发展和丹纳的理论有很深的渊源。其代表性人物左拉（Émile Zola）坦言年轻时正是因为阅读丹纳，才走上实证主义道路。但他认为丹纳的"种族、环境、时代"三要素的论断不够严谨，重点不突出。左拉受达尔文主义影响，提出要做纯粹的自然主义者和纯粹的生理学家。在《实验小说》（"The Experimental Novel"）中，左拉将小说家比作医生，指出医生在医学实验中观察人的身体物质性，文学家则在文学实验创作中观察人类的激情和冲动。小说家需要以医生式的不偏不倚的科学态度观察和记录社会的真实相貌，包括承认其阴暗面以及描写人作为动物的基本冲动。为此，他受到了诸多抨击。比如，他的自然主义立场被当时的法国批评界批评为缺乏道德责任感，他被称为"阴沟里的清道夫"。对此，左拉予以回应，表示自己虽然描写了社会的阴暗面，但是这是为了揭露问题。而且，他认为自然主义的写作不应有禁区，作家应该有创作的自由。当批评界把他和现实主义作家相比较，批评他的作品缺乏广阔的社会视野时，他撰写了《巴尔扎克与我的区别》一文，宣告他不打算像巴尔扎克一样，做一个政治家、哲学家和道德家。他指出，巴尔扎克写《人间喜剧》是要通过描绘三千人物撰写法国风俗史，而他写《卢贡–马卡尔家族》所想描绘的不是当代社会，而是要透过一个家族，看环境对其的影响。

左拉的自然主义主张用解剖者的眼光观察世界，对现实进行科学文献式的记录。美国小说家亨利·詹姆斯（Henry James）则惋惜左拉虽才华出众，却被自然主义创作理念拖累，在小说中罗列过多平庸琐碎的意象，牺牲了差异感和微妙，而且对人物和激情的刻画用力过猛，反而使作品流于混沌。詹姆斯主张以生动性和精确性作为写作规范——这是詹姆斯所看重的"小说的艺术"。他认为人类的经验是如此丰富、如此复杂，唯有对细节进行精心的挑选和精确的呈现，才能在艺术的图案中呈现现实的繁复、精美与生动。驾驭艺术，不能凭技巧，需要的是高度的智性、审美领悟力和文学想象力。实际上，詹姆斯基于艺术性原则，也批判了丹纳。他认为丹纳在其理论中将人类类比为植物或者是机器，剥夺了人的神秘性与神圣性，无法解释人性中各种曲折幽微之处。

托尔斯泰（Leo Tolstoy）的现实主义文学观既不同于左拉近乎冷酷的自然主义，也不同于詹姆斯优雅细腻的小说艺术论。托尔斯泰重视艺术的人民性。他指出，这个社会的主体是普通劳动者，无法让他们喜爱的艺术不是真正的艺术。他反对欧洲文学中的精英主义倾向，认为它所反映的艺术世界虽然精致，却狭隘局促、伪善虚荣。为此，他特别重视艺术的情感之真：普通民众不会欣赏阳春白雪，却会被艺术家的真诚所感染，被诚恳创作的朴素艺术所打动。托尔斯泰认为艺术是全人类共同的崇高精神幸福，"艺术的任务就是建立人类之间兄弟般的团结"。

以上理论家的看法各有侧重点，但总体而言，他们都属于19世纪中叶以来西方文论中影响力最大的现实主义阵营。而欧洲的现实主义，在19世纪下半叶，受到了来自唯美主义的挑战。

在英国，唯美主义的诞生和时代精神危机有关。19世纪下半叶的英国，功利主义、个人主义流行，人们看重物质利益，轻视精神追求。为此，马修·阿诺德撰写《文化与无政府主义》来剖析英国文化时弊。他指出当时社会存在三种人和三种习气：贵族是野蛮人（Barbarians），傲慢自满，自由不羁；中产阶级是非利士人（Philistines），眼界狭隘，唯利是图；平民是群氓（Populace），缺乏独立思考能力，冲动鲁莽好热闹。他们各行其是，致使社会成为一盘散沙，缺乏统一的道德准则作为向心力。为此，阿诺德主张用文化教化团结社会各阶层，认为文化是对完美的追寻，是行善的道德热情和社会热情。他认为要树立正确的文化观，离不开批评界对思想的塑造。在《当今批评的功用》一文中，他主张用无功利性的批评确立公正的文学标准，"建立起思想观念的秩序"，让"最好的思想观念占优势"，引领人们克服心智的迟钝和庸俗的自我满足，重塑心灵的完善，提振社会风气。

在宗教式微的年代，阿诺德实际上把文化视为新的公民宗教。相同的是，唯美主义也对文化寄予了厚望。不同的是，唯美主义认为过度强调文化的道德性，也是一种含功利目标的理性。纯感性的无功利的审美才是对抗时代异化的途径。早期唯美主义者沃尔特·佩特（Walter Pater）在《文艺复兴史研究》中特别强调美的感性和经验性，反对孔德和黑格尔美学的抽象讨论。他在著作中赞颂波提切利、达芬奇、米开朗琪罗的艺术创作，看似高扬古典美学的旗帜，实则提倡具有现代性内涵的"瞬间"美学：人生既异彩纷呈，又倏忽无常，为此，不必在艺术中寻找永恒的价值，相反，要加强观察和接触，获取新的印象，寻求新的体验。佩特喜爱文艺复兴的艺术，因为它的丰盈之美能够瞬间直击人心。在佩特看来，美的意义在于当下性，美携带丰沛的激情，但也稍纵即逝。这种时不我待的审美渴望反映出身处急速变化且失去恒久精神依托的现代世界的焦虑感。

英国唯美主义最负盛名的代表人物奥斯卡·王尔德（Oscar Wilde）深受佩特影响，也主张瞬间美学，而且强化了这种美学中及时行乐的色彩。但是他一方面强调美的经验性，主张生活艺术化，另一方面将美抽象化，主张"为艺术而艺术"，从而使美成为可以寄托永恒价值的精神乌托邦。王尔德在现实主义潮流中高扬唯美主义旗帜，批评现实主义小说家所塑造的被历史潮流裹挟的人缺乏真正的主体性和独立的精神世界。他从艺术中剥离了道德负载和真理言说，弱化了它与现实的关联，只保留它的感性冲动和超验价值，认为美能够为被功利时代所异化的人们提供精神救赎。

"为艺术而艺术"不是王尔德的原创。1835年，法国唯美主义者戈蒂埃（Théophile Gautier）在长篇小说《莫班小姐》的序言中，已提出类似的观点。戈蒂埃继承浪漫主义超验美学，提出美的本质是非功利性。如同一件东西的用途会遮蔽它的美感一样，诗歌一旦与现实生活关联甚密，就失去了它的诗性。艺术唯有以自身为目的，才是自由的和纯粹的。19世纪中叶，法国诗人波德莱尔（Charles Baudelaire）受爱伦·坡的唯美论影响，主张把道德、科学和哲学从艺术中剔除，以打造艺术的自治领域。艺术为自己立法，艺术化丑为美，这是艺术奇妙的特权。《恶之花》便是波德莱尔践行唯美主义艺术观的具体范例。

波德莱尔是唯美主义者，同时也是象征主义者，他在创作中用象征主义的艺术手法传达唯美主义的理念。当个别事物中寓居了超越其个体性的更深广的普遍意义时，它就构成了象征。象征因此具有三重性：它是经验可感知的具体物；它有精神性的内涵；它还蕴含着人类对世界的共通性的体悟和认识。波德莱尔既重视美的感性，也重视美的超验性，这两者在象征中完美地结合。在被称为"象征主义宪章"的诗歌《应和》中，他将世界视为象征组成的森林，其中万物联动，意象相互应和，感受与思想、物质与精神、自我与世界的界限消弭，融为一体。

法国象征主义灵魂人物马拉美（Stéphane Mallarmé）则比波德莱尔更重视象征主义的语言维度，认为象征主义文学应主动挑战语言极限，使阐释具有多种可能性，以扩充文学的意指维度。为此，他主张象征的"暗示"论，在《文学的进化》（"The Evolution of Literature"）中指出："命名一个对象在很大程度上会破坏诗意的快感……理想的做法是暗示对象。正是这种神秘感的完美运用才构成了象征。"他认为象征的意义藏匿于作为其载体的具象之物中，透过线索性的暗示指向多重意义的内涵。问题在于，此类诗歌曲高和寡，复杂意象和艰深语言令普通读者望而生畏。19世纪末，象征主义在法国文坛渐渐没落。但20世纪20年代，它在欧洲迎来了复兴：象征主义以语言的先锋性、神秘主义的美学特征和丰富的文化内涵吸引了里尔克（Rainer Maria Rilke）和叶芝（William Butler Yeats）等现代主义诗人。以叶芝为例，他发现借助象征，"高度主观的艺术能避免因刻意安排而导致的贫乏和浅陋，进入自然的丰富和深沉之中"。他在爱尔兰民间文学和神话的复杂象征体系中吸取养分，找到了既能保持诗人独特个性又能应和自然之力和历史文化传承的象征主义诗歌创作之路。

论述及此，我们已简略通览西方文论从19世纪中叶到20世纪初的变化历程。在这一时期，现实主义是主调，从中演化出自然主义分支；但浪漫主义影响力尤在，随时代演进，形成了唯美主义和象征主义两股支流。事实上，这些流派都以或明或暗的方式，关联着20世纪西方现当代文论：何为现实主义是西方马克思主义的主要议题之一；自然主义文论关注人的生命冲动，始自弗洛伊德的心理分析学派对此有更为系统的论述；唯美主义文论强调艺术本体论，20世纪初的形式主义也有相同关切；象征主义诗学以含混和复杂性为特征，这是欧美新批评所推崇的诗学风格。至此，西方文论即将开启现当代文论的新章。

主要文本阅读

丹纳：《〈英国文学史〉序言》

选文简介

丹纳认为文学是由自然和社会的双重合力孕育而成。具体而言，它牵涉三个决定性因素：内部动力是种族，外部动力是环境，后天动力是时代。种族体现人类的先天性和遗传性倾向，世代积淀的传统经由血脉传承铸就民族性格。环境则是塑造种族的外部力量，它包括气候、地貌等地理环境，也包括宗教信仰、国家制度等社会环境，在它的影响下，不同的民族具有不同的性格。时代则带来变化的动态力量，同一个民族世代居住在同一片土地，可是每一代人有各自的特点。在这三个因素中，丹纳认为种族是主要动力。需要澄清的是，丹纳在法语语境中使用"种族"这个概念时，虽然也指涉生物学意义上的意涵，但主要还是"民族"与"国家"之意。

From Introduction to *History of English Literature*

Hippolyte Taine (1828-1893)

Three different sources contribute to producing this elementary moral state—the race, the surroundings, and the epoch. What we call the *race* are the innate and hereditary dispositions which man brings with him to the light, and which, as a rule, are united with the marked differences in the temperament and structure of the body. They vary with various peoples. There is a natural variety of men, as of oxen and horses, some brave and intelligent, some timid and dependent, some capable of superior conceptions and creations, some reduced to rudimentary ideas and inventions, some more specially fitted to special works, and gifted more richly with particular instincts, as we meet with species of dogs better favored than others—these for hunting, these for fighting, these for the chase, these again for house dogs or shepherds' dogs. We have here a distinct force—so distinct, that amidst the vast deviations which the other two motive forces produce in him, one can recognize it still; and a race, like the old Aryans, scattered from the Ganges as far as the Hebrides, settled in every clime, spread over every grade of civilization, transformed by thirty centuries of revolutions, nevertheless manifests in its tongues, religions, literatures, philosophies, the community of blood and of intellect which to this day binds its offshoots together. Different as they are, their parentage is not obliterated; barbarism, culture and grafting, differences of sky and soil, fortunes good and bad, have labored in vain: the great marks of the original model have remained, and we find again the two or three principal lineaments of the primitive imprint underneath the secondary imprints which time has stamped above them....For as soon as an animal begins to exist, it has to reconcile itself with its surroundings; it breathes after a new fashion, renews itself, is differently affected according to the new changes in air, food, temperature. Different climate and situation bring it various needs, and consequently a different course of actions; and this, again, a different set of habits; and still again, a different set of aptitudes and instincts. Man, forced to accommodate himself to circumstances, contracts a temperament and a character corresponding to them; and his character, like his temperament, is so much more stable, as the external impression is made upon him by more numerous repetitions, and is transmitted to his progeny by a more ancient descent. So that at any moment we may consider the character of a people as an abridgment of all its preceding actions and sensations; that is, as a quantity and as a weight, not infinite, since everything in nature is finite, but disproportioned to the rest, and almost impossible to lift, since every moment of an almost infinite past has contributed to increasing it, and because, in order to raise the scale, one must place in the opposite scale a still greater number of actions and sensations. Such is the first and richest source of these master faculties from which historical events take their rise; and one sees at the outset, that if it be powerful, it is because this is no simple spring, but a kind of lake, a deep reservoir wherein other springs have, for a multitude of centuries, discharged their several streams.

Having thus outlined the interior structure of a race, we must consider the surroundings in which it exists. For man is not alone in the world: nature surrounds him, and his fellow men surround him; accidental and secondary tendencies come to place themselves on his primitive tendencies, and physical or social circumstances disturb or confirm the character committed to their charge. In course of time the climate has had its effect. Though we can follow but obscurely the Aryan peoples from their common fatherland to their final countries, we can yet assert that the profound differences which are manifest between the German races on the one side, and the Greek and Latin on the other arise for the most part from the difference between the countries in which they are settled: some in cold moist lands, deep in black marshy forests or on the shores of a wild ocean, caged in by melancholy or violent sensations, prone to drunkenness and gluttony, bent on a fighting, blood-spilling life; others, again, within a lovely landscape, on a bright and laughing seacoast, enticed to navigation and commerce, exempt from gross cravings of the stomach, inclined from the beginning to social ways, to a settled organization of the state, to feelings and dispositions such as develop the art of oratory, the talent for enjoyment, the inventions of science, letters, arts. Sometimes the state policy has been at work, as in the two Italian civilizations: the first wholly turned to action, conquest, government, legislation, by the original site of its city of refuge, by its borderland emporium, by an armed aristocracy, who, by inviting and drilling the strangers and the conquered, presently set face to face two hostile armies, having no escape from its internal discords and its greedy instincts but in systematic warfare; the other, shut out from unity and any great political ambition by the stability of its municipal character, the cosmopolitan condition of its pope, and the military intervention of neighboring nations, directed the whole of its magnificent, harmonious bent toward the worship of pleasure and beauty....Look around you upon the regulating instincts and faculties implanted in a race—in short, the mood of intelligence in which it thinks and acts at the present time: you will discover most often the work of some one of these prolonged situations, these surrounding circumstances, persistent and gigantic pressures, brought to bear upon an aggregation of men who, singly and together, from generation to generation, are continually molded and modeled by their action; in Spain, an eight-century crusade against the Mussulmans, protracted even beyond and until the exhaustion of the nation by the expulsion of the Moors, the spoliation of the Jews, the establishment of the Inquisition, the Catholic wars; in England, a political establishment of eight centuries, which keeps a man erect and respectful, in independence and obedience, and accustoms him to striving unitedly, under the authority of the law; in France, a Latin organization, which, imposed first upon docile barbarians, then shattered in the universal crash, is reformed from within under a lurking conspiracy of the national instinct, is developed under hereditary kings, ends in a sort of egality republic, centralized, administrative, under dynasties exposed to revolution. These are the most efficacious of the visible causes which mold the primitive man: they are to nations what education, career, condition, abode, are to individuals; and they seem to comprehend everything, since they comprehend all external powers which shape human matter, and by which the external acts on the internal.

There is yet a third rank of causes; for, with the forces within and without, there is the work which they have already produced together, and this work itself contributes to producing that which follows. Beside the permanent impulse and the given surroundings, there is the acquired momentum. When the national character and surrounding circumstances operate, it is not upon a *tabula rasa*, but on a ground on which marks are already impressed. According as one takes the ground at one moment or another, the imprint is different; and this is the cause that the total effect is different. Consider, for instance, two epochs of a literature or an art—French tragedy under Corneille and under Voltaire, the Greek drama under Aeschylus and under Euripides, Italian painting under da Vinci and under Guido. Truly, at either of these two extreme points the general idea has not changed; it is always the same human type which is its subject of representation or painting; the mold of verse, the structure of the drama, the form of body has endured. But among several differences there is this, that the one artist is the precursor, the other the successor; the first has no model, the second has; the first sees objects face to face, the second sees them through the first; that many great branches of art are lost, many details are perfected, that simplicity and grandeur of impression have diminished, pleasing and refined forms have increased— in short, that the first work has outlived the second. So it is with a people as with a plant; the same sap, under the same temperature, and in the same soil, produces, at different steps of its progressive development, different formations, buds, flowers, fruits, seed vessels, in such a manner that the one which follows has always the first for its condition, and grows from its death. And if now you consider no longer a brief epoch, as our own time, but one of those wide intervals which embrace one or more centuries, like the Middle Ages, or our last classic age, the conclusion will be similar. A certain dominant idea has had sway; men, for two, for five hundred years, have taken to themselves a certain ideal model of man: in the Middle Ages, the knight and the monk; in our classic age, the courtier, the man who speaks well. This creative and universal idea is displayed over the whole field of action and thought; and after covering the world with its works, involuntarily systematic, it has faded, it has died away, and lo, a new idea springs up, destined to a like domination, and the like number of creations. And here remember that the second depends in part upon the first, and that the first, uniting its effect with those of national genius and surrounding circumstances, imposes on each new creation its bent and direction. The great historical currents are formed after this law—the long dominations of one intellectual pattern, or a master idea, such as the period of spontaneous creations called the Renaissance, or the period of oratorical models called the Classical Age, or the series of mystical compositions called the Alexandrian and Christian eras, or the series of mythological efflorescences which we meet with in the infancy of the German people, of the Indian and the Greek. Here as elsewhere we have but a mechanical problem; the total effect is a result, depending entirely on the magnitude and direction of the producing causes. The only difference which separates these moral problems from physical ones is that the magnitude and direction cannot be valued or computed in the first as in the second. If a need or a faculty is a quantity, capable of degrees, like a pressure or a weight, this quantity is not measurable like the pressure or the weight. We cannot define it in an exact or approximative formula; we cannot have more, or give more, in respect of it, than a literary impression; we are limited to marking and quoting the salient points by which it is manifested, and which indicate approximately and roughly the part of the scale which is its position. But though the means of notation are not the same in the moral and physical sciences, yet as in both the matter is the same, equally made up of forces, magnitudes, and directions, we may say that in both the final result is produced after the same method....So much we can say with confidence, that the unknown creations toward which the current of the centuries conducts us, will be raised up and regulated altogether by the three primordial forces; that if these forces could be measured and computed, one might deduce from them as from a formula the specialties of future civilization; and that if, in spite of the evident crudeness of our notations, and the fundamental inexactness of our measures, we try now to form some idea of our general destiny, it is upon an examination of these forces that we must ground our prophecy. For in enumerating them, we traverse the complete circle of the agencies; and when we have considered race, circumstance, and epoch, which are the internal mainsprings, the external pressure, and the acquired momentum, we have exhausted not only the whole of the actual cause, but also the whole of the possible causes of motive.

左拉：《实验小说》

选文简介

左拉于1880年发表了《实验小说》来阐述他的自然主义立场。"实验性"这个概念借鉴自贝尔纳（Claude Bernard）的《实验医学研究导论》。左拉希望用医学实验观察的方法使他的小说有"科学真理的严谨"。在小说实验中，小说家设定出特定的环境，将人物置于其中，观察和记录他们的行动，考察遗传、生理、环境诸因素对人物的决定作用。这篇文章的重点可以总结成一句话：自然主义小说是"小说家借助观察对人进行的真正的实验"。但还有另外两点值得注意。首先，左拉在文中反驳了"自然主义没有道德感"的论断。左拉抵制用道德洁癖钳制小说创作自由，他认为对非道德议题避而不谈，只能令人无法厘清问题所在。实验小说家肩负着伦理使命，他需要观察人性弱点的生成原因和过程，找到约束它的规律——这比道德家空谈理想更有的放矢。此外，左拉反驳了"自然主义信奉宿命论"的说法。宿命论中，人们放弃了自由意志，跟随命运的指挥棒麻木行进，对环境等制约性因素毫不在意。左拉指出，自然主义的决定论反对听天由命，主张通过实验，观察和了解各种现象的生成条件和制约因素，清理滋生弊病的环境。小说家的要务是通过实验了解症结所在，以便立法者和管理者采取有效行动。

From "The Experimental Novel"

Émile Zola (1840-1902)

In my literary essays I have often spoken of the application of the experimental method to the novel and to the drama. The return to nature, the naturalistic evolution which marks the century, drives little by little all the manifestation of human intelligence into the same scientific path. Only the idea of a literature governed by science is doubtless a surprise, until explained with precision and understood. It seems to me necessary, then, to say briefly and to the point what I understand by the experimental novel.

I really only need to adapt, for the experimental method has been established with strength and marvelous clearness by Claude Bernard in his *Introduction à l'étude de la médecine experimentale*. This work, by a savant whose authority is unquestioned, will serve me as a solid foundation. I shall here find the whole question treated, and I shall restrict myself to irrefutable arguments and to giving the quotations which may seem necessary to me. This will then be but a compiling of texts, as I intend on all points to entrench myself behind Claude Bernard. It will often be but necessary for me to replace the word *doctor* by the word *novelist*, to make my meaning clear and to give it the rigidity of a scientific truth.

What determined my choice, and made me choose *L'Introduction* as my basis, was the fact that medicine, in the eyes of a great number of people, is still an art, as is the novel. Claude Bernard all his life was searching and battling to put medicine in a scientific path. In his struggle we see the first feeble attempts of a science to disengage itself little by little from empiricism, and to gain a foothold in the realm of truth, by means of the experimental method. Claude Bernard demonstrates that this method, followed in the study of inanimate bodies in chemistry and in physics, should be also used in the study of living bodies, in physiology and medicine. I am going to try and prove for my part that if the experimental method leads to the knowledge of physical life, it should also lead to the knowledge of the passionate and intellectual life. It is but a question of degree in the same path which runs from chemistry to physiology, then from physiology to anthropology and to sociology. The experimental novel is the goal....

Now, to return to the novel, we can easily see that the novelist is equally an observer and an experimentalist. The observer in him gives the facts as he has observed them, suggests the point of departure, displays the solid earth on which his characters are to tread and the phenomena to develop. Then the experimentalist appears and introduces an experiment, that is to say, sets his characters going in a certain story so as to show that the succession of facts will be such as the requirements of the determinism of the phenomena under examination call for. Here it is nearly always an experiment "*pour voir*," as Claude Bernard calls it. The novelist starts out in search of a truth. I will take as an example the character of the Baron Hulot, in *Cousine Bette*, by Balzac. The general fact observed by Balzac is the ravages that the amorous temperament of a man makes in his home, in his family, and in society. As soon as he has chosen his subject he starts from known facts; then he makes his experiment, and exposes Hulot to a series of trials, placing him amid certain surroundings in order to exhibit how the complicated machinery of his passions works. It is then evident that there is not only observation there, but that there is also experiment; as Balzac does not remain satisfied with photographing the facts collected by him, but interferes in a direct way to place his character in certain conditions, and of these he remains the master. The problem is to know what such a passion, acting in such a surrounding and under such circumstances, would produce from the point of view of an individual and of society; and an experimental novel, *Cousine Bette*, for example, is simply the report of the experiment that the novelist conducts before the eyes of the public. In fact, the whole operation consists in taking facts in nature, then in studying the mechanism of these facts, acting upon them, by the modification of circumstances and surroundings, without deviating from the laws of nature. Finally, you possess knowledge of the man, scientific knowledge of him, in both his individual and social relations....

And I reach thus the great reproach with which they think to crush the naturalistic novelists, by treating them as fatalists. How many times have they wished to prove to us that as soon as we did not accept free will, that as soon as man was no more to us than a living machine, acting under the influence of heredity and surroundings, we should fall into gross fatalism, we should debase humanity to the rank of a troop marching under the baton of destiny. It is necessary to define our terms: we are not fatalists, we are determinists, which is not at all the same thing. Claude Bernard explains the two terms very plainly:

> We have given the name of determinism to the nearest or determining cause of phenomena. We never act upon the essence of phenomena in nature, but only on their determinism, and by this very fact, that we act upon it, determinism differs from fatalism, upon which we could not act at all. Fatalism assumes that the appearance of any phenomenon is necessary apart from its conditions, while determinism is just the conditions, essential for the appearance of any phenomenon, and such appearance is never forced. Once the search for the determinism of phenomena is placed as a fundamental principle of the experimental method, there is no longer either materialism, or spiritualism, or inanimate matter, or living matter; there remain but phenomena of which it is necessary to determine the conditions, that is to say, the circumstances which play, by their proximity to these phenomena, the role of nearest cause.

This is decisive. All we do is to apply this method in our novels, and we are the determinists who experimentally try to determine the condition of the phenomena, without departing in our investigations from the laws of nature. As Claude Bernard very truly says, the moment that we can act, and that we do act, on the determining cause of phenomena—by modifying their surroundings, for example—we cease to be fatalists.

Here you have, then, the moral purpose of the experimental novelist clearly defined. I have often said that we do not have to draw a conclusion from our works; and this means that our works carry their conclusion with them. An experimentalist has no need to conclude, because, in truth, experiment concludes for him. A hundred times, if necessary, he will repeat the experiment before the public; he will explain it; but he need neither become indignant nor approve of it personally; such is the truth, such is the way phenomena work; it is for society to produce or not to produce these phenomena, according as the result is useful or dangerous. You cannot imagine, as I have said elsewhere, a savant being provoked with azote because azote is dangerous to life; he suppresses azote when it is harmful, and not otherwise. As our power is not the same as that of a savant, as we are experimentalists without being practitioners, we ought to content ourselves with searching out the determinism of social phenomena, and leaving to legislators and to men of affairs the care of controlling sooner or later these phenomena in such a way as to develop the good and reject the bad, from the point of view of their utility to man.

In our role as experimental moralists we show the mechanism of the useful and the useless, we disengage the determinism of the human and social phenomena so that, in their turn, the legislators can one day dominate and control these phenomena. In a word, we are working with the whole country toward that great object, the conquest of nature and the increase of man's power a hundredfold. Compare with ours the work of the idealistic writers, who rely upon the irrational and the supernatural, and whose every flight upward is followed by a deeper fall into metaphysical chaos. We are the ones who possess strength and morality....

The conclusion to which I wish to come is this: if I were to define the experimental novel I should not say, as Claude Bernard says, that a literary work lies entirely in the personal feeling, for the reason that in my opinion the personal feeling is but the first impulse. Later nature, being there, makes itself felt, or at least that part of nature of which science has given us the secret, and about which we have no longer any right to romance. The experimental novelist is therefore the one who accepts proven facts, who points out in man and in society the mechanism of the phenomena over which science is mistress, and who does not interpose his personal sentiments, except in the phenomena whose determinism is not yet settled, and who tries to test, as much as he can, this personal sentiment, this idea a priori, by observation and experiment.

I cannot understand how our naturalistic literature can mean anything else. I have only spoken of the experimental novel, but I am fairly convinced that the same method, after having triumphed in history and in criticism, will triumph everywhere, on the stage and in poetry even. It is an inevitable evolution. Literature, in spite of all that can be said, does not depend merely upon the author; it is influenced by the nature it depicts and by the man whom it studies. Now if the savants change their ideas of nature, if they find the true mechanism of life, they force us to follow them, to precede them even, so as to play our role in the new hypotheses. The metaphysical man is dead; our whole territory is transformed by the advent of the physiological man. No doubt "Achilles' Anger," "Dido's Love," will last forever on account of their beauty; but today we feel the necessity of analyzing anger and love, of discovering exactly how such passions work in the human being. This view of the matter is a new one; we have become experimentalists instead of philosophers. In short, everything is summed up in this great fact: the experimental method in letters, as in the sciences, is in the way to explain the natural phenomena, both individual and social, of which metaphysics, until now, has given only irrational and supernatural explanations.

詹姆斯:《小说的艺术》

选文简介

詹姆斯的《小说的艺术》一文发表于1884年,是对沃尔特·贝赞特爵士(Sir Walter Besant)在大不列颠皇家研究院的演讲的回应。贝赞特在演讲中指出,小说是一种高贵的艺术,相比绘画等艺术形式以及诗歌等文学形式,小说有它的优势,适合展现广阔的人性。詹姆斯对此深表赞同,但是反对贝赞特在演讲中列出的小说艺术的清单——贝赞特认为人们可以像学习绘画法则一样掌握小说的写作技巧。詹姆斯认为小说需要捕捉生活的真实感,这是总的原则,但是它没有具体配方,因为"人性广袤,现实有无数种形式"。人们对现实的感受凝聚成经验,它是情感、动机和行动等的复杂缠绕,詹姆斯在选文中将它比喻为蛛网:"经验是无穷的,并且永无止境;它是广大的情感,是一种由最精细的丝线织成的巨大蛛网,悬挂在意识的洞穴中,捕捉飘浮到网内的空中微粒。"詹姆斯认为小说的艺术性也是它的形式美,应为表征这种复杂而真实的经验服务。要实现这一点,需要对经验保持开放的心态,尊重艺术和想象的自由,以及培养心智,因为"艺术作品最深层的质量永远是制作者的思想的质量"。

From "The Art of Fiction"

Henry James (1843-1916)

It goes without saying that you will not write a good novel unless you possess the sense of reality; but it will be difficult to give you a recipe for calling that sense into being. Humanity is immense, and reality has a myriad forms; the most one can affirm is that some of the flowers of fiction have the odor of it, and others have not; as for telling you in advance how your nosegay should be composed, that is another affair. It is equally excellent and inconclusive to say that one must write from experience; to our supposititious aspirant such a declaration might savor of mockery. What kind of experience is intended, and where does it begin and end? Experience is never limited, and it is never complete; it is an immense sensibility, a kind of huge spider-web of the finest silken threads suspended in the chamber of consciousness, and catching every air-borne particle in its tissue. It is the very atmosphere of the mind; and when the mind is imaginative—much more when it happens to be that of a man of genius—it takes to itself the faintest hints of life, it converts the very pulses of the air into revelations. The young lady living in a village has only to be a damsel upon whom nothing is lost to make it quite unfair (as it seems to me) to declare to her that she shall have nothing to say about the military. Greater miracles have been seen than that, imagination assisting, she should speak the truth about some of these gentlemen. I remember an English novelist, a woman of genius, telling me that she was much commended for the impression she had managed to give in one of her tales of the nature and way of life of the French Protestant youth. She had been asked where she learned so much about his recondite being, she had been congratulated on her peculiar opportunities. These opportunities consisted in her having once, in Paris, as she ascended a staircase, passed an open door where, in the household of a *pasteur*, some of the young Protestants were seated at table around a finished meal. The glimpse made a picture; it lasted only a moment, but that moment was experience. She had got her direct personal impression, and she turned out her type. She knew what youth was, and what Protestantism; she also had the advantage of having seen what it was to be French, so that she converted these ideas into a concrete image and produced a reality. Above all, however, she was blessed with the faculty which when you give it an inch takes an ell, and which for the artist is a much greater source of strength than any accident of residence or of place in the social scale. The power to guess the unseen from the seen, to trace the implication of things, to judge the whole piece by the pattern, the condition of feeling life in general so completely that you are well on your way to knowing any particular corner of it—this cluster of gifts may almost be said to constitute experience, and they occur in country and in town, and in the most differing stages of education. If experience consists of impressions, it may be said that impressions *are* experience, just as (have we not seen it?) they are the very air we breathe. Therefore, if I should certainly say to a novice, "Write from experience and experience only," I should feel that this was rather a tantalizing monition if I were not careful immediately to add, "Try to be one of the people on whom nothing is lost!"

I am far from intending by this to minimize the importance of exactness—of truth of detail. One can speak best from one's own taste, and I may therefore venture to say that the air of reality (solidity of specification) seems to me to be the supreme virtue of a novel—the merit on which all its other merits (including that conscious moral purpose of which Mr. Besant speaks) helplessly and submissively depend. If it be not there, they are all as nothing, and if these be there, they owe their effect to the success with which the author has produced the illusion of life. The cultivation of this success, the study of this exquisite process, form, to my taste, the beginning and the end of the art of the novelist. They are his inspiration, his despair, his reward, his torment, his delight. It is here in very truth that he competes with life; it is here that he competes with his brother the painter in *his* attempt to render the look of things, the look that conveys their meaning, to catch the color, the relief, the expression, the surface, the substance of the human spectacle....I cannot imagine composition existing in a series of blocks, nor conceive, in any novel worth discussing at all, of a passage of description that is not in its intention narrative, a passage of dialogue that is not in its intention descriptive, a touch of truth of any sort that does not partake of the nature of incident, or an incident that derives its interest from any other source than the general and only source of the success of a work of art—that of being illustrative. A novel is a living thing, all one and continuous, like any other organism, and in proportion as it lives will it be found, I think, that in each of the parts there is something of each of the other parts....There is an old-fashioned distinction between the novel of character and the novel of incident which must have cost many a smile to the intending fabulist who was keen about his work. It appears to me as little to the point as the equally celebrated distinction between the novel and the romance—to answer as little to any reality. There are bad novels and good novels, as there are bad pictures and good pictures; but that is the only distinction in which I see any meaning, and I can as little imagine speaking of a novel of character as I can imagine speaking of a picture of character. When one says picture, one says of character, when one says novel one says of incident, and the terms may be transposed at will. What is character but the determination of incident? What is incident but the illustration of character? What is either a picture or a novel that is *not* of character? What else do we seek in it and find in it? It is an incident for a woman to stand up with her hand resting on a table and look out at you in a certain way; or if it be not an incident I think it will be hard to say what it is. At the same time it is an expression of character. If you say you don't see it (character in *that*—*allons donc*!), this is exactly what the artist who has reasons of his own for thinking he *does* see it undertakes to show you....

So that it comes back very quickly, as I have said, to the liking: in spite of M. Zola, who reasons less powerfully than he represents, and who will not reconcile himself to this absoluteness of taste, thinking that there are certain things that people ought to like, and that they can be made to like. I am quite at a loss to imagine anything (at any rate in this matter of fiction) that people *ought* to like or to dislike. Selection will be sure to take care of itself, for it has a constant motive behind it. That motive is simply experience. As people feel life, so they will feel the art that is most closely related to it. This closeness of relation is what we should never forget in talking of the effort of the novel. Many people speak of it as a factitious, artificial form, a product of ingenuity, the business of which is to alter and arrange the things that surround us, to translate them into conventional, traditional moulds. This, however, is a view of the matter which carries us but a very short way, condemns the art to an eternal repetition of a few familiar *clichés*, cuts short its development, and leads us straight up to a dead wall. Catching the very note and trick, the strange irregular rhythm of life, that is the attempt whose strenuous force keeps Fiction upon her feet. In proportion as in what she offers us we see life *without* rearrangement do we feel that we are touching the truth; in proportion as we see it *with* rearrangement do we feel that we are being put off with a substitute, a compromise and convention....

There is one point at which the moral sense and the artistic sense lie very near together; that is in the light of the very obvious truth that the deepest quality of a work of art will always be the quality of the mind of the producer. In proportion as that intelligence is fine will the novel, the picture, the statue partake of the substance of beauty and truth. To be constituted of such elements is, to my vision, to have purpose enough. No good novel will ever proceed from a superficial mind; that seems to me an axiom which, for the artist in fiction, will cover all needful moral ground: if the youthful aspirant take it to heart it will illuminate for him many of the mysteries of "purpose." There are many other useful things that might be said to him, but I have come to the end of my article, and can only touch them as I pass....But the only condition that I can think of attaching to the composition of the novel is, as I have already said, that it be sincere. This freedom is a splendid privilege, and the first lesson of the young novelist is to learn to be worthy of it.

"Enjoy it as it deserves [I should say to him]; take possession of it, explore it to its utmost extent, publish it, rejoice in it. All life belongs to you, and do not listen either to those who would shut you up into corners of it and tell you that it is only here and there that art inhabits, or to those who would persuade you that this heavenly messenger wings her way outside of life altogether, breathing a superfine air, and turning away her head from the truth of things. There is no impression of life, no manner of seeing it and feeling it, to which the plan of the novelist may not offer a place; you have only to remember that talents so dissimilar as those of Alexandre Dumas and Jane Austen, Charles Dickens and Gustave Flaubert, have worked in this field with equal glory. Do not think too much about optimism and pessimism; try and catch the color of life itself. In France today we see a prodigious effort (that of Émile Zola, to whose solid and serious work no explorer of the capacity of the novel can allude without respect), we see an extraordinary effort vitiated by a spirit of pessimism on a narrow basis. M. Zola is magnificent, but he strikes an English reader as ignorant; he has an air of working in the dark; if he had as much light as energy, his results would be of the highest value. As for the aberrations of a shallow optimism, the ground (of English fiction especially) is strewn with their brittle particles as with broken glass. If you must indulge in conclusions, let them have the taste of a wide knowledge. Remember that your first duty is to be as complete as possible—to make as perfect a work. Be generous and delicate and pursue the prize."

马拉美:《文学的进化》

选文简介

《文学的进化》是儒勒·于莱（Jules Huret）对马拉美的采访报告。马拉美从文学史演进的角度，阐释了象征主义的新意。马拉美认为，当时的时代是缺乏稳定性和统一性的时代，象征主义顺应时代，在诗歌中追求个性化表达，"有史以来，诗人第一次不按照正统的音律来歌唱了"。象征主义诗人不排斥19世纪中叶的帕纳斯派（the Parnassians）法国诗人对严谨诗歌形式的追求，但反对其千篇一律的刻板；不排斥古典格律，但希冀为它加入节奏的变化，使它更自由更灵动。从诗歌内容看，帕纳斯派诗歌遵循摹仿论传统，主张直陈其是；象征主义则认为诗歌不为模仿，不求表达，它"存在于对事物的沉思之中，存在于由事物唤起的退想而自然形成的意象之中"。在此过程中，隐含深意的暗示凝结成了象征。在揣测象征之物的含义时，人们在解码谜团，也在进行想象性创造。马拉美不在乎人们批评象征主义诗歌晦涩难懂。他认为诗歌的魅力在于它的神秘性，平庸之人无法领悟它的美。

From "The Evolution of Literature"

Stéphane Mallarmé (1842-1898)

"We are now witnessing a spectacle," he told me, "which is truly extraordinary, unique in the history of poetry: every poet is going off by himself with his own flute, and playing the songs he pleases. For the first time since the beginning of poetry, poets have stopped singing bass. Hitherto, as you know, if they wished to be accompanied, they had to be content with the great organ of official meter. Well, it was simply overplayed and they got tired of it! I am sure that when the great Hugo died, he was convinced that he had buried all poetry for the next century; and yet Paul Verlaine had already written *Sagesse.* We can forgive Hugo his illusion, when we remember all the miracles he produced; he was simply forgetting the eternal instinct, the perpetual and unavoidable growth of the lyrical. But the essential and undeniable point is this: that in a society without stability, without unity, there can be no stable or definitive art. From that incompletely organized society—which also explains the restlessness of certain minds—the unexplained need for individuality was born. The literary manifestations of today are a direct reflection of that need.

"A more immediate explanation of recent innovations is this: it has finally been understood that the old verse form was *not* the absolute, unique, and changeless form, but just one way to be sure of writing good verse. We say to children: 'Don't steal, and you'll be honest.' That is true, but it is not everything. Is it possible to write poetry without reference to time-honored precepts? Poets have answered this question affirmatively, and I believe that they are right. Poetry is everywhere in language, so long as there is rhythm—everywhere except on posters and the back page of the newspaper. In the genre we call *prose*, there are verses—sometimes admirable verses—of all sorts of rhythms. Actually, there is no such thing as prose: there is the alphabet, and then there are verses which are more or less closely knit, more or less diffuse. So long as there is stylistic effort, there is versification.

"I said a minute ago that today's poetry is, in the main, the result of the poets' boredom with official verse. Even the partisans of official verse share this boredom. Isn't it rather abnormal that, when we open a book of poetry, we should be sure of finding uniform and conventional rhythms throughout? And yet, all the while, the writer hopes to arouse our interest in the essential variety of human feelings! Where is the inspiration in all this! Where is the unforeseen! How tiresome it all is! Official verse must be used only in crisis moments of the soul. Modern poets have understood this. With a fine sense of the delicate and the sparing, they hover around the official Alexandrine, approach it with unusual timidity, almost with fear; and rather than use it as their principle or as a point of departure, they suddenly conjure it up, and with it they crown their poem or period!

"Moreover, the same transformation has taken place in music. Instead of the very clearly delineated melodies of the past, we have an infinity of broken melodies which enrich the poetic texture, and we no longer have the impression of strong cadence."

"Is that how the scission was effected?" I asked.

"Why, yes. The Parnassians were fond of a very formal prosody which has its own beauty, and they failed to realize that the modern poets were simply complementing their work; this also had the advantage of creating a sort of interregnum for the noble Alexandrine which had been at bay, crying for mercy. What we have to realize is that the most recent poetical writings do not tend to suppress the official verse; they tend rather to let a little more air into the poem, to create a kind of fluidity or mobility between long-winded verses, which has heretofore been lacking. In an orchestra, for example, you may suddenly hear very fine bursts of sound from the basses; but you know perfectly well that if there were nothing but that, you would soon have enough of it. Young poets space these bursts so that they will occur only when a total effect is to be produced. In this way, the Alexandrine (which was invented by nobody, but rather poured forth spontaneously from the instrument of language) will get out of its present finicky, sedentary state, and henceforth it will be freer, more sudden, more refreshed. Its value will lie exclusively in its use during the soul's most serious times. And future volumes of poetry will be traversed by a majestic first verse which scatters in its wake an infinity of motifs originating in the individual's sensibility.

"So there has been scission because both sides have been unaware that their points of view are reconcilable rather than mutually destructive. On the one hand, the Parnassians have, in effect, been perfectly obedient servants of verse, and have sacrificed their personalities. The young poets, on the other hand, have anchored their instinct in a variety of modes, as if there were no precedent; actually, all they are doing is reducing here and there the stiffness of the Parnassian structures; and it seems to me that the two points of view are complementary.

"Despite all this, I still believe, personally, that, with the miraculous knowledge of verse and with the superb instinct for rhythmic pause which such masters as Banville possess, the Alexandrine can be infinitely varied and can reproduce all possible shades of human passion. Banville's *Forgeron*, for example, has a number of Alexandrines which seem interminable, yet others which are unbelievably concise.

"But, after all, it was a good thing to give our perfect and traditional poetic instrument a little rest. It had been overworked."

"So much for form," I said. "What about content?"

"As far as content is concerned," he answered, "I feel that the young poets are nearer than the Parnassians to the poetical ideal. The latter still treat their subjects as the old philosophers and orators did: that is, they present things directly, whereas I think that they should be presented allusively. Poetry lies in the *contemplation* of things, in the image emanating from the reveries which things arouse in us. The Parnassians take something in its entirety and simply exhibit it; in so doing, they fall short of mystery; they fail to give our minds that exquisite joy which consists of believing that we are creating something. To *name* an object is largely to destroy poetic enjoyment, which comes from gradual divination. The ideal is to *suggest* the object. It is the perfect use of this mystery which constitutes symbol. An object must be gradually evoked in order to show a state of soul; or else, choose an object and from it elicit a state of soul by means of a series of decodings."

"Now," I said, "we are coming to the big objection I was going to make: obscurity!"

"Yes, it is a dangerous thing," he replied, "regardless of whether it results from the reader's inadequacy or from the poet's. But if you avoid the work it involves, you are cheating. If a person of mediocre intelligence and insufficient literary experience happens to open an obscure book and insists on enjoying it, something is wrong; there has simply been a misunderstanding. There must always be enigma in poetry. The purpose of literature—the *only* purpose—is to *evoke* things."

"Was it you, sir," I asked, "who created the new movement in poetry?"

"I detest 'schools,'" he replied, "and anything resembling schools. The professional attitude toward literature is repugnant to me. Literature is entirely an individual matter. As far as I am concerned, a poet today, in the midst of this society which refuses to let him live, is a man who seeks out solitude in order to sculpture his own tomb. The reason I appear to be the leader of a school, is, first of all, that I have always taken an interest in the ideas of young poets; and second, because of my sincerity in recognizing the originality of what the latest writers have contributed. In reality,

I am a hermit. I believe that poetry should be for the supreme pomp and circumstance of a constituted society in which glory should have its place. Most people seem to have forgotten glory. In our time the poet can only go on strike against society, and turn his back on all the contaminated ways and means that are offered him. For anything that is offered him is necessarily inferior to his ideal and to his secret labor."...

"What do you think of the end of naturalism?"

"Up to now, writers have entertained the childish belief that if they could just choose a certain number of precious stones, for example, and put the names on paper, they would be *making* precious stones. Now, really! That is impossible, no matter how well it is done. Poetry consists of *creation*: we must delve into our souls for states and gleams of such perfect purity, so perfectly sung and illuminated, that they will truly be the jewels of man. When we do that, we have symbol, we have creation, and the word *poetry* has its full meaning. This, in short, is the only possible human creation....

"But to get back to naturalism. It seems to me that when we use that word, we mean the work of Émile Zola; and when he has finished his work, the name will disappear. I have great admiration for Zola. Actually, what he does is not so much literature as evocative art. He depends as little as possible on literary means. True, he uses words, but that is all. Everything else is based on his marvelous sense of organization and has immediate repercussions in the mind of the mob. His talent is truly powerful; consider his tremendous feeling for life, his mob movements, that texture in Nana's skin that every one of us has touched; and he paints it all with prodigious colors. It really is an admirably organized piece of work. But literature is more of an intellectual thing than that. Things already exist, we don't have to create them; we simply have to see their relationships. It is the threads of those relationships which go to make up poetry and music."

"Are you acquainted with the psychological novel?"

"Slightly. After the great works of Flaubert, the Goncourt brothers, and Zola—which are, in a sense, poems—novelists seem to be going back to the old eighteenth century French taste which was much more humble and modest, consisting, as it did, not of a pictorial presentation of the outer form of things but rather of a dissection of the motives of the human soul. But there is the same difference between that and poetry as there is between a corset and a beautiful throat."

思考题

1. 丹纳认为考察文学史，需要注意哪三个决定性因素？它们的具体内容是什么？
2. 左拉为什么称自然主义小说是"实验小说"？
3. 左拉如何看待自然主义小说与道德之间的关系？
4. 詹姆斯在《小说的艺术》中为什么特别强调经验的作用？
5. 马拉美认为象征主义在形式上有什么样的特点？在内容上又有什么样的关注？

讨论题

1. 请比较左拉和詹姆斯对文学道德观的差异性认识。在此基础上，查阅相关资料，讨论在文学与道德的关系这个议题上，现实主义与自然主义的不同立场。
2. 请在19世纪后期到20世纪初期的欧洲象征主义诗歌中选择一首，对其进行赏析。

补充文本选摘与评述

托尔斯泰：《什么是艺术?》
From *What Is Art?*

Leo Tolstoy (1828-1910)

A real work of art destroys in the consciousness of the recipient the separation between himself and the artist, and not that alone, but also between himself and all whose minds receive this work of art. In this freeing of our personality from its separation and isolation, in this uniting of it with others, lies the chief characteristic and the great attractive force of art....

And the degree of the infectiousness of art depends on three conditions: (1) on the greater or lesser individuality of the feeling transmitted; (2) on the greater or lesser clearness with which the feeling is transmitted; (3) on the sincerity of the artist, that is, on the greater or lesser force with which the artist himself feels the emotion he transmits.

The more individual the feeling transmitted the more strongly does it act on the recipient; the more individual the state of soul into which he is transferred the more pleasure does the recipient obtain and therefore the more readily and strongly does he join in it.

Clearness of expression assists infection because the recipient who mingles in consciousness with the author is the better satisfied the more clearly that feeling is transmitted which, as it seems to him, he has long known and felt and for which he has only now found expression....

I have mentioned three conditions of contagion in art, but they may all be summed up into one, the last, sincerity; that is, that the artist should be impelled by an inner need to express his feeling. That condition includes the first; for if the artist is sincere he will express the feeling as he experienced it. And as each man is different from everyone else, his feeling will be individual for everyone else; and the more individual it is—the more the artist has drawn it from the depths of his nature—the more sympathetic and sincere will it be. And this same sincerity will impel the artist to find clear expression for the feeling which he wishes to transmit.

Therefore this third condition—sincerity—is the most important of the three. It is always complied with in peasant art, and this explains why such art always acts so powerfully; but it is a condition almost entirely absent from our upper-class art, which is continually produced by artists actuated by personal aims of covetousness or vanity.

王尔德:《谎言的衰朽》
From "The Decay of Lying"
Oscar Wilde (1854-1900)

CYRIL: Then we must certainly cultivate it at once. But in order to avoid making any error I want you to tell me briefly the doctrines of the new aesthetics.

VIVIAN: Briefly, then, they are these. Art never expresses anything but itself. It has an independent life, just as Thought has, and develops purely on its own lines. It is not necessarily realistic in an age of realism, nor spiritual in an age of faith. So far from being the creation of its time, it is usually in direct opposition to it, and the only history that it preserves for us is the history of its own progress. Sometimes it returns upon its footsteps, and revives some antique form, as happened in the archaistic movement of late Greek Art, and in the pre-Raphaelite movement of our own day. At other times it entirely anticipates its age, and produces in one century work that it takes another century to understand, to appreciate, and to enjoy....

The second doctrine is this. All bad art comes from returning to Life and Nature, and elevating them into ideals. Life and Nature may sometimes be used as part of Art's rough material, but before they are of any real service to art they must be translated into artistic conventions. The moment Art surrenders its imaginative medium it surrenders everything. As a method Realism is a complete failure, and the two things that every artist should avoid are modernity of form and modernity of subject-matter. To us, who live in the nineteenth century, any century is a suitable subject for art except our own. The only beautiful things are the things that do not concern us....M. Zola sits down to give us a picture of the Second Empire. Who cares for the Second Empire now? It is out of date. Life goes faster than Realism, but Romanticism is always in front of Life.

The third doctrine is that Life imitates Art far more than Art imitates Life. This results not merely from Life's imitative instinct, but from the fact that the self-conscious aim of Life is to find expression, and that Art offers it certain beautiful forms through which it may realize that energy. It is a theory that has never been put forward before, but it is extremely fruitful, and throws an entirely new light upon the history of Art.

It follows, as a corollary from this, that external Nature also imitates Art. The only effects that she can show us are effects that we have already seen through poetry, or in paintings. This is the secret of Nature's charm, as well as the explanation of Nature's weakness.

The final revelation is that Lying, the telling of beautiful untrue things, is the proper aim of Art. But of this I think I have spoken at sufficient length.

叶芝:《诗歌的象征主义》
From "The Symbolism of Poetry"
William Butler Yeats (1865-1939)

All sounds, all colors, all forms, either because of their preordained energies or because of long association, evoke indefinable and yet precise emotions, or, as I prefer to think, call down among us certain disembodied powers, whose footsteps over our hearts we call emotions; and when sound, and color, and form are in a musical relation, a beautiful relation to one another, they become, as it were, one sound, one color, one form, and evoke an emotion that is made out of their distinct evocations and yet is one emotion. The same relation exists between all portions of every work of art, whether it be an epic or a song, and the more perfect it is, and the more various and numerous the elements that have flowed into its perfection, the more powerful will be the emotion, the power, the god it calls among us. Because an emotion does not exist, or does not become perceptible and active among us, till it has found its expression, in color or in sound or in form, or in all of these, and because no two modulations or arrangements of these evoke the same emotion, poets and painters and musicians, and in a less degree because their effects are momentary, day and night and cloud and shadow, are continually making and unmaking mankind....

Besides emotional symbols, symbols that evoke emotions alone,—and in this sense all alluring or hateful things are symbols, although their relations with one another are too subtle to delight us fully, away from rhythm and pattern,—there are intellectual symbols, symbols that evoke ideas alone, or ideas mingled with emotions; and outside the very definite traditions of mysticism and the less definite criticism of certain modern poets, these alone are called symbols. Most things belong to one or another kind, according to the way we speak of them and the companions we give them, for symbols, associated with ideas that are more than fragments of the shadows thrown upon the intellect by the emotions they evoke, are the playthings of the allegorist or the pedant, and soon pass away. If I say "white" or "purple" in an ordinary line of poetry, they evoke emotions so exclusively that I cannot say why they move me; but if I bring them into the same sentence with such obvious intellectual symbols as a cross or a crown of thorns, I think of purity and sovereignty. Furthermore, innumerable meanings, which are held to "white" or to "purple" by bonds of subtle suggestion, and alike in the emotions and in the intellect, move visibly through my mind, and move invisibly beyond the threshold of sleep, casting lights and shadows of an indefinable wisdom on what had seemed before, it may be, but sterility and noisy violence. It is the intellect that decides where the reader shall ponder over the procession of the symbols, and if the symbols are merely emotional, he gazes from amid the accidents and destinies of the world; but if the symbols are intellectual too, he becomes himself a part of pure intellect, and he is himself mingled with the procession....So, too, if one is moved by Shakespeare, who is content with emotional symbols that he may come the nearer to our sympathy, one is mixed with the whole spectacle of the world; while if one is moved by Dante, or by the myth of Demeter, one is mixed into the shadow of God or of a goddess.

选文评述

托尔斯泰认为艺术可以促进人与人之间的联系，打破阶级隔膜，传递价值观，所以他特别重视艺术的感染力。在《什么是艺术？》中，他认为感染力是衡量艺术价值的唯一标准。托尔斯泰认为有感染力的艺术需要具备三个条件：1）它所传递的是独特的情感，越是独特，越能让感受者印象深刻；2）它所传递的是清晰的情感，越是清晰，越能让感受者有豁然开朗之感；3）它所传递的是真诚的情感，艺术家的诚意能打动人心，引发共鸣。托尔斯泰指出，三个条件中，"真诚"是核心。它是艺术家创作时的天然内驱力，它把个体从自身的孤独中解放出来，使人能够通过艺术与他人情感相通。托尔斯泰本人有强烈的宗教情怀，他期待艺术能如宗教一样，触及每个人的灵魂，团结人类共同前进，引领人性走向完善，减少世间的苦难。

托尔斯泰谈艺术的真诚与道德性，王尔德则谈艺术的非真实性（好作惊人之语的王尔德称其为"谎言"）——这反映了现实主义和唯美主义的本质区别。《谎言的衰朽》采用对话体，王尔德借助认真严肃的西里尔和放浪不羁的维维安的讨论，指出艺术与政治和道德等没有必然联系，是一种自主的人类活动，有独立的目标和评价标准。在他看来，艺术体现人类寻求表达的本能追求，不应落入现实主义的束缚，所以他在选文中强调"生活对艺术的模仿远远多于艺术对生活的模仿"，认为艺术世界在人类的日常经验世界之上，而美构成了这个艺术世界的永恒现实。王尔德的美学观中有新柏拉图主义的色彩，即美是一种理想。但是他没有将它供奉在超验的神坛上，而是要求以它为法则，对经验世界进行修改，指导和定义我们对生活和对自然世界的感觉，使它变成现实中的美学实践。这种艺术与现实、美与真之间的缠绕关系使王尔德的唯美主义观具有复杂性。

叶芝的《诗歌的象征主义》由五部分组成，对象征主义的诸多要素、和谐性原则以及音韵性特征等进行了讨论。此处选文关涉象征的分类。叶芝将象征分为情感象征和理智象征。前者是诸多感性体验积淀与融合后浑然而成的象征；后者传达纯粹的或者部分纯粹的观念，是寓言中常用的手法。他认为莎士比亚戏剧中有较多的情感象征，能够唤起我们的同情心，而但丁的史诗以理智象征为主。有趣的是，叶芝谈理智象征的时候，没有刻意将其彻底抽象化，他承认此类象征有时会是混杂性的，有情感附着其上。由此可见，叶芝的象征分类法注意到了象征在情感维度与观念维度的不同运作方式，但没有为它们设定固定的边界，而是允许象征体系自由地征调感性与理性的力量。

关键术语释例

1. **现实主义（Realism）**：现实主义有广义和狭义两种定义方式。从广义定义看，现实主义泛指用忠实于生活的方式再现人类的经验。在各个时期的文学中都能看到现实主义的脉动，它的艺术能量来自人类对自己熟悉的生活世界和日常经验的关注。从文论角度看，亚里士多德的摹仿论奠定了广义现实主义的根基。从狭义定义看，现实主义特指19世纪中叶到20世纪初的西方文学运动，它的初始诉求是抵制浪漫主义后期对想象力的滥用、过度的情感主义以及以自我为中心的表现论美学，要求"按如其所是的样态来看待事物"，代表人物有英国的狄更斯、法国的巴尔扎克、美国的豪威尔斯等。总体而言，这一时期的现实主义关注外部环境对人的塑造，描写人的具体经验历程，反映其所身处的历史和社会的总体图景。20世纪初，随着现代主义文学向人的内部心灵世界的转向，狭义的现实主义退出历史舞台，但它的传统不断被吸收、嫁接和混合，出现了超现实主义、魔幻现实主义、新现实主义等分支。

2. **象征（symbol）**："象征"在希腊语中的原意是将一块木板一分为二，两方各持一半作为信物，后来指参与神秘活动的人彼此相认时使用的标识和密语。象征作为修辞手法，特指通过言说此物，传达彼意。"以物达情""以物寓理"等手法古已有之。早在人类文明肇始时期，原始人就在借助象征，用已知之物比附、解释与表达未知之物。原始人的巫术与艺术中随处可见象征符号的应用。古希腊时期，象征是神话和史诗的重要元素。中世纪时，象征被赋予基督教的神秘性，人们借感性直观物体比喻超验的神的存在。在近现代的浪漫主义和象征主义诗歌中，象征以有形寓无形，以有限表无限，拓展了诗学语言的肌理层次，提高了文学对生命体验的表征能力。在20世纪，弗洛伊德的释梦理论和荣格的集体无意识理论都离不开对象征进行编码与解码的表意体系。

推荐书目

Baldick, Chris. *The Social Mission of English Criticism 1848-1932*. Oxford: Clarendon Press, 1983.

Carroll, Joseph. *Reading Human Nature: Literary Darwinism in Theory and Practice*. Albany: State University of New York Press, 2011.

Chadwick, Charles. *Symbolism*. London: Routledge, 2017.

Docherty, Thomas. *The Politics of Realism*. London: Bloomsbury Academic, 2021.

Furst, Lilian R., and Peter N. Skrine. *Naturalism*. London: Routledge, 2017.

Gal, Michalle. *Aestheticism: Deep Formalism and the Emergence of Modernist Aesthetics*. Bern: Peter Lang, 2015.

Habib, M. A. R. *The Cambridge History of Literary Criticism. Vol. 6: The Nineteenth Century, c. 1830-1914*. Cambridge: Cambridge University Press, 2013.

Johnson, R. V. *Aestheticism*. London: Routledge, 2017.

Lukács, György. *Studies in European Realism: A Sociological Survey of the Writings of Balzac, Stendhal, Zola, Tolstoy, Gorki and Others*. London: Merlin Press, 1972.

蒋承勇:《19世纪西方文学思潮研究:第二卷 现实主义》。北京:北京大学出版社,2022年。

王守仁等:《战后世界进程与外国文学进程研究:1 战后现实主义文学研究》。南京:译林出版社,2019年。

第二部分
现当代文论

第五章
俄国形式主义与英美新批评

概述

20世纪上半叶的现代西方文论领域，重要事件之一是俄国形式主义和英美新批评的兴起。它们起源于不同的国家，彼此没有重大相互影响，却默契地展现出某些相似的诉求：反对文学的外部研究，提倡文学本体论。具体而言，俄国形式主义和英美新批评强调"文学性"，重点考察文学的内在规律；关注文本的自足性，视其为文学价值所在；重视文学的语言维度，分析修辞、文体、叙事结构等文本性元素。因以上共性，它们被一起归入了广义的"形式主义"的行列。

事实上，广义的形式主义关注是西方文论发展史中一条从未中断过的线索。在文本层面，形式指语言、修辞、媒介等表现要素及情节和文类等组织结构方式；在艺术层面，形式指作品的文体特征和美学特质等。亚里士多德的戏剧情节论、朗吉努斯的崇高文体论、浪漫主义的诗学语言观等都反映了形式主义倾向。然而，古典文论和近代文论中，形式需要服务于其他目的：摹仿论中，形式被视为表征世界的手段；功能论中，形式被视为打动读者心灵、促进教化的工具；表现论中，形式被视为作者的艺术选择，是其创造力的证明。俄国形式主义和英美新批评的特殊之处在于它们将目光投注于形式本身，形式被视为文学的本质和考察形式，不必依赖外在因素，由形式构成的文本成了文学研究的核心。这种转向延续了19世纪末的唯美主义和象征主义对实证主义的反对和向文学内部研究的回归，但比唯美主义和象征主义的印象式批评更具野心。为了彰显文学的特异性，使其有别于历史、哲学等人文社会科学学科，俄国形式主义和英美新批评均有意识地建构批评话语体系。由于两个流派诞生的时空语境不同，其理论内部存在差异，所以需要分开论述。在此，先从俄国形式主义谈起。

维克托·厄利希（Victor Erlich）在其经典之作《俄国形式主义》（*Russian Formalism: History-Doctrine*，1955）中，对俄国形式主义进行了时间线梳理，将其分为三个时期：1916—1920年是"斗争与论战的年代"；1921—1926年是"狂飙突进的年代"；1926—1930年是"危机与溃败的年代"。俄国形式主义诞生在动荡的历史时代。1914年，俄国卷入第一次世界大战；1917年，二月革命、沙皇退位、十月革命相继发生；1918年起，苏俄陷入内战，其间还有协约国的外国武装势力介入，战火不断，直到1922年苏维埃社会主义共和国联盟（简称"苏联"）真正成立，才迎来了和平。表面看，俄国形式主义者研究普遍意义的文学属性，不谈历史和政治，具保守倾向，有"遁世"之嫌。实质上，他们的精神内核属于这个革命的时代，与活跃在这一时期的先锋艺术家们相互欣赏，尤其和俄国未来派文学家有很多互动。俄国未来派由以马雅可夫斯基（Vladimir Mayakovsky）为首的现代艺术家组成。他们拥抱革命，反对权威，主张破旧迎新，探索诗歌等艺术语言的极限表达形式，在1912年发表的《给公众趣味的一记耳光》中，甚至提出要把普希金、陀思妥耶夫斯基和托尔斯泰从现代轮船上抛下去。

俄国未来派作家向文学旧传统宣战，俄国形式主义学者则寻求文学研究的革新之路。彼时的俄国学术界将钻故纸堆、爬梳作者生平与历史细节视为学问之道。俄国形式主义者则接受胡塞尔（Edmund Husserl）等欧陆哲学家、库尔德内（Baudouin de Courtenay）为首的喀山语言学派和索绪尔（Ferdinand de Saussure）为首的日内瓦语言学派的影响，向传记研究、历史研究和社会研究等学术体制内的主导范式发起挑战，开启了形式主义的文学内部研究转向。

俄国形式主义的火种点燃于大学校园之内，是"双城故事"：一个中心是圣彼得堡大学，1916年该校的青年学生们组成了"诗歌语言研究会"（缩略语为Opoyaz，音译为"奥波亚兹"）；另一个中心是莫斯科大学，1915年"莫斯科语言学小组"（Moscow Linguistic Circle）成立。前者的核心人物是什克洛夫斯基（Viktor Shklovsky）。他也是整个俄国形式主义运动的灵魂人物。他认为诗歌与注重身体姿态的舞蹈和注重视觉冲击力的绘画一样，其艺术性源于特殊形式带来的审美体验。为此，他在《作为手法的艺术》（"Art as Technique"，1917）中，提炼出"陌生化"的概念，指出形式的创新不是为了表达新的内容，而是为了取代已经丧失艺术性的旧形式，用"陌生化"带来惊奇新颖的审美悸动。他视艺术的形式特征为文学的灵魂，在《散文理论》的序言中坦承地表示，"文学理论中我所从事的是其内部规律的研究，若用工厂生产来类比，那么我关心的不是世界面纱市场的行情，不是托拉斯的政策，而是棉纱的支数及其纺织方式"。

同属"奥波亚兹"的埃亨巴乌姆（Boris Eichenbaum）在《"形式主义方法"的理论》（"The Theory of the 'Formal Method'"，1926）中，将什克洛夫斯基的"内部规律研究"细化为"以文学材料为研究对象"，以科学性为原则，使诗学重新回到研究事实的道路上来。在这篇总结形式主义纲领的文章中,他澄清了对形式主义的诸多偏见,指出形式主义不是真理性的刻板规条,它提倡科学实证主义,重视具体语境,其理论可以进行自我修正;它不否认日常语言的重要性,但是以研究文学本体为目标,所以关心诗性语言;它不否认内容和形式之间的联系,但坚持对形式进行研究的必要性和重要性。以埃亨巴乌姆本人的文学批评实践为例,在《论悲剧与悲剧性》中,他指出怜悯之情是生活经验的一部分,不是悲剧专属。人们观看悲剧,不是为了与悲剧人物共情,也不是为了体悟戏剧的故事内涵,而是为了感受戏剧家通过艺术手法营造出的感染力。艺术的价值不在于其唤起的情感,而在于唤起这种情感的特殊艺术形式。艺术的成功取决于其表现手法。人们被艺术的独具匠心的设置所吸引。艺术手法越精巧,越不易被人觉察,其感染力就越强烈,艺术性就越高。

俄国形式主义另外一脉起源于"莫斯科语言学小组"。"奥波亚兹"多为文学批评家,他们关注文学语言与技巧的审美功能。而"莫斯科语言学小组"的成员主要是语言学家,他们所感兴趣的是如何从语言学视角解释诗歌的特殊性。其核心人物是雅各布森(Roman Jakobson)。1920年他应邀到捷克斯洛伐克讲学,后定居布拉格,1926年建立了布拉格语言学学会,将俄国形式主义的影响带到了欧洲。雅各布森在《什么是诗歌?》中指出,在日常交流中,符号和意指对象是一致的,这可以促进顺畅的交流。诗歌语言中,符号与它的所指不完全相同,语词不再被用于表征客体或者表达情感,而是进行着自我指涉。当语词及其组合、意义、内外形式有了自身的分量和价值,诗性也随之而来。作家就是借助对语言媒介的有意识调用,使诗歌具有文学性。他的学生穆卡若夫斯基(Jan Mukarovsky)则在《标准语言和诗歌语言》一文中指出,诗歌语言理论有别于常规语言理论之处在于,前者关注诗歌语言和常规语言的差异,后者则主要关注两者的相同点。诗歌语言偏离和扭曲了常规语言,使语言被"前置"到了醒目的位置,突出了语言的审美功能。

俄国形式主义的理论活力充分说明了对文学内部诸要素进行考察的必要性,但它对文学外部因素的刻意忽略也引发了争议,其中比较有代表性的是托洛茨基(Leon Trotsky)在《文学与革命》中从马克思主义立场对其提出的批评。托洛茨基指出,新的艺术形式产生于新的历史需要,形式主义漠视历史和社会的物质基础,有唯心主义倾向。此外,文学从来不是与世隔绝的自治领地,虽然艺术形式具独立性,但作为艺术形式生产者的艺术家以及欣赏艺术形式的公众都生活在社会现实之中。托洛茨基的批评是有道理的,形式主义持有激进的文艺学立场,割裂文学内外部研究,对文学的内容与意义的阐释有偏颇之处。这是造成俄国形式主义衰落的重要内部原因,而衰落的外部因素来自时代风气的转变。形式主义发展到后期,恰逢苏俄文学研究向机械的意识形态决定论转变的时期，唯政治论的转向剥夺了形式主义参与讨论的学术空间。1930年，什克洛夫斯基撰文《给科学上的错误立个纪念碑》，承认自己将文艺中立化，使其独立于社会，这是政治立场上的错误。他的自我检讨标志着俄国形式主义从文学理论主阵地中退场。

英美新批评和俄国形式主义的起始时期相近，但绵延的历史更长，有半个世纪之久。它的先驱之一是诗人T. S. 艾略特。艾略特反对浪漫主义的情感表现论，认为它过于强调诗人的中心地位，使诗歌的视野受局限，且情感泛滥。为此，他在《传统与个人才能》("Tradition and the Individual Talent"，1919）中提出"非个人化"（impersonality）理论，认为艺术家只有"不断地牺牲自己，不断地消灭自己的个性"，才能附身伟大，令创作摆脱个人的小格局，汇入文学传统的漫长传承。他言及的"传统"是整体性的长线历史，淡化了具体当下历史境遇的重要性。他希冀通过以上立场，使文学摆脱作者中心论和时代决定论，令文学研究聚焦在文学文本自身。

英国批评家I. R. 瑞恰慈（I. R. Richards）也主张文学研究以文本为中心。但他采用的是实证研究的方式，有别于艾略特的文学家视角。他和俄国形式主义者一样，关注文学和语言的关系，但分类原则不同：俄国形式主义者关心日常语言和文学语言的区别，瑞恰慈关心科学语言与文学语言的区别。在《文学批评原理》（*Principles of Literary Criticism*，1924）中，他提出科学语言指涉明确，有现实对应，可被检验，存在正确与谬误之分；文学语言的真实性与现实无关，指涉性是它的辅助功能，情感传达是它的主要功能，所以是"准陈述"。瑞恰慈用"准陈述"来指涉文学的虚构本质，不是为了贬低文学的作用。相反，他认为文学描摹幻想的世界，提供情感表达的渠道，符合人类的心理需要。因此，文学是独立的领地，诗性思维有其内部逻辑。他很重视文学阅读经验。在《实用批评》（*Practical Criticism*，1929）中，他用"文献记录法"，收集了高校学生阅读文学文本时千差万别的评论，对其进行分析，期待由此寻找更好的文学教学方法，帮助学生提高阅读和理解文本的能力。

英国批评家威廉·燕卜荪（William Empson）是瑞恰慈的学生，他继承了瑞恰慈对批评实践的重视，其代表作是1930年出版的《含混七型》（*Seven Types of Ambiguity*）。在这本著作中，他对"含混"进行了全方位的考察，指出"任何语义上的差别，无论如何细微，只要它使一句话有可能引起不同反应"，便是含混。含混有多重亚类，包括隐喻、双关，也有上下文造成的意义叠加、矛盾冲突，甚至是含义背离等。燕卜荪的分类很细，但依然有批评家指责他的研究不够科学缜密。其实，含混是如此暧昧纠缠，如何分类都很难穷尽它在具体语境中生发出的复杂性。燕卜荪著作的真正价值在于它对含混的全面而立体的批评解读实践。他在书中分析了四十多位作家作品中的两百多个段落，其中相当数量的作品出自文艺复兴时代的古典作家，体现了高妙的艺术鉴赏力和广博的文学视野。

英国的几位新批评代表人物都对西方批评史有重要贡献，但是艾略特、瑞恰慈和燕卜荪的学术路径不同，未形成合力，相对而言，英国新批评的影响力有一定局限。与之相比，新批评的美国脉络议题更为集中，批评家更有凝聚力，影响力也更大。美国新批评的发起者和倡导者是约翰·克罗·兰色姆（John Crowe Ransom）和他的学生艾伦·泰特（Allen Tate）、罗伯特·佩恩·沃伦（Robert Penn Warren）、克林斯·布鲁克斯（Cleanth Brooks）。这些学者都曾经在田纳西的范德比尔特大学（Vanderbilt University）执教或求学，有共同的南方背景，认同南方农业社会的传统价值观，反对工业社会的工具理性和消费主义，认为艺术是抵抗现代异化的避难所。他们一边从事文学创作，撰写诗歌和小说，一边给杂志撰稿，表述自己的文学研究主张，在此过程中，逐渐赢得了学界关注。1938年，布鲁克斯和沃伦合著的《理解诗歌》（*Understanding Poetry*）出版。1943年，他们合著的《理解小说》（*Understanding Fiction*）出版。这两本著作用新批评的方法解读文学作品，迅速受到美国高校教师和学生的热烈欢迎，在此后数十年多次再版，成为美国经典文学教材，在普及新批评研究方法方面发挥了重要作用。自20世纪40年代后期开始，布鲁克斯和沃伦在耶鲁大学任教，与勒内·韦勒克（René Wellek）、W. K. 维姆萨特（W. K. Wimsatt）等一起组成了"耶鲁集团"，将新批评的影响力推至全美乃至西方世界，使之成为战后影响力最持久的文学理论学派之一。

美国新批评和英国新批评相比，本体论色彩更强。英国批评家中，艾略特重视历史性，瑞恰慈将心理学作为研究工具，燕卜荪的研究糅合了传记和历史研究。而美国"新批评"这个概念的提出者兰色姆则坚持较为纯粹的文学本体论。在1941年出版的著作《新批评》（*The New Criticism*）的结尾，兰色姆指出，文学不是逻辑、感情和道德的同义词，必须将文学世界与其他世界——包括科学世界——区别开来。他反对瑞恰慈的文学是"准陈述"的观点，认为其他世界都是文学世界的简化和删减。诗歌的意义在于它能唤起我们对复杂难知的世界的感知，它所提供的是一种特殊的知识，寻求对世界最深刻的理解。

新批评的本体论立场要求它聚焦文学文本，深入挖掘它的意义。在此前提下，维姆萨特和门罗·比尔兹利（Monroe Beardsley）提出了意图谬见论和情感谬见论。在《意图谬见》（"The Intentional Fallacy"，1946）中，他们指出研究文学不必关注作者，不能将诗歌与其生产过程相混淆。从写诗的心理因素中推导的批评标准会陷入"传记式批评与相对主义"。在《情感谬见》（"The Affective Fallacy"，1949）中，他们认为不能将诗歌和它的阅读效果混为一谈，否则容易陷入印象式批评，这也是一种相对主义。为了克服两种谬见,应该只考察作品语言及其技巧等文学因素,这样方能实现批评客观和公正的科学性。

不同于俄国形式主义,新批评提倡的科学性不以抽象思辨的能力提炼文学普遍规律。新批评要求批评者不带主观色彩地观察每个文本的文学表征,准确理解它所反映的具体生命经验。比如,兰色姆提出文学文本具有"架构"(structure)和"肌质"(texture)两重性:前者是其逻辑框架,可类比为房屋的构架;后者则是繁复的细节,使文学世界有血有肉、丰满生动。所以诗歌的特异性存在于它的"肌质"而非它的"架构"。

由此,不难理解为什么新批评理论家偏爱"悖论"(paradox)、"反讽"(irony)、"含混"(ambiguity)等与明晰的科学语言相反的文学概念。它们的多重意涵只有在"肌质"中才能被真正领会。布鲁克斯认为反讽是字面义和深意之间的差距造成的内容的自我消解,悖论则是同一语境中相反意义的共存。简而言之,悖论是"似非而是",反讽是"口是心非",它们均在文本内部构造出冲突性。布鲁克斯没有简单地从修辞角度来解读反讽和悖论,而是认为它们既体现在具体的语言表达层面,又具有对篇章进行结构化的框架性功能,还携带意指内涵。以上立场挑战了形式—内容的二分模式,将形式纳入整体语境进行思考。在其经典著作《精致的瓮》(*The Well Wrought Urn: Studies in the Structure of Poetry*,1947)的最后一章"释义异说"("The Heresy of Paraphrase")中,布鲁克斯强调诗歌是通过戏剧过程而非逻辑过程来实现它的整体性,诗歌通过命题、隐喻和象征等形成多方张力,既展现冲突,也体现平衡。

泰特的"张力说"(tension)也符合这种包容对立冲突的文学观念。泰特认为诗歌意义可分为"内涵"(intension)和"外延"(extension):前者指语言的暗示意义以及附属于文辞上的感情色彩;后者指词语的字面意义和概念意义。好的诗歌是"内涵和外延的统一"。不同流派虽各有所长,但都应该有这种内部张力,既需要由内涵来提供艺术性联想与情感力量,又需要具备外延的意义明晰性。他指出玄学派诗人作为理性主义者,写诗起笔偏向外延的一端;浪漫主义或象征主义写诗的契机则源自情之所系的内涵。两个诗歌派别出发点不同,但都在诗歌表达的动态过程中,力图达成内涵与外延的平衡,实现整体性的艺术之美。

无论是兰色姆的肌质说、布鲁克斯的反讽结构论,还是泰特的张力说,这些理论都认为文本的整体性依赖于细节的精细组织安排。为此,他们以"细读"法作为核心的研究方法,认为文学批评不需要收集外部材料,没必要检索历史以及钩沉作者生平,但需要以精致入微的洞察力和对语言的敏感度,对文本进行逐字逐句的解读,由此获得对文本的完整意义的认识。在新批评理论家看来,细读不仅是一种阅读技能,也体现了综合性的人文素养。用泰特的话说，在理解诗歌时，我们需要动用"由经验、文化以及我们的人道主义赋予的才能"，而阅读诗歌也有助于以上能力的培养。

至此，我们可以看出英美新批评和俄国形式主义的区别。英美新批评擅长具体的文学批评实践，反对抽象思辨，强调形式的重要性，但拒绝割裂形式和内容的有机联系，其根基深植在人文主义传统之中。俄国形式主义则更看重科学话语的提炼概括，重点考察具文学特异性的语言、手法和结构等形式要素。这两个文论流派的相同点，即它们对文学内部世界的关注，放在20世纪上半叶的语境来看，是具有开创性意义的。文学研究终于不必向历史、哲学、伦理学等借力，获得了人文科学研究的独立合法地位。这两个文论流派的差异，则在二战后当代文论的"结构主义"和"解构主义"思潮中，留下了各自的影响痕迹，形成了错综复杂的谱系关系。综合来看，俄国形式主义和英美新批评是现当代西方文学理论当之无愧的重要起点。

主要文本阅读

什克洛夫斯基：《作为手法的艺术》

| 选文简介

《作为手法的艺术》被视为俄国形式主义的宣言。什克洛夫斯基用驳论法开篇，直击象征主义信奉的"艺术就是用形象来思维"的流行观点，指出形象是固定的、停滞的，无法解释文学的变化，而且形象思维的适用面太窄，能概括象征主义，但无法解释其他类型的文学艺术。他认为艺术的目的是审美，本质上依赖能激活审美感知力的手法。选文即围绕这一主要观点展开。

理解什克洛夫斯基艺术手法观的关键词是"陌生化"。他指出人们对日常生活中的事物习以为常，这种感知的"自动化"是程式性的、无意识的。陌生化的手法旨在克服自动化，恢复人的感受力，把事物从习惯的遮蔽中召唤出来，"使石头展现石头的属性"。在什克洛夫斯基看来，"艺术是体验事物的艺术性的一种方式，而事物本身不重要"。这体现了他重形式、轻内容的形式主义立场。他认为诗歌的文学性来自语言的陌生化策略：日常的语言是便捷的、准确的、直接的、晓畅的、得体的；而诗性语言是形式化的语言，诗人通过俗语、方言、外国语等方式，偏离惯常语言范式，强化审美感知。

From "Art as Technique"

Viktor Shklovsky (1893-1984)

If we start to examine the general laws of perception, we see that as perception becomes habitual, it becomes automatic. Thus, for example, all of our habits retreat into the area of the unconsciously automatic; if one remembers the sensations of holding a pen or of speaking in a foreign language for the first time and compares that with his feeling at performing the action for the ten thousandth time, he will agree with us. Such habituation explains the principles by which, in ordinary speech, we leave phrases unfinished and words half expressed. In this process, ideally realized in algebra, things are replaced by symbols. Complete words are not expressed in rapid speech; their initial sounds are barely perceived. Alexander Pogodin offers the example of a boy considering the sentence "The Swiss mountains are beautiful" in the form of a series of letters: *T, S, m, a, b.*

This characteristic of thought not only suggests the method of algebra, but even prompts the choice of symbols (letters, especially initial letters). By this "algebraic" method of thought we apprehend objects only as shapes with imprecise extensions; we do not see them in their entirety but rather recognize them by their main characteristics. We see the object as though it were enveloped in a sack. We know what it is by its configuration, but we see only its silhouette. The object, perceived thus in the manner of prose perception, fades and does not leave even a first impression; ultimately even the essence of what it was is forgotten. Such perception explains why we fail to hear the prose word in its entirety (see Leo Jakubinsky's article) and, hence, why (along with other slips of the tongue) we fail to pronounce it. The process of "algebrization," the over-automatization of an object, permits the greatest economy of perceptive effort. Either objects are assigned only one proper feature—a number, for example—or else they function as though by formula and do not even appear in cognition:

> I was cleaning and, meandering about, approached the divan and couldn't remember whether or not I had dusted it. Since these movements are habitual and unconscious I could not remember and felt that it was impossible to remember—so that if I had dusted it and forgot—that is, had acted unconsciously, then it was the same as if I had not. If some conscious person had been watching, then the fact could be established. If, however, no one was looking, or looking on unconsciously, if the whole complex lives of many people go on unconsciously, then such lives are as if they had never been.

And so life is reckoned as nothing. Habitualization devours work, clothes, furniture, one's wife, and the fear of war. "If the whole complex lives of many people go on unconsciously, then such lives are as if they had never been." And art exists that one may recover the sensation of life; it exists to make one feel things, to make the stone *stony*. The purpose of art is to impart the sensation of things as they are perceived and not as they are known. The technique of art is to make objects "unfamiliar," to make forms difficult, to increase the difficulty and length of perception because the process of perception is an aesthetic end in itself and must be prolonged. *Art is a way of experiencing the artfulness of an object: the object is not important....*

After we see an object several times, we begin to recognize it. The object is in front of us and we know about it, but we do not see it—hence we cannot say anything significant about it. Art removes objects from the automatism of perception in several ways. Here I want to illustrate a way used repeatedly by Leo Tolstoy, that writer who, for Merezhkovsky at least, seems to present things as if he himself saw them, saw them in their entirety, and did not alter them.

Tolstoy makes the familiar seem strange by not naming the familiar object. He describes an object as if he were seeing it for the first time, an event as if it were happening for the first time. In describing something he avoids the accepted names of its parts and instead names corresponding parts of other objects. For example, in "Shame" Tolstoy "defamiliarizes" the idea of flogging in this way: "to strip people who have broken the law, to hurl them to the floor, and to rap on their bottoms with switches," and, after a few lines, "to lash about on the naked buttocks." Then he remarks:

> Just why precisely this stupid, savage means of causing pain and not any other—why not prick the shoulders or any part of the body with needles, squeeze the hands or the feet in a vise, or anything like that?

I apologize for this harsh example, but it is typical of Tolstoy's way of pricking the conscience. The familiar act of flogging is made unfamiliar both by the description and by the proposal to change its form without changing its nature....

The technique of defamiliarization is not Tolstoy's alone. I cited Tolstoy because his work is generally known.

Now, having explained the nature of this technique, let us try to determine the approximate limits of its application. I personally feel that defamiliarization is found almost everywhere form is found.... An image is not a permanent referent for those mutable complexities of life which are revealed through it, its purpose is not to make us perceive meaning, but to create a special perception of the object—*it creates a vision of the object instead of serving as a means for knowing it*....

Such constructions as "the pestle and the mortar," or "Old Nick and the infernal regions" (*Decameron*) are also examples of the technique of defamiliarization. And in my article on plot construction I write about defamiliarization in psychological parallelism. Here, then, I repeat that the perception of disharmony in a harmonious context is important in parallelism. The purpose of parallelism, like the general purpose of imagery, is to transfer the usual perception of an object into the sphere of new perception—that is, to make a unique semantic modification.

In studying poetic speech in its phonetic and lexical structure as well as in its characteristic distribution of words and in the characteristic thought structures compounded from the words, we find everywhere the artistic trademark—that is, we find material obviously created to remove the automatism of perception; the author's purpose is to create the vision which results from that deautomatized perception. A work is created "artistically" so that its perception is impeded and the greatest possible effect is produced through the slowness of the perception. As a result of this lingering, the object is perceived not in its extension in space, but, so to speak, in its continuity. Thus "poetic language" gives satisfaction....Leo Jakubinsky has demonstrated the principle of phonetic "roughening" of poetic language in the particular case of the repetition of identical sounds. The language of poetry is, then, a difficult, roughened, impeded language.

In a few special instances the language of poetry approximates the language of prose, but this does not violate the principle of "roughened" form.

> Her sister was called Tatyana
> For the first time we shall
> Willfully brighten the delicate
> Pages of a novel with such a name

wrote Pushkin. The usual poetic language for Pushkin's contemporaries was the elegant style of Derzhavin; but Pushkin's style, because it seemed trivial then, was unexpectedly difficult for them. We should remember the consternation of Pushkin's contemporaries over the vulgarity of his expressions. He used the popular language as a special device for prolonging attention, just as his contemporaries generally used Russian words in their usually French speech (see Tolstoy's examples in *War and Peace*).

Just now a still more characteristic phenomenon is under way. Russian literary language, which was originally foreign to Russia, has so permeated the language of the people that it has blended with their conversation. On the other hand, literature has now begun to show a tendency toward the use of dialects (Remizov, Klyuyev, Essenin, and others, so unequal in talent and so alike in language, are intentionally provincial) and/or barbarisms (which gave rise to the Severyanin group). And currently Maxim Gorky is changing his diction from the old literary language to the new literary colloquialism of Leskov. Ordinary speech and literary language have thereby changed places (see the work of Vyacheslav Ivanov and many others). And finally, a strong tendency, led by Khlebnikov, to create a new and properly poetic language has emerged. In the light of these developments we can define poetry as *attenuated*, *tortuous* speech. Poetic speech is *formed speech*. Prose is ordinary speech—economical, easy, proper, the goddess of prose [*dea prosae*] is a goddess of the accurate, facile type, of the "direct" expression of a child. I shall discuss roughened form and retardation as the general *law* of art at greater length in an article on plot construction.

埃亨巴乌姆：《"形式主义方法"的理论》

选文简介

人们对俄国形式主义常有这样的误解：俄国形式主义重语言、重手法技巧、重结构形式，只有共时性研究，没有历时性研究。事实上，文学史也是俄国形式主义的重点关注之一。这也是本篇选文的主题。埃亨巴乌姆反对历史主义文学史观，认为它是历史事实的堆砌，忽略了文学的当代性。他也反对象征主义文学史观，认为它流于主观印象，空谈当代品味。他认为形式主义文学史观兼具历史性、客观性、文学性和当代性：关心文学范式变化的客观事实，立足当代的文学现象，以不受外部因素干扰的文学内部因素为依据，梳理文学史的发展脉络。这种内在进化论聚焦文学的形式演化进程，勾勒出的不是和平渐变的文学史，而是各个时期文学范式推陈出新的复杂斗争史，反映了历史性与文学性兼具的方法立场。

From "The Theory of the 'Formal Method'"

Boris Eichenbaum (1886-1959)

Earlier I noted that the problem of the diffusion and change of form—the problem of literary evolution—is raised naturally along with theoretical problems. The problem of literary evolution arises in connection with a reconsideration of Veselovsky's view of *skaz* motifs and devices; the answer ("new form is not to express new content, but to replace old form") led to a new understanding of form. If form is understood as the very content, constantly changing according to its dependence upon previous images, then we naturally had to approach it without abstract, ready-made, unalterable, classical schemes; and we had to consider specifically its historical sense and significance. The approach developed its own kind of dual perspective: the perspective of theoretical study (like Shklovsky's *Development of Plot* and my *Verse Melody*), which centered on a given theoretical problem and its applicability to the most diverse materials, and the perspective of historical studies—studies of literary evolution as such. The combination of these two perspectives, both organic to the subsequent development of the formal school, raised a series of new and very complex problems, many of which are still unsolved and even undefined.

Actually, the original attempt of the Formalists to take a particular structural device and to establish its identity in diverse materials became an attempt to differentiate, to understand, the *function* of a device in each given case. This notion of functional significance was gradually pushed toward the foreground and the original idea of the device pushed into the background. This kind of sorting out of its own general ideas and principles has been characteristic of our work throughout the evolution of the formal method.

We have no dogmatic position to bind us and shut us off from facts. We do not answer for our schematizations; they may require change, refinement, or correction when we try to apply them to previously unknown facts. Work on specific materials compelled us to speak of functions and thus to revise our idea of the device. The theory itself demanded that we turn to history.

Here again we were confronted with the traditional academic sciences and the preferences of critics. In our student days the academic history of literature was limited chiefly to biographical and psychological studies of various writers—only the "greats," of course. Critics no longer made attempts to construct a history of Russian literature as a whole, attempts which evidenced the intention of bringing the great historical materials into a system; nevertheless, the traditions established by earlier histories (like A. N. Pypin's *History of Russian Literature*) retained their scholarly authority, the more so because the following generation had decided not to pursue such broad themes. Meanwhile, the chief role was played by such general and somewhat vague notions as realism and romanticism (realism was said to be better than romanticism); evolution was understood as gradual perfection, as progress (from romanticism to realism); succession [of literary schools] as the peaceful transfer of the inheritance from father to son. But generally, there was no notion of literature as such; material taken from the history of social movements, from biography, etc. had replaced it entirely.

This primitive historicism, which led away from literature, naturally provoked the Symbolist theoreticians and critics into a denial of any kind of historicism. Their own discussions of literature, consequently, developed into impressionistic "*études*" and "silhouettes," and they indulged in a widespread "modernization" of old writers, transforming them into "eternal companions." The history of literature was silently (and sometimes aloud) declared unnecessary.

We had to demolish the academic tradition and to eliminate the bias of the journalists [the Symbolist theoreticians]. We had to advance against the first a new understanding of literary evolution and of literature itself—without the idea of progress and peaceful succession, without the ideas of realism and romanticism, without materials foreign to literature—as a specific order of phenomena, a specific order of material. We had to act against the second by pointing out concrete historical facts, fluctuating and changing forms, by pointing to the necessity of taking into account the specific functions of this or that device—in a word, we had to draw the line between the literary work as a definite historical fact and a free interpretation of it from the standpoint of contemporary literary needs, tastes, or interests. Thus the basic passion for our historical-literary work had to be a passion for destruction and negation, and such was the original tone of our theoretical attacks; our work later assumed a calmer note when we went on to solutions of particular problems.

That is why the first of our historical-literary pronouncements came in the form of theses expressed almost against our will in connection with some specific material. A particular question would unexpectedly lead to the formulation of a general problem, a problem that inextricably mixed theoretical and historical considerations....

In his *Rozanov*, Shklovsky showed, almost in the absence of basic themes, a whole theory of literary evolution which even then reflected the current discussion of such problems in *Opoyaz*. Shklovsky showed that literature moves forward in a broken line.

> In each literary epoch there is not one literary school, but several. They exist simultaneously, with one of them representing the high point of the current orthodoxy. The others exist uncanonized, mutely; in Pushkin's time, for example, the courtly tradition of [Wilhelm] Kuchelbecker and [Alexander] Griboyedov existed simultaneously with the tradition of Russian vaudeville verse and with such other traditions as that of the pure adventure novel of Bulgarin.

The moment the old art is canonized, new forms are created on a lower level. A "young line" is created which

> grows up to replace the old, as the vaudevillist Belopyatkin is transformed into a Nekrasov (see Brik's discussion of the relationship); a direct descendant of the eighteenth century, Tolstoy, creates a new novel (see the work of Boris Eichenbaum); Blok makes the themes and times of the gypsy ballad acceptable, and Chekhov introduces the "alarm clock" into Russian literature. Dostoevsky introduced the devices of the dime novel into the mainstream of literature. Each new literary school heralds a revolution, something like the appearance of a new class. But, of course, this is only an analogy. The vanquished line is not obliterated; it does not cease to exist. It is only knocked from the crest; it lies dormant and may again arise as a perennial pretender to the throne. Moreover, in reality the matter is complicated by the fact that the new hegemony is usually not a pure revival of previous forms but

is made more complex by the presence of features of the younger schools and with features, now secondary, inherited from its predecessors on the throne.

Shklovsky is discussing the dynamism of genres, and he interprets Rozanov's books as embodiments of a new genre, as a new type of novel in which the parts are unconnected by motivation. "Thematically, Rozanov's books are characterized by the elevation of new themes; compositionally, by the revealed device." As part of this general theory, we introduced the notion of the dialectical self-creation of new forms, that is, hidden in the new form we saw both analogies with other kinds of cultural development and proof of the independence of the phenomena of literary evolution. In a simplified form, this theory quickly changed hands and, as always happens, became a simple and fixed scheme—very handy for critics. Actually, we have here only a general outline of evolution surrounded by a whole series of complicated conditions. From this general outline the Formalists moved on to a more consistent solution of historical-literary problems and facts, specifying and refining their original theoretical premises.

Given our understanding of literary evolution as the dialectical change of forms, we did not go back to the study of those materials which had held the central position in the old-fashioned historical-literary work. We studied literary evolution insofar as it bore a distinctive character and only to the extent that it stood alone, quite independent of other aspects of culture. In other words, we stuck exclusively to facts in order not to pass into an endless number of indefinite connections and correspondences which would do nothing at all to explain literary evolution. We did not take up questions of the biography and psychology of the artist because we assumed that these questions, in themselves serious and complex, must take their places in other sciences. We felt it important to find indications of historical regularity in evolution—that is why we ignored all that seemed, from this point of view, circumstantial, not concerned with [literary] history. We were interested in the very process of evolution, in the very *dynamics* of literary form, insofar as it was possible to observe them in the facts of the past. For us, the central problem of the history of literature is the problem of evolution without personality—the study of literature as a *self-formed social phenomenon*....

...The Formalists, then, characteristically had a close interest in contemporary literature and also reconciled criticism and scholarship. The earlier literary historians had, to a great extent, kept themselves aloof from contemporary literature; the Symbolists had subordinated scholarship to criticism. We saw in the history of literature not so much a special theoretical *subject* as a special *approach*, a special cross section of literature. The character of our historical-literary work involved our being drawn not only to historical conclusions, but also to theoretical conclusions—to the posing of new theoretical problems and to the testing of old.

布鲁克斯:《释义异说》

选文简介

选文出自《精致的瓮》的最后一章。作者布鲁克斯指出，诗歌不适合用释义法进行解读。释义法用简明的逻辑对经验进行概括或者是抽象，而真正的诗歌是对现实的拟像，是对经验的完整捕捉。因此，要理解作品的立场，必须考虑具体语境，才能把握文本各种因素相互碰撞和相互施压所达到的平衡和统一。在选文的后半程中，布鲁克斯重点讨论了诗歌中的反讽（irony）。他重视反讽，因为反讽不是意义的——明晰对应，而是意义之间的冲突与不协调。以反讽为结构的诗歌充满张力，能充分体现多重意义的潜在能量。他以玄学派诗人约翰·多恩（John Donne）的诗歌为例探讨了反讽。多恩是一位擅长思辨的诗人，他在诗歌中巧设反讽，以缜密的逻辑为非逻辑的立场张目，揭示出日常观念或逻辑的虚假之处。需要补充的是，布鲁克斯等新批评理论家们普遍推崇玄学派的诗歌，是他们让这个很长一段时间内被浪漫主义诗歌的光芒所掩盖的17世纪诗歌流派重新回到英国文学研究的主流视野。

From "The Heresy of Paraphrase"

Cleanth Brooks (1906-1994)

But to deny that the coherence of a poem is reflected in a logical paraphrase of its "real meaning" is not, of course, to deny coherence to poetry; it is rather to assert that its coherence is to be sought elsewhere. The characteristic unity of a poem (even of those poems which may accidentally possess a logical unity as well as this poetic unity) lies in the unification of attitudes into a hierarchy subordinated to a total and governing attitude. In the unified poem, the poet has "come to terms" with his experience. The poem does not merely eventuate in a logical conclusion. The conclusion of the poem is the working out of the various tensions—set up by whatever means—by propositions, metaphors, symbols. The unity is achieved by a dramatic process, not a logical; it represents an equilibrium of forces, not a formula. It is "proved" as a dramatic conclusion is proved: by its ability to resolve the conflicts which have been accepted as the *données* of the drama.

Thus, it is easy to see why the relation of each item to the whole context is crucial, and why the effective and essential structure of the poem has to do with the complex of attitudes achieved. A scientific proposition can stand alone. If it is true, it is true. But the expression of an attitude, apart from the occasion which generates it and the situation which it encompasses, is meaningless....

We have already seen the ease with which the statement "Beauty is truth, truth beauty" becomes detached from its context, even in the hands of able critics; and we have seen the misconceptions that ensue when this detachment occurs. To take one more instance: the last stanza of Herrick's *Corinna*, taken in isolation, would probably not impress the average reader as sentimental nonsense. Yet it would suffer quite as much by isolation from its context as would the lines from Keats' *Ode*. For, as mere statement, it would become something flat and obvious—of course our lives are short! And the conclusion from the fact would turn into an obvious truism for the convinced pagan, and, for the convinced Christian, equally obvious, though damnable, nonsense.

Perhaps this is why the poet, to people interested in hard-and-fast generalizations, must always seem to be continually engaged in blurring out distinctions only after provoking and unnecessary delays. But this last position is merely another variant of the paraphrastic heresy: to assume it is to misconceive the end of poetry—to take its meanderings as negative, or to excuse them (with the comfortable assurance that the curved line is the line of beauty) because we can conceive the purpose of a poem to be only the production, in the end, of a proposition—of a statement.

But the meanderings of a good poem (they are meanderings only from the standpoint of the prose paraphrase of the poem) are not negative, and they do not have to be excused; and most of all, we need to see what their positive function is; for unless we can assign them a positive function, we shall find it difficult to explain why one divergence from "the prose line of the argument" is not as good as another. The truth is that the apparent irrelevancies which metrical pattern and metaphor introduce do become relevant when we realize that they function in a good poem to modify, qualify, and develop the total attitude which we are to take in coming to terms with the total situation.

If the last sentence seems to take a dangerous turn toward some special "use of poetry"—some therapeutic value for the sake of which poetry is to be cultivated—I can only say that I have in mind no special ills which poetry is to cure. Uses for poetry are always to be found, and doubtless will continue to be found. But my discussion of the structure of poetry is not being conditioned at this point by some new and special role which I expect poetry to assume in the future or some new function to which I would assign it. The structure described—a structure of "gestures" or attitudes—seems to me to describe the essential structure of both the *Odyssey* and *The Waste Land*. It seems to be the kind of structure which the ten poems considered in this book possess in common.

If the structure of poetry is a structure of the order described, that fact may explain (if not justify) the frequency with which I have had to have recourse, in the foregoing chapters, to terms like *irony* and *paradox*. By using the term *irony*, one risks, of course, making the poem seem arch and self-conscious, since irony, for most readers of poetry, is associated with satire, *vers de société*, and other "intellectual" poetries. Yet, the necessity for some such terms ought to be apparent; and *irony* is the most general term that we have for the kind of qualification which the various elements in a context receive from the context. This kind of qualification, as we have seen, is of tremendous importance in any poem. Moreover, *irony* is our most general term for indicating that recognition of incongruities—which, again, pervades all poetry to a degree far beyond what our conventional criticism has been heretofore willing to allow.

Irony in this general sense, then, is to be found in Tennyson's *Tears, Idle Tears* as well as in Donne's *Canonization*. We have, of course, been taught to expect to find irony in Pope's *Rape of the Lock*, but there is a profound irony in Keats' *Ode on a Grecian Urn*; and there is irony of a very powerful sort in Wordsworth's *Intimations* ode. For the thrusts and pressures exerted by the various symbols in this poem are not avoided by the poet: they are taken into account and played, one against the other. Indeed, the symbols—from a scientific point of view—are used perversely: it is the child who is the best philosopher; it is from a kind of darkness—from something that is "shadowy"—that the light proceeds; growth into manhood is viewed, not as an extrication from, but as an incarceration within, a prison.

There should be no mystery as to why this must be so. The terms of science are abstract symbols which do not change under the pressure of the context. They are pure (or aspire to be pure) denotations; they are defined in advance. They are not to be warped into new meanings. But where is the dictionary which contains the terms of a poem? It is a truism that the poet is continually forced to remake language. As Eliot has put it, his task is to "dislocate language into meaning." And, from the standpoint of a scientific vocabulary, this is precisely what he performs: for, rationally considered, the ideal language would contain one term for each meaning, and the relation between term and meaning would be constant. But the word, as the poet uses it, has to be conceived of, not as a discrete particle of meaning, but as potential of meaning, a nexus or cluster of meanings.

What is true of the poet's language in detail is true of the larger wholes of poetry. And therefore, if we persist in approaching the poem as primarily a rational statement, we ought not to be surprised if the statement seems to be presented to us always in the ironic mode. When we consider the statement immersed in the poem, it presents itself to us, like the stick immersed in the pool of water, warped and bent. Indeed, whatever the statement, it will always show itself as deflected away from a positive, straightforward formulation.

It may seem perverse, however, to maintain, in the face of our revived interest in Donne, that the essential structure of poetry is not logical. For Donne has been appealed to of late as the great master of metaphor who imposes a clean logic on his images beside which the ordering of the images in Shakespeare's sonnets is fumbling and loose. It is perfectly true that Donne makes a great show of logic; but two matters need to be observed. In the first place, the elaborated and "logical" figure is not Donne's only figure or even his staple one. "Telescoped" figures like "Made one another's hermitage" are to be found much more frequently than the celebrated comparison of the souls of the lovers to the legs of a pair of compasses. In the second place, where Donne uses "logic," he regularly uses it to justify illogical positions. He employs it to overthrow a conventional position or to "prove" an essentially illogical one.

Logic, as Donne uses it, is nearly always an ironic logic to state the claims of an idea or attitude which we have agreed, with our everyday logic, is false. This is not to say, certainly, that Donne is not justified in using his logic so, or that the best of his poems are not "proved" in the only senses in which poems can be proved.

But the proof is not a logical proof. *The Canonization* will scarcely prove to the hard-boiled naturalist that the lovers, by giving up the world, actually attain a better world. Nor will the argument advanced in the poem convince the dogmatic Christian that Donne's lovers are really saints.

In using logic, Donne as a poet is fighting the devil with fire. To adopt Robert Penn Warren's metaphor (which, though I lift it somewhat scandalously out of another context, will apply to this one):

> The poet, somewhat less spectacularly [than the saint], proves his vision by submitting it to the fires of irony—to the drama of the structure—in the hope that the fires will refine it. In other words, the poet wishes to indicate that his vision has been earned, that it can survive reference to the complexities and contradictions of experience.

The same principle that inspires the presence of irony in so many of our great poems also accounts for the fact that so many of them seem to be built around paradoxes. Here again the conventional associations of the term may prejudice the reader just as the mention of Donne may prejudice him. For Donne, as one type of reader knows all too well, was of that group of poets who wished to impress their audience with their cleverness. All of us are familiar with the censure passed upon Donne and his followers by Dr. Johnson, and a great many of us still retain it as our own, softening only the rigor of it and the thoroughness of its application, but not giving it up as a principle.

Yet there are better reasons than that of rhetorical vain-glory that have induced poet after poet to choose ambiguity and paradox rather than plain, discursive simplicity. It is not enough for the poet to analyze his experience as the scientist does, breaking it up into parts, distinguishing part from part, classifying the various parts. His task is finally to unify experience. He must return to us the unity of the experience itself as man knows it in his own experience. The poem, if it be a true poem, is a simulacrum of reality—in this sense, at least, it is an "imitation"—by *being* an experience rather than any mere statement about experience or any mere abstraction from experience.

Tennyson cannot be content with *saying* that in memory the poet seems both dead *and* alive; he must dramatize its life-in-death for us, and his dramatization involves, necessarily, ironic shock and wonder. The dramatization demands that the antithetical aspects of memory be coalesced into one entity which—if we take it on the level of statement—is a paradox, the assertion of the union of opposites. Keats' Urn must express a life which is above life and its vicissitudes, but it must also bear witness to the fact that its life is not life at all but is a kind of death. To put it in other terms, the Urn must, in its role as historian, assert that myth is truer than history. Donne's lovers must reject the world in order to possess the world....

If the poet, then, must perforce dramatize the oneness of the experience, even though paying tribute to its diversity, then his use of paradox and ambiguity is seen as necessary. He is not simply trying to spice up, with a superficially exciting or mystifying rhetoric, the old stale stockpot (though doubtless this will be what the inferior poet does generally and what the real poet does in his lapses). He is rather giving us an insight which preserves the unity of experience and which, at its higher and more serious levels, triumphs over the apparently contradictory and conflicting elements of experience by unifying them into a new pattern.

维姆萨特、比尔兹利：《意图谬见》

选文简介

维姆萨特和比尔兹利反对作者中心论的意图谬见，即反对"为了判断诗人的表现，我们必须知道他的意图"。他们指出，现实生活中，为了准确获取信息，我们需要对言说者的意图进行正确推断；欣赏文学，则不必如此，也不该如此。文学以文字为媒介，通过风格技巧等传达复杂的意义。诗人内心的构思和计划是什么？对自己的作品是什么态度？动笔的原因是什么？这些问题关乎作者意图，但与文本价值无关。作品一旦完成，就不再属于作者，而是属于公众。作品成功与否，仅仅取决于它自身的艺术性，所以应以文本为中心，进行客观的批评。

From "The Intentional Fallacy"

W. K. Wimsatt (1907-1975), Monroe Beardsley (1915-1985)

The claim of the author's "intention" upon the critic's judgment has been challenged in a number of recent discussions, notably in the debate entitled *The Personal Heresy*, between Professors Lewis and Tillyard. But it seems doubtful if this claim and most of its Romantic corollaries are as yet subject to any widespread questioning. The present writers, in a short article entitled *Intention* for a dictionary of literary criticism, raised the issue but were unable to pursue its implications at any length. We argued that the design or intention of the author is neither available nor desirable as a standard for judging the success of a work of literary art, and it seems to us that this is a principle which goes deep into some differences in the history of critical attitudes. It is a principle which accepted or rejected points to the polar opposites of classical "imitation" and Romantic expression. It entails many specific truths about inspiration, authenticity, biography, literary history and scholarship, and about some trends of contemporary poetry, especially its allusiveness. There is hardly a problem of literary criticism in which the critic's approach will not be qualified by his view of "intention."

Intention, as we shall use the term, corresponds to *what he intended* in a formula which more or less explicitly has had wide acceptance. "In order to judge the poet's performance, we must know *what he intended*." Intention is design or plan in the author's mind. Intention has obvious affinities for the author's attitude toward his work, the way he felt, what made him write.

We begin our discussion with a series of propositions summarized and abstracted to a degree where they seem to us axiomatic.

1. A poem does not come into existence by accident. The words of a poem, as Professor Stoll has remarked, come out of a head, not out of a hat. Yet to insist on the designing intellect as a *cause* of a poem is not to grant the design or intention as a *standard* by which the critic is to judge the worth of the poet's performance.

2. One must ask how a critic expects to get an answer to the question about intention. How is he to find out what the poet tried to do? If the poet succeeded in doing it, then the poem itself shows what he was trying to do. And if the poet did not succeed, then the poem is not adequate evidence, and the critic must go outside the poem—for evidence of an intention that did not become effective in the poem. "Only one caveat must be borne in mind," says an eminent intentionalist in a moment when his theory repudiates itself; "the poet's aim must be judged at the moment of the creative act, that is to say, by the art of the poem itself."

3. Judging a poem is like judging a pudding or a machine. One demands that it work. It is only because an artifact works that we infer the intention of an artificer. "A poem should not mean but be." A poem can *be* only through its *meaning*—since its medium is words—yet it *is*, simply *is*, in the sense that we have no excuse for inquiring what part is intended or meant. Poetry is a feat of style by which a complex of meaning is handled all at once. Poetry succeeds because all or most of what is said or implied is relevant; what is irrelevant has been excluded, like lumps from pudding and "bugs" from machinery. In this respect poetry differs from practical messages, which are successful if and only if we correctly infer the intention. They are more

abstract than poetry.

4. The meaning of a poem may certainly be a personal one, in the sense that a poem expresses a personality or state of soul rather than a physical object like an apple. But even a short lyric poem is dramatic, the response of a speaker (no matter how abstractly conceived) to a situation (no matter how universalized). We ought to impute the thoughts and attitudes of the poem immediately to the dramatic *speaker*, and if to the author at all, only by an act of a biographical inference.

5. There is a sense in which an author, by revision, may better achieve his original intention. But it is a very abstract sense. He intended to write a better work, or a better work of a certain kind, and now has done it. But it follows that his former concrete intention was not his intention. "He's the man we were in search of, that's true," says Hardy's rustic constable, "and yet he's not the man we were in search of. For the man we were in search of was not the man we wanted."

"Is not a critic," asks Professor Stoll, "a judge, who does not explore his own consciousness, but determines the author's meaning or intention, as if the poem were a will, a contract, or the constitution? The poem is not the critic's own." He has accurately diagnosed two forms of irresponsibility, one of which he prefers. Our view is yet different. The poem is not the critic's own and not the author's (it is detached from the author at birth and goes about the world beyond his power to intend about it or control it). The poem belongs to the public. It is embodied in language, the peculiar possession of the public, and it is about the human being, an object of public knowledge. What is said about the poem is subject to the same scrutiny as any statement in linguistics or in the general science of psychology.

A critic of our dictionary article, Ananda K. Coomaraswamy, has argued that there are two kinds of inquiry about a work of art: (1) whether the artist achieved his intentions; (2) whether the work of art "ought ever to have been undertaken at all" and so "whether it is worth preserving." Number 2, Coomaraswamy maintains, is not "criticism of any work of art qua work of art," but is rather moral criticism; number 1 is artistic criticism. But we maintain that 2 need not be moral criticism: that there is another way of deciding whether works of art are worth preserving and whether, in a sense, they "ought" to have been undertaken, and this is the way of objective criticism of works of art as such, the way which enables us to distinguish between a skillful murder and a skillful poem. A skillful murder is an example which Coomaraswamy uses, and in his system the difference between the murder and the poem is simply a "moral" one, not an "artistic" one, since each if carried out according to plan is "artistically" successful. We maintain that 2 is an inquiry of more worth than 1, and since 2 and not 1 is capable of distinguishing poetry from murder, the name "artistic criticism" is properly given to 2.

思考题

1. 请结合《作为手法的艺术》的选文，解释什么是"陌生化"手法，它的意义何在。

2. 埃亨巴乌姆为什么批评传统的历史主义文学史观？他为什么批评象征主义文学史观？他如何从形式主义的立场解释文学史的变迁？
3. 布鲁克斯为什么认为诗歌无法用"释义法"进行概括？他主张什么样的研究方法？
4. 布鲁克斯为什么重视诗歌中反讽的运用？选文中，他如何解读约翰·多恩诗歌中的反讽？
5. 什么是维姆萨特和比尔兹利所指的"意图谬见"？他们为什么称其为谬见？

讨论题

1. 请仔细阅读所选的文本，适当进行课外拓展阅读，查阅相关资料，在此基础上，对俄国形式主义和英美新批评进行比较，讨论两者的共性和差异。
2. 请从莎士比亚、多恩、华兹华斯、埃米莉·狄金森或罗伯特·弗罗斯特等人的诗作中，选取一首符合新批评诗学标准的诗作，采用"细读"的方法，对其进行文本分析与解读。

补充文本选摘与评述

艾略特：《传统与个人才能》
From "Tradition and the Individual Talent"

T. S. Eliot (1888-1965)

No poet, no artist of any art, has his complete meaning alone. His significance, his appreciation is the appreciation of his relation to the dead poets and artists. You cannot value him alone; you must set him, for contrast and comparison, among the dead. I mean this as a principle of aesthetic, not merely historical, criticism....

...I have tried to point out the importance of the relation of the poem to other poems by other authors, and suggested the conception of poetry as a living whole of all the poetry that has ever been written. The other aspect of this impersonal theory of poetry is the relation of the poem to its author. And I hinted, by an analogy, that the mind of the mature poet differs from that of the immature one not precisely in any valuation of "personality," not being necessarily more interesting, or having "more to say," but rather by being a more finely perfected medium in which special, or very varied, feelings are at liberty to enter into new combinations.

The analogy was that of the catalyst. When the two gases previously mentioned are mixed in the presence of a filament of platinum, they form sulfurous acid. This combination takes place only if the platinum is present; nevertheless the newly formed acid contains no trace of platinum, and the platinum itself is apparently unaffected; has remained inert, neutral, and unchanged. The mind of the poet is the shred of platinum. It may partly or exclusively operate upon the experience of the man himself; but, the more perfect the artist, the more completely separate in him will be the man who suffers and the mind which creates; the more perfectly will the mind digest and transmute the passions which are its material....

...There are many people who appreciate the expression of sincere emotion in verse, and there is a smaller number of people who can appreciate technical excellence. But very few know when there is an expression of *significant* emotion, emotion which has its life in the poem and not in the history of the poet. The emotion of art is impersonal. And the poet cannot reach his impersonality without surrendering himself wholly to the work to be done. And he is not likely to know what is to be done unless he lives in what is not merely the present, but the present moment of the past, unless he is conscious; not of what is dead, but of what is already living.

雅各布森:《主导因素》
From "The Dominant"

Roman Jakobson (1896-1982)

The first three stages of Formalist research have been briefly characterized as follows: (1) analysis of the sound aspects of a literary work; (2) problems of meaning within the framework of poetics; (3) integration of sound and meaning into an inseparable whole. During this latter stage, the concept of the *dominant* was particularly fruitful; it was one of the most crucial, elaborated, and productive concepts in Russian Formalist theory. The dominant may be defined as the focusing component of a work of art: it rules, determines, and transforms the remaining components. It is the dominant which guarantees the integrity of the structure....

...In contrast to one-sided monism and one-sided pluralism, there exists a point of view which combines an awareness of the multiple functions of a poetic work with a comprehension of its integrity, that is to say, that function which unites and determines the poetic work. From this point of view, a poetic work cannot be defined as a work fulfilling neither an exclusively aesthetic function nor an aesthetic function along with other functions; rather, a poetic work is defined as a verbal message whose aesthetic function is its dominant. Of course, the marks disclosing the implementation of the aesthetic function are not unchangeable or always uniform. Each concrete poetic canon, every set of temporal poetic norms, however, comprises indispensable, distinctive elements without which the work cannot be identified as poetic.

The definition of the aesthetic function as the dominant of a poetic work permits us to determine the hierarchy of diverse linguistic functions within the poetic work. In the referential function, the sign has a minimal internal connection with the designated object, and therefore the sign in itself carries only a minimal importance; on the other hand, the expressive function demands a more direct, intimate relationship between the sign and the object, and therefore a greater attention to the internal structure of the sign. In comparison with referential language, emotive language, which primarily fulfills an expressive function, is as a rule closer to poetic language (which is directed precisely toward the sign as such). Poetic language and emotional language often overlap each other, and therefore these two varieties of language are often quite erroneously identified. If the aesthetic function is the dominant in a verbal message, then this message may certainly use many devices of expressive language; but these components are then subject to the decisive function of the work, i.e. they are transformed by its dominant.

Inquiry into the dominant had important consequences for Formalist views of literary evolution. In the evolution of poetic form it is not so much a question of the disappearance of certain elements and the emergence of others as it is the question of shifts in the mutual relationship among the diverse components of the system, in other words, a question of the shifting dominant.

燕卜荪:《含混七型》
From *Seven Types of Ambiguity*

William Empson (1906-1984)

Thus a word may have several distinct meanings; several meanings connected with one another; several meanings which need one another to complete their meaning; or several meanings which unite together so that the word means one relation or one process. This is a scale which might be followed continuously. "Ambiguity" itself can mean an indecision as to what you mean, an intention to mean several things, a probability that one or other or both of two things has been meant, and the fact that a statement has several meanings. It is useful to be able to separate these if you wish, but it is not obvious that in separating them at any particular point you will not be raising more problems than you solve. Thus I shall often use the ambiguity of "ambiguity," and pronouns like "one," to make statements covering both reader and author of a poem, when I want to avoid raising irrelevant problems as to communication. To be less ambiguous would be like analyzing the sentence about the cat into a course of anatomy. In the same way the words of the poet will, as a rule, be more justly words, what they represent will be more effectively a unit in the mind, than the more numerous words with which I shall imitate their meaning so as to show how it is conveyed....

...Most of the ambiguities I have considered here seem to me beautiful; I consider, then, that I have shown by example, in showing the nature of the ambiguity, the nature of the forces which are adequate to hold it together. It would seem very artificial to do it the other way around, and very tedious to do it both ways at once. I wish only, then, to say here that such vaguely imagined "forces" are essential to the totality of a poem, and that they cannot be discussed in terms of ambiguity, because they are complementary to it. But by discussing ambiguity, a great deal may be made clear about them. In particular, if there is contradiction, it must imply tension; the more prominent the contradiction, the greater the tension; in some way other than by the contradiction, the tension must be conveyed, and must be sustained.

An ambiguity, then, is not satisfying in itself, nor is it, considered as a device on its own, a thing to be attempted; it must in each case arise from, and be justified by, the peculiar requirements of the situation. On the other hand, it is a thing which the more interesting and valuable situations are more likely to justify.

选文评述

艾略特是西方现代主义的代表诗人，他的《传统与个人才能》则展现出其文学观中古典主义的一面。他明确批判了浪漫主义的天才论和情感论，也隐秘地反对同时代作家与传统决裂的先锋姿态。此外，他也反对对个人经验的过度倚重。在他看来，伟大的文学的共同性大于个性差异，好的作家放弃了个性，历史文脉得以传承。他将这种"非个人化"形容为"催化剂"效应：把铂金丝放入贮有氧气和二氧化硫的玻璃瓶，会引发化学反应，生成亚硫酸，铂金丝却未有任何改变。诗人就如同铂金丝，文学创作离不开他的参与，但是作品中找不到他的个体生命经验的印痕。文章讨论的是文学创作观，其实也在建构客观主义的文学观，反映了艾略特的文学本体论的立场：文学与作者的生平经历以及喜怒哀乐无关，反映的是人类普遍意义上的经验和情感，艺术的价值需要在传统中加以评价。值得注意的是，艾略特看重传统，强调历史意识，其实他所说的历史意识是"非历史性的"，即它取消了过去和现在的差异，用统一性的永恒取代了具体的时代。文学的世界既在时间长河之内，又超然独立，拥有自治权。

《主导因素》中，雅各布森对"主导因素"做出了如下定义：主导因素是"一件艺术品的核心成分，其他部分由它支配、决定和变更。正是主导因素保证了结构的完整性"。雅各布森用主导因素来解释他的诗性语言观。他既反对一元论，即诗性语言为文学所独有，也反对多元论，即诗性语言和指称性语言等其他性质的语言没有区别。他认为，文学作为语言艺术，以诗性语言为主导因素，而在其他非文学文体中，诗性语言是辅助性的。他还用主导因素来解释文学史的变化，提出文学史的发展是由艺术手法的淘汰更新所推动。他从系统角度看待文学，认为文学中的主导因素变了，系统的组织原则变了，各诗学形式要素之间的相互关系也要随之变化，有的沉入传统，有的成为崭新潮流。这是一种历时性和共时性兼具的整体性文学观。

《含混七型》中，燕卜荪指出含混是意义的复数形态，它可以是多重意义的叠加，也可能是双重意义的悬而未决。这些无法用概念清晰呈现的含混，赋予文本意义以不确定性、多义性、冲突性，进而给作品带来矛盾中的紧张感和充满深意的复杂感。燕卜荪用了大量篇幅解读含混，但他反对过度的条分缕析，将含混和具体生成的语境相剥离。在他看来，是不同的力量在文本中因缘际会带来了含混的艺术效果。需要强调的是，在《含混七型》的结尾，也就是目前选文第二、三段，燕卜荪指出含混是艺术的手段，不是艺术的目标。在著作中，他也曾数次提及文学创作不必刻意追求含混，意义不是越复杂越好。他称含混是"美丽的"，但它的前提是运用得当，只有这样才能为文本增加魅力和内涵。

关键术语释例

1. **陌生化（defamiliarization）**："陌生化"是俄国形式主义的重要概念，由什克洛夫斯基在《作为手法的艺术》中提出。什克洛夫斯基认为，"艺术的手法就是使对象陌生化，使形式变得困难，增加感知的难度和时间长度"，以实现增强审美感知的艺术目标。需要澄清的是，所谓"使形式变得困难"，不是指文辞越艰深、越复杂、越晦涩越好。陌生化也不追求"语不惊人死不休"。只要艺术手法运用得当，能带来耳目一新的审美体验，就符合陌生化的标准。在语言层面，陌生化体现在文学语言对标准语言的偏离。在艺术手法方面，陌生化意味着对新颖表征方式的探索。从文学史角度看，陌生化是激励文学范式与潮流转变的动力之一。德国戏剧家布莱希特（Bertolt Brecht）则从俄国形式主义陌生化理论中看到了文学的政治动能。他改造陌生化理论，提出戏剧"间离效果"，在创作的戏剧中对日常生活进行陌生化表征，阻断观众的习惯性认同，逼迫他们重新感知、重新思考和发现问题，激发出改造世界的思想动力。

2. **细读（close reading）**：细读有广义和狭义两种定义。广义而言，细读是人类常用的阅读方式之一。读者认真发掘文本内部字里行间的深意，从而更加准确地提炼信息、理解文意。狭义而言，细读特指新批评倡导的文学研究方法。它聚焦文学内部因素，以文本的措辞、修辞、象征、肌质、结构、文体等为分析对象，通过对文本细节的详细阐释，勾勒出文本整体性的复杂图案，助力理解文本与人类丰富生命经验相连通的深层内涵。燕卜荪的《含混七型》、布鲁克斯的《精致的瓮》都是运用新批评方法解读文学文本的经典之作。新批评理论衰落以后，细读仍是文学阅读最常用的范式，而且不断被解构主义、新历史主义、文化批评等理论流派所借鉴和化用。

推荐书目

Bann, Stephen, and John E. Bowlt. *Russian Formalism: A Collection of Articles and Texts in Translation*. Edinburgh: Scottish Academic Press, 1973.

Bennett, Tony. *Formalism and Marxism*. London: Methuen, 1979.

Childs, Donald J. *The Birth of New Criticism: Conflict and Conciliation in the Early Work of William Empson, I. A. Richards, Laura Riding, and Robert Graves*. Montreal: McGill-Queen's University Press, 2013.

Davis, Garrick. *Praising It New: The Best of the New Criticism*. Athens, Ohio: Ohio University Press, 2008.

Erlich, Victor. *Russian Formalism: History-Doctrine*. New York: Mouton, 1980.

Jancovich, Mark. *The Cultural Politics of the New Criticism*. Cambridge: Cambridge University Press, 1993.

Steiner, Peter. *Russian Formalism: A Metapoetics*. Ithaca: Cornell University Press, 1984.

Thompson, Ewa M. *Russian Formalism and Anglo-American New Criticism: A Comparative Study*. The Hague: Mouton, 1971.

赵宪章，张辉，王雄：《西方形式美学：关于形式的美学研究》。南京：南京大学出版社，2008年。

赵毅衡：《重访新批评》。成都：四川文艺出版社，2013年。

第六章
精神分析与神话原型批评

概述

　　精神分析流派的诞生，是19世纪后期到20世纪上半叶的变革所促成的。在生物学领域，达尔文的物种进化论指明人类与动物的亲缘关系，承认了人类的本能和生物欲望。从文化语境看，以尼采为代表的哲学家发出"上帝死了"的宣言，批评基督教伦理的束缚性，强调生命意志，为人的非理性提供了思想支持。从社会语境看，资本主义不再强调封建制中家庭身份和私人身份的深度捆绑，家庭结构的日益松散化赋予每个人独立的身份，其个人化的精神世界也越来越受到重视。从历史语境看，欧洲在这一时期历经繁荣与危机后，两次陷入世界大战，现代人在巨变的时代承受多重的精神痛苦。这些因素使人们越来越关注人的欲望本能、非理性之思、个人的心灵世界以及精神的困境，聚焦于这些议题的精神分析应运而生。精神分析既观照人类的生理本能，也重视人的精神世界和社会文化属性，用探察的目光发现心灵的深邃秘密。

　　西格蒙德·弗洛伊德（Sigmund Freud）是精神分析的奠基者。他是奥地利人，毕业于维也纳大学医学专业，专攻神经病理学。1885年，弗洛伊德参加了沙尔科（Jean-Martin Charcot）在巴黎举办的讲习班。当时人们普遍将歇斯底里症视为器官性病变，沙尔科则认为这是心理疾病，在讲习班展示如何用催眠术治疗歇斯底里症。弗洛伊德深受启发，但他比沙尔科思考得更深：为什么催眠术能够治疗精神疾病？他对问题的追问使他发现了无意识的存在：无意识是无法浮现在表层意识的深层心理积累。

　　对于普通人来说，窥见无意识存在的场合是梦境。在《梦的解析》（The Interpretation of Dreams，1899）中，弗洛伊德指出，人在做梦时心理监审机制会放松，允许"梦的工作"（dreamwork）对无意识领域的欲望进行改头换面的编码，通过压缩（condensation）和置换（displacement）机制，将触碰禁忌的内容包装成合法形式，呈现在梦中。弗洛伊德指出心灵中的意识体验有三个层面：意识（the conscious）、前意识（the preconscious）、无意识（the unconscious）。梦的内容属于前意识的待定区域，醒来时大部分会被压抑，回归无意识之中，因此我们往往记不清做过的梦，但留下少量内容留在意识领域，成为窥见无意识的欲望的线索。这种三分法的心灵结构论可以用冰山的地形图进行类比：无意识是水面之下深不可测的庞然山体，前意识是冰山与水面的交界地带，而意识是浮现在水面上的冰山尖角。

弗洛伊德另外一组重要的理论概念是他在《自我与本我》（*The Ego and the Id*，1923）等著作中提出的本我（id）、自我（ego）和超我（superego）。本我将身体接受的本能需求反映在心理层面，是激情涌动的混沌状态，听命于唯乐原则（the pleasure principle）。自我的知觉—意识负责感知心理世界和外部现实世界，然后根据现实原则（the reality principle）应对社会规训，维护个体生存，争取以安全的方式实现本我的要求。超我则是社会道德规范在人格结构中的内化，它塑造自我理想（ego ideal），构成了人的良知。弗洛伊德认为自我特别辛苦，它有"三个暴虐的主人"：外部世界、本我和超我。主人们的要求截然不同，自我由此体会到各种焦虑：面对外部世界时的现实焦虑，面对超我时的规范焦虑，面对本我激情的力量时的精神焦虑。这也是各类神经症的成因。

值得注意的是，弗洛伊德特别强调，本我—自我—超我的人格结构与无意识—前意识—意识的心灵结构不是一一对应的关系。人类心理是复杂领域，没有清晰界限划定固定疆界，弗洛伊德认为它们之间的关系可以类比为色彩区域的相互延伸相互融合。自我虽然在意识领域，但和无意识领域的本我牵涉甚深。超我由社会伦理系统塑造，但它的惩罚机制能导致自杀等极端行为，联动着无意识领域的自我攻击本能。

弗洛伊德在精神分析实践中发现，成人的精神疾病的症结往往深藏在儿童时期。他视童年为人格形成的关键期，在《性学三论》（*Three Essays on the Theory of Sexuality*，1905）等著作中考察儿童性心理的发展，将其分为五个阶段。从出生到十八个月是口唇期（oral stage），婴儿从吮吸母亲乳房获得口唇愉悦。这一时期的欲望未获满足或者是过于餍足，会造成成年期的依恋型人格，以及吸烟、嗜酒等成瘾性行为模式。一般说来，两到三岁属于肛门期（anal stage），孩子的愉悦来自排便时的肛门刺激。在父母的监督和外界的要求下，孩子无法随心所欲，必须学会规律排便。强迫症、施虐欲和受虐欲等成年性格趋向与这一阶段相关。第三个阶段是性器期（phallic stage，或译为"性蕾期"），儿童开始意识到男女的生理差异，快感区转移到性器官。性瘾、性冷淡等问题可以追溯到这一时期。第四阶段是从六岁到青春期之间的潜伏期（latency stage），性冲动被压抑，儿童在同龄人群体里成长，探索自己的兴趣爱好。第五阶段是伴随青春期而来的生殖期（genital stage），性冲动萌动，追求性交的快感。

弗洛伊德的性意识阶段论认为，儿童从第三阶段性器期的性好奇进入第四阶段潜伏期的性压抑，是由"俄狄浦斯情结"（Oedipus Complex）引发"阉割焦虑"所造成的。弗洛伊德认为，女性在社会中的弱势地位会让儿童将母亲缺少阴茎的生理事实解读为被强势的父亲阉割的结果。儿童天生有恋母情结，欲望对象是孕育和抚养自己的母亲。所以，男孩内心渴望如希腊神话中的俄狄浦斯王一样，杀父娶母。他和父亲、和兄弟姐妹间存在竞争，要独占母亲的爱。但在阉割焦虑的威胁下，他会放弃对母亲的欲望，认同父亲的权威，服从社会的规范，以便在成年后获得属于自己的女性伴侣。女孩则会在这一时期意识到女性的软弱，转向恋慕父亲。弗洛伊德将"恋父情结"命名为"伊莱克特拉情结"（Electra Complex），但他很快承认对女性欲望理解不足，放弃了这一模式。弗洛伊德最有名的文学批评实践是运用俄狄浦斯情结对莎士比亚名剧《哈姆雷特》进行解读。弗洛伊德在《梦的解析》中指出，哈姆雷特迟迟不肯杀死叔父，是因为叔父杀了他父亲，娶了他母亲，实现了哈姆雷特隐秘的乱伦欲望。而在《创造性作家与白日梦》（"Creative Writers and Daydreaming"，1908）中，弗洛伊德指出，文学创作的冲动与儿童时期的游戏冲动同源：儿童通过游戏实现无意识的愿望满足；成年人则通过写作，用白日梦的想象（fantasy）绕过禁忌的监控，满足被压抑的欲望。

在弗洛伊德的人格结构论和儿童性心理阶段论中，本能、冲动、欲望都是关键词。在弗洛伊德看来，这些概念关联人类生命的本质驱动力，他将其命名为"力比多"（libido），即以性爱为核心的爱的力量。弗洛伊德主张正视生命的本能冲动，认为歇斯底里症、精神分裂等神经症都源于对欲望的过度压抑。事实上，压抑是人类文明社会的普遍现实：被压抑的欲望通过升华等机制转化为社会认可的心理能量，创造出人类的文明。

弗洛伊德除了关心个人的精神世界，力图为精神疾病提供疗愈以外，也重视考察人类心理与人类社会文明发展之间的关系。在《图腾与禁忌》（*Totem and Taboo*，1913）中，他从"禁忌之下，必有欲望"的精神分析视角出发，考察原始文化的图腾禁忌，指出它源于血亲兄弟们在俄狄浦斯情结的驱动下，共同参与的弑父之举。弑父后的罪恶感让他们将死者奉为图腾，订立了不可弑父和不可乱伦的律法，缔造出文明社会。在《超越唯乐原则》（*Beyond the Pleasure Principle*，1920）中，他提出生命本能（Eros，或译为"爱欲"）以保存生命为宗旨，趋利避害，追求快乐，为性爱和繁衍后代提供动力，促进群体发展。死亡本能（Thanatos，或译为"死亡欲望"）是有机生命重返最初的无机物状态的无意识冲动，具有自我攻击性，可以造成自责、自残，甚至是自杀。当将这种攻击性引向外部对象时，则表现为仇恨、侵略性和破坏力。在《文明及其不满》（Civilization and Its Discontents, 1930）中，弗洛伊德指出文明的过度压抑会激发人类的攻击性，引起社会撕裂，引发人与人之间的冲突、族群之间的争斗、国与国之间的战争。他的思考反映了他对第一次世界大战的追问，隐含着他对当时欧洲反犹主义倾向的焦虑，也显示出他预感到了二战阴影的逼近。

弗洛伊德的理论既是对神经症的科学研究，也包含对人类身体、精神、社会和文明的深刻洞察。经由弗洛伊德的奠基，精神分析成为人文学科的重要组成部分。在弗洛伊德去世后，精神分析学派分裂出多个分支。其中，20世纪40年代到60年代，"自我心理学"（Ego Psychology）的影响力最大，代表性理论家有安娜·弗洛伊德（Anna Freud）、海因茨·哈特曼（Heinz Hartmann）和戴维·拉帕波特（David Rapaport）等。他们基于弗洛伊德的人格论，在精神疾苦的疗愈中，主张以自我为核心，调和其与本我、超我和现实的关系，按照社会规范的要求，加强自我的社会适应性。

这种自我心理学令法国理论家雅克·拉康（Jacques Lacan）深感不满，拉康认为它背叛了弗洛伊德的精神。在20世纪50年代，他提出"回归弗洛伊德"（Return to Freud）的口号，认为弗洛伊德的无意识论是其思想精髓，重申弗洛伊德对人的本能、驱力和欲望的分析的重要意义，举办了近三十年的讲习班，对弗洛伊德的文本进行细读和再阐释。拉康拒绝把精神分析视为驯化心灵的工具，注重考察个人欲望与社会规范之间的冲突，继承了弗洛伊德理论的反思深度和批判棱角。

拉康的重要理论贡献之一是"镜像阶段"的主体生成论。拉康在1949年发表的《精神分析经验所显示的镜像阶段对"我"的功能形成的影响》（"The Mirror Stage as Formative of the Function of the I as Revealed in Psychoanalytic Experience"，简称《镜像阶段》）一文中指出，六到十八个月大的婴儿会迷恋照镜子，因为在其有限视域中的支离破碎的身体在镜中被"整形"为完整的独立的形象，婴儿在此基础上形成对主体的感知和认同。然而，拉康指出，这种主体认同其实是"误认"：镜中的自我是虚像。镜像阶段的感知、认同与错觉同时发生，这也是其关联的"想象界"的精神维度的特点。

拉康认为人类心理界域存在三种秩序（Orders），可以据此分为想象界（the Imaginary）、象征界（the Symbolic）和实在界（the Real）。想象界的秩序反映在镜像阶段的主体形成机制，它源于自恋，构筑幻象，遮蔽异化。象征界则是法的领域，是主体性的决定秩序，反映社会规范的召唤和约束，承担社会的结构性功能。拉康的实在界则关涉婴儿刚出生时的混沌经验——主体尚未形成，不懂得区分自己、他人和世界，只懂得追求本能需要的满足。这种心理动能源自胎儿孕育在母亲子宫时感受到的与母亲亲如一人的圆满——人类自出生剪断脐带，就无法重回这种圆满，终生被匮乏感困扰。实在界破坏了想象界的自恋想象，拒绝接受象征界的规训，挑战主体的稳定性，逃逸出语言的命名和法的捕捉。

需要注意的是，拉康的三界说不遵循弗洛伊德的口唇期—肛门期—性器期的线性时间逻辑，三界之间是拓扑学意义上相互纠缠相互依存的关系。以镜像阶段为例，婴儿对镜像的想象性认同，是基于父母用语言所予以的肯定性指认："镜中像就是你。"这种指认意味着象征秩序的介入：在成为主体之前，"我是谁"的主体位置已经被家庭秩序和语言系统标定。想象界所无法认同的内容（比如婴儿对自己的身体性的混乱感知）、象征界视为非法和禁忌的内容（比如对母亲的欲望），都被置于实在界。拉康在早期理论中用"原质"（the Thing），后期用"小对象a"（*objet petit a*）的概念来表达这些被排斥、被压抑的不可言说不可表征之物。

拉康的心理分析理论受索绪尔影响，重视语言符号的功能。弗洛伊德理论中逼迫孩子放弃恋母欲望的父亲，变成了拉康理论中具有象征性功能的"父亲的名义"（the Name of the Father，或译"父亲之名"）。儿童阉割焦虑所关涉的不是阴茎（penis）这一男性生殖器官，而是菲勒斯（Phallus，或译为"阳具"）——菲勒斯是符号化的阴茎，具有想象维度和象征意义。儿童在俄狄浦斯阶段，畏惧想象中的阉割，把菲勒斯视为权力的象征，服从"父亲的名义"所颁布的法的规范。拉康认为语言也是法的规则的一部分。当主体言说欲望时，受语言和法规的限制，能指无法真正抵达所指，只能关联另一个能指，在符号链条上让意义不断滑动，使欲望言说似是而非、言不及义。

虽然拉康对弗洛伊德理论进行了不少改造，但拉康将这些改造置于"回归弗洛伊德"的旗帜之下。以梅拉妮·克莱因（Melanie Klein）和唐纳德·伍兹·温尼科特（Donald Woods Winnicott）等为代表的英国精神分析学家，虽深受弗洛伊德的影响，但也不讳言对弗洛伊德理论的修改。克莱因关注儿童的神经症研究，反对弗洛伊德的俄狄浦斯情结论，认为无论是男孩还是女孩，他们先天的欲望对象都是母亲，对母亲的占有欲会滋生各种负面情绪，人类的爱、恨、负疚感等复杂情绪皆源于此。温尼科特反对弗洛伊德的个体模式的心理成长机制，认为人始终处于关系中，人的心理构成离不开周围世界对人的塑造和影响。外界影响，尤其是母亲的影响，既是儿童成长的先决条件，也是儿童需要学会恰当应对，以形成独立人格的关键之一。

在弗洛伊德的众多分歧者中，最为知名的当属神话原型批评理论的奠基者卡尔·荣格（Carl Jung）。荣格曾热情追随弗洛伊德，但后来与弗洛伊德产生分歧，创建分析心理学（Analytic Psychology）学派。荣格是瑞士人，父亲是神职人员，家庭宗教氛围浓厚，因此无法接受弗洛伊德对性驱动力的强调。弗洛伊德的无意识理论关注个体心理世界的形成，关注后天经历带来的压抑和创伤。荣格则将无意识分成了两个层面：表层是生活中各种难解情结（complex）组成的个体无意识；深层是集体无意识。荣格认为集体无意识不是个人后天获得的，而是具有遗传的性质，是先天的固有的直觉形式，形成了知觉与领悟的原型。

荣格认为人类在漫长历史中，经历过多少种典型境遇，就会有多少种相应的原型。比如，"人格面具"（the Persona）的原型是人类为了应对社会压力，压抑不被认可的原始冲动，按照外界期待所戴上的表演性假面。"阴影"（the Shadow）的原型中隐藏着人类极力想要否定的情绪和欲望等因素，比如愤怒、嫉妒、性欲、攻击性等。"自性"原型（the Self，或译为"自我"原型）是心灵整合的原型，反映人格的理想和谐。荣格认为宗教中常见的曼陀罗图案——对称、平衡、具有整体性、层次丰富——是此类原型的图示。在两性关系中，荣格认为每个性别均有嵌套其中的异性原型。对女性来说，她的男性特质构成了"阿尼玛斯"原型（Animus）。男性则有女性特质的"阿尼玛"原型（Anima）。一对男女一见钟情，是因为符合彼此的阿尼玛/阿尼玛斯原型，所以才会一见如故，彼此倾心。

如何证明集体无意识的存在？荣格认为神话提供了证据。荣格的观点受到英国人类学家詹姆斯·乔治·弗雷泽（James George Frazer）的影响。弗雷泽在《金枝》中比较了世界上不同文明的神话模式，发现它们存在相似性。荣格从心理分析的角度来解释这种相似性，他把原型（archetype）和原始意象（primordial image）相联系，指出原型是人类与生俱来的心理模式，是具体内容有待填充的基本形式；原始意象则是原型与具体文学意象等感性材料相结合的载体，每一个原始意象中都有着人类精神和人类命运的一块碎片，反映着人类在漫长历史中的情感积淀。不同神话中共同的象征和意象反映了人类的集体无意识，在不同时代的文学作品中反复出现。

荣格对文学创作的动机也是从集体无意识的角度进行解释的。他在《论分析心理学与诗歌的关系》（"On the Relation of Analytical Psychology to Poetry"，1922）中解析了艺术的生成与人类的集体无意识的联系。荣格指出，有些文学作品反映作者的个人情感和经验；但有些文学作品，作者的灵感来自对集体无意识的直觉捕捉，讲述的不仅是个人的故事，也是人类共同的故事——此类作品更能打动读者的心灵。荣格很喜欢讨论神话、幻想、梦等具有神秘主义色彩的内容。他反对启蒙理性，也反对现代性的进步史观，认为作家对集体无意识的展示，能够唤醒身处时代洪流中的人们，拯救西方现代文明的心理失调。在他看来，一个民族失去了神话，也就失去了它的精神根系。

当代神话原型批评理论的代表人物是加拿大批评家诺思罗普·弗莱（Northrop Frye）。弗莱称自己是文学人类学家，受荣格的神话原型论的启发，关注文学母题和神话叙事。此外，他受结构主义影响，把文学视为一系列基础程式构成的复合体。他将原型视为这些程式的基础，认为原型统摄文学表征中的原型意象，是文学文本的叙事结构的基本原则。

在代表作《批评的剖析》（*Anatomy of Criticism*，1957）中，弗莱将典型的原型意象分为三类：神启意象，展现天堂以及人类得到救赎的理想世界；魔怪意象，表现地狱、暴政、死亡等负面因素；类比意象，介于两者之间，既非纯真也非邪恶，贴近现实世界。弗莱以人物行动力的差异为依据，将叙事模式分为五类：在神话模式中，人物超越自然规律的束缚，是高高在上的神；在浪漫传奇模式中，主人公具有超凡能力，但是人非神；高模仿模式反映帝王将相和英雄人物在现实世界里的命运；低模仿模式中，普通人和世俗世界成为主角；如果主人公的智力或者行动力不如普通人，则是反讽模式。弗莱在叙事模式基础上提出他的文学史观，认为文学史沿着神话到反讽的顺序，周而复始地进行模式循环。比如，现代小说以反讽模式为经典，改编自荷马史诗的乔伊斯的《尤利西斯》是其代表作。当代文坛则出现了科幻小说热——弗莱认为科幻小说属于神话模式，科幻小说热潮说明了神话的回归。

在当代，神话原型批评理论较多运用在文学人类学、文化人类学、比较文学与世界文学等领域。而精神分析理论的影响力更为广泛，不仅是解读文学文本和文化文本的基础理论工具，也对西方马克思主义、女性主义、后殖民主义等流派的理论发现有重要的启发作用。综合来看，精神分析理论和神话原型批评关注人类经验中的无意识层面，为人类理解自我和理解社会拓展出极其重要的维度，为把握文学与艺术的创作动力和阐释文学与艺术文本的深层意义提供了富有穿透力的视角。

主要文本阅读

弗洛伊德：《创造性作家与白日梦》

| 选文简介

弗洛伊德在《创造性作家与白日梦》中提出了这样一个问题：为什么作家能够通过他的作品在我们的内心唤起那么强烈的情感？他发现这是因为作家的创作符合人类的想象性的创造本能。这种本能我们在童年时期人人都有："每个在游戏的儿童的举止都像一个创造性的作家"，儿童热情地投入游戏，愉快地创造着符合他的想象的世界。成年人无法再像孩子一样游戏，但是他记得游戏时的快乐，于是通过白日梦来模糊想象和现实的界限。艺术创作就是这种白日梦：通过变形和掩饰等手法，在作品中打造幻想的世界，劝诱内心放松监审尺度，对令人不满的现实进行裁剪，让现实中无法满足的愿望得以实现。我们喜爱有创造力的作家，因为他们既在作品中表达了个人的隐秘欲望，又以高超的审美技巧，软化我们对触碰禁忌的反感。这些作品能让我们放松内心的紧张感，让我们也能"无须自责也无须羞耻地欣赏我们自己的白日梦"。

From "Creative Writers and Daydreaming"

Sigmund Freud (1856-1939)

We laymen have always been intensely curious to know—like the cardinal who put a similar question to Ariosto—from what sources that strange being, the creative writer, draws his material, and how he manages to make such an impression on us with it and to arouse in us emotions of which, perhaps, we had not even thought ourselves capable. Our interest is only heightened the more by the fact that, if we ask him, the writer himself gives us no explanation, or none that is satisfactory; and it is not at all weakened by our knowledge that not even the clearest insight into the determinants of his choice of material and into the nature of the art of creating imaginative form will ever help to make creative writers of *us*.

If we could at least discover in ourselves or in people like ourselves an activity which was in some way akin to creative writing! An examination of it would then give us a hope of obtaining the beginnings of an explanation of the creative work of writers. And, indeed, there is some prospect of this being possible. After all, creative writers themselves like to lessen the distance between their kind and the common run of humanity; they so often assure us that every man is a poet at heart and that the last poet will not perish till the last man does.

Should we not look for the first traces of imaginative activity as early as in childhood? The child's best-loved and most intense occupation is with his play or games. Might we not say that every child at play behaves like a creative writer, in that he creates a world of his own, or, rather, rearranges the things of his world in a new way which pleases him? It would be wrong to think he does not take that world seriously; on the contrary, he takes his play very seriously and he expends large amounts of emotion on it. The opposite of play is not what is serious but what is real. In spite of all the emotion with which he cathects his world of play, the child distinguishes it quite well from reality; and he likes to link his imagined objects and situations to the tangible and visible things of the real world. This linking is all that differentiates the child's "play" from "fantasying."

The creative writer does the same as the child at play. He creates a world of fantasy which he takes very seriously—that is, which he invests with large amounts of emotion—while separating it sharply from reality. Language has preserved this relationship between children's play and poetic creation. It gives the name of *Spiel* ["play"] to those forms of imaginative writing which require to be linked to tangible objects and which are capable of representation. It speaks of a *Lustspiel* or *Trauerspiel* ["comedy" or "tragedy"] and describes those who carry out the representation as *Schauspieler* ["players"]. The unreality of the writer's imaginative world, however, has very important consequences for the technique of his art; for many things which, if they were real, could give no enjoyment, can do so in the play of fantasy, and many excitements which, in themselves, are actually distressing, can become a source of pleasure for the hearers and spectators at the performance of a writer's work....

As people grow up, then, they cease to play, and they seem to give up the yield of pleasure which they gained from playing. But whoever understands the human mind knows that hardly anything is harder for a man than to give up a pleasure which he has once experienced. Actually, we can never give anything up; we only exchange one thing for another. What appears to be a renunciation is really the formation of a substitute or surrogate. In the same way, the growing child, when he stops playing, gives up nothing but the link with real objects; instead of playing, he now fantasies. He builds castles in the air and creates what are called daydreams. I believe that most people construct fantasies at times in their lives. This is a fact which has long been overlooked and whose importance has therefore not been sufficiently appreciated.

People's fantasies are less easy to observe than the play of children. The child, it is true, plays by himself or forms a closed psychical system with other children for the purposes of a game; but even though he may not play his game in front of the grown-ups, he does not, on the other hand, conceal it from them. The adult, on the contrary, is ashamed of his fantasies and hides them from other people. He cherishes his fantasies as his most intimate possessions, and as a rule he would rather confess his misdeeds than tell anyone his fantasies. It may come about that for that reason he believes he is the only person who invents such fantasies and has no idea that creations of this kind are widespread among other people. This difference in the behavior of a person who plays and a person who fantasies is accounted for by the motives of these two activities, which are nevertheless adjuncts to each other.

A child's play is determined by wishes: in point of fact by a single wish—one that helps in his upbringing—the wish to be big and grown up. He is always playing at being "grown up," and in his games he imitates what he knows about the lives of his elders. He has no reason to conceal this wish. With the adult, the case is different. On the one hand, he knows that he is expected not to go on playing or fantasying any longer, but to act in the real world; on the other hand, some of the wishes which give rise to his fantasies are of a kind which it is essential to conceal. Thus he is ashamed of his fantasies as being childish and as being unpermissible....

Let us make ourselves acquainted with a few of the characteristics of fantasying. We may lay it down that a happy person never fantasies, only an unsatisfied one. The motive forces of fantasies are unsatisfied wishes, and every single fantasy is the fulfillment of a wish, a correction of unsatisfying reality. These motivating wishes vary according to the sex, character, and circumstances of the person who is having the fantasy; but they fall naturally into two main groups. They are either ambitious wishes, which serve to elevate the subject's personality; or they are erotic ones....

I cannot pass over the relation of fantasies to dreams. Our dreams at night are nothing else than fantasies like these, as we can demonstrate from the interpretation of dreams. Language, in its unrivaled wisdom, long ago decided the question of the essential nature of dreams by giving the name of *daydreams* to the airy creations of fantasy. If the meaning of our dreams usually remains obscure to us in spite of this pointer, it is because of the circumstance that at night there also arise in us wishes of which we are ashamed; these we must conceal from ourselves, and they have consequently been repressed, pushed into the unconscious. Repressed wishes of this sort and their derivatives are only allowed to come to expression in a very distorted form. When scientific work had succeeded in elucidating this factor of *dream distortion*, it was no longer difficult to recognize that night dreams are wish-fulfillments in just the same way as daydreams—the fantasies which we all know so well.

So much for fantasies. And now for the creative writer. May we really attempt to compare the imaginative writer with the "dreamer in broad daylight," and his creations with daydreams? Here we must begin by making an initial distinction. We must separate writers who, like the ancient authors of epics and tragedies, take over their material ready-made, from writers who seem to originate their own material. We will keep to the latter kind, and, for the purposes of our comparison, we will choose not the writers most highly esteemed by the critics, but the less pretentious authors of novels, romances and short stories, who nevertheless have the widest and most eager circle of readers of both sexes. One feature above all cannot fail to strike us about the creations of these story-writers: each of them has a hero who is the center of interest, for whom the writer tries to win our sympathy by every possible means and whom he seems to place under the protection of a special providence. If, at the end of one chapter of my story, I leave the hero unconscious and bleeding from severe wounds, I am sure to find him at the beginning of the next being carefully nursed and on the way to recovery; and if the first volume closes with the ship he is in going down in a storm at sea, I am certain, at the opening of the second volume, to read of his miraculous rescue—a rescue without which the story could not proceed. The feeling of security with which I follow the hero through his perilous adventures is the same as the feeling with which a hero in real life throws himself into the water to save a drowning man or exposes himself to the enemy's fire in order to storm a battery. It is the true heroic feeling, which one of our best writers has expressed in an inimitable phrase: "Nothing can happen to *me*!" It seems to me, however, that through this revealing characteristic of invulnerability we can immediately recognize His Majesty the Ego, the hero alike of every daydream and of every story.

Other typical features of these egocentric stories point to the same kinship. The fact that all the women in the novel invariably fall in love with the hero can hardly be looked on as a portrayal of reality, but it is easily understood as a necessary constituent of a daydream. The same is true of the fact that the other characters in the story are sharply divided into good and bad, in defiance of the variety of human characters that are to be observed in real life. The "good" ones are the helpers, while the "bad" ones are the enemies and rivals, of the ego which has become the hero of the story....

You will remember how I have said that the daydreamer carefully conceals his fantasies from other people because he feels he has reasons for being ashamed of them. I should now add that even if he were to communicate them to us he could give us no pleasure by his disclosures. Such fantasies, when we learn them, repel us or at least leave us cold. But when a creative writer presents his plays to us or tells us what we are inclined to take to be his personal daydreams, we experience a great pleasure, and one which probably arises from the confluence of many sources. How the writer accomplishes this is his innermost secret; the essential *ars poetica* [art of poetry] lies in the technique of overcoming the feeling of repulsion in us which is undoubtedly connected with the barriers that rise between each single ego and the others. We can guess two of the methods used by this technique. The writer softens the character of his egoistic daydreams by altering and disguising it, and he bribes us by the purely formal—that is, aesthetic—yield of pleasure which he offers us in the presentation of his fantasies. We give the name of an *incentive bonus*, or a *forepleasure*, to a yield of pleasure such as this, which is offered to us so as to make possible the release of still greater pleasure arising from deeper psychical sources. In my opinion, all the aesthetic pleasure which a creative writer affords us has the character of a forepleasure of this kind, and our actual enjoyment of an imaginative work proceeds from a liberation of tensions in our minds. It may even be that not a little of this effect is due to the writer's enabling us thenceforward to enjoy our own daydreams without self-reproach or shame. This brings us to the threshold of new, interesting, and complicated inquiries; but also, at least for the moment, to the end of our discussion.

荣格：《论分析心理学与诗歌的关系》

选文简介

荣格和弗洛伊德的艺术观存在重要区别：弗洛伊德在个人的私密精神生活中寻找艺术创作的线索；荣格则认为这种做法将诗人与艺术品当作临床科学的案例，而且这种做法也贬低了艺术的价值，仿佛艺术只能言说个人欲望。在《论分析心理学与诗歌的关系》中，荣格集中讨论了艺术创作、艺术作品、艺术家三者之间的关系。他发现有的文学作品中，作家仿佛拥有神来之笔，能写出令他自己也吃惊的伟大作品。荣格用"自主情结"来形容这种艺术创造力，认为它反映了集体无意识的存在，使艺术具有超越个人经验的精神升腾力。在文学作品中，经典神话象征反复出现，原型被激活，也是集体无意识的体现，"就好像我们身上从未响起过的和弦被敲响了……我们不再是个人，而是种族；全人类的声音在我们身上响起"。值得注意的是，荣格反对将原型理解为一成不变的模板，他认为文学创作以原型为底本，可以与时代相交融，有创作变化的自由，只是这些变化具有万变不离其宗的共性。

From "On the Relation of Analytical Psychology to Poetry"

Carl Jung (1875-1961)

The school of medical psychology inaugurated by Freud has undoubtedly encouraged the literary historian to bring certain peculiarities of a work of art into relations with the intimate, personal life of the poet. But this is nothing new in principle, for it has long been known that the scientific treatment of art will reveal the personal threads that the artist, intentionally or unintentionally, has woven into his work. The Freudian approach may, however, make possible a more exhaustive demonstration of the influences that reach back into earliest childhood and play their part in artistic creation. To this extent the psychoanalysis of art differs in no essential from the subtle psychological nuances of a penetrating literary analysis. The difference is at most a question of degree, though we may occasionally be surprised by indiscreet references to things which a rather more delicate touch might have passed over if only for reasons of tact. This lack of delicacy seems to be a professional peculiarity of the medical psychologist, and the temptation to draw daring conclusions easily leads to flagrant abuses. A slight whiff of scandal often lends spice to a biography, but a little more becomes a nasty inquisitiveness—bad taste masquerading as science. Our interest is insidiously deflected from the work of art and gets lost in the labyrinth of psychic determinants, the poet becomes a clinical case and, very likely, yet another addition to the curiosa of *psychopathia sexualis*. But this means that the psychoanalysis of art has turned aside from its proper objective and strayed into a province that is as broad as mankind, that is not in the least specific to the artist and has even less relevance to his art....

The reductive method of Freud is a purely medical one, and the treatment is directed at a pathological or otherwise unsuitable formation which has taken the place of the normal functioning. It must therefore be broken down, and the way cleared for healthy adaptation. In this case, reduction to the common human foundation is altogether appropriate. But when applied to a work of art it leads to the results I have described. It strips the work of art of its shimmering robes and exposes the nakedness and drabness of *Homo sapiens*, to which species the poet and artist also belong. The golden gleam of artistic creation—the original object of discussion—is extinguished as soon as we apply to it the same corrosive method which we use in analyzing the fantasies of hysteria....

In order to do justice to a work of art, analytical psychology must rid itself entirely of medical prejudice; for a work of art is not a disease, and consequently requires a different approach from the medical one. A doctor naturally has to seek out the causes of a disease in order to pull it up by the roots, but just as naturally the psychologist must adopt exactly the opposite attitude toward a work of art. Instead of investigating its typically human determinants, he will inquire first of all into its meaning, and will concern himself with its determinants only insofar as they enable him to understand it more fully....

...There are literary works, prose as well as poetry, that spring wholly from the author's intention to produce a particular result....He is wholly at one with the creative process, no matter whether he has deliberately made himself its spearhead, as it were, or whether it has made him its instrument so completely that he has lost all consciousness of this fact. In either case, the artist is so identified with his work that his intentions and his faculties are indistinguishable from the act of creation itself. There is no need, I think, to give examples of this from the history of literature or from the testimony of the artists themselves.

Nor need I cite examples of the other class of works which flow more or less complete and perfect from the author's pen. They come as it were fully arrayed into the world, as Pallas Athene sprang from the head of Zeus. These works positively force themselves upon the author; his hand is seized, his pen writes things that his mind contemplates with amazement. The work brings with it its own form; anything he wants to add is rejected, and what he himself would like to reject is thrust back at him. While his conscious mind stands amazed and empty before this phenomenon, he is overwhelmed by a flood of thoughts and images which he never intended to create and which his own will could never have brought into being. Yet in spite of himself he is forced to admit that it is his own self speaking, his own inner nature revealing itself and uttering things which he would never have entrusted to his tongue. He can only obey the apparently alien impulse within him and follow where it leads, sensing that his work is greater than himself, and wields a power which is not his and which he cannot command. Here the artist is not identical with the process of creation; he is aware that he is subordinate to his work or stands outside it, as though he were a second person; or as though a person other than himself had fallen within the magic circle of an alien will....

...I am assuming that the work of art we propose to analyze, as well as being symbolic, has its source not in the personal unconscious of the poet, but in a sphere of unconscious mythology whose primordial images are the common heritage of mankind. I have called this sphere the *collective unconscious*, to distinguish it from the personal unconscious. The latter I regard as the sum total of all those psychic processes and contents which are capable of becoming conscious and often do, but are then suppressed because of their incompatibility and kept subliminal. Art receives tributaries from this sphere too, but muddy ones; and their predominance, far from making a work of art a symbol, merely turns it into a symptom. We can leave this kind of art without injury and without regret to the purgative methods employed by Freud.

In contrast to the personal unconscious, which is a relatively thin layer immediately below the threshold of consciousness, the collective unconscious shows no tendency to become conscious under normal conditions, nor can it be brought back to recollection by an analytical technique, since it was never repressed or forgotten. The collective unconscious is not to be thought of as a self-subsistent entity; it is no more than a potentiality handed down to us from primordial times in the specific form of mnemonic images or inherited in the anatomical structure of the brain. There are no inborn ideas, but there are inborn possibilities of ideas that set bounds to even the boldest fantasy and keep our fantasy activity within certain categories: *a priori* ideas, as it were, the existence of which cannot be ascertained except from their effects. They appear only in the shaped material of art as the regulative principles that shape it; that is to say, only by inferences drawn from the finished work can we reconstruct the age-old original of the primordial image.

The primordial image, or archetype, is a figure—be it a demon, a human being, or a process—that constantly recurs in the course of history and appears wherever creative fantasy is freely expressed. Essentially, therefore, it is a mythological figure. When we examine these images more closely, we find that they give form to countless typical experiences of our ancestors. They are, so to speak, the psychic residua of innumerable experiences of the same type. They present a picture of psychic life in the average, divided up and projected into the manifold figures of the mythological pantheon. But the mythological figures are themselves products of creative fantasy and still have to be translated into conceptual language. Only the beginnings of such a language exist, but once the necessary concepts are created they could give us an abstract, scientific understanding of the unconscious processes that lie at the roots of the primordial images. In each of these images there is a little piece of human psychology and human fate, a remnant of the joys and sorrows that have been repeated countless times in our ancestral history, and on the average follow ever the same course. It is like a deeply graven river-bed in the psyche, in which waters of life, instead of flowing along as before in a broad but shallow stream, suddenly swell into a mighty river. This happens whenever that particular set of circumstances is encountered which over long periods of time has helped to lay down the primordial image.

The moment when this mythological situation reappears is always characterized by a peculiar emotional intensity; it is as though chords in us were struck that had never resounded before, or as though forces whose existence we never suspected were unloosed. What makes the struggle for adaptation so laborious is the fact that we have constantly to be dealing with individual and atypical situations. So it is not surprising that when an archetypal situation occurs we suddenly feel an extraordinary sense of release, as though transported, or caught up by an overwhelming power. At such moments we are no longer individuals, but the race; the voice of all mankind resounds in us. The individual man cannot use his powers to the full unless he is aided by one of those collective representations we call ideals, which releases all the hidden forces of instinct that are inaccessible to his conscious will. The most effective ideals are always fairly obvious variants of an archetype, as is evident from the fact that they lend themselves to allegory....

The impact of an archetype, whether it takes the form of immediate experience or is expressed through the spoken word, stirs us because it summons up a voice that is stronger than our own. Whoever speaks in primordial images speaks with a thousand voices; he enthralls and overpowers, while at the same time he lifts the idea he is seeking to express out of the occasional and the transitory into the realm of the ever-enduring. He transmutes our personal destiny into the destiny of mankind, and evokes in us all those beneficent forces that ever and anon have enabled humanity to find a refuge from every peril and to outlive the longest night.

That is the secret of great art, and of its effect upon us. The creative process, so far as we are able to follow it at all, consists in the unconscious activation of an archetypal image, and in elaborating and shaping this image into the finished work. By giving it shape, the artist translates it into the language of the present, and so makes it possible for us to find our way back to the deepest springs of life. Therein lies the social significance of art: it is constantly at work educating the spirit of the age, conjuring up the forms in which the age is most lacking. The unsatisfied yearning of the artist reaches back to the primordial image in the unconscious which is best fitted to compensate the inadequacy and one-sidedness of the present. The artist seizes on this image, and in raising it from deepest unconsciousness he brings it into relation with conscious values, thereby transforming it until it can be accepted by the minds of his contemporaries according to their powers.

拉康：《镜像阶段》

选文简介

《镜像阶段》的初稿写于1936年，正式发表于1949年，是拉康被引用最多的理论文章。文章篇幅不长，但是讨论了非常重要的议题：人类主体是如何形成的？拉康借用动物学的发现作为引题，指出猩猩一旦认识到镜中像是自己，就会失去照镜子的乐趣。六到十八个月大的婴儿则相反，当婴儿辨认出自己的镜中像，反而会更入迷地照镜子。拉康询问产生这种表现差异的心理动因，认为镜像阶段发生在婴儿自我意识形成期。当时的婴儿行动笨拙，对身体的感受混乱，镜中映像从视觉和行动力的角度全面重塑了婴儿对自我的认识。婴儿对镜子的迷恋，体现了其对镜像的"理想自我"（Ideal-I）的自恋式认同。这种认同发生时，婴儿也在镜中看到了周围的世界与自己的关系，认识到何为自己、何为他人、何为世界，在此基础上建立起主体性，实现"内在世界"和"外在世界"的统一。拉康的镜像阶段的主体观动摇了启蒙主义以来以笛卡尔的"我思故我在"为代表的理性主体观，揭露出人的主体性建立在无意识的意象（imago）之上，依赖于想象与误认等机制，根基处隐含着裂隙。

From "The Mirror Stage as Formative of the Function of the I as Revealed in Psychoanalytic Experience"

Jacques Lacan (1901-1981)

The conception of the mirror stage that I introduced at our last congress, thirteen years ago, has since become more or less established in the practice of the French group. However, I think it worthwhile to bring it again to your attention, especially today, for the light it sheds on the formation of the I as we experience it in psychoanalysis. It is an experience that leads us to oppose any philosophy directly issuing from the *Cogito*.

Some of you may recall that this conception originated in a feature of human behavior illuminated by a fact of comparative psychology. The child, at an age when he is for a time, however short, outdone by the chimpanzee in instrumental intelligence, can nevertheless already recognize as such his own image in a mirror. This recognition is indicated in the illuminative mimicry of the *Aha-Erlebnis*, which Köhler sees as the expression of situational apperception, an essential stage of the act of intelligence.

This act, far from exhausting itself, as in the case of the monkey, once the image has been mastered and found empty, immediately rebounds in the case of the child in a series of gestures in which he experiences in play the relation between the movements assumed in the image and the reflected environment, and between this virtual complex and the reality it reduplicates—the child's own body, and the persons and things, around him.

This event can take place, as we have known since Baldwin, from the age of six months, and its repetition has often made me reflect upon the startling spectacle of the infant in front of the mirror. Unable as yet to walk, or even to stand up, and held tightly as he is by some support, human or artificial (what, in France, we call a "*trotte-bébé*"), he nevertheless overcomes, in a flutter of jubilant activity, the obstructions of his support and, fixing his attitude in a slightly leaning-forward position, in order to hold it in his gaze, brings back an instantaneous aspect of the image.

For me, this activity retains the meaning I have given it up to the age of eighteen months. This meaning discloses a libidinal dynamism, which has hitherto remained problematic, as well as an ontological structure of the human world that accords with my reflections on paranoiac knowledge.

We have only to understand the mirror stage *as an identification*, in the full sense that analysis gives to the term: namely, the transformation that takes place in the subject when he assumes an image—whose predestination to this phase-effect is sufficiently indicated by the use, in analytic theory, of the ancient term *imago*.

This jubilant assumption of his specular image by the child at the *infans* stage, still sunk in his motor incapacity and nursing dependence, would seem to exhibit in an exemplary situation the symbolic matrix in which the *I* is precipitated in a primordial form, before it is objectified in the dialectic of identification with the other, and before language restores to it, in the universal, its function as subject.

This form would have to be called the Ideal-I, if we wished to incorporate it into our usual register, in the sense that it will also be the source of secondary identifications, under which term I would place the functions of libidinal normalization. But the important point is that this form situates the agency of the ego, before its social determination, in a fictional direction, which will always remain irreducible for the individual alone, or rather, which will only rejoin the coming-into-being (*le devenir*) of the subject asymptotically, whatever the success of the dialectical syntheses by which he must resolve as *I* his discordance with his own reality.

The fact is that the total form of the body by which the subject anticipates in a mirage the maturation of his power is given to him only as *Gestalt*, that is to say, in an exteriority in which this form is certainly more constituent than constituted, but in which it appears to him above all in a contrasting size (*un relief de stature*) that fixes it and in a symmetry that inverts it, in contrast with the turbulent movements that the subject feels are animating him. Thus, this *Gestalt*—whose pregnancy should be regarded as bound up with the species, though its motor style remains scarcely recognizable—by these two aspects of its appearance, symbolizes the mental permanence of the *I*, at the same time as it prefigures its alienating destination; it is still pregnant with the correspondences that unite the *I* with the statue in which man projects himself, with the phantoms that dominate him, or with the automaton in which, in an ambiguous relation, the world of his own making tends to find completion.

Indeed, for the *imagos*—whose veiled faces it is our privilege to see in outline in our daily experience and in the penumbra of symbolic efficacity—the mirror-image would seem to be the threshold of the visible world, if we go by the mirror disposition that the *imago of one's own body* presents in hallucinations or dreams, whether it concerns its individual features, or even its infirmities, or its object-projections; or if we observe the role of the mirror apparatus in the appearances of the *double*, in which psychical realities, however heterogeneous, are manifested.

That a *Gestalt* should be capable of formative effects in the organism is attested by a piece of biological experimentation that is itself so alien to the idea of psychical causality that it cannot bring itself to formulate its results in these terms. It nevertheless recognizes that it is a necessary condition for the maturation of the gonad of the female pigeon that it should see another member of its species, of either sex; so sufficient in itself is this condition that the desired effect may be obtained merely by placing the individual within reach of the field of reflection of a mirror. Similarly, in the case of the migratory locust, the transition within a generation from the solitary to the gregarious form can be obtained by exposing the individual, at a certain stage, to the exclusively visual action of a similar image, provided it is animated by movements of a style sufficiently close to that characteristic of the species. Such facts are inscribed in an order of homeomorphic identification that would itself fall within the larger question of the meaning of beauty as both formative and erogenic.

But the facts of mimicry are no less instructive when conceived as cases of heteromorphic identification, in as much as they raise the problem of the signification of space for the living organism—psychological concepts hardly seem less appropriate for shedding light on these matters than ridiculous attempts to reduce them to the supposedly supreme law of adaptation. We have only to recall how Roger Caillois (who was then very young, and still fresh from his breach with the sociological school in which he was trained) illuminated the subject by using the term "*legendary psychasthenia*" to classify morphological mimicry as an obsession with space in its derealizing effect.

I have myself shown in the social dialectic that structures human knowledge as paranoiac why human knowledge has greater autonomy than animal knowledge in relation to the field of force of desire, but also why human knowledge is determined in that "little reality" (*ce peu de réalité*), which the Surrealists, in their restless way, saw as its limitation. These reflections lead me to recognize in the spatial captation manifested in the mirror-stage, even before the social dialectic, the effect in man of an organic insufficiency in his natural reality—in so far as any meaning can be given to the word "nature."

I am led, therefore, to regard the function of the mirror-stage as a particular case of the function of the *imago*, which is to establish a relation between the organism and its reality —or, as they say, between the *Innenwelt* and the *Umwelt*.

In man, however, this relation to nature is altered by a certain dehiscence at the heart of the organism, a primordial Discord betrayed by the signs of uneasiness and motor uncoordination of the neo-natal months. The objective notion of the anatomical incompleteness of the pyramidal system and likewise the presence of certain humoral residues of the maternal organism confirm the view I have formulated as the fact of a real *specific prematurity of birth* in man.

It is worth noting, incidentally, that this is a fact recognized as such by embryologists, by the term *foetalization*, which determines the prevalence of the so-called superior apparatus of the neurax, and especially of the cortex, which psycho-surgical operations lead us to regard as the intra-organic mirror.

This development is experienced as a temporal dialectic that decisively projects the formation of the individual into history. The mirror stage is a drama whose internal thrust is precipitated from insufficiency to anticipation— and which manufactures for the subject, caught up in the lure of spatial identification, the succession of fantasies that extends from a fragmented body-image to a form of its totality that I shall call orthopedic—and, lastly, to the assumption of the armor of an alienating identity, which will mark with its rigid structure the subject's entire mental development. Thus, to break out of the circle of the *Innenwelt* into the *Umwelt* generates the inexhaustible quadrature of the ego's verifications.

This fragmented body—which term I have also introduced into our system of theoretical references—usually manifests itself in dreams when the movement of the analysis encounters a certain level of aggressive disintegration in the individual. It then appears in the form of disjointed limbs, or of those organs represented in exoscopy, growing wings and taking up arms for intestinal persecutions— the very same that the visionary Hieronymus Bosch has fixed, for all time, in painting, in their ascent from the fifteenth century to the imaginary zenith of modern man. But this form is even tangibly revealed at the organic level, in the lines of "fragilization" that define the anatomy of fantasy, as exhibited in the schizoid and spasmodic symptoms of hysteria.

Correlatively, the formation of the I is symbolized in dreams by a fortress, or a stadium—its inner arena and enclosure, surrounded by marshes and rubbish-tips, dividing it into two opposed fields of contest where the subject flounders in quest of the lofty, remote inner castle whose form (sometimes juxtaposed in the same scenario) symbolizes the id in a quite startling way. Similarly, on the mental plane, we find realized the structures of fortified works, the metaphor of which arises spontaneously, as if issuing from the symptoms themselves, to designate the mechanisms of obsessional neurosis—inversion, isolation, reduplication, cancellation and displacement.

弗莱:《文学的原型》

选文简介

《文学的原型》最初发表于《凯尼恩评论》(*Kenyon Review*)，后来其主要思想被收入《批评的剖析》(*Anatomy of Criticism*)。弗莱在文中批评两种理论倾向：他反对新批评的"细读法"对具体文本的精耕细作的阐释，认为这是"只见树木，不见森林"；他也反对批评理论"寄生虫"般依附于社会学、哲学、心理学、历史学等学科，失去了文学研究的独立性。在《文学的原型》中可见弗莱的兴趣焦点：他将文学视为自足体系，关注文学的共性和文学史长时段的变化规律。他从弗雷泽的文化人类学和荣格的神话原型概念中汲取灵感，指出文学诞生于人类早期文明的各种仪式实践，和仪式一样，受人类集体无意识的影响，遵循大自然的律动规则，体现神话原型的基本模式。弗莱将一日之不同时段、一年之四季变化、人一生的生命历程、神话的不同阶段和文学文类的变化发展进行类比，指出浪漫主义、喜剧、悲剧和反讽分别对应春、夏、秋、冬的自然周期，各有主题，各有典型人物。

From "The Archetypes of Literature"

Northrop Frye (1912-1991)

Some arts move in time, like music; others are presented in space, like painting. In both cases the organizing principle is recurrence, which is called rhythm when it is temporal and pattern when it is spatial. Thus we speak of the rhythm of music and the pattern of painting; but later, to show off our sophistication, we may begin to speak of the rhythm of painting and the pattern of music. In other words, all arts may be conceived both temporally and spatially. The score of a musical composition may be studied all at once; a picture may be seen as the track of an intricate dance of the eye. Literature seems to be intermediate between music and painting: its words form rhythms which approach a musical sequence of sounds at one of its boundaries, and form patterns which approach the hieroglyphic or pictorial image at the other. The attempts to get as near to these boundaries as possible form the main body of what is called experimental writing. We may call the rhythm of literature the narrative, and the pattern, the simultaneous mental grasp of the verbal structure, the meaning or significance. We hear or listen to a narrative, but when we grasp a writer's total pattern we "see" what he means.

The criticism of literature is much more hampered by the representational fallacy than even the criticism of painting. That is why we are apt to think of narrative as a sequential representation of events in an outside "life," and of meaning as a reflection of some external "idea." Properly used as critical terms, an author's narrative is his linear movement; his meaning is the integrity of his completed form. Similarly an image is not merely a verbal replica of an external object, but any unit of a verbal structure seen as part of a total pattern or rhythm. Even the letters an author spells his words with form part of his imagery, though only in special cases (such as alliteration) would they call for critical notice. Narrative and meaning thus become respectively, to borrow musical terms, the melodic and harmonic contexts of the imagery.

Rhythm, or recurrent movement, is deeply founded on the natural cycle, and everything in nature that we think of as having some analogy with works of art, like the flower or the bird's song, grows out of a profound synchronization between an organism and the rhythms of its environment, especially that of the solar year. With animals some expressions of synchronization, like the mating dances of birds, could almost be called rituals. But in human life a ritual seems to be something of a voluntary effort (hence the magical element in it) to recapture a lost rapport with the natural cycle. A farmer must harvest his crop at a certain time of year, but because this is involuntary, harvesting itself is not precisely a ritual. It is the deliberate expression of a will to synchronize human and natural energies at that time which produces the harvest songs, harvest sacrifices and harvest folk customs that we call rituals. In ritual, then, we may find the origin of narrative, a ritual being a temporal sequence of acts in which the conscious meaning or significance is latent: it can be seen by an observer, but is largely concealed from the participators themselves. The pull of ritual is toward pure narrative, which, if there could be such a thing, would be automatic and unconscious repetition. We should notice too the regular tendency of ritual to become encyclopedic. All the important recurrences in nature, the day, the phases of the moon, the seasons and solstices of the year, the crises of existence from birth to death, get rituals attached to them, and most of the higher religions are equipped with a definitive total body of rituals suggestive, if we may put it so, of the entire range of potentially significant actions in human life.

Patterns of imagery, on the other hand, or fragments of significance, are oracular in origin, and derive from the epiphanic moment, the flash of instantaneous comprehension with no direct reference to time, the importance of which is indicated by Cassirer in *Language and Myth*. By the time we get them, in the form of proverbs, riddles, commandments, and etiological folk tales, there is already a considerable element of narrative in them. They too are encyclopedic in tendency, building up a total structure of significance, or doctrine, from random and empiric fragments. And just as pure narrative would be an unconscious act, so pure significance would be an incommunicable state of consciousness, for communication begins by constructing narrative.

The myth is the central informing power that gives archetypal significance to the ritual and archetypal narrative to the oracle. Hence the myth is the archetype, though it might be convenient to say myth only when referring to narrative, and archetype when speaking of significance. In the solar cycle of the day, the seasonal cycle of the year, and the organic cycle of human life, there is a single pattern of significance, out of which myth constructs a central narrative around a figure who is partly the sun, partly vegetative fertility and partly a god or archetypal human being. The crucial importance of this myth has been forced on literary critics by Jung and Frazer in particular, but the several books now available on it are not always systematic in their approach, for which reason I supply the following table of its phases:

1. The dawn, spring, and birth phase. Myths of the birth of the hero, of revival and resurrection, of creation and (because the four phases are a cycle) of the defeat of the powers of darkness, winter and death. Subordinate characters: the father and the mother. The archetype of romance and of most dithyrambic and rhapsodic poetry.

2. The zenith, summer, and marriage or triumph phase. Myths of apotheosis, of the sacred marriage, and of entering into Paradise. Subordinate characters: the companion and the bride. The archetype of comedy, pastoral, and idyll.

3. The sunset, autumn, and death phase. Myths of fall, of the dying god, of violent death and sacrifice and of the isolation of the hero. Subordinate characters: the traitor and the siren. The archetype of tragedy and elegy.

4. The darkness, winter, and dissolution phase. Myths of the triumph of these powers; myths of floods and the return of chaos, of the defeat of the hero, and Götterdämmerung myths. Subordinate characters: the ogre and the witch. The archetype of satire (see, for instance, the conclusion of *The Dunciad*).

The quest of the hero also tends to assimilate the oracular and random verbal structures, as we can see when we catch the chaos of local legends that results from prophetic epiphanies consolidating into a narrative mythology of departmental gods. In most of the higher religions this in turn has become the same central quest-myth that emerges from ritual, as the Messiah myth became the narrative structure of the oracles of Judaism. A local flood may beget a folk tale by accident, but a comparison of flood stories will show how quickly such tales become examples of the myth of dissolution. Finally, the tendency of both ritual and epiphany to become encyclopedic is realized in the definitive body of myth which constitutes the sacred scriptures of religions. These sacred scriptures are consequently the first documents that the literary critic has to study to gain a comprehensive view of his subject. After he has understood their structure, then he can descend from archetypes to genres, and see how the drama emerges from the ritual side of myth and lyric from the epiphanic or fragmented side, while the epic carries on the central encyclopedic structure.

Some words of caution and encouragement are necessary before literary criticism has clearly staked out its boundaries in these fields. It is part of the critic's business to show how all literary genres are derived from the quest-myth, but the derivation is a logical one within the science of criticism: the quest-myth will constitute the first chapter of whatever future handbooks of criticism may be written that will be based on enough organized critical knowledge to call themselves "introductions" or "outlines" and still be able to live up to their titles. It is only when we try to expound the derivation chronologically that we find ourselves writing pseudo-prehistorical fictions and theories of mythological contact. Again, because psychology and anthropology are more highly developed sciences, the critic who deals with this kind of material is bound to appear, for some time, a dilettante of those subjects. These two phases of criticism are largely undeveloped in comparison with literary history and rhetoric, the reason being the later development of the sciences they are related to. But the fascination which *The Golden Bough* and Jung's book on libido symbols have for literary critics is not based on dilettantism, but on the fact that these books are primarily studies in literary criticism, and very important ones.

In any case the critic who is studying the principles of literary form has a quite different interest from the psychologist's concern with states of mind or the anthropologist's with social institutions. For instance: the mental response to narrative is mainly passive; to significance mainly active. From this fact Ruth Benedict's *Patterns of Culture* develops a distinction between "Apollonian" cultures based on obedience to ritual and "Dionysiac" ones based on a tense exposure of the prophetic mind to epiphany. The critic would tend rather to note how popular literature which appeals to the inertia of the untrained mind puts a heavy emphasis on narrative values, whereas a sophisticated attempt to disrupt the connection between the poet and his environment produces the Rimbaud type of *illumination*, Joyce's solitary epiphanies, and Baudelaire's conception of nature as a source of oracles. Also how literature, as it develops from the primitive to the self-conscious, shows a gradual shift of the poet's attention from narrative to significant values, this shift of attention being the basis of Schiller's distinction between naive and sentimental poetry.

思考题

1. 在弗洛伊德看来，儿童和艺术家之间有什么共性？
2. 弗洛伊德为什么说创造性艺术家所写的是白日梦？
3. 荣格为什么反对从诗人的个人生活经历来解读文学？荣格用什么证据来说明艺术创作中有集体无意识的驱动？
4. 拉康所说的"镜像阶段"特指什么阶段？它在人格形成中的重要意义是什么？
5. 弗莱将文学叙事的神话模式分为几个阶段？分别对应什么样的自然周期？有哪些具体内容？

讨论题

1. 弗洛伊德的艺术观和荣格的艺术观的主要区别是什么？为什么会有这样的区别？请根据选文以及课外资料进行综合讨论。
2. 请选择一位文学作品中的主人公，比如《麦克白》中的麦克白、《儿子与情人》中的保罗·莫雷尔、《红字》中的海丝特·白兰、《了不起的盖茨比》中的盖茨比等，讨论作者如何描写这个人物的欲望，分析文本所反映的人物的意识与无意识之间的冲突，解释造成这种冲突的社会文化原因。

补充文本选摘与评述

布鲁姆：《影响的焦虑》
From *The Anxiety of Influence: A Theory of Poetry*

Harold Bloom (1930-2019)

Oedipus, blind, was on the path to oracular godhood, and the strong poets have followed him by transforming their blindness toward their precursors into the revisionary insights of their own work. The six revisionary movements that I will trace in the strong poet's life-cycle could as well be more, and could take quite different names than those I have employed. I have kept them to six, because these seem to be minimal and essential to my understanding of how one poet deviates from another. The names, though arbitrary, carry on from various traditions that have been central in Western imaginative life, and I hope can be useful.

The greatest poet in our language is excluded from the argument of this book for several reasons. One is necessarily historical; Shakespeare belongs to the giant age before the flood, before the anxiety of influence became central to poetic consciousness. Another has to do with the contrast between dramatic and lyric form. As poetry has become more subjective, the shadow cast by the precursors has become more dominant. The main cause, though, is that Shakespeare's prime precursor was Marlowe, a poet very much smaller than his inheritor. Milton, with all his strength, yet had to struggle, subtly and crucially, with a major precursor in Spenser, and this struggle both formed and malformed Milton. Coleridge, ephebe of Milton and later of Wordsworth, would have been glad to find his Marlowe in Cowper (or in the much weaker Bowles), but influence cannot be willed. Shakespeare is the largest instance in the language of a phenomenon that stands outside the concern of this book: the absolute absorption of the precursor. Battle between strong equals, father and son as mighty opposites, Laius and Oedipus at the crossroads; only this is my subject here, though some of the fathers, as will be seen, are composite figures. That even the strongest poets are subject to influences not poetical is obvious even to me, but again my concern is only with *the poet in a poet*, or the aboriginal poetic self.

A change like the one I propose in our ideas of influence should help us read more accurately any group of past poets who were contemporary with one another. To give one example, as misinterpreters of Keats, *in their poems*, the Victorian disciples of Keats most notably include Tennyson, Arnold, Hopkins, and Rossetti. That Tennyson triumphed in his long, hidden contest with Keats, no one can assert absolutely, but his clear superiority over Arnold, Hopkins, and Rossetti is due to his relative victory or at least holding of his own in contrast to their partial defeats. Arnold's elegiac poetry uneasily blends Keatsian style with anti-Romantic sentiment, while Hopkins' strained intensities and convolutions of diction and Rossetti's densely inlaid art are also at variance with the burdens they seek to alleviate in their own poetic selves. Similarly, in our time we need to look again at Pound's unending match with Browning, as at Stevens' long and largely hidden civil war with the major poets of English and American Romanticism—Wordsworth, Keats, Shelley, Emerson, and Whitman. As with the Victorian Keatsians, these are instances among many, if a more accurate story is to be told about poetic history.

穆尔维:《视觉快感与叙事电影》
From "Visual Pleasure and Narrative Cinema"

Laura Mulvey (1941-   )

This paper intends to use psychoanalysis to discover where and how the fascination of film is reinforced by pre-existing patterns of fascination already at work within the individual subject and the social formations that have moulded him. It takes as starting point the way film reflects, reveals and even plays on the straight, socially established interpretation of sexual difference which controls images, erotic ways of looking and spectacle. It is helpful to understand what the cinema has been, how its magic has worked in the past, while attempting a theory and a practice which will challenge this cinema of the past. Psychoanalytic theory is thus appropriated here as a political weapon, demonstrating the way the unconscious of patriarchal society has structured film form....

The psychoanalytic background that has been discussed in this article is relevant to the pleasure and unpleasure offered by traditional narrative film. The scopophilic instinct (pleasure in looking at another person as an erotic object), and, in contradistinction, ego libido (forming identification processes) act as formations, mechanisms, which this cinema has played on. The image of woman as (passive) raw material for the (active) gaze of man takes the argument a step further into the structure of representation, adding a further layer demanded by the ideology of the patriarchal order as it is worked out in its favorite cinematic form—illusionistic narrative film. The argument returns again to the psychoanalytic background in that woman as representation signifies castration, inducing voyeuristic or fetishistic mechanisms to circumvent her threat. None of these interacting layers is intrinsic to film, but it is only in the film form that they can reach a perfect and beautiful contradiction, thanks to the possibility in the cinema of shifting the emphasis of the look. It is the place of the look that defines cinema, the possibility of varying it and exposing it. This is what makes cinema quite different in its voyeuristic potential from, say, striptease, theater, shows, etc. Going far beyond highlighting a woman's to-be-looked-at-ness, cinema builds the way she is to be looked at into the spectacle itself. Playing on the tension between film as controlling the dimension of time (editing, narrative) and film as controlling the dimension of space (changes in distance, editing), cinematic codes create a gaze, a world, and an object, thereby producing an illusion cut to the measure of desire. It is these cinematic codes and their relationship to formative external structures that must be broken down before mainstream film and the pleasure it provides can be challenged.

卡鲁斯:《无法言说的经历》
From *Unclaimed Experience: Trauma, Narrative, and History*

Cathy Caruth (1955-   )

The return of the traumatic experience in the dream is not the signal of the direct experience but, rather, of the attempt to overcome the fact that it was *not* direct, to attempt to master what was never fully grasped in the first place. Not having truly known the threat of death in the past, the survivor is forced, continually, to confront it over and over again. For consciousness then, the act of survival, as the experience of trauma, is the repeated confrontation with the necessity and impossibility of grasping the threat to one's own life. It is because the mind cannot confront the possibility of its death directly that survival becomes for the human being, paradoxically, an endless testimony to the impossibility of living.

From this perspective, the survival of trauma is not the fortunate passage beyond a violent event, a passage that is accidentally interrupted by reminders of it, but rather the endless *inherent necessity* of repetition, which ultimately may lead to destruction. The examples of repetition compulsion that Freud offers—the patient repeating painful events in analysis, the woman condemned repeatedly to marry men who die, the soldier Tancred in Tasso's poem wounding his beloved again—all seem to point to the necessity by which consciousness, once faced with the possibility of its death, can do nothing but repeat the destructive event over and over again. Indeed, these examples suggest that the shape of individual lives, the history of the traumatized individual, is nothing other than the determined repetition of the event of destruction.

In modern trauma theory as well, there is an emphatic tendency to focus on the destructive repetition of the trauma that governs a person's life. As modern neurobiologists point out, the repetition of the traumatic experience in the flashback can itself be retraumatizing; if not life-threatening, it is at least threatening to the chemical structure of the brain and can ultimately lead to deterioration. And this would also seem to explain the high suicide rate of survivors, for example, survivors of Vietnam or of concentration camps, who commit suicide only after they have found themselves completely in safety. As a paradigm for the human experience that governs history, then, traumatic disorder is indeed the apparent struggle to die. The postulation of a drive to death, which Freud ultimately introduces in *Beyond the Pleasure Principle*, would seem only to recognize the reality of the destructive force that the violence of history imposes on the human psyche, the formation of history as the endless repetition of previous violence.

| 选文评述

布鲁姆在《影响的焦虑》中，化用弗洛伊德的俄狄浦斯情结，用它来描述诗人之间的代际传承与竞争关系。诗人与前辈诗人是"子"与"父"的竞争关系，与同辈诗人是兄弟间的竞争关系。诗人在继承传统的同时，如果想要克服"影响的焦虑"

（anxiety of influence），就必须与先驱者角力，对其进行误读（misreading）、错释（misinterpretation）和曲解（misprision），从而找到突破点，胜过前人，形成自己的风格。文学的变化来自诗人对前辈诗人的创造性的误读，文学史的发展轨迹展现出文学传统始终是在继承与反叛中进行修正性调整。

穆尔维在《视觉快感与叙事电影》中分析了观影快感的由来：它体现了弗洛伊德所说的窥视欲（voyeurism）。窥视欲源于婴儿期对性器官的好奇，随着孩子的成长，被部分升华为求知欲，但欲望动力仍在，驱动着成人观影的乐趣——在漆黑的影院中，观众是隐身的、不受监视的，窥视着屏幕上的世界。这种快感也源于拉康镜像阶段的视觉认同机制。荧幕相当于镜子，观众将自己投射到影片人物身上，将他们看作自我的化身。好莱坞电影的特点是征用窥视欲与镜像凝视为父权制的视觉政治服务，提供男性视角的窥视欲的快感，将女人身体化，变成男人凝视的欲望对象。穆尔维的文章揭秘了好莱坞电影中男性观看/女性被看的意识形态框架，是女性主义电影研究的经典之作。

卡鲁斯在《无法言说的经历》中聚焦创伤经历的叙事特征，指出创伤叙事具有重复性特点。为了避免创伤性暴力带来的无法承受的伤害，创伤事件会被经历者封存在记忆中，但这种封存会持续释放心理压力，逼迫受害者为了理解它而不断在心理层面重新经历它。幸存者的高自杀率说明创伤性心理疾病是与死亡做斗争，而卡鲁斯由此联想到弗洛伊德的死亡欲望（Thanatos）。她指出弗洛伊德的死亡驱力概念展现出人类历史是暴力的叠加和重复，历史记忆的暴力性会对人类心灵造成持续的破坏力。卡鲁斯的理论对文学研究的启示在于，我们往往能够在文学表征的重复言说或者沉默空白中窥见创伤性经历的印痕。文学语言的曲折性、含混性，以及擅长留白，恰为揭秘被遮蔽却不肯愈合的历史创伤提供了合适的媒介。

关键术语释例

1. 防御机制（defense mechanism）：弗洛伊德发现，人们为了规避痛苦，面对焦虑、内疚和超我谴责等来自心灵内部的压力时，以及面对危及安全感的来自外部世界的压力时，会采取防御性的方法寻求心理保护。弗洛伊德将其命名为"防御机制"，指人们面对可能对自我造成威胁的刺激时所产生的心理反应，以及所采取的应对性策略。为了把不可接受的内容阻挡在意识之外，人们或对它们进行压抑或否认，或对它们进行掩饰、伪装，或绕过它们，进行自我欺骗。但自我防御也有负面效果：它会扭曲现实，带来虚假感受，所以过度的自我防御会引发心理疾病。常见的心理防御机制包括压抑（repression）、否定（denial）、合理化（rationalization）、理想化（idealization）、隔离（isolation）、分裂（dissociation）、歪曲（distortion）、转移（displacement）、投射（projection）和升华（sublimation）等。

2. **认同（identification）**：认同是指人们通过模仿他人来塑造自己。人们通过想象自己是他人，或者通过在自己内心塑造一个他人的形象，将它作为理想模型来建构自己的身份。弗洛伊德认为认同不是主体主动选择的结果。从他的"本我""超我"和"自我"的人格结构论中，可以看到主体是在欲望的挤压、社会的律令和自我的模仿中生成的。拉康通过"想象界"和"象征界"进一步说明了主体认同机制的复杂性。在想象性认同中，主体将镜中虚像视为理想自我（ideal ego）；在象征性认同中，主体在社会期待和权威压制下，向自我理想（ego ideal）靠近。人们的身份（identity）随着主体性认同得以确立，而身份危机的诸多隐患，也潜藏在这种认同机制之中。

推荐书目

Ellmann, Maud. *Psychoanalytic Literary Criticism*. London: Longman, 1994.

Felman, Shoshana. *Jacques Lacan and the Adventure of Insight: Psychoanalysis in Contemporary Culture*. Cambridge, Mass.: Harvard University Press, 1987.

Gay, Peter. *Freud: A Life for Our Time*. New York: W. W. Norton, 1988.

Gill, Glen. *Northrop Frye and the Phenomenology of Myth*. Toronto: University of Toronto Press, 2006.

Lee, Alvin A., and Robert D. Denham. *The Legacy of Northrop Frye*. Toronto: University of Toronto Press, 1995

Rabaté, Jean-Michel. *The Cambridge Introduction to Literature and Psychoanalysis*. Cambridge: Cambridge University Press, 2014.

Rowland, Susan. *C. G. Jung and Literary Theory: The Challenge from Fiction*. New York: St. Martin's Press, 1999.

Wright, Elizabeth. *Psychoanalytic Criticism: Theory in Practice*. London: Methuen, 1984.

马元龙：《欲望的变奏：精神分析的文学反射镜》。北京：北京大学出版社，2021。

第七章

西方马克思主义

概述

德国学者卡尔·科尔施（Karl Korsch）在《"马克思主义与哲学"问题的现状》（"The Present State of the Problem of 'Marxism and Philosophy'", 1930）中，用"西方马克思主义"指有别于苏联模式的西欧马克思主义。后来，这个概念的意义不断扩宽，目前泛指西方资本主义国家知识分子对马克思主义的吸纳和重新阐释。

学术界一般将1923年捷尔吉·卢卡奇（György Lukács，或Georg Lukács）的《历史与阶级意识》（*History and Class Consciousness*）的出版视为西方马克思主义的起点事件。卢卡奇出生于匈牙利，是哲学家和文学批评家，1919—1929年间曾担任匈牙利共产主义运动的领导人，之后的十几年定居苏联。他反对第二国际用"正统论"将马克思主义奉为不可更改的经典，使其教条化。他尖锐地指出这是对马克思主义的庸俗化。他认为马克思主义的精髓是辩证法和总体历史观，是"关于社会（作为总体）发展的科学"。因此，卢卡奇重视考察文学作品中人的具体经验与总体性的生存境遇之间的关联，赞美人类创造历史的能动性，强调文学家的责任意识。他在早期代表作《小说理论》（*The Theory of the Novel*，1916）中指出，小说诞生于现代社会，和古典史诗时代相比，这个时代缺乏古希腊人面对世界的家园感、领悟生命意义的方向感和人与人之间的联结感。现代人与外部世界之间的关系是割裂的，他们的生活是个体性的、碎片化的、茫然的。小说家以这种现代个体为主人公，在作品中勾勒主人公意识发展的心路历程，反映他与外部世界的矛盾，展现他寻找生命总体意义的努力。

出于同样的立场，卢卡奇在现实主义和现代主义的美学之争中，撰写了《报道或描绘?》（"Reportage or Portrayal?"，1932）、《表现主义》（"Expressionism: Its Significance and Decline"，1934）、《平衡的现实主义》（"Realism in the Balance"，

1938)等文章,高扬现实主义旗帜,对以布莱希特为代表的表现主义先锋派提出批评。卢卡奇认为,无产阶级在资本主义社会中被物化,无法形成阶级意识,无法认识到自己被剥削被压迫的现实,因此丧失了革命积极性。他推崇巴尔扎克、托尔斯泰等现实主义作家,认为他们笔下的人物具有历史典型性,刻画的世界符合历史发展的规律,而且蕴含着变革和希望的力量。他称赞托尔斯泰的小说"向往一种依偎于自然的不朽韵律的生活,向往一种伴随着自然生生死死节拍而动的生活,一种摒弃了一切狭隘的、分离的、破碎的、僵硬的、非自然形式的生活"。卢卡奇批评布莱希特等现代主义作家,认为他们用先锋手法揭示了资本主义社会的症候,但在作品中未能为人类命运探索出路,以悲观主义和虚无主义为基调。

面对卢卡奇的指责,布莱希特撰写了系列文章,予以回应。他认为现实主义没有定规和范本,时代在变化,现实主义的概念也应拓展,引进新形式,反映新的生活世界和精神状态。而且,布莱希特认为自己的戏剧具有人民性。当他用艺术手法打破了舞台的专制时,他在邀请观众加入演出行动。这种实验戏剧的内核是生机勃勃的现实主义,是真正意义上的人民文学。

对于布莱希特的先锋探索,德国哲学家瓦尔特·本雅明(Walter Benjamin)给予了积极肯定。他在《什么是史诗剧?》("What Is Epic Theater?",1939)中指出,传统戏剧制造真实的幻象,操纵着观众的反应,对他们进行思想灌输,让他们在愉悦慵懒中接受世界的既定规则。布莱希特的史诗剧拒绝营造戏剧环境的舒适感,迫使观众行动起来,且在这一过程中激发积极思考,这是对传统剧场政治的有力挑战。

在《什么是史诗剧?》中,有处细节值得细读。本雅明写道:"史诗剧的形式和新的技术形式——电影和广播——相类似。史诗剧适应于现代的技术水平。"实际上,本雅明对艺术手法的革新有着异乎寻常的敏锐感知。在《作为生产者的作者》("The Author as Producer",1934)、《机械复制时代的艺术作品》("The Work of Art in the Age of Mechanical Reproduction",1935)、《讲故事的人》("The Storyteller",1936)等发于20世纪30年代的论著中,本雅明从生产力与生产关系的角度,分析技术革新与艺术生产之间的关系,指出"对于作为生产者的作家来说,技术的进步也是他政治进步的基础"。他所指的技术,既包括文学艺术的表现手法,也包括照相机、摄影机等新型媒介。事实上,他是少数率先对摄影和电影等新型媒介艺术进行深入研究的学者。然而,他对这些艺术及其技术的看法很复杂。比如,讨论印刷术和摄影术的普及时,他既为此前无缘看真迹的普罗大众可以通过技术复制品欣赏名画而欣喜,也为艺术品失去了凝结在真品上的令人着迷的"光晕"而忧虑。

本雅明是西方马克思主义法兰克福学派（Frankfurt School）的重要成员。法兰克福学派是以德国法兰克福大学社会研究所的社会学家和哲学家为主体的学术共同体，代表人物有马克斯·霍克海默尔（Max Horkheimer）、西奥多·W. 阿多尔诺（Theodor W. Adorno）、赫伯特·马尔库塞（Herbert Marcuse）以及他们的朋友本雅明。研究所成立于1923年，后因纳粹崛起，德国政治环境恶化，曾经迁至美国。二战结束后，部分成员返回欧洲。

法兰克福学派理论家和卢卡奇等前辈的思想差异在于，他们不再强调阶级意识，而是集中力量对资本主义进行文化与思想史的综合考察。他们的方法论是"批判理论"（critical theory）。依霍克海默尔之见，"哲学的真正社会功能在于它对流行的东西进行批判"，以防止人们"在现存社会组织慢慢灌输给它的成员的观点和行为中迷失方向"。在经典著作《启蒙辩证法》（*Dialectic of Enlightenment*，1944）中，霍克海默尔和阿多尔诺追问两次世界大战和纳粹极权主义的起因，批判启蒙现代性。他们指出，启蒙的理想是解放人性、反抗压迫、追求自由和实现人的全面发展。科学理性本应是达成这些理想的重要手段，但却被资本主义制度利用，变成了对人进行控制、使其服务于工业化和商业化进程的工具。这导致了人的自我异化——人性中与理性不相符的部分被舍弃，也导致了人的高度同质化——理性成了无人质疑的真理。此时，理性其实已经变成了非理性，因为它违反了真正的人性。战争的技术逻辑和极权主义的政治逻辑都是以此为基础。

在《启蒙辩证法》中，有一个章节的标题是"文化工业：欺骗大众的启蒙"，由阿多尔诺执笔。社会研究所二战期间搬迁到美国，让阿多尔诺对美国发达的娱乐产业有了直观认识。他洞察到资本主义在用软性手段，在文化领域制造垄断，用商业法则刺激大众文化产品的批量生产，进而通过这些文化产品来塑造人的思想，将其变成社会规范所需要的样子。读广告、看电影、听广播，人们随时都身处文化工业的影响之中。

应该如何抵制千人一面的同质化社会，抵抗工具理性，反抗文化工业的垄断？阿多尔诺在《否定的辩证法》（*Negative Dialectics*，1966）中提出了哲学方案。传统辩证法用否定之否定终止了对立项的相互质疑，是不彻底的否定，实质仍是对同一性的肯定。他主张采用"否定的辩证法"，不断地进行怀疑和否定，不畏惧矛盾，推进批判性思考的深入。与此同时，阿多尔诺也将精神救赎的希望寄托在艺术领域，在《美学理论》（*Aesthetic Theory*，1970）中指出艺术应保持其独立性，承担起反对社会的功能，摒弃"对社会有用"的原则，承担起批判的责任。他认为卡夫卡、普鲁斯特、乔伊斯的小说都体现了审美自律的独立性和独特性。

对同一性的批判也是马尔库塞的理论出发点之一，从他的著作《单向度的人》

(*One-Dimensional Man: Studies in the Ideology of Advanced Industrial Society*，1964)的标题就能看出这一点。马尔库塞发现，资本主义进入发达工业阶段后，生产力水平提高，物质财富增加，人们的个人需要得到满足，可是这种以狭隘的理性为原则的进步压制了生活的多样性和个人的认识能力和感知能力，使人们看不到自己失去自主性的事实，变成了单向度的人，无法进行质疑和批判，只能顺从和接受社会现实。马尔库塞和阿多尔诺的分歧在于，马尔库塞积极介入社会运动，支持街头抵抗。在《爱欲与文明》(*Eros and Civilization: A Philosophical Inquiry into Freud*，1955)中，他呼吁释放被文明压抑的爱欲，将其转化为革命能量，为生命而战，为爱欲而战，为政治而战。在《单向度的人》中，马尔库塞指出新工人阶级已经被资本主义收编，而大学生尚未进入社会，没有被其同化，所以有反抗旧体制的激情。他的理论成为美国20世纪60年代风起云涌的学生运动的重要思想资源。

法兰克福学派的意识形态批判聚焦资本主义及现代性进程等议题，有清晰的历史文化语境。法国哲学家路易·阿尔都塞(Louis Althusser)的意识形态批判则受到结构主义共时性研究方法影响，关注意识形态的系统功能。阿尔都塞的著名论断之一是"意识形态无历史"：虽然各个时代的意识形态有基于具体历史时期的阶级斗争的历史，但是从绝对的角度看，意识形态贯穿于人类历史的各个阶段，是恒常的社会基础，具体内容或随时而变，但结构和功能始终如一。在阿尔都塞看来，意识形态的核心功能之一是生成主体。他受拉康镜像阶段论的启发，指出意识形态对主体的建构依赖于可欲求的想象性自我投射。我们主动认领主体身份，殊不知这是意识形态"询唤"(interpellation)的结果。主体的自主认同使其无法觉察误认中发生的"异化"。意识形态通过塑造主体维护既有秩序，保证生产关系的再生产和劳动力的再生产。阿尔都塞不赞同苏俄马克思主义的意识形态经济决定论，他认为社会是一个整体，意识形态不是单纯依附于基础结构，它的法律、政治和文化等机制均有自身的能动性和物质实践性，和资本主义再生产的各个环节密切关联。在《意识形态与意识形态国家机器》("Ideology and Ideological State Apparatuses"，1970)中，他提出了意识形态国家机器(Ideological State Apparatuses，简称ISAs)的概念，用它揭秘资本主义如何通过教育、宗教、科学、文化等机制塑造主体，巩固秩序，维护体制稳定。

意识形态可以对既有的生产关系进行再生产，是稳定资本主义制度的重要力量。安东尼奥·葛兰西(Antonio Gramsci)对此也早有觉察，所以提出了"霸权"(hegemony)理论。事实上，葛兰西的霸权论早于阿尔都塞的意识形态论，而阿尔都塞也承认自己受到葛兰西的巨大启发。葛兰西是意大利共产党的重要思想领袖，曾经组织无产阶级城市暴动，革命失败后被捕入狱，1937年因病去世，留下了《狱中笔记》(Prison Notebooks)。他在笔记中记录对城市革命失败的反思，提出了"霸权"概念。"霸权"指的是特定社会中主导阶层的文化领导权。葛兰西认为欧洲国家未能走上俄国革命的道路，是因为市民社会保证了资本主义意识形态的延续。葛兰西所说的市民社会，由政治团体、商业联盟、教会、媒体等组成。它们植根于民众的日常生活，形成特定的思想框架，发挥潜移默化的影响，比国家强权的效果更广泛持久。资本主义的文化霸权便以市民社会为依托。值得强调的是，葛兰西虽然承认霸权的强大，但是，他的霸权理论支持反抗和革命——这是葛兰西霸权论和阿尔都塞意识形态论的重要区别。霸权的形成需要民众的认可，因此霸权不是牢不可破的。葛兰西指出，革命者不仅要发动"运动战"，用暴力革命推翻既有政权，也要在思想领域打响"阵地战"，以长期的决心和坚韧，组织和教育民众，获得民众的拥护，赢得文化领导权。

葛兰西的文化霸权理论深刻影响了雷蒙·威廉斯（Raymond Williams）、特里·伊格尔顿（Terry Eagleton）和弗雷德里克·詹姆逊（Fredric Jameson）等英美左翼马克思主义批评家。这些理论家的思想来源还包括卢卡奇的总体论、阿尔都塞的意识形态论，以及法兰克福学派的批判理论等。英美马克思主义文学批评的共性特点是关注文化政治。

英国批评家威廉斯来自工人家庭。靠着奖学金，威廉斯得以进入剑桥大学读书。他的家庭背景使他对当时学院派的F. R. 利维斯（F. R. Leavis）式的经典文本阅读法不感兴趣。他受20世纪50年代英国新左派思想的影响，研究以"文化"为关键词，融合了文学、历史、政治等视域，有唯物主义特点，重点考察文化的意义生产和物质实践。在《文化与社会》(Culture and Society, 1958)中，他梳理了1780到1950年间数十位主要思想家围绕"工业""民主""阶级""艺术"和"文化"所进行的论述，让我们看到思想文化变迁如何与工业革命带来的社会物质实践相互激发、相互影响。在《马克思主义与文学》(Marxism and Literature, 1977)中，他反对过分强调文学文本的价值，也反对将文学视为对社会和文化的简单反映，提倡从文化唯物主义的立场，以更具综合性的视角来理解文学、文化和社会的相互塑造。

伊格尔顿是威廉斯的学生，受老师影响，在文学研究中重视文学与社会文化历史的交叉互动。但他亲近欧陆哲学与美学理论，和威廉斯的经验主义的研究方法有一定差异，理论色彩更浓一些。此外，他受阿尔都塞的影响，比威廉斯更重视意识形态分析。伊格尔顿在撰写其经典文论教材《文学理论导论》(Literary Theory: An Introduction, 1983)时，在对文论不同流派分章介绍之前，用一章的篇幅详细分析了英语兴起的历史动因，批驳了中性的语言观和无功利的文学观，指出英语的兴起是19世纪信仰危机的表现。以马修·阿诺德为首的知识分子希望通过将英语提高到类似宗教的高度，使它担负起原先宗教所承担的整合国民思想的意识形态功能，英国文学的"伟大的传统"（F. R. 利维斯语）实则由此而来。

在美国的马克思主义文学理论家中，詹姆逊最有影响力。他有敏锐的理论眼光和广阔的文学视野，对推进西方马克思主义文论做出了重要贡献。在《语言的牢笼》（*The Prison-House of Language: A Critical Account of Structuralism and Russian Formalism*，1972）中，詹姆逊反思形式主义和结构主义文论的缺陷，指出索绪尔在语言哲学体系建构中，把共时性和历时性对立，导致结构性和历史性对立，迫使结构研究抛弃历史。受其影响很深的结构主义和俄国形式主义也有同样的缺憾，在文学研究中无法形成辩证历史观。在《政治无意识》（*The Political Unconscious: Narrative as a Socially Symbolic Act*，1981）中，詹姆逊开篇就直陈历史意识的重要性："永远历史化！"他受卢卡奇影响，将历史视为过去、当下与未来的统一体，认为文学作品不可能凭空而生，它始终牢牢镶嵌在历史之中。所以，阐释文本时，不应只关注作品的表层故事，必须深入阐释它的历史性和政治性。在《未来的考古学》（*Archaeologies of the Future: The Desire Called Utopia and Other Science Fictions*，2005）中，詹姆逊对科幻小说文类的政治无意识进行了探讨。他指出，无论小说的故事情节是什么，当小说家选定科幻文类进行创作时，该文类的未来向度以及乌托邦冲动都已被编码进小说。而且，科幻的乌托邦冲动是对当下的警示：之所以想象未来新方案，是因为对历史和现状不满。詹姆逊对乌托邦的讨论有激进政治色彩。

当代西方马克思主义思想家中，法国哲学家雅克·朗西埃（Jacques Rancière）也以激进政治立场著称。理解朗西埃思想的关键词是"平等"。在《无知的教师》（*The Ignorant Schoolmaster: Five Lessons in Intellectual Emancipation*，1987）中，朗西埃以约瑟夫·雅科托（Joseph Jacotot）的教育实验为引线，讨论激发学生智识自主性的重要意义，进而将视野扩展到政治领域，提出人类解放的前提是"智识平等"。朗西埃在这一点上和他的老师阿尔都塞有分歧。阿尔都塞认为劳动者需要知识分子的精神引领，朗西埃则呼吁"平等者的共同体"，所以两人决裂。在美学领域，朗西埃也秉承反精英主义立场，批评阿多尔诺对高雅美学的推崇。朗西埃在早期作品《劳工之夜》（*The Nights of Labor: The Workers' Dream in Nineteenth-Century France*，1989）中，展示了19世纪巴黎劳工所写的日记、诗歌、虚构创作等，让人们听见这个阶级群体的声音，感受到他们的创造力。他在《当代艺术与美学的政治》（"Contemporary Art and the Politics of Aesthetics"，2009）中指出，审美和政治的相通之处在于它们都以人的感性为基础条件，建构"感觉的共同体"

（community of sense）。人人有感官，能感受世界，产生爱憎好恶，爱美的愉悦形成了审美，对好恶的感受则是政治的动因。美学机制的规定性，体现在它可以对可感性（the sensible）进行分配，推动共享。被审美领域排斥的，未必不美，但它失去了可感性，我们无法看到它、理解它。朗西埃让我们意识到，让不可见的变得可见，让静默者被人听到，让"丑"的进入美的视域，这既是审美，也是政治。

从20世纪20年代至今，西方马克思主义文论已有百年历史。它让人们认识到文学和艺术的意识形态功能，重视审美的政治性。它拓展了文学研究的领域，文化和历史成为批评阐释中必须考察的要素。它彰显出文学批评反思时代的能动性，帮助人们更好地剖析资本主义症候，构想社会新形态。与此同时，西方马克思主义反抗压迫，追求公正、平等、自由的诉求，使它成为被压迫、被剥削、被边缘化的各个群体装配自身理论武器的重要资源。近半个世纪以来，在女性主义、后殖民主义、生态批评以及文化批评等的理论场域中，我们不断能够听到它们与西方马克思主义的深层对话。

主要文本阅读

霍克海默尔、阿多尔诺：《启蒙辩证法》

| 选文简介

《启蒙辩证法》撰写于20世纪40年代，选文出自序言部分。霍克海默尔和阿多尔诺在书中反思启蒙传统，发现欧洲启蒙的初衷是"祛魅"：将人们从神话与迷信中拯救出来，从封建等级秩序的压迫中解放出来。然而，启蒙理想很快发生了褪变：以人性论、价值论和形而上学为基础的人文理性被抛弃了；以孔德的实证主义为基础的科学精神和技术理性被奉为信仰，推动着资本主义工业社会的快速发展，建构出进步的新"神话"。这种进步以人性为代价：早期启蒙所推崇的批判精神受到了压制，想象力被驱逐，资本逻辑控制了文化产品的标准化生产，世界失去了百家争鸣的声音。更可怕的是，纳粹极权主义以"理性"之名登场，造就奥斯维辛的地狱。在霍克海默尔和阿多尔诺看来，启蒙的"进步"神话是破坏性的，带来的是文明的倒退。

From *Dialectic of Enlightenment*

Max Horkheimer (1895-1973), Theodor W. Adorno (1903-1969)

While attentive cultivation and investigation of the scientific heritage—especially when positivist new brooms have swept it away as useless lumber—does represent one moment of knowledge, in the present collapse of bourgeois civilization not only the operations but the purpose of science have become dubious. The tireless self-destruction of enlightenment hypocritically celebrated by implacable fascists and implemented by pliable experts in humanity compels thought to forbid itself its last remaining innocence regarding the habits and tendencies of the *Zeitgeist*. If public life has reached a state in which thought is being turned inescapably into a commodity and language into celebration of the commodity, the attempt to trace the sources of this degradation must refuse obedience to the current linguistic and intellectual demands before it is rendered entirely futile by the consequence of those demands for world history.

If the only obstacles were those arising from the oblivious instrumentalization of science, thought about social questions could at least attach itself to tendencies opposed to official science. Those tendencies, too, however, are caught up in the general process of production. They have changed no less than the ideology they attacked. They suffer the fate which has always been reserved for triumphant thought. If it voluntarily leaves behind its critical element to become a mere means in the service of an existing order, it involuntarily tends to transform the positive cause it has espoused into something negative and destructive. The eighteenth-century philosophy which, defying the funeral pyres for books and people, put the fear of death into infamy, joined forces with it under Bonaparte. Finally, the apologetic school of Comte usurped the succession to the uncompromising *encyclopédistes*, extending the hand of friendship to all those whom the latter had opposed. Such metamorphoses of critique into affirmation do not leave theoretical content untouched; its truth evaporates. Today, however, motorized history is rushing ahead of such intellectual developments, and the official spokesmen, who have other concerns, are liquidating the theory to which they owe their place in the sun before it has time to prostitute itself completely.

In reflecting on its own guilt, therefore, thought finds itself deprived not only of the affirmative reference to science and everyday phenomena but also of the conceptual language of opposition. No terms are available which do not tend toward complicity with the prevailing intellectual trends, and what threadbare language cannot achieve on its own is precisely made good by the social machinery. The censors voluntarily maintained by the film factories to avoid greater costs have their counterparts in all other departments. The process to which a literary text is subjected, if not in the automatic foresight of its producer then through the battery of readers, publishers, adapters, and ghost writers inside and outside the editorial office, outdoes any censor in its thoroughness. To render their function entirely superfluous appears, despite all the benevolent reforms, to be the ambition of the educational system. In the belief that without strict limitation to the observation of facts and the calculation of probabilities the cognitive mind would be overreceptive to charlatanism and superstition, that system is preparing arid ground for the greedy acceptance of charlatanism and superstition.

Just as prohibition has always ensured the admission of the poisonous product, the blocking of the theoretical imagination has paved the way for political delusion. Even when people have not already succumbed to such delusion, they are deprived by the mechanisms of censorship, both the external ones and those implanted within them, of the means of resisting it.

The aporia which faced us in our work thus proved to be the first matter we had to investigate: the self-destruction of enlightenment. We have no doubt—and herein lies our *petitio principii*—that freedom in society is inseparable from enlightenment thinking. We believe we have perceived with equal clarity, however, that the very concept of that thinking, no less than the concrete historical forms, the institutions of society with which it is intertwined, already contains the germ of the regression which is taking place everywhere today. If enlightenment does not assimilate reflection on this regressive moment, it seals its own fate. By leaving consideration of the destructive side of progress to its enemies, thought in its headlong rush into pragmatism is forfeiting its sublating character, and therefore its relation to truth. In the mysterious willingness of the technologically educated masses to fall under the spell of any despotism, in its self-destructive affinity to nationalist paranoia, in all this uncomprehended senselessness the weakness of contemporary theoretical understanding is evident.

We believe that in these fragments we have contributed to such understanding by showing that the cause of enlightenment's relapse into mythology is to be sought not so much in the nationalist, pagan, or other modern mythologies concocted specifically to cause such a relapse as in the fear of truth which petrifies enlightenment itself. Both these terms, enlightenment and truth, are to be understood as pertaining not merely to intellectual history but also to current reality. Just as enlightenment expresses the real movement of bourgeois society as a whole from the perspective of the idea embodied in its personalities and institutions, truth refers not merely to rational consciousness but equally to the form it takes in reality. The loyal son of modern civilization's fear of departing from the facts, which even in their perception are turned into clichés by the prevailing usages in science, business, and politics, is exactly the same as the fear of social deviation. Those usages also define the concept of clarity in language and thought to which art, literature, and philosophy must conform today. By tabooing any thought which sets out negatively from the facts and from the prevailing modes of thought as obscure, convoluted, and preferably foreign, that concept holds mind captive in ever deeper blindness. It is in the nature of the calamitous situation existing today that even the most honorable reformer who recommends renewal in threadbare language reinforces the existing order he seeks to break by taking over its worn-out categorial apparatus and the pernicious power-philosophy lying behind it. False clarity is only another name for myth. Myth was always obscure and luminous at once. It has always been distinguished by its familiarity and its exemption from the work of concepts.

The enslavement to nature of people today cannot be separated from social progress. The increase in economic productivity which creates the conditions for a more just world also affords the technical apparatus and the social groups controlling it a disproportionate advantage over the rest of the population. The individual is entirely nullified in face of the economic powers. These powers are taking society's domination over nature to unimagined heights. While individuals as such are vanishing before the apparatus they serve, they are provided for by that apparatus and better than ever before. In the unjust state of society the powerlessness and pliability of the masses increase with the quantity of goods allocated to them. The materially considerable and socially paltry rise in the standard of living of the lower classes is reflected in the hypocritical propagation of intellect. Intellect's true concern is a negation of reification. It must perish when it is solidified into a cultural asset and handed out for consumption purposes. The flood of precise information and brand-new amusements make people smarter and more stupid at once.

What is at issue here is not culture as a value, as understood by critics of civilization such as Huxley, Jaspers, and Ortega y Gasset, but the necessity for enlightenment to reflect on itself if humanity is not to be totally betrayed. What is at stake is not conservation of the past but the fulfillment of past hopes. Today, however, the past is being continued as destruction of the past. If, up to the nineteenth century, respectable education was a privilege paid for by the increased sufferings of the uneducated, in the twentieth the hygienic factory is bought with the melting down of all cultural entities in the gigantic crucible. That might not even be so high a price as those defenders of culture believe if the bargain sale of culture did not contribute to converting economic achievements into their opposite.

Under the given circumstances the gifts of fortune themselves become elements of misfortune. If, in the absence of the social subject, the volume of goods took the form of so-called overproduction in domestic economic crises in the preceding period, today, thanks to the enthronement of powerful groups as that social subject, it is producing the international threat of fascism: progress is reverting to regression. That the hygienic factory and everything pertaining to it, Volkswagen and the sports palace, are obtusely liquidating metaphysics does not matter in itself, but that these things are themselves becoming metaphysics, an ideological curtain, within the social whole, behind which real doom is gathering, does matter. That is the basic premise of our fragments.

阿尔都塞：《意识形态与意识形态国家机器》

选文简介

主体论是阿尔都塞意识形态论的重要议题。阿尔都塞认为离开了主体，意识形态就无从谈起，意识形态就是为主体生成服务的。选文中，为了说明意识形态主体生成的"询唤"机制（interpellation），阿尔都塞举了个通俗的例子。警察在街上叫某位路人："嘿，那个你！"对方十有八九会意识到警察询唤的是他，进而转身进行确认。他转身的动作立刻将他和其他人区别开来，他回应询唤，成为独一无二的主体。阿尔都塞认为意识形态的目的就是让具体的个体主动去做此类接受询唤的主体认同。实际上，在人成为个体之前，已经在主体的生成之中。在家庭意识形态体系中，孩子出生前已经获得了父族的姓氏。日常生活中，意识形态认同仪式更是无所不在，不停塑造着我们看似具体的、个性化的、有辨识度的、不可替代的主体性，而掩盖了主体的建构本质。阿尔都塞揭示了"主体"（subject）这个概念的两面性：主体是行动的施为者，没有人强迫他违背意愿行事；主体也是服从者（subject本就有"臣服""臣属"之意），主动遵从意识形态的规定。阿尔都塞认为个体的自由掩盖了强制性的现实——主体是其必须所是。

From "Ideology and Ideological State Apparatuses"

Louis Althusser (1918-1990)

This thesis is simply a matter of making my last proposition explicit: there is no ideology except by the subject and for subjects. Meaning, there is no ideology except for concrete subjects, and this destination for ideology is only made possible by the subject: meaning, *by the category of the subject* and its functioning.

By this I mean that, even if it only appears under this name (the subject) with the rise of bourgeois ideology, above all with the rise of legal ideology, the category of the subject (which may function under other names: e.g. as the soul in Plato, as God, etc.) is the constitutive category of all ideology, whatever its determination (regional or class) and whatever its historical date—since ideology has no history.

I say: the category of the subject is constitutive of all ideology, but at the same time and immediately I add that *the category of the subject is only constitutive of all ideology insofar as all ideology has the function (which defines it) of "constituting" concrete individuals as subjects*. In the interaction of this double constitution exists the functioning of all ideology, ideology being nothing but its functioning in the material forms of existence of that functioning....

As St. Paul admirably put it, it is in the "Logos," meaning in ideology, that we "live, move and have our being." It follows that, for you and for me, the category of the subject is a primary "obviousness" (obviousnesses are always primary): it is clear that you and I are subjects (free, ethical, etc....). Like all obviousnesses, including those that make a word "name a thing" or "have a meaning" (therefore including the obviousness of the "transparency" of language), the "obviousness" that you and I are subjects—and that that does not cause any problems—is an ideological effect, the elementary ideological effect. It is indeed a peculiarity of ideology that it imposes (without appearing to do so, since these are "obviousnesses") obviousnesses as obviousnesses, which we cannot *fail to recognize* and before which we have the inevitable and natural reaction of crying out (aloud or in the "still, small voice of conscience"): "That's obvious! That's right! That's true!"

At work in this reaction is the ideological *recognition* function which is one of the two functions of ideology as such (its inverse being the function of *misrecognition—méconnaissance*).

To take a highly "concrete" example, we all have friends who, when they knock on our door and we ask, through the door, the question "Who's there?" answer (since "it's obvious") "It's me." And we recognize that "it is him," or "her." We open the door, and "it's true, it really was she who was there." To take another example, when we recognize somebody of our (previous) acquaintance ([*re*]-*connaissance*) in the street, we show him that we have recognized him (and have recognized that he has recognized us) by saying to him "Hello, my friend," and shaking his hand (a material ritual practice of ideological recognition in everyday life—in France, at least; elsewhere, there are other rituals).

In this preliminary remark and these concrete illustrations, I only wish to point out that you and I are *always already* subjects, and as such constantly practice the rituals of ideological recognition, which guarantee for us that we are indeed concrete, individual, distinguishable and (naturally) irreplaceable subjects. The writing I am currently executing and the reading you are currently performing are also in this respect rituals of ideological recognition, including the "obviousness" with which the "truth" or "error" of my reflections may impose itself on you.

But to recognize that we are subjects and that we function in the practical rituals of the most elementary everyday life (the handshake, the fact of calling you by your name, the fact of knowing, even if I do not know what it is, that you "have" a name of your own, which means that you are recognized as a unique subject, etc.)—this recognition only gives us the "consciousness" of our incessant (eternal) practice of ideological recognition—its consciousness, i.e. its *recognition*—but in no sense does it give us the (scientific) *knowledge* of the mechanism of this recognition. Now it is this knowledge that we have to reach, if you will, while speaking in ideology, and from within ideology we have to outline a discourse which tries to break with ideology, in order to dare to be the beginning of a scientific (i.e. subjectless) discourse on ideology.

Thus in order to represent why the category of the "subject" is constitutive of ideology, which only exists by constituting concrete subjects as subjects, I shall employ a special mode of exposition: "concrete" enough to be recognized, but abstract enough to be thinkable and thought, giving rise to a knowledge.

As a first formulation I shall say: *all ideology hails or interpellates concrete individuals as concrete subjects*, by the functioning of the category of the subject.

This is a proposition which entails that we distinguish for the moment between concrete individuals on the one hand and concrete subjects on the other, although at this level concrete subjects only exist insofar as they are supported by a concrete individual.

I shall then suggest that ideology "acts" or "functions" in such a way that it "recruits" subjects among the individuals (it recruits them all), or "transforms" the individuals into subjects (it transforms them all) by that very precise operation which I have called *interpellation* or hailing, and which can be imagined along the lines of the most commonplace everyday police (or other) hailing: "Hey, you there!"

Assuming that the theoretical scene I have imagined takes place in the street, the hailed individual will turn around. By this mere one-hundred-and-eighty-degree physical conversion, he becomes a *subject*. Why? Because he has recognized that the hail was "really" addressed to him, and that "it was *really him* who was hailed" (and not someone else). Experience shows that the practical telecommunication of hailings is such that they hardly ever miss their man: verbal call or whistle, the one hailed always recognizes that it is really him who is being hailed. And yet it is a strange phenomenon, and one which cannot be explained solely by "guilt feelings," despite the large numbers who "have something on their consciences."

Naturally for the convenience and clarity of my little theoretical theater I have had to present things in the form of a sequence, with a before and an after, and thus in the form of a temporal succession. There are individuals walking along. Somewhere (usually behind them) the hail rings out: "Hey, you there!" One individual (nine times out of ten it is the right one) turns around, believing/suspecting/knowing that it is for him, i.e. recognizing that "it really is he" who is meant by the hailing. But in reality these things happen without any succession. The existence of ideology and the hailing or interpellation of individuals as subjects are one and the same thing....

Thus ideology hails or interpellates individuals as subjects. As ideology is eternal, I must now suppress the temporal form in which I have presented the functioning of ideology, and say: ideology has always-already interpellated individuals as subjects, which amounts to making it clear that individuals are always-already interpellated by ideology as subjects, which necessarily leads us to one last proposition: *individuals are always-already subjects*. Hence individuals are "abstract" with respect to the subjects which they always-already are. This proposition might seem paradoxical.

That an individual is always-already a subject, even before he is born, is nevertheless the plain reality, accessible to everyone and not a paradox at all. Freud shows that individuals are always "abstract" with respect to the subjects they always-already are, simply noting the ideological ritual that surrounds the expectation of a "birth," that "happy event." Everyone knows how much and in what way an unborn child is expected. Which amounts to saying, very prosaically, if we agree to drop the "sentiments," i.e. the forms of family ideology (paternal/maternal/conjugal/fraternal) in which the unborn child is expected: it is certain in advance that it will bear its Father's name, and will therefore have an identity and be irreplaceable. Before its birth, the child is therefore always-already a subject, appointed as a subject in and by the specific familial ideological configuration in which it is "expected" once it has been conceived. I hardly need add that this familial ideological configuration is, in its uniqueness, highly structured, and that it is in this implacable and more or less "pathological" (presupposing that any meaning can be assigned to that term) structure that the former subject-to-be will have to "find" "its" place, i.e. "become" the sexual subject (boy or girl) which it already is in advance. It is clear that this ideological constraint and pre-appointment, and all the rituals of rearing and then education in the family, have some relationship with what Freud studied in the forms of the pre-genital and genital "stages" of sexuality, i.e. in the "grip" of what Freud registered by its effects as being the unconscious.

威廉斯：《马克思主义与文学》

选文简介

威廉斯的文化观是动态文化观，强调文化的复杂性。他将一个时代的文化分为三类：社会决定性因素所确定的主导文化，由旧时代的文化思想及其实践组成的残余文化，以及刚刚涌现的新兴文化。残余文化不等于过时了的文化，历史性的因素在当下仍在发挥作用；新兴文化也不是骤然横空出世，它在社会变化进程中有复杂的生成机制；主导文化在不停吸纳新兴文化，与此同时，它的某些因素演变成了残余文化的组成部分。从威廉斯的分类，我们能够看到他的"超越决定论"的立场。他认为每个时代都有其主导性的文化特征，这由经济基础与上层建筑之间的关系所决定。但主导文化不是霸权永固，而是不断与另两种文化形态进行着领导权的争夺，相互吸纳，相互推动。整体性的文化发展，离不开多重历史因素和社会力量的共同塑造和综合影响。

From *Marxism and Literature*

Raymond Williams (1921-1988)

The complexity of a culture is to be found not only in its variable processes and their social definitions—traditions, institutions, and formations—but also in the dynamic interrelations, at every point in the process, of historically varied and variable elements. In what I have called "epochal" analysis, a cultural process is seized as a cultural system, with determinate dominant features: feudal culture or bourgeois culture or a transition from one to the other. This emphasis on dominant and definitive lineaments and features is important and often, in practice, effective. But it then often happens that its methodology is preserved for the very different function of historical analysis, in which a sense of movement within what is ordinarily abstracted as a system is crucially necessary, especially if it is to connect with the future as well as with the past. In authentic historical analysis it is necessary at every point to recognize the complex interrelations between movements and tendencies both within and beyond a specific and effective dominance. It is necessary to examine how these relate to the whole cultural process rather than only to the selected and abstracted dominant system. Thus "bourgeois culture" is a significant generalizing description and hypothesis, expressed within epochal analysis by fundamental comparisons with "feudal culture" or "socialist culture." However, as a description of cultural process, over four or five centuries and in scores of different societies, it requires immediate historical and internally comparative differentiation. Moreover, even if this is acknowledged or practically carried out, the "epochal" definition can exert its pressure as a static type against which all real cultural process is measured, either to show "stages" or "variations" of the type (which is still historical analysis) or, at its worst, to select supporting and exclude "marginal" or "incidental" or "secondary" evidence.

Such errors are avoidable if, while retaining the epochal hypothesis, we can find terms which recognize not only "stages" and "variations" but the internal dynamic relations of any actual process. We have certainly still to speak of the "dominant" and the "effective," and in these senses of the hegemonic. But we find that we have also to speak, and indeed with further differentiation of each, of the "residual" and the "emergent," which in any real process, and at any moment in the process, are significant both in themselves and in what they reveal of the characteristics of the "dominant."

By "residual" I mean something different from the "archaic," though in practice these are often very difficult to distinguish. Any culture includes available elements of its past, but their place in the contemporary cultural process is profoundly variable. I would call the "archaic" that which is wholly recognized as an element of the past, to be observed, to be examined, or even on occasion to be consciously "revived," in a deliberately specializing way. What I mean by the "residual" is very different. The residual, by definition, has been effectively formed in the past, but it is still active in the cultural process, not only and often not at all as an element of the past, but as an effective element of the present. Thus certain experiences, meanings, and values which cannot be expressed or substantially verified in terms of the dominant culture, are nevertheless lived and practiced on the basis of the residue—cultural as well as social—of some previous social and cultural institution or formation. It is crucial to distinguish this aspect of the residual, which may have an alternative or even oppositional relation to the dominant culture, from that active manifestation of the residual (this being its distinction from the archaic) which has been wholly or largely incorporated into the dominant culture....

A residual cultural element is usually at some distance from the effective dominant culture, but some part of it, some version of it—and especially if the residue is from some major area of the past—will in most cases have had to be incorporated if the effective dominant culture is to make sense in these areas. Moreover, at certain points the dominant culture cannot allow too much residual experience and practice outside itself, at least without risk. It is in the incorporation of the actively residual—by reinterpretation, dilution, projection, discriminating inclusion and exclusion—that the work of the selective tradition is especially evident. This is very notable in the case of versions of "the literary tradition," passing through selective versions of the character of literature to connecting and incorporated definitions of what literature now is and should be. This is one among several crucial areas, since it is in some alternative or even oppositional versions of what literature is (has been) and what literary experience (and in one common derivation, other significant experience) is and must be, that, against the pressures of incorporation, actively residual meanings and values are sustained.

By "emergent" I mean, first, that new meanings and values, new practices, new relationships and kinds of relationship are continually being created. But it is exceptionally difficult to distinguish between those which are really elements of some new phase of the dominant culture (and in this sense "species-specific") and those which are substantially alternative or oppositional to it: emergent in the strict sense, rather than merely novel. Since we are always considering relations within a cultural process, definitions of the emergent, as of the residual, can be made only in relation to a full sense of the dominant. Yet the social location of the residual is always easier to understand, since a large part of it (though not all) relates to earlier social formations and phases of the cultural process, in which certain real meanings and values were generated. In the subsequent default of a particular phase of a dominant culture there is then a reaching back to those meanings and values which were created in actual societies and actual situations in the past, and which still seem to have significance because they represent areas of human experience, aspiration, and achievement which the dominant culture neglects, undervalues, opposes, represses, or even cannot recognize.

The case of the emergent is radically different. It is true that in the structure of any actual society, and especially in its class structure, there is always a social basis for elements of the cultural process that are alternative or oppositional to the dominant elements. One kind of basis has been valuably described in the central body of Marxist theory: the formation of a new class, the coming to consciousness of a new class, and within this, in actual process, the (often uneven) emergence of elements of a new cultural formation. Thus the emergence of the working class as a class was immediately evident (for example, in nineteenth-century England) in the cultural process. But there was extreme unevenness of contribution in different parts of the process. The making of new social values and institutions far outpaced the making of strictly cultural institutions, while specific cultural contributions, though significant, were less vigorous and autonomous than either general or institutional innovation. A new class is always a source of emergent cultural practice, but while it is still, as a class, relatively subordinate, this is always likely to be uneven and is certain to be incomplete. For new practice is not, of course, an isolated process. To the degree that it emerges, and especially to the degree that it is oppositional rather than alternative, the process of attempted incorporation significantly begins. This can be seen, in the same period in England, in the emergence and then the effective incorporation of a radical popular press. It can be seen in the emergence and incorporation of working-class writing, where the fundamental problem of emergence is clearly revealed, since the basis of incorporation, in such cases, is the effective predominance of received literary forms—an incorporation, so to say, which already conditions and limits the emergence. But the development is always uneven. Straight incorporation is most directly attempted against the visibly alternative and oppositional class elements: trade unions, working-class political parties, working-class life styles (as incorporated into "popular" journalism, advertising, and commercial entertainment). The process of emergence, in such conditions, is then a constantly repeated, an always renewable, move beyond a phase of practical incorporation: usually made much more difficult by the fact that much incorporation looks like recognition, acknowledgment, and thus a form of *acceptance*. In this complex process there is indeed regular confusion between the locally residual (as a form of resistance to incorporation) and the generally emergent.

Cultural emergence in relation to the emergence and growing strength of a class is then always of major importance, and always complex. But we have also to see that it is not the only kind of emergence. This recognition is very difficult, theoretically, though the practical evidence is abundant. What has really to be said, as a way of defining important elements of both the residual and the emergent, and as a way of understanding the character of the dominant, is that *no mode of production and therefore no dominant social order and therefore no dominant culture ever in reality includes or exhausts all human practice, human energy, and human intention.* This is not merely a negative proposition, allowing us to account for significant things which happen outside or against the dominant mode. On the contrary it is a fact about the modes of domination, that they select from and consequently exclude the full range of human practice. What they exclude may often be seen as the personal or the private, or as the natural or even the metaphysical. Indeed it is usually in one or other of these terms that the excluded area is expressed, since what the dominant has effectively seized is indeed the ruling definition of the social.

詹姆逊：《政治无意识》

选文简介

詹姆逊在《政治无意识》的第一章点明了他的写作目标：论证文学文本政治阐释的重要性。他反对将社会和政治的文化文本与非社会和非政治的文化文本区别开来，认为人们想要逃避无所不在的历史和社会影响，寄希望于划分公私界限，在个人的自由王国里建构避难所，寻求心理救赎，这其实是徒劳。必须清醒认识到"一切事物都是社会的和历史的。事实上，一切事物'说到底'都是政治"。从政治角度看，历史由人类的斗争所创造，是人类集体的故事。每个具体历史事件，每个具体的人，都是人类尚在发展中的总体史的一部分。所以，文学的历史性是其语义生成的先决条件，有三层同心圆式的框架：第一层是狭窄的政治历史，由具体事件构成，牵动身处其中的具体个人；第二层是社会历史，时间线相对长，反映特定的社会秩序中不同阶级之间的斗争；第三层是从史前时代一直延伸到未来的总体历史，不同社会模式均在其中。与之对应的是文学的三重"语义视域"：第一层视域中，文学文本是特定历史时期的个人书写；第二层视域中，文学文本反映社会矛盾，是阶级性的集体书写；第三层视域中，在总体历史的参照系里，文学文本的符码系统关联着社会的生产方式，显现出文学形式也具意识形态性。

From *The Political Unconscious*

Fredric Jameson (1934-)

This book will argue the priority of the political interpretation of literary texts. It conceives of the political perspective not as some supplementary method, not as an optional auxiliary to other interpretive methods current today—the psychoanalytic or the mythcritical, the stylistic, the ethical, the structural—but rather as the absolute horizon of all reading and all interpretation.

This is evidently a much more extreme position than the modest claim, surely acceptable to everyone, that certain texts have social and historical—sometimes even political—resonance. Traditional literary history has, of course, never prohibited the investigation of such topics as the Florentine political background in Dante, Milton's relationship to the schismatics, or Irish historical allusions in Joyce. I would argue, however, that such information—even where it is not recontained, as it is in most instances, by an idealistic conception of the history of ideas—does not yield interpretation as such, but rather at best its (indispensable) preconditions.

Today this properly antiquarian relationship to the cultural past has a dialectical counterpart which is ultimately no more satisfactory; I mean the tendency of much contemporary theory to rewrite selected texts from the past in terms of its own aesthetic and, in particular, in terms of a modernist (or more properly post-modernist) conception of language. I have shown elsewhere the ways in which such "ideologies of the text" construct a straw man or inessential term—variously called the "readerly" or the "realistic" or the "referential" text—over against which the essential term—the "writerly" or modernist or "open" text, *écriture* or textual productivity—is defined and with which it is seen as a decisive break. But Croce's great dictum that "all history is contemporary history" does not mean that all history is *our* contemporary history; and the problems begin when your epistemological break begins to displace itself in time according to your own current interests, so that Balzac may stand for unenlightened representationality when you are concerned to bring out everything that is "textual" and modern in Flaubert, but turns into something else when, with Roland Barthes in *S/Z*, you have decided to rewrite Balzac as Philippe Sollers, as sheer text and *écriture*.

This unacceptable option, or ideological double bind, between antiquarianism and modernizing "relevance" or projection demonstrates that the old dilemmas of historicism—and in particular, the question of the claims of monuments from distant and even archaic moments of the cultural past on a culturally different present—do not go away just because we choose to ignore them. Our presupposition, in the analyses that follow, will be that only a genuine philosophy of history is capable of respecting the specificity and radical difference of the social and cultural past while disclosing the solidarity of its polemics and passions, its forms, structures, experiences, and struggles, with those of the present day....

My position here is that only Marxism offers a philosophically coherent and ideologically compelling resolution to the dilemma of historicism evoked above. Only Marxism can give us an adequate account of the essential *mystery* of the cultural past, which, like Tiresias drinking the blood, is momentarily returned to life and warmth and allowed once more to speak, and to deliver its long-forgotten message in surroundings utterly alien to it. This mystery can be reenacted only if the human adventure is one; only thus—and not through the hobbies of antiquarianism or the projections of the modernists—can we glimpse the vital claims upon us of such long-dead issues as the seasonal alternation of the economy of a primitive tribe, the passionate disputes about the nature of the Trinity, the conflicting models of the *polis* or the universal Empire, or, apparently closer to us in time, the dusty parliamentary and journalistic polemics of the nineteenth century nation states. These matters can recover their original urgency for us only if they are retold within the unity of a single great collective story; only if, in however disguised and symbolic a form, they are seen as sharing a single fundamental theme—for Marxism, the collective struggle to wrest a realm of Freedom from a realm of Necessity; only if they are grasped as vital episodes in a single vast unfinished plot: "The history of all hitherto existing society is the history of class struggles: freeman and slave, patrician and plebeian, lord and serf, guildmaster and journeyman—in a word, oppressor and oppressed—stood in constant opposition to one another, carried on an uninterrupted, now hidden, now open fight, a fight that each time ended, either in a revolutionary reconstitution of society at large or in the common ruin of the contending classes." It is in detecting the traces of that uninterrupted narrative, in restoring to the surface of the text the repressed and buried reality of this fundamental history, that the doctrine of a political unconscious finds its function and its necessity.

From this perspective the convenient

working distinction between cultural texts that are social and political and those that are not becomes something worse than an error: namely, a symptom and a reinforcement of the reification and privatization of contemporary life. Such a distinction reconfirms that structural, experiential, and conceptual gap between the public and the private, between the social and the psychological, or the political and the poetic, between history or society and the "individual," which—the tendential law of social life under capitalism—maims our existence as individual subjects and paralyzes our thinking about time and change just as surely as it alienates us from our speech itself. To imagine that, sheltered from the omnipresence of history and the implacable influence of the social, there already exists a realm of freedom—whether it be that of the microscopic experience of words in a text or the ecstasies and intensities of the various private religions—is only to strengthen the grip of Necessity over all such blind zones in which the individual subject seeks refuge, in pursuit of a purely individual, a merely psychological, project of salvation. The only effective liberation from such constraint begins with the recognition that there is nothing that is not social and historical—indeed, that everything is "in the last analysis" political.

The assertion of a political unconscious proposes that we undertake just such a final analysis and explore the multiple paths that lead to the unmasking of cultural artifacts as socially symbolic acts. It projects a rival hermeneutic to those already enumerated; but it does so, as we shall see, not so much by repudiating their findings as by arguing its ultimate philosophical and methodological priority over more specialized interpretive codes whose insights are strategically limited as much by their own situational origins as by the narrow or local ways in which they construe or construct their objects of study....

...Marxist critical insights will therefore here be defended as something like an ultimate *semantic* precondition for the intelligibility of literary and cultural texts. Even this argument, however, needs a certain specification: in particular we will suggest that such semantic enrichment and enlargement of the inert givens and materials of a particular text must take place within three concentric frameworks, which mark a widening out of the sense of the social ground of a text through the notions, first, of political history, in the narrow sense of punctual event and a chroniclelike sequence of happenings in time; then of society, in the now already less diachronic and time-bound sense of a constitutive tension and struggle between social classes; and, ultimately, of history now conceived in its vastest sense of the sequence of modes of production and the succession and destiny of the various human social formations, from prehistoric life to whatever far future history has in store for us.

These distinct semantic horizons are, to be sure, also distinct moments of the process of interpretation, and may in that sense be understood as dialectical equivalents of what Frye has called the successive "phases" in our reinterpretation—our rereading and rewriting—of the literary text. What we must also note, however, is that each phase or horizon governs a distinct reconstruction of its object, and construes the very structure of what can now only in a general sense be called "the text" in a different way.

Thus, within the narrower limits of our first, narrowly political or historical, horizon, the "text," the object of study, is still more or less construed as coinciding with the individual literary work or utterance. The difference between the perspective enforced and enabled by this horizon, however, and that of ordinary *explication de texte*, or individual exegesis, is that here the individual work is grasped essentially as a *symbolic* act.

When we pass into the second phase, and find that the semantic horizon within which we grasp a cultural object has widened to include the social order, we will find that the very object of our analysis has itself been thereby dialectically transformed, and that it is no longer construed as an individual "text" or work in the narrow sense, but has been reconstituted in the form of the great collective and class discourses of which a text is little more than an individual *parole* or utterance. Within this new horizon, then, our object of study will prove to be the *ideologeme*, that is, the smallest intelligible unit of the essentially antagonistic collective discourses of social classes.

When finally, even the passions and values of a particular social formation find themselves placed in a new and seemingly relativized perspective by the ultimate horizon of human history as a whole, and by their respective positions in the whole complex sequence of the modes of production, both the individual text and its ideologemes know a final transformation, and must be read in terms of what I will call the *ideology of form*, that is, the symbolic messages transmitted to us by the coexistence of various sign systems which are themselves traces or anticipations of modes of production....

History is therefore the experience of Necessity, and it is this alone which can forestall its thematization or reification as a mere object of representation or as one master code among many others. Necessity is not in that sense a type of content, but rather the inexorable *form* of events; it is therefore a narrative category in the enlarged sense of some properly narrative political unconscious which has been argued here, a retextualization of History which does not propose the latter as some new representation or "vision," some new content, but as the formal effects of what Althusser, following Spinoza, calls an "absent cause." Conceived in this sense, History is what hurts, it is what refuses desire and sets inexorable limits to individual as well as collective praxis, which its "ruses" turn into grisly and ironic reversals of their overt intention. But this History can be apprehended only through its effects, and never directly as some reified force. This is indeed the ultimate sense in which History as ground and untranscendable horizon needs no particular theoretical justification: we may be sure that its alienating necessities will not forget us, however much we might prefer to ignore them.

思考题

1. 霍克海默尔和阿多尔诺为什么说启蒙变成了神话？启蒙神话的核心是什么？它带来的问题是什么？
2. 根据阿尔都塞的理论，意识形态是如何将个体"询唤"为主体的？
3. 威廉斯将一个时代中的文化分为哪三类？每一类的特点是什么？
4. 詹姆逊为什么认为在文学阐释中必须重视历史维度？
5. 詹姆逊所说的"语义视域"（semantic horizons）共有几个层次？分别是什么？

讨论题

1. 请查阅资料，了解法兰克福学派批判理论的内涵，结合霍克海默尔和阿多尔诺的《启蒙辩证法》的选文，讨论法兰克福学派对现代性的反思。
2. 请从外国文学名著中挑选一部小说，比如《鲁滨逊漂流记》《德伯家的苔丝》《嘉莉妹妹》等，结合阿尔都塞的意识形态理论，讨论意识形态对人的主体性的影响，在小组中分享口头报告。

补充文本选摘与评述

卢卡奇:《平衡的现实主义》
From "Realism in the Balance"

György Lukács (1885-1971)

The development of literature, particularly in capitalist society, and particularly at capitalism's moment of crisis, is extraordinarily complex. Nevertheless, to offer a crude oversimplification, we may still distinguish three main currents in the literature of our age; these currents are not of course entirely distinct but often overlap in the development of individual writers:

1) Openly anti-realist or pseudo-realist literature which is concerned to provide an apologia for, and a defense of, the existing system. Of this group we shall say nothing here.

2) So-called avant-garde literature (we shall come to authentic modern literature in due course) from Naturalism to Surrealism. What is its general thrust? We may briefly anticipate our findings here by saying that its main trend is its growing distance from, and progressive dissolution of, realism.

3) The literature of the major realists of the day. For the most part these writers do not belong to any literary set; they are swimming against the mainstream of literary development, in fact, against the two currents noted above. As a general pointer to the complexion of this contemporary form of realism, we need only mention the names of Gorky, Thomas and Heinrich Mann and Romain Rolland....

...If literature is a particular form by means of which objective reality is reflected, then it becomes of crucial importance for it to grasp that reality as it truly is, and not merely to confine itself to reproducing whatever manifests itself immediately and on the surface. If a writer strives to represent reality as it truly is, i.e. if he is an authentic realist, then the question of totality plays a decisive role, no matter how the writer actually conceives the problem intellectually. Lenin repeatedly insisted on the practical importance of the category of totality: "In order to know an object thoroughly, it is essential to discover and comprehend all of its aspects, its relationships and its 'mediations.' We shall never achieve this fully, but *insistence on all-round knowledge* will protect us from errors and inflexibility."...

...Great realism, therefore, does not portray an immediately obvious aspect of reality but one which is permanent and objectively more significant, namely man in the whole range of his relations to the real world, above all those which outlast mere fashion. Over and above that, it captures tendencies of development that only exist incipiently and so have not yet had the opportunity to unfold their entire human and social potential. To discern and give shape to such underground trends is the great historical mission of the true literary avant-garde.

葛兰西：《狱中笔记》
From *Prison Notebooks*
Antonio Gramsci (1891-1937)

The relationship between the intellectuals and the world of production is not as direct as it is with the fundamental social groups but is, in varying degrees, "mediated" by the whole fabric of society and by the complex of superstructures, of which the intellectuals are, precisely, the "functionaries." It should be possible both to measure the "organic quality" [*organicità*] of the various intellectual strata and their degree of connection with a fundamental social group, and to establish a gradation of their functions and of the superstructures from the bottom to the top (from the structural base upward). What we can do, for the moment, is to fix two major superstructural "levels": the one that can be called "civil society," that is the ensemble of organisms commonly called "private," and that of "political society" or "the State." These two levels correspond on the one hand to the function of "hegemony" which the dominant group exercises throughout society and on the other hand to that of "direct domination" or command exercised through the State and "juridical" government. The functions in question are precisely organizational and connective. The intellectuals are the dominant group's "deputies" exercising the subaltern functions of social hegemony and political government. These comprise:

1) The "spontaneous" consent given by the great masses of the population to the general direction imposed on social life by the dominant fundamental group; this consent is "historically" caused by the prestige (and consequent confidence) which the dominant group enjoys because of its position and function in the world of production.

2) The apparatus of state coercive power which "legally" enforces discipline on those groups who do not "consent" either actively or passively. This apparatus is, however, constituted for the whole of society in anticipation of moments of crisis of command and direction when spontaneous consent has failed.

伊格尔顿：《马克思主义与文学批评》
From *Marxism and Literary Criticism*
Terry Eagleton (1943-)

The question of how to describe this relationship within art between "base" and "superstructure," between art as production and art as ideological, seems to me one of the most important questions which Marxist literary criticism has now to confront. Here, perhaps, it may learn something from Marxist criticism of the other arts. I am thinking in particular about John Berger's comments on oil painting in his *Ways of Seeing* (1972). Oil painting, Berger claims, only developed as an artistic *genre* when it was needed to express a certain ideological way of seeing the world, a way of seeing for which other techniques were inadequate. Oil painting creates a certain density, luster and solidity in what it depicts; it does to the world what capital does to social relations, reducing everything to the equality of objects. The painting itself becomes an object—a commodity to be bought and possessed; it is itself a piece of property, and represents the world in those terms. We have here, then, a whole set of factors to be interrelated. There is the stage of economic production of the society in which oil painting first grew up, as a particular technique of artistic production. There is the set of social relations between artist and audience (producer/consumer, vendor/purchaser) with which that technique is bound up. There is the relation between those artistic property-relations, and property-relations in general. And there is the question of how the ideology which underpins those property-relations embodies itself in a certain form of painting, a certain way of seeing and depicting objects. It is this kind of argument, which connects modes of production to a facial expression captured on canvas, which Marxist literary criticism must develop in its own terms.

There are two important reasons why it must do so. First, because unless we can relate past literature, however indirectly, to the struggle of men and women against exploitation, we shall not fully understand our own present and so will be less able to change it effectively. Secondly, because we shall be less able to *read* texts, or to produce those art forms which might make for a better art and a better society. Marxist criticism is not just an alternative technique for interpreting *Paradise Lost* or *Middlemarch*. It is part of our liberation from oppression, and that is why it is worth discussing at book length.

| 选文评述

卢卡奇《平衡的现实主义》一文的写作背景是卢卡奇和同时代思想家布洛赫（Ernst Bloch）围绕表现主义展开的论战。布洛赫也是马克思主义者，他的重要贡献是在乌托邦理论领域。他和卢卡奇一样，认识到艺术是抵抗资本主义意识形态的有力武器。但他推崇现代主义，认为以布莱希特为代表的表现主义者的艺术创新呼应了时代变化，反映了当下性，揭露出现实弊病。卢卡奇反对布洛赫的论断，认为布莱希特的先锋戏剧和乔伊斯的意识流小说对现实的反映局限于眼前，停留在浅薄的表层刻画，背离了现实主义的"真实性"原则——卢卡奇所认为的"真实"是总体性的现实感,它基于过去,关注当下,且思考未来。在选文中,卢卡奇列举了他所欣赏的艺术家:高尔基、托马斯·曼和罗曼·罗兰等。他认为这些作家能够深入到日常生活的表象之下,发现隐藏其中的社会客观发展规律。卢卡奇认为文学的先锋性应该体现在对人与世界的各种关系的全面洞察,作家的责任是对萌芽中的社会发展潜能进行敏锐捕捉。

葛兰西的选文出自《狱中笔记》,关键词有三个:上层建筑、霸权以及知识分子。葛兰西认为上层建筑可以分为两个层面:市民社会层面以及政体和国家层面。市民社会是私人领域,它的意识形态性体现在"霸权"这个概念。因为统治阶级既有经济权力,又有历史威望,所以民众自发同意统治阶级的文化霸权。政体和国家层面是公共领域,司法体系直接维护统治,其强制性针对不肯膺服霸权的少数人。葛兰西指出,知识分子不是外在于统治阶级或者被统治阶级的独立阶级,而是深深嵌于这些基本社会群体之中,扮演着中介性的角色,在意识形态塑造中发挥作用,参与上层建筑自下而上的逐层建构与确立。葛兰西的笔记写于狱中,文稿要受官方审查,所以有些话无法明白表达。实际上,他在讨论市民社会和文化霸权时,专门提及知识分子,其潜台词是,由于被统治阶级的大多数民众自愿认可统治阶级领导权,革命意识很难在市民社会的层面产生,所以他希冀知识分子积极赢取民众认可,在市民社会建立新的文化领导权,打破资产阶级的霸权统治。

伊格尔顿的选文出自《马克思主义与文学批评》。伊格尔顿反对简单套用马克思主义理论,重视文学批评对人类经验的复杂性的呈现。他在书中倡导对艺术生产的"经济基础"与艺术的意识形态的"上层建筑"之间的联动进行深入探察。他认为唯有如此,才能透彻理解历史,明白当下从何而来,应向何处去;才能正确理解艺术品,更好地推动艺术的发展。选文中,他以英国公共知识分子兼艺术评论家约翰·伯格的批评实践作为马克思主义文艺批评的范例。伯格在《观看之道》中聚焦油画这一艺术品类别,对油画的诞生历史、商品属性、艺术家与观众和购买者的复杂关系、油画的意识形态功能等进行了解析,揭示出观看艺术品的审美活动中多重要素的复杂作用。

关键术语释例

1. **物化(reification)**:"物化"概念的提出者是卢卡奇,他用其揭秘资本主义社会中人的异化。人通过劳动创造了物,人与物之间是主客体关系。然而,在现代社会,经由物化,人与物的关系发生了颠倒:物独立于人,被视为自然的事实或神圣意志的表现，进而对人进行主宰和支配；人丧失了主体性，被客体化为物，需要遵从物的法则。卢卡奇的物化概念脱化于马克思的商品拜物教理论。在《资本论》中，马克思指出，在资本主义经济中人与人之间的关系被物与物之间的关系所替代。商品和货币被神秘化了，变成了人们膜拜的对象。卢卡奇的物化论也借鉴了德国社会学家马克斯·韦伯（Max Weber）的理论。韦伯注意到现代社会的理性原则要求对一切无法纳入其体系的因素——包括人性中与理性相冲突的因素——进行"合理化"的抛弃。卢卡奇指出，物化对人性的钳制构成了现代人生存的普遍境遇。在当代，法兰克福学派第三代理论家阿克塞尔·霍耐特（Axel Honneth）对卢卡奇的物化理论进行了进一步阐释。他认为导致物化的核心是主体间性的缺失，即人与人之间未能实现对彼此主体地位的承认。

2. **意识形态国家机器（Ideological State Apparatuses，简称ISAs）**：在经典马克思主义国家学说中，国家机器包括政府机关、军队、警察、法庭和监狱等，通过镇压手段维护社会政治秩序。阿尔都塞受葛兰西的文化领导权理论的影响，认为维护国家政权的意识形态也具有国家机器的功能，他称其为意识形态国家机器。意识形态国家机器包括一系列机制，涵盖宗教（各种教会体系）、教育（公立私立学校体系）、家庭、法律、政治（不同政党在内的政治体系）、工会、信息（出版物、广播电视等）、文化（文学、艺术、体育等）等领域。此前，这些机制中的大多数被认为隶属于市民社会领域。阿尔都塞却认为它们承担意识形态职能，是国家机器的有机部分。相比镇压性国家机器，意识形态国家机器形式灵活多样，各自相对独立，负责从不同侧面向大众进行意识形态的宣传、灌输和教育，将公民塑造为符合统治阶级国家意志的个人主体。ISAs理论是解析资本主义文化政治的有力工具。比如，阿尔都塞发现教育机器已经取代教会，在资本主义社会发挥着主导性的作用。

推荐书目

Bronner, Stephen E., and Douglas Kellner. *Critical Theory and Society: A Reader*. New York: Routledge, 1989.

Eagleton, Terry, and Drew Milne. *Marxist Literary Theory: A Reader*. Oxford: Blackwell Publishers, 1996.

Foley, Barbara. *Marxist Literary Criticism Today*. London: Pluto Press, 2019.

Jameson, Fredric. *Marxism and Form: Twentieth-Century Dialectical Theories of Literature*. Princeton: Princeton University Press, 1974.

Jay, Martin. *The Dialectical Imagination: A History of the Frankfurt School and the Institute of Social Research, 1923-1950*. Berkeley: University of California Press, 1996.

Lukács, Georg. *The Theory of the Novel: A Historico-Philosophical Essay on the Forms of Great Epic Literature*. Cambridge, Mass.: The MIT Press, 1974.

Mulhern, Francis. *Contemporary Marxist Literary Criticism*. New York: Longman, 1992.

程巍:《否定性思维:马尔库塞思想研究》。北京:北京大学出版社,2001年。

赵勇:《法兰克福学派内外:知识分子与大众文化》。北京:北京大学出版社,2016年。

第八章
结构主义与叙事学

概述

二战之后，在法国率先兴起的结构主义思潮，从亲缘关系看，接续的是俄国形式主义理论。二者都希冀在纷繁多样的文本中寻找共性规律。而且，二者思想体系中都能看到索绪尔现代语言学理论的影响印痕。但俄国形式主义利用索绪尔理论讨论何为文学的语言，法国结构主义看重的则是索绪尔对符号系统的论述，将其运用在人类学、社会学、精神分析、文化研究以及文学批评等更为广泛的领域，引领了人文社科研究的全面范式转变。

结构主义兴起于战后的法国，有具体的历史文化原因。二战期间以及战后的法国思想界，存在主义哲学一度独领风骚。存在主义哲学推崇"自为的存在"，主张超越性的激进自由；法国结构主义者则反思存在主义自由是否可能，追问社会机制用何种原则对人进行规训，讨论社会文化的组织结构，分析它们对人类思维和行为的决定性影响。所以克洛德·列维–施特劳斯（Claude Lévi-Strauss）引入索绪尔语言学的关系论，讨论人类文明的基础模式。拉康将弗洛伊德的精神分析和索绪尔的符号论对接，讨论人类意识、无意识与语言之间的关系（见第六章）。阿尔都塞在拉康理论的启发下，对意识形态机制进行结构性分析（见第七章）。罗兰·巴特（Roland Barthes）以符号学为理论工具，对日常文化生活现象进行解读。这些理论家的研究兴趣不同，但均注重透过表层现象辨析深层结构，揭秘社会文化体系内部的基本原则以及意义的生产与转换机制。

在结构主义思潮影响下，文学理论家们和形式主义者一样重视文学内部研究，但落脚点既不是新批评的"细读"，也不是俄国形式主义的"文学性"，而是文学整体性的结构范式。我们在第六章中介绍过诺思罗普·弗莱用神话原型批评解读文学史的演进，他的文学整体观深具结构主义特点。我们将在本章介绍的叙事学，其经典时期隶属结构主义文论，后经典叙事理论则是对结构主义的反思。

对结构主义来说，索绪尔的语言学提供了研究方法论的基础。索绪尔是20世纪初最伟大的语言学家，他的《普通语言学教程》（*Course in General Linguistics*）1916年出版，是现代语言学的奠基之作。在索绪尔之前，语言学研究国别语言以及语言史。索绪尔认为在不同国别的语言和不同时代的语言的变化背后，是语言表意系统的共性特征。他细化了传统意义上的"语言"（language）概念，将它分为语言（langue）和言语（parole）两个层面。语言（langue）是包括词汇、语法规则等在内的整体性符号系统，言语（parole）则是具体言说，是个体化的行为。在两者关系中，语言决定着和规范着言语，索绪尔认为科学研究的重点应是前者。

索绪尔语言学研究的切入点是作为表意单元的"符号"（sign）。他指出符号是由两个部分组成的，即能指（signifier）和所指（signified）。能指是声音形象（sound-image）；所指是概念（concept）。索绪尔将能指和所指之间的关系比作白纸的两面，声音唤起的心理印象与概念合二为一，形成符号。索绪尔还提炼出语言符号的两个重要特征，其一是符号的任意性。例如，同样是"树"的概念，它在英文中是tree，在法文中是arbor。传统的语言观认为词语和事物之间存在天然的联系，命名是落实这种实质联系。索绪尔的符号论则让我们认识到语言是独立体系，不是由实物世界决定。某个概念用何种声音形象和语言符号来加以表达，源于集体的共识性认同，由此形成惯例。对于个体来说，语言是强制机制，言说要有意义，必须符合语言共同体约定俗成的规范。

索绪尔认为符号的第二个特征是符号构成的线性序列：能指属听觉性质，只在时间上展开。言说时，一次只能说出一个词语要素，它们的音位先后相继，组成线性表意链条。值得注意的是，当符号被写下来时，会拥有空间性，每个符号占据句段线条中的一个点位，与前后项相对立。每个符号的价值意涵，源自它与其他符号发音上的区别和在句段中的点位差异。这种符号之间的"是此非彼"的对立，体现了语言体系的差异性原则。

索绪尔语言系统论不仅关注差异性，也强调关系性。索绪尔认为人类的言说是一种社会心理行为，能在符号间搭建两种关系：句段关系和联想关系。句段关系是水平轴向的，词语串起来形成一定长度的话语言说，有历时性的特点；联想关系是垂直轴向的，当选择一个词时，大脑里与之相关的词语集合式地聚在一起，有共时性的特点。事实上，在历时性和共时性的对立项中，索绪尔更重视后者。在语言研究中，他认为应排除历史干扰，探究静态系统的结构原理。语言是符号体系中的一种。为此他还积极主张将语言学的整体性、结构性和共时性的范式运用于研究其他社会文化符号体系，推动人文社科研究新发展。

俄国形式主义的发展充分体现了索绪尔理论对文学研究领域的影响。这种影响力继而辐射到了法国思想界，结构主义由此而来。在思想的传递承继中，雅各布森起到了桥梁作用。第五章中，我们重点了解了雅各布森的诗性语言观。实际上，雅各布森从莫斯科移居布拉格后，研究兴趣已从对语言的研究，扩展到了对整个表意系统的研究，早在1929年就率先使用了"结构主义"这一概念。二战期间，雅各布森移居美国纽约教书，与列维-施特劳斯相遇。通过雅各布森，列维-施特劳斯了解了索绪尔理论，将其引入人类学研究，开创了法国结构主义的风气之先。

人类学的研究对象是不同部族的宗教信仰、社会机制、文化习俗等，目标是在考察和比较中获得对人类的全面理解。人类学家通过田野调查认识到每种文明的特殊性、地方性和历史性。然而，如何解释文明之间的共性？列维-施特劳斯从索绪尔理论中受到了启发。在《结构人类学》（*Structural Anthropology*，1958）中，他先介绍了音位学研究方法：关注有意识的语言现象背后的无意识的基础结构，重视语言单元之间的关系，聚焦系统及其结构，发现其一般运作规律。他继而指出，这种方法也应为人类学研究所采用，使社会文化的杂多现象经由系统的结构性原则得以解释。列维-施特劳斯之所以主张系统性的共时性研究，不是因为他轻视历史，忽略具体性，而是他想要从普遍人性的角度出发，寻求对西方中心主义框架的突破，发现不同文明之间的连接。在《野性的思维》（*The Savage Mind*，1962）中，他质疑野蛮人和文明人的差距，指出原始部落的修补匠人和西方世界的工程师的思考方式异曲同工，人类思维有相同的结构。在《亲属关系的基本结构》（*The Elementary Structures of Kinship*，1949）中，他对不同社会不同文化的亲属关系进行研究，发现人类亲属关系的本质不是血脉传承，而是"交换"——通过交换女性，进行家庭乃至部落之间的联姻。他在《结构人类学》中进一步指出，交换原则反映在社会诸多层面："交换总是在三个层面上完成：妇女的交换、商品和服务的交换、信息的交换。"亲属关系、经济学和语言学看似三个不同领域，却有相似原则。

神话也是列维-施特劳斯的研究领域。列维-施特劳斯曾经在美洲部落做过田野调查，收集了大量的神话故事。此外，他也非常熟悉包括俄狄浦斯系列故事在内的欧洲神话。在《神话结构研究》（"The Structural Study of Myth"，1955）等著述中，他阐述了他的神话研究方法。列维-施特劳斯将每则神话看作单个的"言语"，将整个神话体系看作集体的"语言"。他通过对神话体系的基础结构的探究，发现矛盾性因素经常成对地出现在神话中。每则神话中的矛盾，具体内容或许不相同，却都反映二元对立的冲突性价值观。他认为神话的生成，源于化解两难困境的愿望。在人类社会中，神话的真正意义在于对两极化的立场进行调和，起到斡旋调解的作用。

法国结构主义另外一位关键理论家罗兰·巴特则用符号学进行文化批评。《神话学》(*Mythologies*, 1957)是其代表性著作。书中的"神话"(myth)不是荣格和列维-施特劳斯所指的反映人类族群经验的集体故事,而是携带意识形态信息的特殊话语术,所以也可译为"迷思"。神话的话语建构依赖于双重符号化过程。在第一层中,能指和所指在具体的语境中结合成具有特定意义的符号。第二层中,这个符号被当作能指,重新编码,编码的过程虚化了符号的历史具体性,自然化了它的意识形态内涵,导致人们把它视为历来如此的"神话",不加质疑地接受。比如,法国人喜欢看摔跤比赛。当摔跤手登上角力场,观众期待看到的是一场类似于古希腊戏剧的表演。摔跤手们被赋予了"正义"与"邪恶"的不同身份,通过对抗性的夸张的表演,展示摔跤的"正邪之争"的"神话"意义。

《神话学》中,巴特对摔跤比赛、儿童玩具、红酒消费、政治家的竞选照片等法国日常生活现象进行了灵动而犀利的分析。他的《流行体系》(*The Fashion System*, 1967)则从符号学角度,集中讨论了时装杂志如何塑造流行体系的议题。巴特在研究中,既需要分析穿着搭配的符码系统,看衣饰的选择和组合逻辑的内在"语法"规范;也需要探察变幻不定的流行风尚的建构机制,看流行体系如何通过符号生产范式来制造流行元素,引导时尚的迭代变化。巴特运用符号学方法,对时装杂志文章进行分析,勾勒出资本主义社会以服装为代表的流行产业的全景图:杂志文章塑造潮流符码;潮流符码影响现实中服装的生产和消费;流行体系推陈出新,刺激人们对时尚的欲望,为新一轮的服饰生产和消费提供动力。事实上,好的结构主义批评从来不是干瘪抽象的讨论,它能让人对复杂体系的神秘运行法则形成更为本质的认识。

法国结构主义思潮中,不仅有列维-施特劳斯、罗兰·巴特等理论家在人文科学大语境中进行开拓性探索,也有一些理论家继续在文学传统领域进行研究。他们的结构主义转向促进了叙事学的诞生。

1969年,法国学者茨维坦·托多洛夫(Tzvetan Todorov)在《〈十日谈〉语法》(*Grammar of the Decameron*)中写道:"这部著作属于一门尚未存在的科学,我们暂且将这门科学取名为叙事学,即关于叙事作品的科学。"虽然"叙事学"到此时才被提出,其探索在俄国形式主义时期就已经出现。1928年,弗拉基米尔·普罗普(Vladimir Propp)基于对俄罗斯民间故事的研究写成的《故事形态学》(*Morphology of the Folktale*)出版。普罗普在研究中发现,民间神奇故事中的人物千差万别,但他们在行动过程承担的角色功能却只有七种,即主人公、对头(加害者)、赠予者(提供者)、相助者、公主(要找的人)、派遣人和伪主人公。普罗普还总结了角色功能项的聚合排列的三十一种范式,包括主人公离家远行、与对头交锋、打败对头、回到家乡等经典叙事范式。

普罗普以"形态学"命名自己的研究方法，特地指出这个词不是结构主义意义上的，而是来自歌德的思想，旨在说明文学和世界是一个整体。但他探索文本的普遍规律，注重功能项之间的关系性，这说明他的研究和结构主义思想之间存在共鸣。这也是法国学者视他为先驱者，受他启发，发展出结构主义叙事学的原因。

1966年，法国学者A. J. 格雷马斯（Algirdas Julien Greimas）出版了《结构语义学》（*Structural Semantics: An Attempt at a Method*），提出"行动元"的概念。行动元和行动者不同，它具有普罗普式的功能性色彩，所以行动元可以是一组人物，而单个角色可以隶属于多个行动元。但格雷马斯比普罗普更重视角色间的关系，他将普罗普的分类简化为三组六种行动元：主体/客体、发送者/接受者、辅助者/反对者。行动元的深层逻辑是二元对立。主体对客体的期待与欲求是神话叙事的核心，其他两组行动元也以这组行动元为中心。格雷马斯认为具体的叙事表达相当于索绪尔语言学中的"言语"（parole），它受制于叙事的内在体系（immanent system），即"语言"（langue）。在内在体系的规范中，行动元及其叙事模式是表层结构，人类的思维模式和世界观等是深层结构。格雷马斯认为叙事动力来自深层结构，在表层结构被叙事语法所规范，继而形成外显的各不相同的叙事话语。

格雷马斯的叙事学有很重的符号学色彩，重视叙事表意体系的结构性原则。热拉尔·热奈特（Gérard Genette）则关心"故事如何讲"，对叙事的表现形式与相关基本概念进行了系统而细致的讨论，为叙事学的发展做出了奠基性的贡献。热奈特提出，为了更好地讨论"叙事"，需要澄清三个概念：故事，即叙述的内容；叙事话语，即能指或叙述文本本身；以及叙事行为。举个古典文学的例子。史诗《奥德赛》的故事始于主人公奥德修斯在特洛伊战争之后踏上了归家之路，而史诗的叙事话语则始于诗人叙述者的吟诵。在叙述者的吟诵中，我们得知奥德修斯已在归乡路上漂泊多年，此刻正困于女神卡吕普索的海岛，但他终于获得神明允许，可以返回家乡。

因为故事和叙事话语之间存在差异和张力，热奈特在其叙事理论中，特别重视辨析叙事话语对故事的呈现方式。在经典之作《叙事话语》（*Narrative Discourse: An Essay in Method*，1972）中，他分五个板块，对时序（order）、时距（duration）、时频（frequency）、语式（mood）和语态（voice）逐一进行了深入讨论。其中，时间性议题占据了著作大半篇幅。热奈特指出，叙事中时间具有双重性：有故事时间和叙事时间两个维度。时序关涉叙事时间以倒叙、预叙等形式对故事时间进行的重新排序。时距反映阅读叙事所花费时间与故事事件本身持续时间之间的差异：叙事时间中轻轻一句"百年已过"，阅读时间只是数秒，故事时间却已经进入下个世纪。时频则反映叙述中故事的讲述次数。只讲一次和反复讲述的区别很大，后者体现出叙述者的念念不忘。

热奈特关于语式和语态的讨论，则都与叙述者的讲述行为有关。语式讨论叙述的距离远近以及叙述视角的不同。热奈特反对用"谁说"来定义叙述者，主张以"谁看"（后修正为"谁感知"）为分类标准，提出用叙事聚焦（focalization）这个概念，取代视点（point of view）的传统概念，将叙事中的聚焦按照与故事中人物的关系，分为三类：上帝视角的全知是无聚焦；叙述者即人物，其所知所见有限，这是内聚焦；摄影机式的视角，对人物内心一无所知，这是外聚焦。热奈特的语态则关涉故事、叙事话语和叙事行为的相互关联。比如同一个文本中，可能存在不同的叙事层面，形成各种时间嵌套，联动叙事时间顺序的变化，叙述者处在不同叙述层级，视角也可能随之而变。

叙事学的理论源头可以一直追溯到亚里士多德的《诗学》。在漫长的历史发展中，其线索从未中断，却也未能真正成为体系。进入20世纪，形式主义对文学艺术手法倍加关注，这为叙事学的诞生准备了良好的条件。在二战后，当结构主义带来了有效理论工具时，叙事学在法国顺势而生。始于法国的叙事学，很快吸引了米克·巴尔（Mieke Bal）、杰拉德·普林斯（Gerald Prince）、西摩·查特曼（Seymour Chatman）等国际学者的目光。他们在该领域进行的探索，丰富了其概念体系的建构和理论内涵的深化，汇流成经典叙事学理论。

由于叙事学对人们如何阅读文学文本有重大指导意义，它自成为独立学科以来，不断吸引着新的研究者加入和拓展研究的视域。经典叙事学重视文学的内部研究，以文本为中心，讨论文学世界的叙事编码体系。进入20世纪中后期，这种结构主义的框架受到了越来越多的研究者的质疑。反思结构主义传统，拓展新的研究领域，构成了后经典叙事学的重要发展动力。

在后经典叙事理论中，修辞叙事学是重要分支。西方的修辞学始于古希腊罗马时代，亚里士多德、西塞罗、昆体良、朗吉努斯等都是修辞学的经典理论家。修辞学的核心目标是用文学手段打动人心，激发读者与听众的反应，实现教化的效果。作为叙事学和修辞学的结合，修辞叙事学反对经典叙事学对文本性的过度关注，主张叙事学应探察作者、文本、读者三者之间的互动，代表人物是彼得·拉比诺维茨（Peter Rabinowitz）、詹姆斯·费伦（James Phelan）等。其先声是芝加哥学派的韦恩·布斯（Wayne Booth）。二战后，在美国新批评当道的时代，芝加哥学派反对新批评的文本中心论，认为文学是人与人进行交流的形式，具有公共性，蕴含伦理意义。为此，布斯在《小说修辞学》（*The Rhetoric of Fiction*，1961）中提出"隐含作者"（implied author）的概念。布斯和新批评学者一样，认为文学阅读无须关注现实作者，但他关注现实作者在文本叙事中建构的隐含作者，认为现实作者借隐含作者传达其道德立场，对读者施加影响。读者则通过在作品中发现隐含作者，获得深入理解文本的线索。

费伦是布斯的学生，也是当代修辞叙事学的代表理论家。和老师布斯相比，费伦更重视读者的作用，认为我们不能笼统地理解读者概念，而应该认识到它有四个层面：现实世界有血有肉的读者是"实际的读者"；作者心中假设的理想读者是"作者的读者"；叙事世界为实际的读者提供的观察者设定是"叙事的读者"；叙述者叙说的接受者是"受述者"。他主张叙事学应细致考察读者在阅读过程中如何受到文本影响，如何形成阐释判断、伦理判断和审美判断。在《阅读人物，阅读情节》(Reading People, Reading Plots: Character, Progression, and the Interpretation of Narrative，1989)、《体验小说》(Experiencing Fiction: Judgments, Progressions, and the Rhetorical Theory of Narrative，2007)等著作中，费伦超越经典叙事理论的情节论，提出"叙事进程"(narrative progression)的概念，用它讨论叙事的动态变化及其互动因素。费伦认为叙事进程是个双动力系统，既有从开头经由中间再到结尾的"文本动力"支配叙事运动，也有"读者动力"的参与推动。文学要求读者投身于阅读，将叙事世界当成自己的世界，在此过程中，读者动力不可或缺。对于费伦的叙事进程论，我国学者申丹给予了积极肯定，但也指出它存在局限：费伦的叙事进程论是单一进程论。申丹发现有些文学文本叙事中除了情节的发展进程，还存在一股叙事的暗流，形成与情节平行的独立的叙事运动，她将之称为"隐性进程"(covert progression)，在此基础上提出了双重叙事进程(dual progression)理论。

什洛米斯·里蒙-凯南(Shlomith Rimmon-Kenan)在《叙事小说》(Narrative Fiction: Contemporary Poetics，1983)中指出，叙事学的理论化模式是开放的、动态的、永远没有尽头的。这正是当代叙事学理论异彩纷呈的原因。后经典叙事学除了上文详细介绍的修辞叙事学，还有其他一些值得关注的研究领域。女性主义叙事学重视对文本的历史语境的考察，讨论女性叙事与父权意识形态的冲突，代表人物有苏珊·兰瑟(Susan Lanser)等。后殖民叙事学将对形式结构的美学关注与文化批评相结合，分析后殖民小说和族裔身份政治，代表人物有玛丽昂·吉姆尼希(Marion Gymnich)等。认知叙事学借鉴认知科学领域的最新成果，从人的身心结构角度理解叙事，代表人物有戴维·赫尔曼(David Herman)、帕特里克·科尔姆·霍根(Patrick Colm Hogan)等。当代科幻小说热潮、生态主义引发对动植物叙事的关注等，都推动了非自然叙事学的发展，代表理论家有布赖恩·理查森(Brian Richardson)等。以玛丽-劳里·瑞安(Marie-Laure Ryan)为代表的跨媒介叙事学的学者们，则在当今数字信息时代，研究叙事如何应对各种新媒介的挑战，创造新的意义。

概而述之，结构主义继承了形式主义的文学本体论关注，但对文学的考察，从对文本世界的具象分析，迁移到文学系统层面，为理解文学的文化符号本质和结构性特征提供了整体性的视角。结构主义的另一个特点是长于分析综合性的文本体系，是神话体系研究、文学文类研究等的有效理论工具。结构主义的另一重要理论贡献是促成了叙事学的学科体系发展。目前，叙事学已经超越了经典时期的结构主义地平线，后经典叙事学响应文学创作与文化现象的新变化，不断拓展研究领域。同时，叙事学也打开视野，向跨学科领域汲取理论灵感，以丰富理论思想的内涵。在21世纪的今天，叙事学是最富有活力的理论研究领域之一。

主要文本阅读

列维-施特劳斯：《神话结构研究》

选文简介

《神话结构研究》一文1955年登载于《美国民俗学杂志》（*Journal of American Folklore*）。列维-施特劳斯在研究中发现，每个神话故事内容不同，彼此没有连续性，但世界各地的神话却仿佛遥相呼应，存在某种相似性。如何解释这种相似性？荣格从集体无意识角度出发，提出了神话原型解读。列维-施特劳斯却予以反对，认为心理学方法不重视神话之间的关系性，主张以语言学方法对神话体系进行考察。选文中，他以俄狄浦斯系列神话为例，示范了如何用结构主义方法解读神话：他将俄狄浦斯系列神话视为一个整体，将其中的各则神话按照最小意义单元——他称之为"神话素"（mytheme）——进行切分。每则神话中彼此承继的神话素，按照叙事顺序排成一个横列；不同神话故事中遥相呼应的神话素，按照同类原则，列在各自纵列。在横列和纵列组成的结构图表中，我们可以看到俄狄浦斯系列神话反映了"过度重视亲缘关系"和"过度漠视亲缘关系"、"过度亲近土地根系"和"过度漠视土地根系"的对立关系。这说明神话以二元对立为结构性原则。

From "The Structural Study of Myth"

Claude Lévi-Strauss (1908-2009)

To sum up the discussion at this point, we have so far made the following claims: (1) If there is a meaning to be found in mythology, it cannot reside in the isolated elements which enter into the composition of a myth, but only in the way those elements are combined. (2) Although myth belongs to the same category as language, being, as a matter of fact, only part of it, language in myth exhibits specific properties. (3) Those properties are only to be found *above* the ordinary linguistic level, that is, they exhibit more complex features than those which are to be found in any other kind of linguistic expression.

If the above three points are granted, at least as a working hypothesis, two consequences will follow: (1) Myth, like the rest of language, is made up of constituent units. (2) These constituent units presuppose the constituent units present in language when analyzed on other levels—namely, phonemes, morphemes, and sememes—but they, nevertheless, differ from the latter in the same way as the latter differ among themselves; they belong to a higher and more complex order. For this reason, we shall call them *gross constituent units*.

How shall we proceed in order to identify and isolate these gross constituent units or mythemes? We know that they cannot be found among phonemes, morphemes, or sememes, but only on a higher level; otherwise myth would become confused with any other kind of speech. Therefore, we should look for them on the sentence level. The only method we can suggest at this stage is to proceed tentatively, by trial and error, using as a check the principles which serve as a basis for any kind of structural analysis: economy of explanation; unity of solution; and ability to reconstruct the whole from a fragment, as well as later stages from previous ones.

The technique which has been applied so far by this writer consists in analyzing each myth individually, breaking down its story into the shortest possible sentences, and writing each sentence on an index card bearing a number corresponding to the unfolding of the story.

Practically each card will thus show that a certain function is, at a given time, linked to a given subject. Or, to put it otherwise, each gross constituent unit will consist of a *relation*.

However, the above definition remains highly unsatisfactory for two different reasons. First, it is well known to structural linguists that constituent units on all levels are made up of relations, and the true difference between our *gross* units and the others remains unexplained; second, we still find ourselves in the realm of a non-reversible time, since the numbers of the cards correspond to the unfolding of the narrative. Thus the specific character of mythological time, which as we have seen is both reversible and non-reversible, synchronic and diachronic, remains unaccounted for. From this springs a new hypothesis, which constitutes the very core of our argument: the true constituent units of a myth are not the isolated relations but *bundles of such relations*, and it is only as bundles that these relations can be put to use and combined so as to produce a meaning. Relations pertaining to the same bundle may appear diachronically at remote intervals, but when we have succeeded in grouping them together we have reorganized our myth according to a time referent of a new nature, corresponding to the prerequisite of the initial hypothesis, namely a two-dimensional time referent which is simultaneously diachronic and synchronic, and which accordingly integrates the characteristics of *langue* on the one hand, and those of *parole* on the other. To put it in even more linguistic terms, it is as though a phoneme were always made up of all its variants....

Now for a concrete example of the method we propose. We shall use the Oedipus myth, which is well known to everyone. I am well aware that the Oedipus myth has only reached us under late forms and through literary transmutations concerned more with esthetic and moral preoccupations than with religious or ritual ones, whatever these may have been. But we shall not interpret the Oedipus myth in literal terms, much less offer an explanation acceptable to the specialist. We simply wish to illustrate—and without reaching any conclusions with respect to it—a certain technique, whose use is probably not legitimate in this particular instance, owing to the problematic elements indicated above. The "demonstration" should therefore be conceived, not in terms of what the scientist means by this term, but at best in terms of what is meant by the street peddler, whose aim is not to achieve a concrete result, but to explain, as succinctly as possible, the functioning of the mechanical toy which he is trying to sell to the onlookers.

The myth will be treated as an orchestra score would be if it were unwittingly considered as a unilinear series; our task is to re-establish the correct arrangement. Say, for instance, we were confronted with a sequence of the type: 1, 2, 4, 7, 8, 2, 3, 4, 6, 8, 1, 4, 5, 7, 8, 1, 2, 5, 7, 3, 4, 5, 6, 8..., the assignment being to put all the 1's together, all the 2's, the 3's, etc.; the result is a chart:

1	2		4			7	8
	2	3	4		6		8
1			4	5		7	8
1	2			5		7	
		3	4	5	6		8

We shall attempt to perform the same kind of operation on the Oedipus myth, trying out several arrangements of the mythemes until we find one which is in harmony with the principles enumerated above. Let us suppose, for the sake of argument, that the best arrangement is the following (although it might certainly be improved with the help of a specialist in Greek mythology):

Cadmos seeks his sister Europa, ravished by Zeus			
		Cadmos kills the dragon	
	The Spartoi kill one another		
			Labdacos (Laios' father) = *lame* (?)
	Oedipus kills his father, Laios		Laios (Oedipus' father) = *left-sided* (?)
		Oedipus kills the Sphinx	
			Oedipus = *swollen-foot* (?)
Oedipus marries his mother, Jocasta			
	Eteocles kills his brother, Polynices		
Antigone buries her brother, Polynices, despite prohibition			

We thus find ourselves confronted with four vertical columns, each of which includes several relations belonging to the same bundle. Were we to *tell* the myth, we would disregard the columns and read the rows from left to right and from top to bottom. But if we want to *understand* the myth, then we will have to disregard one half of the diachronic dimension (top to bottom) and read from left to right, column after column, each one being considered as a unit.

All the relations belonging to the same column exhibit one common feature which it is our task to discover. For instance, all the events grouped in the first column on the left have something to do with blood relations which are overemphasized, that is, are more intimate than they should be. Let us say, then, that the first column has as its common feature the *overrating of blood relations*. It is obvious that the second column expresses the same thing, but inverted: *underrating of blood relations*. The third column refers to monsters being slain. As to the fourth, a few words of clarification are needed. The remarkable connotation of the surnames in Oedipus' father-line has often been noticed. However, linguists usually disregard it, since to them the only way to define the meaning of a term is to investigate all the contexts in which it appears, and personal names, precisely because they are used as such, are not accompanied by any context. With the method we propose to follow the objection disappears, since the myth itself provides its own context. The significance is no longer to be sought in the eventual meaning of each name, but in the fact that all the names have a common feature: all the hypothetical meanings (which may well remain hypothetical) refer to *difficulties in walking straight and standing upright*.

What then is the relationship between the two columns on the right? Column three refers to monsters. The dragon is a chthonian being which has to be killed in order that mankind be born from the Earth; the Sphinx is a monster unwilling to permit men to live. The last unit reproduces the first one, which has to do with the *autochthonous origin* of mankind. Since the monsters are overcome by men, we may thus say that the common feature of the third column is *denial of the autochthonous origin of man*.

This immediately helps us to understand the meaning of the fourth column. In mythology it is a universal characteristic of men born from the Earth that at the moment they emerge from the depth they either cannot walk or they walk clumsily. This is the case of the chthonian beings in the mythology of the Pueblo: Muyingwu, who leads the emergence, and the chthonian Shumaikoli are lame ("bleeding-foot," "sore-foot"). The same happens to the Koskimo of the Kwakiutl after they have been swallowed by the chthonian monster, Tsiakish: when they returned to the surface of the Earth "they limped forward or tripped side ways." Thus the common feature of the fourth column is *the persistence of the autochthonous origin of man*. It follows that column four is to column three as column one is to column two. The inability to connect two kinds of relationships is overcome (or rather replaced) by the assertion that contradictory relationships are identical inasmuch as they are both self-contradictory in a similar way. Although this is still a provisional formulation of the structure of mythical thought, it is sufficient at this stage.

Turning back to the Oedipus myth, we may now see what it means. The myth has to do with the inability, for a culture which holds the belief that mankind is autochthonous, to find a satisfactory transition between this theory and the knowledge that human beings are actually born from the union of man and woman. Although the problem obviously cannot be solved, the Oedipus myth provides a kind of logical tool which relates the original problem—born from one or born from two?—to the derivative problem: born from different or born from same? By a correlation of this type, the overrating of blood relations is to the underrating of blood relations as the attempt to escape autochthony is to the impossibility to succeed in it. Although experience contradicts theory, social life validates cosmology by its similarity of structure. Hence cosmology is true.

巴特：《神话学》

选文简介

《神话学》是巴特为法国文化杂志撰写的文章的合集。第一部分是对法国的各种流行文化现象的深入读解；第二部分是一篇名为"今日神话"的长文，对神话的意义生成机制进行了符号学解析，选文即出自这一部分。理解这一部分选文，需要紧扣两个隐含的关键词。第一个关键词是"符号性"。在巴特看来，神话是一种双重编码的符号体系，在能指、所指和符号均有清晰对应的第一重符号意义生成基础上，对符号进行再编码，叠加新意涵。这一机制在选文的符号图表中被揭示得十分清晰。第二个关键词是"意识形态"。巴特解剖神话，是为了揭秘日常生活中无处不在的意识形态符号体系。他发现，在诸多司空见惯的文化现象中，有神话的双重编码机制在发挥作用。这种机制掏空了符号意指的历史性，将意识形态"伪自然化"，使其能更好地发挥"神话"般的影响力。巴特的神话学提供了"去神秘化"的批判视角，是当代文化研究的重要理论工具。他在选文中，对来自当时法属殖民地的有色人种士兵向法国国旗敬礼的照片进行了详细分析，此分析已成为当代视觉文化批评的经典范例。

From *Mythologies*

Roland Barthes (1915-1980)

Let me therefore restate that any semiology postulates a relation between two terms, a signifier and a signified. This relation concerns objects which belong to different categories, and this is why it is not one of equality but one of equivalence. We must here be on our guard for despite common parlance which simply says that the signifier *expresses* the signified, we are dealing, in any semiological system, not with two, but with three different terms. For what we grasp is not at all one term after the other, but the correlation which unites them: there are, therefore, the signifier, the signified and the sign, which is the associative total of the first two terms. Take a bunch of roses: I use it to *signify* my passion. Do we have here, then, only a signifier and a signified, the roses and my passion? Not even that: to put it accurately, there are here only "passionified" roses. But on the plane of analysis, we do have three terms; for these roses weighted with passion perfectly and correctly allow themselves to be decomposed into roses and passion: the former and the latter existed before uniting and forming this third object, which is the sign. It is as true to say that on the plane of experience I cannot dissociate the roses from the message they carry, as to say that on the plane of analysis I cannot confuse the roses as signifier and the roses as sign: the signifier is empty, the sign is full, it is a meaning. Or take a black pebble: I can make it signify in several ways, it is a mere signifier; but if I weigh it with a definite signified (a death sentence, for instance, in an anonymous vote), it will become a sign. Naturally, there are between the signifier, the signified and the sign, functional implications (such as that of the part to the whole) which are so close that to analyze them may seem futile; but we shall see in a moment that this distinction has a capital importance for the study of myth as semiological schema.

Naturally these three terms are purely formal, and different contents can be given to them. Here are a few examples: for Saussure, who worked on a particular but methodologically exemplary semiological system—the language or *langue*—the signified is the concept, the signifier is the acoustic image (which is mental) and the relation between concept and image is the sign (the word, for instance), which is a concrete entity. For Freud, as is well known, the human psyche is a stratification of tokens or representatives. One term (I refrain from giving it any precedence) is constituted by the manifest meaning of behavior, another, by its latent or real meaning (it is, for instance, the substratum of the dream); as for the third term, it is here also a correlation of the first two: it is the dream itself in its totality, the parapraxis (a mistake in speech or behavior) or the neurosis, conceived as compromises, as economies effected thanks to the joining of a form (the first term) and an intentional function (the second term). We can see here how necessary it is to distinguish the sign from the signifier: a dream, to Freud, is no more its manifest datum than its latent content: it is the functional union of these two terms. In Sartrean criticism, finally (I shall keep to these three well-known examples), the signified is constituted by the original crisis in the subject (the separation from his mother for Baudelaire, the naming of the theft for Genet); literature as discourse forms the signifier; and the relation between crisis and discourse defines the work, which is a signification. Of course, this tri-dimensional pattern, however constant in its form, is actualized in different ways: one cannot therefore say too often that semiology can have its unity only at the level of forms, not contents; its field is limited, it knows only one operation: reading, or deciphering.

In myth, we find again the tri-dimensional pattern which I have just described: the signifier, the signified and the sign. But myth is a peculiar system, in that it is constructed from a semiological chain which existed before it: it is a *second-order semiological system*. That which is a sign (namely the associative total of a concept and an image) in the first system, becomes a mere signifier in the second. We must here recall that the materials of mythical speech (the language itself, photography, painting, posters, rituals, objects, etc.), however different at the start, are reduced to a pure signifying function as soon as they are caught by myth. Myth sees in them only the same raw material; their unity is that they all come down to the status of a mere language. Whether it deals with alphabetical or pictorial writing, myth wants to see in them only a sum of signs, a global sign, the final term of a first semiological chain. And it is precisely this final term which will become the first term of the greater system which it builds and of which it is only a part. Everything happens as if myth shifted the formal system of the first significations sideways. As this lateral shift is essential for

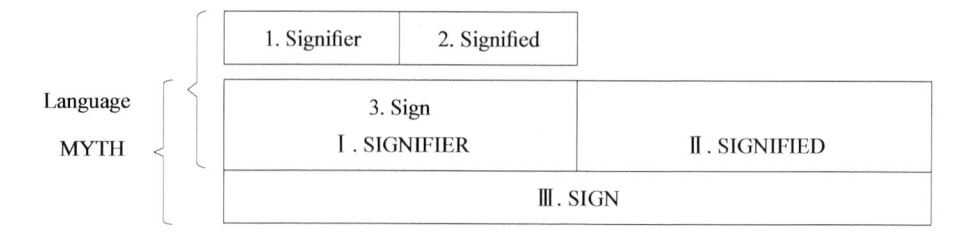

	1. Signifier	2. Signified	
Language / MYTH	3. Sign / I. SIGNIFIER		II. SIGNIFIED
	III. SIGN		

the analysis of myth, I shall represent it in the following way, it being understood, of course, that the spatialization of the pattern is here only a metaphor:

It can be seen that in myth there are two semiological systems, one of which is staggered in relation to the other: a linguistic system, the language (or the modes of representation which are assimilated to it), which I shall call the *language-object*, because it is the language which myth gets hold of in order to build its own system; and myth itself, which I shall call *metalanguage*, because it is a second language, *in which* one speaks about the first. When he reflects on a metalanguage, the semiologist no longer needs to ask himself questions about the composition of the language-object, he no longer has to take into account the details of the linguistic schema; he will only need to know its total term, or global sign, and only inasmuch as this term lends itself to myth. This is why the semiologist is entitled to treat in the same way writing and pictures: what he retains from them is the fact that they are both *signs*, that they both reach the threshold of myth endowed with the same signifying function, that they constitute, one just as much as the other, a language-object.

It is now time to give one or two examples of mythical speech. I shall borrow the first from an observation by Valery. I am a pupil in the second form in a French *lycée*. I open my Latin grammar, and I read a sentence, borrowed from Aesop or Phaedrus: *quia ego nominor leo*. I stop and think. There is something ambiguous about this statement: on the one hand, the words in it do have a simple meaning: *because my name is lion*. And on the other hand, the sentence is evidently there in order to signify something else to me. Inasmuch as it is addressed to me, a pupil in the second form, it tells me clearly: I am a grammatical example meant to illustrate the rule about the agreement of the predicate. I am even forced to realize that the sentence in no way *signifies* its meaning to me, that it tries very little to tell me something about the lion and what sort of name he has; its true and fundamental signification is to impose itself on me as the presence of a certain agreement of the predicate. I conclude that I am faced with a particular, greater, semiological system, since it is co-extensive with the language: there is, indeed, a signifier, but this signifier is itself formed by a sum of signs, it is in itself a first semiological system (*my name is lion*). Thereafter, the formal pattern is correctly unfolded: there is a signified (*I am a grammatical example*) and there is a global signification, which is none other than the correlation of the signifier and the signified; for neither the naming of the lion nor the grammatical example are given separately.

And here is now another example: I am at the barber's, and a copy of *Paris-Match* is offered to me. On the cover, a young Negro in a French uniform is saluting, with his eyes uplifted, probably fixed on a fold of the tricolor. All this is the *meaning* of the picture. But, whether naively or not, I see very well what it signifies to me: that France is a great Empire, that all her sons, without any color discrimination, faithfully serve under her flag, and that there is no better answer to the detractors of an alleged colonialism than the zeal shown by this Negro in serving his so-called oppressors. I am therefore again faced with a greater semiological system: there is a signifier, itself already formed with a previous system (*a black soldier is giving the French salute*); there is a signified (it is here a purposeful mixture of Frenchness and militariness); finally, there is a presence of the signified through the signifier.

Before tackling the analysis of each term of the mythical system, one must agree on terminology. We now know that the signifier can be looked at, in myth, from two points of view: as the final term of the linguistic system, or as the first term of the mythical system. We therefore need two names. On the plane of language, that is, as the final term of the first system, I shall call the signifier: *meaning* (*my name is lion, a Negro is giving the French salute*); on the plane of myth, I shall call it: *form*. In the case of the signified, no ambiguity is possible: we shall retain the name *concept*. The third term is the correlation of the first two: in the linguistic system, it is the *sign*; but it is not possible to use this word again without ambiguity, since in myth (and this is the chief peculiarity of the latter), the signifier is already formed by the *signs* of the language. I shall call the third term of myth the *signification*. This word is here all the better justified since myth has in fact a double function: it points out and it notifies, it makes us understand something and it imposes it on us.

热奈特：《叙事话语》

选文简介

在《叙事话语》中，热奈特以时间性议题开篇，解释了叙事话语中时间复杂性的由来：时间是双重性的，存在故事时间和叙事时间的差异。这种差异使叙述中的时间畸变随时可能发生。选文重点讨论了"时间倒错"（anachrony），即故事时间与叙事时间顺序之间的各种不协调。其中涉及两个概念：倒叙（analepsis）和预叙（prolepsis）。倒叙有助于营造高潮感，增加戏剧性，还可以起到解释的作用。预叙的好处是可以制造悬疑，揭出事实的冰山一角，引起读者的好奇心。在叙事文本中，预叙比倒叙少见，但《伊利亚特》《奥德赛》和《埃涅阿斯纪》等经典史诗，都用了预叙的手法，用预期性的总结，传达宿命论的讯息。叙事时间通过倒叙与预叙等手法，摆脱了对客观时间的依赖，有利于文学作品从时间性角度体现生命的丰富意蕴。《叙事话语》中，热奈特不断用他的理论体系来解读《追忆似水年华》这部意识流小说。《追忆似水年华》在叙事时间、叙事分层、叙事视角等方面的现代主义叙事探索，是热奈特思考和建构叙事理论的动力之一。

From *Narrative Discourse*

Gérard Genette (1930-2018)

Narrative Time?

Narrative is a...doubly temporal sequence....There is the time of the thing told and the time of the narrative (the time of the signified and the time of the signifier). This duality not only renders possible all the temporal distortions that are commonplace in narratives (three years of the hero's life summed up in two sentences of a novel or in a few shots of a "frequentative" montage in film, etc.). More basically, it invites us to consider that one of the functions of narrative is to invent one time scheme in terms of another time scheme. [Christian Metz, *Film Language: A Semiotics of the Cinema.*]

The temporal duality so sharply emphasized here, and referred to by German theoreticians as the opposition between *erzählte Zeit* (story time) and *Erzählzeit* (narrative time), is a typical characteristic not only of cinematic narrative but also of oral narrative, at all its levels of aesthetic elaboration, including the fully "literary" level of epic recitation or dramatic narration (the narrative of Théramène, for example). It is less relevant perhaps in other forms of narrative expression, such as the *roman-photo* or the comic strip (or a pictorial strip, like the predella of Urbino, or an embroidered strip, like the "tapestry" of Queen Matilda), which, while making up sequences of images and thus requiring a successive or diachronic reading, also lend themselves to, and even invite, a kind of global and synchronic look—or at least a look whose direction is no longer determined by the sequence of images. The status of written literary narrative in this respect is even more difficult to establish. Like the oral or cinematic narrative, it can only be "consumed," and therefore actualized, in a *time* that is obviously reading time, and even if the sequentiality of its components can be undermined by a capricious, repetitive, or selective reading, that undermining nonetheless stops short of perfect analexia: one can run a film backward, image by image, but one cannot read a text backward, letter by letter, or even word by word, or even sentence by sentence, without its ceasing to be a text. Books are a little more constrained than people sometimes say they are by the celebrated *linearity* of the linguistic signifier, which is easier to deny in theory than eliminate in fact. However, there is no question here of identifying the status of written narrative (literary or not) with that of oral narrative. The temporality of written narrative is to some extent conditional or instrumental; produced in time, like everything else, written narrative exists in space and as space, and the time needed for "consuming" it is the time needed for *crossing* or *traversing* it, like a road or a field. The narrative text, like every other text, has no other temporality than what it borrows, metonymically, from its own reading.

This state of affairs, we will see below, has certain consequences for our discussion, and at times we will have to correct, or try to correct, the effects of metonymic displacement; but we must first take that displacement for granted, since it forms part of the narrative game, and therefore accept literally the quasi-fiction of *Erzählzeit*, this false time standing in for a true time and to be treated—with the combination of reservation and acquiescence that this involves—as a *pseudo-time*.

Having taken these precautions, we will study relations between the time of the story and the (pseudo-) time of the narrative according to what seem to me to be three essential determinations: connections between the temporal *order* of succession of the events in the story and the pseudo-temporal order of their arrangement in the narrative, which will be the subject of the first chapter; connections between the variable *duration* of these events or story sections and the pseudo-duration (in fact, length of text) of their telling in the narrative—connections, thus, of *speed*—which will be the subject of the second chapter; finally, connections of *frequency*, that is (to limit myself to an approximate formulation), relations between the repetitive capacities of the story and those of the narrative, relations to which the third chapter will be devoted.

Anachronies

To study the temporal order of a narrative is to compare the order in which events or temporal sections are arranged in the narrative discourse with the order of succession these same events or temporal segments have in the story, to the extent that story order is explicitly indicated by the narrative itself or inferable from one or another indirect clue. Obviously this reconstitution is not always possible, and it becomes useless for certain extreme cases like the novels of Robbe-Grillet, where temporal reference is deliberately sabotaged. It is just as obvious that in the classical narrative, on the other hand, reconstitution is most often not only possible, because in those texts narrative discourse never inverts the order of events without saying so, but also necessary, and precisely for the same reason: when a narrative segment begins with an indication like "Three months earlier..." we must take into account both that this scene comes *after* in the narrative, and that it is supposed to have come *before* in the story: each of these, or rather the relationship between them (of contrast or of dissonance), is basic to the narrative text, and suppressing this relationship by eliminating one of its members is not only not sticking to the text, but is quite simply killing it.

Pinpointing and measuring these narrative *anachronies* (as I will call the various types of discordance between the two orderings of story and narrative) implicitly assume the existence of a kind of zero degree that would be a condition of perfect temporal correspondence between narrative and story. This point of reference is more hypothetical than real. Folklore narrative habitually conforms, at least in its major articulations, to chronological order, but our (Western) literary tradition, in contrast, was inaugurated by a characteristic effect of anachrony. In the eighth line of the *Iliad*, the narrator, having evoked the quarrel between Achilles and Agamemnon that he proclaims as the starting point of his narrative (*ex hou de ta prôta*), goes back about ten days to reveal the cause of the quarrel in some 140 retrospective lines (affront to Chryses—Apollo's anger—plague). We know that this beginning in *medias res*, followed by an expository return to an earlier period of time, will become one of the formal topoi of epic, and we also know how faithfully the style of novelistic narration follows in this respect the style of its remote ancestor, even in the heart of the "realistic" nineteenth century....We will thus not be so foolish as to claim that anachrony is either a rarity or a modern invention. On the contrary, it is one of the traditional resources of literary narration....

Analepses

Every anachrony constitutes, with respect to the narrative into which it is inserted—onto which it is grafted—a narrative that is temporally second, subordinate to the first in a sort of narrative syntax that we met in the analysis we undertook above of a very short fragment from *Jean Santeuil*. We will henceforth call the temporal level of narrative with respect to which anachrony is defined as such, "first narrative." Of course—and this we have already verified—the embeddings can be more complex, and an anachrony can assume the role of first narrative with respect to another that it carries; and more generally, with respect to an anachrony the totality of the context can be taken as first narrative....

This distinction is not as useless as it might seem at first sight. In effect, external analepses and internal analepses (or the internal part of mixed analepses) function for purposes of narrative analysis in totally different ways, at least on one point that seems to me essential. External analepses, by the very fact that they are external, never at any moment risk interfering with the first narrative, for their only function is to fill out the first narrative by enlightening the reader on one or another "antecedent." This is obviously the case with some of the examples already mentioned and it is also, and just as typically, the case with *Un amour de Swann* in the *Recherche du temps perdu*. The case is otherwise with internal analepses: since their temporal field is contained within the temporal field of the first narrative, they present an obvious risk of redundancy or collision....

We have seen how the determination of *reach* allowed us to divide analepses into two classes, external and internal, depending on whether the point to which they reach is located outside or inside the temporal field of the first narrative. The mixed class—not, after all, much resorted to—is in fact determined by a characteristic of *extent*, since this class consists of external analepses prolonged to rejoin and pass beyond the starting point of the first narrative....

Prolepses

Anticipation, or temporal prolepsis, is clearly much less frequent than the inverse figure, at least in the Western narrative tradition—although each of the three great early epics, the *Iliad*, the *Odyssey*, and the *Aeneid*, begins with a sort of anticipatory summary that to a certain extent justifies the formula Todorov applied to Homeric narrative: "plot of predestination." The concern with narrative suspense that is characteristic of the "classical" conception of the novel ("classical" in the broad sense, and whose center of gravity is, rather, in the nineteenth century) does not easily come to terms with such a practice. Neither, moreover, does the traditional fiction of a narrator who must appear more or less to discover the story at the same time that he tells it. Thus we will find very few prolepses in a Balzac, a Dickens, or a Tolstoy, even if the common practice, as we have already seen, of beginning *in medias res* (or yet, I may venture to say, *in ultimas res*), sometimes gives the illusion of it. It goes without saying that a certain load of "predestination" hangs over the main part of the narrative in *Manon Lescaut* (where we know, even before Des Grieux opens his story, that it ends with a deportation), or *a fortiori* in *The Death of Ivan Ilych*, which begins with its epilogue.

The "first-person" narrative lends itself better than any other to anticipation, by the very fact of its avowedly retrospective character, which authorizes the narrator to allude to the future and in particular to his present situation, for these to some extent form part of his role. Robinson Crusoe can tell us almost at the beginning that the lecture his father gave to turn him aside from nautical adventures was "truly prophetic," even though at the time he had no idea of it, and Rousseau, with the episode of the combs, does not fail to vouch for not only his past innocence but also the vigor of his retrospective indignation: "In writing this I feel my pulse quicken yet." Nonetheless, the *Recherche du temps perdu* uses prolepsis to an extent probably equaled in the whole history of narrative, even autobiographical narrative, and is thus privileged territory for the study of this type of narrative anachrony....

The importance of "anachronic" narrative in the *Recherche du temps perdu* is obviously connected to the retrospectively synthetic character of Proustian narrative, which is totally present in the narrator's mind at every moment. Ever since the day when the narrator in a trance perceived the unifying significance of his story, he never ceases to hold all of its threads simultaneously, to apprehend simultaneously all of its places and all of its moments, to be capable of establishing a multitude of "telescopic" relationships amongst them: a ubiquity that is spatial but also temporal, an "omnitemporality."

费伦：《体验小说》

选文简介

《体验小说》是费伦修辞性叙事理论体系建构中的重要著作。在这本书中，他在继续强调"叙事进程"论的基础上，提出"叙事判断"论，指出读者在阅读中形成的叙事判断反映了叙事形式、叙事伦理、叙事审美的交叉。选文出自这本著作的前言部分。费伦在选文中总结了虚构叙事的三个命题和五个原则，这是他著作中讨论叙事判断的前提。他认为叙事是修辞行为，以作者主体、文本现象（包括文本关系）和读者反应之间的循环关系为基础，不断相互反馈，形成回路。在作者、文本和读者的多层次交流中，读者调动智力，也牵动情感。此外，读者的道德价值观与审美价值观也在发挥作用。这些都说明叙事判断至关重要。

From *Experiencing Fiction*

James Phelan (1951-)

When we first begin reading narratives (or have them read to us), we learn both that they typically have good guys (or gals), e.g. Cinderella and the Prince, and bad guys (or gals), e.g. Cinderella's stepmother and her stepsisters, and that the narrative itself signals which characters are which....One of the main arguments of this book will be that these judgments are as crucial for the kinds of engagements we make with these sophisticated narratives as our judgments in "Cinderella" are for our engagement with the fairy tale.

To take another example, consider this passage from Ring Lardner's "Haircut," in which Lardner's narrator, Whitey the barber, tells his new customer from out of town a little about Jim Kendall and his wife:

> As I say, she'd of divorced Jim, only she seen that she couldn't support herself and the kids and she was always hopin' that some day Jim would cut out his habits and give her

more than two or three dollars a week. They was a time when she would go to whoever he was workin' for and ask them to give her his wages, but after she done this once or twice, he beat her to it by borrowin' most of his pay in advance. He told it all around town, how he had outfoxed his Missus. He certainly was a caution!

What stands out here is not only that we judge Jim much more negatively than Whitey does (we recognize Jim's selfishness and meanness; Whitey regards him as an entertaining trickster), but also that we judge Whitey negatively too (though not mean and selfish himself, he is so morally imperceptive that he does not recognize Jim's meanness and selfishness). But as we judge this character and this narrator negatively, we are also approving the moral vision of the implied Ring Lardner because we feel he is guiding us to make those judgments. In addition, we are tacitly registering Lardner's skill in communicating these judgments to us while using only Whitey's discourse. Consequently, our engagement is similar to but more complicated than it is in "Cinderella." We regard Kendall as cruel and therefore dangerous, Whitey as obtuse and perhaps therefore dangerous, and Lardner as a skilled practitioner with whom we'd like to collaborate further.

We could of course continue up the ladder of sophisticated narratives to look at cases in which our moral discriminations among characters and our corresponding engagements are much more nuanced than they are in "Haircut"—and even to narratives that don't seem to give sufficient signals for us to make clear and firm discriminations. Later in this book I will climb that ladder, but now I want to pause at Lardner's rung because it is sufficiently high to allow me to lay out the threefold thesis of this book. (1) The judgments we readers of narrative make about characters and tellers (both narrators and authors) are crucial to our experience—and understanding—of narrative form. By form I mean the particular fashioning of the elements, techniques, and structure of a narrative in the service of a set of readerly engagements that lead to particular final effects on the implied audience. (2) Narrative form, in turn, is experienced through the temporal process of reading and responding to narrative. Consequently, to account for that experience of form we need to focus on narrative progression, that is, the synthesis of both the textual dynamics that govern the movement of narrative from beginning through middle to end and the readerly dynamics—what I have so far been calling our engagement—that both follow from and influence those textual dynamics. (3) As key elements of narrative experience, narrative judgments and narrative progressions are responsible for the various components of that experience, especially the significant interrelation of form, ethics, and aesthetics—even as judgments and progressions do not totally explain everything we might want to know about ethics and aesthetics.

This threefold thesis itself is best understood within a broader rhetorical approach to narrative that can be sketched through a discussion of its five main principles. The first principle is that narrative can be fruitfully understood as a rhetorical act: somebody telling somebody else on some occasion and for some purpose(s) that something happened. In fictional narrative, the rhetorical situation is doubled: the narrator tells her story to her narratee for her purposes, while the author communicates to her audience for her own purposes both that story and the narrator's telling of it. As I argue in *Living to Tell About It*, recognizing the consequences of this doubled communicative situation (one text, more than one teller, more than one audience, more than one purpose) is fundamental to a rhetorical understanding of character narration....

Second, the approach assumes a recursive relationship (or feedback loop) among authorial agency, textual phenomena (including intertextual relations), and reader response. In other words, for the purposes of interpreting narratives, the approach assumes that texts are designed by authors in order to affect readers in particular ways; that those designs are conveyed through the words, techniques, structures, forms, and dialogic relations of texts as well as the genres and conventions readers use to understand them; and that reader responses are a function of and, thus, a guide to how designs are created through textual and intertextual phenomena. At the same time, reader responses are also a test of the efficacy of those designs.

Third, the model of audience behind the approach's conception of reader response is the one developed by Peter J. Rabinowitz that I have modified slightly. This model identifies four main audiences: the flesh-and-blood or actual reader, the authorial audience (the author's ideal reader or what I have called the implied reader above), the narrative audience (the observer position within the narrative world that the flesh-and-blood reader assumes), and the narratee (the audience addressed by the narrator). The model assumes that the flesh-and-blood (or actual) reader seeks to enter the authorial audience; hence, when I speak of what "we" readers do in response to a narrative text, I am referring to the activities of the authorial audience....

Methodologically, the feedback loop among author, text, and reader means that the rhetorical critic may begin the interpretive inquiry from any one of these points on the rhetorical triangle, but the inquiry will necessarily consider how each point both influences and can be influenced by the other two....

Fourth, audiences will develop interests and responses of three kinds, each related to a particular component of the narrative: mimetic, thematic, and synthetic. Responses to the mimetic component involve an audience's interest in the characters as possible people and in the narrative world as like our own, that is, hypothetically or conceptually possible; responses to the mimetic component include our evolving judgments and emotions, our desires, hopes, expectations, satisfactions, and disappointments. Responses to the thematic component involve an interest in the ideational function of the characters and in the cultural, ideological, philosophical, or ethical issues being addressed by the narrative. Responses to the synthetic component involve an audience's interest in and attention to the characters and to the larger narrative as artificial constructs. The relationship among an audience's relative interests in these different components will vary from narrative to narrative depending on the nature of its progression. Some narratives are dominated by mimetic interests, some by thematic, and others by synthetic, but developments in the progression can generate new relations among those interests. Furthermore, there is no necessary reason why a narrative cannot make two or even all three interests important....

Fifth, the approach assumes that the rhetorical act of telling a story entails a multileveled communication from author to audience, one involving the audience's intellect, emotions, and values (both moral and aesthetic), and that these levels interact with each other.

思考题

1. 列维-施特劳斯是如何解读俄狄浦斯系列神话的？他的发现是什么？
2. 巴特所说的"神话"指的是什么？它和列维-施特劳斯所说的"神话"有什么不同？
3. 巴特从符号学角度解读"神话"机制。他这样做的目的是什么？
4. 热奈特为什么说叙事中时间具有双重性？双重性具体指什么？
5. 热奈特所说的"时间倒错"是什么？他在选文中讨论了哪些时间倒错的形式？它们各自有什么作用？
6. 费伦在选文中概括了他对修辞叙事学的认识，它包含三个命题和五个主要原则。它们分别是什么？

讨论题

1. 请根据巴特的"神话"理论，选择一部你认为含有"神话"因素的文学作品或影视作品，或者选择一种你认为具有"神话"功能的文化现象（照片、广告等），对其进行解读。
2. 请选择一部现代主义小说，比如约瑟夫·康拉德的《黑暗的心》、威廉·福克纳的《喧哗与骚动》等，运用热奈特的叙事时间理论，对其中的时间倒错现象进行分析，解读其意图。

补充文本选摘与评述

索绪尔：《普通语言学教程》
From *Course in General Linguistics*

Ferdinand de Saussure (1857-1913)

Chapter V: Syntagmatic and Associative Relations

1. Definitions

In a language-state everything is based on relations. How do they function?

Relations and differences between linguistic terms fall into two distinct groups, each of which generates a certain class of values. The opposition between the two classes gives a better understanding of the nature of each class. They correspond to two forms of our mental activity, both indispensable to the life of language.

In discourse, on the one hand, words acquire relations based on the linear nature of language because they are chained together. This rules out the possibility of pronouncing two elements simultaneously. The elements are arranged in sequence on the chain of speaking. Combinations supported by linearity are *syntagms*. The syntagm is always composed of two or more consecutive units (e.g. French *relire* "re-read," *contre tous* "against everyone," *la vie humaine* "human life," *Dieu est bon* "God is good," *s'il fait beau temps, nous sortirons* "if the weather is nice, we'll go out," etc.). In the syntagm a term acquires its value only because it stands in opposition to everything that precedes or follows it, or to both.

Outside discourse, on the other hand, words acquire relations of a different kind. Those that have something in common are associated in the memory, resulting in groups marked by diverse relations. For instance, the French word *enseignement* "teaching" will unconsciously call to mind a host of other words (*enseigner* "teach," *renseigner* "acquaint," etc.; or *armement* "armament," *changement* "amendment," etc.; or *éducation* "education," *apprentissage* "apprenticeship," etc.). All those words are related in some way.

We see that the co-ordinations formed outside discourse differ strikingly from those formed inside discourse. Those formed outside discourse are not supported by linearity. Their seat is in the brain; they are a part of the inner storehouse that makes up the language of each speaker. They are *associative relations*.

The syntagmatic relation is *in praesentia*. It is based on two or more terms that occur in an effective series. Against this, the associative relation unites terms *in absentia* in a potential mnemonic series.

From the associative and syntagmatic viewpoint a linguistic unit is like a fixed part of a building, e.g. a column. On the one hand, the column has a certain relation to the architrave that it supports; the arrangement of the two units in space suggests the syntagmatic relation. On the other hand, if the column is Doric, it suggests a mental comparison of this style with others (Ionic, Corinthian, etc.) although none of these elements is present in space: the relation is associative.

巴赫金:《小说的话语》
From "Discourse in the Novel"

Mikhail Bakhtin (1895-1975)

Heteroglossia, once incorporated into the novel (whatever the forms for its incorporation), is *another's speech in another's language*, serving to express authorial intentions but in a refracted way. Such speech constitutes a special type of *double-voiced discourse*. It serves two speakers at the same time and expresses simultaneously two different intentions: the direct intention of the character who is speaking, and the refracted intention of the author. In such discourse there are two voices, two meanings and two expressions. And all the while these two voices are dialogically interrelated, they—as it were—know about each other (just as two exchanges in a dialogue know of each other and are structured in this mutual knowledge of each other); it is as if they actually hold a conversation with each other. Double-voiced discourse is always internally dialogized. Examples of this would be comic, ironic or parodic discourse, the refracting discourse of a narrator, refracting discourse in the language of a character and finally the discourse of a whole incorporated genre—all these discourses are double-voiced and internally dialogized. A potential dialogue is embedded in them, one as yet unfolded, a concentrated dialogue of two voices, two world views, two languages....

The double-voicedness one finds in prose is of another sort altogether. There—on the rich soil of novelistic prose—double-voicedness draws its energy, its dialogized ambiguity, not from *individual* dissonances, misunderstandings or contradictions (however tragic, however firmly grounded in individual destinies); in the novel, this double-voicedness sinks its roots deep into a fundamental, socio-linguistic speech diversity and multi-languagedness. True, even in the novel heteroglossia is by and large always personified, incarnated in individual human figures, with disagreements and oppositions individualized. But such oppositions of individual wills and minds are submerged in *social* heteroglossia, they are reconceptualized through it. Oppositions between individuals are only surface upheavals of the untamed elements in social heteroglossia, surface manifestations of those elements that play *on* such individual oppositions, make them contradictory, saturate their consciousness and discourses with a more fundamental speech diversity....

If the art of poetry, as a utopian philosophy of genres, gives rise to the conception of a purely poetic, extrahistorical language, a language far removed from the petty rounds of everyday life, a language of the gods—then it must be said that the art of prose is close to a conception of languages as historically concrete and living things. The prose art presumes a deliberate feeling for the historical and social concreteness of living discourse, as well as its relativity, a feeling for its participation in historical becoming and in social struggle; it deals with discourse that is still warm from that struggle and hostility, as yet unresolved and still fraught with hostile intentions and accents; prose art finds discourse in this state and subjects it to the dynamic-unity of its own style.

瑞安:《故事的变身》
From *Avatars of Story*

Marie-Laure Ryan (1946-)

I regard narratology as an unfinished project, and if classical narratology fails the test of interactive textuality, this does not necessarily mean that interactive textuality fails the test of narrativity. It rather means that narratology must expand beyond its original territory. In this chapter I propose to investigate what needs to be done to allow narratology to deal with interactive digital texts. Needless to say, the development of a digital narratology will be a long-term collaborative project, and I can only sketch here what I consider to be its most urgent concerns....

Yet if interactivity is the property that makes the greatest difference between old and new media, it does not facilitate storytelling, because narrative meaning presupposes the linearity and unidirectionality of time, logic, and causality, while a system of choices involves a nonlinear or multilinear branching structure, such as a tree, a rhizome, or a network. Narrative meaning, moreover, is the product of the top-down planning of a storyteller or designer, while interactivity requires a bottom-up input from the user. It will consequently take a seamless (some will say miraculous) convergence of bottom-up input and top-down design to produce well-formed narrative patterns. This convergence requires a certain type of textual architecture and a certain kind of user involvement. It would be of course easy to constrain the user's choices in such a way that they will always fit into a predefined narrative pattern; but the aesthetics of interactive narrative demand a choice sufficiently broad to give the user a sense of freedom, and a narrative pattern sufficiently adaptable to those choices to give the impression of being generated on the fly. The ideal top-down design should disguise itself as an emergent story, giving users both confidence that their efforts will be rewarded by a coherent narrative and the feeling of acting of their own free will, rather than being the puppets of the designer.

选文评述

《普通语言学教程》选文中，索绪尔讨论了符号体系内部的两种关系。一是句段关系：语言要素遵从线性规则，连续排列，组成有一定长度的句段。二是联想关系：某些方面具有共性的词汇，通过记忆汇成集合。句段关系发生在话语之内，语言要素具有在场性；联想关系发生在话语之外，缺席的潜在的要素之间存在相互关联。为了说明这两种关系，索绪尔用建筑学进行类比：语言单位就像建筑物的柱子。柱子和柱顶过梁这两个空间要素的排列体现了句段关系。柱子的陶立克式风格让人想到爱奥尼亚式、科林斯式等其他风格的柱子，这时起作用的是联想关系。句段关系将联想关系中存在的多种可能性变成了唯一的言说事实，体现了语言的实践应用与语言体系之间的结构性关联。

《小说的话语》的作者巴赫金是俄国最重要的文学理论家之一。他的理论立场深具复杂性：他对文学形式的关注源自俄国形式主义；同时，他强调文学的历史性和意识形态性，这反映了他的马克思主义立场。本章收录他的选文，是为了提示他的思想与结构主义乃至下一章要讨论的去中心化的后结构主义也存在亲缘关系。比如他著名的复调理论（dialogism）就是如此。选文中，巴赫金讨论了小说的话语特征。俄国形式主义重视诗性语言，巴赫金则重视小说话语。巴赫金认为，现实社会中语言具有多样性，即杂语性。"杂语"在小说中引发表达的"双声性"：同时有两个言说者，展现了两种表达方式、两种意图、两种世界观，它们彼此竞争，使小说内部出现对话性。这也体现了小说与诗歌在话语层面的本质区别：诗歌艺术远离日常生活的琐碎，用诗性的超越历史的语言建构乌托邦；小说的话语是历史性的、鲜活的、多声部的，渗透着历史意识和斗争意识，形成了动态的统一。

《故事的变身》中,瑞安指出,叙事学应根据时代新媒介的变化主动应对互动数字文本的挑战。互动数字文本多种多样,不仅包括超文本小说,而且还包括基于文本的历险游戏、互动戏剧、单用户电子游戏、多用户网络角色扮演游戏等。它们的共同特点是用户享有叙事的选择权——唯有选择才能带来互动。为了提供选择,互动文本的系统需要采用树枝状、根茎状、网络状等非线性或多线性的分岔结构;但叙事的意义生成,需要遵循历时性顺序,时间、逻辑、因果都是单向性的。这构成第一组矛盾。根据互动性原则,用户要求的是自下而上的输入方式;而互动脚本只能源于脚本作者自上而下的叙事设计。这构成第二组矛盾。为了应对矛盾带来的挑战,瑞安认为互动叙事美学需要提供多样性的选择,使用户既能在互动中享受连贯的叙事,又能行使自由意志。后文中,瑞安对互动叙事学的文本架构、互动性的类型、参数建构等进行了讨论。随着互动数字技术日新月异的发展,瑞安的技术讨论在部分细节上已过时,但这也恰好说明瑞安所倡导的跨媒介叙事研究深具必要性。

关键术语释例

1. 二元对立(binary opposition):二元对立是结构主义的重要概念,指二元项的意义生成于彼此的对立关系之中。索绪尔语言学中,能指/所指、历时性/共时性等概念,体现了符号系统的二元对立原则。列维–施特劳斯的人类学分析则揭示出人类的二元对立思维范式。格雷马斯的行动元叙事学,也以二元对立为基础。事实上,在人类语言、文学、社会文化生活等诸多领域,都能看到二元对立的思维模式在发挥结构性作用。但意识形态常常会利用二元对立,将其中一项拔高,确立为优势项,使对立项自然而然地受到贬低和压制。比如,父权体制中,男性与女性看似平等,事实上,男性享有主导特权,女性则是顺从者。此外,二元对立是封闭结构,二元项摒除了其他项存在的可能性,容易导致意义的窄化。为此,有必要对以二元对立为主导的结构体系进行慎重反思。

2. 视点(point of view,或译为"视角""叙述眼光"):视点指叙述者在叙事交流中的位置和功能,站在什么位置、看到多少、理解了什么、能讲什么、讲了什么,都与此有关。眼光不同的人物处在不同的观察角度,在叙述同一事件时,会讲出不同的版本。亨利·詹姆斯指出,观察视点的限制会对叙事构成挑战。珀西·卢伯克(Percy Lubbock)将此概念按照第一人称、第三人称、内在性、外在性与全知性进行了分类。热奈特则反对卢伯克的分类,认为这些分类不能清晰显示谁是叙述者、谁是观察角度的提供者。为此，他提出要用"聚焦"（focalization）替代"视点"概念，以凸显观察者的目光所在。

推荐书目

Bal, Mieke. *Narratology: Introduction to the Theory of Narrative*. Toronto: University of Toronto Press, 2017.

Culler, Jonathan. *Structuralist Poetics: Structuralism, Linguistics and the Study of Literature*. London: Routledge, 2022.

Dosse, François. *History of Structuralism*. Trans. Deborah Glassman. Minneapolis: University of Minnesota Press, 1997.

Hawkes, Terence. *Structuralism and Semiotics*. London: Routledge, 2003.

Herman, David. *The Cambridge Companion to Narrative*. Cambridge: Cambridge University Press, 2007.

Scholes, Robert, James Phelan, and Robert Kellogg. *The Nature of Narrative.* Oxford: Oxford University Press, 2006.

Sturrock, John. *Structuralism.* Malden: Wiley-Blackwell, 2003.

傅修延：《听觉叙事研究》。北京：北京大学出版社，2021年。

李幼蒸：《理论符号学导论》。北京：中国人民大学出版社，2007年。

申丹：《双重叙事进程研究》。北京：北京大学出版社，2021年。

第九章

后结构主义与后现代主义

概述

后结构主义以"后"为前缀,既表示时间线性顺序,指其在结构主义之后,也表达着对结构主义的质疑和寻求区别。随着结构主义的发展,理论家们逐渐意识到它的盲区:过分强调系统性,忽略了个性和差异;过分强调结构性,忽略了能动性;过分强调共时性,忽略了历史性;过分看重科学性,对意识形态的关注不够。与之相对,后结构主义警惕宏大叙事,重视差异性,剖析社会结构背后的权力运作,关注理论的政治、文化和伦理维度,是更为多元化的思想场域。

后结构主义理论的一部分能量来自批评家自我立场的修改。以罗兰·巴特为例,他的思想轨迹经历了从结构主义向后结构主义的调整。事实上,在他早期所写的文章《结构主义活动》("The Activity of Structuralism",1963)中,已可见后结构主义思想的端倪。他将结构主义定义为创造"拟像"客体的活动。此处的结构主义"拟像"和传统摹仿论中的"拟像"不同:后者用模仿的方式再现现实,前者则用模型来展现结构性的功能与规律。从一开始,巴特就注意到了结构主义的建构本质。在早期作品中,他关注结构的原理性,从符号学角度,将社会文化现象视为文本,探讨其表征范式和生成动因。巴特在后期则致力于拆解结构,解放被结构所压抑的人类经验的多样性。他向后结构主义转向的代表作之一是《S/Z》(*S/Z*,1970)这部解读巴尔扎克的短篇小说《萨拉辛》的著作。他在书中把小说《萨拉辛》的文本分割为五百六十一个单元,按照阐释符码、情节符码、意义符码、象征符码、文化符码进行分类,对其进行读解,使文本意义不断增生,将阐释活动变成一场语言游戏。在《文之悦》(*The Pleasure of the Text*,1973)、《恋人絮语》(*A Lover's Discourse: Fragments*,1977)等作品中,他进一步提出了"可读性文本"和"可写性文本"的区别:前一类文本以作者为权威,读者追随作者意图;后一类文本中,读者将自身欲望带入阅读体验，与文本互动，生产出文本的意义。巴特重视阅读的情感效应，将阅读的快感分为两种：文之悦是一种温和的愉悦感，是我们阅读经典文学作品时体会到的快乐；文之醉则是极限的体验——在阅读先锋性的文本时，读者被文本中不可预测的偶然、混沌不明的暧昧以及不断跳跃震荡的游戏性等所吸引和驱动，在失序感中体会迷醉的狂喜。

与巴特相比，雅克·德里达（Jacques Derrida）从学术生涯的起点就在质疑结构主义。1966年，在美国约翰·霍普金斯大学召开的学术会议上，结构主义作为理论新潮，风头正劲。年轻的德里达却宣读了题为《人文科学话语中的结构、符号和游戏》（"Structure, Sign, and Play in the Discourse of the Human Sciences"）的论文，直击结构主义问题的内核。他指出，在西方科学和哲学中占支配地位的结构概念，其生成和自由运转离不开一个本源性的确定的中心。结构内部的要素可变，中心不可变。它非但不受结构法则的约束，而且为结构提供组织原则。德里达的解构论从拆散中心入手，通过去中心化，挑战权威和确定性，包容流动性、变化性和多样性。在《书写与差异》（*Writing and Difference*，1967）、《声音与现象》（*Speech and Phenomena*，1967）、《论文字学》（*Of Grammatology*，1967）等早期著作中，他揭秘西方形而上学中的逻各斯中心主义（logocentrism）的运作方式，指出逻各斯的原意是神的言说，它既具神的权力，也反映言说的力量。在西方传统中，逻各斯是"道"，它是神学体系中的上帝，是启蒙思想中的理性，是父权制中的男性至上。世界围绕逻各斯建立起等级制的结构，中心享有特权，边缘受到压制和剥削。

德里达对逻各斯中心主义的批判具有政治意义。此外，这个概念还承载了他对语言的思考。逻各斯有语音中心主义（phonocentrism）的特征，强调意义的即时性和直接性。德里达认为索绪尔的符号论以声音形象为基础，也有逻各斯中心主义的倾向。索绪尔认为言说是本源性的，书写是其缺席时的增补手段。问题是索绪尔又不得不承认人们依赖于书写来认识语言，书写的"增补"（supplément）不可或缺，是表意系统的基础条件。对索绪尔的再审视也让德里达提出了"延异"（différance）的概念。索绪尔在符号的能指/所指二元论中，以所指作为意义的决定因素。其实离开了能指，不可能有所指。举个简单的例子：当我们查词典想弄清楚一个词的确切含义时，会在释义中看到更多的词，而弄清释义的每个词，又会牵涉更多的新词和新释义。"延异"就是这种意义在差异中不断产生与延宕的过程。所以德里达主张用"痕迹"（trace）的概念替代符号——每个词的意义中都缠绕着其他词的影子，它们既在场，又不在场。如果试图追溯源头，则会带来更多的痕迹叠加，造成进一步的意义的"撒播"（dissemination）。

从德里达所创造的"延异""增补""痕迹""撒播"等概念，我们可以看到德里达解构论的特点：解构既不是翻转二元对立，颠倒对立项的主从关系；也不是简单地将对立项视为平等项；更不是彻底颠覆机制，捣毁系统，用相对主义的虚无性替代真理性。解构意在从系统和真理的内部入手，质疑中心性，拆解对立结构，批判权力等级，解放多元项，承认个性和差异，为边缘群体赋能，为独立个体赋能。德里达沿着这一逻辑，在晚期著作中关心伦理及其政治议题。在《友爱的政治学》（*The Politics of Friendship*，1994）中，德里达批评西方政治传统所标榜的民主有明显的局限性，它的共同体想象依赖于男性之间的友谊，将女性以及其他边缘人群排除在共同体之外，缺乏包容性。在《论好客》（*Of Hospitality*，2000）中，他紧扣"好客"这个与接纳异己者有关的概念，揭秘其中隐含的主客相异、内外有别、敌我不同的二元对立机制，讨论应采用何种"好客"原则来面对异乡的移民和流离失所的难民等门口的陌生人。在《动物故我在》（*The Animal That Therefore I am*，2006）中，德里达将思考范围扩展到动物，重新审视人与动物的关系设定，承认动物的主体性和独特性，同时追问何为人类。

德里达的解构论是当代西方文论最有影响力的理论之一。它引发了20世纪60年代和70年代美国学界的解构主义思潮。美国本土的理论传统是新批评，它和德里达的解构思想有天然的亲近感。新批评推崇文本细读，这和德里达的文本解读策略很相似；新批评喜欢对含混、张力、矛盾、悖论等修辞的复杂意涵进行分析，这和德里达重视文本的复义性很契合。但新批评畏惧冲突导致的不和谐和不可相容，为了调和内部张力，提出了文本的总体有机论。而德里达的语言观则拒绝这种折中姿态，要求更为自由和解放的立场，这对已厌倦了新批评保守性的美国学界来说，非常有吸引力。保罗·德曼（Paul de Man）、J. 希利斯·米勒（J. Hillis Miller）、哈罗德·布鲁姆（Harold Bloom）和杰弗里·哈特曼（Geoffrey Hartman）等耶鲁大学的学者受德里达解构论中的语言论的启发，形成了具有美国特色的解构主义流派。

在耶鲁解构主义者中，德曼的影响力最大。德曼重视德里达的"延异"论，在此基础上提出解构主义应直面语言的不稳定性，承认以语言为载体的文学无法呈现真实的世界，不把文学和历史挂钩，不追求文学的审美功效，摆脱摹仿论传统，聚焦文学自身，深入探索语言组成的多元异质性的文本世界。在《盲视与洞见》（*Blindness and Insight: Essays in the Rhetoric of Contemporary Criticism*，1971）中，德曼指出，文学的基本特征是文本的多义性，这是语言"言此意彼"的修辞性决定的。所以，阅读中的盲视可能意味着洞见，而洞见亦可能是盲视。比如，新批评在浪漫主义中已经洞见性地看到了修辞性带来的悖论与含混，却非要用整体和谐的有机论的"洞见"进行解释，造成了真正的盲视。在《阅读的寓言》（*Allegories of Reading: Figural Language in Rousseau, Nietzsche, Rilke, and Proust*，1979）中，德曼继续对"言此意彼"的分裂进行剖析。人们在阅读时，总想在字面义下找寓意，殊不知言说总是多义的，没有字面义和寓意的区分。在这本书的后半部分，德曼用数章篇幅详细解读了卢梭的《忏悔录》。卢梭说自己写《忏悔录》的目的是通过坦白来悔罪，但卢梭也借着坦白来言说欲望，彰显欲望。怎么区别两者谁是真意？谁是假意？实际上，德曼去世后，他对《忏悔录》的读解被重新审视。有学者在研究德曼的学术历程时，发现他年轻时曾为纳粹撰文。他在战后定居美国，直到去世，对这段反犹历史讳莫如深。或许德曼谈卢梭，是为了借用言说卢梭的忏悔表达他自己的忏悔，但他用寓言式的书写回避了真正的忏悔，拒绝公开承担伦理责任。他在解构主义理论中屏蔽历史，只谈文本，这种立场的动机是可疑的。

看重文学的语言维度，这的确是美国解构主义者的共性。事实上，解构主义理论家在写理论文章时，风格也带有语言游戏的特点，在不断反转中，让文本层层袒露出内蕴的复杂性。米勒的《作为寄生虫的批评家》（"The Critic as Host"，1977）就是一个典型例子。米勒在文中用大量篇幅对"寄生虫"与"寄主"这两个词进行词源学的追溯，在溯源过程中，不停进行意义的"撒播"，最终说明了这两个词看似矛盾，实则含义相通。他由此笔锋一转，进入文学批评与文学作品的关系的讨论。长期以来，人们总在说文学作品是原创，批评是寄生虫。但是，批评家从文学文本中挑出各种片段，让它们寄生在批评文本中，使它们进入不同的语境，获得了新的滋养。米勒的文章展现了解构主义有魅力的一面：语言游戏不是为了纸面上的狂欢，而是为了激发新的认识。解构的意义不在于破坏，而在于催生新的可能性。

后结构主义理论家的思想频谱上，既有偏向语言一端的美国解构主义者，也有偏向社会历史一端的理论家，后者的代表是米歇尔·福柯（Michel Foucault）。福柯曾经做过一个题为《结构主义和文学分析》（"Structuralism and Literary Analysis"，1967）的演讲。在演讲中，他分析了法国当时的结构主义方法论的局限性，认为结构主义的贡献在于发现了值得研究的对象——人类不断生成不断积淀的符号集合形成的各种"文献集"（masse documentaire）。但福柯反对结构主义用过于倚重语言学的方法对其进行研究。福柯认为这就像考察文学，仅从修辞学入手是一种偏狭的视角。文学研究必须关注外在语境，因为任何言说的意义都由其语境所决定。此外，也应关注文学的述行性，认识到文学言说中隐含着权力和行动力。实际上，他的立场也反映在《什么是作者？》（"What Is an Author?"，1969）这篇文章中。他关注的不是作家如何创作作品，以及作品有什么样的书写特点，而是当作品归于作者名下时，作者承担何种功能，如何被权力征用，如何受权力的规训等一系列问题。

实际上，对这些问题的思考，反映了福柯对"文献集"及其背后的权力关系的关注。福柯用话语（discourse）这个概念来指代"文献集"，重点考察其诞生的语境和反映的权力关系。

在他的博士论文《古典时代疯狂史》(*Madness and Civilization: A History of Insanity in the Age of Reason*,1961)中,福柯围绕"疯狂"/"精神病"这组关键词,爬梳文献,看人类是如何通过对疯癫的标定来确立理性原则,一步步从古典走向现代性。有关疯癫的科学讨论与社会机制联动,负责制定规范、甄别正常与反常、划定中心与边缘。这些都体现着话语的功能。福柯对话语的研究视野很广,在《临床医学的诞生》(*The Birth of the Clinic: An Archaeology of Medical Perception*,1963)中,他分析医学话语在18世纪和19世纪的实证转向,看临床医学如何努力消除人体疾病的一切"晦暗之处",确立诊断式凝视的权威性,重塑医患之间的权力关系,促成新型医学管理方式的出现,将健康、身体和生命纳入社会治理的领域。在《规训与惩罚》(*Discipline and Punish: The Birth of the Prison*,1975)中,福柯关心现代监狱如何诞生于全景敞视结构,后者又如何成为现代公共空间的经典范式之一。在边沁的全景敞视结构中,监狱是环形设置,中间是瞭望塔,确保囚牢中的犯人时刻能感受到瞭望塔上看守的凝视。犯人们由此自觉守规矩,监狱管理效率得到了提高。在当代,此类空间设定已得到推广,运用于工厂、写字楼等处,借以塑造自我规训自我监控的主体。在《性经验史》(*The History of Sexuality*,1976)中,福柯研究同性恋的禁忌话语,看权力的触角如何通过性话语伸向最个人化的身体私密领域。福柯的话语—权力论彰显出权力的无所不在,它比意识形态的弥散性还强,以各种话语的形式全方位地影响着日常生活实践和人的主体性的塑造。但是,福柯认为反抗始终存在,话语会催生出反话语。在福柯看来,权力斗争模式不是自上而下的镇压模式,而是微观权力的网状样态,在不同的点位会出现此消彼长的抗争。

至此,我们可以看到后结构主义思潮的内部差异很大:一方面,游戏、自由、迷醉、多元性、解构等概念勾勒出了乌托邦的愿景;另一方面,全景敞视机制、微观权力论等理论联动着冷峻的现实。其实,我们也会在后现代主义理论中看到类似的冲突和类似的关键词。这种相似性很容易理解——后现代主义深受后结构主义思潮滋养,而后结构主义的文化社会语境主要是后现代主义意义上的。这种亲密关系意味着我们不可能将理论家们分为泾渭分明的两个阵营。此处分而述之,是为了各有侧重。我们需要认真审视后现代社会以及作为其社会文化表征的后现代主义。

二战后,西方社会逐步迈入了后工业化阶段。如何面对这一时期的晚期资本主义、全球化、消费主义、信息技术发展等现象的挑战?对此,理论家们进行了探索性的思考。

让-弗朗索瓦·利奥塔(Jean-François Lyotard)是后现代主义理论家中的代表人物。他影响力最大的著作是《后现代状态》(*The Postmodern Condition: A Report on Knowledge*，1979），其议题是科学话语这一与我们当代社会息息相关的概念。利奥塔指出，现代社会中，"科学知识"被视为真理标准，是社会建构的重要力量，以理性压制人性，用宏大叙事扼杀多样性和可能性。其实，我们应认清它的话语本质。它的合法性最初来自两种叙事：政治上的启蒙解放叙事和哲学上的精神思辨叙事。但这些神话已破产，它现在靠的是资本和高等教育体制的支持，但也因此沦为庸俗的实用主义。利奥塔认为这恰是我们启动科学知识的后现代话语机制的机会——用反系统、反决定论和反实用主义的立场抵制科学的真理化，让科学知识变成"语言游戏"一样开放的充满争论的领域，使它不再是压制性的力量，始终保持对未知性的探索。在《定义后现代》（"Defining the Postmodern"，1986）中，他强调先锋艺术的意义，认为先锋艺术在现代主义内部不断进行反思和突破，其后现代的特征反映在艺术生成的不竭动力中。

对探索的渴望和对生命潜能的观照也是吉勒·德勒兹（Gilles Deleuze）和皮埃尔-费利克斯·瓜塔里（Pierre-Félix Guattari）这两位法国理论家的核心议题。在《反俄狄浦斯》（*Anti-Oedipus*，1972）中，他们抨击弗洛伊德以核心家庭为基础的"俄狄浦斯情结"论，认为弗洛伊德在用精神分析的科学话语，对人的生命能量进行结构化和等级化，压制无意识的欲望生产，将它限定为家庭伦理剧，使力比多困于家庭投注，而无力进行社会投注，丧失了进行革命和创造的能力——而这恰是资本主义所喜闻乐见和积极倡导的。德勒兹和瓜塔里提倡精神分裂分析，反对统一的精神分析意义上的意识主体，意在对抗精神分析与资本主义的共谋，恢复欲望机器的生产机制，让生命恢复奔放不羁，以造化万千。

《千高原》（*A Thousand Plateaus*，1980）是《反俄狄浦斯》的续篇，全书由十五座"高原"（章）组成。德勒兹和瓜塔里表示，读者可以随心所欲地选择任何一座"高原"作为入口，开启阅读之旅。这种"高原"式的差异性的排列是去中心性和反逻辑性的，类似于德勒兹和瓜塔里所推崇的"块茎"的组织方式：具生成式、连接式和多元性特征。此处的块茎形态，对应的是树状形态——树状形态根茎叶层级分明，以根为本源，向上线性有序生长，是西方形而上学结构的典型形态。而在地下连绵蔓延生长的块茎和在千高原上的游牧空间互为呼应，对抗的是格栅化的纹理空间。纹理空间是现代社会的重要空间组织和管理形态，它将现代人的生活限定在公寓房和写字楼的一个个格子间。德勒兹和瓜塔里认为生命是拒绝格栅化的，它总在逃逸中，也总在生成中。实际上，德勒兹在英美文学中找到了"逃逸线"。他认同D. H. 劳伦斯的观点，认为文学的最高目标是离开和逃跑，是穿过地平线，探索新的生命形式。他批评法国文学缺乏这种自由，而在英美文学中，他发现这样的作家比比皆是，除了劳伦斯，还有托马斯·哈代、赫尔曼·麦尔维尔、弗吉尼亚·伍尔夫、F. S. 菲茨杰拉德、杰克·凯鲁亚克等。

当德勒兹和瓜塔里歌颂艺术的能动性和逃逸性时，美国西方马克思主义理论家弗雷德里克·詹姆逊则批判后现代先锋艺术。他发现它正在失去先锋艺术的核心价值，不再关心人类解放的议题，被抽干了历史性，表征出后现代主义的症候。詹姆逊批评美国波普艺术家安迪·沃霍尔（Andy Warhol）。沃霍尔招牌式的艺术手法是将一系列流行文化中的意象复制、叠加和拼贴在一起。金宝汤罐头、可口可乐瓶、玛丽莲·梦露、猫王都出现在他的画作中。在《后现代主义或晚期资本主义的文化逻辑》（Postmodernism, or, The Cultural Logic of Late Capitalism，1991）中，詹姆逊对比了梵高的《农民的鞋》和沃霍尔的《钻石灰尘鞋》。在梵高笔下，农民劳作后脱下来的鞋子以鲜艳的色彩占据画面的视野中心，人、鞋、劳动与大地联系在一起。而沃霍尔的鞋子则看起来是一堆随意凑合起来的死物。它们排列起来，好比一串被人遗弃的萝卜，漫不经心地挂在画布上，仿佛跟那个孕育它们的人间完全切断了关系。詹姆逊认为此类波普艺术所捕捉到的恰是后现代主义文化的破碎感、平面化、缺乏历史深度以及情感淡漠。

法国理论家让·鲍德里亚（Jean Baudrillard）也和詹姆逊一样，是后现代主义的批评者。他早期受西方马克思主义影响，后来将之融入对社会学和符号学的关注。在《消费社会》（The Consumer Society，1970）、《符号政治经济学批判》（For a Critique of the Political Economy of the Sign，1972）和《象征交换和死亡》（Symbolic Exchange and Death，1976）等一系列作品中，鲍德里亚剖析了当代消费社会中的异化现象。他指出，工业社会的商品崇拜在当代已变成了对商品的符号价值的崇拜。消费不再与物的使用有关，而与消费者对商品的符号价值的认同有关。由此，穿什么牌子的衣服、开什么牌子的车，这些消费行为都和消费者的"自我实现"与"自我价值"捆绑在一起。问题是，消费者通过消费所获得的主体感和自由感其实是虚幻的。用鲍德里亚在《消费社会》里的话来说，"需求实际上是生产的结果"，资本主义为了维持消费社会的繁荣以牟利，在源源不断地创造新符号，刺激新消费，造成了自然资源的浪费，也消耗着人类的生命价值。

鲍德里亚从消费社会制造虚假需求的角度出发，开始关心"仿真"的议题。他在《拟像与仿真》（Simulacra and Simulation，1981）中，对其机制进行了深入阐释。鲍德里亚注意到当代社会的媒介技术在不断通过仿真创造"超真实"，但这种真实不是像风景和海洋这样的现成之物，而是人为生产或再生产出来的真实，是一种精雕细琢的显得比真实更为真实的虚拟存在。鲍德里亚指出，迪士尼乐园就是这种超真实的体现。在海湾战争战火正酣时，他还语出惊人地声称：海湾战争没发生，人们通过电视、新闻报道等各种媒介所看到的战争，是大众传媒仿真、军事演习言论和超越真实世界的界限和实际可能性的想象的结果。他以虚无主义的态度对待战争的残酷现实，受到学界的广泛批评。但他焦虑于媒介技术对人们认知的改造和操控，是有道理的。如今，技术的发展已经让"超真实"高度融入人类的日常生活，面对虚拟性的扩张，鲍德里亚的理论依然值得关注。

除了上述关心哲学和社会维度的后现代理论家之外，还有一些理论家将目光投向后现代主义文学领域。埃及裔美国文学批评家伊哈布·哈桑（Ihab Hassan）是最早注意到后现代主义文学的特殊性的理论家，他以"后现代转向"为之命名，通过《肢解俄耳甫斯》（*The Dismemberment of Orpheus: Toward a Postmodern Literature*，1971）、《超批评》（*Paracriticisms: Seven Speculations of the Times*，1975）、《后现代转向》（*The Postmodern Turn: Essays in Postmodern Theory and Culture*，1987）等著作对它进行了理论化。在哈桑看来，后现代有反形式、自由游戏、延异、反讽、无政府主义等诸多表征，其核心是不确定性和内在性。不确定性表达了含混、断裂与相对主义，消解了历史和真实的维度，反映着总体性的危机；而内在性的生命力则反映在语言游戏的自我指涉性的狂欢及其跃动在文学作品中的对自由和解放的渴望。两者交织着，形成了后现代主义的立体面貌。

加拿大理论家琳达·哈琴（Linda Hutcheon）是另一位关注后现代文学的理论家。她和詹姆逊在如何看待后现代主义的问题上存在分歧。她部分认同詹姆逊对后现代主义历史无根感的批判，但认为我们有必要从后现代视角对历史修撰的叙事本质有所认识。她在《后现代主义诗学》（*A Poetics of Postmodernism: History, Theory, Fiction*，1988）中对历史编撰元小说（historiographic metafiction）进行了深入研究，指出该文类呈现出更为丰富的时间维度和更为复杂的历史立场。此外，哈琴也很重视后现代主义先锋性有别于现代主义的新特点。她注意到现代主义先锋性强调审美和艺术自主，带有精英主义的傲慢；后现代作品将精英文化探索和流行文化元素结合，杂糅的力量里既有自我消解的成分，也隐含革命的契机。

至此，虽然本章有关后结构主义和后现代主义理论的概述即将结束，我们依然很难对后结构主义和后现代主义进行清晰的定义，因为它们内部有众多冲突的声音，而且，这两个理论流派之间也有大量的对话和合流。从这个角度来看，它们各自名称中的"后"字的使用，既带有作为权宜之计的无奈之意，也体现了鲜明的问题意识。它们的核心都深具反思性：反思结构主义所勾连的整个西方形而上学传统，反思我们身处的这个复杂时代。

主要文本阅读

德里达：《人文科学话语中的结构、符号和游戏》

选文简介

选文出自1966年10月德里达在约翰·霍普金斯大学举办的会议上的发言，后被收入《书写与差异》。德里达在文中指出，结构主义主张结构之内的各个要素具有可替换性，却忽略了这样一个事实：结构的中心不参与自由替换。唯有中心保持不变，才能保证内部要素围绕中心的范式。这造成了结构主义的悖论：中心在结构内，是其起源，为其提供平衡，对其进行组织；但它又脱离结构性，不遵从结构的自由游戏的基本原则。实际上，在结构主义范式中，中心不需要占据结构中的具体点位，它的在场是功能性的，源自人类对结构的本源和基准的欲求与依赖。西方各个时期的思想结构中都能找到中心性的设定。在宗教世界中，上帝是中心；在启蒙时代，理性是中心；在精神分析领域，意识是中心。德里达的解构理论就从质疑中心的合法性入手，认为结构一旦去中心化，就会坍塌。值得注意的是，德里达不认为我们可以超越中心谈结构。中心就嵌套在结构中，没有中心就没有结构。这个道理如同我们不可能脱离符号谈符号一样。换而言之，在德里达看来，解构只能在结构内部进行。

From "Structure, Sign, and Play in the Discourse of the Human Sciences"

Jacques Derrida (1930-2004)

Perhaps something has occurred in the history of the concept of structure that could be called an "event," if this loaded word did not entail a meaning which it is precisely the function of structural—or structuralist—thought to reduce or to suspect. But let me use the term "event" anyway, employing it with caution and as if in quotation marks. In this sense, this event will have the exterior form of a *rupture* and a *redoubling*.

It would be easy enough to show that the concept of structure and even the word "structure" itself are as old as the *epistemé*—that is to say, as old as Western science and Western philosophy—and that their roots thrust deep into the soil of ordinary language, into whose deepest recesses the *epistemé* plunges to gather them together once more, making them part of itself in a metaphorical displacement. Nevertheless, up until the event which I wish to mark out and define, structure—or rather the structurality of structure—although it has always been involved, has always been neutralized or reduced, and this by a process of giving it a center or referring it to a point of presence, a fixed origin. The function of this center was not only to orient, balance, and organize the structure—one cannot in fact conceive of an unorganized structure—but above all to make sure that the organizing principles of the structure would limit what we might call the *freeplay* of the structure. No doubt that by orienting and organizing the coherence of the system, the center of a structure permits the freeplay of its elements inside the total form. And even today the notion of a structure lacking any center represents the unthinkable itself.

Nevertheless, the center also closes off the freeplay it opens up and makes possible. *Qua* center, it is the point at which the substitution of contents, elements, or terms is no longer possible. At the center, the permutation or the transformation of elements (which may of course be structures enclosed within a structure) is forbidden. At least this permutation has always remained *interdicted* (I use this word deliberately). Thus it has always been thought that the center, which is by definition unique, constituted that very thing within a structure which governs the structure, while escaping structurality. This is why classical thought concerning structure could say that the center is, paradoxically, *within* the structure and *outside* it. The center is at the center of the totality, and yet, since the center does not belong to the totality (is not part of the totality), the totality *has its center elsewhere*. The center is not the center. The concept of centered structure—although it represents coherence itself, the condition of the *epistemé* as philosophy or science—is contradictorily coherent. And, as always, coherence in contradiction expresses the force of a desire. The concept of centered structure is in fact the concept of a freeplay based on a fundamental ground, a freeplay which is constituted upon a fundamental immobility and a reassuring certitude, which is itself beyond the reach of the freeplay. With this certitude anxiety can be mastered, for anxiety is invariably the result of a certain mode of being implicated in the game, of being caught by the game, of being as it were from the very beginning at stake in the game....

The event I called a rupture, the disruption I alluded to at the beginning of this paper, would presumably have come about when the structurality of structure had to begin to be thought, that is to say, repeated, and this is why I said that this disruption was repetition in all of the senses of this word. From then on it became necessary to think the law which governed, as it were, the desire for the center in the constitution of structure and the process of signification prescribing its displacements and its substitutions for this law of the central presence—but a central presence which was never itself, which has always already been transported outside itself in its surrogate. The surrogate does not substitute itself for anything which has somehow pre-existed it. From then on it was probably necessary to begin to think that there was no center, that the center could not be thought in the form of being-present, that the center had no natural locus, that it was not a fixed locus but a function, a sort of non-locus in which an infinite number of sign-substitutions came into play. This moment was that in which language invaded the universal problematic; that in which, in the absence of a center or origin, everything became discourse—provided we can agree on this word—that is to say, when everything became a system where the central signified, the original or transcendental signified, is never absolutely present outside a system of differences. The absence of the transcendental signified extends the domain and the interplay of signification *ad infinitum*....

...Freeplay is the disruption of presence. The presence of an element is always a signifying and substitutive reference inscribed in a system of differences and the movement of a chin. Freeplay is always an interplay of absence and presence, but if it is to be radically conceived, freeplay must be conceived of before the alternative of presence and absence; being must be conceived of as presence or absence beginning with the possibility of freeplay and not the other way around. If Lévi-Strauss, better than any other, has brought to light the freeplay of repetition and the repetition of freeplay, one no less perceives in his work a sort of ethic of presence, an ethic of nostalgia for origins, an ethic of archaic and natural innocence, of a purity of presence and self-presence in speech—an ethic, nostalgia, and even remorse which he often presents as the motivation of the ethnological project when he moves toward archaic societies—exemplary societies in his eyes. These texts are well known.

As a turning toward the presence, lost or impossible, of the absent origin, this structuralist thematic of broken immediateness is thus the sad, *negative*, nostalgic, guilty, Rousseauist facet of the thinking of freeplay of which the Nietzschean *affirmation*—the joyous affirmation of the freeplay of the world and of the innocence of becoming, the affirmation of a world of signs without fault, without truth, without origin, offered to an active interpretation—would be the other side. *This affirmation then determines the non-center otherwise than as loss of the center.* And it plays the game without security. For there is a *sure* freeplay: that which is limited to the *substitution of given and existing, present,* pieces. In absolute chance, affirmation also surrenders itself to *genetic* indetermination, to the *seminal* adventure of the trace.

There are thus two interpretations of interpretation, of structure, of sign, of freeplay. The one seeks to decipher, dreams of deciphering, a truth or an origin which is free from freeplay and from the order of the sign, and lives like an exile the necessity of interpretation. The other, which is no longer turned toward the origin, affirms freeplay and tries to pass beyond man and humanism, the name man being the name of that being who, throughout the history of metaphysics or of ontotheology—in other words, through the history of all of his history—has dreamed of full presence, the reassuring foundation, the origin and the end of the game. The second interpretation of interpretation, to which Nietzsche showed us the way, does not seek in ethnography, as Lévi-Strauss wished, the "inspiration of a new humanism."

There are more than enough indications today to suggest we might perceive that these two interpretations of interpretation—which are absolutely irreconcilable even if we live them simultaneously and reconcile them in an obscure economy—together share the field which we call, in such a problematic fashion, the human sciences.

For my part, although these two interpretations must acknowledge and accentuate their difference and define their irreducibility, I do not believe that today there is any question of *choosing*—in the first place because here we are in a region (let's say, provisionally, a region of historicity) where the category of choice seems particularly trivial; and in the second, because we must first try to conceive of the common ground, and the *différance* of this irreducible difference. Here there is a sort of question, call it historical, of which we are only glimpsing today the *conception, the formation, the gestation, the labor*. I employ these words, I admit, with a glance toward the business of childbearing—but also with a glance toward those who, in a company from which I do not exclude myself, turn their eyes away in the face of the as yet unnameable which is proclaiming itself and which can do so, as is necessary whenever a birth is in the offing, only under the species of the non-species, in the formless, mute, infant, and terrifying form of monstrosity.

福柯:《什么是作者?》

选文简介

我们日常经验中谈到作者,要么将他看作具体作品的创作者,要么从传记角度或历史角度来理解他的写作。福柯却提出这样一个问题:人们即便不知道作者是谁,也一样能够进行阅读,那么为什么作品还需要与作者挂钩?此时,福柯关注的是作者功能,即作者是如何为自己名下的作品提供保障,确定其同质性、关联性、真实性,为阐释提供基础,为权力的介入提供保证。在《什么是作者?》中,福柯讨论了作者功能的四个特点:1)作者功能与裁决和立法体系相联系。以作品所有权为例,明确了作者之后,如果作品犯禁违规,可以将他绳之以法;如果作品售卖,作者的经济利益可以得到保障。2)不同时代不同话语体系中,作者功能是不同的。在古代,人们乐于吟诵无名氏的作品,但读科学作品时却需要知悉作者,比如:希波克拉底这样的专家写的作品要比普通医生有分量。在现代社会,科学领域的著述具有真理效应,没人深究数学书的作者;文学作品却需要作者为它增加影响力。3)确定谁是作者需要一系列复杂运作,也会产生相应后果。比如不同文本一旦被确定属于同一作者,文本间的差异性就会被同质性所取代。4)作者功能可以是复数性的,为文本中的不同的主体设定提供服务。

From "What Is an Author?"

Michel Foucault (1926-1984)

It would seem that the author's name, unlike other proper names, does not pass from the interior of a discourse to the real and exterior individual who produced it; instead, the name seems always to be present, marking off the edges of the text, revealing, or at least characterizing, its mode of being. The author's name manifests the appearance of a certain discursive set and indicates the status of this discourse within a society and a culture. It has no legal status, nor is it located in the fiction of the work; rather, it is located in the *break* that founds a certain discursive construct and its very particular mode of being. As a result, we could say that in a civilization like our own there are a certain number of discourses that are endowed with the "author-function," while others are deprived of it. A private letter may well have a signer—it does not have an author; a contract may well have a guarantor—it does not have an author. An anonymous text posted on a wall probably has a writer—but not an author. The author-function is therefore characteristic of the mode of existence, circulation, and functioning of certain discourses within a society.

Let us analyze this "author-function" as we have just described it. In our culture, how does one characterize a discourse containing the author-function? In what way is this discourse different from other discourses? If we limit our remarks to the author of a book or a text, we can isolate four different characteristics.

First of all, discourses are objects of

appropriation. The form of ownership from which they spring is of a rather particular type, one that has been codified for many years. We should note that, historically, this type of ownership has always been subsequent to what one might call penal appropriation. Texts, books, and discourses really began to have authors (other than mythical, "sacralized" and "sacralizing" figures) to the extent that authors became subject to punishment, that is, to the extent that discourses could be transgressive. In our culture (and doubtless in many others), discourse was not originally a product, a thing, a kind of goods; it was essentially an act—an act placed in the bipolar field of the sacred and the profane, the licit and the illicit, the religious and the blasphemous. Historically, it was a gesture fraught with risks before becoming goods caught up in a circuit of ownership....

The author-function does not affect all discourses in a universal and constant way, however. This is its second characteristic. In our civilization, it has not always been the same types of texts which have required attribution to an author. There was a time when the texts that we today call "literary" (narratives, stories, epics, tragedies, comedies) were accepted, put into circulation, and valorized without any question about the identity of their author; their anonymity caused no difficulties since their ancientness, whether real or imagined, was regarded as a sufficient guarantee of their status. On the other hand, those texts that we now would call scientific—those dealing with cosmology and the heavens, medicine and illnesses, natural sciences and geography—were accepted in the Middle Ages, and accepted as "true," only when marked with the name of their author. "Hippocrates said," "Pliny recounts," were not really formulas of an argument based on authority; they were the markers inserted in discourses that were supposed to be received as statements of demonstrated truth.

A reversal occurred in the seventeenth or eighteenth century. Scientific discourses began to be received for themselves, in the anonymity of an established or always redemonstrable truth; their membership in a systematic ensemble, and not the reference to the individual who produced them, stood as their guarantee. The author-function faded away, and the inventor's name served only to christen a theorem, proposition, particular effect, property, body, group of elements, or pathological syndrome. By the same token, literary discourses came to be accepted only when endowed with the author-function. We now ask of each poetic or fictional text: from where does it come, who wrote it, when, under what circumstances, or beginning with what design? The meaning ascribed to it and the status or value accorded to it depend upon the manner in which we answer these questions. And if a text should be discovered in a state of anonymity—whether as a consequence of an accident or the author's explicit wish—the game becomes one of rediscovering the author....

The third characteristic of this author-function is that it does not develop spontaneously as the attribution of a discourse to an individual. It is, rather, the result of a complex operation which constructs a certain rational being that we call "author." Critics doubtless try to give this intelligible being a realistic status, by discerning, in the individual, a "deep" motive, a "creative" power, or a "design," the milieu in which writing originates. Nevertheless, these aspects of an individual which we designate as making him an author are only a projection, in more or less psychologizing terms, of the operations that we force texts to undergo, the connections that we make, the traits that we establish as pertinent, the continuities that we recognize, or the exclusions that we practice. All these operations vary according to periods and types of discourse. We do not construct a "philosophical author" as we do a "poet," just as, in the eighteenth century, one did not construct a novelist as we do today. Still, we can find through the ages certain constants in the rules of author-construction....

Modern literary criticism, even when—as is now customary—it is not concerned with questions of authentification, still defines the author the same way: the author provides the basis for explaining not only the presence of certain events in a work, but also their transformations, distortions, and diverse modifications (through his biography, the determination of his individual perspective, the analysis of his social position, and the revelation of his basic design). The author is also the principle of a certain unity of writing—all differences having to be resolved, at least in part, by the principles of evolution, maturation, or influence. The author also serves to neutralize the contradictions that may emerge in a series of texts: there must be—at a certain level of his thought or desire, of his consciousness or unconscious—a point where contradictions are resolved, where incompatible elements are at last tied together or organized around a fundamental or originating contradiction. Finally, the author is a particular source of expression that, in more or less completed forms, is manifested equally well, and with similar validity, in works, sketches, letters, fragments, and so on....

But the author-function is not a pure and simple reconstruction made secondhand from a text given as passive material. The text always contains a certain number of signs referring to the author. These signs, well known to grammarians, are personal pronouns, adverbs of time and place, and verb conjugation. Such elements do not play the same role in discourses provided with the author-function as in those lacking it. In the latter, such "shifters" refer to the real speaker and to the spatio-temporal coordinates of his discourse (although certain modifications can occur, as in the operation of relating discourses in the first person). In the former, however, their role is more complex and variable. Everyone knows that, in a novel narrated in the first person, neither the first person pronoun, nor the present indicative refer exactly either to the writer or to the moment in which he writes, but rather to an alter ego whose distance from the author varies, often changing in the course of the work. It would be just as wrong to equate the author with the real writer as to equate him with the fictitious speaker; the author-function is carried out and operates in the scission itself, in this division and this distance.

One might object that this is a characteristic peculiar to novelistic or poetic discourse, a "game" in which only "quasi-discourses" participate. In fact, however, all discourses endowed with the author-function do possess this plurality of self. The self that speaks in the preface to a treatise on mathematics—and that indicates the circumstances of the treatise's composition—is identical neither in its position nor in its functioning to the self that speaks in the course of a demonstration, and that appears in the form of "I conclude" or "I suppose." In the first case, the "I" refers to an individual without an equivalent who, in a determined place and time, completed a certain task; in the second, the "I" indicates an instance and a level of demonstration which any individual could perform provided that he accept the same system of symbols, play of axioms, and set of previous demonstrations. We could also, in the same treatise, locate a third self, one that speaks to tell the work's meaning, the obstacles encountered, the results obtained, and the remaining problems; this self is situated in the field of already existing or yet-to-appear mathematical discourses. The author-function is not assumed by the first of these selves at the expense of the other two, which would then be nothing more than a fictitious splitting in two of the first one. On the contrary, in these discourses the author-function operates so as to effect the dispersion of these three simultaneous selves.

No doubt analysis could discover still more characteristic traits of the author-function. I will limit myself to these four, however, because they seem both the most visible and the most important. They can be summarized as follows: (1) the author-function is linked to the juridical and institutional system that encompasses, determines, and articulates the universe of discourses; (2) it does not affect all discourses in the same way at all times and in all types of civilization; (3) it is not defined by the spontaneous attribution of a discourse to its producer, but rather by a series of specific and complex operations; (4) it does not refer purely and simply to a real individual, since it can give rise simultaneously to several selves, to several subjects—positions that can be occupied by different classes of individuals....

...[The] author is not an indefinite source of significations which fill a work; the author does not precede the works, he is a certain functional principle by which, in our culture, one limits, excludes, and chooses; in short, by which one impedes the free circulation, the free manipulation, the free composition, decomposition, and recomposition of fiction. In fact, if we are accustomed to presenting the author as a genius, as a perpetual surging of invention, it is because, in reality, we make him function in exactly the opposite fashion. One can say that the author is an ideological product, since we represent him as the opposite of his historically real function. (When a historically given function is represented in a figure that inverts it, one has an ideological production.) The author is therefore the ideological figure by which one marks the manner in which we fear the proliferation of meaning....

All discourses, whatever their status, form, value, and whatever the treatment to which they will be subjected, would then develop in the anonymity of a murmur. We would no longer hear the questions that have been rehashed for so long: "Who really spoke? Is it really he and not someone else? With what authenticity or originality? And what part of his deepest self did he express in his discourse?" Instead, there would be other questions, like these: "What are the modes of existence of this discourse? Where has it been used, how can it circulate, and who can appropriate it for himself? What are the places in it where there is room for possible subjects? Who can assume these various subject-functions?" And behind all these questions, we would hear hardly anything but the stirring of an indifference: "What difference does it make who is speaking?"

利奥塔：《定义后现代》

选文简介

1986年，利奥塔撰文，加入对后现代概念引发的争议的探讨。在选文中，他主要讨论了三个议题。第一个议题关乎现代主义和后现代主义的关系。利奥塔不认为后现代的"后"是超越现代性之后的重新开始。后现代主义喜欢使用拼贴技巧，对现代主义进行重复引用，这种策略说明二者之间没有清晰边界。第二个议题有关后现代面临的挑战。在利奥塔看来，后现代既要面对现代性带来的如奥斯维辛集中营这样的灾难，也要面对当代科学技术的发展带来的新威胁。前者关乎人类亘古不变的生存需求，后者则是当代人必须应对的复杂局面。第三个议题关涉人文艺术。利奥塔看重先锋艺术的作用，认为它不是现代主义所独有，应从时间延续的角度看待人类通过艺术表达的求变求新的渴望。后现代主义正在继续着先锋性的艺术探索。简而言之，在利奥塔看来，后现代的"后"不是撤退，不是闪回，也不是重复。它既负责分析，也承接记忆，体现反思性，将历史与当下连接，突破界限的束缚，具有开放性。

From "Defining the Postmodern"

Jean-François Lyotard (1924-1998)

I should like to make only a small number of observations, in order to point to—and not at all to resolve—some problems surrounding the term "postmodern." My aim is not to close the debate, but to open it, to allow it to develop by avoiding certain confusions and ambiguities, as far as this is possible.

There are many debates implied by, and implicated in, the term "postmodern." I will distinguish three of them.

First, the opposition between postmodernism and modernism, or the Modern Movement (1910–1945), in architectural theory. According to Paolo Portoghesi, there is a rupture or break, and this break would be the abrogation of the hegemony of Euclidean geometry, which was sublimated in the plastic poetry of the movement known as De Stijl, for example. According to Victorio Gregotti, another Italian architect, the difference between the two periods is characterized by what is possibly a more interesting fissure. There is no longer any close linkage between the architectural project and socio-historical progress in the realization of human emancipation on the larger scale. Postmodern architecture is condemned to generate a multiplicity of small transformations in the space it inherits, and to give up the project of a last rebuilding of the whole space occupied by humanity. In this sense, a perspective is opened in the larger landscape.

In this account there is no longer a horizon of universalization, of general emancipation before the eyes of the postmodern man, or in particular, of the postmodern architect. The disappearance of this idea of progress within rationality and freedom would explain a certain tone, style or modus which is specific to postmodern architecture. I would say a sort of *bricolage*: the high frequency of quotations of elements from previous styles or periods (classical or modern), giving up the consideration of environment, and so on.

Just a remark about this aspect. The "post-," in the term "postmodernist" is in this case to be understood in the sense of a simple succession, of a diachrony of periods, each of them clearly identifiable. Something like a conversion, a new direction after the previous one. I should like to observe that this idea of chronology is totally modern. It belongs to Christianity, Cartesianism, Jacobinism. Since we are beginning something completely new, we have to re-set the hands of the clock at zero. The idea of modernity is closely bound up with this principle that it is possible and necessary to break with tradition and to begin a new way of living and thinking. Today we can presume that this "breaking" is, rather, a manner of forgetting or repressing the past. That's to say of repeating it. Not overcoming it.

I would say that the quotation of elements of past architectures in the new one seems to me to be the same procedure as the use of remains coming from past life in the dream-work as described by Freud, in the *Interpretation of Dreams*. This use of repetition or quotation, be it ironical or not, cynical or not, can be seen in the trends dominating contemporary painting, under the name of "transavantgardism" (Achille Bonito Oliva) or under the name of neo-expressionism. I'll come back to this question in my third point.

The second point. A second connotation of the term "postmodern," and I admit that I am at least partly responsible for the misunderstanding associated with this meaning.

The general idea is a trivial one. One can note a sort of decay in the confidence placed by the last two centuries in the idea of progress. This idea of progress as possible, probable or necessary was rooted in the certainty that the development of the arts, technology, knowledge and liberty would be profitable to mankind as a whole. To be sure, the question of knowing which was the subject truly victimized by the lack of development—whether it was the poor, the worker, the illiterate—remained open during the 19th and 20th centuries. There were disputes, even wars, between liberals, conservatives and leftists over the very name of the subject we are to help to become emancipated. Nevertheless, all the parties concurred in the same belief that enterprises, discoveries and institutions are legitimate only insofar as they contribute to the emancipation of mankind.

After two centuries, we are more sensitive to signs that signify the contrary....Following Theodor Adorno, I use the name of Auschwitz to point out the irrelevance of empirical matter, the stuff of recent past history, in terms of the modern claim to help mankind to emancipate itself. What kind of thought is able to sublate (*Aufheben*) Auschwitz in a general (either empirical or speculative) process toward a universal emancipation? So there is a sort of sorrow in the *Zeitgeist*. This can express itself by reactive or reactionary attitudes or by utopias, but never by a positive orientation offering a new perspective.

The development of techno-sciences has become a means of increasing disease, not of fighting it. We can no longer call this development by the old name of progress. This development seems to be taking place by itself, by an autonomous force or "motricity." It doesn't respond to a demand coming from human needs. On the contrary, human entities (individual or social) seem always to be destabilized by the results of this development. The intellectual results as much as the material ones. I would say that mankind is in the condition of running after the process of accumulating new objects of practice and thought. In my view it is a real and obscure question to determine the reason of this process of complexification. It's something like a destiny toward a more and more complex condition. Our demands for security, identity and happiness, coming from our condition as living beings and even social beings, appear today irrelevant in the face of this sort of obligation to complexify, mediate, memorize and synthesize every object, and to change its scale. We are in this techno-scientific world like Gulliver: sometimes too big, sometimes too small, never at the right scale. Consequently, the claim for simplicity, in general, appears today that of a barbarian.

From this point, it would be necessary to consider the division of mankind into two parts: one part confronted with the challenge of complexity; the other with the terrible ancient task of survival. This is a major aspect of the failure of the modern project (which was, in principle, valid for mankind as a whole).

The third argument is more complex, and I shall present it as briefly as possible. The question of postmodernity is also the question of the expressions of thought: art, literature, philosophy, politics. You know that in the field of art for example, and more especially the plastic arts, the dominant idea is that the big movement of avant-gardism is over. There seems to be general agreement about laughing at the avant-gardes, considered as the expression of an obsolete modernity. I don't like the term avant-garde any more than anyone else, because of its military connotations. Nevertheless I would like to observe that the very process of avant-gardism in painting was in reality a long, obstinate and highly responsible investigation of the presuppositions implied in modernity. The right approach, in order to understand the work of painters from, say, Manet to Duchamp or Barnett Newman, is to compare their work with the anamnesis which takes place in psychoanalytical therapy. Just as the patient elaborates his present trouble by freely associating the more imaginary, immaterial, irrelevant bits with past situations, so discovering hidden meanings of his life, we can consider the work of Cézanne, Picasso, Delaunay, Kandinsky, Klee, Mondrian, Malevitch and finally Duchamp as a working through—what Freud called *Durcharbeitung*—operated by modernity on itself. If we give up this responsibility, it is certain that we are condemned to repeat, without any displacement, the modern neurosis, the Western schizophrenia, paranoia, and so on. This being granted, the "post-" of postmodernity does not mean a process of coming back or flashing back, feeding back, but of *ana*-lyzing, *ana*-mnesing, of reflecting.

鲍德里亚：《拟像与仿真》

选文简介

选文开篇处，鲍德里亚引用了博尔赫斯的一则小说。小说中，一个已湮灭在历史长河中的国家，其地图流传了下来，变成了图纸上的真实。鲍德里亚以这个故事作为楔子，引入了"超真实"的概念——它特指拟像机制生成的没有本源或现实的真实。在超真实的框架下，不是先有国土，才有地图，用地图表征真实；而是先有地图，才有国土，是地图生成真实。在鲍德里亚看来，我们已经迈入仿真时代。这个时代的空间不再由真实和真理的经纬织就，真实指涉物被清除了，复活的是符号系统产生的人工指涉物，用有关真实的符号代替了真实。鲍德里亚在选文中详细说明了仿真所依托的拟像机制，它包括四个阶段：1）它是对某种基本真实的反映；2）它遮蔽以及篡改这种基本的真实；3）它遮蔽了基本真实的缺席；4）它与任何真实都没有联系，纯粹是自身的拟像。在鲍德里亚看来，美国的迪士尼乐园就是这种以仿真逻辑运行的超真实世界。

From *Simulacra and Simulation*

Jean Baudrillard (1929-2007)

If we were able to take as the finest allegory of simulation the Borges tale where the cartographers of the Empire draw up a map so detailed that it ends up exactly covering the territory (but where the decline of the Empire see this map become frayed and finally ruined, a few shreds still discernible in the deserts—the metaphysical beauty of this ruined abstraction, bearing witness to an imperial pride and rotting like a carcass, returning to the substance of the soil, rather as an aging double ends up being confused with the real thing)—then this fable has come full circle for us, and now has nothing but the discrete charm of second-order simulacra.

Abstraction today is no longer that of the map, the double, the mirror or the concept. Simulation is no longer that of a territory, a referential being or a substance. It is the generation by models of a real without origin or reality: a hyperreal. The territory no longer precedes the map, nor survives it. Henceforth, it is the map that precedes the territory—PRECESSION OF SIMULACRA—it is the map that engenders the territory and if we were to revive the fable today, it would be the territory whose shreds are slowly rotting across the map. It is the real, and not the map, whose vestiges subsist here and there, in the deserts which are no longer those of the Empire, but our own. *The desert of the real itself.*

In fact, even inverted, the fable is useless. Perhaps only the allegory of the Empire remains. For it is with the same Imperialism that present-day simulators try to make the real, all the real, coincide with their simulation models. But it is no longer a question of either maps or territory. Something has disappeared: the sovereign difference between them that was the abstraction's charm. For it is the difference which forms the poetry of the map and the charm of the territory, the magic of the concept and the charm of the real. This representational imaginary, which both culminates in and is engulfed by the cartographer's mad project of an ideal coextensivity between the map and the territory, disappears with simulation—whose operation is nuclear and genetic, and no longer specular and discursive. With it goes all of metaphysics. No more mirror of being and appearances, of the real and its concept. No more imaginary coextensivity: rather, genetic miniaturization is the dimension of *simulation*. The real is produced from miniaturized units, from matrices, memory banks and command models—and with these it can be reproduced an indefinite number of times. It no longer has to be rational, since it is no longer measured against some ideal or negative instance. It is nothing more than operational. In fact, since it is no longer enveloped by an imaginary, it is no longer real at all. It is a hyperreal, the product of an irradiating synthesis of combinatory models in a hyperspace without atmosphere.

In this passage to a space whose curvature is no longer that of the real, nor of truth, the age of simulation thus begins with a liquidation of all referentials—worse: by their artificial resurrection in systems of signs, a more ductile material than meaning, in that it lends itself to all systems of equivalence, all binary oppositions and all combinatory algebra. It is no longer a question of imitation, nor of reduplication, nor even of parody. It is rather a question of substituting signs of the real for the real itself, that is, an operation to deter every real process by its operational double, a metastable, programmatic, perfect descriptive machine which provides all the signs of the real and short-circuits all its vicissitudes. Never again will the real have to be produced—this is the vital function of the model in a system of death, or rather of anticipated resurrection which no longer leaves any chance even in the event of death. A hyperreal henceforth sheltered from the imaginary, and from any distinction between the real and the imaginary, leaving room only for the orbital recurrence of models and the simulated generation of difference.

The Divine Irreference of Images

To dissimulate is to feign not to have what one has. To simulate is to feign to have what one hasn't. One implies a presence, the other an absence. But the matter is more complicated, since to simulate is not simply to feign: "Someone who feigns an illness can simply go to bed and make believe he is ill. Some[one] who simulates an illness produces in himself some of the symptoms." Thus, feigning or dissimulating leaves the reality principle intact: the difference is always clear, it is only masked; whereas simulation threatens the difference between "true" and "false," between "real" and "imaginary." Since the simulator produces "true" symptoms, is he ill or not? He cannot be treated objectively either as ill, or as not-ill. Psychology and medicine stop at this point, before a thereafter undiscoverable truth of the illness. For if any symptom can be "produced," and can no longer be accepted as a fact of nature, then every illness may be considered as simulatable and simulated, and medicine loses its meaning since it only knows how to treat "true" illnesses by their objective causes. Psychosomatics evolves in a dubious way on the edge of the illness principle. As for psychoanalysis, it transfers the symptom from the organic to the unconscious order: once again, the latter is held to be true, more true than the former—but why should simulation stop at the portals of the unconscious? Why couldn't the "work" of the unconscious be "produced" in the same way as any other symptom in classical medicine? Dreams already are.

The alienist, of course, claims that "for each form of the mental alienation there is a particular order in the succession of symptoms, of which the simulator is unaware and in the absence of which the alienist is unlikely to be deceived." This (which dates from 1865) in order to save at all cost the truth principle, and to escape the specter raised by simulation—namely that truth, reference and objective causes have ceased to exist. What can medicine do with something which floats on either side of illness, on either side of health, or with the reduplication of illness in a discourse that is no longer true or false? What can psychoanalysis do with the reduplication of the discourse of the unconscious in a discourse of simulation that can never be unmasked, since it isn't false either?...

So it is with simulation, insofar as it is opposed to representation. The latter starts from the principle that the sign and the real are equivalent (even if this equivalence is utopian, it is a fundamental axiom). Conversely, simulation starts from *the utopia* of this principle of equivalence, *from the radical negation of the sign as value*, from the sign as reversion and death sentence of every reference. Whereas representation tries to absorb simulation by interpreting it as false representation, simulation envelops the whole edifice of representation as itself a simulacrum.

This would be the successive phases of the image:

—it is the reflection of a basic reality

—it masks and perverts a basic reality

—it masks the *absence* of a basic reality

—it bears no relation to any reality whatever: it is its own pure simulacrum.

In the first case, the image is a *good* appearance—the representation is of the order of sacrament. In the second, it is an *evil* appearance—of the order of malefice. In the third, it *plays at being* an appearance—it is of the order of sorcery. In the fourth, it is no longer in the order of appearance at all, but of simulation.

The transition from signs which dissimulate something to signs which dissimulate that there is nothing, marks the decisive turning point. The first implies a theology of truth and secrecy (to which the notion of ideology still belongs). The second inaugurates an age of simulacra and simulation, in which there is no longer any God to recognize his own, nor any last judgment to separate true from false, the real from its artificial resurrection, since everything is already dead and risen in advance.

When the real is no longer what it used to be, nostalgia assumes its full meaning. There is a proliferation of myths of origin and signs of reality; of second-hand truth, objectivity and authenticity. There is an escalation of the true, of the lived experience; a resurrection of the figurative where the object and substance have disappeared. And there is a panic-stricken production of the real and the referential, above and parallel to the panic of material production: this is how simulation appears in the phase that concerns us—a strategy of the real, neo-real and hyperreal, whose universal double is a strategy of deterrence....

Hyperreal and Imaginary

Disneyland is a perfect model of all the entangled orders of simulation. To begin with it is a play of illusions and phantasms: Pirates, the Frontier, Future World, etc. This imaginary world is supposed to be what makes the operation successful. But what draws the crowds is undoubtedly much more the social microcosm, the miniaturized and *religious* reveling in real America, in its delights and drawbacks. You park outside, queue up inside, and are totally abandoned at the exit. In this imaginary world the only phantasmagoria is in the inherent warmth and affection of the crowd, and in that sufficiently excessive number of gadgets used there to specifically maintain the multitudinous affect. The contrast with the absolute solitude of the parking lot—a veritable concentration camp—is total. Or rather: inside, a whole range of gadgets magnetize the crowd into direct flows—outside, solitude is directed onto a single gadget: the automobile. By an extraordinary coincidence (one that undoubtedly belongs to the peculiar enchantment of this universe), this deep-frozen infantile world happens to have been conceived and realized by a man who is himself now cryogenized: Walt Disney, who awaits his resurrection at minus 180 degrees centigrade.

The objective profile of America, then, may be traced throughout Disneyland, even down to the morphology of individuals and the crowd. All its values are exalted here, in miniature and comic strip form. Embalmed and pacified. Whence the possibility of an ideological analysis of Disneyland (L. Marin does it well in *Utopies, jeux d'espaces*): digest of the American way of life, panegyric to American values, idealized transposition of a contradictory reality. To be sure. But this conceals something else, and that "ideological" blanket exactly serves to cover over a *third-order simulation*: Disneyland is there to conceal the fact that it is the "real" country, all of "real" America, which *is* Disneyland (just as prisons are there to conceal the fact that it is the social in its entirety, in its banal omnipresence, which is carceral). Disneyland is presented as imaginary in order to make us believe that the rest is real, when in fact all of Los Angeles and the America surrounding it are no longer real, but of the order of the hyperreal and of simulation. It is no longer a question of a false representation of reality (ideology), but of concealing the fact that the real is no longer real, and thus of saving the reality principle.

思考题

1. 德里达是如何从"中心"这个概念入手，批驳结构主义的自相矛盾之处的？他这样做的意义是什么？
2. 福柯的"作者"概念和我们平常所说的"作者"概念有什么不同？
3. 福柯认为作者功能具有哪些特点？
4. 利奥塔在选文中讨论了哪些与后现代有关的议题？他的主要观点是什么？
5. 鲍德里亚认为"拟像"是如何形成的？请详细解释它的四个步骤。
6. 鲍德里亚如何从"超真实"的角度理解美国的迪士尼乐园？

讨论题

1. 德里达批判逻各斯中心主义，利奥塔批判宏大叙事。请查阅资料，进行延伸阅读，在此基础上，讨论两位理论家批判视角的共通之处以及他们的立场给我们带来的思想启示。
2. 请从《美丽新世界》《仿生人会梦见电子羊吗？》《神经漫游者》等科幻小说，或者《黑客帝国》《楚门的世界》《西部世界》等影视作品中选择一部，参考鲍德里亚的"超真实"理论，对其进行讨论。

补充文本选摘与评述

德曼：《阅读的寓言》
From *Allegories of Reading*

Paul de Man (1919-1983)

Let me begin by considering what is perhaps the most commonly known instance of an apparent symbiosis between a grammatical and a rhetorical structure, the so-called rhetorical question, in which the figure is conveyed directly by means of a syntactical device. I take the first example from the sub-literature of the mass media: asked by his wife whether he wants to have his bowling shoes laced over or laced under, Archie Bunker answers with a question. He asks, "What's the difference?" Being a reader of sublime simplicity, his wife replies by patiently explaining the difference between lacing over and lacing under, whatever this may be, but provokes only ire. "What's the difference?" did not ask for difference but meant instead "I don't give a damn what the difference is." The same grammatical pattern engenders two meanings that are mutually exclusive: the literal meaning asks for the concept (difference) whose existence is denied by the figurative meaning. As long as we are talking about bowling shoes, the consequences are relatively trivial; Archie Bunker, who is a great believer in the authority of origins (as long, of course, as they are the right origins), muddles along in a world where literal and figurative meanings get in each other's way, though not without discomforts. But if a *de*-Bunker rather than a Bunker, a de-bunker of the *arché* (origin), an "Archie Debunker" such as Nietzsche or Jacques Derrida, asks the question "What is the Difference?" we cannot even tell from his grammar whether he "really" wants to know "what" difference is or is merely telling us that we should not even try to find out. Confronted with the question of the difference between grammar and rhetoric, grammar allows us to ask the question, but the sentence by means of which we ask it may deny the very possibility of asking. For what is the use of asking, I ask, when we cannot even authoritatively decide whether a question asks or doesn't ask?

The point is as follows. A perfectly clear syntactical paradigm (the question) engenders a sentence that has at least two meanings, one which asserts and the other which denies its own illocutionary mode. It is not that there are simply two meanings, one literal and the other figural, and that we have to decide which one of these meanings is the right one in this particular situation. The confusion can only be cleared up by the intervention of an extratextual intention, such as Archie Bunker setting his wife straight; but the very anger he displays is indicative of more than impatience: it reveals his despair when confronted with a structure of linguistic meaning that he cannot control and that holds the discouraging prospect of an infinity of similar future confusions, all of them potentially catastrophic in their consequences. Nor is this intervention really a part of the minitext constituted by the figure, which holds our attention only as long as it remains suspended and unresolved. I follow the usage of common speech in calling this semiological enigma "rhetorical." The grammatical model of the question becomes rhetorical not when we have, on the one hand, a literal meaning and, on the other hand, a figural meaning, but when it is impossible to decide by grammatical or other linguistic devices which of the two meanings (that can be entirely contradictory) prevails. Rhetoric radically suspends logic and opens up vertiginous possibilities of referential aberration. And although it would perhaps be somewhat more remote from common usage, I would not hesitate to equate the rhetorical, figural potentiality of language with literature itself....

...The deconstruction is not something we have added to the text; it constituted the text in the first place. A literary text simultaneously asserts and denies the authority of its own rhetorical mode; and, by reading the text as we did, we were only trying to come closer to being as rigorous a reader as the author had to be in order to write the sentence in the first place. Poetic writing is the most advanced and refined mode of deconstruction; it may differ from critical or discursive writing in the economy of its articulation, but it is not different in kind.

德勒兹、瓜塔里:《千高原》
From *A Thousand Plateaus*
Gilles Deleuze (1925-1995), Pierre-Félix Guattari (1930-1992)

Let us summarize the principal characteristics of a rhizome: unlike trees or their roots, the rhizome connects any point to any other point, and its traits are not necessarily linked to traits of the same nature; it brings into play very different regimes of signs, and even nonsign states. The rhizome is reducible neither to the One nor the multiple. It is not the One that becomes Two or even directly three, four, five, etc. It is not a multiple derived from the One, or to which One is added ($n + 1$). It is composed not of units but of dimensions, or rather directions in motion. It has neither beginning nor end, but always a middle (*milieu*) from which it grows and which it overspills. It constitutes linear multiplicities with n dimensions having neither subject nor object, which can be laid out on a plane of consistency, and from which the One is always subtracted ($n - 1$). When a multiplicity of this kind changes dimension, it necessarily changes in nature as well, undergoes a metamorphosis. Unlike a structure, which is defined by a set of points and positions, with binary relations between the points and biunivocal relationships between the positions, the rhizome is made only of lines: lines of segmentarity and stratification as its dimensions, and the line of flight or deterritorialization as the maximum dimension after which the multiplicity undergoes metamorphosis, changes in nature. These lines, or lineaments, should not be confused with lineages of the arborescent type, which are merely localizable linkages between points and positions. Unlike the tree, the rhizome is not the object of reproduction: neither external reproduction as image-tree nor internal reproduction as tree-structure. The rhizome is an antigenealogy. It is a short-term memory, or antimemory. The rhizome operates by variation, expansion, conquest, capture, offshoots. Unlike the graphic arts, drawing, or photography, unlike tracings, the rhizome pertains to a map that must be produced, constructed, a map that is always detachable, connectable, reversible, modifiable, and has multiple entryways and exits and its own lines of flight. It is tracings that must be put on the map, not the opposite. In contrast to centered (even polycentric) systems with hierarchical modes of communication and preestablished paths, the rhizome is an acentered, nonhierarchical, nonsignifying system without a General and without an organizing memory or central automaton, defined solely by a circulation of states. What is at question in the rhizome is a relation to sexuality—but also to the animal, the vegetal, the world, politics, the book, things natural and artificial—that is totally different from the arborescent relation: all manner of "becomings."

哈琴:《后现代主义诗学》
From *A Poetics of Postmodernism*

Linda Hutcheon (1947-   )

The paradoxes of postmodernism work to instruct us in the inadequacies of totalizing systems and of fixed institutionalized boundaries (epistemological and ontological). Historiographic metafiction's parody and self-reflexivity function both as markers of the literary and as challenges to its limitations. Its contradictory "contamination" of the self-consciously literary with the verifiably historical and referential challenges the borders we accept as existing between literature and the extra-literary narrative discourses which surround it: history, biography, autobiography. This challenge to the limitations of the humanist privileging (and simultaneous marginalizing) of the literary has had repercussions that have intersected with feminist and other "minoritarian" contestings of the canon as a stable, fixed body of eternally and universally accepted "great" works. The point of intersection here is in the realization shared by both theory and practice that "literariness depends crucially not on the formal properties of a text in themselves but on the position which those properties establish for the text within the matrices of the prevailing ideological field."

Instead of a "poetics," then, perhaps what we have here is a "problematics": a set of problems and basic issues that have been created by the various discourses of postmodernism, issues that were not particularly problematic before but certainly are now. For example we now query those boundaries between the literary and the traditionally extra-literary, between fiction and non-fiction, and ultimately, between art and life. We can interrogate these borders, though, only because we still posit them. We think we know the difference. The paradoxes of postmodernism serve to call to our attention both our continuing postulation of that difference and also a newer epistemological doubt. (*Do* we know the difference? *Can* we?) The focus of this doubt in postmodern art and theory is often on the historical, as we have seen. How can we know the past today? The question of historical knowledge is obviously not a new one, but the powerful and unignorable conjunction of multiple challenges to any unproblematic concept of it in art and in theory today is one of those intersections that, I think, define the postmodern....

Considerations of this postmodern poetics or problematics would also include the many issues which result from these challenges to the knowing and writing of history, issues such as the textuality of the archive and the inevitable intertextuality of all writing. And it is not only literature that is involved in this contesting. What Renato Barilli (1986) has dubbed the art of the "Nuovi Nuovi" (New New) in Italian painting is reappraising the past of both local and international art and its relation to global informational mass culture. Similarly postmodern architecture's parodic return to the history of architectural form is an ironic (not nostalgic) reworking of both the structural and ideological inheritance that was deliberately wiped out of architectural memory by high modernism. Parody is the ironic mode of intertextuality that enables such revisitations of the past. Such self-reflexive, parodic interrogating of history has also brought about a questioning of the assumptions beneath both modernist aesthetic autonomy and unproblematic realist reference. The entire notion of reference in art has been problematized by the postmodern mingling of the historical and the self-reflexive.

选文评述

在《阅读的寓言》中，德曼从电视剧中挑选了一个带有文学性的场景进行解读：妻子问丈夫打算怎么系鞋带，要从上面系还是从下面系。丈夫答："有什么区别？"妻子仔细解释了区别。丈夫懊恼地反问："有什么区别？"从语法来看，这是个特殊疑问句，但丈夫把它当作设问句来使用。有什么区别？没什么区别，鞋带怎么系都可以。这个例子里，语法也变成了修辞的一部分，相互矛盾的意义同时存在。在德曼看来，这反映了语言的本质：语言与它的指涉不是明晰对应的关系，存在诸多解读的可能性。德曼认为无须从文本之外引入解构立场，解构就内嵌于文本之中。

德勒兹和瓜塔里在合著的《千高原》中详细讨论了"块茎"的概念。德勒兹和瓜塔里批评西方的形而上学传统对具有固定结构的"树状"或"根状"模式的依赖。他们有感于块茎植物根系蔓生的特点，决定用"块茎"来隐喻非中心性的非等级制的非意指的空间样态。德勒兹和瓜塔里指出，各块茎之间既相互连接又相互隔开，既是一，也是多，是多元体。此外，块茎无起源无终结，不断生长，有不同的伸展领域，其空间维度具有反辖域化的逃逸特征。究其本质，块茎反映了德勒兹和瓜塔里所推崇的"生成"观，是生命能量的多样多姿的体现。

在《后现代主义诗学》的选文中，哈琴聚焦后现代主义诗学的跨边界特征。她以历史编撰元小说为例，指出该文类跨越了文学与历史、传记等非虚构作品的区分，且倚重于互文性，具有对话性和杂糅性。此外，后现代艺术还擅长使用反讽手法，在互文基础上进行反思。如果我们将德曼的选文和哈琴的相比较，可以看出秉承解构立场的德曼认为文学是自治领域；而哈琴虽然也承认文学语言的自我指涉性，但她认为文学和历史等其他文类之间是有联系的，跨界带来的是对边界的重新定义。

关键术语释例

1. **延异（différance）**：延异是德里达自创的词，具有两面性含义。它既表示差异，也表达延迟。前者具有空间性，后者具有时间性。德里达的延异观是对索绪尔的符号论的质疑。索绪尔的符号论也是兼具时间性和空间性。索绪尔认为符号在表意链上的各占其位，决定了符号意义的差异。当能指沿着时间线性顺序，遵循句法规则，与所指形成一一对应时，意义由此生成。德里达却认为索绪尔用能指和所指的匹配掩盖了二者之间不可调和的差异本质。而且，当能指在表意链条上滑动，它不断指向的是新的能指，而不是抵达所指。德里达用延异的概念来展现意义总在延宕中，这种悬而未决中的能量正在推动差异性带来新的意义的生成。

2. **宏大叙事**（grand narrative）：宏大叙事指试图为社会提供全面的普适性的真理言说的叙事。在这个概念的提出者利奥塔看来，基督教的神学体系、黑格尔的哲学体系以及当代社会的科学技术体系都具有宏大叙事的特点。宏大叙事的问题在于，它追求大一统的言说，压制了个体的声音和普遍的生命力。而且，它特别容易被权力所利用，被意识形态所收编，变成社会压迫机制。利奥塔主张在后现代语境中反思宏大叙事包罗万象的野心，用带有地方性和个性的小叙事来对抗宏大叙事。

推荐书目

Best, Steven, and Douglas Kellner. *Postmodern Theory: Critical Interrogations*. New York: Guilford Press, 1991.

Bloom, Harold, et al. *Deconstruction and Criticism*. New York: Seabury Press, 1979.

Butler, Christopher. *Postmodernism: A Very Short Introduction*. Oxford: Oxford University Press, 2002.

Culler, Jonathan. *On Deconstruction: Theory and Criticism After Structuralism*. Ithaca: Cornell University Press, 1982.

Currie, Mark. *The Invention of Deconstruction*. New York: Palgrave Macmillan, 2013.

Jameson, Fredric. *Postmodernism, or, The Cultural Logic of Late Capitalism*. Durham: Duke University Press, 1991.

Norris, Christopher. *Deconstruction: Theory and Practice*. London: Routledge, 2002.

Zima, Peter V. *Modern/Postmodern: Society, Philosophy, Literature*. London: Continuum, 2010.

盛宁：《人文困惑与反思：西方后现代主义思潮批判》。北京：三联书店，1997年。

汪民安：《福柯的界线》。开封：河南大学出版社，2018年。

第十章
接受理论与读者反应批评

概述

文学作品由作者创作，以文本的形式存在，由读者来阅读。对作者、文本和读者三要素的考察构成文学理论的重要议题。从古典时代到近现代，作为文本创造者的作者一直在三要素中最受瞩目，围绕作者的创作动机、文学想象力、写作技巧、道德立场、历史语境的讨论从未停止。进入20世纪，"作者中心论"受到挑战，取而代之的是"文本中心论"，无论是俄国形式主义、英美新批评，还是结构主义和解构主义，都重视文学本体论研究。相比而言，虽然没人否定作为三要素之一的读者的重要性——读者是作者的写作对象，是阅读文本的人，但无论是在作者中心论的语境，还是在文本中心论的语境，读者的作用往往被低估、被窄化，仿佛读者仅是作者意图的传达对象以及文本信息的被动接受者。从20世纪60年代开始，读者才真正进入西方文论中心视域。战后德国兴起的接受理论（reception theory）认识到了读者在文学作品意义建构中的主体作用。它启发了美国学界对读者的阅读能力、心理机制、社会属性以及读者与文本的互动性等问题的研究关注，促进了读者反应批评（reader-response criticism）流派的发展。文学理论自此不仅关心"谁在写""为什么写""写什么"以及"如何写"，也关心"谁在读""为什么读""如何读"以及"读到什么"。

现当代西方理论界的"读者转向"始于德国接受理论的诞生。战后德国笼罩在二战之罪的阴影之下，学界风气保守谨慎，文学研究拘泥于文本的形式主义解读，畏惧深入的历史反思，否认文学介入现实的能力。以汉斯·罗伯特·姚斯（Hans Robert Jauss）和沃尔夫冈·伊瑟尔（Wolfgang Iser）为首的康斯坦茨大学的新锐学者们抨击这种学术立场的狭隘性，主张恢复文学研究与历史和现实的联系。他们把理论切入点放在读者身上，认识到读者置身于社会文化的具体语境之中，是文本世界与现实世界的接驳纽带。由此，康斯坦茨学派提出聚焦读者理解与阐释经验的接受理论。

接受理论既孵化于德国战后的历史文化语境，也深受欧陆哲学思想的滋养。仔细辨析，它有阐释学和现象学两条理论脉络。我们先看第一条脉络。西方历来就有阐释学传统，阐释学的英文hermeneutics源自Hermes，即希腊神话中的宙斯之子赫尔墨斯。赫尔墨斯负责向凡人传达神的指令，凡人听不懂神语，赫尔墨斯传令时少不了阐释的环节，"赫尔墨斯之学"也就是阐释之学。在中世纪，阐释传统在神学领域发挥重要作用。阐释学和语文学有很深的联系，认识到语言的复义与含混会增加理解的难度，探索正确解读《圣经》的方法，对《圣经》的奥义进行阐释，寻求对神的真正意涵的把握。进入启蒙时代后，阐释学不再仅为宗教服务，而是开始应用于世俗世界的各领域，近现代阐释学由此诞生。德国神学家、哲学家施莱尔马赫（Friedrich Schleiermacher）是其奠基性人物。施莱尔马赫从认识论角度定义阐释学，指出误解是普遍存在的，阐释学是正确理解他人话语的技艺，理解是阐释的基础。施莱尔马赫注意到理解的过程是言说过程的反转：言说时，思想化为表达；理解时，则从表达入手，还原言说者的所思所想。为此，阐释者需要克服可能会带来偏见的主观性，以实现阐释的忠诚。德国哲学家狄尔泰（Wilhelm Dilthey）发扬施莱尔马赫的阐释理论，将它推广为人文科学研究的普遍方法，而且还将理解和阐释的精神活动与生命哲学的宏观视角相联系，指出理解是通向作家和作品的生命世界的途径。他和施莱尔马赫一样重视阐释的忠实性，视阐释者和被阐释者的时代差距为干扰因素，主张阐释者应培养历史意识，跳出自己的认识框架，在阐释中尽可能贴近作者的语境。

施莱尔马赫和狄尔泰都承认阐释者的重要性，认为阐释者是理解和解释的主体。问题在于，他们要求阐释者摒弃自身的历史性和主观性，这其实是无法实现的。海德格尔（Martin Heidegger）认识到这种要求的盲区，提出不应只在认识论意义上谈阐释学，还要从本体论意义上理解何为阐释。阐释者的"此在"是"在世之在"。阐释活动中，阐释者、文本和世界不是各自独立，而是相互勾连的共在。而且，"此在"的当下性联系历时性和历史性，阐释活动中，当下视域与历史视域交汇。

德国哲学家伽达默尔（Hans-Georg Gadamer）在海德格尔的启发下，深入讨论阐释者的作用。在《真理与方法》（*Truth and Method*，1960）中，伽达默尔指出，阐释者在阐释开始前，头脑中已经有了由以往经验和预设观念组成的"前理解"（pre-understanding）。如果这种"前理解"意味着"成见"（prejudice），那么"成见"不是遮蔽理解的屏障，而是进入文本的认识起点，反映着读者的体验能力，决定着我们如何对世界敞开，是阐释的最初视野。进入阐释进程后，阐释者的个人视域与文本视域碰撞，对整体的理解与对各部分的理解相互依存、相互纠偏。在伽达默尔看来，理解既不能过度依赖个人主观立场，也不能实现绝对的客观性。阐释具有动态性和对话性，是一种循环往复的进程，推动阐释者不断调整视域、修正立场；阐释体现关系性，关联文本的部分与整体、内部世界与外部世界；阐释具有历史性，勾连过去和当下；阐释蕴含创造性和开放性，理解传统的同时，用新的阐释推动传统的演进，为传统注入鲜活的动力。

德国接受理论的代表理论家姚斯深受伽达默尔的影响，将阐释学方法论引入文学研究，强调读者在文本阐释中的主体作用，重点考察读者对文本的接受。与此同时，他期待以读者为引线，把历史带回文学研究的中心舞台。姚斯眼中的读者，不可能随心所欲，但也不会被文本彻底框定，有接受力，也有能动性。文学阐释的过程中，读者既被动接收文本信息，同时也主动理解和建构文本意义。而且，读者将"前理解"带入阐释，这意味着他的阅读必定有历史维度，在与文本的视域融合中，可能激发新的变化。姚斯认为形式主义建立静态的文学自治领的主张是徒劳而错误的，文学作品的意义是在与读者的历史对话中创造出来的，文学史的写作应该记录这种对话。

姚斯在《作为文学理论的挑战的文学史》("Literary History as a Challenge to Literary Theory"，1969)中指出，传统文学史书写有两种模式：关注客观历史的文学史书写注重对文学文本相关事实的罗列，是不断增加的"文学资料"的堆积，做的是收集与分类工作，缺乏真正的历史视野；经典文学史写作则太看重经典建构，缺少批判性。姚斯主张用文学史记录文学与读者的相互塑造。每个时代特有的审美感知倾向构成文学阐释的"期待视野"(horizon of expectations)。通俗文学和流行文学所迎合的是主流的期待视野。当作品具有先锋性和实验性，和读者预期之间存在审美距离时，读者的既有视野会受到挑战，激发其创造出新的视野，推动文学的新发展。在姚斯看来，文学史反映社会历史的过程，也展现了读者从旧的束缚中解脱出来的过程，从中可见人类的创造性和超越性。

德国接受理论的另外一位重要代表人物是伊瑟尔。伊瑟尔在其代表作《阅读行为》(*The Act of Reading: A Theory of Aesthetic Response*，1976)的中文版序言中，谈及接受理论有两个研究方向：接受研究考察读者在接受文本过程中所持有的立场、所做出的反应，倚重历史学和社会学的方法；反应研究关心读者如何受到文本结构的启示、调度和影响，倚重文本分析的方法。两个研究方向的结合构成了接受理论的全貌。从伊瑟尔所说的这两个方向，可以看出姚斯和伊瑟尔的区别：姚斯以接受研究为主，有宏观视野；伊瑟尔以反应研究为主，重视读者的阅读经验。深究区别的原因，可以发现姚斯受伽达默尔的阐释学思想影响，而伊瑟尔则受到了波兰哲学家英伽登（Roman Ingarden）的现象学角度的文学艺术论的启发。

从伊瑟尔这里，我们能够追溯到接受理论的另外一条思想源流，即现象学源流。现象学诞生于20世纪初，奠基人胡塞尔（Edmund Husserl）有感于当时西方思想界的认识论危机，反对自然主义对独立于意识的客观事物的确信立场，也反对心理主义的相对主义。此外，他还反对西方传统中唯理论对事物的抽象概念化。为此，他提出"悬置"的概念，把事物的客观存在放入括号中，搁置不论，转而关心人类意识活动的"意向性"。胡塞尔注意到当意识活动指向对象时，人的心灵结构与外部世界、主观思维和客观对象联系在了一起。胡塞尔的现象学的落脚点在"现象"，看事物在人类意识活动的知觉体验中的显现，主张不谈抽象概念，回到事物本身。英伽登是胡塞尔的学生，他将现象学引入艺术研究，从艺术本体论出发，讨论艺术家的意向性如何在艺术品的创造中得以实现，艺术品以何种方式显现，以及艺术品如何能够使欣赏者获得审美愉悦。英伽登在《文学的艺术作品》（*The Literary Work of Art*，1931）中，聚焦文学的艺术审美议题。他指出，文学作品的显现方式具有多层次的结构性，召唤着读者按照结构图式进行阐释。但结构间也留有"未定点"，等待读者将它具体化，读者具体化的过程，也是感受、想象和创造的过程，这是文学作品艺术吸引力的来源。

伊瑟尔的读者论聚焦反应研究，有两个核心议题：一是文学作品如何调动读者的能动作用，促使他进行个性化加工；二是文本如何为这种加工活动提供预设结构。这两个问题显然都和英伽登的艺术现象学理论一脉相承。比如，伊瑟尔认为文学阅读能动性体现在读者对文本"空白"的填空。伊瑟尔的"空白"概念受英伽登的"未定点"影响，但是，伊瑟尔专门解释过这两个概念的不同意涵：英伽登的"未定点"是文本结构的具体设置；而伊瑟尔的"空白"概念，与文本整体图式生成有关。在《文本与读者的互动》（"Interaction Between Text and Reader"，1980）中，伊瑟尔指出文本叙事中暗藏着四种视角：叙述者视角、人物视角、情节视角和虚构读者视角。视角之间的冲突和差异会导致文本网络出现"空白"。读者需要深度参与文本阐释，不断调整立足点，才能逐渐看到全局，通过想象、感受、思考等活动对空白进行填充。空白的"消失"意味着读者对文本形成了整体性的把握。

从伊瑟尔的第二个议题看，他和英伽登一样，关注文本结构对读者的预设和引导。但他比英伽登更关注读者的实践，考察文本的预设如何在读者的阅读进程中变成现实。他提出了"隐含读者"（implied reader）的概念，作为文本召唤结构和现实读者之间的枢纽。隐含读者是作品的主题、观点、叙述方式、语言风格等各种因素交织成的全局性的视点。当现实中的读者进入文本，开始阅读，他会受文本的引导，走向隐含读者所占据的制高点，看到作品的全面意义。需要强调的是，伊瑟尔反对抬高隐含读者，贬低现实读者。没有现实世界里的读者阅读，隐含读者只能停留在文本层面，无法激发意义生成。在伊瑟尔看来，现实读者向作者通过文本结构设置的隐含读者靠拢，是在贴近作者的创作历程，体验对文本的再创造。

当德国接受理论将读者问题作为文学研究的核心问题加以考察时，它在大洋彼岸的美国学界引起了强烈响应。美国学界之所以欢迎读者论，显性原因是20世纪60年代美国学界开始反思新批评和结构主义的文学本体论立场的局限性，而读者论为突破文本中心主义提供了新思路。隐性原因则是进入20世纪以来，美国文学研究领域一直重视读者阅读实践。美国本土影响力最大的新批评理论的确在法理上批判"情感谬见"，主张切断文本与读者的联系，但是它强调文本"细读法"，将其推广到美国各个层次的文学阅读教育之中，有效促进了读者阅读文本的实践活动，为读者转向提供了现实依托。因此，美国读者反应批评和德国接受理论相比，哲学思辨色彩淡，但高度关注读者的现实境遇，对读者阅读兴趣、阅读能力、阅读进程和文学共同体等问题进行考察，拓展了读者研究的视野。

美国读者反应批评的先锋人物是路易丝·罗森布拉特（Louise Rosenblatt）。1938年，罗森布拉特在《文学作为探索》（*Literature as Exploration*）中指出，读者通过与文学文本相互作用（interaction），拓展了个人经验，提升了敏感性、想象力和感悟力。1978年，她在《读者·文本·诗歌》（*The Reader, the Text, the Poem: The Transactional Theory of the Literary Work*）中修改了自己的观点，提出了交互式阅读（transactive reading）的概念。她认为"互动"（interaction）概念默认了读者和文本是两个独立实体，它们之间仿佛两粒台球一样在进行机械碰撞；而交互式阅读是事件性的，有具体情境，读者和文本进行来回往复的商讨交换。她将阅读进一步细分为输出阅读（efferent reading）和审美阅读（aesthetic reading）：前者关心对文本输出信息的准确掌握，阅读科学文献便是如此；后者旨在获得审美经验，文学阅读更偏向这一类。印在纸上的诗行构成的只是文本，经过阅读，读者的心理影像、情感和联想等均被唤起，这些文本才成为真正意义上的诗。罗森布拉特看重读者阅读文学时的经验性、审美愉悦和能动性，其理论对文学教学有重要影响。

文学阅读中的读者也是美国理论家乔纳森·卡勒（Jonathan Culler）的关注对象。在《结构主义诗学》（*Structuralist Poetics: Structuralism, Linguistics, and the Study of Literature*，1975）中，他设专章讨论"文学能力"。他注意到读者遇到文学作品时，会以特定的程式进行阅读。如果按照德国接受理论来看，这种程式化的反应源自文本结构的召唤。卡勒则从读者身上找原因，认为这是因为读者具备"文学能力",即了解文学的运作模式,能识别文学的惯例、符号和规则,将其用于阐释。卡勒认为文学理论是文学能力的重要组成部分。他还指出,结构主义文论其实是一种阅读理论:它生成于对文学现象的提炼,也为读者提供了解析文学的有效工具。

卡勒谈文学能力的建构性,而美国读者反应批评的另外一位重要理论家斯坦利·费什(Stanley Fish)则专注于对这种建构性进行解构分析。他用"有见识的读者"(informed reader)来指称具备足够知识储备、拥有文学能力的读者。这些读者的"见识",看似帮助他们"正确"认识文本,其实是向读者提供了进行文本意义生产的工具。在收录在《这个课堂有文本吗?》(*Is There a Text in This Class? The Authority of Interpretive Communities*,1980)这部文集中的《如何看到一首诗时知道它是诗》("How to Recognize a Poem When You See One")一文中,费什讲了一则课堂轶事。语言学课后,黑板上留下的板书写着几位语言学家的名字。在接下来的文学课上,文学专业的学生纷纷把板书解读为一首诗,对它的深意进行了各种挖掘。费什用这个例子说明文本内部无意义,意义由读者生成,且离不开特定阐释策略的运用。他反对伊瑟尔的文本特意留白等待读者发现与补充的观点。在他看来,不同读者的期待视野、阅读假设、解读策略都不一样,文本给定了什么取决于读者发现和补充了什么、读出了什么。那么,该如何解释不同读者会对同一个文本形成相似的看法?费什认为读者分属各自的"阐释共同体"(interpretive communities),在同一个共同体里的读者有相似的立场和阐释策略,他们的解读必定是同质化的。"人以群分",读者评价相左,是因为他们的阐释共同体相异。费什认为文本解读没有标准答案,也不存在误读,只有特定解读范式受到了学术以及权威机制的加持,被视为"标准答案"。

费什分析阐释共同体的主观立场,戴维·布莱希(David Bleich)则关心作为个体的读者,提出了"主观性读者"(subjective reader)的概念。布莱希认为写作是作者对自己的生活经验的回应,阐释是读者对自己的阅读经验的回应。我们的心灵是我们进行文学体验的根基所在。每位读者进入文本的诉求不同,个人经验不同,与作者的共鸣不同,对文本的反应因而具有多元化的特点。布莱希指出,检验文学批评解读的标准是它的社会生存力,有生存力的批评体现了读者的主观感受的普遍性,反映着群体性的价值观。

关注读者个体性的还有荷兰学者诺曼·霍兰德(Norman Holland)。他的落脚点是在个人阅读时的心理维度。在《同一文本五个读者》(*5 Readers Reading*,1975)中,霍兰德请五位读者共同阅读三篇短篇小说并写出他们的感受。他以精神分析的核心概念"身份"为线索,来解释五位读者阅读同一个文本后出现个性化解读的原因。霍兰德不是拉康学派的理论家，他对"身份"的理解更偏向传统，认为我们每个人心理层面都有相对稳定的连续性的身份意识。他用音乐术语做类比，指出身份是一种个人风格，有鲜明的主旋律，但也有各种动态的调性变化。阅读中，个人的爱憎好恶决定了读者对文本内容是接受还是排斥，而文本带来的冲击，也令个性化身份做出调整。在《交互式批评》("Transactive Criticism: Re-Creation Through Identity"，1976）一文中，霍兰德指出，读者在阅读文本过程中，防御（defense）、期待（expectation）、幻想（fantasy）和转化（transformation）等一系列心理机制（合称为DEFT）都在起作用，牵涉焦虑、恐惧、希冀、憧憬、愿望等心理能量。自我身份驱动阅读反应，也被阅读的作品所构筑。

　　从方法论来看，霍兰德的读者理论以精神分析为主，但他关心读者阅读进程和自我认识，因此他的理论也具备一些认知诗学的特点。实际上，他后来的研究兴趣也转向了认知诗学。在21世纪的当代，认知诗学是读者理论新发展的方向之一。认知诗学是研究文学如何与人类认知过程相交互的学科，它将心理学、神经科学、人类学等学科的理论和方法应用于文学研究中。普通读者为什么要阅读小说？如何阅读小说？在阅读过程中，有什么样的认知发现？美国理论家莉萨·詹塞恩（Lisa Zunshine）的《我们为什么读小说》（*Why We Read Fiction: Theory of Mind and the Novel*，2006）对此类问题进行了探索性的回答。詹塞恩提出，小说对普通读者的吸引力源于它们可以激发心智理论（Theory of Mind，简称ToM）这一基本认知能力。在日常生活中，我们遇到和陌生人打交道、处理复杂人际问题、寻求合作等情境时，经常会调用心智理论的认知能力，通过对他人的信念、愿望和情感的归因，来理解和预测他们的行为。在詹塞恩看来，人们之所以热爱阅读文学作品，也是基于这种认知他人心理的渴望。小说叙事提供了独特的平台，能让读者用"读心术"理解角色的思想、感情和意图，且在阅读中不断评判和校正理解的准确度。读者获得审美愉悦时，心智理论也得到了加强。

　　综上所述，我们可以看到读者理论在二战后的发展丰富了文学研究的内涵。德国接受理论揭示出作品—读者的复杂联动和历史维度。美国的读者反应批评拓展了对读者的身份、意图、阐释策略、主观能动性等议题的讨论。事实上，读者问题紧密关联文学意义的生成，涉及读者如何理解自我、作品、历史和世界，以及在此基础上进行创造。读者理论关注我们作为读者如何在阅读中将文学与人类生命经验、现实世界和历史纵深连接在一起，这种连接中既有个体心灵的震颤，也有集体性的回旋共鸣以及新声初绽。

主要文本阅读

姚斯:《作为文学理论的挑战的文学史》

选文简介

姚斯在《作为文学理论的挑战的文学史》的开篇阐明了全文问题意识的由来:他注意到在过去的一百五十年中,文学史研究日趋衰落。19世纪语文学家的最高理想是写一部民族文学史,进入20世纪,文学史书写却成了被遗忘的领域。姚斯认为这种衰落不可避免,因为旧式的文学史研究方法存在缺陷:百年来,文学史研究要么忙于提供编年体的事实罗列,忽视了对文学价值的关注;要么拘泥于伟大作家的生平和作品的主线,缺乏整体性和社会性的文学史观。在选文中,姚斯反对以上鼓吹"客观性"的文学史研究方法,提出文学史应反映读者和文本的对话,勾勒读者对文学作品的接受史,记录每一代读者的期待视野随时代发展和文学创新而出现的调整与变化。姚斯的文学史观是动态史观,作品的社会文化价值和审美价值生成于读者在当下语境对凝结着历史的作品的解读,也等待着后来者续写传承。

From "Literary History as a Challenge to Literary Theory"

Hans Robert Jauss (1921-1997)

For the critic who judges a new work, the writer who conceives of his work in light of positive or negative norms of an earlier work and the literary historian who classifies a work in his tradition and explains it historically are also readers before their reflex relationship to literature can become productive again. In the triangle of author, work and reading public the latter is no passive part, no chain of mere reactions, but even history-making energy. The historical life of a literary work is unthinkable without the active participation of its audience. For it is only through the process of its communication that the work reaches the changing horizon of experience in a continuity in which the continual change occurs from simple reception to critical understanding, from passive to active reception, from recognized aesthetic norms to a new production which surpasses them. The historicity of literature as well as its communicative character presupposes a relation of work, audience and new work which takes the form of a dialogue as well as a process, and which can be understood in the relationship of message and receiver as well as in the relationship of question and answer, problem and solution. The circular system of production and of representation within which the methodology of literary criticism has mainly moved in the past must therefore be widened to include an aesthetics of reception and impact if the problem of understanding the historical sequence of literary works as a continuity of literary history is to find a new solution....

Literary history can be rewritten on this premise, and the following remarks suggest seven theses that provide a systematic approach to such rewriting.

I

If literary history is to be rejuvenated, the prejudices of historical objectivism must be removed and the traditional approach to literature must be replaced by an aesthetics of reception and impact. The historical relevance of literature is not based on an organization of literary works which is established *post factum* but on the reader's past experience of the "literary data." This relationship creates a dialogue that is the first condition for a literary history. For the literary historian must first become a reader again himself before he can understand and classify a work; in other words, before he can justify his own evaluation in light of his present position in the historical progression of readers.

...A literary work is not an object which stands by itself and which offers the same face to each reader in each period. It is not a monument which reveals its timeless essence in a monologue. It is much more like an orchestration which strikes ever new chords among its readers and which frees the text from the substance of the words and makes it meaningful for the time: "words which must, at the same time that they speak to him, create an interlocutor capable of listening." A literary work must be understood as creating a dialogue, and philological scholarship has to be founded on a continuous re-reading of texts, not on mere facts. Philological scholarship is continuously dependent upon interpretation, which must have as its goal, along with learning about the object, the reflection upon and description of the perfection of this knowledge as an impulse to new understanding.

History of literature is a process of aesthetic reception and production which take place in realization of literary texts on the part of the receptive reader, the reflective critic and the author in his continued creativity. The continuously growing "literary data" which appear in the conventional literary histories are merely left over from this process; they are only the collected and classified past and therefore not history at all, but pseudo-history. Anyone who considers such literary data as history confuses the eventful character of a work of art with that of historical matter-of-factness....

II

The analysis of the literary experience of the reader avoids the threatening pitfalls of psychology if it describes the response and the impact of a work within the definable frame of reference of the reader's expectations: this frame of reference for each work develops in the historical moment of its appearance from a previous understanding of the genre, from the form and themes of already familiar works, and from the contrast between poetic and practical language....

A literary work, even if it seems new, does not appear as something absolutely new in an informational vacuum, but predisposes its readers to a very definite type of reception by textual strategies, overt and covert signals, familiar characteristics or implicit allusions. It awakens memories of the familiar, stirs particular emotions in the reader and with its "beginning" arouses expectations for the "middle and end," which can then be continued intact, changed, re-oriented or even ironically fulfilled in the course of reading according to certain rules of the genre or type of text. The psychical process in the assimilation of a text on the primary horizon of aesthetic experience is by no means only a random succession of merely subjective impressions, but the carrying out of certain directions in a process of directed perception which can be comprehended from the motivations which constitute it and the signals which set it off and which can be described linguistically....The new text evokes for the reader (listener) the horizon of expectations and rules familiar from earlier texts, which are then varied, corrected, changed or just reproduced. Variation and correction determine the scope, alteration and reproduction of the borders and structure of the genre. The interpretative reception of a text always presupposes the context of experience of aesthetic perception. The question of the subjectivity of the interpretation and the taste of different readers or levels of readers can be asked significantly only after it has been decided which transsubjective horizon of understanding determines the impact of the text.

The ideal cases of the objective capability of such literary frames of reference are works which, using the artistic standards of the reader, have been formed by conventions of genre, style, or form. These purposely evoke responses so that they can frustrate them. This can serve not only a critical purpose but can even have a poetic effect. Thus Cervantes in *Don Quixote* fosters the expectations of the old tales of knighthood, which the adventures of his last knight then parody seriously....

There is also the possibility of objectifying the expectations in works which are historically less sharply delineated. For the specific reception which the author anticipates from the reader for a particular work can be achieved, even if the explicit signals are missing, by three generally acceptable means: first, by the familiar standards or the inherent poetry of the genre; second, by the implicit relationships to familiar works of the literary-historical context; and third, by the contrast between fiction and reality, between the poetic and the practical function of language, which the reflective reader can always realize while he is reading. The third factor includes the possibility that the reader of a new work has to perceive it not only within the narrow horizon of his literary expectations but also within the wider horizon of his experience of life....

III

If the horizon of expectations of a work is reconstructed in this way, it is possible to determine its artistic nature by the nature and degree of its effect on a given audience. If the "aesthetic distance" is considered as the distance between the given horizon of expectations and the appearance of a new work, whose reception results in a "horizon change" because it negates familiar experience or articulates an experience for the first time, this aesthetic distance can be measured historically in the spectrum of the reaction of the audience and the judgment of criticism (spontaneous success, rejection or shock, scattered approval, gradual or later understanding).

The way in which a literary work satisfies, surpasses, disappoints, or disproves the expectations of its first readers in the historical moment of its appearance obviously gives a criterion for the determination of its aesthetic value. The distance between the horizon of expectations and the work, between the familiarity of previous aesthetic experiences and the "horizon change" demanded by the response to new works, determines the artistic nature of a literary work along the lines of the aesthetics of reception: the smaller this distance, which means that no demands are made upon the receiving consciousness to make a change on the horizon of unknown experience, the closer the work comes to the realm of "culinary" or light reading. This last phrase can be characterized from the point of view of the aesthetics of reception in this way: it demands no horizon change but actually fulfills expectations, which are prescribed by a predominant taste, by satisfying the demand for the reproduction of familiar beauty, confirming familiar sentiments, encouraging dreams, making unusual experiences palatable as "sensations" or even raising moral problems, but only to be able to "solve" them in an edifying manner when the solution is already obvious. On the other hand, if the artistic character of a work is to be measured by the aesthetic distance with which it confronts the expectations of its first readers, it follows that this distance, which at first is experienced as a happy or distasteful new perspective, can disappear for later readers to the same degree to which the original negativity of the work has become self-evident and, as henceforth familiar expectation, has even become part of the horizon of future aesthetic experience.

伊瑟尔:《文本与读者的互动》

选文简介

伊瑟尔认为，读者对文本结构所做出的反应构成了读者的阅读行为。伊瑟尔重视阅读行为，因为它关联文学作品的两个极点：作者创作的文本是"艺术的极点"；需要读者来实现的是"审美的极点"。文学作品不是独立领域，而是这两个极点之间的虚拟态，既具有文本性，也在等待读者给它赋予现实生命力。在选文中，伊瑟尔重点讨论了阅读行为的复杂进程。他指出，文学文本由叙述者视角、人物视角、情节视角和虚构读者视角的多视点交汇而成，阅读进程中不同视角的文本片段陆续浮现、相互交织，形成了不断呼应又不断背离的阐释张力。面对文本世界，读者需要在文本中穿行，形成综合视野，才能觅得真意。阅读就是协调视角、填充空白、否定成见和发现新的意义——读者的能动性必然伴随着阅读行为的整个过程，文本结构为读者设下的挑战促使读者进行观察、思考和创造。

From "Interaction Between Text and Reader"

Wolfgang Iser (1926-2007)

Central to the reading of every literary work is the interaction between its structure and its recipient. This is why the phenomenological theory of art has emphatically drawn attention to the fact that the study of a literary work should concern not only the actual text but also, and in equal measure, the actions involved in responding to that text. The text itself simply offers "schematized aspects" through which the aesthetic object of the work can be produced.

From this we may conclude that the literary work has two poles, which we might call the artistic and the aesthetic: the artistic pole is the author's text, and the aesthetic is the realization accomplished by the reader. In view of this polarity, it is clear that the work itself cannot be identical with the text or with its actualization but must be situated somewhere between the two. It must inevitably be virtual in character, as it cannot be reduced to the reality of the text or to the subjectivity of the reader, and it is from this virtuality that it derives its dynamism. As the reader passes through the various perspectives offered by the text, and relates the different views and patterns to one another, he sets the work in motion, and so sets himself in motion, too....

Communication in literature, then, is a process set in motion and regulated, not by a given code, but by a mutually restrictive and magnifying interaction between the explicit and the implicit, between revelation and concealment. What is concealed spurs the reader into action, but this action is also controlled by what is revealed; the explicit in its turn is transformed when the implicit has been brought to light. Whenever the reader bridges the gaps, communication begins. The gaps function as a kind of pivot on which the whole text-reader relationship revolves. Hence, the structured blanks of the text stimulate the process of ideation to be performed by the reader on terms set by the text. There is, however, another place in the textual system where text and reader converge, and that is marked by the various types of negation which arise in the course of the reading. Blanks and negations both control the process of communication in their own different ways: the blanks leave open the connection between textual perspectives, and so spur the reader into coordinating these perspectives and patterns—in other words, they induce the reader to perform basic operations *within* the text. The various types of negation invoke familiar and determinate elements or knowledge only to cancel them out. What is cancelled, however, remains in view, and thus brings about modifications in the reader's attitude toward what is familiar or determinate—in other words, he is guided to adopt a position *in relation* to the text.

In order to spotlight the communication process we shall confine our consideration to how the blanks trigger off and simultaneously control the reader's activity. Blanks indicate that the different segments and patterns of the text are to be connected even though the text itself does not say so. They are the unseen joints of the text, and as they mark off schemata and textual perspectives from one another, they simultaneously prompt acts of ideation on the reader's part. Consequently when the schemata and perspectives have been linked together, the blanks "disappear."

If we are to grasp the unseen structure that regulates but does not formulate the connection or even the meaning, we must bear in mind the various forms in which the textual segments are presented to the reader's viewpoint in the reading process. Their most elementary form is to be seen on the level of the story. The threads of the plot are suddenly broken off, or continued in unexpected directions. One narrative section centers on a particular character and is then continued by the abrupt introduction of new characters. These sudden changes are often denoted by new chapters and so are clearly distinguished; the object of this distinction, however, is not separation so much as a tacit invitation to find the missing link. Furthermore, in each articulated reading moment, only segments of textual perspectives are presented to the reader's wandering viewpoint.

In order to become fully aware of the implication, we must bear in mind that a narrative text, for instance, is composed of a variety of perspectives, which outline the author's view and also provide access to what the reader is meant to visualize. As a rule, there are four main perspectives in narration: those of the narrator, the characters, the plot, and the fictitious reader. Although these may differ in order of importance, none of them on its own is identical to the meaning of the text, which is to be brought about by their constant intertwining through the reader in the reading process. An increase in the number of blanks is bound to occur through the frequent subdivisions of each of the textual perspectives; thus the narrator's perspective is often split into that of the implied author's set against that of the author as narrator. The hero's perspective may be set against that of the minor characters. The fictitious reader's perspective may be divided between the explicit position ascribed to him and the implicit attitude he must adopt to that position.

As the reader's wandering viewpoint travels between all these segments, its constant switching during the time flow of reading intertwines them, thus bringing forth a network of perspectives, within which each perspective opens a view not only of others, but also of the intended imaginary object. Hence no single textual perspective can be equated with this imaginary object, of which it forms only one aspect. The object itself is a product of interconnection, the structuring of which is to a great extent regulated and controlled by blanks.

In order to explain this operation, we shall first give a schematic description of how the blanks function, and then we shall try to illustrate this function with an example. In the time flow of reading, segments of the various perspectives move into focus and are set off against preceding segments. Thus the segments of characters, narrator, plot, and fictitious reader perspectives are not only marshaled into a graduated sequence but are also transformed into reciprocal reflectors. The blank as an empty space between segments enables them to be joined together, thus constituting a field of vision for the wandering viewpoint. A referential field is always formed when there are at least two positions related to and influencing one another—it is the minimal organizational unit in all processes of comprehension, and it is also the basic organizational unit of the wandering viewpoint.

The first structural quality of the blank, then, is that it makes possible the organization of a referential field of interacting textual segments projecting themselves one upon another. Now, the segments present in the field are structurally of equal value, and the fact that they are brought together highlights their affinities and their differences. This relationship gives rise to a tension that has to be resolved, for, as Arnheim has observed in a more general context: "It is one of the functions of the third dimension to come to the rescue when things get uncomfortable in the second." The third dimension comes about when the segments of the referential field are given a common framework, which allows the reader to relate affinities and differences and so to grasp the patterns underlying the connections. But this framework is also a blank, which requires an act of ideation in order to be filled. It is as if the blank in the field of the reader's viewpoint had changed its position. It began as the empty space between perspective segments, indicating their connectability, and so organizing them into projections of reciprocal influence. But with the establishment of this connectability the blank, as the unformulated framework of these interacting segments, now enables the reader to produce a determinate relationship between them. We may infer already from this change in position that the blank exercises significant control over all the operations that occur within the referential field of the wandering viewpoint.

Now we come to the third and most decisive function of the blank. Once the segments have been connected and a determinate relationship established, a referential field is formed which constitutes a particular reading moment, and which in turn has a discernible structure. The grouping of segments within the referential field comes about, as we have seen, by making the viewpoint switch between the perspective segments. The segment on which the viewpoint focuses in each particular moment becomes the theme. The theme of one moment becomes the background against which the next segment takes on its actuality, and so on. Whenever a segment becomes a theme, the previous one must lose its thematic relevance and be turned into a marginal, thematically vacant position, which can be and usually is occupied by the reader so that he may focus on the new thematic segment.

In this connection it might be more appropriate to designate the marginal or horizontal position as a vacancy and not as a blank; blanks refer to suspended connectability in the text, vacancies refer to non-thematic segments within the referential field of the wandering viewpoint. Vacancies, then, are important guiding devices for building up the aesthetic object, because they condition the reader's view of the new theme, which in turn conditions his view of previous themes. These modifications, however, are not formulated in the text—they are to be implemented by the reader's ideational activity. And so these vacancies enable the reader to combine segments into a field by reciprocal modification, to form positions from those fields, and then to adapt each position to its successor and predecessors in a process that ultimately transforms the textual perspectives, through a whole range of alternating themes and background relationships, into the aesthetic object of the text.

霍兰德:《交互式批评》

选文简介

如果询问精神分析派批评家霍兰德为什么一千个读者眼中会有一千个哈姆雷特,他的回答大概会是因为一千个读者在《哈姆雷特》里看到的不是丹麦王子,而是一千个读者自己。霍兰德认为身份构成了人类存在的根本,是万变不离其宗的整体性的个人意识。当读者阅读文学时,身份个性决定了其理解文学时的独特反应。需要注意的是,霍兰德的身份论很强调关系性。我们拥有个人身份,用它与世界打交道。捍卫什么、欲求什么、想象什么,都与我们的身份有关,而在捍卫、欲求、想象中,我们也在不断将外部世界的内容化为己有,将互动引发的变化融入有关身份的统一叙事中。这也是霍兰德所说的文学阅读DEFT机制的由来:阅读中,我们带着关联着欲望的期待(expectation)进入新文本;启动防御机制(defense)来处理与期待相符合或者相违背的内容;用幻想(fantasy)吸纳满足欲望的内容;通过对这些无意识的幻想的转化(transformation),生成思想、社会、伦理或者审美意义。以上四个机制不是按照线性顺序逐一开启,而是同时发挥作用。交互式批评模糊了读者和文本的主客体关系。对DEFT机制的认识,使读者在阅读中更清晰地了解自己,也使读者懂得如何向世界敞开。

From "Transactive Criticism"

Norman Holland (1927-2017)

I know about myself, for example, that my feelings about books and people, the things that turn me on sexually, the way I walk and talk and write essays—all these express certain central themes in my character. One can learn to look at oneself this way through psychoanalysis; one can also learn it simply through living. As Proust sagely puts it: "What we call experience is merely the revelation to our own eyes of a trait in our character...." "The human plagiarism which it is most difficult to avoid...is the plagiarism of ourselves."

One can look at those themes within a personality quite systematically. From the millions of ego choices which constitute a human being, facts as visible as words on a page, I can abstract subordinate patterns and themes and combine them until I arrive at a single unifying theme for that life, a way of stating the sameness or "identity" of the person living it. Operationally, I can arrive at a centering identity for the series of ego choices which manifest a particular person by the same method of interpretation which led me to a theme for the series of ego choices which is *Macbeth. Identity is the unity I find in a person if I look at him as if he were a text.*

Identity *de*scribes a person; it does not *pre*scribe one. No one has succeeded in using identity to predict what a person will do, only to show how what he is doing now fits in with what he has done before. To be sure, identity defines a personal style which sets constraints as well as possibilities. Yet the individual is free to act in any way that will fit into the style. We are all in some sense free to choose, to change, and to do the very opposite of what others predict of us (particularly if we know what it is). Identity is a way to be you or me, and only in that sense is it limiting.

Identity, moreover, is not unique. Just as the theme I derived for Macbeth might describe many other literary works, so the same identity theme might describe several different persons. Further, it may not even *be there*. Identity in this operational sense is a way of looking at a person, not necessarily something *in* them.

Although there may be a "primary identity" in Lichtenstein's sense, we cannot know it. Instead, we abstract from surface data to arrive at the essence of a given text or a person. When I do so, I engage in an act which becomes part of my own identity. And so do you. Each of us will bring different kinds of background information to bear. Each will seek out the particular issues that concern him. Each will have different ways of giving the person (or text) a satisfying coherence and significance....

The unity we find in texts or persons is impregnated with the personality that finds that unity. *Interpretation is a function of identity*, identity being defined operationally as what is found in a person by looking for a unity in him, in other words, by interpretation. We seem to be caught in a circular argument, but it is not the argument which is circular—it is the human condition in which we cannot extricate an "objective" reality from our "subjective" perception of it. What is not circular, of course, is the method of interpretation toward a unity. That remains fixed, although the interpretations resulting will vary according to the interpreter.

The idea that an interpretation expresses the character of the person doing the interpreting does not, of course, imply that all interpretations are equally good. True, they all may equally well fulfill the needs of the interpreters, but that does not imply that they will work equally well for other people besides the interpreter. Others might find, for example, that my interpretation of *Macbeth* leaves out certain features of the play or that they cannot follow the connections I made between details or themes—they may seem far-fetched to those with other critical styles, backgrounds, or identities.

Again, the position may seem solipsistic, but it is not. Unlike Berkeley, the transactive critic recognizes a real difference between saying, "It's terribly hot today," and "I find it terribly hot today." Or between saying, "*Macbeth* is a play about supernatural and natural things mixing in a man's mind," and saying, "As I interpret it, *Macbeth* is a play about supernatural and natural things mixing in a man's mind." The difference, however, is not in what they say about the weather or the play, but in the claims made by the critic. Saying "It's terribly hot today" implies not only that the speaker finds it hot, but that anyone else taking the air that day will also find it hot. Similarly, the critic who simply says "*Macbeth* is a play about..." implies that anyone else interpreting the play will come to the same conclusion about its theme that he has. But, of course, that is not true, as the never-ending stream of Shakespearean criticism proves. Such a claim cannot stand up against either the evidence—the great variation in interpretations even by equally skilled readers—or the general psychological principles: perception is a constructive act; interpretation is a function of identity.

Our next question is clear enough: If interpretation is a function of identity, what is that function? In the course of an "experiment" relating readers' comments on short stories to their identity themes (discovered through interviews and testing), I have arrived at four principles which I think govern the relationship between the reader's personality and the creation and re-creation of literary and other experiences. You can remember the four by an acronym—readers are DEFT in shaping literary works by means of *defense, expectation, fantasy*, and *transformation*. Although I must describe them sequentially, obviously all four go on together.

Expectation: each of us brings to a new experience a cluster of needs, hopes, fears, wishes, and so on, directed toward that yet-to-happen event. While these will at any given moment be quite specific (think, for example, of your expectations at the end of a scene of *Macbeth*), in a general way, we hope to gain as much pleasure as we can with as little pain or psychological effort. Our means for doing so are *defenses*, the mechanisms by which we ward off anxiety. The word is useful because it brings in a well-established clinical tradition and vocabulary, but I intend to include here all of an individual's characteristic ego strategies for making the world gratify his expectations. Reading literature, we construct our defenses from the verbal structures the literary work gives us—at least we do if we feel satisfied by it. If we do not have that feeling, its absence is a signal that we are not matching our defensive and adaptive strategies from the work, and we begin to defend against it, pushing the work away totally. If we do feel satisfaction, however, it is a signal that we are matching our characteristic defenses by means of the work, and taking it in. As we take it in, we invest it with *fantasy*, our characteristic clusters of wish and desire. (These are the oedipal and other wishes that psychoanalytic critics customarily talk about.) Finally—although, of course, all these four transactions take place as one— we *transform* those unconscious fantasies by means of the defensive strategies we have built up from the work toward an intellectual, social, ethical, or aesthetic meaning.

I would like to go into these four modalities more fully. Elsewhere, in *Poems in Persons* (1973) and *5 Readers Reading* (1975), I have described the total transaction at length, and, in an earlier work, *The Dynamics of Literary Response* (1968), which has more literary analysis and less psychology, I have described the fantasy and transformation parts of the transaction in great detail. Here in a limited space, we can compress all four principles into one over-arching one: identity re-creates itself or, it is perhaps clearer to say, personal style creates itself. One can think of these four separate principles as emphases on one aspect or another of a single transaction: shaping an experience to fit one's identity and in doing so, (D) avoiding anxiety, (F) gratifying unconscious wishes, (E) absorbing the event as part of a sequence of events, and (T) shaping it with that sequence into a meaningful totality. Through each and all of these, we use the literary work to symbolize and finally to replicate ourselves. We take the work into ourselves and make it part of our own psychic economy—identity re-creates itself.

费什:《这个课堂有文本吗?》

选文简介

在《这个课堂有文本吗?》中,费什表达了他的解构主义立场,认为文本的符号系统具有复义性和含混性,读者对文本的解读离不开对语境的理解,也离不开阐释策略的运用。所以文本不存在独立的权威释义,不同读者的解读之间会形成竞争。选文中,费什批驳了艾布拉姆斯等人对文本"正解"的执念,认为文学不是机械学或者数学,没有标准答案。文学意义的生成离不开规范和语境,而这二者本身是生成性的和流变性的。规范在变,阐释的策略在变,文本的意义也在变。此外,他认为艾布拉姆斯等人对阐释多样性会造成相对主义和唯我主义的担忧是多余的。没有一个人的解读可以是纯粹主观的,因为人无法脱离社会文化语境,无法脱离规范限制。无人能真正自说自话,大家分属于不同的"阐释共同体"。所以个性阅读不会妨碍共同交流,但它也不会导向确定性的权威共识。

From *Is There a Text in This Class?*

Stanley Fish (1938-)

Let me recall you to it by recalling the contention of Abrams and others that authority depends upon the existence of a determinate core of meanings because in the absence of such a core there is no normative or public way of construing what anyone says or writes, with the result that interpretation becomes a matter of individual and private construings none of which is subject to challenge or correction. In literary criticism this means that no interpretation can be said to be better or worse than any other, and in the classroom this means that we have no answer to the student who says my interpretation is as valid as yours. It is only if there is a shared basis of agreement at once guiding interpretation and providing a mechanism for deciding between interpretations that a total and debilitating relativism can be avoided.

But the point of my analysis has been to show that while "Is there a text in this class?" does not have a determinate meaning, a meaning that survives the sea change of situations, in any situation we might imagine the meaning of the utterance is either perfectly clear or capable, in the course of time, of being clarified. What is it that makes this possible, if it is not the "possibilities and norms" already encoded in language? How does communication ever occur if not by reference to a public and stable norm? The answer, implicit in everything I have already said, is that communication occurs within situations and that to be in a situation is already to be in possession of (or to be possessed by) a structure of assumptions, of practices understood to be relevant in relation to purposes and goals that are already in place; and it is within the assumption of these purposes and goals that any utterance is *immediately* heard. I stress immediately because it seems to me that the problem of communication, as someone like Abrams poses it, is a problem only because he assumes a distance between one's receiving of an utterance and the determination of its meaning—a kind of dead space when one has only the words and then faces the task of construing them. If there were such a space, a moment before interpretation began, then it would be necessary to have recourse to some mechanical and algorithmic procedure by means of which meanings could be calculated and in relation to which one could recognize mistakes. What I have been arguing is that meanings come already calculated, not because of norms embedded in the language but because language is always perceived, from the very first, within a structure of norms. That structure, however, is not abstract and independent but social; and therefore it is not a single structure with a privileged relationship to the process of communication as it occurs in any situation but a structure that changes when one situation, with its assumed background of practices, purposes, and goals, has given way to another. In other words, the shared basis of agreement sought by Abrams and others is never not already found, although it is not always the same one.

Many will find in this last sentence, and in the argument to which it is a conclusion, nothing more than a sophisticated version of the relativism they fear. It will do no good, they say, to speak of norms and standards that are context specific, because this is merely to authorize an infinite plurality of norms and standards, and we are still left without any way of adjudicating between them and between the competing systems of value of which they are functions. In short, to have many standards is to have no standards at all.

On one level this counterargument is unassailable, but on another level it is finally beside the point. It is unassailable as a general and theoretical conclusion: the positing of context- or institution-specific norms surely rules out the possibility of a norm whose validity would be recognized by everyone, no matter what his situation. But it is beside the point for any particular individual, for since everyone is situated somewhere, there is no one for whom the absence of an asituational norm would be of any practical consequence, in the sense that his performance or his confidence in his ability to perform would be impaired. So that while it is generally true that to have many standards is to have none at all, it is not true for anyone in particular (for there is no one in a position to speak "generally"), and therefore it is a truth of which one can say "it doesn't matter."

In other words, while relativism is a position one can entertain, it is not a position one can occupy. No one can *be* a relativist, because no one can achieve the distance from his own beliefs and assumptions which would result in their being no more authoritative *for him* than the beliefs and assumptions held by others, or, for that matter, the beliefs and assumptions he himself used to hold. The fear that in a world of indifferently authorized norms and values the individual is without a basis for action is groundless because no one is indifferent to the norms and values that enable his consciousness. It is in the name of personally held (in fact they are doing the holding) norms and values that the individual acts and argues, and he does so with the full confidence that attends belief. When his beliefs change, the norms and values to which he once gave unthinking assent will have been demoted to the status of opinions and become the objects of an analytical and critical attention; but that attention will itself be enabled by a new set of norms and values that are, for the time being, as unexamined and undoubted as those they displace. The point is that there is never a moment when one believes nothing, when consciousness is innocent of any and all categories of thought, and whatever categories of thought are operative at a given moment will serve as an undoubted ground.

Here, I suspect, a defender of determinate meaning would cry "solipsist" and argue that a confidence that had its source in the individual's categories of thought would have no public value. That is, unconnected to any shared and stable system of meanings, it would not enable one to transact the verbal business of everyday life; a shared intelligibility would be impossible in a world where everyone was trapped in the circle of his own assumptions and opinions. The reply to this is that an individual's assumptions and opinions are not "his own" in any sense that would give body to the fear of solipsism. That is, *he* is not their origin (in fact it might be more accurate to say that they are his); rather, it is their prior availability which delimits in advance the paths that his consciousness can possibly take. When my colleague is in the act of construing his student's question ("Is there a text in this class?"), none of the interpretive strategies at his disposal are uniquely his, in the sense that he thought them up; they follow from his preunderstanding of the interests and goals that could possibly animate the speech of someone functioning within the institution of academic America, interests and goals that are the particular property of no one in particular but which link everyone for whom their assumption is so habitual as to be unthinking. They certainly link my colleague and his student, who are able to communicate and even to reason about one another's intentions, not, however, because their interpretive efforts are constrained by the shape of an independent language but because their shared understanding of what could possibly be at stake in a classroom situation results in language appearing to them in the same shape (or successions of shapes). That shared understanding is the basis of the confidence with which they speak and reason, but its categories are their own only in the sense that as actors within an institution they automatically fall heir to the institution's way of making sense, its systems of intelligibility. That is why it is so hard for someone whose very being is defined by his position within an institution (and if not this one, then some other) to explain to someone outside it a practice or a meaning that seems to him to require no explanation, because he regards it as natural. Such a person, when pressed, is likely to say, "but that's just the way it's done" or "but isn't it obvious" and so testify that the practice or meaning in question is community property, as, in a sense, he is too.

We see then that (1) communication does occur, despite the absence of an independent and context-free system of meanings, that (2) those who participate in this communication do so confidently rather than provisionally (they are not relativists), and that (3) while their confidence has its source in a set of beliefs, those beliefs are not individual-specific or idiosyncratic but communal and conventional (they are not solipsists).

Of course, solipsism and relativism are what Abrams and Hirsch fear and what lead them to argue for the necessity of determinate meaning. But if, rather than acting on their own, interpreters act as extensions of an institutional community, solipsism and relativism are removed as fears because they are not possible modes of being. That is to say, the condition required for someone to be a solipsist or relativist, the condition of being independent of institutional assumptions and free to originate one's own purposes and goals, could never be realized, and therefore there is no point in trying to guard against it.

思考题

1. 姚斯认为文学史写作应该关注什么内容？为什么？
2. 伊瑟尔如何理解文学阅读行为？他为什么很重视文本中的"空白"？
3. 霍兰德认为在阅读文学时，我们会启动DEFT机制。它具体包含哪些环节？
4. 什么是费什所说的"阐释共同体"？
5. 艾布拉姆斯等批评家认为费什的读者反应批评理论会导致文学阐释的相对主义。费什是如何批驳这一观点的？

讨论题

1. 请根据本章选文，结合课外拓展性的阅读，对姚斯、伊瑟尔、霍兰德和费什对读者与文本之间的关系的理解进行简要综述。
2. 从华兹华斯和柯尔律治的《抒情歌谣集》、马克·吐温的《哈克贝利·费恩历险记》、塞缪尔·贝克特的《等待戈多》和约瑟夫·海勒的《第二十二条军规》等文学作品中任选一部，查找相关资料，结合文学史，讨论该作品的出现如何挑战了当时时代的"期待视野"，以及对新视野的生成产生了什么样的影响。

补充文本选摘与评述

伽达默尔：《真理与方法》
From *Truth and Method*

Hans-Georg Gadamer (1900-2002)

The anticipation of meaning that governs our understanding of a text is not an act of subjectivity, but proceeds from the communality that binds us to the tradition. But this is contained in our relation to tradition, in the constant process of education. Tradition is not simply a precondition into which we come, but we produce it ourselves, inasmuch as we understand, participate in the evolution of tradition and hence further determine it ourselves. Thus the circle of understanding is not a "methodological" circle, but describes an ontological structural element in understanding.

The significance of this circle, which is fundamental to all understanding, has a further hermeneutic consequence which I may call the "fore-conception of completion." But this, too, is obviously a formal condition of all understanding. It states that only what really constitutes a unity of meaning is intelligible. So when we read a text we always follow this complete presupposition of completion, and only when it proves inadequate, i.e. the text is not intelligible, do we start to doubt the transmitted text and seek to discover in what way it can be remedied....

...Hermeneutics must start from the position that a person seeking to understand something has a relation to the object that comes into language in the transmitted text and has, or acquires, a connection with the tradition out of which the text speaks. On the other hand, hermeneutical consciousness is aware that it cannot be connected with this object in some self-evident, unquestioned way, as is the case with the unbroken stream of a tradition. There is a polarity of familiarity and strangeness on which hermeneutic work is based: only that this polarity is not to be seen, psychologically, with Schleiermacher, as the tension that conceals the mystery of individuality, but truly hermeneutically, i.e. in regard to what has been said: the language in which the text addresses us, the story that it tells us. Here too there is a tension. The place between strangeness and familiarity that a transmitted text has for us is that intermediate place between being a historically intended separate object and being part of a tradition. The true home of hermeneutics is in this intermediate area.

罗森布拉特：《读者·文本·诗歌》
From *The Reader, the Text, the Poem*

Louise Rosenblatt (1904-2005)

The reading of a text is an event occurring at a particular time in a particular environment at a particular moment in the life history of the reader. The transaction will involve not only the past experience but also the present state and present interests or preoccupations of the reader. This suggests the possibility that printed marks on a page may even become different linguistic symbols by virtue of transactions with different readers. Just as a knowing is the process linking a knower and a known, so a poem should not be thought of as an object, an entity, but rather as an active process lived through during the relationship between a reader and a text. This experience may be the object of thought, like any other experience in life, but it should not be confused with an object in the sense of an entity existing apart from author or reader.

The danger is that the transactional view may be misunderstood as focusing too narrowly on "the mind" of the reader isolated from anything outside himself. Recall that the text is more than mere paper and ink. The transaction is basically between the reader and what he senses the words as pointing to. The paradox is that he must call forth from memory of his world what the visual or auditory stimuli symbolize for him, yet he feels the ensuing work as part of the world outside himself. The physical signs of the text enable him to reach through himself and the verbal symbols to something sensed as outside and beyond his own personal world.

The boundary between inner and outer world breaks down, and the literary work of art, as so often remarked, leads us into a new world. It becomes part of the experience which we bring to our future encounters in literature and in life.

This has perforce been a very sketchy initial presentation of only the broadest view of the reading of a poem. Many aspects of the reading process and many problems of critical theory remain to be treated. The following chapters will offer answers to such questions, among others, as the following: How do we distinguish the reading event that yields a poem from other kinds of reading? (chap. 3). What are the reader's activities during the process of evoking a poem from a text? (chap. 4). How does the text function in the transaction? (chap. 5). If literary works are events in time, how can we agree on something called *Hamlet* or *The Waste Land*? (chap. 6). How does the reader produce an interpretation of the work? What are the implications of the transactional nature of the poem for evaluation? for literary criticism, literary analysis, literary history? (chap. 7). The complexity of these questions is such that the transactional theory of the reading process will not be fully developed until the final chapter.

詹塞恩:《我们为什么读小说》
From *Why We Read Fiction*

Lisa Zunshine (1968-)

Our Theory of Mind allows us to make sense of fictional characters by investing them with an inexhaustible repertoire of states of mind, but the price that this arrangement may extract from us is that we begin to feel that fictional people do indeed have an inexhaustible repertoire of states of mind. Our pleasant illusion that there are at least *some* minds in our messy social world that we know well is thus tarnished by our suspicion that even those ostensibly transparent minds harbor some secrets. (Who knows, after all, what *exactly* went through Mr. Darcy's mind when he was introduced to Elizabeth's uncle and aunt?)

In other words, we may see the pleasure afforded by fictional narratives as grounded in our awareness of the successful testing of our mind-reading adaptations, in the respite that such a testing offers us from our everyday mind-reading uncertainties, or in some combination of the two. No matter which explanation or combination of explanations we lean toward, however, we have to remember that the joys of reading fictional minds are subject to some of the same instabilities that render our real-life mind-reading both exciting and exasperating.

If this is not complex enough, throw in some aesthetics. Some writers are willing to construct rather breathtaking tests of our mind-reading ability—provided we are willing to take those tests. (This "we," by the way, is a complex cultural compound, for it denotes a particularly historically situated reader with a particular individual taste.) After all, the story of Little Red Riding Hood tests our ToM quite well—with all the attributions of states of mind to the grandma, to the trusting little girl, and to the Big Bad Wolf that it requires from its readers/listeners. Still, as we grow older, we begin to hanker for different mind-reading fare. For literary critic Wayne Booth, for example, it has to be Henry James, and not just any James, but the one in his later period. Toward *that* James, Booth ends up feeling a profound "gratitude"—gratitude of a self-conscious reader of fiction at a certain point in his life toward an author who succeeded in making him try on a poignantly rich suit of mental states....

If you happen to be a sneaky cognitive literary theorist, you are only too delighted to hear Booth wondering "how can [he] express [his] conviction that it is good for [him] to be required to go through all this." Why (so you pipe in happily), if a reader's mind-reading profile is constituted like Booth's, there is no doubt that it is "good" for him or her to be "tested" by *The Wings of the Dove*. At every step, the book is telling such a reader, as it were: "*These* immensely complex, multi-leveled, ethically ambiguous, class-conscious, mutually reflecting and mutually distorting states of mind you are capable of navigating. *This* is how good you are at this maddening and exhilarating social game. Did you know it? *Now* you know it!"

选文评述

伽达默尔的《真理与方法》是一部从哲学角度深入讨论阐释学的著作。选文中，伽达默尔关注作为阐释基础的理解，认为理解的议题关涉的不是方法论，而是本体论，与人类的意识结构和认识范式有关。他指出，理解不是凭空而来，而是受传统影响，受人类思维结构的制约。前者使读者进入文本时，不断依据传统对文本进行语境化；后者意味着读者会在阅读中追求意义的完整性，遇到他者文本带来的阐释困境时，会努力理解文本，进行意义建构。伽达默尔认为阐释的循环中，有"成见"的读者遭遇陌生的文本，在阐释的循环中逐步加深理解。理解行为沟通着读者和文本、个体与社会、当下与历史。阐释学的家园在中间地带，一边是作为独立对象的文本，另一边是文本和读者所寄身的传统。

罗森布拉特在《读者·文本·诗歌》的选文中，将阅读理解为"事件"：它发生在特定时刻、特定环境。而读者也处在特定人生阶段，有特定的诉求。所以同样的文本符号，对不同的读者来说，意义不同，影响也不同。在罗森布拉特的交互式阅读理论中，文本不是独立的外在客体，读者的阅读也不是个人的心灵活动。阅读打破了内部世界和外部世界的界限，激发读者的反应，使读者跳出自己的小世界、进入新世界，因此是经验拓展的过程。

詹塞恩在《我们为什么读小说》中，从认知角度讨论我们阅读小说的体验。她注意到，我们在日常生活中经常不清楚自己是否真正理解他人所思所想，"读心术"既带来探究的乐趣，也带来不知何为真相的不确定感。小说世界为读者施展"读心术"提供了丰富的素材，为读者磨砺认知能力提供了各式各样的挑战。童年时代，我们通过阅读《小红帽》等简单的童话故事，学习分辨真相。成年之后，文学审美的乐趣在于深入亨利·詹姆斯这样的作家创造的复杂文学世界。当我们能读懂詹姆斯作品中人物内心的幽微之处，理解小说的道德意涵，看透其中的阶级意识形态时，我们的"心智理论"也在参透社会游戏的秘密。

关键术语释例

1. **视域融合（fusion of horizons）**：视域融合是伽达默尔的阐释学理论的基础概念。伽达默尔重视阐释行为的历史性，指出文本和阐释者各有诞生的具体语境，两者时间距离和历史情境的不同，造成了阐释者和文本的视域差异。阐释者无法摆脱自身的历史文化印记，带着"成见"进入文本视域，阐释者和阐释对象的视域彼此碰撞。伽达默尔反对阐释时以作品为中心，也反对以读者为中心。他主张将阐释活动视为视域的融合。虽然两种视域无法替代彼此，但通过融合，文本和读者可以突破各自的局限性。视域融合中既有文本和读者的交互作用，也有历史意义的互动，文本的历史性沾染了当下性，阐释者则获得了更宽阔的历史意识。

2. **情感文体学（affective stylistics）**：费什在1970年的文章《读者中的文学》（"Literature in the Reader: Affective Stylistics"）中提出了"情感文体学"的概念。它是对新批评理论家维姆萨特的"情感谬见"说的驳论。维姆萨特认为读者在阅读中会产生情感牵动，使本应客观的文本批评沦为印象化的评述。费什却认为阅读不应以文本为中心，而应关注读者对文本的体验，文学寓身于读者，旨在唤起读者感受,是读者的内在体验使文学具有意义。在费什看来,情感文体学的作用在于,它唤起了读者的自我意识,这种自我意识会让读者更好地进行文本细读,成为更有领悟力的阅读者。

推荐书目

Bennett, Andrew. *Readers and Reading*. London: Longman, 1995.

Davis, Todd F., and Kenneth Womack. *Formalist Criticism and Reader-Response Theory*. New York: Palgrave, 2002.

Freund, Elizabeth. *The Return of the Reader: Reader-Response Criticism*. London: Routledge, 2003.

Goldstein, Philip, and James L. Machor. *New Directions in American Reception Study*. Oxford: Oxford University Press, 2008.

Holub, Robert C. *Reception Theory: A Critical Introduction*. London: Methuen, 1984.

Palmer, Richard E. *Hermeneutics: Interpretation Theory in Schleiermacher, Dilthey, Heidegger, and Gadamer*. Evanston: Northwestern University Press, 1969.

Tompkins, Jane P. *Reader-Response Criticism: From Formalism to Post-Structuralism*. Baltimore: Johns Hopkins University Press, 1980.

Zimmermann, Jens. *Hermeneutics: A Very Short Introduction*. Oxford: Oxford University Press, 2015.

张隆溪:《道与逻各斯:东西方文学阐释学》,冯川译。南京:江苏教育出版社,2006年。

朱立元:《接受美学导论》。合肥:安徽教育出版社,2004年。

第十一章
女性主义

概述

女性主义理论的动力之源是女性在父权社会中为争取平等权利和自由解放所做的不懈抗争。它从历史进程、现实境遇以及社会文化实践等角度，对女性所遭受的各种形式的歧视与压迫进行解析，对女性追求社会公正和性别平等道路上的经验教训进行总结，旨在唤醒女性的自觉意识和主体能动性，为自身权益而战斗。它希冀通过对关乎女性的个体生命和集体诉求的各种议题的思考，促进社会变革，构筑不同性别之间和谐平等共生的未来。

女性主义思想的隐形线索可追溯到古希腊时代的女诗人萨福（Sappho）的诗作中闪烁的女性意识。文艺复兴时期，皮桑（Christine de Pisan）尝试在《女人城之书》（*The Book of the City of Ladies*，1405）中构想女性乌托邦。但女性主义真正意义的萌芽出现于18世纪末期。受启蒙运动的感召，女性开始从人权角度思考父权制对女性的歧视、奴役与权利剥夺，尝试为自己发声，反抗父权社会的暴政。1791年，法国女作家德古热（Olympe de Gouges）受法国大革命的影响，撰写了《女权和女公民权宣言》（*Declaration of the Rights of Woman and of the [Female] Citizen*），为女性争取教育权、就业权、财产权等基本权利。英国思想家玛丽·沃尔斯通克拉夫特（Mary Wollstonecraft）撰写了《女权辩护》（*A Vindication of the Rights of Woman*，1792），批评父权社会用柔弱、感性、顺从等"美德"标签束缚女性发展，要求男性承认女性在智识和道德上的平等，尊重女性的人权。她将反父权和反君权视为一体，将女性的解放和人类共同解放联系在一起。

进入19世纪，两性平权的诉求激励着女性，她们开始踏入公共领域，发动妇女运动。1848年，在伊丽莎白·卡迪·斯坦顿（Elizabeth Cady Stanton）等的倡导下，大约三百名代表在美国塞内卡福尔斯召开的大会（Seneca Falls Convention）上齐聚一堂，其中的一百名代表签署了《情感宣言》（Declaration of Sentiments），套用美国《独立宣言》中的"所有人生而平等"的概念，指明了"所有的男人和女人都生而平等"，鼓励女性争取政治、经济、教育、宗教等领域的基本权利。19世纪下半叶，以争取女性选举权为重点任务的妇女运动蓬勃发展。经过半个多世纪的努力，英国于1918年通过了《国民参政法案》（Representation of the People Act），给予三十岁以上有一定财产的女性投票权。1920年，美国也通过宪法第十九修正案（The Nineteenth Amendment to the United States Constitution），给予女性参加选举的资格。

20世纪上半叶，虽然女性赢得了参政权，也在教育、工作、婚姻等方面赢得了一定的基本权利，但父权思想的霸权地位未被撼动，社会结构未发生实质变化。英国的弗吉尼亚·伍尔夫（Virginia Woolf）在1929年出版的《一间自己的房间》（A Room of One's Own）中，形象地阐释了父权制的问题所在。她假设莎士比亚有一个与他一样才华横溢的妹妹。如果她和哥哥一样，来到伦敦戏剧界追寻梦想，只会落得被人始乱终弃、陷入癫狂的结局。在莎士比亚的时代，女性的才华反而是不幸的根源：要释放出她脑子里的东西（不论是什么），须有一种心境，然而她的全部生活条件，她所有的本能，都与那种心境相冲突。伍尔夫认为20世纪初的女性，其境遇没有实质性改变。女性被捧成了"家中天使"，被鼓励任劳任怨地为丈夫和家庭做奉献，却无人关心她该如何追求自我。为此，她直白地写道："想要写小说或诗歌，你每年必须有五百镑的收入，以及一间带锁的房间。""五百镑"意味着经济和物质保障，令女性不必依附于男性生活；"一间带锁的房间"可以把丈夫和孩子隔在门外，使女性拥有独立的心灵空间和创作空间。

二战期间，因男性参战，后方岗位空缺，女性得以广泛参与社会建设，自我意识进一步觉醒。二战后，法国哲学家波伏娃（Simone de Beauvoir）出版了被奉为"女性主义的《圣经》"的《第二性》（The Second Sex, 1949）。在两卷本中，她先以开阔的视野纵览世界文明历史进程，揭秘父权制如何得以确立，如何对女性进行定义和掌控；之后又以细腻的分析，解读女性在生命历程中如何被父权制所压迫，关涉女童、少女、妻子、母亲、老妇人等各个阶段，论及性经验、工作、家庭生活等各个方面。波伏娃发现，"一个人不是天生为女人的，而毋宁说是变成女人的"：父权制将男性塑造成独立完整的人，有本真的主体性；将女性定义为劣一等级的第二性，鼓励她们自愿服从于男性意志，培养宜家宜室的"女性气质"，令她们丧失超越环境的行动能力。波伏娃认为女性必须识破父权制迷障，为自由而斗争。

在女性主义思想史中，波伏娃从文化、历史、心理、生理角度对女性境遇进行综合分析，和第二次浪潮中的理论家们形成呼应。第二次女性主义浪潮的导火索是女性对父权保守主义思潮的抵制，先驱者是美国社会活动家贝蒂·弗里丹（Betty

Friedan）。1963年，弗里丹出版了《女性的奥秘》（*The Feminine Mystique*）。写书的契机是她参加大学同学聚会，发现不少在家相夫教子的"幸福的女人"正因"无名的问题的困扰"而焦虑不安。弗里丹继而对更多家庭主妇进行了调查，发现她们的焦虑源自广告、杂志、电视节目所宣扬的"女性奥秘论"："女子的本性只有通过性被动、受男性支配以及培育母爱才能实现。"在家庭这个"舒适的集中营"中，女性体会不到自身的生命价值所在。为此，弗里丹号召女性走出家庭，进入公共空间，投身于工作和社会实践。她自己也身体力行，参与美国全国妇女组织（NOW）的建设，担任了第一任主席。弗里丹在《女性的奥秘》中聚焦中产阶级女性，强调女性与男性的共性，以此作为平权斗争的基础，她的观点属于自由主义女性主义（Liberal Feminism）的范畴。

20世纪70年代的女性主义理论发展具有多样性的特点。舒拉米斯·费尔斯通（Shulamith Firestone）是激进女性主义（Radical Feminism）的先驱。在1970年出版的《性的辩证法》（*The Dialectic of Sex: The Case for Feminist Revolution*）中，她要求消灭男性和女性的性别分类，提倡性自由，将女性生殖和育儿视为奴役，主张用技术手段解决生育问题。朱丽叶·米切尔（Juliet Mitchell）则是精神分析女性主义（Psychoanalytical Feminism）的奠基人之一。在《精神分析与女性主义》（*Psychoanalysis and Feminism: Freud, Reich, Laing, and Women*，1974）中，她一方面指出弗洛伊德的"阴茎嫉妒"（penis envy）等观点在解释女性经验和心理维度时存在含混性和盲区，一方面指出精神分析理论有助于我们了解父权家庭结构和社会结构对性别角色的塑造。

米切尔同时隶属于马克思主义女性主义（Marxist Feminism）的阵营。在《妇女的地位》（*Women's Estate*，1971）中，米切尔分析了父权秩序如何在工作、生育、性和儿童社会化四个方面对女性实施控制，将其纳入资本主义生产体系。这一阵营的新生代代表是意大利学者西尔维娅·费代里奇（Silvia Federici）。她在2004年出版的《凯列班与女巫》（*Caliban and the Witch: Women, the Body and Primitive Accumulation*）中，分析了封建主义向资本主义转型期间，男性如何借助猎巫运动将在外打工的妇女描绘成荡妇和女巫，通过污名化策略剥夺其工作权，迫使她们只能在家庭内部当生育机器，做免费保姆。

如果说马克思主义女性主义关心的是性别与阶级议题的交织，非裔美国女性主义（African-American Feminism）则在此基础上加上了"种族"这个关键词。非裔美国女性主义的历史可以追溯到19世纪的废奴运动。它是20世纪60年代末，在与黑人民权运动和以白人为主的妇女解放运动的对话中逐渐蓬勃发展起来的。纵观半个世纪的理论发展史，以芭芭拉·史密斯（Barbara Smith）、帕特里夏·希尔·柯林斯（Patricia Hill Collins）、贝尔·胡克斯（bell hooks）为代表的理论家们坚持反对笼统的"女性"观，警惕妇女运动中白人中产阶级女性价值观的普世化。诚如胡克斯在《女性主义理论》（*Feminist Theory: From Margin to Center*，1984）中所指出，这种白人视角的女性主义，使她频频遇到这样的提问：作为黑人女性主义者，黑人身份和女性身份哪个更重要？她的回应是加入女性主义运动，不等于没有权利参加其他政治领域的斗争。在胡克斯等非裔美国女性主义者看来，黑人女性面临的压迫是多重性的：父权制、种族主义与阶级剥削制度在联合发挥作用。因黑人男性同时也是种族制度的受害者，黑人女性应该如何反抗黑人男性的父权身份，同时与他们一起战斗，对抗种族主义，这样的议题在白人的理论框架内无法得到充分讨论。为此，胡克斯等理论家主张黑人女性之间的团结、与白人女性以及其他少数族裔女性的联盟，以及与受压迫的男性的相互支持，认为妇女解放的实现和反抗种族主义、反抗剥削以及追求社会正义的斗争密切相关。

20世纪70至80年代也是女性主义开始启发文学批评，进而成为重要文学批评流派的时代。1970年，凯特·米利特（Kate Millett）出版了《性政治》（*Sexual Politics*），批评亨利·米勒、诺曼·梅勒和D. H. 劳伦斯等男性作家笔下的两性关系体现了"男性与生俱来有统治女性的特权"。1979年，桑德拉·吉尔伯特（Sandra Gilbert）和苏珊·古芭（Susan Gubar）的《阁楼上的疯女人》（*The Madwoman in the Attic: The Woman Writer and the Nineteenth-Century Literary Imagination*）出版。这部著作关注女性作家笔下反复出现的疯女人形象，指出疯癫是女性的愤怒、创造力和性欲望的外化，体现着她们对"家中天使"的性别规范的激烈反抗，也反映着父权制对女性进行迫害所导致的症候。在这一时期的女性主义文学理论中，伊莱恩·肖瓦尔特（Elaine Showalter）的《她们自己的文学》（*A Literature of Their Own: British Women Novelists from Brontë to Lessing*，1978）是一部里程碑式的著作。肖瓦尔特在书中讨论了一百多位英国女性作家，勾勒出她们之间的文学史传承，将其分为三个阶段：1840—1880年的"女人气"阶段（the Feminine phase），女性作家模仿男性作家的创作，期待获得认可；1880—1920年的"女权主义"阶段（the Feminist phase），女性作家抗议男性作家作品中的性别不平等，捍卫自身立场；始于1920年的"女性"阶段（the Female phase），女性作家不再关注男性评价体系，开始了"自我发现"的探索。

肖瓦尔特是美国学者。在《荒野中的女性主义批评》（"Feminist Criticism in the Wilderness"，1981）中，她总结了美国、英国和法国女性主义者的研究的不同侧重点：美国学者重视文本，关注表达（expression），致力于书写女性文学传统；英国学者的马克思主义色彩比美国浓，批判压迫（oppression），思考社会正义；法国学者在方法论上偏向于精神分析，关注压抑（repression）机制。肖瓦尔特的总结有一定道理，但法国和英美的根本分歧在于：英美学派认为我们需要从具体的历史社会语境入手，才能理解女性的真正境遇，懂得她们想说什么；以埃莱娜·西苏（Hélène Cixous）、朱莉娅·克里斯蒂娃（Julia Kristeva）和吕斯·伊里加雷（Luce Irigaray）为代表的法国女性主义者则认为我们必须跳出具体历史，才能看清父权社会的结构性压迫，才能理解女性的自我表达之难。

进入西苏理论世界的关键词之一是"女性书写"。西苏指出，女性总是受制于语言背后的父权逻辑，女性在言说时，很难逃脱对男性欲望的依从。她反对以阴茎（penis）/笔（pen）为隐喻的"阳性书写"，认为它过度倚重理性，太强调线性叙事。她主张感性的、直觉性的和非线性的"阴性写作"，以女性的"白色墨水"（乳汁）为隐喻，歌颂女性的创造力。她在《美杜莎的笑声》（"The Laugh of the Medusa"，1975）一文中批评男性对女性力量的畏惧。美杜莎的笑声是对父权制的嘲讽，也宣告着女性与男性传统的决裂，体现了女性创造新未来的信心。

克里斯蒂娃和西苏一样，也关注语言与书写议题。克里斯蒂娃是语言学家。她从符号学角度，结合女性主义立场，在《诗性语言的革命》（*Revolution in Poetic Language*，1974）、《恐怖的权力》（*Powers of Horror: An Essay on Abjection*，1980）等著作中，反思人类的意指系统，指出它有两种状态："象征态"（the symbolic）是符合语法等语言系统的规定，受社会认可的语言形态；"记号态"（the semiotic）是尚未被语言规则编码的碎片化的、流动的、复义性的形态。象征态遵循法的原则，反映父权秩序，体现逻各斯中心主义。记号态打破了约定俗成的意指边界，无视禁忌，是巫术、狂欢和神秘主义使用的言说。诗歌中的节奏、韵律和语调也属于记号态。克里斯蒂娃认为记号态产生于前镜像阶段，那时俄狄浦斯情结尚未出现，婴儿与母亲紧密相连。她从柏拉图的《蒂迈欧篇》（*Timaeus*）中借用了"穹若"（chora）的概念，赋予它多重空间内涵：它是孕育个体生命的母亲的身体，是容纳万物的混沌空间，是记号态的表意空间。"穹若"有女性子宫的意思，它是生命律动的原初来源。记号态的诗性语言也反映这种律动，具物质性、独异性和狂迷感，与追求澄澈抽象的普遍意义的象征态形成对比。值得注意的是，克里斯蒂娃反对将象征态和记号态归类于男性书写与女性书写的二元对立体系。她认为记号态不是女性写作的特权，马拉美（Stéphane Mallarmé）和洛特雷阿蒙（Comte de Lautréamont）等男性作家的先锋写作是其范例。

法国女性主义三杰中，西苏是文学家，克里斯蒂娃有语言学背景，而伊里加雷则是哲学家。她从女性角度对西方形而上学传统发起挑战。理解伊里加雷的核心词是"差异"（difference）。在她看来，所谓的普遍话语，已经以男性的方式被性化

(sexualized)。人类社会由两性组成，其普遍性应该是二元论的，而非一元论。在《他者女人的窥镜》(Speculum of the Other Woman，1974)和《此性非一》(This Sex Which Is Not One，1977)中，她详细分析了女性的身体性以及女性的欲望感知方式，指出女性比男性有更复杂和更多样化的体验，无法套用男性框架。在《性差异的伦理学》(An Ethics of Sexual Difference，1984)中，她批评父权制哲学体系用"同一性逻辑"来生成"支配—服从"模式的伦理关系，提倡尊重两性间不可化约的本体性差异。在《我的爱，向你》(I Love to You: Sketch for a Felicity Within History，1990)中，她提出主体间性观，即各自的独立性，主张放弃对"我"（主体）的执念和对"你"（客体，他者）的掌控。为此她主张将"我爱你"(I love you)改为"我的爱，向你"。这既保留了"我"的主体性，又经由介词"向"，令"我"向他人的主体性敞开，期待着相遇带来的变化。

经历了20世纪70至80年代的快速发展，女性主义与各种形式的妇女运动相互配合，促进了女性地位的快速提升。正因如此，20世纪80年代末90年代初，在影视、小说与广告等流行文化领域，出现了后女性主义(Postfeminism)的声音。后女性主义认为女性主义已取得胜利，是时候放下对男性的敌意，避免上纲上线的意识形态批判，让女性依从个性快乐生活了。这种后学声浪的推动因素之一是新自由主义。它在收编女性，将其塑造为独立奋斗的个体，从而自觉为资本主义体系服务，放弃集体行动，不再追问性别结构中的深层不平等。

有感于此，瑞贝卡·沃克（Rebecca Walker）于1992年在《女士》(Ms.)杂志上撰写文章，提出"我不是后女性主义者，我是第三次浪潮"，拉开了新一代女性主义者参与斗争的序幕。第三次浪潮的中坚力量普遍出生于20世纪60至70年代，是全球化时代的新生代。这些理论家既关注身份政治——这是女性团结斗争的基础，也对其局限性怀有警惕。沃克呼吁人们摆脱对固着不变的身份立场的选择，反对设立女性与男性、黑人与白人、被压迫者与压迫者、好人与坏人这样的对立选项。为此，这次浪潮中的女性主义者多采用跨地区、跨阶级、跨学科的立场，同时积极吸纳其他领域的理论资源。有关女性主义批评与阶级、种族、资本主义等议题的交叉讨论在前文已有论述，此处重点关注性别议题。第三次浪潮中的性别概念，深受朱迪斯·巴特勒（Judith Butler）等理论家的影响，不再仅强调生理性别(sex)和社会性别(gender)的区别，而是更具流变性和多元性。

巴特勒是塑造当代性别研究(gender studies)的核心理论家。她承认男性和女性在生理上的差异，但是反对将生理性别理解为天然的不涉性别政治的生物事实。她在《身体之重》(Bodies That Matter: On the Discursive Limits of "Sex"，1993)中指出，婴儿出生之际，宣布"这是个女孩儿！"不仅是在陈述眼前所见的事实，在这句话里，一个性别属性被指派向了一个物质性的身体。语言表述所执行的是施事话语的功能，要求个体去引用构建在异性恋基础上的性别规范，构筑主体性认同。在父权制社会中，相对稳定的性别化的身体根据"男性"和"女性"的异性恋规范，选择与各自性别相符的发型、着装、身体姿态等，经日常生活中的反复操演而逐步形成。鉴于性别化的身体是操演出来的，缺乏本质的属性，它可以通过颠覆规范、故意错误引用等方式进行消解。在巴特勒之前，女性主义倚重女性有别于男性的身体性，将其视为女性力量的来源。巴特勒在《消解性别》(*Undoing Gender*, 2004) 中提出，如果想要根除父权制，需要拒绝将性别限定在男性/女性的二分法，看到性别规范的建构与流变，进而跨越规范，接受性别的不同表达方式，承认性别的光谱具有多样性。

在巴特勒看来，承认性别多样性意味着对身体自主权和生命自由权的尊重。巴特勒的思想启发了伊夫·科索夫斯基·赛吉维克（Eve Kosofsky Sedgwick）、朱迪斯·霍伯斯坦（Judith Halberstam）等理论家。这些理论家投身性别研究，推动了对LGTB、酷儿等群体的深入认识，为抵制性别歧视、推进性别平等、尊重性别自由进行了深入探索。

近年来，有学者提出女性主义第四次浪潮已来到。21世纪是数字时代，互联网平台和移动手机应用为女性抗争提供了新的发声场所和新的表达形式。人们从文化、权力与法律等角度讨论性骚扰、代孕、色情业等现象，从性别的角度看赛博空间、媒介研究和数字技术。线上世界的热议和线下世界的社会实践相互呼应，学院派的声音和草根大众的声音相互交织。实际上，进入21世纪，不断有理论家提倡以现实为基点，反思学院派精英主义倾向，呼吁集体性社会动员和知行合一的个人行动。以萨拉·艾哈迈德（Sara Ahmed）为例。她曾是伦敦大学金史密斯学院教授，以情感研究领域的理论著作蜚声国际。2016年，她不满学校对性骚扰的包庇，愤然辞职。她意识到大学校园里的高妙理论和女性的日常生活有脱节之处，因此决定扎根现实境遇，探讨女性主义的立场。2017年出版的《过一种女性主义的生活》(*Living a Feminist Life*) 展现了艾哈迈德成为独立学者后结合实践的理论探索。与此同时，在21世纪的女性主义研究中，理论家们越来越提倡全球视野。在非洲、亚洲和拉丁美洲的某些地区，女性面临的问题与西方国家女性所面临的问题不同。她们还在对抗贫困、饥馑、种姓制度、战争等威胁，还在争取基本生存权。女性主义须跳出西方框架，克服文化偏见，通过跨文化、跨地域、跨民族的联合，为不同群体的女性应对不同挑战提供支持。

女性主义理论不是象牙塔里的思想游戏。它在漫长的历史进程中萌芽与发展；它在解读社会现象时反思、阐释与深化认识；它在特定议题中发现困惑、进行争辩、选择不同的道路……以上种种理论探索，无一不和女性在这个世界的感受、思考与实践息息相关。女性主义是复数性的，因阶级、种族、性属、国家等的不同，形成不同的流派，各有所愿，但中心诉求是一致的：消灭性别歧视和性别剥削，建设平等、自由而公正的社会。如何将此愿景变成现实？人类仍在探索。这也意味着女性主义理论的新拓展不会停歇。

主要文本阅读

西苏：《美杜莎的笑声》

选文简介

西苏在《美杜莎的笑声》中重写美杜莎，指出她不是男性笔下面目可憎的恶魔，她是美丽的，她在笑。西苏在美杜莎发出的笑声和女性书写的自我表达中发现了共通性：美杜莎挑战男性权威，女性书写挑战逻各斯中心主义；美杜莎的笑声发自她的身体，女性书写的动力是女性身体性的生命律动。西苏认为女性通过书写可以打破男性范式，找回被男性压制的身体驱动力，突破被禁言的沉默，用力发声，将自己融入文本、融入世界、融入历史，去预言和构筑未来。《美杜莎的笑声》采用了女性书写的文体，跳出了传统意义上理论著作的结构严谨的说理范式，行文摇曳生姿，是散文，也有诗情，意象十分生动。比如，在选文中，西苏以飞翔比喻女性写作——在语言中飞翔，让语言飞翔。她号召女性联合起来，共同抵制父权制，但是她珍视女性作为个体的独特性，不愿用同质化的集体身份抹杀女性群体内部的丰富性，也不愿将女性写作进行理论化编码，主张自由的表达，保持个性、活力和开放性。

From "The Laugh of the Medusa"

Hélène Cixous (1937-   )

I shall speak about women's writing: about *what it will do*. Woman must write her self: must write about women and bring women to writing, from which they have been driven away as violently as from their bodies—for the same reasons, by the same law, with the same fatal goal. Woman must put herself into the text—as into the world and into history—by her own movement.

The future must no longer be determined by the past. I do not deny that the effects of the past are still with us. But I refuse to strengthen them by repeating them, to confer upon them an irremovability the equivalent of destiny, to confuse the biological and the cultural. Anticipation is imperative.

Since these reflections are taking shape in an area just on the point of being discovered, they necessarily bear the mark of our time—a time during which the new breaks away from the old, and, more precisely, the (feminine) new from the old (*la nouvelle de l'ancien*). Thus, as there are no grounds for establishing a discourse, but rather an arid millennial ground to break, what I say has at least two sides and two aims: to break up, to destroy; and to foresee the unforeseeable, to project....

She must write her self, because this is the invention of a *new insurgent* writing which, when the moment of her liberation has come, will allow her to carry out the indispensable ruptures and transformations in her history, first at two levels that cannot be separated.

(1) Individually. By writing her self, woman will return to the body which has been more than confiscated from her, which has been turned into the uncanny stranger on display—the ailing or dead figure, which so often turns out to be the nasty companion, the cause and location of inhibitions. Censor the body and you censor breath and speech at the same time.

Write your self. Your body must be heard. Only then will the immense resources of the unconscious spring forth. Our naphtha will spread, throughout the world, without dollars—black or gold—nonassessed values that will change the rules of the old game....

(2) An act that will also be marked by woman's *seizing* the occasion to *speak*, hence her shattering entry into history, which has always been based *on her suppression*. To write and thus to forge for herself the antilogos weapon. To become *at will* the taker and initiator, for her own right, in every symbolic system, in every political process.

It is time for women to start scoring their feats in written and oral language.

Every woman has known the torment of getting up to speak. Her heart racing, at times entirely lost for words, ground and language slipping away—that's how daring a feat, how great a transgression it is for a woman to speak—even just open her mouth—in public. A double distress, for even if she transgresses, her words fall almost always upon the deaf male ear, which hears in language only that which speaks in the masculine.

It is by writing, from and toward women, and by taking up the challenge of speech which has been governed by the phallus, that women will confirm women in a place other than that which is reserved in and by the symbolic, that is, in a place other than silence. Women should break out of the snare of silence. They shouldn't be conned into accepting a domain which is the margin or the harem.

Listen to a woman speak at a public gathering (if she hasn't painfully lost her wind). She doesn't "speak," she throws her trembling body forward; she lets go of herself, she flies; all of her passes into her voice, and it's with her body that she vitally supports the "logic" of her speech. Her flesh speaks true. She lays herself bare. In fact, she physically materializes what she's thinking; she signifies it with her body. In a certain way she inscribes what she's saying, because she doesn't deny her drives the intractable and impassioned part they have in speaking. Her speech, even when "theoretical" or political, is never simple or linear or "objectified," generalized: she draws her story into history....

It is impossible to *define* a feminine practice of writing, and this is an impossibility that will remain, for this practice can never be theorized, enclosed, coded—which doesn't mean that it doesn't exist. But it will always surpass the discourse that regulates the phallocentric system; it does and will take place in areas other than those subordinated to philosophico-theoretical domination. It will be conceived of only by subjects who are breakers of automatisms, by peripheral figures that no authority can ever subjugate....

In body. —More so than men who are coaxed toward social success, toward sublimation, women are body. More body, hence more writing. For a long time it has been in body that women have responded to persecution, to the familial-conjugal enterprise of domestication, to the repeated attempts at castrating them. Those who have turned their tongues 10,000 times seven times before not speaking are either dead from it or more familiar with their tongues and their mouths than anyone else. Now, I-woman am going to blow up the Law: an explosion henceforth possible and ineluctable; let it be done, right now, in language.

Let us not be trapped by an analysis still encumbered with the old automatisms. It's not to be feared that language conceals an invincible adversary, because it's the language of men and their grammar. We mustn't leave them a single place that's any more theirs alone than we are.

If woman has always functioned "within" the discourse of man, a signifier that has always referred back to the opposite signifier which annihilates its specific energy and diminishes or stifles its very different sounds, it is time for her to dislocate this "within," to explode it, turn it around, and seize it; to make it hers, containing it, taking it in her own mouth, biting that tongue with her very own teeth to invent for herself a language to get inside of. And you'll see with what ease she will spring forth from that "within"— the "within" where once she so drowsily crouched—to overflow at the lips she will cover the foam.

Nor is the point to appropriate their instruments, their concepts, their places, or to begrudge them their position of mastery. Just because there's a risk of identification doesn't mean that we'll succumb. Let's leave it to the worriers, to masculine anxiety and its obsession with how to dominate the way things work—knowing "how it works" in order to "make it work." For us the point is not to take possession in order to internalize or manipulate, but rather to dash through and to "fly."

Flying is woman's gesture—flying in language and making it fly. We have all learned the art of flying and its numerous techniques; for centuries we've been able to possess anything only by flying; we've lived in flight, stealing away, finding, when desired, narrow passageways, hidden crossovers. It's no accident that *voler* has a double meaning, that it plays on each of them and thus throws off the agents of sense. It's no accident: women take after birds and robbers just as robbers take after women and birds. They (*illes*) go by, fly the coop, take pleasure in jumbling the order of space, in disorienting it, in changing around the furniture, dislocating things and values, breaking them all up, emptying structures, and turning propriety upside down.

What woman hasn't flown/stolen? Who hasn't felt, dreamt, performed the gesture that jams sociality? Who hasn't crumbled, held up to ridicule, the bar of separation? Who hasn't inscribed with her body the differential, punctured the system of couples and opposition? Who, by some act of transgression, hasn't overthrown successiveness, connection, the wall of circumfusion?

A feminine text cannot fail to be more than subversive. It is volcanic; as it is written it brings about an upheaval of the old property crust, carrier of masculine investments; there's no other way. There's no room for her if she's not a he. If she's a her-she, it's in order to smash everything, to shatter the framework of institutions, to blow up the law, to break up the "truth" with laughter.

肖瓦尔特:《走向一种女性主义诗学》

选文简介

《走向一种女性主义诗学》是肖瓦尔特于1978年在牛津大学所做演讲的发言稿,于1979年发表。肖瓦尔特发现,20世纪70年代英语文学研究方法中,女性主义最受孤立,有男性批评家指责:女性主义借文学之名宣扬妇女解放运动,和文学关联不大。肖瓦尔特则认为:女性主义具有跨学科视野,深化了我们对文学的理解,意义重大。它有两种范式:女权主义批评范式(feminist critique)和女性主义批评范式(gynocritics,或gynocriticism)。前者以女性读者为主体,揭秘男性作家作品中的性别密码,批评男性作家和批评家对女性进行的基于刻板印象的误读,具政治性;后者聚焦女性作家,发掘被男性评价体系所遮蔽的女性文学传统,展现女性创造力,具实验性。根据肖瓦尔特的梳理,英国女性文学发展史可以分为三个阶段:以模仿男性作家为主调的女人气阶段,以反抗为主旨的女权主义阶段和以女性自我发现为主题的女性阶段。她认为书写女性文学传统不是为了和男性对抗竞争,而是为了让我们听到被消音的女性的言说。

From "Toward a Feminist Poetics"

Elaine Showalter (1941-   )

Feminist criticism can be divided into two distinct varieties. The first type is concerned with *woman as reader*—with woman as the consumer of male-produced literature, and with the way in which the hypothesis of a female reader changes our apprehension of a given text, awakening us to the significance of its sexual codes. I shall call this kind of analysis the *feminist critique*, and like other kinds of critique it is a historically grounded inquiry which probes the ideological assumptions of literary phenomena. Its subjects include the images and stereotypes of women in literature, the omissions of and misconceptions about women in criticism, and the fissures in male-constructed literary history. It is also concerned with the exploitation and manipulation of the female audience, especially in popular culture and film; and with the analysis of woman-as-sign in semiotic systems. The second type of feminist criticism is concerned with *woman as writer*—with woman as the producer of textual meaning, with the history, themes, genres, and structures of literature by women. Its subjects include the psychodynamics of female creativity; linguistics and the problem of a female language; the trajectory of the individual or collective female literary career; literary history; and, of course, studies of particular writers and works. No term exists in English for such a specialized discourse, and so I have adapted the French term *la gynocritique*: "gynocritics" (although the significance of the male pseudonym in the history of women's writing also suggested the term "georgics").

The feminist critique is essentially political and polemical, with theoretical affiliations to Marxist sociology and aesthetics; gynocritics is more self-contained and experimental, with connections to other modes of new feminist research. In a dialogue between these two positions, Carolyn Heilbrun, the writer, and Catharine Stimpson, editor of the journal *Signs: Women in Culture and Society*, compare the feminist critique to the Old Testament, "looking for the sins and errors of the past," and gynocritics to the New Testament, seeking "the grace of imagination." Both kinds are necessary, they explain, for only the Jeremiahs of the feminist critique can lead us out of the "Egypt of female servitude" to the promised land of the feminist vision. That the discussion makes use of these Biblical metaphors points to the connections between feminist consciousness and conversion narratives which often appear in women's literature; Carolyn Heilbrun comments on her own text, "When I talk about feminist criticism, I am amazed at how high a moral tone I take."

The Feminist Critique: Hardy

Let us take briefly as an example of the way a feminist critique might proceed, Thomas Hardy's *The Mayor of Casterbridge*, which begins with the famous scene of the drunken Michael Henchard selling his wife and infant daughter for five guineas at a country fair. In his study of Hardy, Irving Howe has praised the brilliance and power of this opening scene:

> To shake loose from one's wife; to discard that drooping rag of a woman, with her mute complaints and maddening passivity; to escape not by a slinking abandonment but through the public sale of her body to a stranger, as horses are sold at a fair; and thus to wrest, through sheer amoral wilfulness, a second chance out of life—it is with this stroke, so insidiously attractive to male fantasy, that *The Mayor of Casterbridge* begins.

It is obvious that a woman, unless she has been indoctrinated into being very deeply identified indeed with male culture, will have a different experience of this scene. I quote Howe first to indicate how the fantasies of the male critic distort the text; for Hardy tells us very little about the relationship of Michael and Susan Henchard, and what we see in the early scenes does not suggest that she is drooping, complaining, or passive. Her role, however, is a passive one; severely constrained by her womanhood, and further burdened by her child, there is no way that *she* can wrest a second chance out of life. She cannot master events, but only accommodate herself to them....

The emotional center of *The Mayor of Casterbridge* is neither Henchard's relationship to his wife nor his superficial romance with Lucetta Templeman, but his slow appreciation of the strength and dignity of his wife's daughter, Elizabeth-Jane. Like the other women in the book, she is governed by her own heart—man-made laws are not important to her until she is taught by Henchard himself to value legality, paternity, external definitions, and thus in the end to reject him. A self-proclaimed "woman-hater," a man who has felt at best a "supercilious pity" for womankind, Henchard is humbled and "unmanned" by the collapse of his own virile façade, the loss of his mayor's chain, his master's authority, his father's rights. But in Henchard's alleged weakness and "womanishness," breaking through in moments of tenderness, Hardy is really showing us the man at his best. Thus Hardy's female characters in *The Mayor of Casterbridge*, as in his other novels, are somewhat idealized and melancholy projections of a repressed male self.

As we see in this analysis, one of the problems of the feminist critique is that it is male-oriented. If we study stereotypes of women, the sexism of male critics, and the limited roles women play in literary history, we are not learning what women have felt and experienced, but only what men have thought women should be....

Gynocritics and Female Culture

In contrast to this angry or loving fixation on male literature, the program of gynocritics is to construct a female framework for the analysis of women's literature, to develop new models based on the study of female experience, rather than to adapt male models and theories. Gynocritics begins at the point when we free ourselves from the linear absolutes of male literary history, stop trying to fit women between the lines of the male tradition, and focus instead on the newly visible world of female culture. This is comparable to the ethnographer's effort to render the experience of the "muted" female half of a society, which is described in Shirley Ardener's collection *Perceiving Women*. Gynocritics is related to feminist research in history, anthropology, psychology, and sociology, all of which have developed hypotheses of a female subculture including not only the ascribed status, and the internalized constructs of feminity, but also the occupations, interactions, and consciousness of women. Anthropologists study the female subculture in the relationships between women, as mothers, daughters, sisters, and friends; in sexuality, reproduction, and ideas about the body; and in rites of initiation and passage, purification ceremonies, myths, and taboos. Michelle Rosaldo writes in *Woman, Culture, and Society*

> The very symbolic and social conceptions that appear to set women apart and to circumscribe their activities may be used by women as a basis for female solidarity and worth. When men live apart from women, they in fact cannot control them, and unwittingly they may provide them with the symbols and social resources on which to build a society of their own.

Thus in some women's literature, feminine values penetrate and undermine the masculine systems that contain them; and women have imaginatively engaged the myths of the Amazons, and the fantasies of a separate female society, in genres from Victorian poetry to contemporary science fiction....

Feminine, Feminist, Female

All of these themes have been important to feminist literary criticism in the 1960s and 1970s, but we have approached them with more historical awareness. Before we can even begin to ask how the literature of women would be different and special, we need to reconstruct its past, to rediscover the scores of women novelists, poets, and dramatists whose work has been obscured by time, and to establish the continuity of the female tradition from decade to decade, rather than from Great Woman to Great Woman. As we re-create the chain of writers in this tradition, the patterns of influence and response from one generation to the next, we can also begin to challenge the periodicity of orthodox literary history and its enshrined canons of achievement. It is because we have studied women writers in isolation that we have never grasped the connections between them. When we go beyond Austen, the Brontës, and Eliot, say, to look at a hundred and fifty or more of their sister novelists, we can see patterns and phases in the evolution of a female tradition which correspond to the developmental phases of any subcultural art. In my book on English women writers, *A Literature of Their Own*, I have called these the Feminine, Feminist, and Female stages. During the Feminine phase, dating from about 1840 to 1880, women wrote in an effort to equal the intellectual achievements of the male culture, and internalized its assumptions about female nature. The distinguishing sign of this period is the male pseudonym, introduced in England in the 1840s, and a national characteristic of English women writers. In addition to the famous names we all know—George Eliot, Currer, Ellis, and Acton Bell—dozens of other women chose male pseudonyms as a way of coping with a double literary standard. This masculine disguise goes well beyond the title page; it exerts an irregular pressure on the narrative, affecting tone, diction, structure, and characterization....

In the Feminist phase, from about 1880 to 1920, or the winning of the vote, women are historically enabled to reject the accommodating postures of femininity and to use literature to dramatize the ordeals of wronged womanhood. The personal sense of injustice which feminine novelists such as Elizabeth Gaskell and Frances Trollope expressed in their novels of class struggle and factory life become increasingly and explicitly feminist in the 1880s, when a generation of New Women redefined the woman artist's role in terms of responsibility to suffering sisters. The purest examples of this phase are the Amazon utopias of the 1890s, fantasies of perfected female societies set in an England or an America of the future, which were also protests against male government, male laws, and male medicine. One author of Amazon utopias, the American Charlotte Perkins Gilman, also analyzed the preoccupations of masculine literature with sex and war, and the alternative possibilities of an emancipated feminist literature....

In the Female phase, ongoing since 1920, women reject both imitation and protest—two forms of dependency—and turn instead to female experience as the source of an autonomous art, extending the feminist analysis of culture to the forms and techniques of literature. Representatives of the formal Female Aesthetic, such as Dorothy Richardson and Virginia Woolf, begin to think in terms of male and female sentences, and divide their work into "masculine" journalism and "feminine" fictions, redefining and sexualizing external and internal experience. Their experiments were both enriching and imprisoning retreats into the celebration of consciousness; even in Woolf's famous definition of life: "a luminous halo, a semi-transparent envelope surrounding us from the beginning of consciousness to the end," there is a submerged metaphor of uterine withdrawal and containment. In this sense, the Room of One's Own becomes a kind of Amazon utopia, population 1.

胡克斯:《女性主义理论》

选文简介

胡克斯的本名是格洛丽亚·简·沃特金斯（Gloria Jean Watkins）。她以bell hooks为笔名进行创作。这个笔名的选择承载着她对曾外祖母Bell Blair Hooks的敬意，体现着女性的传承。将姓名首字母小写，也是对男性确立的书写规范的挑战。而且，她也希望用这种方式来淡化作者，让作品自己说话。《女性主义理论》是非裔美国女性主义的经典著作。在这部作品中，胡克斯关切性别压迫、种族压迫、阶级压迫的相互扭结，让我们看到黑人女性作为边缘化女性群体所面对的复杂现实。选文中，胡克斯分析了黑人女性主义者与当时占主流的自由主义女性主义者之间的冲突。后者以白人中产阶级女性为主，她们出于自身的阶级优势地位和种族优越感，看不到黑人女性深陷贫困和被剥夺了自由选择权的现实处境，所宣扬的解放目标与黑人女性的真实诉求相脱节。胡克斯认为这是当时流行的女性主义对黑人妇女没有感召力的原因。她同时也批判黑人男性虽然也是种族主义的受害者，但性别歧视使他们成为女性的剥削者和压迫者。她认为黑人妇女处在种族主义、阶级主义、性别歧视的最底层，对以上霸权性结构有最为深切的体会，应该积极发声，为重塑女性主义理论做出贡献。

From *Feminist Theory*

bell hooks (1952-2021)

We resist hegemonic dominance of feminist thought by insisting that it is a theory in the making, that we must necessarily criticize, question, re-examine, and explore new possibilities. My persistent critique has been informed by my status as a member of an oppressed group, experience of sexist exploitation and discrimination, and the sense that prevailing feminist analysis has not been the force shaping my feminist consciousness. This is true for many women. There are white women who had never considered resisting male dominance until the feminist movement created an awareness that they could and should. My awareness of feminist struggle was stimulated by social circumstance. Growing up in a Southern, black, father-dominated, working-class household, I experienced (as did my mother, my sisters, and my brother) varying degrees of patriarchal tyranny, and it made me angry—it made us all angry. Anger led me to question the politics of male dominance and enabled me to resist sexist socialization. Frequently, white feminists act as if black women did not know sexist oppression existed until they voiced feminist sentiment. They believe they are providing black women with "the" analysis and "the" program for liberation. They do not understand, cannot even imagine, that black women, as well as other groups of women who live daily in oppressive situations, often acquire an awareness of patriarchal politics from their lived experience, just as they develop strategies of resistance (even though they may not resist on a sustained or organized basis).

These black women observed white feminist focus on male tyranny and women's oppression as if it were a "new" revelation, and felt such a focus had little impact on their lives. To them it was just another indication of the privileged living conditions of middle- and upper-class white women that they would need a theory to "inform them that they were oppressed." The implication being that people who are truly oppressed know it even though they may not be engaged in organized resistance or are unable to articulate in written form the nature of their oppression. These black women saw nothing liberatory in party-line analyses of women's oppression. Neither the fact that black women have not organized collectively in huge numbers around the issues of "feminism" (many of us do not know or use the term) nor the fact that we have not had access to the machinery of power that would allow us to share our analyses or theories about gender with the American public negates its presence in our lives or places us in a position of dependency in relationship to those white and non-white feminists who address a larger audience....

When I participated in feminist groups, I found that white women adopted a condescending attitude toward me and other non-white participants. The condescension they directed at black women was one of the means they employed to remind us that the women's movement was "theirs"—that we were able to participate because they allowed it, even encouraged it; after all, we were needed to legitimate the process. They did not see us as equals. They did not treat us as equals. And though they expected us to provide first-hand accounts of black experience, they felt it was their role to decide if these experiences were authentic. Frequently, college-educated black women (even those from poor and working-class backgrounds) were dismissed as mere imitators. Our presence in movement activities did not count, as white women were convinced that "real" blackness meant speaking the patois of poor black people, being uneducated, streetwise, and a variety of other stereotypes. If we dared to criticize the movement or to assume responsibility for reshaping feminist ideas and introducing new ideas, our voices were tuned out, dismissed, silenced. We could be heard only if our statements echoed the sentiments of the dominant discourse.

Attempts by white feminists to silence black women are rarely written about. All too often they have taken place in conference rooms, classrooms, or the privacy of cozy living-room settings, where one lone black woman faces the racist hostility of a group of white women. From the time the women's liberation movement began, individual black women went to groups. Many never returned after a first meeting. Anita Cornwall is correct in "Three for the Price of One: Notes from a Gay Black Feminist" when she states, "...sadly enough, fear of encountering racism seems to be one of the main reasons that so many black women refuse to join the women's movement." Recent focus on the issue of racism has generated discourse but has had little impact on the behavior of white feminists toward black women. Often the white women who are busy publishing papers and books on "unlearning racism" remain patronizing and condescending when they relate to black women. This is not surprising given that frequently their discourse is aimed solely in the direction of a white audience and the focus solely on changing attitudes rather than addressing racism in a historical and political context. They make us the "objects" of their privileged discourse on race. As "objects," we remain unequals, inferiors. Even though they may be sincerely concerned about racism, their methodology suggests they are not yet free of the type of paternalism endemic to white supremacist ideology. Some of these women place themselves in the position of "authorities" who must mediate communication between racist white women (naturally they see themselves as having come to terms with their racism) and angry black women who they believe are incapable of rational discourse. Of course, the system of racism, classism, and educational elitism must remain intact if they are to maintain their authoritative positions....

Privileged feminists have largely been unable to speak to, with, and for diverse groups of women because they either do not understand fully the interrelatedness of sex, race, and class oppression or refuse to take this interrelatedness seriously. Feminist analyses of woman's lot tend to focus exclusively on gender and do not provide a solid foundation on which to construct feminist theory. They reflect the dominant tendency in Western patriarchal minds to mystify woman's reality by insisting that gender is the sole determinant of woman's fate. Certainly it has been easier for women who do not experience race or class oppression to focus exclusively on gender. Although socialist feminists focus on class and gender, they tend to dismiss race, or they make a point of acknowledging that race is important and then proceed to offer an analysis in which race is not considered.

As a group, black women are in an unusual position in this society, for not only are we collectively at the bottom of the occupational ladder, but our overall social status is lower than that of any other group. Occupying such a position, we bear the brunt of sexist, racist, and classist oppression. At the same time, we are the group that has not been socialized to assume the role of exploiter/oppressor in that we are allowed no institutionalized "other" that we can exploit or oppress. (Children do not represent an institutionalized other even though they may be oppressed by parents.) White women and black men have it both ways. They can act as oppressor or be oppressed. Black men may be victimized by racism, but sexism allows them to act as exploiters and oppressors of women. White women may be victimized by sexism, but racism enables them to act as exploiters and oppressors of black people. Both groups have led liberation movements that favor their interests and support the continued oppression of other groups. Black male sexism has undermined struggles to eradicate racism just as white female racism undermines feminist struggle. As long as these two groups or any group defines liberation as gaining social equality with ruling-class white men, they have a vested interest in the continued exploitation and oppression of others.

Black women with no institutionalized "other" that we may discriminate against, exploit, or oppress often have a lived experience that directly challenges the prevailing classist, sexist, racist social structure and its concomitant ideology. This lived experience may shape our consciousness in such a way that our world view differs from those who have a degree of privilege (however relative within the existing system). It is essential for continued feminist struggle that black women recognize the special vantage point our marginality gives us and make use of this perspective to criticize the dominant racist, classist, sexist hegemony as well as to envision and create a counter-hegemony. I am suggesting that we have a central role to play in the making of feminist theory and a contribution to offer that is unique and valuable. The formation of a liberatory feminist theory and praxis is a collective responsibility, one that must be shared. Though I criticize aspects of feminist movement as we have known it so far, a critique which is sometimes harsh and unrelenting, I do so not in an attempt to diminish feminist struggle but to enrich, to share in the work of making a liberatory ideology and a liberatory movement.

巴特勒:《性别麻烦》

选文简介

在《性别麻烦》中，巴特勒用trouble这个蕴含"麻烦"和"困扰"双重含义的词，对"性别"概念进行了问题化，指出性别缺乏天生的固定不变的本体论基础，我们须回归身体性议题，审视社会规范如何铭写在身体之上。她指出我们身体的性别化关涉三个维度：解剖学意义上的性别（sex）、性别身份（gender identity）和性别操演（gender performance）。每个维度都有社会话语的介入，对其按照异性恋的性别范式进行塑造。问题在于，这种话语塑造是一种编造，只能对身体表面进行构型，无法确保三个维度之间存在必然的一致性。巴特勒举例指出，变装表演（drag）就利用了生理身体、性别认同和性别操演之间的差异，以戏仿的方式，令性别诸维度之间的关系更加错综复杂。巴特勒借此批驳性别本质主义，解构性别二元性。她的性别操演论既揭示出性别身份"表演"中个体意向性和公共规范性的交织，也展现了身体如何通过重复的仪式性的"操练"，在行动中形成性别化的风格。

From *Gender Trouble: Feminism and the Subversion of Identity*

Judith Butler (1956-)

According to the understanding of identification as an enacted fantasy or incorporation, however, it is clear that coherence is desired, wished for, idealized, and that this idealization is an effect of a corporeal signification. In other words, acts, gestures, and desire produce the effect of an internal core or substance, but produce this *on the surface* of the body, through the play of signifying absences that suggest, but never reveal, the organizing principle of identity as a cause. Such acts, gestures, enactments, generally construed, are *performative* in the sense that the essence or identity that they otherwise purport to express are *fabrications* manufactured and sustained through corporeal signs and other discursive means. That the gendered body is performative suggests that it has no ontological status apart from the various acts which constitute its reality. This also suggests that if that reality is fabricated as an interior essence, that very interiority is an effect and function of a decidedly public and social discourse, the public regulation of fantasy through the surface politics of the body, the gender border control that differentiates inner from outer, and so institutes the "integrity" of the subject. In other words, acts and gestures, articulated and enacted desires create the illusion of an interior and organizing gender core, an illusion discursively maintained for the purposes of the regulation of sexuality within the obligatory frame of reproductive heterosexuality. If the "cause" of desire, gesture, and act can be localized within the "self" of the actor, then the political regulations and disciplinary practices which produce that ostensibly coherent gender are effectively displaced from view. The displacement of a political and discursive origin of gender identity onto a psychological "core" precludes an analysis of the political constitution of the gendered subject and its fabricated notions about the ineffable interiority of its sex or of its true identity.

If the inner truth of gender is a fabrication and if a true gender is a fantasy instituted and inscribed on the surface of bodies, then it seems that genders can be neither true nor false, but are only produced as the truth effects of a discourse of primary and stable identity.

In *Mother Camp: Female Impersonators in America*, anthropologist Esther Newton suggests that the structure of impersonation reveals one of the key fabricating mechanisms through which the social construction of gender takes place. I would suggest as well that drag fully subverts the distinction between inner and outer psychic space and effectively mocks both the expressive model of gender and the notion of a true gender identity. Newton writes:

> At its most complex, [drag] is a double inversion that says, "appearance is an illusion." Drag says [Newton's curious personification] "my 'outside' appearance is feminine, but my essence 'inside' [the body] is masculine." At the same time it symbolizes the opposite inversion; "my appearance 'outside' [my body, my gender] is masculine but my essence 'inside' [myself] is feminine."

Both claims to truth contradict one another and so displace the entire enactment of gender significations from the discourse of truth and falsity.

The notion of an original or primary gender identity is often parodied within the cultural practices of drag, cross-dressing, and the sexual stylization of butch/femme identities. Within feminist theory, such parodic identities have been understood to be either degrading to women, in the case of drag and cross-dressing, or an uncritical appropriation of sex-role stereotyping from within the practice of heterosexuality, especially in the case of butch/femme lesbian identities. But the relation between the "imitation" and the "original" is, I think, more complicated than that critique generally allows. Moreover, it gives us a clue to the way in which the relationship between primary identification—that is, the original meanings accorded to gender—and subsequent gender experience might be reframed. The performance of drag plays upon the distinction between the anatomy of the performer and the gender that is being performed. But we are actually in the presence of three contingent dimensions of significant corporeality: anatomical sex, gender identity, and gender performance. If the anatomy of the performer is already distinct from the gender of the performer, and both of those are distinct from the gender of the performance, then the performance suggests a dissonance not only between sex and performance, but sex and gender, and gender and performance. As much as drag creates a unified picture of "woman" (what its critics often oppose), it also reveals the distinctness of those aspects of gendered experience which are falsely naturalized as a unity through the regulatory fiction of heterosexual coherence. *In imitating gender, drag implicitly reveals the imitative structure of gender itself—as well as its contingency.* Indeed, part of the pleasure, the giddiness of the performance is in the recognition of a radical contingency in the relation between sex and gender in the face of cultural configurations of causal unities that are regularly assumed to be natural and necessary. In the place of the law of heterosexual coherence, we see sex and gender denaturalized by means of a performance which avows their distinctness and dramatizes the cultural mechanism of their fabricated unity....

If the body is not a "being," but a variable boundary, a surface whose permeability is politically regulated, a signifying practice within a cultural field of gender hierarchy and compulsory heterosexuality, then what language is left for understanding this corporeal enactment, gender, that constitutes its "interior" signification on its surface? Sartre would perhaps have called this act "a style of being," Foucault, "a stylistics of existence." And in my earlier reading of

Beauvoir, I suggest that gendered bodies are so many "styles of the flesh." These styles all never fully self-styled, for styles have a history, and those histories condition and limit the possibilities. Consider gender, for instance, as *a corporeal style*, an "act," as it were, which is both intentional and performative, where "*performative*" suggests a dramatic and contingent construction of meaning.

Wittig understands gender as the workings of "sex," where "sex" is an obligatory injunction for the body to become a cultural sign, to materialize itself in obedience to a historically delimited possibility, and to do this, not once or twice, but as a sustained and repeated corporeal project. The notion of a "project," however, suggests the originating force of a radical will, and because gender is a project which has cultural survival as its end, the term *strategy* better suggests the situation of duress under which gender performance always and variously occurs. Hence, as a strategy of survival within compulsory systems, gender is a performance with clearly punitive consequences. Discrete genders are part of what "humanizes" individuals within contemporary culture; indeed, we regularly punish those who fail to do their gender right. Because there is neither an "essence" that gender expresses or externalizes nor an objective ideal to which gender aspires, and because gender is not a fact, the various acts of gender create the idea of gender, and without those acts, there would be no gender at all....

In what senses, then, is gender an act? As in other ritual social dramas, the action of gender requires a performance that is *repeated*. This repetition is at once a reenactment and reexperiencing of a set of meanings already socially established; and it is the mundane and ritualized form of their legitimation. Although there are individual bodies that enact these significations by becoming stylized into gendered modes, this "action" is a public action. There are temporal and collective dimensions to these actions, and their public character is not inconsequential; indeed, the performance is effected with the strategic aim of maintaining gender within its binary frame—an aim that cannot be attributed to a subject, but, rather, must be understood to found and consolidate the subject.

Gender ought not to be construed as a stable identity or locus of agency from which various acts follow; rather, gender is an identity tenuously constituted in time, instituted in an exterior space through a *stylized repetition of acts*. The effect of gender is produced through the stylization of the body and, hence, must be understood as the mundane way in which bodily gestures, movements, and styles of various kinds constitute the illusion of an abiding gendered self. This formulation moves the conception of gender off the ground of a substantial model of identity to one that requires a conception of gender as a constituted *social temporality*. Significantly, if gender is instituted through acts which are internally discontinuous, then the *appearance of substance* is precisely that, a constructed identity, a performative accomplishment which the mundane social audience, including the actors themselves, come to believe and to perform in the mode of belief. Gender is also a norm that can never be fully internalized; "the internal" is a surface signification, and gender norms are finally phantasmatic, impossible to embody. If the ground of gender identity is the stylized repetition of acts through time and not a seemingly seamless identity, then the spatial metaphor of a "ground" will be displaced and revealed as a stylized configuration, indeed, a gendered corporealization of time. The abiding gendered self will then be shown to be structured by repeated acts that seek to approximate the ideal of a substantial ground of identity, but which, in their occasional *dis*continuity, reveal the temporal and contingent groundlessness of this "ground." The possibilities of gender transformation are to be found precisely in the arbitrary relation between such acts, in the possibility of a failure to repeat, a deformity, or a parodic repetition that exposes the phantasmatic effect of abiding identity as a politically tenuous construction.

If gender attributes, however, are not expressive but performative, then these attributes effectively constitute the identity they are said to express or reveal. The distinction between expression and performativeness is crucial. If gender attributes and acts, the various ways in which a body shows or produces its cultural signification, are performative, then there is no preexisting identity by which an act or attribute might be measured; there would be no true or false, real or distorted acts of gender, and the postulation of a true gender identity would be revealed as a regulatory fiction. That gender reality is created through sustained social performances means that the very notions of an essential sex and a true or abiding masculinity or femininity are also constituted as part of the strategy that conceals gender's performative character and the performative possibilities for proliferating gender configurations outside the restricting frames of masculinist domination and compulsory heterosexuality.

Genders can be neither true nor false, neither real nor apparent, neither original nor derived. As credible bearers of those attributes, however, genders can also be rendered thoroughly and radically *incredible*.

思考题

1. 西苏所主张的女性书写有什么样的特点？
2. 西苏的女性主义理论为什么特别重视身体性？
3. 肖瓦尔特认为女权主义批评和女性主义批评这两个范式的区别是什么？
4. 肖瓦尔特认为英国女性文学发展史经历了哪三个阶段？
5. 胡克斯认为白人女性主义者和黑人女性主义者的境遇有什么差别？这些差别如何影响她们的女性主义立场？
6. 请简述巴特勒的性别操演理论。

讨论题

1. 请在阅读选文的基础上，查阅相关课外资料，讨论西苏、胡克斯和巴特勒的性别观的侧重点有什么不同。
2. 请选择一位英国女性小说家，讨论她的写作应该属于肖瓦尔特所说的女性文学传统中的哪个阶段。在此基础上，选取这位小说家的一部作品，从女性主义角度对其进行解读。

补充文本选摘与评述

波伏娃:《第二性》
From *The Second Sex*

Simone de Beauvoir (1908-1986)

Woman as Other

But first we must ask: what is a woman? "*Tota mulier in utero*," says one, "woman is a womb." But in speaking of certain women, connoisseurs declare that they are not women, although they are equipped with a uterus like the rest. All agree in recognizing the fact that females exist in the human species; today as always they make up about one half of humanity. And yet we are told that femininity is in danger; we are exhorted to be women, remain women, become women. It would appear, then, that every female human being is not necessarily a woman; to be so considered she must share in that mysterious and threatened reality known as femininity. Is this attribute something secreted by the ovaries? Or is it a Platonic essence, a product of the philosophic imagination? Is a rustling petticoat enough to bring it down to earth? Although some women try zealously to incarnate this essence, it is hardly patentable....

If her functioning as a female is not enough to define woman, if we decline also to explain her through "the eternal feminine," and if nevertheless we admit, provisionally, that women do exist, then we must face the question: what is a woman?

To state the question is, to me, to suggest, at once, a preliminary answer. The fact that I ask it is in itself significant. A man would never get the notion of writing a book on the peculiar situation of the human male. But if I wish to define myself, I must first of all say: "I am a woman"; on this truth must be based all further discussion. A man never begins by presenting himself as an individual of a certain sex; it goes without saying that he is a man. The terms *masculine* and *feminine* are used symmetrically only as a matter of form, as on legal papers. In actuality the relation of the two sexes is not quite like that of two electrical poles, for man represents both the positive and the neutral, as is indicated by the common use of *man* to designate human beings in general; whereas woman represents only the negative, defined by limiting criteria, without reciprocity....

Thus humanity is male and man defines woman not in herself but as relative to him; she is not regarded as an autonomous being.... And she is simply what man decrees; thus she is called "the sex," by which is meant that she appears essentially to the male as a sexual being. For him she is sex—absolute sex, no less. She is defined and differentiated with reference to man and not he with reference to her; she is the incidental, the inessential as opposed to the essential. He is the Subject, he is the Absolute—she is the Other.

吉利根：《不同的声音》

From *In a Different Voice: Psychological Theory and Women's Development*

Carol Gilligan (1936-   )

The equation of human with male was assumed in the Platonic and in the Enlightenment tradition as well as by psychologists who saw all-male samples as "representative" of human experience. The equation of care with self-sacrifice is in some ways more complex. The premise of self-interest assumes a conflict of interest between self and other manifest in the opposition of egoism and altruism. Together, the equations of male with human and of care with self-sacrifice form a circle that has had a powerful hold on moral philosophy and psychology. The conjunction of women and moral theory thus challenges the traditional definition of human and calls for a reconsideration of what is meant by both justice and care....

It is easy to understand the ascendance of justice reasoning and of justice-focused moral theories in a society where care is associated with personal vulnerability in the form of economic disadvantage. But another way of thinking about the ascendance of justice reasoning and also about sex differences in moral development is suggested in the novel *Masks*, written by Fumiko Enchi, a Japanese woman. The subject is spirit possession, and the novel dramatizes what it means to be possessed by the spirits of others. Writing about the Rokujo lady in *Tales of Genji*, Enchi's central character notes that

> her soul alternates uncertainly between lyricism and spirit possession, making no philosophical distinction between the self alone and in relation to others, and is unable to achieve the solace of a religious indifference.

The option of transcendence, of a religious indifference or a philosophical detachment, may be less available to women because women are more likely to be possessed by the spirits and the stories of others. The strength of women's moral perceptions lies in the refusal of detachment and depersonalization, and insistence on making connections that can lead to seeing the person killed in war or living in poverty as someone's son or father or brother or sister, or mother, or daughter, or friend. But the liability of women's development is also underscored by Enchi's novel in that women, possessed by the spirits of others, also are more likely to be caught in a chain of false attachments. If women are at the present time the custodians of a story about human attachment and interdependence, not only within the family but also in the world at large, then questions arise as to how this story can be kept alive and how moral theory can sustain this story. In this sense, the relationship between women and moral theory itself becomes one of interdependence.

By rendering a care perspective more coherent and making its terms explicit, moral theory may facilitate women's ability to speak about their experiences and perceptions and may foster the ability of others to listen and to understand. At the same time, the evidence of care focus in women's moral thinking suggests that the study of women's development may provide a natural history of moral development in which care is ascendant, revealing the ways in which creating and sustaining responsive connection with others becomes or remains a central moral concern. The promise in joining women and moral theory lies in the fact that human survival, in the late twentieth century, may depend less on formal agreement than on human connection.

艾哈迈德:《过一种女性主义的生活》
From *Living a Feminist Life*

Sara Ahmed (1969-)

In this first part of the book, I explore the process of becoming a feminist. Reflecting on this process can offer a way of doing feminist theory, a way of generating new insights into how gender works, as a social system, or as machinery that tends to spit some bodies out. Insights into gender as well as race are worldly. Becoming a feminist involves coming up against the world.

What's my feminist story? Like you, I have many. As I will try to show, my own feminist biography is entangled with other aspects of my biography; how could it not be; how messy life is. I start this part of the book very simply, staying in chapter 1 as close to home as I can, beginning by recalling things that happened. I return to experiences that were painful and difficult, but that were animating, that gave me life because they were how I was directed along a feminist path. If we start close to home, we open ourselves out. I will try to show how, in making sense of things that happen, we also draw on histories of thought and activism that precede us. Throughout I thus reflect on how feminism itself can be understood as an affective inheritance; how our own struggles to make sense of realities that are difficult to grasp become part of a wider struggle, a struggle to be, to make sense of being.

In the process of describing how I became a feminist, this opening part of the book also offers a feminist approach to some key areas of concern within feminist theory and beyond: the role of sensation in knowledge formation; the sociality of emotions; how power operates through directionality and orientation; and how to think about happiness, as well as the relationship between will and force. I show how becoming feminist is also about generating ideas about the worlds we encounter. Feminist theory, in other words, comes out of the sense-making process of becoming feminist and navigating a way through a world.

The figures of the feminist killjoy and willful subject are considered in this part of the book primarily in terms of how they relate to some of my early experiences of becoming and being a feminist. These figures will pop up all over the place. They are everywhere.

| 选文评述

波伏娃是存在主义哲学家,主张超越限制,反对被定义的人生,强调自由的重要性,所以她强烈反对父权制,因为它是"对一半人类的奴隶制"。在《第二性》中,波伏娃深入剖析女性在父权社会所受到的压迫,希冀唤起女性自身以及全社会对妇女解放的关注。选文出自《第二性》的开篇,波伏娃借"什么是女人?"这个提问,来阐发她的女性观。她既反对父权制用生理构造来定义女性,也反对部分女性主义者从抽象意义上理解女性。在她看来,前者是父权制的阴谋,将女性等同于子宫,贬低她的生命价值,视她为从属于男性的第二性;后者看似拔高女性,说女性和男性一样,都是人，但这里的"人"的概念是以男性为范本，而且男女平等的论调听起来悦耳，但现实中父权社会的风俗习惯仍是主流，女性依然饱受歧视。波伏娃认为女性若想要超越目前的境遇，既需要尊重自己有别于男性的生命体验，也需要拒绝由父权制定义的"女性气质"的绑架，做独立自主的女性，实现生命的完整意义。

吉利根在《不同的声音》中，立足于女性经验，结合心理学视角，考察伦理价值的范式生成。她指出，男性将与他人的联系视为自主性和独立性的阻碍。他们的伦理观以正义为关键词，重视规范，批评女性只会自我牺牲，缺乏道德原则，是软弱的、易受伤害的。吉利根反对将男性正义论作为唯一道德范式，认为女性重视人与人之间的联系，坚持从关系的角度理解自身的伦理责任，这不是女性的弱点，而是女性的力量。她倡导关怀伦理，主张以更具连接性和责任感的态度来护持这个世界。

《过一种女性主义的生活》是一本理论著作，但读起来却有传记色彩。这反映了作者艾哈迈德的立场：她认为女性主义必须是活生生的，主张向世界开放，与女性主义传承进行呼应，在现实中发现问题，用理论推动认识。值得注意的是，她在选文中谈到了"扫兴鬼"（killjoy）这个概念。这和她的"生存可以是一种抗议"的立场密切相连。她准备做"任性的主体"（willful subject），在遭遇父权制被默认为惯例的行为时，与之"较真"，拒绝不受重视，将对父权制的抵制进行到底。

关键术语释例

1. **交叉性**（intersectionality）："交叉性"的概念首次出现在非裔美国女性学者金伯利·克伦肖（Kimberlé Crenshaw）于1989年发表的论文《种族和性别的交叉性的去边缘化》。她在文中反对将种族和性别视为相互排斥的经验，主张从多重维度理解身份议题。其实贝尔·胡克斯在1984年的《女性主义理论》中，就已经在使用"交叉"（intersect）这个动词来描述性别歧视和种族歧视的交织。在当代，许多理论家在研究性别问题时，会主动运用交叉性理论，把种族、阶级、性取向等变量同时纳入考量，倾听群体内部的差异性诉求，分析多种结构性因素的相互影响和共同作用。实际上，交叉性概念也被广泛应用在后殖民主义、生态批评、老龄叙事研究等领域。

2. **女性主义认识论**（feminist epistemology）：认识论的中心议题是人类如何认识世界以及如何获取知识。传统认识论强调以科学理性的方法认识世界，追求知识的客观性和真理性。女性主义批评家则注意到了这种认识论的男性中心主义立场：在父权社会中，认知的主体是男性，女性受到众多歧视，被认为缺乏客观性，是不合格的认知者；女性被认为理性不足，思辨能力不够，没有资格进入科学、前沿技术、哲学等研究领域；而且女性即便作为认知客体，也无法得到男性尊重，男性已习惯于武断地给女性下定义。女性主义认识论是对以上传统的反拨，认为知识和真理是情境性的，应将认知者的主观立场和具体处境纳入考量；鼓励女性积极参与科学与知识的建构，为其加入女性视角，以纠正男性偏见，为人类感知和理解世界提供新方法；反对认识论不公（epistemological injustice），反对男性在认知领域为女性设限，致力于让女性从认识论的边缘地带走向中心。代表性理论家有伊丽莎白·安德森（Elizabeth Anderson）、唐娜·哈拉维（Donna Haraway）、米兰达·弗里克（Miranda Fricker）等。

推荐书目

Braidotti, Rosi. *Nomadic Subjects: Embodiment and Sexual Difference in Contemporary Feminist Theory.* New York: Columbia University Press, 2011.

Cooke, Jennifer. *The New Feminist Literary Studies*. Cambridge: Cambridge University Press, 2020.

Eagleton, Mary. *Feminist Literary Theory: A Reader*. Malden: Wiley-Blackwell, 2011.

Felski, Rita. *Doing Time: Feminist Theory and Postmodern Culture*. New York: New York University Press, 2000.

Goodman, Robin Truth. *The Bloomsbury Handbook of 21st-Century Feminist Theory*. London: Bloomsbury Academic, 2019.

Halberstam, Judith. *Female Masculinity*. Durham: Duke University Press, 1998.

Moi, Toril. *Sexual/Textual Politics: Feminist Literary Theory*. London: Methuen, 1985.

Sedgwick, Eve Kosofsky. *Epistemology of the Closet*. Berkeley: University of California Press, 1990.

Smith, Bonnie G., and Nova Robinson. *The Routledge Global History of Feminism*. London: Routledge, 2022.

金莉等：《当代美国女权文学批评家研究》。北京：北京大学出版社，2014年。

第十二章

后殖民主义

概述

后殖民主义兴起于20世纪70年代，体现理论领域的历史转向和文化转向，是对殖民主义、解殖运动及其当代影响的全面回应。后殖民主义中的"后"反映一种时间意识。自15世纪末哥伦布发现美洲大陆以来，西班牙、葡萄牙、法国、英国等西方列强逐渐用武力征服和文化霸权建构帝国体制和殖民模式，其后四百年间，将亚洲、非洲、美洲和大洋洲的很多地区纳入其统治版图。但帝国殖民进程也始终伴随着殖民地的反抗。19世纪末到20世纪60年代，解殖运动一浪高似一浪，各殖民地纷纷摆脱宗主国，走上独立之路。后殖民主义回顾殖民主义和帝国主义的历史，关切解殖进程，跟踪当代相关议题。与此同时，后殖民主义中的"后"也反映着批判思维和超越意识。在殖民地获得独立后，人们认识到去殖民的工作才完成了第一阶段，殖民的结构性因素在经济、政治、社会、文化等领域皆有存留，要想清除这些因素，任重且道远。为此，后殖民理论家主张对殖民主义和帝国主义的负面影响进行彻底审视，呼吁西方摒弃以其为中心的全球霸权构想，也呼吁亚非拉等地区的人民自主探索发展之路，希冀多方合作，共同建设新的世界图景。

后殖民主义的思想先驱之一是弗朗茨·法农（Frantz Fanon）。他出生于法属马提尼克岛，成年后到法国学习精神病学，后在阿尔及利亚行医，参与了当地的独立解放运动。法农的精神分析背景使他敏锐地发现自己故乡的居民有复杂的心理状态：他们为自己是法国公民而骄傲，认为自己比其他黑人更尊贵；面对白人时，他们却有自卑情结。他在《黑皮肤，白面具》（*Black Skin, White Masks*，1952）中指出，黑人将白人"他者"内化进自己的精神结构，向往戴上"白面具"，通过说地道的法语、与白人结婚、遵照法国礼仪行事等方式，来实现"漂白"。但黑皮肤是无法改变的生理事实，与白面具之间构成矛盾，妨碍了黑人健全人格的形成，甚至会造成神经症。法农在《大地上的苦难者》(*The Wretched of the Earth*，1961)中指出，黑人一旦对自己的命运有所觉醒，自然会追问"我是谁？"这个问题。他号召黑人放弃成为白人的幻想，立足自身，与"我们的有色人种兄弟"形成认同，发动暴力革命，打破不公的殖民体系。他期待黑人团结一致，在推翻殖民制度的战斗中找到黑人身份的立足点，翻开历史新篇章，努力创造跳出旧框架的新黑人的概念。

20世纪70年代末，后殖民主义理论在英美等国家的兴起，离不开爱德华·萨义德（Edward Said）这位关键理论家。他来自巴勒斯坦地区，曾经在埃及求学，后在美国的大学任教。他的传记《格格不入》(*Out of Place: A Memoir*，1999)的标题说明了他对自己身份复杂性的体悟：他来自巴勒斯坦，来自伊斯兰教占主导地位的阿拉伯国家，是一名基督徒，不断在异域漂泊，后成为美国公民，而美国在巴勒斯坦问题上持有亲近以色列的立场，这令他的身份更为尴尬。在他与故乡、自我与真正的家园感之间"存在着无法愈合的伤口"。跨东西方的视角促使他于1978年出版了《东方学》(*Orientalism*)。书中的东方，不是地理意义上的东方（the East），而是西方知识体系中的东方（the Orient），反映了西方掺杂了欲望、压抑和自我投射的"东方化"意图——西方将自我理想化，设为"普世价值"的标准，将东方贬低为它的反面，建构起西方理性、和平宽仁、有道德感的形象和东方非理性、专制狭隘、纵欲而邪恶的形象，用这种二元对立赋予西方殖民事业合法性。看似中立的东方学在这种思维的驱动下，在帝国的资助下应运而生。它的学科体系服务于殖民体制的需要，分支学科深入历史学、语文学、政治学、地理学等各个领域。无论是殖民地社会政体的构造、官方语言的选择，还是风俗传统的革新，甚至是博物馆的陈列布展，处处可见东方学的话语体系与帝国殖民权力的勾连——东方学既塑造着殖民者和被殖民者的思想和知识结构，也影响着具体的社会历史实践。

在《文化与帝国主义》(*Culture and Imperialism*，1993)中，萨义德将研究关注转向文学和文化领域。他反对将作家的写作与意识形态、阶级、经济历史的驱使直接挂钩。但他指出作者身处自己的社会时代之中，不同程度上参与了对历史和社会经验的塑造，同时也在被历史和经验所塑造。所以当我们阅读奥斯汀、狄更斯等的作品时，如果将其放入英国的帝国主义大图景中进行考察，就会看到作家的文学想象和帝国主义之间存在着或明或暗的联系。萨义德主张用平行性的"对位阅读法"（contrapuntal reading）解读小说家们所描绘的英国日常生活与帝国遥远的殖民地之间的和声交织，看殖民主义如何全面渗透进英国本土文化，又如何煽动着帝国公民的欲望,帮助帝国拓展其世界版图。

萨义德在上述著作中揭秘无处不在的西方中心主义意识。印度裔理论家霍米·巴巴(Homi Bhabha)则在《文化的位置》(*The Location of Culture*,1994)中分析殖民者与被殖民者之间的交锋与互动。他引入被殖民者视角,讨论地方性对帝国体系的挑战,要求西方正视被殖民者的形式多样的抵抗。巴巴认为殖民空间是"第三空间"(the Third Space),殖民者与被殖民者的文化在此相遇,空间呈现出杂糅性(hybridity)。这种杂糅性不仅体现文化多元性,而且也构成殖民地的抵抗策略。被殖民者顺从殖民者指令,学习和模拟宗主国的文化、语言和行为,但在重复模仿中,不断混入本土异质性元素,使殖民者的版本失去权威性。实际上,巴巴的主体观也体现杂糅性:身份不是固定而单一的,在流变中始终有抗争的可能性。

抗争的努力也反映在殖民地以及前殖民地的作家们抵制西方文化帝国主义、寻找自我表达的文学创作实践中。比尔·阿希克洛夫特(Bill Ashcroft)、格瑞斯·格里菲斯(Gareth Griffiths)、海伦·蒂芬(Helen Tiffin)在合著的《逆写帝国》(*The Empire Writes Back: Theory and Practice in Post-Colonial Literatures*,1989)中提出,(前)殖民地作家有意识地运用杂交与融合的模式,将帝国的语言放入殖民地的语境,表达本土经验,造就"后殖民文学"。著作标题中的"逆写"是语言的逆写——将像英语这样的帝国语言本土化,形成小写的复数的英语,颠覆语言霸权;"逆写"也是对宗主国文学经典传统的逆写——颠覆西方的文化领导权,让小写的多样性的英语文学从(前)殖民地的边缘地带走向世界文学舞台的中心。

后殖民文学要求我们从全球维度破除西方"正统"文学标准,肯定去中心化的地方性书写。罗伯特·杨(Robert Young)的历史与文化研究也在呼应这种后殖民主体立场。在《白色神话》(*White Mythologies: Writing History and the West*,1990)中,他指出殖民地从边缘处提供的是进入历史的新视角,是对单一、线性以及理性的西方进步史观的挑战。西方用现代性进程的同质化历史观来评判亚非拉地区的地方历史,以"前现代"和"现代"的分野认定西方是先进的、发展的、文明的,其他地区是原始的、停滞的、未开化的。杨指出,西方应该认识到自己的现代性优势建立在殖民剥削体制的全球掠夺上,而且,这种现代性叙事也在影响着全球化的历史进程,制造更多的压迫和不公。印度裔理论家阿吉兹·阿罕默德(Aijaz Ahmad)则将去西方中心主义的审视投射到后殖民理论自身。《在理论内部》(*In Theory: Classes, Nations, Literatures*,1992)中,他指出后殖民主义理论生长于西方知识语境,过度重视文化批评,导致文本主义。我们应该对其保持警惕,避免将对殖民主义与帝国主义的批判从帝国战争、政治经济剥削等领域撤离,避免仅仅围绕文学表征与文化立场做文章。他主张尊重社会实质和历史诉求，回到马克思主义的唯物史观。为此，阿罕默德批评萨义德的《东方学》，认为虽然《东方学》揭秘了西方对东方的话语建构，但是萨义德避而不谈真正的东方，阻断了对殖民体系的深层次追问。与之相比，他赞扬萨义德后期积极投身社会活动，著书立说，为巴勒斯坦发声。

加亚特里·查克拉沃蒂·斯皮瓦克（Gayatri Chakravorty Spivak）的后殖民批评也有理论和实践的双重聚焦。她关注反抗者的能动性问题。在引起广泛关注的长文《庶民能说话吗？》（"Can the Subaltern Speak?"，1988）中，她以"庶民"为核心词，在批判殖民者的文化霸权的同时，也批判了被殖民者内部层级差异导致的话语权不平等。庶民概念（the subaltern，或译为"属下""从属阶层""底层人"）的最初使用者是西方马克思主义理论家葛兰西。葛兰西坐牢时进行写作，无法在文本中直接指称无产阶级，就用subaltern这个在军队中表示"属下""下级"的术语进行指代。他有时也用subaltern泛指下层社会集团。相比葛兰西，斯皮瓦克重点强调"庶民"是和"精英阶层"形成对比的底层大众。印度殖民体系除了白人殖民者是精英阶层，被殖民者内部的上层权贵和地方名流也是精英，与庶民阶层拉开了距离。精英阶层替庶民阶层发言，真正的庶民却被挡在话语体系之外。斯皮瓦克以印度寡妇火焚殉葬的萨提风俗来说明庶民发声之难。白人精英认为萨提风俗反映了印度文明的蒙昧本质，他们颁布法令，废除萨提制，洋洋自得于从男性棕色人种手中/落后殖民地拯救了女性棕色人种。可从具体语境看，英国禁止萨提制是为了维护帝国政治利益。而从印度传统文化角度看，只有贤惠的妻子才会甘于承受火焚之苦，在男性家长口中，她们的行为带有英雄主义色彩。棕色女人身处"西方"与"东方"、"现代"与"传统"、"文明"与"蒙昧"的话语夹缝之中，缄默无语，听从白人或和她们同肤色的印度男性替她们发声。

斯皮瓦克在1999年将该文章收入专著《后殖民理性批判》（*A Critique of Postcolonial Reason: Toward a History of the Vanishing Present*）时，对之前的立场进行了补充说明。她强调庶民的底层独异性，认为不可滥用概念，将所有被殖民者都视为庶民。庶民是无法发声的，但当庶民和从事社会运动的知识分子进行接触，踏上了争取公民权和政治权的道路，就将摆脱庶民性，拥有能动性。在这一过程中，要警惕精英阶层用知识暴力（epistemic violence）代替其言说。斯皮瓦克持有启蒙立场，主张通过教育为底层大众赋能。然而，她也注意到教育体制内部的权力不对称性，要求知识阶层保持高度自省。实际上，自20世纪80年代开始，斯皮瓦克一直在积极践行自己的理论，如在印度贫困地区做基础教育的普及工作。在《斯皮瓦克访谈录》（*Conversations with Gayatri Chakravorty Spivak*，2006）中，她提出教育的目的不是建构某种理想的庶民主体，而是建构"庶民的主体性"（the subjectivity of the subaltern），使庶民摆脱无言沉默，进入公共领域自主言说。

斯皮瓦克在讨论庶民问题时，选取印度女性殉葬制度为聚焦案例，体现出她的后殖民理论的女性主义立场。同样有女性主义与后殖民主义交叉立场的是钱德拉·塔尔帕德·莫汉蒂（Chandra Talpade Mohanty）。莫汉蒂也来自印度，目前在美国的大学执教。她以非西方的主体立场，敏锐捕捉到西方女性主义研究中的殖民意识。在《西方视野之下》（"Under Western Eyes: Feminist Scholarship and Colonial Discourses"，1984）中，她批评西方女性主义理论家一边宣称全世界女性以姐妹情谊联结，有共同的利益和愿望，一边在研究中不断塑造和巩固第三世界女性的刻板印象，称这些女性未受教育，习惯依附他人，被传统和家庭束缚。西方女性主义者笔下的第三世界女性的形象越发衬托出西方女性的优越：西方女性是世俗的、自由的，对自己的生活拥有控制权。莫汉蒂指出，西方女性主义者的话语术是一种知识暴力，通过对第三世界女性复杂多样的具体境遇进行均质化的概括，掩盖了第三世界女性作为劳动力被帝国主义剥削和压迫的现实，保护了西方女性从殖民体系中获得的既得利益。2003年，莫汉蒂撰写了《再访〈西方视野之下〉》（"'Under Western Eyes' Revisited: Feminist Solidarity Through Anticapitalist Struggles"），澄清自己批评西方女性主义，不是为了在女性主义内部制造第一世界和第三世界的鸿沟，而是为了肃清欧洲中心主义的影响。同时，她也反对美国高校流行的"重视差异"的文化相对主义观，认为它是资本主义全球化的障眼法，捍卫着西方的国际等级秩序。她主张正视不同女性主义群体之间的差异，以开阔的视野和善于自我反思的精神建立联盟，共同抵抗资本主义跨国跨文化的全球化殖民扩张。

斯皮瓦克和莫汉蒂都来自第三世界，同样是后殖民女性理论家的格洛丽亚·阿扎尔杜亚（Gloria Anzaldúa）则来自第一世界。她出生于美国，但她是奇卡诺人，血统混杂，文化身份多元，而且有酷儿身份。所以她从自身出发的理论立场既有从边缘看中心的反思性，也有跨界的前沿性，反映出西方理论阵营内部也具多样性。阿扎尔杜亚住在美国得克萨斯州南部与墨西哥交界的里奥格兰德河谷地区。在《边土》（Borderlands/La Frontera: The New Mestiza，1987）中，她展现出这片边疆土地的张力：一边是种族主义、殖民主义和帝国主义对边界线的强势捍卫，一边是混杂居住带来的边界突破、弥合与新生。她是奇卡诺人，日常的语言交融了英语、西班牙语、北墨西哥方言、得州墨西哥方言等多种语言。美国人反对其中的西班牙语语汇，西班牙人嫌弃其中的美墨边境方言，而当地人以说一口纯正的英语为荣。阿扎尔杜亚则选择以语言血统的混杂性为荣，让语言相互授粉、焕发活力，形成"边疆的语言"。她用这种语言，从自己身处的美国和墨西哥边境的生存处境出发，描写这片土地上的剥削、压迫、仇恨、愤怒，但也歌颂这片土地上的生命力、流动性和创造性。她反对将家园浪漫化和纯粹化。在她看来，家园不是舒适的理想居所，但它是她的栖息之地。

同样关心后殖民跨界议题的还有保罗·吉尔罗伊（Paul Gilroy）。他是加勒比海移民的后裔，师从斯图尔特·霍尔（Stuart Hall），是英国当代最重要的族裔理论家。在《黑色大西洋》（*The Black Atlantic: Modernity and Double Consciousness*，1993）中，吉尔罗伊用大西洋这一连接非洲、南美洲和欧洲的空间概念，勾连起奴隶贸易、殖民体系建构、帝国疆域拓展以及资本主义制度扩张的黑色历史。在背井离乡的迁移中，黑人承受苦难，但是吉尔罗伊反对将黑人视为无所作为的受害者。他关注非洲文化在流散过程中对欧洲文化的深刻影响，也关注黑人对欧洲文化的主动吸纳。他反对将族裔身份与国别身份严格绑定，用跨国主义（transnationality）视角呈现流散中的黑人既不同于非洲也不同于欧洲的种族身份重塑和文化创造力，以及黑人为寻求自身解放、寻求公民身份所进行的各种斗争。在他看来，黑色大西洋文化是文化综合体，反映非洲、美洲、加勒比和不列颠文化的多重源流的交汇。2022年，在为《黑色大西洋》中文版所写的序言中，吉尔罗伊强调，他的著作议题具有开源性的特点，虽然三十年后的今日与当初写作时的具体语境有差异，但是问题意识未变，继续关切对种族主义和殖民主义的各种各样新变体的追踪和批判。他反对局限于一地一时，主张把世界看作一个整体，从行星的尺度（the planetary scale）进行思考、对话和展望。

我们已经进入21世纪，目前的时代依然充满对立、纷争、不平等和剥削。其中许多问题，比如种族主义问题、南北贫富差距问题、东西方文化冲突问题，都可以归类于殖民体系的历史遗留问题。后殖民批判意识仍是有力的思想武器，促使我们从个人、社群、国族、全球的维度进行全面思考。它也在提示我们继续努力的方向：超越西方中心主义思维，支持文化和文学的多元表达；重视后殖民空间中各个层面、各个群体、各种形式的抵抗和创新；寻求社会正义、环境正义（本书第十四章将讨论后殖民生态主义）；在尊重的基础上加强对话和合作，克服东西方分歧，弥补南北差距，跨越国族差异，共同构筑公正平等的未来。

主要文本阅读

萨义德:《东方学》

选文简介

萨义德来自巴勒斯坦,在美国教书。对比阿拉伯地区和美国两种学术体制,他发现了这样一个问题:阿拉伯国家的东方学研究无人关注,举步维艰;西方的东方学却蓬勃发展。西方人为什么会对东方学感兴趣?这个学科的发展是在为谁服务?他在追溯西方的东方学建构历史时,发现帝国主义和殖民体制是其强有力的推手。东方学关注的不是地理和国家意义上的东方,而是西方创造的一整套促进殖民主义推广的话语体系和实践体系。它不是凭空捏造的文化想象,而是历史思想、词汇观念等组成的话语集合,为西方的社会、政治、经济利益服务,影响着社会实践,契合西方霸权宰制,塑造着西方的优越和东方的落后。这个看似独立的学术领域,生产出符合西方利益的"东方",内容琳琅满目,关注议题深入历史、文化、政治等各个领域,反映出西方殖民意识形态的辐射力之广。

From *Orientalism*

Edward Said (1935-2003)

I have begun with the assumption that the Orient is not an inert fact of nature. It is not merely *there*, just as the Occident itself is not just *there* either. We must take seriously Vico's great observation that men make their own history, that what they can know is what they have made, and extend it to geography: as both geographical and cultural entities—to say nothing of historical entities—such locales, regions, geographical sectors as "Orient" and "Occident" are man-made. Therefore as much as the West itself, the Orient is an idea that has a history and a tradition of thought, imagery, and vocabulary that have given it reality and presence in and for the West. The two geographical entities thus support and to an extent reflect each other.

Having said that, one must go on to state a number of reasonable qualifications. In the first place, it would be wrong to conclude that the Orient was *essentially* an idea, or a creation with no corresponding reality. When Disraeli said in his novel *Tancred* that the East was a career, he meant that to be interested in the East was something bright young Westerners would find to be an all-consuming passion; he should not be interpreted as saying that the East was *only* a career for Westerners. There were—and are—cultures and nations whose location is in the East, and their lives, histories, and customs have a brute reality obviously greater than anything that could be said about them in the West. About that fact this study of Orientalism has very little to contribute, except to acknowledge it tacitly. But the phenomenon of Orientalism as I study it here deals principally, not with a correspondence between Orientalism and Orient, but with the internal consistency of Orientalism and its ideas about the Orient (the East as career) despite or beyond any correspondence, or lack thereof, with a "real" Orient. My point is that Disraeli's statement about the East refers mainly to that created consistency, that regular constellation of ideas as the pre-eminent thing about the Orient, and not to its mere being, as Wallace Stevens' phrase has it.

A second qualification is that ideas, cultures, and histories cannot seriously be understood or studied without their force, or more precisely their configurations of power, also being studied. To believe that the Orient was created—or, as I call it, "Orientalized"—and to believe that such things happen simply as a necessity of the imagination, is to be disingenuous. The relationship between Occident and Orient is a relationship of power, of domination, of varying degrees of a complex hegemony, and is quite accurately indicated in the title of K. M. Panikkar's classic *Asia and Western Dominance*. The Orient was Orientalized not only because it was discovered to be "Oriental" in all those ways considered commonplace by an average nineteenth-century European, but also because it *could be*—that is, submitted to being—*made* Oriental. There is very little consent to be found, for example, in the fact that Flaubert's encounter with an Egyptian courtesan produced a widely influential model of the Oriental woman; she never spoke of herself, she never represented her emotions, presence, or history. *He* spoke for and represented her. He was foreign, comparatively wealthy, male, and these were historical facts of domination that allowed him not only to possess Kuchuk Hanem physically but to speak for her and tell his readers in what way she was "typically Oriental." My argument is that Flaubert's situation of strength in relation to Kuchuk Hanem was not an isolated instance. It fairly stands for the pattern of relative strength between East and West, and the discourse about the Orient that it enabled.

This brings us to a third qualification. One ought never to assume that the structure of Orientalism is nothing more than a structure of lies or of myths which, were the truth about them to be told, would simply blow away. I myself believe that Orientalism is more particularly valuable as a sign of European-Atlantic power over the Orient than it is as a veridic discourse about the Orient (which is what, in its academic or scholarly form, it claims to be). Nevertheless, what we must respect and try to grasp is the sheer knitted-together strength of Orientalist discourse, its very close ties to the enabling socio-economic and political institutions, and its redoubtable durability. After all, any system of ideas that can remain unchanged as teachable wisdom (in academies, books, congresses, universities, foreign-service institutes) from the period of Ernest Renan in the late 1840s until the present in the United States must be something more formidable than a mere collection of lies. Orientalism, therefore, is not an airy European fantasy about the Orient, but a created body of theory and practice in which, for many generations, there has been a considerable material investment. Continued investment made Orientalism, as a system of knowledge about the Orient, an accepted grid for filtering through the Orient into Western consciousness, just as that same investment multiplied—indeed, made truly productive—the statements proliferating out from Orientalism into the general culture.

Gramsci has made the useful analytic distinction between civil and political society in which the former is made up of voluntary (or at least rational and noncoercive) affiliations like schools, families, and unions, the latter of state institutions (the army, the police, the central bureaucracy) whose role in the polity is direct domination. Culture, of course, is to be found operating within civil society, where the influence of ideas, of institutions, and of other persons works not through domination but by what Gramsci calls consent. In any society not totalitarian, then, certain cultural forms predominate over others, just as certain ideas are more influential than others; the form of this cultural leadership is what Gramsci has identified as *hegemony*, an indispensable concept for any understanding of cultural life in the industrial West. It is hegemony, or rather the result of cultural hegemony at work, that gives Orientalism the durability and the strength I have been speaking about so far. Orientalism is never far from what Denys Hay has called the idea of Europe, a collective notion identifying "us" Europeans as against all "those" non-Europeans, and indeed it can be argued that the major component in European culture is precisely what made that culture hegemonic both in and outside Europe: the idea of European identity as a superior one in comparison with all the non-European peoples and cultures. There is in addition the hegemony of European ideas about the Orient, themselves reiterating European superiority over Oriental backwardness, usually overriding the possibility that a more independent, or more skeptical, thinker might have had different views on the matter.

In a quite constant way, Orientalism depends for its strategy on this flexible *positional* superiority, which puts the Westerner in a whole series of possible relationships with the Orient without ever losing him the relative upper hand. And why should it have been otherwise, especially during the period of extraordinary European ascendancy from the late Renaissance to the present? The scientist, the scholar, the missionary, the trader, or the soldier was in, or thought about, the Orient because he *could be there*, or could think about it, with very little resistance on the Orient's part. Under the general heading of knowledge of the Orient, and within the umbrella of Western hegemony over the Orient during the period from the end of the eighteenth century, there emerged a complex Orient suitable for study in the academy, for display in the museum, for reconstruction in the colonial office, for theoretical illustration in anthropological, biological, linguistic, racial, and historical theses about mankind and the universe, for instances of economic and sociological theories of development, revolution, cultural personality, national or religious character. Additionally, the imaginative examination of things Oriental was based more or less exclusively upon a sovereign Western consciousness out of whose unchallenged centrality an Oriental world emerged, first according to general ideas about who or what was an Oriental, then according to a detailed logic governed not simply by empirical reality but by a battery of desires, repressions, investments, and projections....

Much of the personal investment in this study derives from my awareness of being an "Oriental" as a child growing up in two British colonies. All of my education, in those colonies (Palestine and Egypt) and in the United States, has been Western, and yet that deep early awareness has persisted. In many ways my study of Orientalism has been an attempt to inventory the traces upon me, the Oriental subject, of the culture whose domination has been so powerful a factor in the life of all Orientals. This is why for me the Islamic Orient has had to be the center of attention. Whether what I have achieved is the inventory prescribed by Gramsci is not for me to judge, although I have felt it important to be conscious of trying to produce one. Along the way, as severely and as rationally as I have been able, I have tried to maintain a critical consciousness, as well as employing those instruments of historical, humanistic, and cultural research of which my education has made me the fortunate beneficiary. In none of that, however, have I ever lost hold of the cultural reality of, the personal involvement in having been constituted as, "an Oriental."

The historical circumstances making such a study possible are fairly complex, and I can only list them schematically here. Anyone resident in the West since the 1950s, particularly in the United States, will have lived through an era of extraordinary turbulence in the relations of East and West. No one will have failed to note how "East" has always signified danger and threat during this period, even as it has meant the traditional Orient as well as Russia. In the universities a growing establishment of area-studies programs and institutes has made the scholarly study of the Orient a branch of national policy. Public affairs in this country include a healthy interest in the Orient, as much for its strategic and economic importance as for its traditional exoticism. If the world has become immediately accessible to a Western citizen living in the electronic age, the Orient too has drawn nearer to him, and is now less a myth perhaps than a place crisscrossed by Western, especially American, interests....

The nexus of knowledge and power creating "the Oriental" and in a sense obliterating him as a human being is therefore not for me an exclusively academic matter. Yet it is an *intellectual* matter of some very obvious importance. I have been able to put to use my humanistic and political concerns for the analysis and description of a very worldly matter, the rise, development, and consolidation of Orientalism. Too often literature and culture are presumed to be politically, even historically innocent; it has regularly seemed otherwise to me, and certainly my study of Orientalism has convinced me (and I hope will convince my literary colleagues) that society and literary culture can only be understood and studied together.

巴巴:《文化的位置》

选文简介

选文摘自《文化的位置》第四章"模拟与人:殖民话语的矛盾情感",此前曾于1984年以期刊论文形式发表。巴巴所说的"模拟",指的是被殖民者接受殖民列强教化时采取的策略。白人教育当地人,要求他们模仿白人的规条,将其内化为行动准则。有意思的是,当地人三心二意地执行殖民者的意图,靠模拟实现了变色龙适应环境式的伪装。巴巴在选文中解析了模拟的机制,指出它是一种"讽刺性的妥协"(ironic compromise),生成不了殖民者所期待的理想他者。虽然模拟有顺从之意,以殖民者的版本为模本,进行着一次次重复性操演,但模拟的版本暗藏差异,当地人用挪用、戏仿和变形等策略,掏空了白人模版的内核,形成似是而非的新版。由此可见,在殖民者的收编中,被殖民者具有一定的能动性。表面化的模拟甚至具有威胁性——新版可以对殖民者的文化原版进行污染,使后者失去本真性和优越性。事实上,殖民体制无法彻底驯服被殖民者,当地人在用杂糅的方式创造自己的文化属性。

From *The Location of Culture*

Homi Bhabha (1949-)

Of Mimicry and Man: The Ambivalence of Colonial Discourse

The discourse of post-Enlightenment English colonialism often speaks in a tongue that is forked, not false. If colonialism takes power in the name of history, it repeatedly exercises its authority through the figures of farce. For the epic intention of the civilizing mission, "human and not wholly human" in the famous words of Lord Rosebery, "writ by the finger of the Divine" often produces a text rich in the traditions of *trompe-l'œil*, irony, mimicry and repetition. In this comic turn from the high ideals of the colonial imagination to its low mimetic literary effects mimicry emerges as one of the most elusive and effective strategies of colonial power and knowledge.

Within that conflictual economy of colonial discourse which Edward Said describes as the tension between the synchronic panoptical vision of domination—the demand for identity, stasis—and the counter-pressure of the diachrony of history—change, difference—mimicry represents an *ironic* compromise. If I may adapt Samuel Weber's formulation of the marginalizing vision of castration, then colonial mimicry is the desire for a reformed, recognizable Other, *as a subject of a difference that is almost the same, but not quite*. Which is to say, that the discourse of mimicry is constructed around an *ambivalence*; in order to be effective, mimicry must continually produce its slippage, its excess, its difference. The authority of that mode of colonial discourse that I have called mimicry is therefore stricken by an indeterminacy: mimicry emerges as the representation of a difference that is itself a process of disavowal. Mimicry is, thus the sign of a double articulation; a complex strategy of reform, regulation and discipline, which "appropriates" the Other as it visualizes power. Mimicry is also the sign of the inappropriate, however, a difference or recalcitrance which coheres the dominant strategic function of colonial power, intensifies surveillance, and poses an immanent threat to both "normalized" knowledges and disciplinary powers.

The effect of mimicry on the authority of colonial discourse is profound and disturbing. For in "normalizing" the colonial state or subject, the dream of post-Enlightenment civility alienates its own language of liberty and produces another knowledge of its norms. The ambivalence which thus informs this strategy is discernible, for example, in Locke's *Second Treatise* which *splits* to reveal the limitations of liberty in his double use of the word "slave": first simply, descriptively as the locus of a legitimate form of ownership, then as the trope for an intolerable, illegitimate exercise of power. What is articulated in that distance between the two uses is the absolute, imagined difference between the "Colonial" State of Carolina and the Original State of Nature.

It is from this area between mimicry and mockery, where the reforming, civilizing mission is threatened by the displacing gaze of its disciplinary double, that my instances of colonial imitation come. What they all share is a discursive process by which the excess or slippage produced by the *ambivalence* of mimicry (almost the same, *but not quite*) does not merely "rupture" the discourse, but becomes transformed into an uncertainty which fixes the colonial subject as a "partial" presence. By "partial" I mean both "incomplete" and "virtual." It is as if the very emergence of the "colonial" is dependent for its representation upon some strategic limitation or prohibition *within* the authoritative discourse itself. The success of colonial appropriation depends on a proliferation of inappropriate objects that ensure its strategic failure, so that mimicry is at once resemblance and menace.

A classic text of such partiality is Charles Grant's "Observations on the State of Society Among the Asiatic Subjects of Great Britain" (1792) which was only superseded by James Mills' *History of India* as the most influential early nineteenth-century account of Indian manners and morals. Grant's dream of an evangelical system of mission education conducted uncompromisingly in the English language, was partly a belief in political reform along Christian lines and partly an awareness that the expansion of company rule in India required a system of subject formation—a reform of manners, as Grant put it—that would provide the colonial with "a sense of personal identity as we know it." Caught between the desire for religious reform and the fear that the Indians might become turbulent for liberty, Grant paradoxically implies that it is the "partial" diffusion of Christianity, and the "partial" influence of moral improvements which will construct a particularly appropriate form of colonial subjectivity. What is suggested is a process of reform through which Christian doctrines might collude with divisive caste practices to prevent dangerous political alliances. Inadvertently, Grant produces a knowledge of Christianity as a form of social control which conflicts with the enunciatory assumptions that authorize his discourse. In suggesting, finally, that "partial reform" will produce an empty form of "the *imitation* [my emphasis] of English manners which will induce them [the colonial subjects] to remain under our protection." Grant mocks his moral project and violates the Evidence of Christianity—a central missionary tenet— which forbade any tolerance of heathen faiths.

The absurd extravagance of Macaulay's "Minute" (1835)—deeply influenced by Charles Grant's "Observations"—makes a mockery of Oriental learning until faced with the challenge of conceiving of a "reformed" colonial subject. Then, the great tradition of European humanism seems capable only of ironizing itself. At the intersection of European learning and colonial power, Macaulay can conceive of nothing other than "a class of interpreters between us and the millions whom we govern—a class of persons Indian in blood and color, but English in tastes, in opinions, in morals and in intellect"—in other words a mimic man raised "through our English School," as a missionary educationist wrote in 1819, "to form a corps of translators and be employed in different departments of Labor." The line of descent of the mimic man can be traced through the works of Kipling, Forster, Orwell, Naipaul, and to his emergence, most recently, in Benedict Anderson's excellent work on nationalism, as the anomalous Bipin Chandra Pal. He is the effect of a flawed colonial mimesis, in which to be Anglicized is *emphatically* not to be English.

The figure of mimicry is locatable within what Anderson describes as "the inner compatibility of empire and nation." It problematizes the signs of racial and cultural priority, so that the "national" is no longer naturalizable. What emerges between mimesis and mimicry is a *writing*, a mode of representation, that marginalizes the monumentality of history, quite simply mocks its power to be a model, that power which supposedly makes it imitable. Mimicry *repeats* rather than *re-presents* and in that diminishing perspective emerges Decoud's displaced European vision of Sulaco in Conrad's *Nostromo* as:

> the endlessness of civil strife where folly seemed even harder to bear than its ignominy…the lawlessness of a populace of all colors and races, barbarism, irremediable tyranny…. America is ungovernable.

Or Ralph Singh's apostasy in Naipaul's *The Mimic Men*:

> We pretended to be real, to be learning, to be preparing ourselves for life, we mimic men of the New World, one unknown corner of it, with all its reminders of the corruption that came so quickly to the new.

Both Decoud and Singh, and in their different ways Grant and Macaulay, are the parodists of history. Despite their intentions and invocations they inscribe the colonial text erratically, eccentrically across a body politic that refuses to be representative, in a narrative that refuses to be representational. The desire to emerge as "authentic" through mimicry—through a process of writing and repetition—is the final irony of partial representation.

What I have called mimicry is not the familiar exercise of *dependent* colonial relations through narcissistic identification so that, as Fanon has observed, the black man stops being an actional person for only the white man can represent his self-esteem. Mimicry conceals no presence or identity behind its mask: it is not what Césaire describes as "colonization-thingification" behind which there stands the essence of the *présence Africaine*. The *menace* of mimicry is its *double* vision which in disclosing the ambivalence of colonial discourse also disrupts its authority. And it is a double vision that is a result of what I've described as the partial representation/recognition of the colonial object. Grant's colonial as partial imitator, Macaulay's translator, Naipaul's colonial politician as play-actor, Decoud as the scene setter of the *opéra bouffe* of the New World, these are the appropriate objects of a colonialist chain of command, authorized versions of otherness. But they are also, as I have shown, the figures of a doubling, the part-objects of a metonymy of colonial desire which alienates the modality and normality of those dominant discourses in which they emerge as "inappropriate" colonial subjects. A desire that, through the repetition of *partial presence*, which is the basis of mimicry, articulates those disturbances of cultural, racial and historical difference that menace the narcissistic demand of colonial authority. It is a desire that reverses "in part" the colonial appropriation by now producing a partial vision of the colonizer's presence; a gaze of otherness, that shares the acuity of the genealogical gaze which, as Foucault describes it, liberates marginal elements and shatters the unity of man's being through which he extends his sovereignty….

In mimicry, the representation of identity and meaning is rearticulated along the axis of metonymy. As Lacan reminds us, mimicry is like camouflage, not a harmonization of repression of difference, but a form of resemblance, that differs from or defends presence by displaying it in part, metonymically. Its threat, I would add, comes from the prodigious and strategic production of conflictual, fantastic, discriminatory "identity effects" in the play of a power that is elusive because it hides no essence, no "itself."

斯皮瓦克:《庶民能说话吗?》

选文简介

斯皮瓦克曾经和印度庶民研究小组合作,共同关注殖民霸权下的阶级问题。但是斯皮瓦克和庶民研究小组的分歧在于,后者以男性研究者为主,不关注女性境遇。斯皮瓦克的《庶民能说话吗?》混合了女性主义、马克思主义、后结构主义、文化研究等多重理论视角,从性别、族裔和阶级角度切入对殖民权力结构的批判。斯皮瓦克的"庶民"不同于无产阶级,无后者的认识能力、自主觉悟和行动能力——庶民是不懂抗争的社会底层。斯皮瓦克认为殖民体系由占统治地位的外来殖民精英、本土精英(含国家精英和地方精英)和庶民组成。而庶民中的底层是该阶层的女性。她们既受殖民主义压迫,也受本土父权制的奴役,同时,因为印度属于第三世界,这些女性劳工也是世界资本体系的剥削对象。在选文中,斯皮瓦克重点讨论了没有办法进入殖民主义和父权制的话语体系的庶民阶层为何在白人殖民者和印度精英的代言中始终缄默,无法拥有言说的能力。

"Can the Subaltern Speak?"

Gayatri Chakravorty Spivak (1942-)

I am thinking of the general nonspecialist, nonacademic population across the class spectrum, for whom the episteme operates its silent programming function. Without considering the map of exploitation, on what grid of "oppression" would they place this motley crew?

Let us now move to consider the margins (one can just as well say the silent, silenced center) of the circuit marked out by this epistemic violence, men and women among the illiterate peasantry, the tribals, the lowest strata of the urban subproletariat. According to Foucault and Deleuze (in the First World, under the standardization and regimentation of socialized capital, though they do not seem to recognize this) the oppressed, if given the chance (the problem of representation cannot be bypassed here), and on the way to solidarity through alliance politics (a Marxist thematic is at work here) *can speak and know their conditions*. We must now confront the following question: on the other side of the international division of labor from socialized capital, inside *and* outside the circuit of the epistemic violence of imperialist law and education supplementing an earlier economic text, *can the subaltern speak?*...

The first part of my proposition—that the phased development of the subaltern is complicated by the imperialist project—is confronted by a collective of intellectuals who may be called the "Subaltern Studies" group. They *must* ask, Can the subaltern speak? Here we are within Foucault's own discipline of history and with people who acknowledge his influence. Their project is to rethink Indian colonial historiography from the perspective of the discontinuous chain of peasant insurgencies during the colonial occupation.

This is indeed the problem of "the permission to narrate" discussed by Said. As Ranajit Guha argues,

> The historiography of Indian nationalism has for a long time been dominated by elitism—colonialist elitism and bourgeois-nationalist elitism...shar[ing] the prejudice that the making of the Indian nation and the development of the consciousness—nationalism—which confirmed this process were exclusively or predominantly elite achievements. In the colonialist and neo-colonialist historiographies these achievements are credited to British colonial rulers, administrators, policies, institutions, and culture; in the nationalist and neo-nationalist writings—to Indian elite personalities, institutions, activities and ideas.

Certain varieties of the Indian elite are at best native informants for first-world intellectuals interested in the voice of the Other. But one must nevertheless insist that the colonized subaltern *subject* is irretrievably heterogeneous.

Against the indigenous elite we may set what Guha calls "the *politics* of the people," both outside ("this was an *autonomous* domain, for it neither originated from elite politics nor did its existence depend on the latter") and inside ("it continued to operate vigorously in spite of [colonialism], adjusting itself to the conditions prevailing under the Raj and in many respects developing entirely new strains in both form and content") the circuit of colonial production. I cannot entirely endorse this insistence on determinate vigor and full autonomy, for practical historiographic exigencies will not allow such endorsements to privilege subaltern consciousness. Against the possible charge that his approach is essentialist, Guha constructs a definition of the people (the place of that essence) that can be only an identity-in-differential. He proposes a dynamic stratification grid describing colonial social production at large. Even the third group on the list, the buffer group, as it were, between the people and the great macrostructural dominant groups, is itself defined as a place of in-betweenness, what Derrida has described as an "*antre*":

elite
1. Dominant foreign groups.
2. Dominant indigenous groups on the all-India level.
3. Dominant indigenous groups at the regional and local levels.
4. The terms "people" and "subaltern classes" have been used as synonymous throughout this note. The social groups and elements included in this category represent *the demographic difference between the total Indian population and all those whom we have described as the "elite."*

Consider the third item on this list—the *antre* of situational indeterminacy these careful historians presuppose as they grapple with the question, Can the subaltern speak? "*Taken as a whole and in the abstract* this...category...was *heterogeneous* in its composition and thanks to the uneven character of regional economic and social developments, *differed from area to area*. The same class or element which was dominant in one area...could be among the dominated in another. This could and did create many ambiguities and contradictions in attitudes and alliances, especially among the lowest strata of the rural gentry, impoverished landlords, rich peasants and upper-middle-class peasants all of whom belonged, *ideally speaking*, to the category of people or subaltern classes."

"The task of research" projected here is "to investigate, identify and measure the *specific* nature and degree of the *deviation* of [the] elements [constituting item 3] from the ideal and situate it historically." "Investigate, identify, and measure the specific": a program could hardly be more essentialist and taxonomic. Yet a curious methodological imperative is at work. I have argued that, in the Foucault-Deleuze conversation, a postrepresentationalist vocabulary hides an essentialist agenda. In subaltern studies, because of the violence of imperialist epistemic, social, and disciplinary inscription, a project understood in essentialist terms must traffic in a radical textual practice of differences. The object of the group's investigation, in the case not even of the people as such but of the floating buffer zone of the regional elite-subaltern, is a *deviation* from an *ideal*—the people or subaltern—which is itself defined as a difference from the elite. It is toward this structure that the research is oriented, a predicament rather different from the self-diagnosed transparency of the first-world radical intellectual. What taxonomy can fix such a space? Whether or not they themselves perceive it—in fact Guha sees his definition of "the people" within the master-slave dialectic—their text articulates the difficult task of rewriting its own conditions of impossibility as the conditions of its possibility.

"At the regional and local levels [the dominant indigenous groups]...if belonging to social strata hierarchically inferior to those of the dominant all-Indian groups *acted in the interests of the latter and not in conformity to interests corresponding truly to their own social being*." When these writers speak, in their essentializing language, of a gap between interest and action in the intermediate group, their conclusions are closer to Marx than to the self-conscious naiveté of Deleuze's pronouncement on the issue. Guha, like Marx, speaks of interest in terms of the social rather than the libidinal being. The Name-of-the-Father imagery in *The Eighteenth Brumaire* can help to emphasize that, on the level of class or group action, "true correspondence to own being" is as artificial or social as the patronymic.

So much for the intermediate group marked in item 3. For the "true" subaltern group, whose identity is its difference, there is no unrepresentable subaltern subject that can know and speak itself; the intellectual's solution is not to abstain from representation. The problem is that the subject's itinerary has not been traced so as to offer an object of seduction to the representing intellectual. In the slightly dated language of the Indian group, the question becomes, How can we touch the consciousness of the people, even as we investigate their politics? With what voice-consciousness can the subaltern speak? Their project, after all, is to rewrite the development of the consciousness of the Indian nation. The planned discontinuity of imperialism rigorously distinguishes this project, however old-fashioned its articulation, from "rendering visible the medical and juridical mechanisms that surrounded the story [of Pierre Riviere]." Foucault is correct in suggesting that "to make visible the unseen can also mean a change of level, addressing oneself to a layer of material which had hitherto had no pertinence for history and which had not been recognized as having any moral, aesthetic or historical value." It is the slippage from rendering visible the mechanism to rendering vocal the individual, both avoiding "any kind of analysis of [the subject] whether psychological, psychoanalytical or linguistic," that is consistently troublesome....

When we come to the concomitant question of the consciousness of the subaltern, the notion of what the work *cannot* say becomes important. In the semioses of the social text, elaborations of insurgency stand in the place of "the utterance." The sender— "the peasant"—is marked only as a pointer to an irretrievable consciousness. As for the receiver, we must ask who is "the real receiver" of an "insurgency?" The historian, transforming "insurgency" into "text for knowledge," is only one "receiver" of any collectively intended social act. With no possibility of nostalgia for that lost origin, the historian must suspend (as far as possible) the clamor of his or her own consciousness (or consciousness-effect, as operated by disciplinary training), so that the elaboration of the insurgency, packaged with an insurgent-consciousness, does not freeze into an "object of investigation," or, worse yet, a model for imitation. "The subject" implied by the texts of insurgency can only serve as a counterpossibility for the narrative sanctions granted to the colonial subject in the dominant groups. The postcolonial intellectuals learn that their privilege is their loss. In this they are a paradigm of the intellectuals.

It is well known that the notion of the feminine (rather than the subaltern of imperialism) has been used in a similar way within deconstructive criticism and within certain varieties of feminist criticism. In the former case, a figure of "woman" is at issue, one whose minimal predication as indeterminate is already available to the phallocentric tradition. Subaltern historiography raises questions of method that would prevent it from using such a ruse. For the "figure" of woman, the relationship between woman and silence can be plotted by women themselves; race and class differences are subsumed under that charge. Subaltern historiography must confront the impossibility of such gestures. The narrow epistemic violence of imperialism gives us an imperfect allegory of the general violence that is the possibility of an episteme.

Within the effaced itinerary of the subaltern subject, the track of sexual difference is doubly effaced. The question is not of female participation in insurgency, or the ground rules of the sexual division of labor, for both of which there is "evidence." It is, rather, that, both as object of colonialist historiography and as subject of insurgency, the ideological construction of gender keeps the male dominant. If, in the context of colonial production, the subaltern has no history and cannot speak, the subaltern as female is even more deeply in shadow.

莫汉蒂:《再访〈西方视野之下〉》

选文简介

莫汉蒂在《西方视野之下》中批评西方女性主义者在研究第三世界女性时,运用知识暴力将其塑造成缺乏主体性的蒙昧客体,为自身利益容忍西方帝国主义对第三世界女性的剥削压迫。2003年,莫汉蒂重访旧文,继续强调旧文中提及的对西方女性主义的批判立场;继续主张女性主义者在进行跨边界研究时,从微观政治层面关注具体的语境、主体性和斗争,以及从宏观政治层面关注全球政治经济体制及其变化进程;继续呼吁尊重不同地区女性的差异,在此基础上建构非殖民模式的女性主义同盟。但她也对自己的立场进行了补充,提出当下的关键词是"团结"。在莫汉蒂看来，真正的团结不是忽略差异，强行推行"普世价值"，而是认识到差异是普遍存在的现实，尊重各自的诉求，积极促进对话，实现合作。她认为跨边界的女性主义的集体行动有团结一致的目标：反对资本主义的全球化，因为资本主义是当今社会包括种族主义、父权制、阶级剥削、性别歧视等各种形式的压迫的根源。

From "'Under Western Eyes' Revisited"

Chandra Talpade Mohanty (1955-)

I wrote "Under Western Eyes" to discover and articulate a critique of "Western feminist" scholarship on Third World women via the discursive colonization of Third World women's lives and struggles. I also wanted to expose the power-knowledge nexus of feminist cross-cultural scholarship expressed through Eurocentric, falsely universalizing methodologies that serve the narrow self-interest of Western feminism. As well, I thought it crucial to highlight the connection between feminist scholarship and feminist political organizing while drawing attention to the need to examine the "political implications of our analytic strategies and principles." I also wanted to chart the location of feminist scholarship within a global political and economic framework dominated by the "First World."

My most simple goal was to make clear that cross-cultural feminist work must be attentive to the micropolitics of context, subjectivity, and struggle, as well as to the macropolitics of global economic and political systems and processes....

I did not write "Under Western Eyes" as a testament to the impossibility of egalitarian and noncolonizing cross-cultural scholarship, nor did I define "Western" and "Third World" feminism in such oppositional ways that there would be no possibility of solidarity between Western and Third World feminists. Yet, this is often how the essay has been read and utilized. I have wondered why such a sharp opposition has developed in this form. Perhaps mapping the intellectual and institutional context in which I wrote back then and the shifts that have affected its reading since would clarify the intentions and claims of the essay.

Intellectually, I was writing in solidarity with the critics of Eurocentric humanism who drew attention to its false universalizing and masculinist assumptions. My project was anchored in a firm belief in the importance of the particular in relation to the universal—a belief in the local as specifying and illuminating the universal. My concerns drew attention to the dichotomies embraced and identified with this universalized framework, the critique of "white feminism" by women of color and the critique of "Western feminism" by Third World feminists working within a paradigm of decolonization. I was committed, both politically and personally, to building a noncolonizing feminist solidarity across borders. I believed in a larger feminist project than the colonizing, self-interested one I saw emerging in much influential feminist scholarship and in the mainstream women's movement.

My newly found teaching position at a primarily white US academic institution also deeply affected my writing at this time. I was determined to make an intervention in this space in order to create a location for Third World, immigrant, and other marginalized scholars like myself who saw themselves erased or misrepresented within the dominant Euro-American feminist scholarship and their communities. It has been a source of deep satisfaction that I was able to begin to open an intellectual space to Third World/immigrant women scholars, as was done at the international conference I helped organize, "Common Differences: Third World Women and Feminist Perspectives" (Urbana, Illinois, 1983). This conference allowed for the possibility of a decolonized, cross-border feminist community and cemented for me the belief that "common differences" can form the basis of deep solidarity, and that we have to struggle to achieve this in the face of unequal power relations among feminists....

...In 1984 my priority was on difference, but now I want to recapture and reiterate its fuller meaning, which was always there, and that is its connection to the universal. In other words, this discussion allows me to reemphasize the way that differences are never just "differences." In knowing differences and particularities, we can better see the connections and commonalities because no border or boundary is ever complete or rigidly determining. The challenge is to see how differences allow us to explain the connections and border crossings better and more accurately, how specifying difference allows us to theorize universal concerns more fully. It is this intellectual move that allows for my concern for women of different communities and identities to build coalitions and solidarities across borders....

While my earlier focus was on the distinctions between "Western" and "Third World" feminist practices, and while I downplayed the commonalities between these two positions, my focus now...is on what I have chosen to call an anticapitalist transnational feminist practice—and on the possibilities, indeed on the necessities, of crossnational feminist solidarity and organizing against capitalism. While "Under Western Eyes" was located in the context of the critique of Western humanism and Eurocentrism and of white, Western feminism, a similar essay written now would need to be located in the context of the critique of global capitalism (on antiglobalization), the naturalization of the values of capital, and the unacknowledged power of cultural relativism in cross-cultural feminist scholarship and pedagogies.

"Under Western Eyes" sought to make the operations of discursive power visible, to draw attention to what was left out of feminist theorizing, namely, the material complexity, reality, and agency of Third World women's bodies and lives. This is in fact exactly the analytic strategy I now use to draw attention to what is unseen, undertheorized, and left out in the production of knowledge about globalization. While globalization has always been a part of capitalism, and capitalism is not a new phenomenon, at this time I believe the theory, critique, and activism around antiglobalization has to be a key focus for feminists. This does not mean that the patriarchal and racist relations and structures that accompany capitalism are any less problematic at this time, or that antiglobalization is a singular phenomenon. Along with many other scholars and activists, I believe capital as it functions now depends on and exacerbates racist, patriarchal, and heterosexist relations of rule....

It is especially on the bodies and lives of women and girls from the Third World/South—the Two-Thirds World—that global capitalism writes its script, and it is by paying attention to and theorizing the experiences of these communities of women and girls that we demystify capitalism as a system of debilitating sexism and racism and envision anticapitalist resistance. Thus any analysis of the effects of globalization needs to centralize the experiences and struggles of these particular communities of women and girls.

Drawing on Arif Dirlik's notion of "place consciousness as the radical other of global capitalism," Grace Lee Boggs makes an important argument for place-based civic activism that illustrates how centralizing the struggles of marginalized communities connects to larger antiglobalization struggles. Boggs suggests that "[p]lace consciousness...encourages us to come together around common, local experiences and organize around our hopes for the future of our communities and cities. While global capitalism doesn't give a damn about the people or the natural environment of any particular place because it can always move on to other people and other places, place-based civic activism is concerned about the health and safety of people and places." Since women are central to the life of neighborhood and communities they assume leadership positions in these struggles. This is evident in the example of women of color in struggles against environmental racism in the United States, as well as in Shiva's example of tribal women in the struggle against deforestation and for an intellectual commons. It is then the lives, experiences, and struggles of girls and women of the Two-Thirds World that demystify capitalism in its racial and sexual dimensions—and that provide productive and necessary avenues of theorizing and enacting anticapitalist resistance.

I do not wish to leave this discussion of capitalism as a generalized site without contextualizing its meaning in and through the lives it structures. Disproportionately, these are girls' and women's lives, although I am committed to the lives of all exploited peoples. However, the specificity of girls' and women's lives encompasses the others through their particularized and contextualized experiences. If these particular gendered, classed, and racialized realities of globalization are unseen and undertheorized, even the most radical critiques of globalization effectively render Third World/South women and girls as absent. Perhaps it is no longer simply an issue of Western eyes, but rather how the West is inside and continually reconfigures globally, racially, and in terms of gender. Without this recognition, a necessary link between feminist scholarship/analytic frames and organizing/activist projects is impossible. Faulty and inadequate analytic frames engender ineffective political action and strategizing for social transformation.

What does the above analysis suggest? That we—feminist scholars and teachers—must respond to the phenomenon of globalization as an urgent site for the recolonization of peoples, especially in the Two-Thirds World. Globalization colonizes women's as well as men's lives around the world, and we need an anti-imperialist, anticapitalist, and contextualized feminist project to expose and make visible the various, overlapping forms of subjugation of women's lives. Activists and scholars must also identify and reenvision forms of collective resistance that women, especially, in their different communities enact in their everyday lives. It is their particular exploitation at this time, their potential epistemic privilege, as well as their particular forms of solidarity that can be the basis for reimagining a liberatory politics for the start of this century.

思考题

1. 什么是萨义德所说的东方学？它与西方殖民体系有什么关系？
2. 巴巴为什么说模拟是一种"讽刺性的妥协"？在巴巴的模拟论中，殖民者和被殖民者之间是什么关系？
3. 斯皮瓦克为什么关心庶民问题？斯皮瓦克认为庶民能说话吗？为什么？
4. 莫汉蒂为什么说西方女性主义对第三世界女性的论述是一种"话语殖民"？
5. 《西方视野之下》的核心议题是什么？《再访〈西方视野之下〉》的核心议题有什么变化？其核心关键词是什么？

讨论题

1. 请结合萨义德、巴巴、斯皮瓦克和莫汉蒂的选文，讨论西方殖民者如何通过二元对立模式，巩固西方中心主义的意识形态，塑造被殖民者的刻板印象。
2. 请在约瑟夫·康拉德、J. M. 库切、V. S. 奈保尔、托妮·莫里森等现当代小说家的作品中挑选一部，结合后殖民理论进行主题阐释，或者结合某个人物的刻画进行人物形象分析。

补充文本选摘与评述

法农：《黑皮肤，白面具》
From *Black Skin, White Masks*

Frantz Fanon (1925-1961)

The black man among his own in the twentieth century does not know at what moment his inferiority comes into being through the other. Of course I have talked about the black problem with friends, or, more rarely, with American Negroes. Together we protested, we asserted the equality of all men in the world. In the Antilles there was also that little gulf that exists among the almost-white, the mulatto, and the nigger. But I was satisfied with an intellectual understanding of these differences. It was not really dramatic. And then...

And then the occasion arose when I had to meet the white man's eyes. An unfamiliar weight burdened me. The real world challenged my claims. In the white world the man of color encounters difficulties in the development of his bodily schema. Consciousness of the body is solely a negating activity. It is a third-person consciousness. The body is surrounded by an atmosphere of certain uncertainty. I know that if I want to smoke, I shall have to reach out my right arm and take the pack of cigarettes lying at the other end of the table. The matches, however, are in the drawer on the left, and I shall have to lean back slightly. And all these movements are made not out of habit but out of implicit knowledge. A slow composition of my *self* as a body in the middle of a spatial and temporal world—such seems to be the schema. It does not impose itself on me; it is, rather, a definitive structuring of the self and of the world-definitive because it creates a real dialectic between my body and the world....

"Look, a Negro!" It was an external stimulus that flicked over me as I passed by. I made a tight smile.

"Look, a Negro!" It was true. It amused me.

"Look, a Negro!" The circle was drawing a bit tighter. I made no secret of my amusement.

"Mama, see the Negro! I'm frightened!" Frightened! Frightened! Now they were beginning to be afraid of me. I made up my mind to laugh myself to tears, but laughter had become impossible....

My body was given back to me sprawled out, distorted, recolored, clad in mourning in that white winter day. The Negro is an animal, the Negro is bad, the Negro is mean, the Negro is ugly; look, a nigger, it's cold, the nigger is shivering, the nigger is shivering because he is cold, the little boy is trembling because he is afraid of the nigger, the nigger is shivering with cold, that cold that goes through your bones, the handsome little boy is trembling because he thinks that the nigger is quivering with rage, the little white boy throws himself into his mother's arms: Mama, the nigger's going to eat me up.

All around me the white man, above the sky tears at its navel, the earth rasps under my feet, and there is a white song, a white song. All this whiteness that burns me.

阿希克洛夫特、格里菲斯、蒂芬:《逆写帝国》
From *The Empire Writes Back*

Bill Ashcroft (1946-), Gareth Griffiths (1943-) and Helen Tiffin (1945-)

More english than English

The contemporary art, philosophy, and literature produced by postcolonial societies are in no sense continuations or simple adaptations of European models. This book has argued that a much more profound interaction and appropriation has taken place. Indeed, the process of cultural decolonization has involved a radical dismantling of the European codes and a post-colonial subversion and appropriation of the dominant European discourses.

This dismantling has been frequently accompanied by the demand for an entirely new or wholly recovered pre-colonial "reality." Such a demand, given the nature of the relationship between colonizer and colonized, its social brutality and cultural denigration, is perfectly comprehensible. But, as we have argued, it cannot be achieved. Postcolonial culture is inevitably a hybridized phenomenon involving a dialectical relationship between the "grafted" European cultural systems and an indigenous ontology, with its impulse to create or recreate an independent local identity. Such construction or reconstruction only occurs as a dynamic interaction between European hegemonic systems and "peripheral" subversions of them. It is not possible to return to or to rediscover an absolute pre-colonial cultural purity, nor is it possible to create national or regional formations entirely independent of their historical implication in the European colonial enterprise.

Hence it has been the project of post-colonial writing to interrogate European discourse and discursive strategies from its position within and between two worlds; to investigate the means by which Europe imposed and maintained its codes in its colonial domination of so much of the rest of the world. Thus the rereading and the rewriting of the European historical and fictional record is a vital and inescapable task at the heart of the post-colonial enterprise. These subversive maneuvers, rather than the construction of essentially national or regional alternatives, are the characteristic features of the post-colonial text. Post-colonial literatures/cultures are constituted in counter-discursive rather than homologous practices.

What is more, post-colonial literature and its study is essentially political in that its development and the theories which accompany this development radically question the apparent axioms upon which the whole discipline of English has been raised. Not only the canon of "classical texts," the disruption of which by new, "exotic" texts can be easily countered by a strategy of incorporation from the center, but the very idea of English Literature as a study which occludes its own specific national, cultural, and political grounding and offers itself as a new system for the development of "universal" human values, is exploded by the existence of the post-colonial literatures.

杨:《后殖民存留》
From "Postcolonial Remains"

Robert Young (1950-)

What remains of the postcolonial? Has it already perished, leaving only its earthly relics, forgotten books, abandoned articles floating in cyberspace, remnants of yellowing conference programs? So one might think on reading the obituary announced by *PMLA* in 2007: "The End of Postcolonial Theory?" There, a group of apparently former postcolonial critics pronounced "it" over....

The desire to pronounce postcolonial theory dead on both sides of the Atlantic suggests that its presence continues to disturb and provoke anxiety: the real problem lies in the fact that the postcolonial remains. Why does it continue to unsettle people so much? The aspiring morticians of the postcolonial concur in scarcely relating it to the world from which it comes and for which it claims to speak: that outside Europe and North America. The desired dissolution of postcolonial theory does not mean that poverty, inequality, exploitation, and oppression in the world have come to an end, only that some people in the U.S. and French academies have decided they do not want to have to think about such things any longer and do not want to be reminded of those distant invisible contexts which continue to prompt the transformative energies of the postcolonial.

"Postcolonialism" is not just a disciplinary field, nor is it a theory which has or has not come to an end. Rather, its objectives have always involved a wide-ranging political project—to reconstruct Western knowledge formations, reorient ethical norms, turn the power structures of the world upside down, refashion the world from below. The postcolonial has always been concerned with interrogating the interrelated histories of violence, domination, inequality, and injustice, with addressing the fact that, and the reasons why, millions of people in this world still live without things that most of those in the West take for granted....

The postcolonial remains: it lives on, ceaselessly transformed in the present into new social and political configurations. One marker of its continuing relevance is the degree to which the power of the postcolonial perspective has spread across almost all the disciplines in the humanities and social sciences, from classics to development theory to law to medieval studies to theology—even sociology, under the encouragement of postcolonial-minded scholars such as Arjun Appadurai and Paul Gilroy, has abandoned its former narrow national focus to turn to an interest in globalization in the present. So many disciplines have been, so to speak, postcolonialized, along with the creation of related subdisciplines such as diaspora and transnational studies, that this remarkable dispersal of intellectual and political influence now makes it difficult to locate any kind of center of postcolonial theory: reaching into almost every domain of contemporary thought, it has become part of the consciousness of our era.

选文评述

法农在《黑皮肤，白面具》中，除了从精神分析的角度讨论殖民价值体系对黑人心理的影响，还从哲学的角度讨论种族主义凝视下黑人主体性的异化。黑人作为主体，其身体感知是协调而自在的，但是在白人的注目下，却会手足无措，为自己无法丢弃的肤色而深深惭愧。法农用文学的笔法描写了他在巴黎街头遇到白人小男孩的经历："妈妈，看这个黑人！我害怕！"孩子对黑皮肤的害怕，源于白人对黑人的贬低和妖魔化。"黑人是动物，黑人是坏人，黑人是凶恶的，黑人是丑陋的"——这些标签被黑人内化进自己的人格。黑人为什么喜欢白面具？因为他们以为变白了就可以获得白人的尊重。法农有关白人凝视的讨论，是后殖民视觉文化研究的重要理论资源。

阿希克洛夫特等人合著的《逆写帝国》是对萨义德在《文化与帝国主义》中所论议题的重要补充。后者旨在揭示西方宗主国文学中的帝国主义意识，以批判为主旨；前者转向倾听殖民地人民的本土之声。选文出自《逆写帝国》的结语。作者指出，解殖后，本土文学不可能回归殖民前的"纯粹"，这是因为欧洲文化体系被嫁接到了本土，本土文化已经产生了杂糅。所以后殖民文学只能是"两个世界之间"的文学。它的主体性反映在它对外来文化体系的创造性的拆解和挪用：后殖民文学没有跟着宗主国亦步亦趋，拒绝同质性重构，主动进行改写，形成对抗性话语。如选文中的小标题所示，"地方英语胜于英国英语"，后殖民英语文学是对标准英语规范的突破，推翻了英语经典的"普世价值"规范，而且文本具复杂性。

杨的《后殖民存留》是篇期刊论文，发表于2012年。当时，有学者宣称是时候让后殖民主义寿终正寝了。杨则认为后殖民主义不是一个学科领域，不是一种会过时的理论思潮，只要贫困、不平等、剥削、压迫等后殖民问题没有解决，后殖民主义就不会消亡。后殖民主义的价值在于唤起人们的政治觉醒，放弃西方模式的"普世价值"标准，重新建构知识结构和伦理的范式，自下而上重塑这个世界。事实上，后殖民的视角已经弥散到整个人文学科各领域，全面渗透进了当代思想，成为我们的时代意识的一部分。

关键术语释例

1. **流散（diaspora）**："流散"是空间意义上的大迁徙，它源自希腊语，曾用来指犹太人被逐出家园后在世界各地栖居。在古代，流散总是与政治、经济、宗教或战争等原因有关，是流离失所的艰辛跋涉，贯穿着民族、种族、国家等身份焦虑，所以流散族群普遍有原乡情绪，心系家园，往往以传统文化为根基，寻求在新的栖居地保持族裔独立性。在当下的全球化语境中，流散不再被视为绝对的创伤，它也含有跨文化的含义，兼具杂糅性和流动性。

2. **接触地带（contact zone）**：玛丽·路易丝·普拉特（Mary Louise Pratt）在《帝国之眼》（*Imperial Eyes: Travel Writing and Transculturation*）中将外来定居者与原住民相互关联的空间称为"接触地带"。在这里，迥然不同的文化彼此遭遇，相互冲突，引发对抗与角力。普拉特特别注意到，在这种接触中存在着非对称的支配与从属关系。比如，从殖民模式看，殖民者和原住民的权力不对等，殖民者有文化方面或者军事政治方面的优势，试图对原住民进行霸权宰制。但普拉特不认为在接触地带的弱势一方会毫无作为。面对文化霸权，弱势一方依然有行动空间。理想的接触地带是"文化互化"（transculturation）的场域，不同文化相互影响，相互丰富。

推荐书目

Ahmad, Aijaz. *In Theory: Classes, Nations, Literatures*. London: Verso, 1992.
Lazarus, Neil. *The Cambridge Companion to Postcolonial Literary Studies*. Cambridge: Cambridge University Press, 2004.
Loomba, Ania. *Colonialism/Postcolonialism.* London: Routledge, 2005.
Moore-Gilbert, Bart. *Postcolonial Theory: Contexts, Practices, Politics*. London: Verso, 1997.
Nayar, Pramod K. *Postcolonial Studies: An Anthology*. Chichester: Wiley-Blackwell, 2015.
Pratt, Mary Louise. *Imperial Eyes: Travel Writing and Transculturation*. London: Routledge, 2008.
Young, Robert. *Postcolonialism: A Very Short Introduction*. Oxford: Oxford University Press, 2003.
罗钢，刘象愚：《后殖民主义文化理论》。北京：中国社会科学出版社，1999年。
赵稀方：《后殖民理论》。北京：北京大学出版社，2009年。

第十三章
新历史主义与文化研究

概述

新历史主义是美国学界20世纪最后二十年涌现出的文论思潮之一。它与女性主义和后殖民主义对政治、文化、阶级、性属等议题的历史反思形成应和。新历史主义中的"新"字，则显示着它与历史主义既有深刻关联，又与其传统存在差异。传统历史主义者认为历史书写是对真实事件的客观记录，关心宏观层面的历史脉络，普遍持有进步史观，认为历史事件有因有果，社会发展沿着时间线性轨道不断向前。但他们避而不谈历史修撰对档案材料的依赖和对历史事件的筛选，忽略修撰者的个性和处境，淡化历史书写的叙事属性。进入20世纪，尤其是进入20世纪下半叶，这种历史观不断面临挑战：阐释学要求关注历史言说者的主观立场；后结构主义要求探察历史书写中的权力话语系统；后现代主义要求反思进步史观的宏大叙事对历史偶然性和差异性的遮蔽。以上趋势造就了历史研究的新转向，而史学领域的变革也影响了文学理论界，带来了新历史主义的兴起。

在史学界，历史研究新转向的代表人物是海登·怀特（Hayden White）。他在代表作《元历史》(*Metahistory: The Historical Imagination in Nineteenth-Century Europe*，1973）中提出"元历史"的概念，认为历史学必须反思历史叙事的符码机制，重新审视历史学所标榜的"真实性""客观性"和"科学性"。历史事件虽然真实发生，但即便是亲历者讲述历史，也会受个人视角和立场的影响。而后人修撰历史时，必须在前人史书和历史档案基础上爬梳材料，分辨真伪，进行言说。怀特指出，叙事性是历史的必然维度，对历史事件的记忆、转写、删减、补白、阐释，都离不开书写者的理解与建构。而且，历史学家在修撰历史时，也和文学家一样，在调用"浪漫""悲剧""喜剧""讽刺"等情节类型以及"隐喻""换喻""提喻""反讽"等语言表述模式。同一历史事件，通过不同的情节编排，可能呈现截然相反的意义。换一个作者，一出悲剧可能会变成一则闹剧。怀特的元历史论不是历史虚无主义。他不否定历史事件的客观存在，但他认为应对历史修撰的话语维度保持充分认识，认清历史书写不是真理言说，警惕宏大叙事的"正统"历史，重视历史叙事的复数性和对话性。

历史学领域的转向，也启发了文学研究的学者。他们从怀特的元历史理论中看到了拆除文学与历史之间界墙的契机，由此拓展出文学研究的新方向。他们既反对形式主义者将文学视为自治的领域，也反对传统历史主义研究者将单数的大写的历史视为文学的生成背景。用路易斯·蒙特罗斯（Louis Montrose）的话来说，新历史主义研究既重视文本的历史性（the historicity of texts），也重视历史的文本性（the textuality of history）。文本的历史性指的是文本的书写，无论是文学文本还是文化文本，都离不开它的历史具体性，都渗透着时代的社会能量。而历史的文本性指的是我们无法离开历史修撰空谈历史，作为文本的历史既带有历史修撰者的个人色彩，也铭刻权力话语的烙印。新历史主义者主张将历史文本和文学文本等量齐观。正如其代表人物斯蒂芬·格林布拉特（Stephen Greenblatt）所言，批评家们需要挑战将艺术生产和其他社会生产截然分开的立场。文学研究不应局限于虚构性的文学文本领域，而应该包括对传记、日记、游记、政治宣传手册等许多原先隶属于历史范畴的文本文献的考察。

新历史主义者拆除了文学和历史的分界，文学文本和历史言说同属于特定时代的话语系统，各种社会文化力量汇聚其中，形成复杂互动，共同参与文化网络的建构。在此视域下，如何才能形成对文学及其隶属的复杂语义场的全面认识？新历史主义者主张自下而上，由细节入手，进行考察。此处可见新批评的细读传统的影响，也可见当代文化人类学理论的影响。美国人类学家克利福德·格尔茨（Clifford Geertz）反对结构主义传统，提出"厚描"（thick description）的方法论，主张人类学研究不能只从结构主义角度关注宏观系统，而应沉降到细节的肌理，不放过对具体行动的动机、过程等的体察，以领悟文化的多层意涵。新历史主义从厚描理论中获得启发，主张文学批评实践从小处破题，用具有特殊性的历史轶事作引子。按照格林布拉特和凯瑟琳·加拉格尔（Catherine Gallagher）在《实践新历史主义》（*Practicing New Historicism*，2000）一书中的解释，这种轶事主义特别提醒人们，不要看到正统历史叙事的大门便长驱直入，而应顿住脚步，沿着看似无关紧要的细节，去追寻特定时代的文学、历史、文化、经济等不同领域的文本的关联，发现由它们共同织就的时代全貌。所以，新历史主义者绘制的历史社会文化图景充满了丰盈的细节。比如，格林布拉特在《炼狱中的哈姆雷特》（*Hamlet in Purgatory*，2002）一书中，用16世纪末一篇呈给亨利八世的名不见经传的请愿文开篇，引入当时的天主教和新教在仪轨议题上的分歧，围绕"炼狱"这个带有天主教色彩的意象，对莎士比亚名剧《哈姆雷特》中的幽灵形象进行了解读。通过格林布拉特的旁征博引，墓碑上的碑铭、弥撒祈祷词、威廉·廷代尔的宗教论述、约翰·多恩的诗歌、托马斯·莫尔的著作、莎士比亚的其他名剧，这些不同类属的文本和它们隐含的意义逐一浮现，构筑出莎士比亚身处的立体世界，揭示出隐藏在《哈姆雷特》的幽灵阴影中的天主教与新教、官方立场与民间传统、社会规训与个人主体意识之间的缠斗。

细看新历史主义的批评实践，虽然讨论的文本类型各异，分属不同社会层面，且有跨学科性，但是关键词都是"权力"：新历史主义关注文本的生成和流通是如何受到权力的影响，意识形态如何或明或暗地在这些文本中体现。传统历史研究从宏观社会结构理解权力，权力是统治阶级的手段。而新历史主义受葛兰西的霸权论和福柯的微观权力论的影响，认为权力不是自上而下的统治，而是弥散在社会的各个层面，牵动着所有社会成员的行动逻辑，也影响着包括历史书写和文学书写在内的各种社会文化实践。以蒙特罗斯的《"伊莱扎，牧羊人女王"和权力的田园诗》（"'Eliza, Queene of shepheardes,' and the Pastoral of Power"，1980）为例。蒙特罗斯解析了伊丽莎白一世时代的田园诗的意识形态功能，发现它参与了对伊丽莎白女王形象的塑造，促进了民众对女王的认同。女王在牧歌中，以亲民的平凡人的形象与民同乐。她是英国的精神领袖，引领着被比喻为牧羊人的朝臣和被比喻为羊群的民众。田园诗赞美卑微者的日常生活，歌颂貌视权力的平民世界，却被转用成对王权的礼赞。文学中的权力诗学体现出政治能量在上至女王下至百姓的各个阶层的流通。

在新历史主义的阐释中，文学作品孕育着颠覆性元素，但是这些元素往往被权力收编，被主流意识形态所含纳。不少情况下，颠覆恰恰是权力机制留下的陷阱，它给予人们宣泄的渠道，而宣泄的目的，或许是为了使人们更心甘情愿地被吸纳进社会的运作体系之中。这也是格林布拉特的《文艺复兴时期的自我塑造》（*Renaissance Self-Fashioning: From More to Shakespeare*，1980）和《莎士比亚的协商》（*Shakespearean Negotiations: The Circulation of Social Energy in Renaissance England*，1988）等作品的议题。格林布拉特在这些著作中详细剖析了文艺复兴时代，现代意义上的人的主体性的生成如何被权力所影响，主人公们的反抗其实受权力逻辑的支配。

值得注意的是，格林布拉特早期研究中的"颠覆/含纳说"（subversion/containment）旨在提醒我们要认识到反抗权力操控的复杂性和艰难性，但他在中后期越来越关注能动性，认为文学作品不可避免地受时代制约，但伟大的作品会以文学独有的方式冲击时代文化的疆界。格林布拉特以莎士比亚的《暴风雨》为例，指出这部戏虽然塑造了作为殖民者的普洛斯彼罗在小岛呼风唤雨的魔法师形象，但也用土人卡利班的诅咒在质疑和消解着普洛斯彼罗的权力。他提出文化批评既需要阐释普洛斯彼罗的权力，也需要让我们能够听到卡利班的声音。

新历史主义的研究兴趣不在搭建理论体系，而在具体批评实践。他们打掉了文学与历史的界墙，将文学纳入文化之网进行综合考察，拓展了文学研究的领域。实际上，对于新历史主义这个命名，格林布拉特持有保留态度。他认为自己的研究是"文化诗学"（poetics of culture）——文学书写与历史修撰都是文化的符号系统的有机组成部分。事实上，新历史主义与有更漫长传统的文化研究一样，体现了当代文学研究的文化转向。

什么是文化研究？对于这个问题，首先要回应的是：什么是文化？文化研究的文化，不是传统意义上的大写的精英主义的文化，它更偏向于人类学意义上的文化观：文化是人类的生活方式的总和。文化研究的方法论要求文学研究走出经典作品的狭窄领域，走出高雅艺术的自治领，关注文学是如何嵌合在日常社会文化生活实践之中。这种以小写的复数的文化为切入点的文化研究，其传统的开创源自英国战后的伯明翰学派。

1964年，英国伯明翰大学成立当代文化研究中心（The Centre for Contemporary Cultural Studies，简称CCCS）。根据中心主任理查德·霍加特（Richard Hoggart）的设想，该中心的研究将综合历史、哲学、社会学和文学的视野，以跨学科方法对文化进行研究。雷蒙·威廉斯以及E. P. 汤普森（E. P. Thompson）等理论家因认同这种研究立场，也被归于伯明翰学派。这批学者和法兰克福学派的霍克海默尔、阿多尔诺、马尔库塞等理论家一样，都深受西方马克思主义传统影响，关心文化与社会结构、意识形态以及阶级意识的关联。但法兰克福学派的文化观有精英主义色彩，对大众文化持批判态度，在现代主义先锋艺术中寻找抵抗异化的精神力量。对此，本书第七章已有详细论述，不再赘言。而伯明翰学派的学者普遍熟悉工人阶级的生活方式和思想世界，主张从大众的角度理解文化。本书第七章重点讨论的英国西方马克思主义的代表人物雷蒙·威廉斯就是文化研究的开创者之一。他提出文化是普通的，这与英国传统的精英文化观形成了对比。他以此来倡导文化研究走进社会生活的现实。在这方面，霍加特于1957年出版的《识字的用途》（*The Uses of Literacy*）是英国文化研究的奠基之作。霍加特在书中分析了二战前工人阶级的文化如何帮助工人阶级建构身份认同、家庭关系以及邻里社区的联系。与此对比，战后工人阶级虽然通过受教育，能够识文断字，但是在流行杂志等大众文化产品的影响下，丧失了自身的文化属性。汤普森也和霍加特一样关注工人阶级的文化意识。在他的经典著作《英国工人阶级的形成》（*The Making of the English Working Class*，1963）中，汤普森分析了文化如何在工人阶级的阶级意识觉醒以及争取尊严的斗争中发挥重要作用。在《共有的习惯》（*Customs in Common: Studies in Traditional Popular*

Culture，1991）一书中，他讨论了18世纪社会转型时代，平民的风俗习惯如何在与贵族的博弈中逐渐形成。从汤普森的平民文化解读中，可以看到英国早期现代性的形成进程以及工人阶级诞生的社会文化氛围。在该书第六章"时间、工作纪律和工业资本主义"中，汤普森分析了18世纪工厂时间对自然时间的替代，它如何破坏闲暇文化传统，将劳动者的生命时间纳入了资本主义的生产体系。汤普森此处的讨论是21世纪文化研究中有关时间加速、时间异化等议题的先声。

相比伯明翰学派第一代学者，以斯图尔特·霍尔（Stuart Hall）为首的第二代学者将考察重点从阶级议题扩展到族裔和性别领域。霍尔出生于牙买加，获奖学金到牛津大学留学，后定居英国。他的族裔身份令他对族裔和女性等边缘群体更为关注。他将研究视野投注在大众文化，即被精英和正统文化所排斥的底层阶级和被压迫者的文化。

从方法论看，第一代理论家重视历史实证研究，而霍尔是战后结构主义与后结构主义思想浪潮中成长起来的批评家，他将阿尔都塞的意识形态论、葛兰西的霸权论、巴特的符号学理论等结合起来，作为分析文化系统意义生成机制的有力工具。他在媒介研究领域有重要理论贡献。法兰克福学派率先对电视的大众文化媒介属性进行分析，从电视节目的同质化倾向造就"单向度的人"的角度，对其进行意识形态批判。霍尔则将意识形态批判与符号学混合，对媒介文化的表意系统进行了更细致的分析。在《编码/解码》（"Encoding/Decoding"，1980）一文中，他指出观众解读电视媒介有三种不同的方式：主动接受主流意识形态是"霸权式解读"；基本顺从主流意识形态，但是保留个人立场是"协商式解读"；面对主流意识形态讯息，反其道而行是"对抗式解读"。霍尔同意法兰克福学派的结论，即电视媒介是主流意识形态进行思想灌输的好方式，但霍尔认为个体有能动性，可以主动建构自己的版本。他的文化观更具开放性。这也体现在他的接合（articulation）理论上。接合理论反对阶级决定论和经济决定论，主张个体在发声的同时，与他人形成对话，进而通过"接合"，寻找结盟的可能性。接合理论反映了霍尔对个体与群体关系的浓厚兴趣。这也是霍尔关注英国青年亚文化运动的原因。在其主编的论文集《通过仪式抵抗》(Resistance Through Rituals: Youth Subcultures in Post-War Britain，1976）中，霍尔指出，青年亚文化的兴起是当代英国文化最独特、最引人注目的文化现象。青年人如何建构独立文化身份，如何表达集体抗争，抗争与社会权力管控之间会形成怎样的互动，这些是霍尔青年亚文化研究的思考题。

对亚文化进行深入理论化，使其成为当代文化研究的重要领域，这是霍尔的学生迪克·赫伯迪格（Dick Hebdige）的贡献。20世纪上半叶，美国芝加哥学派在社会学领域率先关注亚文化议题。他们对城市中移民等边缘团体的亚文化进行田野调查，从社会规范与行为越轨的角度，对其社会属性进行分析。伯明翰学派的青年亚文化研究，则关注青年新势力的崛起，解读亚文化符号系统的反叛意义。赫伯迪格在《亚文化》（Subculture: The Meaning of Style，1979）中，将亚文化称作为弱者发出的"噪声"。弱者反抗强权，以"噪声"——打断常规的冒犯之音——进行言说。亚文化运动重视群体身份建构。它征用既有文化符号体系，对其进行僭越和改写，以创造新风格。它以挑战常识为乐，特别擅长用穿着、饰品、姿态、口号等彰显差异，突破禁忌。朋克、无赖青年、摩登族、光头党等英国青年亚文化都有这个特点。赫伯迪格提醒，不能将亚文化简单等同于反主流文化，它与主流文化之间的关系更为复杂。亚文化不直接挑战霸权，而是通过风格隐晦地进行反抗。但它的反抗主要是在文化符号层面，所以不断被媒介手段和消费主义侵蚀和收编。亚文化群体特立独行的文化符号，如发型、衣饰等，纷纷被收录到流行文化符号库，融入资本主义生产体系，其颠覆性被吸纳。

如何抵抗资本主义社会机制的收编，在文化领域保持对意识形态渗透的反抗，这是文化研究高度关注的议题。法国学者米歇尔·德赛图（Michel de Certeau）试图从日常生活的文化实践角度寻找突破口。德赛图赞扬福柯理论的微观权力论对社会治理术进行了清晰揭秘，但是他反对福柯的弥散性的无处逃逸的权力观。福柯从微观权力角度在《规训与惩罚》一书中将现代社会描绘成监狱，德赛图却认为铁笼有缝隙。他区别了反抗的两种策略：战略（strategies）层面的反抗旨在推翻体系性的规则，这需要弱势者积攒巨大力量，才能取得胜利；战术（tactics）层面的反抗则争取在体系内部钻规则的空子，每个人都可以通过花招，为自己争取自由。在德赛图看来，战术层面的斗争有广阔的空间。在《日常生活实践》（The Practice of Everyday Life，1980）一书中，德赛图指出在栖居、散步、吃饭、阅读等看似寻常的行动中，处处存在抵抗权力规训的可能性。以阅读为例，启蒙以降，教育本应启发民智，社会权力阶层却通过教育机制和图书出版机制来钳制读者的思想，告诉他们在阅读中要听从权威人士的阐释。德赛图则指出，读者可以做文本盗猎者，进入禁猎区，在文本中寻找自己想要的内容，以游戏的态度追寻思想逃逸的自由。在德赛图看来，个人是抵抗的根据地。

法国社会学家皮埃尔·布尔迪厄（Pierre Bourdieu）也关心包括衣食住行和文化教育在内的日常生活实践，但是他没有德赛图的乐观态度。理解布尔迪厄的关键词之一是"资本"。他对这个概念进行了详细甄别，指出不能将资本简单理解为金钱。根据布尔迪厄的分类，资本可以分为由金钱和财产构成的经济资本，由社会声誉和名人头衔构成的社会资本，通过馈赠、特权和威望得以彰显的象征资本，以及体现在文化志趣和教育文凭等方面的文化资本。经济资本是所有资本的根本，但只有认识到资本的多样态以及相互的转化，才能理解资本主义社会如何全面形塑人的心智行动，影响人的主体意识、身体经验和行动力。以文化资本为例，它的身体化形态表现为精神和身体的"持久性情"，反映在趣味、教养、气质等方面。它的物质性形态包括字画、书籍、唱片等。布尔迪厄最关心的是教育体系的文化资本生产。在《教育、社会和文化的再生产》（Reproduction in Education, Society and Culture，1970）和《国家精英》（The State Nobility: Elite Schools in the Field of Power，1989）等作品中，布尔迪厄讨论了法国高等教育背后的经济资本以及社会资本向文凭和教养等文化资本的转换，指出高等教育将学业的优势解释为天赋造就，用文凭的神圣性掩盖了优势阶层的特权。在《区分》（Distinction: A Social Critique of the Judgment of Taste，1979）一书中，布尔迪厄深入到生活的日常肌理，详细分析了穿衣风格、饮食习惯、体育运动、艺术欣赏等方面的品味差异如何体现在个人的身体化和心智化的惯习（habitus）之中，成为社会分层的标识。

　　进入21世纪，关注历史和关注文化已经成为文学研究的惯用范式。这种规范的建立，离不开新历史主义和文化研究的影响。在其理论观照下，历史不再只是文学的背景板，文学不再只是历史的镜子，文化不再只是精英的特权。文学研究推开象牙塔之门，与历史互动，与文化对话，跨越不同学科，与每个人感受历史的方式、经验世界的方式、自我塑造的方式、寻求反抗的方式形成更密切的关联，也敦促人们对权力、政治、他人、社会、世界等宏大议题进行更为细致的思考。

主要文本阅读

怀特：《元历史》

选文简介

　　怀特的《元历史》的主体部分有思想史的特点，重点介绍了19世纪欧洲八位主要的史学家与历史哲学家的历史观。在《元历史》的导言部分，他阐述了自己的理论立场：不应从外部寻找原因来解释历史学家修撰风格的差异；著史者历史思维的不同，源于对历史叙事的结构原则和诗学原则的不同选择。怀特的这一主张是对此前的历史研究方法的重大挑战。他未将历史视为科学，而是明确提出人们需要正视历史修撰的叙事本质。在选文中，怀特讨论了历史叙事中编年纪事和故事这两个结构性要素的区别。编年纪事将有待选择和整理的"原始素材"按照事件发生的时间顺序进行排列；

故事则在编年史基础上，设定叙事主题基调，据此对过往事件进行筛选，添加开头、中间和结尾，将开放的可以一直续写的编年史变成了有头有尾的完整故事。在此过程中，历史学家会像文学家一样，征用浪漫、悲剧、喜剧和讽喻的情节模式。而这四种情节模式，对应着形式论、机械论、有机论和情景论四种历史解释模式，反映着无政府主义、激进主义、保守主义和自由主义的意识形态区别。

From *Metahistory*

Hayden White (1928-2018)

This book is a *history* of historical consciousness in nineteenth-century Europe, but it is also meant to contribute to the current discussion of the *problem of historical knowledge*. As such, it represents both an account of the development of historical thinking during a specific period of its evolution and a general theory of the structure of that mode of thought which is called "historical."...

My own analysis of the deep structure of the historical imagination of nineteenth-century Europe is intended to provide a new perspective on the current debate over the nature and function of historical knowledge....

My method, in short, is formalist. I will not try to decide whether a given historian's work is a better, or more correct, account of a specific set of events or segment of the historical process than some other historian's account of them; rather, I will seek to identify the structural components of those accounts....

In sum, considered purely as formal verbal structures, the histories produced by the master historians of the nineteenth century display radically different conceptions of what "the historical work" *should* consist of. In order, therefore, to identify the family characteristics of the different kinds of historical thinking produced by the nineteenth century, it is first necessary to make clear what the ideal-typical structure of the "historical work" *might* consist of. Once such an ideal-typical structure has been worked out, I will have a criterion for determining which aspects of any given historical work or philosophy of history must be considered in the effort to identify its *unique* structural elements. Then, by tracing transformations in the ways historical thinkers characterize those elements and dispose them in a specific narrative in order to gain an "explanatory affect," I should be able to chart the fundamental changes in the deep structure of the historical imagination for the period under study. This, in turn, will permit one to characterize the different historical thinkers of the period in terms of their shared status as participants in a distinctive universe of discourse within which different "styles" of historical thinking were possible.

The Theory of the Historical Work

I begin by distinguishing among the following levels of conceptualization in the historical work: (1) chronicle; (2) story; (3) mode of emplotment; (4) mode of argument; and (5) mode of ideological implication. I take "chronicle" and "story" to refer to "primitive elements" in the *historical account*, but both represent processes of selection and arrangement of data from the *unprocessed historical record* in the interest of rendering that record more comprehensible to an *audience* of a particular kind. As thus conceived, the historical work represents an attempt to mediate among what I will call the *historical field*, the unprocessed *historical record*, *other historical accounts*, and an *audience.*

First the elements in the historical field are organized into a chronicle by the arrangement of the events to be dealt with in the temporal order of their occurrence; then the chronicle is organized into a story by the further arrangement of the events into the components of a "spectacle" or process of happening, which is thought to possess a discernible beginning, middle, and end. This *transformation of chronicle into story* is effected by the characterization of some events in the chronicle in terms of inaugural motifs, of others in terms of terminating motifs, and of yet others in terms of transitional motifs. An event which is simply reported as having happened at a certain time and place is transformed into an inaugurating event by its characterization as such: "The king went to Westminster on June 3, 1321. There the fateful meeting occurred between the king and the man who was ultimately to challenge him for his throne, though at the time the two men appeared to be destined to become the best of friends...." A transitional motif, on the other hand, signals to the reader to hold his expectations about the significance of the events contained in it in abeyance until some terminating motif has been provided: "While the king was journeying to Westminster, he was informed by his advisers that his enemies awaited him there, and that the prospects of a settlement advantageous to the crown were meager." A terminating motif indicates the apparent end or resolution of a process or situation of tension: "On April 6, 1333, the Battle of Balybourne was fought. The forces of the king were victorious, the rebels routed. The resulting Treaty of Howth Castle, June 7, 1333, brought peace to the realm—though it was to be an uneasy peace, consumed in the flames of religious strife seven years later." When a given set of events has been motifically encoded, the reader has been provided with a story; the chronicle of events has been transformed into a *completed* diachronic process, about which one can then ask questions as if he were dealing with a *synchronic structure* of relationships.

Historical *stories* trace the sequences of events that lead from inaugurations to (provisional) terminations of social and cultural processes in a way that *chronicles* are not required to do. Chronicles are, strictly speaking, open-ended. In principle they have no *inaugurations*; they simply "begin" when the chronicler starts recording events. And they have no culminations or resolutions; they can go on indefinitely. Stories, however, have a discernible form (even when that form is an image of a state of chaos) which marks off the events contained in them from the other events that might appear in a comprehensive chronicle of the years covered in their unfoldings....

The arrangement of selected events of the chronicle into a story raises the kinds of questions the historian must anticipate and answer in the course of constructing his narrative. These questions are of the sort: "What happened next?" "How did that happen?" "Why did things happen this way rather than that?" "How did it all come out in the end?" These questions determine the narrative tactics the historian must use in the construction of his story. But such questions about the connections between events which make of them elements in a *followable* story should be distinguished from questions of another sort: "What does it all add up to?" "What is the point of it all?" These questions have to do with the structure of the *entire set of events* considered as a *completed* story and call for a synoptic judgment of the relationship between a given story and other stories that might be "found," "identified," or "uncovered" in the chronicle. They can be answered in a number of ways. I call these ways (1) explanation by emplotment, (2) explanation by argument, and (3) explanation by ideological implication....

The Problem of Historiographical Styles

Having distinguished among the three levels on which historians work to gain an explanatory affect in their narratives, I will now consider the problem of historiographical styles. In my view, a historiographical style represents a particular *combination* of modes of emplotment, argument, and ideological implication. But the various modes of emplotment, argument, and ideological implication cannot be indiscriminately combined in a given work. For example, a Comic emplotment is not compatible with a Mechanistic argument, just as a Radical ideology is not compatible with a Satirical emplotment. There are, as it were, elective affinities among the various modes that might be used to gain an explanatory affect on the different levels of composition. And these elective affinities are based on the structural homologies which can be discerned among the possible modes of emplotment, argument, and ideological implication. The affinities can be represented graphically as follows:

Mode of Emplotment	*Mode of Argument*	*Mode of Ideological Implication*
Romantic	Formist	Anarchist
Tragic	Mechanistic	Radical
Comic	Organicist	Conservative
Satirical	Contextualist	Liberal

These affinities are not to be taken as *necessary* combinations of the modes in a given historian. On the contrary, the dialectical tension which characterizes the work of every master historian usually arises from an effort to wed a mode of emplotment with a mode of argument or of ideological implication which is inconsonant with it. For example, as I will show, Michelet tried to combine a Romantic emplotment and a Formist argument with an ideology that is explicitly Liberal. So, too, Burckhardt used a Satirical emplotment and a Contextualist argument in the service of an ideological position that is explicitly Conservative and ultimately Reactionary. Hegel emplotted history on two levels—Tragic on the microcosmic, Comic on the macrocosmic—both of which are justified by appeal to a mode of argument that is Organicist, with the result that one can derive either Radical or Conservative ideological implications from a reading of his work.

格林布拉特：《文艺复兴时期的自我塑造》

| 选文简介

格林布拉特钟情于文艺复兴时代的研究，被早期现代性社会中的冲突性力量之间的张力所吸引。在《文艺复兴时期的自我塑造》一书中，他聚焦这一时代人的自我意识的形成，发现自我塑造往往发生在受到权威的胁迫、与陌生的他者相遇，或者自身面临身份瓦解的危机时刻。选文中，他以莎士比亚的《奥赛罗》为例，对此进行了阐释。奥赛罗和苔丝狄蒙娜的婚姻是跨种族的僭越行为，他们借此确立独特的自我，这是他们激情的基础。但苔丝狄蒙娜的激情带有情欲的力量，这在当时被视为罪恶，奥赛罗为此产生了性焦虑。他要防止自己受妻子影响而沉沦于欲望，而且担心会被妻子的激情吞噬，于是用杀妻来实现净化、捍卫自我。实际上，这部剧不仅展现了奥赛罗的主体行动如何受到意识形态的影响，而且从中也能够看到描写这种游走在禁忌边缘的情感的剧作家莎士比亚的自我塑造。莎士比亚不像同时代的马洛那样叛逆，也没有全心全意迎合主流意识形态。他的戏剧与权力之间的关系呈现出一种含混复杂的样态。

From *Renaissance Self-Fashioning*

Stephen Greenblatt (1943-)

In the Augustinian conception, as elaborated by Raymond of Peñafort, William of Rennes, and others, there are four motives for conjugal intercourse: to conceive offspring; to render the marital debt to one's partner so that he or she might avoid incontinency, to avoid fornication oneself; and to satisfy desire. The first two motives are without sin and excuse intercourse; the third is a venial sin; the fourth—to satisfy desire—is mortal. Among the many causes that underlie this institutional hostility to desire is the tenacious existence, in various forms, of the belief that pleasure constitutes a legitimate release from dogma and constraint....

It should not surprise us that churchmen, Catholic and Protestant alike, would seek to crush such dangerous notions, nor that they would extend their surveillance and discipline to married couples and warn that excessive pleasure in the marriage bed is at least a potential violation of the Seventh Commandment....

These anxieties, rich in implication for *Othello*, are frequently tempered in Protestant writings by a recognition of the joyful ardor of young married couples, but there remains a constant fear of excess, and, as Ambrose observed centuries earlier, even the most plausible excuse for sexual passion is shameful in the old: "Youths generally assert the desire for generation. How much more shameful for the old to do what is shameful for the young to confess." Othello himself seems eager to ward off this shame; he denies before the Senate that he seeks

> To please the palate of my appetite,
> Nor to comply with heat, the young affects
> In me defunct....
>
> (1.3.262–4)

But Desdemona makes no such disclaimer; indeed her declaration of passion is frankly, though by no means exclusively, sexual:

> That I did love the Moor, to live with him,
> My downright violence, and scorn of fortunes,
> May trumpet to the world: my heart's subdued
> Even to the utmost pleasure of my lord.
>
> (1.3.248–51)

This moment of erotic intensity, this frank acceptance of pleasure and submission to her spouse's pleasure, is, I would argue, as much as Iago's slander the cause of Desdemona's death, for it awakens the deep current of sexual anxiety in Othello, anxiety that with Iago's help expresses itself in quite orthodox fashion as the perception of adultery. Othello unleashes upon Cassio—"Michael Cassio,/That came a-wooing with you" (3.3.71–72)—the fear of pollution, defilement, brutish violence that is bound up with his own experience of sexual pleasure, while he must destroy Desdemona both for her excessive experience of pleasure and for awakening such sensations in himself. Like Guyon in the Bower of Bliss, Othello transforms his complicity in erotic excess and his fear of engulfment into a "purifying," saving violence:

> Like to the Pontic sea,
> Whose icy current and compulsive course
> Ne'er feels retiring ebb, but keeps due on
> To the Propontic and the Hellespont,
> Even so my bloody thoughts, with violent pace,
> Shall ne'er look back, ne'er ebb to humble love,
> Till that a capable and wide revenge
> Swallow them up.
>
> (3.3.460–7)

His insupportable sexual experience has been, as it were, displaced and absorbed by the act of revenge which can swallow up not only the guilty lovers but—as the syntax suggests—his own "bloody thoughts."

Such is the achievement of Iago's improvisation on the religious sexual doctrine in which Othello believes; true to that doctrine, pleasure itself becomes for Othello pollution, a defilement of his property in Desdemona and in himself. It is at the level of this dark, sexual revulsion that Iago has access to Othello, access assured, as we should expect, by the fact that beneath his cynical modernity and professed self-love Iago reproduces in himself the same psychic structure....

To an envious contemporary like Robert Greene, Shakespeare seems a kind of greenroom Iago, appropriating for himself the labors of others. In *Othello* Shakespeare seems to acknowledge, represent, and explore his affinity to the malicious improviser, but, of course, his relation to the theater and to his culture is far more complex than such an affinity could suggest. There are characters in his works who can improvise without tragic results, characters who can embrace a mobility of desire—one of whose emblems is the male actor playing a female character dressed up as a male—that neither Iago, nor Othello, nor Desdemona can endure. Destructive violence is not Shakespeare's only version of these materials, and even in *Othello*, Iago is not the playwright's only representation of himself. Still, at the least we must grant Robert Greene that it would have seemed fatal to be imitated by Shakespeare. He possessed a limitless talent for entering into the consciousness of another, perceiving its deepest structures as a manipulable fiction, reinscribing it into his own narrative form. If in the late plays, he experiments with controlled disruptions of narrative, moments of eddying and ecstasy, these invariably give way to reaffirmations of self-fashioning through story.

Montaigne, who shares many of Shakespeare's most radical perceptions, invents in effect a brilliant mode of *non-narrative* self-fashioning: "I cannot keep my subject still. It goes along befuddled and staggering, with a natural drunkenness. I take it in this condition, just as it is at the moment I give my attention to it." Shakespeare by contrast remains throughout his career the supreme purveyor of "empathy," the fashioner of narrative selves, the master improviser. Where Montaigne withdrew to his study, Shakespeare became the presiding genius of a popular, urban art form with the capacity to foster psychic mobility in the service of Elizabethan power; he became the principal maker of what we may see as the prototype of the mass media Professor Lerner so admires.

Finally, we may ask, is this service to power a function of the theater itself or of Shakespeare's relation to his medium? The answer, predictably, is both. The theater is widely perceived in the period as the concrete manifestation of the histrionic quality of life, and, more specifically, of power—the power of the prince who stands as an actor upon a stage before the eyes of the nation, the power of God who enacts His will in the Theater of the World. The stage justifies itself against recurrent charges of immorality by invoking this normative function: it is the expression of those rules that govern a properly ordered society and display visibly the punishment, in laughter and violence, that is meted out upon those who violate the rules. Most playwrights pay at least professional homage to these values; they honor the institutions that enable them to earn their keep and give voice to the ideology that holds together both their "mystery" and the society at large.

In Marlowe, as we have seen, we encounter a playwright at odds with this ideology. If the theater normally reflects and flatters the royal sense of itself as national performance, Marlowe struggles to expose the underlying motives of any performance of power. If the theater normally affirms God's providence, Marlowe explores the tragic needs and interests that are served by all such affirmations. If the Elizabethan stage functions as one of the public uses of spectacle to impose normative ethical patterns on the urban masses, Marlowe enacts a relentless challenge to those patterns and undermines employment of rhetoric and violence in their service.

Shakespeare approaches his culture not, like Marlowe, as rebel and blasphemer, but rather as dutiful servant, content to improvise a part of his own within its orthodoxy. And if after centuries, that improvisation has been revealed to us as embodying an almost boundless challenge to the culture's every tenet, a devastation of every source, the author of *Othello* would have understood that such a revelation scarcely matters. After all, the heart of a successful improvisation lies in concealment, not exposure; and besides, as we have seen, even a hostile improvisation reproduces the relations of power that it hopes to displace and absorb. This is not to dismiss the power of hatred or the significance of distinctions—it matters a great deal whether Othello or Iago, the Lucayans or the Spaniards prevail—only to suggest the boundaries that define the possibility of any improvisational contact, even contact characterized by hidden malice.

I would not want to argue, in any event, that Shakespeare's relation to his culture is defined by hidden malice. Such a case can no doubt be made for many of the plays—stranger things have been said—but it will sound forced and unconvincing, just as the case for Shakespeare as an unwavering, unquestioning apologist for Tudor ideology sounds forced and unconvincing. The solution here is not, I suggest, that the truth lies somewhere in between. Rather the truth itself is radically unstable and yet constantly stabilized, as unstable as those male authorities that affirm themselves only to be undermined by subversive women and then to be reconstituted in a different guise. If any reductive generalization about Shakespeare's relation to his culture seems dubious, it is because his plays offer no single timeless affirmation or denial of legitimate authority and no central, unwavering authorial presence. Shakespeare's language and themes are caught up, like the medium itself, in unsettling repetitions, committed to the shifting voices and audiences, with their shifting aesthetic assumptions and historical imperatives, that govern a living theater.

霍尔:《编码/解码》

选文简介

本文的底本是1973年霍尔题名为《电视话语中的编码与解码》("Encoding and Decoding in the Television Discourse")的演讲。1980年他对讲稿进行了删改,以《编码/解码》为题发表。修改稿淡化了具体文本分析,强化了概念的普适性,成为大众传播话语理论的经典之作。在文中,霍尔批评此前的大众传播模式论,认为它将传播过程简化为"发送者—信息—接收者",无法概括传播在现实社会中的复杂维度。为此,霍尔提出传播过程论,认为它由生产、流通、分配/消费、再生产等相互关联的实践组成。霍尔指出,电视话语意义的生产与流通先要经历三个阶段:制作者对原材料进行"编码";意义镶嵌进节目文本形成"成品";观众收看节目,进行意义再生产的"解码"。选文主要讨论了观众解码的三种模式。在霸权式解读中,观众受编码者控制,全盘接受文本的意识形态信息。在协商式解读中,观众基本认可编码者的意义输入,但在具体情境层面持有保留观点。在对抗式解读中,观众明了编码者的意涵,但是决定采用对立准则,进行相反的解读。霍尔的理论显示出他非常重视受众的政治能动性。

From "Encoding/Decoding"

Stuart Hall (1932-2014)

Traditionally, mass-communications research has conceptualized the process of communication in terms of a circulation circuit or loop. This model has been criticized for its linearity—sender/message/receiver—for its concentration on the level of message exchange and for the absence of a structured conception of the different moments as a complex structure of relations. But it is also possible (and useful) to think of this process in terms of a structure produced and sustained through the articulation of linked but distinctive moments—production, circulation, distribution/consumption, reproduction. This would be to think of the process as a "complex structure in dominance," sustained through the articulation of connected practices, each of which, however, retains its distinctiveness and has its own specific modality, its own forms and conditions of existence. This second approach, homologous to that which forms the skeleton of commodity production offered in Marx's *Grundrisse* and in *Capital*, has the added advantage of bringing out more sharply how a continuous circuit—production-distribution-production—can be sustained through a "passage of forms." It also highlights the specificity of the forms in which the product of the process "appears" in each moment, and thus what distinguishes discursive "production" from other types of production in our society and in modern media systems.

The "object" of these practices is

meanings and messages in the form of sign-vehicles of a specific kind organized, like any form of communication or language, through the operation of codes within the syntagmatic chain of a discourse. The apparatuses, relations and practices of production thus issue, at a certain moment (the moment of "production/circulation") in the form of symbolic vehicles constituted within the rules of "language." It is in this discursive form that the circulation of the "product" takes place. The process thus requires, at the production end, its material instruments—its "means"—as well as its own sets of social (production) relations—the organization and combination of practices within media apparatuses. But it is in the *discursive* form that the circulation of the product takes place, as well as its distribution to different audiences. Once accomplished, the discourse must then be translated—transformed, again—into social practices if the circuit is to be both completed and effective. If no "meaning" is taken, there can be no "consumption." If the meaning is not articulated in practice, it has no effect. The value of this approach is that while each of the moments, in articulation, is necessary to the circuit as a whole, no one moment can fully guarantee the next moment with which it is articulated. Since each has its specific modality and conditions of existence, each can constitute its own break or interruption of the "passage of forms" on whose continuity the flow of effective production (that is, "reproduction") depends.

Thus while in no way wanting to limit research to "following only those leads which emerge from content analysis," we must recognize that the discursive form of the message has a privileged position in the communicative exchange (from the viewpoint of circulation), and that the moments of "encoding" and "decoding," though only "relatively autonomous" in relation to the communicative process as a whole, are *determinate* moments. A "raw" historical event cannot, *in that form*, be transmitted by, say, a television newscast. Events can only be signified within the aural-visual forms of the televisual discourse. In the moment when a historical event passes under the sign of discourse, it is subject to all the complex formal "rules" by which language signifies. To put it paradoxically, the event must become a "story" before it can become a *communicative event*. In that moment the formal sub-rules of discourse are "in dominance," without, of course, subordinating out of existence the historical event so signified, the social relations in which the rules are set to work or the social and political consequences of the event having been signified in this way. The "message form" is the necessary "form of appearance" of the event in its passage from source to receiver. Thus the transposition into and out of the "message form" (or the mode of symbolic exchange) is not a random "moment," which we can take up or ignore at our convenience. The "message form" is a determinate moment; though, at another level, it comprises the surface movements of the communications system only and requires, at another stage, to be integrated into the social relations of the communication process as a whole, of which it forms only a part....

We identify *three* hypothetical positions from which decodings of a televisual discourse may be constructed. These need to be empirically tested and refined. But the argument that decodings do not follow inevitably from encodings, that they are not identical, reinforces the argument of "no necessary correspondence." It also helps to deconstruct the common-sense meaning of "misunderstanding" in terms of a theory of "systematically distorted communication."

The first hypothetical position is that of the *dominant-hegemonic position*. When the viewer takes the connoted meaning from, say, a television newscast or current affairs program full and straight, and decodes the message in terms of the reference code in which it has been encoded, we might say that the viewer *is operating inside the dominant code*. This is the ideal-typical case of "perfectly transparent communication"—or as close as we are likely to come to it "for all practical purposes." Within this we can distinguish the positions produced by the *professional code*. This is the position (produced by what we perhaps ought to identify as the operation of a "metacode") which the professional broadcasters assume when encoding a message which has *already* been signified in a hegemonic manner. The professional code is "relatively independent" of the dominant code, in that it applies criteria and transformational operations of its own, especially those of a technico-practical nature. The professional code, however, operates *within* the "hegemony" of the dominant code. Indeed, it serves to reproduce the dominant definitions precisely by bracketing their hegemonic quality and operating instead with displaced professional codings which foreground such apparently neutral-technical questions as visual quality, news and presentational values, televisual quality, "professionalism" and so on. The hegemonic interpretations of, say, the politics of Northern Ireland, or the Chilean *coup* or the Industrial Relations Bill are principally generated by political and military elites: the particular choice of presentational occasions and formats, the selection of personnel, the choice of images, the staging of debates are selected and combined through the operation of the professional code. How the broadcasting professionals are able *both* to operate with "relatively autonomous" codes of their own *and* to act in such a way as to reproduce (not without contradiction) the hegemonic signification of events is a complex matter which cannot be further spelled out here. It must suffice to say that the professionals are linked with the defining elites not only by the institutional position of broadcasting itself as an "ideological apparatus," but also by the structure of *access* (that is, the systematic "over-accessing" of selective elite personnel and their "definition of the situation" in television). It may even be said that the professional codes serve to reproduce hegemonic definitions specifically by *not overtly* biasing their operations in a dominant direction: ideological reproduction therefore takes place here inadvertently, unconsciously, "behind men's backs." Of course, conflicts, contradictions and even misunderstandings regularly arise between the dominant and the professional significations and their signifying agencies.

The second position we would identify is that of the *negotiated code* or position. Majority audiences probably understand quite adequately what has been dominantly defined and professionally signified. The dominant definitions, however, are hegemonic precisely because they represent definitions of situations and events which are "in dominance" (*global*). Dominant definitions connect events, implicitly or explicitly, to grand totalizations, to the great syntagmatic views-of-the-world: they take "large views" of issues: they relate events to the "national interest" or to the level of geo-politics, even if they make these connections in truncated, inverted or mystified ways. The definition of a hegemonic viewpoint is (1) that it defines within its terms the mental horizon, the universe, of possible meanings, of a whole sector of relations in a society or culture; and (2) that it carries with it the stamp of legitimacy—it appears coterminous with what is "natural," "inevitable," "taken for granted" about the social order. Decoding within the *negotiated version* contains a mixture of adaptive and oppositional elements: it acknowledges the legitimacy of the hegemonic definitions to make the grand significations (abstract), while, at a more restricted, situational (situated) level, it makes its own ground rules—it operates with exceptions to the rule. It accords the privileged position to the dominant definitions of events while reserving the right to make a more negotiated application to "local conditions," to its own more *corporate* positions. This negotiated version of the dominant ideology is thus shot through with contradictions, though these are only on certain occasions brought to full visibility. Negotiated codes operate through what we might call particular or situated logics: and these logics are sustained by their differential and unequal relation to the discourses and logics of power. The simplest example of a negotiated code is that which governs the response of a worker to the notion of an Industrial Relations Bill limiting the right to strike or to arguments for a wages freeze. At the level of the "national interest" economic debate the decoder may adopt the hegemonic definition, agreeing that "we must all pay ourselves less in order to combat inflation." This, however, may have little or no relation to his/her willingness to go on strike for better pay and conditions or to oppose the Industrial Relations Bill at the level of shop-floor or union organization. We suspect that the great majority of so-called "misunderstandings" arise from the contradictions and disjunctures between hegemonic-dominant encodings and negotiated-corporate decodings. It is just these mismatches in the levels which most provoke defining elites and professionals to identify a "failure in communications."

Finally, it is possible for a viewer perfectly to understand both the literal and the connotative inflection given by a discourse but to decode the message in a *globally* contrary way. He/she detotalizes the message in the preferred code in order to retotalize the message within some alternative framework of reference. This is the case of the viewer who listens to a debate on the need to limit wages but "reads" every mention of the "national interest" as "class interest." He/she is operating with what we must call an *oppositional code*. One of the most significant political moments (they also coincide with crisis points within the broadcasting organizations themselves, for obvious reasons) is the point when events which are normally signified and decoded in a negotiated way begin to be given an oppositional reading. Here the "politics of signification"—the struggle in discourse—is joined.

赫伯迪格：《亚文化》

选文简介

赫伯迪格注意到英国亚文化群体的标识度主要来自其醒目的风格特征。这种风格的形成，源于对规范性的表征体系的破坏——打乱服装编码，僭越行为准则，破坏语言规范，突出差异性，以表达底层边缘群体对文化霸权的反抗。青年人的激进姿态和标新立异的形象引发媒体关注，越轨的行为令警察紧张，反社会的立场引发道德恐慌。但赫伯迪格敏锐地指出，以上对正常秩序的突破只是暂时的，越轨行动能够产生一时的轰动效果，但是很难逃出意识形态形式和商品形式双管齐下的招安。媒介在记录亚文化风格时,既描绘它的标新立异,也擅长将亚文化的服饰、音乐等文化符号化为流行元素;市场经济体系敏锐从中看到商业价值,将其商品化,使其失去原有语境和含义;亚文化群体中还会有少数代表人物成为明星,营造出开放社会的假象。从赫伯迪格的讨论可以看出,青年亚文化的奇峰突起,体现了社会矛盾导致的文化领域的斗争。而亚文化群体的逐渐弱化和流散,反映了社会机制合力对亚文化进行"柔性"收编的强大力量。

From *Subculture*

Dick Hebdige (1951-)

Subcultural: The Unnatural Break

Subcultures represent "noise" (as opposed to sound): interference in the orderly sequence which leads from real events and phenomena to their representation in the media. We should therefore not underestimate the signifying power of the spectacular subculture not only as a metaphor for potential anarchy "out there" but as an actual mechanism of semantic disorder: a kind of temporary blockage in the system of representation. As John Mepham has written:

> Distinctions and identities may be so deeply embedded in our discourse and thought about the world whether this be because of their role in our practical lives, or because they are cognitively powerful and are an important aspect of the way in which we appear to make sense of our experience, that the theoretical challenge to them can be quite startling.

Any elision, truncation or convergence of prevailing linguistic and ideological categories can have profoundly disorienting effects. These deviations briefly expose the arbitrary nature of the codes which underlie and shape all forms of discourse....

Predictably then, violations of the authorized codes through which the social world is organized and experienced have considerable power to provoke and disturb. They are generally condemned, in Mary Douglas' words, as "contrary to holiness" and Levi-Strauss has noted how, in certain primitive myths, the mispronunciation of words and the misuse of language are classified along with incest as horrendous aberrations capable of "unleashing storm and tempest." Similarly, spectacular subcultures express forbidden contents (consciousness of class, consciousness of difference) in forbidden forms (transgressions of sartorial and behavioral codes, law breaking, etc.). They are profane articulations, and they are often and significantly defined as "unnatural."...

Two Forms of Incorporation

We have seen how subcultures "breach our expectancies," how they represent symbolic challenges to a symbolic order. But can subcultures always be effectively incorporated and if so, how? The emergence of a spectacular subculture is invariably accompanied by a wave of hysteria in the press. This hysteria is typically ambivalent: it fluctuates between dread and fascination, outrage and amusement. Shock and horror headlines dominate the front page while, inside, the editorials positively bristle with "serious" commentary and the centerspreads or supplements contain delirious accounts of the latest fads and rituals. Style in particular provokes a double response: it is alternately celebrated (in the fashion page) and ridiculed or reviled (in those articles which define subcultures as social problems).

In most cases, it is the subculture's stylistic innovations which first attract the media's attention. Subsequently deviant or "anti-social" acts—vandalism, swearing, fighting, "animal behavior"—are "discovered" by the police, the judiciary, the press; and these acts are used to "explain" the subculture's original transgression of sartorial codes. In fact, either deviant behavior or the identification of a distinctive uniform (or more typically a combination of the two) can provide the catalyst for a moral panic....

As the subculture begins to strike its own eminently marketable pose, as its vocabulary (both visual and verbal) becomes more and more familiar, so the referential context to which it can be most conveniently assigned is made increasingly apparent. Eventually, the mods, the punks, the glitter rockers can be incorporated, brought back into line, located on the preferred "map of problematic social reality" at the point where boys in lipstick are "just kids dressing up," where girls in rubber dresses are "daughters just like yours." The media, as Stuart Hall has argued, not only record resistance, they "situate it within the dominant framework of meanings" and those young people who choose to inhabit a spectacular youth culture are simultaneously *returned*, as they are represented on T.V. and in the newspapers, to the place where common sense would have them fit (as "animals" certainly, but also "in the family," "out of work," "up to date," etc.). It is through this continual process of recuperation that the fractured order is repaired and the subculture incorporated as a diverting spectacle within the dominant mythology from which it in part emanates: as "folk devil," as Other, as Enemy. The process of recuperation takes two characteristic forms:

> (1) the conversion of subcultural signs (dress, music, etc.) into mass-produced objects (i.e. the commodity form);
> (2) the "labeling" and re-definition of deviant behavior by dominant groups—the police, the media, the judiciary (i.e. the ideological form).

The Commodity Form

The first has been comprehensively handled by both journalists and academics. The relationship between the spectacular subculture and the various industries which service and exploit it is notoriously ambiguous. After all, such a subculture is concerned first and foremost with consumption. It operates exclusively in the leisure sphere ("I wouldn't wear my punk outfit for work—there's a time and a place for everything"). It communicates through commodities even if the meanings attached to those commodities are purposefully distorted or overthrown. It is therefore difficult in this case to maintain any absolute distinction between commercial exploitation on the one hand and creativity/originality on the other, even though these categories are emphatically opposed in the value systems of most subcultures. Indeed, the creation and diffusion of new styles is inextricably bound up with the process of production, publicity and packaging which must inevitably lead to the defusion of the subculture's subversive power—both mod and punk innovations fed back directly into high fashion and mainstream fashion. Each new subculture establishes new trends, generates new looks and sounds which feed back into the appropriate industries. As John Clarke has observed:

The diffusion of youth styles from the subcultures to the fashion market is not simply a "cultural process," but a real network or infrastructure of new kinds of commercial and economic institutions. The small-scale record shops, recording companies, the boutiques and one- or two-woman manufacturing companies—these versions of artisan capitalism, rather than more generalized and unspecific phenomena, situate the dialectic of commercial "manipulation."

However, it would be mistaken to insist on the absolute autonomy of "cultural" and commercial processes. As Lefebvre puts it: "Trade is...both a social and an intellectual phenomenon," and commodities arrive at the marketplace already laden with significance. They are, in Marx's words, "social hieroglyphs" and their meanings are inflected by conventional usage.

Thus, as soon as the original innovations which signify "subculture" are translated into commodities and made generally available, they become "frozen." Once removed from their private contexts by the small entrepreneurs and big fashion interests who produce them on a mass scale, they become codified, made comprehensible, rendered at once public property and profitable merchandise. In this way, the two forms of incorporation (the semantic/ideological and the "real"/commercial) can be said to converge on the commodity form. Youth cultural styles may begin by issuing symbolic challenges, but they must inevitably end by establishing new sets of conventions; by creating new commodities, new industries or rejuvenating old ones (think of the boost punk must have given haberdashery!)...

The Ideological Form

The second form of incorporation—the ideological—has been most adequately treated by those sociologists who operate a transactional model of deviant behavior.... As the use of the term "folk devil" suggests, rather too much weight tends to be given to the sensational excesses of the tabloid press at the expense of the ambiguous reactions which are, after all, more typical. As we have seen, the way in which subcultures are represented in the media makes them both more *and less* exotic than they actually are. They are seen to contain both dangerous aliens and boisterous kids, wild animals and wayward pets. Roland Barthes furnishes a key to this paradox in his description of "identification"—one of the seven rhetorical figures which, according to Barthes, distinguish the metalanguage of bourgeois mythology. He characterizes the petit-bourgeois as a person "...unable to imagine the Other...the Other is a scandal which threatens his existence."

Two basic strategies have been evolved for dealing with this threat. First, the Other can be trivialized, naturalized, domesticated. Here, the difference is simply denied ("Otherness is reduced to sameness"). Alternatively, the Other can be transformed into meaningless exotica, a "pure object, a spectacle, a clown." In this case, the difference is consigned to a place beyond analysis. Spectacular subcultures are continually being defined in precisely these terms....

None the less, on other occasions, the opposite line was taken. For whatever reason, the inevitable glut of articles gleefully denouncing the latest punk outrage was counterbalanced by an equal number of items devoted to the small details of punk family life....Throughout the summer of 1977, the *People* and the *News of the World* ran items on punk babies, punk brothers, and punk-ted weddings. All these articles served to minimize the Otherness so stridently proclaimed in punk style, and defined the subculture in precisely those terms which it sought most vehemently to resist and deny.

Once again, we should avoid making any absolute distinction between the ideological and commercial "manipulations" of subculture. The symbolic restoration of daughters to the family, of deviants to the fold, was undertaken at a time when the widespread "capitulation" of punk musicians to market forces was being used throughout the media to illustrate the fact that punks were "only human after all." The music papers were filled with the familiar success stories describing the route from rags to rags and riches—of punk musicians flying to America, of bank clerks becoming magazine editors or record producers, of harassed seamstresses turned overnight into successful business women. Of course, these success stories had ambiguous implications. As with every other "youth revolution" (e.g. the beat boom, the mod explosion and the Swinging Sixties) the relative success of a few individuals created an impression of energy, expansion and limitless upward mobility. This ultimately reinforced the image of the open society which the very presence of the punk subculture—with its rhetorical emphasis on unemployment, high-rise living and narrow options—had originally contradicted. As Barthes has written: "myth can always, as a last resort, signify the resistance which is brought to bear against it" and it does so typically by imposing its own ideological terms, by substituting in this case "the fairy tale of the artist's creativity" for an art form "within the compass of every consciousness," a "music" to be judged, dismissed or marketed for "noise"—a logically consistent, self-constituted chaos.

思考题

1. 怀特认为历史修撰中的编年史层面和故事层面各有什么特点？彼此是什么关系？
2. 怀特认为史学风格的情节模式可以分为哪四种？分别对应什么样的历史解释模式和意识形态意涵？
3. 根据格林布拉特的阐释，奥赛罗杀死苔丝狄蒙娜的深层动机是什么？莎士比亚的戏剧创作反映了他与他所身处的时代的合法权威之间是什么关系？
4. 霍尔认为观众对电视节目的编码信息进行解码时存在三种不同模式。它们分别是什么？
5. 赫伯迪格认为亚文化的风格是如何形成的？社会主流意识形态是如何对它进行收编的？

讨论题

1. 阅读怀特和格林布拉特的选文，在课外查阅相关材料的基础上，讨论传统历史主义和新历史主义在文学研究方法方面的相同之处和不同之处。
2. 请从垮掉派诗歌与嬉皮文化、赛博朋克小说与朋克文化、美国黑人文学与爵士乐传统等议题中选择其一，对文学作品中的亚文化因素及其含义进行分析。

补充文本选摘与评述

蒙特罗斯:《新历史主义》
From "New Historicisms"

Louis Montrose (1946?-   )

There has been no coalescence of the various identifiably new-historicist practices into a systematic and authoritative interpretive paradigm, nor does the emergence of such a paradigm seem either likely or desirable. Instead, what we have been witnessing is the convergence of various special interests on an unstable signifier: *new historicism* has been constituted as a terminological site of intense debate, of multiple appropriations and contestations, not only within Renaissance studies but in other areas of literary criticism, in history and anthropology, and within the cross-disciplinary space of cultural studies....

Inhabiting the discursive spaces currently traversed by the term *new historicism* are some of the most complex, persistent, and unsettling problems that professors of literature attempt to confront or to evade—among them the conflict between essentialist and historically specific perspectives on the category of literature and its relations with other discourses; the possible relations between cultural practices and social, political, and economic institutions and processes; the consequences of poststructuralist theories of textuality for historical or materialist criticism; the means by which ideologies are produced, sustained, and contested; the operations that construct, maintain, destabilize, and alter subjectivity through the shifting conjunctures of multiple subject positions. My point is not that "the new historicism" as a definable project, or the work of individuals identified by themselves or by others as new historicists, can provide even provisional answers to each of these questions but rather that "the new historicism" is currently being invoked in order to bring such problems into play, and to stake out, or to hunt down, specific positions on the ideological terrain mapped by them.

德赛图:《日常生活实践》
From *The Practice of Everyday Life*

Michel de Certeau (1925-1986)

The Concept-city is decaying. Does that mean that the illness afflicting both the rationality that founded it and its professionals afflicts the urban populations as well? Perhaps cities are deteriorating along with the procedures that organized them. But we must be careful here. The ministers of knowledge have always assumed that the whole universe was threatened by the very changes that affected their ideologies and their positions. They transmute the misfortune of their theories into theories of misfortune. When they transform their bewilderment into "catastrophes," when they seek to enclose the people in the "panic" of their discourses, are they once more necessarily right?

Rather than remaining within the field of a discourse that upholds its privilege by inverting its content (speaking of catastrophe and no longer of progress), one can try another path: one can analyze the microbe-like, singular and plural practices which an urbanistic system was supposed to administer or suppress, but which have outlived its decay; one can follow the swarming activity of these procedures that, far from being regulated or eliminated by panoptic administration, have reinforced themselves in a proliferating illegitimacy, developed and insinuated themselves into the networks of surveillance, and combined in accord with unreadable but stable tactics to the point of constituting everyday regulations and surreptitious creativities that are merely concealed by the frantic mechanisms and discourses of the observational organization.

This pathway could be inscribed as a consequence, but also as the reciprocal, of Foucault's analysis of the structures of power. He moved it in the direction of mechanisms and technical procedures, "minor instrumentalities" capable, merely by their organization of "details," of transforming a human multiplicity into a "disciplinary" society and of managing, differentiating, classifying, and hierarchizing all deviances concerning apprenticeship, health, justice, the army or work. "These often miniscule ruses of discipline," these "minor but flawless" mechanisms, draw their efficacy from a relationship between procedures and the space that they redistribute in order to make an "operator" out of it. But what *spatial practices* correspond, in the area where discipline is manipulated, to these apparatuses that produce a disciplinary space? In the present conjuncture, which is marked by a contradiction between the collective mode of administration and an individual mode of reappropriation, this question is no less important, if one admits that spatial practices in fact secretly structure the determining conditions of social life. I would like to follow out a few of these multiform, resistant, tricky and stubborn procedures that elude discipline without being outside the field in which it is exercised, and which should lead us to a theory of everyday practices, of lived space, of the disquieting familiarity of the city.

布尔迪厄:《区分》
From *Distinction*

Pierre Bourdieu (1930-2002)

Although art obviously offers the greatest scope to the aesthetic disposition, there is no area of practice in which the aim of purifying, refining and sublimating primary needs and impulses cannot assert itself, no area in which the stylization of life, that is, the primacy of forms over function, of manner over matter, does not produce the same effects. And nothing is more distinctive, more distinguished, than the capacity to confer aesthetic status on objects that are banal or even "common" (because the "common" people make them their own, especially for aesthetic purposes), or the ability to apply the principles of a "pure" aesthetic to the most everyday choices of everyday life, e.g. in cooking, clothing or decoration, completely reversing the popular disposition which annexes aesthetics to ethics.

In fact, through the economic and social conditions which they presuppose, the different ways of relating to realities and fictions, of believing in fictions and the realities they simulate, with more or less distance and detachment, are very closely linked to the different possible positions in social space and, consequently, bound up with the systems of dispositions (habitus) characteristic of the different classes and class fractions. Taste classifies, and it classifies the classifier. Social subjects, classified by their classifications, distinguish themselves by the distinctions they make, between the beautiful and the ugly, the distinguished and the vulgar, in which their position in the objective classifications is expressed or betrayed. And statistical analysis does indeed show that oppositions similar in structure to those found in cultural practices also appear in eating habits. The antithesis between quantity and quality, substance and form, corresponds to the opposition—linked to different distances from necessity—between the taste of necessity, which favors the most "filling" and most economical foods, and the taste of liberty—or luxury—which shifts the emphasis to the manner (of presenting, serving, eating, etc.) and tends to use stylized forms to deny function.

The science of taste and of cultural consumption begins with a transgression that is in no way aesthetic: it has to abolish the sacred frontier which makes legitimate culture a separate universe, in order to discover the intelligible relations which unite apparently incommensurable "choices," such as preferences in music and food, painting and sport, literature and hairstyle. This barbarous reintegration of aesthetic consumption into the world of ordinary consumption abolishes the opposition, which has been the basis of high aesthetic since Kant, between the "taste of sense" and the "taste of reflection," and between facile pleasure, pleasure reduced to a pleasure of the senses, and pure pleasure, pleasure purified of pleasure, which is predisposed to become a symbol of moral excellence and a measure of the capacity for sublimation which defines the truly human man. The culture which results from this magical division is sacred. Cultural consecration does indeed confer on the objects, persons and situations it touches, a sort of ontological promotion akin to a transubstantiation.

选文评述

蒙特罗斯在《新历史主义》中对新历史主义的生成语境、理论来源、核心关注等进行了讨论。目前的选文较短，蒙特罗斯在选文中重点谈了两点。一是新历史主义具跨学科性。其研究方法不仅被运用在文艺复兴研究中，进而推广到文学研究的其他方向，也被运用在历史学、人类学和文化研究等领域。二是新历史主义的共性来自批评家们共同的问题意识。新历史主义没有统一的纲领，但关注的议题有共性：思考何为文学的本质，思考文学和其他话语之间的关系；关注文化实践，考察它和社会政治经济机制及其变化发展的联动关系；引入后结构主义的文本观，思考其对历史批评和唯物主义批评的影响；考察意识形态的运行手法；关注主体性的生成机制，等等。重视批评实践，拒绝建构系统和权威的阐释范式，强调跨学科性，这是蒙特罗斯在选文中强调的新历史主义的特色。

德赛图撰写《日常生活实践》，既关注日常生活这一人类生存的重要维度，也在其中寻找抵抗社会规训的路径。他反对过度强调霸权威胁，认为这会引发恐慌，摧毁人们抵抗的信心。他也明了全面推翻既有秩序的条件还不成熟。为此，他提倡调动个体能动性：即便是在福柯式的规训社会，医院、监狱、工厂是受监控的区域，但城市空间依然有小路和岔路，供人们尝试迂回的自由行走。德赛图有关城市空间生活实践和抵抗经验的讨论，是城市文化研究领域的重要资源。

布尔迪厄在《区分》中关心品味如何为商品消费和阶级分层提供加持。自康德以降，人们普遍认为需要判断力的审美品味要比满足感官需要的品味高雅，欣赏艺术的人比关心衣食住行的人高尚。布尔迪厄却指出，当今时代，是时候剥掉纯粹审美的光晕，看审美如何为日常消费增加文化附加值了。欣赏音乐、绘画和文学，与享受美食、参加体育运动和做发型，都可以用来体现品味，彰显资本实力。布尔迪厄注意到，满足基础需要的消费被与低品味挂钩，而奢侈的自由的仪式性的消费被视为高品味。这种对品味进行高低分档的等级体系，对人们的爱好与惯习进行评估，区分和标示出社会的不同层级。

关键术语释例

1. **厚描（thick description）**："厚描"的概念由英国哲学家吉尔伯特·赖尔（Gilbert Ryle）提出。他认为"浅描"只描述行为，"厚描"则通过对行为的具体语境的描绘，获得对其意义的准确把握。比如，不同情况下，同一个眨眼的动作，含义可能大不相同。后来，克利福德·格尔茨将赖尔的"厚描"概念引入人类学，指出民族志书写不能满足于对现象和行为进行客观记录，而要深入当地文化生活之中，对其进行细致描绘。在文学理论领域，新历史主义对"厚描"法的运用主要体现在对细节的捕捉、对材料的扎实掌握和对文本的深入阐释，其目的是通过厚描，描绘出特定时代的社会文化网络的复杂纹理。

2. 接合理论（theory of articulation）：接合理论由后马克思主义思想家埃内斯托·拉克劳（Ernesto Laclau）提出。他注意到特定社会阶级成员可能会认同跨阶级的意识形态，他将这种在特定条件下形成的不同层面的连接命名为"接合"。拉克劳用接合理论说明话语内部充满了协商和意义的重构，霸权的形成是多种社会要求相接合的结果。斯图尔特·霍尔将接合的概念引入文化研究，指出文本的意义不是固定的、本质的，不可能都由编码者的意图所控制。英文中的articulation具有复义性：它既指"发声""表述""阐发"，也指"咬合"和"连接"。文本意义的"发声"是多种因素"接合"的结果，显示出意义的多样性与语境化的特征。霍尔认为在文化批评中，接合理论能够体现文化、社会和政治因素在意义生成中的复杂互动，而且接合理论能让我们看到不同群体的差异化的诉求如何透过"接合"形成集体的能动性。

推荐书目

During, Simon. *Cultural Studies: A Critical Introduction*. London: Routledge, 2005.
Elliott, Anthony. *Routledge Handbook of Social and Cultural Theory*. London: Routledge, 2020.
Gallagher, Catherine, and Stephen Greenblatt. *Practicing New Historicism*. Chicago: University of Chicago Press, 2000
Hamilton, Paul. *Historicism*. London: Routledge, 2003.
Parvini, Neema. *Shakespeare and New Historicist Theory*. London: Bloomsbury Arden Shakespeare, 2017.
Smith, Paul. *The Renewal of Cultural Studies*. Philadelphia: Temple University Press, 2011.
Storey, John. *What Is Cultural Studies?: A Reader*. New York: Arnold, 1996.
Veeser, H. Aram. *The New Historicism Reader*. New York: Routledge, 1994.
张进：《新历史主义与历史诗学》。北京：中国社会科学出版社，2004年。
周宪：《文化表征与文化研究（修订本）》。上海：上海人民出版社，2015年。

第十四章
生态批评与后人类主义

概述

在当代西方文论领域，生态批评姗姗来迟。1962年，蕾切尔·卡森（Rachel Carson）的《寂静的春天》（*Silent Spring*）唤起西方社会对环境污染议题的关注。在学术领域，社会学、政治学、人类学、环境科学等学科均开始关注环境议题。在社会层面，自20世纪70年代开始，环保团体成为社会运动的重要力量。但在文学研究领域，生态批评直到80年代末才萌芽。20世纪60年代到70年代，文学研究的主要范式是结构主义和解构主义等，属于文学本体论研究。70年代后期，文学理论对社会现实的关注日益加深，女性主义、后殖民主义和文化批评等流派纷纷强势崛起。相比而言，生态批评的发展是滞后的，晚于这些流派十年时间。这种滞后展现出生态议题在文学研究中被忽略的程度之深，也恰恰说明对其进行关注是何其必要。

生态批评将人类社会面临的生态危机视为人类生活方式、社会组织方式、价值取向和自然观共同作用的结果。它将人类置于生态体系中进行综合考量，关心文学如何描写人类及其栖息的地球以及如何刻画人类与动植物和自然环境之间的关系，主张用文学艺术引领思想改造、重塑人类精神世界、促进生态伦理观的建构。生态批评流派众多，理论出发点各不相同，但是共识性地重视生态议题，持有反人类中心主义的立场——从生态学角度看，人类只是生态链的一环，而非生物链的主宰者。

生态批评的第一次浪潮始于20世纪80年代末90年代初。1991年，乔纳森·贝特（Jonathan Bate）出版了《浪漫主义生态学》（*Romantic Ecology: Wordsworth and the Environmental Tradition*），这是英国生态批评的奠基之作。贝特在书中讨论了华兹华斯对英国自然想象的贡献，指出华兹华斯关注人与自然的深度连接，奠定了浪漫主义的生态主义基调，敦促人们与自然同行，提醒我们要认识到人类的物质世界和心灵世界都离不开绿色的大地。在美国学界，劳伦斯·布伊尔（Lawrence Buell）的《环境想象》（*The Environmental Imagination: Thoreau, Nature Writing, and the Formation of American Culture*，1995）是里程碑式著作。在书中，布伊尔深入阐释梭罗的自然书写的内涵，分析梭罗的自然观如何影响其后的自然文学作家们，如何参与塑造美国人热爱荒野的文化品格。

这一时期的生态批评，在溯源自然文学传统中，重视"大地伦理"（land ethic）的意义。大地伦理呼吁用爱和尊重建立集多样性于一身的"大地共同体"，最早由生态批评先驱者奥尔多·利奥波德（Aldo Leopold）所提出。在代表作《沙乡年鉴》（*A Sand County Almanac: And Sketches Here and There*，1949）中，利奥波德批评人们忘记了大地是人类和其他所有物种的家园，认为伦理不应只关心人与人之间的关系准则，还需要关心生物群落及其栖息地的整体利益，培育生态良心。美国诗人加里·斯奈德（Gary Snyder）指出，现代人的危机来源于家园感的丧失。他呼吁以扎根的方式，在脚下的土地上建立起家园。

这一时期生态批评的另一个理论关键词是"深层生态学"（deep ecology）。这个概念的提出者是挪威哲学家阿恩·内斯（Arne Naess）。内斯认为科学技术的发展解决不了环境问题，称其解决方案为"打补丁"式的"浅层生态学"（shallow ecology）。他主张的深层生态学要求人类以生态为中心，承认所有物种均有内在价值，认识到地球资源的有限性，重视绿色再循环。深层生态学对西方现行的科学和政治体制深表怀疑，不认可环保改良，主张减少科技介入、缩减物质欲望、回归简单生活。

深层生态学的生态中心主义主张与被誉为环境伦理之父的美国哲学家霍姆斯·罗尔斯顿（Holmes Rolston）的立场有所共鸣。罗尔斯顿在《环境伦理学》（*Environmental Ethics: Duties to and Values in the Natural World*，1988）中提出，旧的伦理学仅强调人类的福祉，而新伦理学必须关注构成地球进化进程的几百万物种的生命利益。此外，他推崇荒野美学，珍视自然之于人类文明的意义，认为荒野既是使物种多样性得以保存的空间，也是滋养人类自由与个性的所在。

综上所述，第一次生态批评浪潮的核心词是"自然"与"生态"。然而，随着生态批评的发展，反思的声音越来越多，深层生态学尤其是争议焦点。深层生态学有激进立场，主张物种平等，要求以自然为中心组织社会。问题在于，人类社会自身还被贫困、战争、不平等等问题深深困扰，深层生态学存在乌托邦主义的倾向，现实可行性存疑。此外，第一次浪潮所说的"自然"，往往指的是人类文明之外的"本真"自然，属于前现代性的生态结构，对自然的内涵有所窄化，与城市化和高科技化的当下世界脱节。"什么是自然？""如何从生态角度理解人类的当代经验？""何为人类伦理责任的边界?"对这些问题的讨论催生出生态批评的第二次浪潮。

生态批评的第二次浪潮始于20世纪90年代后期,其关键词是"环境"与"正义"。批评家们认识到"自然"的概念是一套建构在自然与人、自然与文明、自然与文化、自然与社会等二元对立之上的话语体系。为了走出这种话语体系,布伊尔等理论家在《环境批评的未来》(*The Future of Environmental Criticism: Environmental Crisis and Literary Imagination*,2005)等作品中,主张将生态关注的重心落在"环境"这个关键词。"环境"概念弹性大,内涵丰富,既可以包括"自然"概念,也涉及从精神层面到物质层面的各个维度。第二次浪潮的理论焦点不再集中于纯粹的"自然",而是将现代生活中的社会文化、心理世界、物质条件等因素都纳入考量,重视对现实世界的批判和改造,反对对人类和自然的剥削、压迫和控制,追求社会公平正义。

在环境正义观的影响下,生态批评开始探讨毒物以及废弃物叙事、反田园书写、城市空间正义等议题,主张既重视日常生活的具体实践也重视对政治经济等宏观议题的思考。以2001年出版的文集《超越绿色》(*Getting Over the Color Green: Contemporary Environmental Literature of the Southwest*)为例,书中斯科特·斯洛维克(Scott Slovic)等批评家反思第一次生态批评浪潮所倡导的"绿色"主义。与"绿色"自然形成对比的是美国西南部沙漠地区的棕色地域。它被定义为"无人区"和"不毛之地",成为核试验场和废料掩埋地。绿色和棕色的对比,暴露出自然书写的绿色想象中,可能隐藏着中产阶级城市白人男性的集体性的田园幻想,也暴露出给沙漠等人烟稀少之地贴上废弃之地的标签,可能是为了掩盖环境非正义。我们需要认识到沙漠中物种相互依存,有着基于自身复杂生态体系的独特之美。

自生态批评的第二次浪潮以来,生态批评已成为百家争鸣的理论场域。究其原因,一是因为生态问题越来越成为当代核心议题;二是因为生态批评具有跨学科性,需要征用诸学科的理论,丰富其理论资源库。在此,我们未必需要进行第三次浪潮、第四次浪潮的细致区分,但对于该领域的新进展,有必要进行追踪与思考。

生态批评与其他批评方式交叉而成的分支中,生态女性主义影响力很大。生态女性主义认为,要解决生态问题,首先要认清父权制的二元论模式对女性和自然的双重压迫。在这种结构模式下,自然变成了人类的"他者",是人类控制和改造的对象,而女性被等同于自然,是男性征服和驯化的对象。生态女性主义主张清除以压迫、掌控和剥削为核心的父权意识形态,释放被压抑的女性和自然的力量,借鉴承载女性价值的关怀伦理,构建和谐生态观。

后殖民生态主义则批判殖民体系和帝国主义带来的生态后果,其关注焦点包括殖民体系给原住民栖息地的生态体系所带来的灾难,殖民模式对全球生物多样性所造成的威胁，殖民空间的权力不平等所造就的各种环境非正义，等等。此外，后殖民生态主义深具政治意识，从跨民族跨国家的视角，讨论现代性进程在南北半球不同地域造成的影响，关注全球性和地方性之间的冲突和互动，寻求去殖民去帝国主义的世界建构模式。

从全球视角出发，关注生态议题的时间性后果，也是当代生态批评的特点之一。在《缓慢暴力与穷人的环境主义》(*Slow Violence and the Environmentalism of the Poor*, 2011) 中，罗布·尼克松 (Rob Nixon) 提出"缓慢暴力"(slow violence) 的概念，将其定义为一种逐渐发生的不易被觉察的破坏性暴力。它具有时空的分散性和迁延性，是一种通常根本不被视为暴力的消耗性暴力。他指出，在当今社会，引人瞩目的暴力事件有轰动效应，能快速动员社会力量，对其进行关注。但有些生态暴力机制的进程缓慢，不易为人所觉察，造成的伤害却是长期的、不可逆转的。不幸的是，受害者往往来自最脆弱的贫困社区，没有发声抗议的渠道，甚至不能明了周遭发生的一切对自己意味着什么。比如在越南战争期间，美国军方使用了"橙剂"。它的毒性作用在半个世纪后仍然存在，导致数千越南平民或残疾或死亡。类似的"缓慢暴力"案例还有热带雨林的日复一日的采伐，工业排污影响贫困地区的河流体系，等等。它们给当地居民及其后代带来难以消弭的伤害。

环境问题的累积可能会以缓慢的形式进行，因此尼克松的"缓慢暴力"理论要求我们从超越个体生命的角度关注人与环境的时间关系。实际上，当代生态批评中，长时间线的维度越来越受重视，"人类世"概念是其中的重要焦点。

2000年，荷兰化学家保罗·克鲁岑 (Paul Crutzen) 和美国古生态学家尤金·斯特默 (Eugene Stoermer) 提出了"人类世"(Anthropocene) 的概念，认为地球已经从跨度为一万余年的"全新世"(Holocene) 进入了人类活动成为重要外部地质营力的新阶段。克鲁岑在2002年发表的《人类地质学》("Geology of Mankind") 一文中，进一步提出人类世可以从18世纪末的工业革命开始算起，因为从那时起，人类活动对地球系统的影响开始显著增加。全球史研究专家J. R. 麦克尼尔 (J. R. McNeill) 则主张从二战后开始计算人类世。在他看来，1945年具有象征性的意义。在这一年，人类的第一颗原子弹爆炸。它留下的放射性残留会在地球表面产生持续成千上万年的影响。虽然学者们对人类世的起始时间有争议，但他们有核心的共识：人类必须打破人类中心主义迷思，反思现代性进程，才能为人类的生存争取到未来。人类世概念的诞生，迅速引发哲学、文学、地理学、生物学、社会学等领域的多方回应。

人类世的生态危机，其显性例证是全球变暖。人类的活动正在改变地球大气圈层的状态，气候灾变的威胁突出。如何逆转危机？法国哲学家和人类学家布鲁诺·拉图尔（Bruno Latour）主张从重新认识人类与地球的关系入手。20世纪70年代，英国科学家詹姆斯·洛夫洛克（James Lovelock）提出"盖娅假说"（Gaia hypothesis），以希腊神话中的大地女神盖娅为地球命名，指出地球是一个具有自我调节功能的有机体，其中的生物体、大气、海洋和地壳等各个组成部分通过相互作用和反馈机制形成了平衡关系。拉图尔在《面对盖娅》（*Facing Gaia: Eight Lectures on the New Climatic Regime*，2015）中，化用洛夫洛克的"盖娅假说"，提出我们不应该将地球视为客观的无能动性的物质星球，而应该将它视为生命体。在人类世，地球的生态平衡因人类影响而岌岌可危，气候问题是其症候。要克服危机，需要跳出民族和国家的局限，实现政治意义上的全球协作。

美国学者杰森·W. 摩尔（Jason W. Moore）则认为仅从人类世角度理解当下危机，不够切中命题。地球今日的困局是资本主义造成的，所以他提出了"资本世"的概念。在《生命之网中的资本主义》（*Capitalism in the Web of Life: Ecology and the Accumulation of Capital*，2015）中，摩尔指出，资本主义不仅是一种经济机制，也是"世界生态学"：资本主义对自然进行组织，表面看为世界带来繁荣、创新和丰富的消费品，实际上，它在累积资本、追逐利益，将自然、人类自身乃至整个生命网络卷入廉价化的生产机制。在此过程中，它与自然的矛盾也在不断积累，在自然的反作用力下，环境危机会日益严峻。简而言之，资本主义无法为人类带来可持续发展的未来。

资本主义导致的环境问题、全球化进程中的南北贫富差异加剧、全球变暖引发的气候危机……我们面临前所未有的挑战。蒂莫西·莫顿（Timothy Morton）认为，当下的环保主义未能应对这些挑战。在2007年出版的《没有自然的生态》（*Ecology Without Nature: Rethinking Environmental Aesthetics*）中，莫顿批评环境文学是工业社会缓解压力的安慰剂，指出环保主义绿色营销背后有消费主义的操控之手。他认为人类需要对自然的恐怖力量有所认识，超越目前局限性的时空视角，来理解人类行为之于环境的意义。从长线的历史时间来看，未来严重的环境问题可以追责到当下每个个体的行为。悖论在于，人类个体在其有限的生命中以为自己的所作所为无足轻重，意识不到其应当承担的责任。厄休拉·海斯（Ursula Heise）在2008年出版的《地方意识和行星意识》（*Sense of Place and Sense of Planet: The Environmental Imagination of the Global*）中，也在呼吁铸就新的生态观。她主张从人类的空间感受入手，认为环保主义思想需要将其文化想象的核心从地方感转移到不具地方性的行星意识，以便进行系统性的思考。我们以地方性为根基建立起家园感，但我们应认识到行星地球是人类乃至所有生命的家园的共有根基。

从生态批评理论中，我们能够看到一种有别于启蒙主体观的新型主体观，这种主体观具有后人类特点。启蒙主体观中，人是世界的中心、万物的灵长，拥有崇高的理性。而生态批评中的诸多概念，如人类世、行星意识、盖娅假说等，均在反对将人类视为世界的中心，揭秘"人类"概念建构中人与自然、人与其他物种、人与非人等二元对立中的人类中心主义意识形态，质疑启蒙理性的人类主体观。后人类主义与生态批评密切关联，后者要求对人类与地球的关系进行反思，而前者要求先从人类自身的反思做起。

"后人类"概念的诞生与后现代主义对人文传统的撼动有关。后现代主义批评家伊哈布·哈桑（Ihab Hassan）在1977年发表的《作为表现者的普罗米修斯》（"Prometheus as Performer: Toward a Posthumanist Culture?"）一文中指出，随着人文主义转变为后人类主义，五百年来的人文主义面临消亡的危机。人文主义的成就是建立了启蒙主体观，而后人类主义试图跳出此框架。

后人类主义诞生的另外一个语境是当代科学技术和文化思想的迅猛变化。信息技术、人工智能、生物技术等对人的感知和存在所构成的挑战，激励着对"何为人类？"这个问题的追问。1985年，唐娜·哈拉维（Donna Haraway）发表了《赛博格宣言》（"A Manifesto for Cyborgs: Science, Technology, and Socialist Feminism in the 1980s"），指出当今的科幻小说、医学实践以及美国现代战争体系中，随处可见赛博格：赛博格是控制论的有机体，是机器与生物体的混合，既是虚构的生物也是社会现实的生物。赛博格打破了思想和身体、动物和人类、有机体和机器、公共和私有、自然和文化、男人和女人、原始和文明等二元对立，为理解后人类主体性提供了重要视角。N. 凯瑟琳·海勒斯（N. Katherine Hayles）的后人类理论和哈拉维的看法有重合之处，都关心嵌合体技术带来的变革。但是海勒斯的侧重点是技术媒介环境对人类的基本设定的冲击。信息技术时代，人类身体经验被彻底改变。人类与机器的融合以及虚拟技术的应用带来了后人类转向：认知呈分散态势，意识在身体和机器之间切换，在他人意识和自我意识之间切换。这种后人类主体是一种混合物，一种各种异质、异源成分的集合，一个物质—信息的独立实体，持续不断地建构并且重建自己的边界。

与此同时，在哲学领域，罗西·布拉伊多蒂（Rosi Braidotti）的游牧主体论也在冲击人类传统主体观。布拉伊多蒂深受德勒兹和瓜塔里的影响，她既反对二元对立的身份建构逻辑，也反对消弭冲突的中性化的主体观，提出"游牧主体"（nomadic subject）的概念。这种主体拒绝固定的身份，打破主体间的壁垒，主张从关系性、多样性和潜能性的角度来建构主体间的新型伦理关系。自我与他人、思想与身体、人类与自然、人类与其他物种的分界性受到了质疑。

简·班内特（Jane Bennett）和布拉伊多蒂一样提倡开放性的本体论，而她聚焦在"物质性"这个关键词。班内特提出了"活力物质"（vital materiality）理论，指出人类、动物、植物或矿物之间没有本质界限，都体现物质的活力，反映生命、物质和环境等因素的交织。班内特在《活力物质》（*Vibrant Matter: A Political Ecology of Things*，2010）中将人与自然之间的关系形容为两股物质能量流遭遇时的轨迹交叠，其中的涌动不是单向的、顺滑的、统一的，而是孕育着多样性的变化。世界处处有生机，世界处处有联系。

其实，以上后人类理论均含有"非人"（non-human）的维度——"非人"也是后人类理论的关键词。海勒斯的数字主体不是传统意义上的人；班内特的活力物质论进一步解构了人与"非人"的传统区分。而哈拉维在赛博格的"非人"理论之后，提出了"伙伴物种"（companion species）理论。其焦点也是"非人"。哈拉维所说的伙伴物种，不仅包括猫、狗、牛、马等由人类驯化用以为人类服务的伙伴动物，她认为所有的动植物——包括毒蛇、猛兽、树木、蘑菇——都是伙伴物种。这个长名单还包括细菌等微生物生命体。伙伴物种论反映了人类与其他生命形式的相互连接相互依赖，以及相互竞争相互抵制。哈拉维将这种复杂的共生性关系称为亲缘关系（kinship）。在哈拉维看来，地球生物（earthlings）是一个具有聚合（assembling）意味的词，世界万物共生共在。

目前，生态问题的紧迫性使生态批评理论成为21世纪最为活跃的理论领域之一。它综合各个领域的发现，以跨学科的视角，思考人类如何在地球这颗行星上负责任地生存。这些思考也伴随着人类对自己的重新认识，而这正是后人类主义理论的关注点。"什么是人类？""什么是世界？""我们想要什么样的未来？""应该采取什么样的行动？"这些问题既是理论问题，也和人类当下的具体实践息息相关。

主要文本阅读

布伊尔：《环境批评的未来》

选文简介

布伊尔的《环境批评的未来》对生态理论的发展史进行了综合性讨论，分析了它如何回应当代环境问题，吸纳各种批评声音，深化对空间、地方与全球化等概念的理解，进而推进政治关切和伦理关怀。

选文出自著作第一章，关涉理论史梳理。布伊尔指出，从文学史传统看，文学一直都非常关注环境议题。当代生态理论的诞生,是全球化风险社会环境危机日益严重的结果。应对危机,不仅需要科学研究、技术应用和立法监督机制,也需要文学来塑造想象,追问价值观,勾勒愿景,探索走出危机的出路。我们从选文中能看到布伊尔的立场紧扣生态批评第二次浪潮的关键词"环境"。这是因为"环境"的意指是综合性的,包含与人类生活和发展相关的所有因素,比"自然"更能反映人与周围世界的相互塑造。布伊尔倡导"环境批评",期待它能容纳城市经验,观照边缘弱势人群的环境正义议题。但布伊尔反对从对立角度解读第一次浪潮和第二次浪潮的差异,指出无论前者还是后者,均体现对环境的关注,均具有生态意识。

From *The Future of Environmental Criticism*

Lawrence Buell (1939-   )

To burgeon is not necessarily to mature or to prevail. "Ecocriticism," the commonest omnibus term for an increasingly heterogeneous movement, has not yet achieved the standing accorded (say) to gender or postcolonial or critical race studies. Eventually I believe it will; but it is still finding its path, a path bestrewn by obstacles both external and self-imposed.

At first sight, the belatedness and liminality of the recent environmental turn in literary-critical studies seems strange. For creative art and critical reflection have always taken a keen interest in how the material world is engaged, absorbed, and reshaped by theory, imagination, and *techne*. Humankind's earliest stories are of earth's creation, of its transformation by gods or by human ingenuity's "second nature," as Cicero first called it—tales that frame environmental ethics in varied ways. In at least one case they may have significantly influenced the course of world history. The opening chapters of Genesis, the first book in Hebrew and Christian scripture, have been blamed as the root cause of Western technodominationism: God's mandate to man to take "dominion" over the creatures of the sea and earth and "subdue" them. Others retort that this thesis misreads both history and the biblical text: that "cultivate" is the more crucial term, implying pious stewardship rather than transformation. My point in mentioning this debate is not to arbitrate it but merely to call attention to the antiquity and durability of environmental discourse—and its variety both within individual thought traditions and worldwide. By contrast to either reading of Judaeo-Christian thought, for example, Mayan mythography represents the gods as fashioning human beings after several false starts from corn gathered with the help of already-created animals, thereby symbolizing "the collective survival that must exist between humans, plants, and animals," whereas in Māori cosmology, creation is an ongoing process: "humanity and all things of the natural world are always emerging, always unfolding."

All this goes to show that if environmental criticism today is still an emergent discourse it is one with very ancient roots. In one form or another the "idea of nature" has been a dominant or at least residual concern for literary scholars and intellectual historians ever since these fields came into being. That legacy calls into question just how marked a break from previous practice the contemporary movement is....This is a specter that has bedeviled ecocriticism from its birth: the suspicion that it might not boil down to much more than old-fashioned enthusiasms dressed up in new clothes.

Yet the marked increase and sophistication of environmentality as an issue within literary and cultural studies since the 1980s is a countervailing fact, despite the wrangling over what it means and what should be done about it that will surely continue for some time to come. It testifies to the need to correct somehow against the marginalization of environmental issues in most versions of critical theory that dominated literary and cultural studies through the 1980s—even as "the environment" was becoming an increasingly salient public concern and a major topic of research in science, economics, law, and public policy—and certain humanities fields as well, notably history and ethics....

Symptomatic of the mentality I assimilated was U.S. writer Eudora Welty's demure apology at the start of her luminous essay on "Place in Fiction" for place as "one of the lesser angels that watch over the racing hand of fiction" relative to "character, plot, symbolic meaning," and especially "feeling, who in my eyes carries the crown, soars highest of them all and rightly relegates place into the shade."

Why do the discourses of environment seem more crucial today than they did to Welty in the 1940s? The most obvious answer is that during the last third of the twentieth century "the environment" became front-page news. As the prospect of a sooner-or-later apocalypse by unintended environmental disaster came to seem likelier than apocalypse by deliberate nuclear *machismo*, public concern about the state and fate of "the environment" took increasing hold, initially in the West but now worldwide. The award of the 2004 Nobel Peace Prize to Kenyan environmental activist Wangari Maathai is, at this moment of writing, the latest sign of an advancing level of concern, which the "war against terror" since September 11, 2001 has upstaged but by no means suppressed. Underlying the advance has been a growing malaise about modern industrial society's inability to manage its unintended environmental consequences that Ulrich Beck, the Rachel Carson of contemporary social theory, calls "reflexive modernization," meaning in particular the fear that even the privileged classes of the world inhabit a global "risk society" whose hazards cannot be anticipated, calculated, and controlled, much less escaped.

Environmental issues, in turn, have become an increasing provocation both for artists and for academics, giving rise within colleges and universities to cross-disciplinary environmental studies programs often galvanized by student demand as much as by faculty research agendas. Though natural and social scientists have so far been the major players in such programs, considerable numbers of humanists have also been drawn in, many of them bringing preexisting commitments of a citizenly kind to bear in environmentally directed teaching and scholarship....

That the environmental turn in literary studies has been more issue-driven than method or paradigm-driven is one reason why the catchy but totalizing rubric of "ecocriticism" is less indicative than "environmental criticism" or "literary-environmental studies." Being less cumbersome and (so far) much more widely used, "ecocriticism" may well be here to stay. I have found it a convenient shorthand I cannot do without. But the term implies a nonexistent methodological holism. It overstates the degree to which the environmental turn in literary studies was ever a coordinated project....

A more substantive reason for belaboring the terminological issue is the implicit narrowness of the "eco," insofar as it connotes the "natural" *rather than* the "built" environment and, still more specifically, the field of ecology. "Ecocriticism is a name that implies more ecological literacy than its advocates now possess," pithily observes one who hopes to see more. Although attempted reformation of literary studies via *rapprochement* with life sciences has been *one* of the movement's distinctive projects, it is only one such project—and a minority endeavor at that. From the start, and increasingly, the "eco" of practicing so-called ecocritics has been more aesthetic, ethical, and sociopolitical than scientific. The looser rubric of ASLE's flagship journal *ISLE* (Interdisciplinary Studies in Literature and Environment) better fits the actual mix, and all the more so now that environmental criticism's working conception of "environment" has broadened in recent years from "natural" to include also the urban, the interweave of "built" and "natural" dimensions in every locale, and the interpenetration of the local by the global.

On the other hand, "ecocriticism" suffices if—like poet-critic Gary Snyder—one is careful to use the term in mindfulness of its etymology and of its metaphorical stretch. "Ecology" derives etymologically from the Greek *oikos*, household, and in modern usage refers both to "the study of biological interrelationships and the flow of energy through organisms and inorganic matter." Metaphorically, furthermore, "ecology" can be stretched to cover "energy-exchange and interconnection" in "other realms" too: from technology-based communication systems to the "ecology" of thinking or composition. Indeed, "the ecology movement," particularly outside the United States, sometimes serves as a synonym for environmentalism. Looked at this way, a perfectly plausible case can be made for speaking of environmentally valenced work in literature studies as "ecocriticism."...

...Some significant divisions separate first-wave projects to reconnect humans with the natural world from second-wave skepticism "that more can be learned from the 'black hole' of a weasel's eyes than from, say, the just-closed eyes of a child of the ghetto killed by leadpoisoning from ingesting the peeling paint in his/her immediate environment." According to the former way of thinking, the prototypical human figure is a solitary human and the experience in question activates a primordial link between human and nonhuman. According to the latter, the prototypical human figure is defined by social category and the "environment" is artificially constructed. Is there any common ground here to indicate that environmental criticism might grow rather than fall apart from this kind of schism?

I think so. First and foremost because in both instances the understanding of personhood is defined for better or for worse by environmental entanglement. Whether individual or social, being doesn't stop at the border of the skin. If the weasel epiphany sounds too rarefied, set beside the image of the poisoned child this declaration by a Native American writer quoted by an ecocritic/nature writer of more traditional persuasion. "You could cut off my hand, and I would still live....You could take out my eyes, and I would still live....Take away the sun, and I die. Take away the plants and animals, and I die. So why should I think my body is more a part of me than the sun and the earth?" This too has the marks of the first-wave mentality (environment = nature, nature = nurture, the exemplar and the idiom = more or less what one would expect from the paradigmatic "ecological Indian," the model minority sage of green wisdom). But the underlying view of the environment-constructed body, of environmentality as crucial to health or disease, life or death, is quite similar.

The image of the poisoned child is also in its own way as much an idealization as the image of the eco-sensitive indigene. Its underlying valorization of "the natural" tends not to be so different from the first wave's as one might suppose. Second-wave ecocriticism has so far concentrated strongly, for example, on locating vestiges of nature within cities and/or exposing crimes of eco-injustice against society's marginal groups. In this there should be enough shared ground for ongoing conversation if not *rapprochement*. Skittishness at modernization's aggressive, accelerating, inequitable transformations of "natural" into "constructed" space is a common denominator crucial to giving ecocriticism, both waves of it, its edge of critique. This is ecocriticism's equivalent as it were to queer studies, with which some environmental writers and critics have in fact begun to affiliate: to unsettle normative thinking about environmental status quos. Not that there is anything antinormative about environmental concern as such. On the contrary, environmental concern is more mainstream than homophobia. But not as a high-priority issue. The mainstream view, in the United States at least, is that "the environment" will be society's top problem "tomorrow"—a quarter century from now, say—but not today. Environmental concern is normal. But *vehement* concern still looks queer.

That is a consensus environmental criticism of whatever stripe is out to disrupt. To adapt the terms of Niklas Luhmann's model of systems analysis, the insistence on environmentality—whether it be the ecological Indian or the poisoned child—interjects the disruptive "anxiety" element that "cannot be regulated away by any of the function systems" that comprise modernized society (the institution of economics, law, etc.).

哈拉维：《赛博格宣言》

选文简介

选文出自哈拉维的理论名篇《赛博格宣言》。哈拉维的写作充分体现了跨学科性，她在科学、哲学、动物学与女性主义等多种话语体系和问题意识之间自如穿梭，这也和她文章的关键词"赛博格"的杂糅本质、流变特点以及政治意涵形成呼应。在选文中，哈拉维详细讨论了赛博格语境中的三个关键性的边界突破。一是突破了人类和动物之间的边界。进化论是突破的思想推手，生物科技的发展是技术推手。二是突破了有机体与机器之间的边界，模糊了自然与人工、心智与身体、自我发展与外部设计等之间的区别。三是突破了物质性与非物质性的边界。光能技术、微电子技术等为便携性、流动性和虚拟性赋能。哈拉维在上述突破中看到了危险：赛博格可以被用于高精度战争武器的生产，可以提供更具压迫性的社会监控机制。但哈拉维也从中看到了其革命潜能——赛博格的"怪物"僭越了既定的社会法则，为女性主义领域的思想探索提供了启发；赛博格的能动性和机动性为政治领域的实践提供了动力。

From "A Manifesto for Cyborgs"

Donna Haraway (1944-)

A cyborg is a cybernetic organism, a hybrid of machine and organism, a creature of social reality as well as a creature of fiction. Social reality is lived social relations, our most important political construction, a world-changing fiction. The international women's movements have constructed "women's experience," as well as uncovered or discovered this crucial collective object. This experience is a fiction and fact of the most crucial, political kind. Liberation rests on the construction of the consciousness, the imaginative apprehension, of oppression, and so of possibility. The cyborg is a matter of fiction and lived experience that changes what counts as women's experience in the late twentieth century. This is a struggle over life and death, but the boundary between science fiction and social reality is an optical illusion.

Contemporary science fiction is full of cyborgs—creatures simultaneously animal and machine, who populate worlds ambiguously natural and crafted. Modern medicine is also full of cyborgs, of couplings between organism and machine, each conceived as coded devices, in an intimacy and with a power that was not generated in the history of sexuality. Cyborg "sex" restores some of the lovely replicative baroque of ferns and invertebrates (such nice organic prophylactics against heterosexism). Cyborg replication is uncoupled from organic reproduction. Modern production seems like a dream of cyborg colonization work, a dream that makes the nightmare of Taylorism seem idyllic. And modern war is a cyborg orgy, coded by C^3I, command-control-communication-intelligence, an $84 billion item in 1984's U.S. defense budget. I am making an argument for the cyborg as a fiction mapping our social and bodily reality and as an imaginative resource suggesting some very fruitful couplings. Foucault's biopolitics is a flaccid premonition of cyborg politics, a very open field.

By the late twentieth century, our time, a mythic time, we are all chimeras, theorized and fabricated hybrids of machine and organism; in short, we are cyborgs. The cyborg is our ontology; it gives us our politics. The cyborg is a condensed image of both imagination and material reality, the two joined centers structuring any possibility of historical transformation....

I will return to the science fiction of cyborgs at the end of this essay, but now I want to signal three crucial boundary breakdowns that make the following political fictional (political scientific) analysis possible. By the late twentieth century in United States scientific culture, the boundary between human and animal is thoroughly breached. The last beachheads of uniqueness have been polluted if not turned into amusement parks—language, tool use, social behavior, mental events, nothing really convincingly settles the separation of human and animal. And many people no longer feel the need of such a separation; indeed, many branches of feminist culture affirm the pleasure of connection of human and other living creatures. Movements for animal rights are not irrational denials of human uniqueness; they are a clear-sighted recognition of connection across the discredited breach of nature and culture. Biology and evolutionary theories over the last two centuries have simultaneously produced modern organisms as objects of knowledge and reduced the line between humans and animals to a faint trace re-etched in ideological struggle or professional disputes between life and social sciences. Within this framework, teaching modern Christian creationism should be fought as a form of child abuse.

Biological-determinist ideology is only one position opened up in scientific culture for arguing the meanings of human animality. There is much room for radical political people to contest for the meanings of the breached boundary. The cyborg appears in myth precisely where the boundary between human and animal is transgressed. Far from signaling a walling off of people from other living beings, cyborgs signal disturbingly and pleasurably tight coupling. Bestiality has a new status in this cycle of marriage exchange.

The second leaky distinction is between animal-human (organism) and machine. Pre-cybernetic machines could be haunted; there was always the specter of the ghost in the machine. This dualism structured the dialogue between materialism and idealism that was settled by a dialectical progeny, called spirit or history, according to taste. But basically machines were not self-moving, self-designing, autonomous. They could not achieve man's dream, only mock it. They were not man, an author to himself, but only a caricature of that masculinist reproductive dream. To think they were otherwise was paranoid. Now we are not so sure. Late-twentieth-century machines have made thoroughly ambiguous the difference between natural and artificial, mind and body, self-developing and externally designed, and many other distinctions that used to apply to organisms and machines. Our machines are disturbingly lively, and we ourselves frighteningly inert....

The third distinction is a subset of the second: the boundary between physical and non-physical is very imprecise for us. Pop physics books on the consequences of quantum theory and the indeterminacy principle are a kind of popular scientific equivalent to the Harlequin romances as a marker of radical change in American white heterosexuality: they get it wrong, but they are on the right subject. Modern machines are quintessentially microelectronic devices: they are everywhere and they are invisible. Modern machinery is an irreverent upstart god, mocking the Father's ubiquity and spirituality. The silicon chip is a surface for writing; it is etched in molecular scales disturbed only by atomic noise, the ultimate interference for nuclear scores. Writing, power, and technology are old partners in Western stories of the origin of civilization, but miniaturization has changed our experience of mechanism. Miniaturization has turned out to be about power; small is not so much beautiful as pre-eminently dangerous, as in cruise missiles. Contrast the TV sets of the 1950s or the news cameras of the 1970s with the TV wrist bands or hand-sized video cameras now advertised. Our best machines are made of sunshine; they are all light and clean because they are nothing but signals, electromagnetic waves, a section of a spectrum. And these machines are eminently portable, mobile—a matter of immense human pain in Detroit and Singapore. People are nowhere near so fluid, being both material and opaque. Cyborgs are ether, quintessence....

So my cyborg myth is about transgressed boundaries, potent fusions, and dangerous possibilities which progressive people might explore as one part of needed political work. One of my premises is that most American socialists and feminists see deepened dualisms of mind and body, animal and machine, idealism and materialism in the social practices, symbolic formulations, and physical artifacts associated with "high technology" and scientific culture. From *One-Dimensional Man* to *The Death of Nature*, the analytic resources developed by progressives have insisted on the necessary domination of technics and recalled us to an imagined organic body to integrate our resistance. Another of my premises is that the need for unity of people trying to resist worldwide intensification of domination has never been more acute. But a slightly perverse shift of perspective might better enable us to contest for meanings, as well as for other forms of power and pleasure in technologically mediated societies.

From one perspective, a cyborg world is about the final imposition of a grid of control on the planet, about the final abstraction embodied in a Star War apocalypse waged in the name of defense, about the final appropriation of women's bodies in a masculinist orgy of war. From another perspective, a cyborg world might be about lived social and bodily realities in which people are not afraid of their joint kinship with animals and machines, not afraid of permanently partial identities and contradictory standpoints. The political struggle is to see from both perspectives at once because each reveals both dominations and possibilities unimaginable from the other vantage point. Single vision produces worse illusions than double vision or many-headed monsters. Cyborg unities are monstrous and illegitimate; in our present political circumstances, we could hardly hope for more potent myths for resistance and recoupling.

班内特：《活力物质》

选文简介

《活力物质》的核心议题是超越人类中心论，认识"非人"（non-human）的力量，关注物的能动性。在选文中，班内特区别了斯宾诺莎提出的两个概念："被动的自然"（*natura naturata*）和"能动的自然"（*natura naturans*）。斯宾诺莎用前者指上帝意志造就的自然，用后者指涌动的流变的自然。班内特从斯宾诺莎的概念中看到了两种不同的物质观。在"被动的自然"的物质观中，上帝和人类是能动者，物是惰性的存在，是被设计安排的对象，万物各归其位。在"能动的自然"的物质观中，物质世界在不断生成中，它是创造性的、活跃的、流变的。班内特提倡"能动的自然"，认为自然绝不仅仅是构成世界的物质基底，它蕴含着多重位面的活力物质的流动与转化，不受目的论引导，不受因果论限制，人们无法掌握它、限制它，相反，人们必须尊重它所携带的生命能量。我们人类应采取的立场是放弃人类中心主义，从"非人"角度重新认识自己，正视物的能动性，将它作为重要的行动元纳入生态政治的考量。

From *Vibrant Matter*

Jane Bennett (1957-)

Natura Naturans

In lieu of an environment that surrounds human culture, or even a cosmos that cleaves into three ecologies, picture an ontological field without any unequivocal demarcations between human, animal, vegetable, or mineral.

All forces and flows (materialities) are or can become lively, affective, and signaling. And so an affective, speaking human body is not *radically* different from the affective, signaling nonhumans with which it coexists, hosts, enjoys, serves, consumes, produces, and competes.

This field lacks primordial divisions, but it is not a uniform or flat topography. It is just that its differentiations are too protean and diverse to coincide exclusively with the philosophical categories of life, matter, mental, environmental. The consistency of the field is more uneven than that: portions congeal into bodies, but not in a way that makes any one type the privileged site of agency. The source of effects is, rather, always an ontologically diverse assemblage of energies and bodies, of simple and complex bodies, of the physical and the physiological.

In this onto-tale, everything is, in a sense, alive. This liveliness is not capped by an ultimate purpose or grasped and managed through a few simple and timeless (Kantian) categories. What I am calling vital materiality or vibrant matter is akin to what is expressed in one of the many historical senses of the word *nature*. Though nature can refer to a stable substrate of brute matter, the term has also signaled generativity, fecundity, Isis or Aphrodite, or the "Spring" movement of Antonio Vivaldi's *Four Seasons*. This creativity can be purposive or not. The contrast between nature as brute or purposive matter and nature as generativity is nicely captured by the distinction, key to Baruch Spinoza's *Ethics*, between *natura naturata* and *natura naturans*. *Natura naturata* is passive matter organized into an eternal order of Creation; *natura naturans* is the uncaused causality that ceaselessly generates new forms. When the English Romantics and American transcendentalists sought to refine their senses, they did so in part to be able to better detect *natura naturans*. This universal creativity requires a special sensitivity because, as Samuel Taylor Coleridge noted, the productive power is "suspended and, as it were, quenched in the product." Nature as generativity is also emphasized in Alfred North Whitehead's process philosophy, according to which nature is "a continuous stream of occurrence."...

The sense of nature as creativity also seems a part of what the ancient Greeks meant by *phusis*, of which the Latin *natura* is an equivalent. *Phusis* comes from the verb *phuo*, which probably meant to puff, blow, or swell up, conveying the sense of germination or sprouting up, bringing forth, opening out, or hatching. *Phusis* thus speaks of a process of morphing, of formation and deformation, that is to say, of the becoming otherwise of things in motion as they enter into strange conjunctions with one another.

The point is this: an active becoming, a *creative not-quite-human force capable of producing the new*, buzzes within the history of the term nature. This vital materiality congeals into bodies, bodies that seek to persevere or prolong their run....

Blocks to and for a New Self-Interest

The monism I have just described is a story that may or may not resonate with the reader's experience. Even if, I as believe, the vitality of matter is real, it will be hard to discern it, and, once discerned, hard to keep focused on. It is too close and too fugitive, as much wind as thing, impetus as entity, a movement always on the way to becoming otherwise, an effluence that is vital and engaged in trajectories but not necessarily intentions. What is more, my attention will regularly be drawn away from it by deep cultural attachments to the ideas that matter is inanimate and that real agency belongs only to humans or to God, and by the need for an action-oriented perception that must overlook much of the swirling vitality of the world. In composing and recomposing the sentences of this book—especially in trying to choose the appropriate verbs, I have come to see how radical a project it is to think vital materiality. It seems necessary and impossible to rewrite the default grammar of agency, a grammar that assigns activity to people and passivity to things.

Are there more everyday tactics for cultivating an ability to discern the vitality of matter? One might be to allow oneself, as did Charles Darwin, to anthropomorphize, to relax into resemblances discerned across ontological divides: you (mis)take the wind outside at night for your father's wheezy breathing in the next room; you get up too fast and see stars; a plastic topographical map reminds you of the veins on the back of your hand; the rhythm of the cicada's reminds you of the wailing of an infant; the falling stone seems to express a conative desire to persevere. If a green materialism requires of us a more refined sensitivity to the outside-that-is-inside-too, then maybe a bit of anthropomorphizing will prove valuable. Maybe it is worth running the risks associated with anthropomorphizing (superstition, the divinization of nature, romanticism) because it, oddly enough, works against anthropocentrism: a chord is struck between person and thing, and I am no longer above or outside a nonhuman "environment." Too often the philosophical rejection of anthropomorphism is bound up with a hubristic demand that only humans and God can bear any traces of creative agency. To qualify and attenuate this desire is to make it possible to discern a kind of life irreducible to the activities of humans or gods. This material vitality is me, it predates me, it exceeds me, it postdates me.

Another way to cultivate this new discernment might be to elide the question of the human. Postpone for a while the topics of subjectivity or the nature of human interiority, or the question of what really distinguishes the human from the animal, plant, and thing. Sooner or later, these topics will lead down the anthropocentric garden path, will insinuate a hierarchy of subjects over objects, and obstruct freethinking about what agency really entails. One might also try to elide or not get defensive about the perfectly reasonable objection that the "posthumanist" gestures of vital materialism entail a performative contradiction: "Is it not, after all, a self-conscious, language-wielding human who is articulating this philosophy of vibrant matter?" It is not so easy to resist, deflect, or redirect this criticism. One can point out how dominant notions of human subjectivity and agency are belied by the tangles and aporias into which they enter when the topics are explored in philosophical detail. One can invoke bacteria colonies in human elbows to show how human subjects are themselves nonhuman, alien, outside, vital materiality. One can note that the human immune system depends on parasitic helminth worms for its proper functioning or cite other instances of our cyborgization to show how human agency is always an assemblage of microbes, animals, plants, metals, chemicals, word-sounds, and the like—indeed, that insofar as anything "acts" at all, it has already entered an agentic assemblage: for example, Hurricanes-FEMA-GlobalWarming; or StemCells-NIH-Souls; or Worms-Topsoil-Garbage; or Electricity-Deregulation-Fire-Greed; or E.Coli-Abattoirs-Agribusiness.

The voice of reason or habit is, however, unlikely to be mollified by such tactics and will again grasp for that special something that makes *human* participation in assemblages radically *different*. Here one might try to question the question: Why are we so keen to distinguish the human self from the field? Is it because the assumption of a uniquely human agency is, to use Kantian language, a "necessary presupposition" of assertion as such? Or is the quest motivated by a more provincial demand that humans, above all other things on earth, possess souls that make us eligible for eternal salvation? I do not imagine that any of these replies will end the conversation, but some of them together may open up new avenues within it.

There are many other pitfalls on the road to a vital materialism. For example, while I agree with Latour and Guattari that techno-fixes (smart ones that respect the vitality or quasi autonomy of materialities) must be pursued, and that there is nothing intrinsically wrong with them, I am ambivalent about Latour's claim that life (for Americans and Europeans) has simply become too technologized for the idea of pristine nature to wield any inspirational value. As the popularity of Thoreau and his heirs (such as Wendell Berry and Barry Lopez) shows, the ideal of nature as the Wild continues to motivate some people to live more ecologically sustainable lives. But even if Latour is correct in his prediction that the power of this ideal will dwindle, attracting fewer and fewer human bodies to it, he has not thought through all the normative implications of its demise.

Neither, of course, have I. But one thing I have noticed is that as I shift from environmentalism to vital materialism, from a world of nature versus culture to a heterogeneous monism of vibrant bodies, I find the ground beneath my old ethical maxim, "tread lightly on the earth," to be less solid. According to this maxim, I should try to minimize the impact of my actions so as to minimize the damage or destruction of other things with which I share existence. The ecologist James Nash describes this as the "earth-affirming norm" of frugality, a sparing "of the resources necessary for human communities and sparing of the other species that are both values in themselves and instrumental values for human needs." If I live not as a human subject who confronts natural and cultural objects but as one of many conative actants swarming and competing with each other, then frugality is too simple a maxim. Sometimes ecohealth will require individuals and collectives to back off or ramp down their activeness, and sometimes it will call for grander, more dramatic and violent expenditures of human energy. I know that this last point is pitched at a very high level of abstraction or generality (as maxims must be, I suppose). And I know that more needs to be said to specify the normative implications of a vital materialism in specific contexts. I am, for now, at the end of my rope. So I will just end with a litany, a kind of Nicene Creed for would-be vital materialists: "I believe in one matter-energy, the maker of things seen and unseen. I believe that this pluriverse is traversed by heterogeneities that are continually *doing things*. I believe it is wrong to deny vitality to nonhuman bodies, forces, and forms, and that a careful course of anthropomorphization can help reveal that vitality, even though it resists full translation and exceeds my comprehensive grasp. I believe that encounters with lively matter can chasten my fantasies of human mastery, highlight the common materiality of all that is, expose a wider distribution of agency, and reshape the self and its interests."

摩尔:《生命之网中的资本主义》

选文简介

摩尔认为当代包括生态危机在内的各种危机,均源自以无节制的积累和贪婪的逐利为目标的资本主义。他指出,资本主义不是经济体系和社会体系,它深入自然领域,是组织自然的方式。真正意义上的自然是"生命之网",它是小写的、多重的,既内在于我们人类生命,也环绕着我们,是各种涌动的生命之流的汇聚。资本、帝国与科学却塑造出首字母大写的自然(Nature),将它排除在人类的社会属性之外,以方便对自然进行限制和控制。自然被编码和量化,被"合理"利用,服务于经济利益。摩尔认为唯有用政治想象力摆脱资本主义对"自然/社会"的构想,从"世界生命网络"的角度来理解人类、自然和社会的关系,修补资本主义对"生命之网"造成的损害,才能为平等和可持续发展找到出路。

From *Capitalism in the Web of Life*

Jason W. Moore (1971-   )

The Double Internality: History as if Nature Matters

The human prospect in the twenty-first century is not an altogether happy one. From the outset, our future can be specified at two levels of abstraction. The first is humanity-in-nature. Human engagement with the rest of nature has, over the past decade, reached the point "where abrupt global environmental change can no longer be excluded." The second is capitalism-in-nature. The unfolding crisis of neoliberal capitalism—now in between the *signal* crisis of 2008 and the unpredictable but inevitable onset of terminal crisis—suggests we may be seeing something very different from the familiar pattern. That pattern is one in which new technologies and new organizations of power and production emerged after great systemic crises, and resolved the older crises by putting nature to work in powerful new ways. The neoliberal revolution after the 1970s is only the most recent example. Today, however, it is increasingly difficult to get nature—including human nature—to yield its "free gifts" on the cheap. This indicates we may be experiencing not merely a transition from one phase of capitalism to another, but something more epochal: the breakdown of the strategies and relations that have sustained capital accumulation over the past five centuries. *Capitalism in the Web of Life* is about how the mosaic of relations that we call capitalism work *through* nature; and how nature works *through* that more limited zone, capitalism. This double movement—of capitalism through nature, of nature through capitalism—is what I call the "Double Internality."...

..."*The* economy" and "*the* environment" are not independent of each other. Capitalism is not an economic system; it is not a social system; it is *a way of organizing nature.*

We can begin with a guiding distinction about this phrase: "a way of organizing nature."

Capitalism's governing conceit is that it may do with Nature as it pleases, that Nature is external and may be coded, quantified, and rationalized to serve economic growth, social development, or some other higher good. This is capitalism *as a project*. The reality—the *historical process*—is radically different. While the manifold projects of capital, empire, and science are busy making Nature with a capital "N"—external, controllable, reducible—the web of life is busy shuffling about the biological and geological conditions of capitalism's process. The "web of life" is nature as a whole: *nature* with an emphatically lowercase *n*. This is nature as us, as inside us, as around us. It is nature as a flow of flows. Put simply, humans make environments and environments make humans—and human organization.

There is no widely accepted term for the process through which civilizations, themselves forces of nature, are caught up in the co-production of life. And so Green thinkers, even those who pioneered new ways of seeing and thinking humanity's place in nature, have tended to default to an older vocabulary: Society with a capital "S." This is observation more than critique: we are products of our times. And those times are today different, different even from two decades ago. A new paradigm is now possible—it is breaking out all over, especially among younger scholars. I will call that new paradigm *world-ecology*. This book is a contribution to it, though far from an encompassing definition. World-ecology—or whatever name we end up attaching to this paradigm—is not only intellectually, but politically, necessary if we are to meet the challenges of the twenty-first century.

World-ecology makes one old argument, and one new one. On the one hand, the new paradigm unfolds from a rich mosaic of relational thinking about capitalism, nature, power, and history. On the other hand, world-ecology says that the relationality of nature implies a new method that grasps humanity-in-nature as a world-historical process. In this respect, Capra's insistence that the world's crises—debt, biodiversity, poverty, climate—are unified through a "crisis of perception" is correct. But we can take this insistence further. Modernity's structures of knowledge, its dominant relations of power, re/production, and wealth, its patterns of environment-making: these form an organic whole. Power, production, and perception entwine; they cannot be disentangled because they are unified, albeit unevenly and in evolving fashion. World-ecology asks us to put our post-Cartesian worldview to work on the crucible of world-historical transformation—understood not as history from above but as the fundamental co-production of earth-moving, idea-making, and power-creating across the geographical layers of human experience. Our task is to see how these moments fit together, and how their combinations change, quantitatively and qualitatively. From this perspective, I ask the reader to consider capitalism as a *world-ecology*, joining the accumulation of capital, the pursuit of power, and the co-production of nature in dialectical unity. Far from asserting the unfettered primacy of capitalism's capacity to remake planetary natures, capitalism as world-ecology opens up a way of understanding capitalism as already co-produced by manifold species, extending even to our planet's geo-biological shifts, relations, and cycles....

Today, more than forty years after the first Earth Day, there is broad agreement among many environmentally oriented scholars, and most environmentalists, that humans are a part of nature. This is the perspective of humanity-in-nature. What to do with this awareness has been a vexing problem. It is one thing to say that humans are natural forces, and quite another to say that human organizations—

families, empires, corporations, markets, and all the rest—are natural forces. Green Thought has embraced the former and resisted the latter. To say that humans are a part of nature feels good. To say that human organization is a part of nature feels wrong to most environmentalists, inside and outside the universities. For critical scholars—Red, Green, and many blends in between—the consensus is clear: capitalism acts upon a nature that operates independently of humanity. (And vice versa.) For a broader public concerned about climate and sustainability, a cognate consensus now reigns: humanity makes a "footprint" on the earth, which must be reduced.

Is the image of nature as passive mud and dirt—a place where one leaves a footprint—really the best metaphor to capture the vitality of the web of life? I think we can do better. This book tries to show that the hardened dualism of Nature/Society is not the only possible distinction. It is not even the best. To say that humans are a part of nature is to highlight the *specificity* of humanity within the web of life—its specific forms of *sociality*, its capacities for collective memory and symbolic production, and much more.

It has been a rocky road indeed to travel from humanity-in-nature to capitalism-*in*-nature. Does not such a journey deprive us of our ability to distinguish between "good" and "bad" human interactions with the rest of nature? Does it not leave us powerless to explain the specifically human, and the specifically natural, in the contemporary plunge into global crisis?

I do not think so. This book is an effort to explain why. And it is an attempt to show that a view of humanity as natural force allows us to see new connections between human nature, global power and production, and the web of life. In an era of tightly linked transformations of energy, climate, food and agriculture, labor markets, urbanization, financialization, and resource extraction, the imperative is to grasp the inner connections that conduct flows of power, capital, and energy through the grid of capital accumulation—and in so doing, to shed new light on the limits of that very grid.

So the question bears repeating: If not Nature/Society, then *what*? The alternative, long outlined by Green Thought but rarely (*rarely*) practiced, inverts the Cartesian privileging of substances over relations. Instead of a contemporary world produced by two discrete, interacting, substances—Society and Nature—we might instead look at the history of modernity as co-produced, *all the way down and through*. One substance, Humanity, does not co-produce historical change with another substance, Nature. Rather, the species-specificity of humans is already co-produced within the web of life. Everything that humans do is a flow of flows, in which the rest of nature is always moving through us. The forms of sociality that we evolve reflect a species-specificity that is unusually plastic. In this, "consciousness" is not outside but inside. Consciousness itself is a "state of matter." The stories of human organization are co-produced by *bundles* of human and extra-human nature. Humans build empires on their own as much as beavers build dams on their own. Both are "ecosystem engineers." Neither exists in a vacuum.

To "bundle," however, does not carry us nearly far enough. Even this metaphor inadequately grasps the intimacy, porosity, and permeability of humans and human organizations within the web of life. Absent a conceptual vocabulary that names the relations—rather than the end-points of Nature/Society—we will tend to default to a binary that reasserts the independence of human and extra-human natures. We must have a way of naming—and building the conversation through—the relation of life-making. In this relation, species make environments, and environments make species. It is a relation open to inorganic phenomena as well: plate tectonics, orbital variation, meteors, and much more "make" environments too. So we begin with an open conception of life-making, one that views the boundaries of the organic and inorganic as ever-shifting. It is a multi-layered relation through which there are no basic units, only webs within webs of relations: "worlds within worlds."

思考题

1. 布伊尔如何看待生态批评第一次浪潮和第二次浪潮之间的异同？
2. 哈拉维认为赛博格的概念突破了哪些边界？
3. 班内特的活力物质观的核心论点是什么？
4. 根据班内特的活力物质观，我们应该如何理解自然？这种理解对我们的生态意识培养有什么作用？
5. 摩尔如何理解资本主义与生态危机之间的关系？

讨论题

1. 请选择一部具有生态意识的乌托邦小说或者科幻小说，综合运用生态批评理论，对其进行分析。
2. 请结合本章选文和课外自主阅读的相关资料，从"后人类"的角度，对哈拉维的赛博格理论和班内特的活力物质理论进行比较。

补充文本选摘与评述

海勒斯：《我们何以成为后人类》
From *How We Became Posthuman: Virtual Bodies in Cybernetics, Literature, and Informatics*

N. Katherine Hayles (1943-   )

Although in many ways the posthuman deconstructs the liberal humanist subject, it thus shares with its predecessor an emphasis on cognition rather than embodiment. William Gibson makes the point vividly in *Neuromancer* when the narrator characterizes the posthuman body as "data made flesh." To the extent that the posthuman constructs embodiment as the instantiation of thought/information, it continues the liberal tradition rather than disrupts it.

In tracing these continuities and discontinuities between a "natural" self and a cybernetic posthuman, I am not trying to recuperate the liberal subject. Although I think that serious consideration needs to be given to how certain characteristics associated with the liberal subject, especially agency and choice, can be articulated within a posthuman context, I do not mourn the passing of a concept so deeply entwined with projects of domination and oppression. Rather, I view the present moment as a critical juncture when interventions might be made to keep disembodiment from being rewritten, once again, into prevailing concepts of subjectivity. I see the deconstruction of the liberal humanist subject as an opportunity to put back into the picture the flesh that continues to be erased in contemporary discussions about cybernetic subjects. Hence my focus on how information lost its body, for this story is central to creating what Arthur Kroker has called the "flesh-eating 90s." If my nightmare is a culture inhabited by posthumans who regard their bodies as fashion accessories rather than the ground of being, my dream is a version of the posthuman that embraces the possibilities of information technologies without being seduced by fantasies of unlimited power and disembodied immortality, that recognizes and celebrates finitude as a condition of human being, and that understands human life is embedded in a material world of great complexity, one on which we depend for our continued survival.

Perhaps it will now be clear that I mean my title, *How We Became Posthuman*, to connote multiple ironies, which do not prevent it from also being taken seriously. Taken straight, this title points to models of subjectivity sufficiently different from the liberal subject that if one assigns the term "human" to this subject, it makes sense to call the successor "posthuman." Some of the historical processes leading to this transformation are documented here, and in this sense the book makes good on its title. Yet my argument will repeatedly demonstrate that these changes were never complete transformations or sharp breaks; without exception, they reinscribed traditional ideas and assumptions even as they articulated something new. The changes announced by the title thus mean something more complex than "That was then, this is now." Rather, "human" and "posthuman" coexist in shifting configurations that vary with historically specific contexts. Given these complexities, the past tense in the title— "became"—is intended both to offer the reader the pleasurable shock of a double take and to reference ironically apocalyptic visions such as Moravec's prediction of a "postbiological" future for the human race.

拉图尔：《面对盖娅》
From *Facing Gaia*

Bruno Latour (1947-2022)

We should not be surprised that a new form of agency ("it is moved," "it reacts") is just as startling for the established powers as the old one ("it moves"). If the Inquisition was shocked by the announcement that the Earth was nothing more than a billiard ball turning endlessly in the vast universe (remember the scene in which Bertolt Brecht showed young monks making fun of Galileo's heliocentrism by turning in pointless circles in a room in the Vatican), the new Inquisition (henceforth economic rather than religious) is shocked to learn that the Earth has become—has become again!—an active, local, limited, sensitive, fragile, trembling, and easily irritated envelope. We would need a new Brecht to show how, in the climate skeptics' talk shows, a whole gang (for example, the Koch brothers, numerous physicists, many intellectuals, a good number of right-wing politicians, and also some pastors, preachers, gurus, and advisors to princes) makes fun of this new as well as very old animated and fragile Earth.

To depict this first new Earth as a body in free fall among all the other bodies in free fall in the universe, Galileo had to strip it from all forms of movement except one, abandoning all the prevailing notions of climate, animation, and metamorphoses. Thus he freed us from the so-called prescientific vision of the Earth as a cesspool, marked with the sign of death and corruption, from which our ancestors, their eyes fixed on the incorruptible spheres of the suns, the stars, and God, had no chance of escaping except by prayer, contemplation, and knowledge. Now, to discover the new Earth, climatologists are again conjuring up the climate and bringing back the animated Earth to a thin film whose fragility recalls the old feeling of living in what was once called the *sublunary zone*. Galileo's Earth could revolve, but it had no "tipping point," no "planetary frontiers," no "critical zones." It had a *movement*, but not a *behavior*. In other words, it was not yet the Earth of the Anthropocene.

Today, through a sort of counter-Copernican revolution, it is the New Climate Regime that compels us to turn our gaze toward the Earth considered once again with all its processes of transformation and metamorphosis, including generation, dissolution, war, pollution, corruption, and death. But, this time, it is useless to try to escape by means of prayer. Here is a dramatic rebound: from the cosmos to the universe, then back again to the cosmos! Back to the future? Rather, forward to the past!...

For, as of today, the Earth is quaking anew: not because it shifts and moves in its restless, wise orbit, not because it is changing, from its deep plates to its envelope of air, but because it is being *transformed by our doing*. Nature acted as a reference point for ancient law and for modern science *because it had no subject*: objectivity in the legal sense, as in the scientific sense, emanated from *a space without man*, which did not depend on us and on which we depended de jure and de facto. Yet henceforth it *depends so much* on us that it is shaking and that we too are worried by this deviation from expected equilibria. We are disturbing the Earth and making it quake! Now it *has a subject once again*.

...In the era of the counter-Copernican revolution, when we turn toward the old solid ground of natural law, what do we find? The traces of our action, visible everywhere! And not in the old way in which the Western Masculine Subject dominated the wild and impetuous world of nature through his courageous, violent, sometimes disproportionate dream of control, in the style of the Army Corps of Engineers. No, this time, just as happens in prescientific and nonmodern myths, we encounter an agent that takes its label, "subject," from the fact that it can be *subjected* to the whims, the bad moods, the emotions, the reactions, and even the revenge of another agent, which also takes its quality as "subject" *from the fact that it is equally subjected to the action of the other*.

胡根、蒂芬:《后殖民生态批评》
From *Postcolonial Ecocriticism: Literature, Animals, Environment*
Graham Huggan (1958-), Helen Tiffin (1945-)

Despite the recent advances of eco/environmental criticism, English studies in general, and postcolonial studies more particularly, have yet to resituate the species boundary and environmental concerns at the center of their inquiries; yet the need to examine these interfaces between nature and culture, animal and human, is urgent and never more pertinent than it is today. After all, postcolonialism's concerns with conquest, colonization, racism and sexism, along with its investments in theories of indigeneity and diaspora and the relations between native and invader societies and cultures, are also the central concerns of animal and environmental studies. Moreover, as the American environmental historian Donald Worster acknowledges, it is in the myriad relationships between material practices and ideas—especially in cross-cultural contexts—that day-to-day planetary life is lived and futures are governed: practices and ideas that are inseparable from issues of *representation*—as will be made clear throughout this book.

In his historical studies *The Columbian Exchange* (1973) and *Ecological Imperialism* (1986), Alfred Crosby considers the ways in which both materials and ideas were exchanged between Old World and New in a number of anything but even contexts. In the colonies of occupation, these radical inequalities or exchanges seemed most evident—or at least initially—in the military and political arenas, while in the settler colonies it was the results of *environmental* imperialism that were often most immediately clear. Different conceptions of being-in-the-world had indeed long been exchanged by individuals or groups under colonialist circumstances: Eastern religions had intrigued Europeans for several centuries, while the oral cultures of the Pacific Islands and Africa had provoked interest and admiration in many Westerners as well. But in Australia, North America, New Zealand and South Africa, genuine curiosity about and respect for indigenous cultures, philosophies and religions was rare, and even the most well-intentioned of missionaries, settlers and administrators tended to conceive of themselves as conferring (or imposing) the gifts of civilization upon the benighted heathen with little or no interest in receiving his or her philosophical gifts in return. Settlers arrived with crops, flocks and herds, and cleared land, exterminating local ecosystems, while human, animal and plant specimens taken to Europe from these "new" worlds were, by contrast, few and often inert in form. (Interestingly enough, no human, animal or plant, whether wild or domesticated, transported from the colonies to Europe was in a position to wreak comparable havoc on European ecosystems.) Moreover, they did not arrive as part of traditional agricultural or pastoral practices or with the authority of the normative; instead, they were isolated exotics:

> Indians paraded before royal courts; like turkeys and parrots in cages were the innocent signifiers of an otherness that was [...] exotic, that is, non-systematic, carrying no meaning other than that imposed by the culture to which they were exhibited.

European imports to the newly settled colonies—humans, animals, plants—were regarded on the other hand as necessary and "natural" impositions on, or substitutes for, the local bush or wilderness; and even if these invading species were initially difficult to establish or acclimatize, they soon prospered in lands where their control predators were absent. The genuinely natural ways of indigenous ecosystems were irretrievably undone as "wild" lands were cleared for farming or opened up to pastoralism.

选文评述

《我们何以成为后人类》的英文标题中，海勒斯使用了一般过去时。后人类的确已经是人类日常经验的一部分：当我们连上机器，进入虚拟空间，现实中的身体仿佛消失了，而在屏幕上，我们仿佛拥有由信息组成的主体。海勒斯在著作中介绍了控制论和信息技术对虚拟世界主体经验的塑造。虽然书中有大量的技术讨论，但重点依然在人文领域：海勒斯关心后人类主体性与西方自由人文主义主体性之间的关系。她指出，控制论主体是"数据造肉身"，这是对自由人文主义主体的解构，但同时也呼应了传统人文主体对认知和思辨的重视。总体而言，海勒斯认可技术对人类可能性的拓展，但她认为信息技术从未能真正消解人的物质性，虚拟世界的无肉身的不朽是迷梦。

拉图尔的《面对盖娅》提供了以人类世的角度重新认识地球的方法。启蒙时代，伽利略为了应付教会的审查，在描述地球时，不谈它的复杂性，只谈它是一个简单的球体。这也成为启蒙以降地球科学叙事的源头：地球是一颗遵循物理原则运行的球体。在当代，面对气候问题，拉图尔认为我们需要恢复对地球的前现代想象，意识到这个星球上有死亡和腐败，地球会愤怒，有坏脾气。在当代，人们已经没有办法通过向上帝祈祷来平复地球的愤怒。拉图尔认为将地球看作"盖娅"，可以让我们认识到地球有能动性，有生命力，但也很脆弱。人类活动已经在地球上留下了无处不在的印记，而地球也在对这些予以回应。如果不断忽略地球的回应，就会导致灾难性的后果。

《后殖民生态批评》反映了21世纪后殖民主义与生态批评交叉互动的理论新发展，于2010年首版，2015年发行第二版。著作分为两部分：第一部分讨论后殖民文本中的环境议题，第二部分聚焦当代越来越受瞩目的动物学维度。选文出自第二版导言中有关种族主义和物种主义的讨论。选文指出，目前后殖民批评忽视了一个重要议题：殖民体系还会衍生出环境帝国主义。新旧世界之间不仅存在军事、政治、文化和思想交流的不平等，也存在物种交流的不平等。欧洲人来到殖民地，将欧洲的农作物、兽群和牲畜引入当地，改变了当地的环境，破坏了原生生态系统，给殖民地的物种多样性带来不可估量的损失。反思殖民历史，必须将生态因素纳入其中。不能仅讨论人对人的剥削压迫，也要重视殖民体系对环境的改变，对自然、对动物和植物的影响。

关键术语释例

1. **地方（place）**："地方"是指靠经验与感知而被赋予意义的特定空间位置。它有地理、历史、文化和社会的具体语境。按照文化地理学家段义孚（Yi-Fu Tuan）的定义，相比空间的抽象性、匿名性和开放性，地方是具体的、相对固定的。它是家宅，是耕种的田地，是故乡，为人提供安全感和依恋感。但它可能具有封闭性，带有压抑性。在生态批评语境中，地方这一概念具有重要意义。它是地方意识（sense of place）的物质基础，塑造个人和群体的认同感和归属感。它是动态的，在地方性建构（place-making）进程中，居住者与环境相互塑造。与它有关的地方性知识（local knowledge）体现着当地人在历史进程中积累的环境经验，可以为生态可持续发展提供参考。在当代，随着交通工具和信息技术的发展，地方性的空间与更为广阔的全球空间紧密联系在一起。

2. **赛博格（cyborg）**："赛博格"概念由美国科学家曼弗雷德·克莱因斯（Manfred Clynes）和内森·克兰（Nathan Kline）于20世纪60年代首次提出。两位科学家从cybernetic和organism（"控制论"和"有机体"）中各取前三个字母，构造了新词cyborg，即"赛博格"，用以讨论如何使用技术手段增强航天员的体能。赛博格的本义是自然有机生命体和人造机械的混合，后来经由唐娜·哈拉维等理论家的重新阐释，成为跨越物种界限、跨越有机体和机器、跨越不同物质形态的杂糅性概念。赛博格的嵌合体形象反复出现在科幻小说的想象世界中。在21世纪的当下，随着生物、医学、通信、计算机、材料和能源等领域的科学技术的发展，假牙、器官移植、医学起搏器、便携式电子设备等成为人类日常生活的一部分，使人类越来越赛博格化。赛博格的意义不仅在技术和生活层面，也在思想领域。赛博格的概念含有集成性、拼贴性、含混性、越界性，挑战同一性的身份政治，超越人类传统主体设定，蕴含丰富的政治与文化意涵。

推荐书目

Aloi, Giovanni, and Susan McHugh. *Posthumanism in Art and Science: A Reader*. New York: Columbia University Press, 2021.

Cronon, William. *Uncommon Ground: Rethinking the Human Place in Nature*. New York: W. W.

Norton & Co., 1996.

Garrard, Greg. *Ecocriticism*. London: Routledge, 2012.

Glotfelty, Cheryll, and Harold Fromm. *The Ecocriticism Reader: Landmarks in Literary Ecology*. Athens: University of Georgia Press, 1996.

Gormley, Michael J. *The End of the Anthropocene: Ecocriticism, the Universal Ecosystem, and the Astropocene*. Lanham: Lexington Books, 2021.

Huggan, Graham, and Helen Tiffin. *Postcolonial Ecocriticism: Literature, Animals, Environment*. London: Routledge, 2010.

More, Max, and Natasha Vita-More. *The Transhumanist Reader: Classical and Contemporary Essays on the Science, Technology, and Philosophy of the Human Future*. Chichester: Wiley-Blackwell, 2013.

Vint, Sherryl. *After the Human: Culture, Theory and Criticism in the 21st Century*. Cambridge: Cambridge University Press, 2020.

Wolfe, Cary. *What Is Posthumanism?*. Minneapolis: University of Minnesota Press, 2010.

程相占:《当代西方环境美学通论》。北京:人民出版社,2022年。

胡志红:《西方生态批评史》。北京:人民出版社,2015年。